PENGUIN MODERN CLASSICS

1047

POINT COUNTER POINT

ALDOUS HUXLEY

Born in 1894, Aldous Huxley belongs to a family of great talent: he is the grandson of the famous Thomas Henry Huxley, the son of Leonard Huxley, the editor of *The Cornhill Magazine*, and the brother of Sir Julian Huxley. He was educated at Eton and Balliol, and before devoting himself entirely to his own writing worked as a journalist and dramatic critic.

Aldous Huxley first attracted attention with a volume of stories called *Limbo* (1920) and followed this up with his novel *Crome Yellow* (1921). *Antic Hay* and *Those Barren Leaves* followed in 1923 and 1925 respectively. Probably his three best-known novels are *Point Counter Point* (1928), *Brave New World* (1932), and *Eyeless in Gaza* (1936). His travel books include *Jesting Pilate* (1926) and *Beyond the Mexique Bay* (1934).

His most recent books are *Brave New World Revisited* (1959), *Collected Essays* (1960), *On Art and Artists* (1961), and *Island* (1962).

Cover illustration by Leonard Rosoman

BY ALDOUS HUXLEY

*Published in Penguin Books

ALDOUS HUXLEY

POINT COUNTER POINT

A NOVEL

PENGUIN BOOKS

IN ASSOCIATION WITH CHATTO AND WINDUS

Penguin Books Ltd, Harmondsworth, Middlesex
AUSTRALIA: Penguin Books Pty Ltd, 762 Whitehorse Road,
Mitcham, Victoria

—

First published 1928
Published in Penguin Books 1955
Reprinted 1957, 1961, 1963

—

Made and printed in Great Britain
by R. & R. Clark Ltd
Edinburgh
Set in Monotype Fournier

Oh, wearisome condition of humanity,
Born under one law, to another bound,
Vainly begot and yet forbidden vanity,
Created sick, commanded to be sound.
    What meaneth nature by these diverse laws,
    Passion and reason, self-division's cause?

FULKE GREVILLE

POINT COUNTER POINT

*

Chapter One

'You won't be late?' There was anxiety in Marjorie Carling's voice, there was something like entreaty.

'No, I won't be late,' said Walter, unhappily and guiltily certain that he would be. Her voice annoyed him. It drawled a little, it was too refined – even in misery.

'Not later than midnight.' She might have reminded him of the time when he never went out in the evenings without her. She might have done so; but she wouldn't; it was against her principles; she didn't want to force his love in any way.

'Well, call it one. You know what these parties are.' But as a matter of fact, she didn't know, for the good reason that, not being his wife, she wasn't invited to them. She had left her husband to live with Walter Bidlake; and Carling, who had Christian scruples, was feebly a sadist and wanted to take his revenge, refused to divorce her. It was two years now since they had begun to live together. Only two years; and now, already, he had ceased to love her, he had begun to love someone else. The sin was losing its only excuse, the social discomfort its sole palliation. And she was with child.

'Half past twelve,' she implored, though she knew that her importunity would only annoy him, only make him love her the less. But she could not prevent herself from speaking; she loved him too much, she was too agonizingly jealous. The words broke out in spite of her principles. It would have been better for her, and perhaps for Walter too, if she had had fewer principles and given her feelings the violent expression they demanded. But she had been well brought up in habits of the strictest self-control. Only the uneducated, she knew, made 'scenes'. An imploring 'Half past twelve, Walter' was all that managed to break through her principles. Too weak to move him, the feeble outburst would only annoy. She knew it, and yet she could not hold her tongue.

'If I can possibly manage it.' (There; she had done it. There was exasperation in his tone.) 'But I can't guarantee it; don't expect me

7

too certainly.' For of course, he was thinking (with Lucy Tanta-mount's image unexorcizably haunting him), it certainly wouldn't be half past twelve.

He gave the final touches to his white tie. From the mirror her face looked out at him, close beside his own. It was a pale face and so thin that the down-thrown light of the electric lamp hanging above them made a shadow in the hollows below the cheek-bones. Her eyes were darkly ringed. Rather too long at the best of times, her straight nose protruded bleakly from the unfleshed face. She looked ugly, tired and ill. Six months from now her baby would be born. Something that had been a single cell, a cluster of cells, a little sac of tissue, a kind of worm, a potential fish with gills, stirred in her womb and would one day become a man – a grown man, suffering and enjoying, loving and hating, thinking, remembering, imagining. And what had been a blob of jelly within her body would invent a god and worship; what had been a kind of fish would create and, having created, would be-come the battle-ground of disputing good and evil; what had blindly lived in her as a parasitic worm would look at the stars, would listen to music, would read poetry. A thing would grow into a person, a tiny lump of stuff would become a human body, a human mind. The astounding process of creation was going on within her; but Marjorie was conscious only of sickness and lassitude; the mystery for her meant nothing but fatigue and ugliness and a chronic anxiety about the future, pain of the mind as well as discomfort of the body. She had been glad, or at least she had tried to be glad, in spite of her haunting fears of physical and social consequences, when she first recognized the symptoms of her pregnancy. The child, she believed, would bring Walter closer; (he had begun to fade away from her even then). It would arouse in him new feelings which would make up for whatever element it was that seemed to be lacking in his love for her. She dreaded the pain, she dreaded the inevitable difficulties and em-barrassments. But the pains, the difficulties would have been worth while if they purchased a renewal, a strengthening of Walter's attach-ment. In spite of everything, she was glad. And at first her previsions had seemed to be justified. The news that she was going to have a child had quickened his tenderness. For two or three weeks she was happy, she was reconciled to the pains and discomforts. Then, from one day to another, everything was changed; Walter had met that woman. He still did his best, in the intervals of running after Lucy, to keep up a show of solicitude. But she could feel that the solicitude was resentful, that he was tender and attentive out of a sense of duty, that he hated the child for compelling him to be so considerate to its mother. And because he hated it, she too began to hate it. No longer overlaid by happiness, her fears came to the surface, filled her mind. Pain and discomfort – that was all the future held. And meanwhile ugliness, sickness, fatigue. How could she fight her battle when she was in this state?

'Do you love me, Walter?' she suddenly asked.

Walter turned his brown eyes for a moment from the reflected tie and looked into the image of her sad, intently gazing grey ones. He smiled. But if only, he was thinking, she would leave me in peace! He pursed his lips and parted them again in the suggestion of a kiss. But Marjorie did not return his smile. Her face remained unmovingly sad, fixed in an intent anxiety. Her eyes took on a tremulous brightness, and suddenly there were tears on her lashes.

'Couldn't you stay here with me this evening?' she begged, in the teeth of all her heroic resolutions not to apply any sort of exasperating compulsion to his love, to leave him free to do what he wanted.

At the sight of those tears, at the sound of that tremulous and reproachful voice, Walter was filled with an emotion that was at once remorse and resentment; anger, pity, and shame.

'But can't you understand,' that was what he would have liked to say, what he would have said if he had had the courage, 'can't you understand that it isn't the same as it was, that it can't be the same? And perhaps, if the truth be told, it never was what you believed it was – our love, I mean – it never was what I tried to pretend it was. Let's be friends, let's be companions. I like you, I'm very fond of you. But for goodness sake don't envelop me in love, like this; don't force love on me. If you knew how dreadful love seems to somebody who doesn't love, what a violation, what an outrage. ...'

But she was crying. Through her closed eyelids the tears were welling out, drop after drop. Her face was trembling into the grimace of agony. And he was the tormentor. He hated himself. 'But why should I let myself be blackmailed by her tears?' he asked, and, asking, he hated her also. A drop ran down her long nose. 'She has no right to do this sort of thing, no right to be so unreasonable. Why can't she be reasonable?'

'Because she loves me.'

'But I don't want her love, I don't want it.' He felt the anger mounting up within him. She had no business to love him like that;

not now, at any rate. 'It's a blackmail,' he repeated inwardly, 'a black-mail. Why must I be blackmailed by her love and the fact that once I loved too – or did I ever love her, really?'

Marjorie took out a handkerchief and began to wipe her eyes. He felt ashamed of his odious thoughts. But she was the cause of his shame; it was her fault. She ought to have stuck to her husband. They could have had an affair. Afternoons in a studio. It would have been romantic.

'But after all, it was I who insisted on her coming away with me.'

'But she ought to have had the sense to refuse. She ought to have known that it couldn't last for ever.'

But she had done what he had asked her; she had given up every-thing, accepted social discomfort for his sake. Another piece of black-mail. She blackmailed him with sacrifice. He resented the appeal which her sacrifices made to his sense of decency and honour.

'But if *she* had some decency and honour,' he thought, 'she wouldn't exploit mine.'

But there was the baby.

'Why on earth did she ever allow it to come into existence?'

He hated it. It increased his responsibility towards its mother, increased his guiltiness in making her suffer. He looked at her wiping her tear-wet face. Being with child had made her so ugly, so old. How could a woman expect …? But no, no, no! Walter shut his eyes, gave an almost imperceptible shuddering shake of the head. The ignoble thought must be shut out, repudiated.

'How can I think such things?' he asked himself.

'Don't go,' he heard her repeating. How that refined and drawling shrillness got on his nerves! 'Please don't go, Walter.'

There was a sob in her voice. More blackmail. Ah, how could he be so base? And yet, in spite of his shame and, in a sense, because of it, he continued to feel the shameful emotions with an intensity that seemed to increase rather than diminish. His dislike of her grew because he was ashamed of it; the painful feelings of shame and self-hatred, which she caused him to feel, constituted for him yet another ground of dislike. Resentment bred shame, and shame in its turn bred more resentment.

'Oh, why can't she leave me in peace?' He wished it furiously, in-tensely, with an exasperation that was all the more savage for being suppressed. (For he lacked the brutal courage to give it utterance; he was sorry for her, he was fond of her in spite of everything; he was incapable of being openly and frankly cruel – he was cruel only out of weakness, against his will.)

'Why can't she leave me in peace?' He would like her so much more if only she left him in peace; and she herself would be so much happier. Ever so much happier. It would be for her own good. … But suddenly he saw through his own hypocrisy. 'But all the same, why the devil can't she let me do what I want?'

What he wanted? But what he wanted was Lucy Tantamount. And he wanted her against reason, against all his ideals and principles, madly, against his own wishes, even against his own feelings – for he didn't like Lucy; he really hated her. A noble end may justify shameful means. But when the end is shameful, what then? It was for Lucy that he was making Marjorie suffer – Marjorie, who loved him, who had made sacrifices for him, who was unhappy. But her unhappiness was blackmailing him.

'Stay with me this evening,' she implored once more.

There was a part of his mind that joined in her entreaties, that wanted him to give up the party and stay at home. But the other part was stronger. He answered her with lies – half lies, that were worse, for the hypocritically justifying element of truth in them, than frank whole lies.

He put his arm round her. The gesture was in itself a falsehood.

'But my darling,' he protested in the cajoling tone of one who implores a child to behave reasonably, 'I really must go. You see, my father's going to be there.' That was true. Old Bidlake was always at the Tantamounts' parties. 'And I must have a talk with him. About business,' he added vaguely and importantly, releasing with the magical word a kind of smoke-screen of masculine interests between himself and Marjorie. But the lie, he reflected, must be transparently visible through the smoke.

'Couldn't you see him some other time?'

'It's important,' he answered, shaking his head. 'And besides,' he added, forgetting that several excuses are always less convincing than one, 'Lady Edward's inviting an American editor specially for my sake. He might be useful; you know how enormously they pay.' Lady Edward had told him that she would invite the man if he hadn't started back to America – she was afraid he had. 'Quite preposterously much,' he went on, thickening his screen with impersonal irrelevancies. 'It's the only place in the world where it's possible for a writer to be overpaid.' He made an attempt at laughter. 'And I really need a bit of overpaying to make up for all this two-guineas-a-thousand business.' He tightened his embrace, he bent down to kiss her. But Marjorie averted her face. 'Marjorie,' he implored. 'Don't cry. Please.' He felt guilty and unhappy. But oh! why couldn't she leave him in peace, in peace?

'I'm not crying,' she answered. But her cheek was wet and cold to his lips.

'Marjorie, I won't go, if you don't want me to.'

'But I *do* want you to,' she answered, still keeping her face averted.

'You don't. I'll stay.'

'You mustn't.' Marjorie looked at him and made an effort to smile. 'It's only my silliness. It would be stupid to miss your father and that American man.' Returned to him like this, his excuses sounded peculiarly vain and improbable. He winced with a kind of disgust.

'They can wait,' he answered, and there was a note of anger in his voice. He was angry with himself for having made such lying excuses (why couldn't he have told her the crude and brutal truth straight out? she knew it, after all); and he was angry with her for reminding him of them. He would have liked them to fall directly into the pit of oblivion, to be as though they had never been uttered.

'No, no; I insist. I was only being silly. I'm sorry.'

He resisted her at first, refused to go, demanded to stay. Now that there was no danger of his having to stay, he could afford to insist. For Marjorie, it was clear, was serious in her determination that he should go. It was an opportunity for him to be noble and self-sacrificing at a cheap rate, gratis even. What an odious comedy! But he played it. In the end he consented to go, as though he were doing her a special favour by not staying. Marjorie tied his scarf for him, brought him his silk hat and his gloves, kissed him good-bye lightly, with a brave show of gaiety. She had her pride and her code of amorous honour; and in spite of unhappiness, in spite of jealousy, she stuck to her principles – he *ought* to be free; she had no right to interfere with him. And besides it was the best policy not to interfere. At least, she hoped it was the best policy.

Walter shut the door behind him and stepped out into the cool of the night. A criminal escaping from the scene of his crime, escaping from the spectacle of the victim, escaping from compassion and remorse, could not have felt more profoundly relieved. In the street he drew a deep breath. He was free. Free from recollection and anticipation. Free, for an hour or two, to refuse to admit the existence of past or future. Free to live only now and here, in the place where his body happened at each instant to be. Free – but the boast was idle; he went on remembering. Escape was not so easy a matter. Her voice pursued him. 'I insist on your going.' His crime had been a fraud as well as a murder. 'I insist.' How nobly he had protested! How magnanimously given in at last! It was card-sharping on top of cruelty.

'God!' he said almost aloud. 'How could I?' He was astonished at himself as well as disgusted. 'But if only she'd leave me in peace!' he went on. 'Why can't she be reasonable?' The weak and futile anger exploded again within him.

He thought of the time when his wishes had been different. Not to be left in peace by her had once been his whole ambition. He had encouraged her devotion. He remembered the cottage they had lived in, alone with one another, month after month, among the bare downs. What a view over Berkshire! But it was a mile and a half to the nearest village. Oh, the weight of that knapsack full of provisions! The mud when it rained! And that bucket you had to wind up from the well. The well was more than a hundred feet deep. But even when he wasn't doing something tiresome, like winding up the bucket, had it really been very satisfactory? Had he ever really been happy with Marjorie – as happy, at any rate, as he had imagined he was going to be, as he ought to have been in the circumstances? It should have been like *Epipsychidion*; but it wasn't – perhaps because he had too consciously wanted it to be, because he had deliberately tried to model his feelings and their life together on Shelley's poetry.

'One shouldn't take art too literally.' He remembered what his brother-in-law, Philip Quarles, had said one evening, when they were talking about poetry. 'Particularly where love is concerned.'

'Not even if it's true?' Walter had asked.

'It's apt to be too true. Unadulterated, like distilled water. When truth is nothing but the truth, it's unnatural, it's an abstraction that resembles nothing in the real world. In nature there are always so many other irrelevant things mixed up with the essential truth. That's why art moves you – precisely because it's unadulterated with all the irrelevancies of real life. Real orgies are never so exciting as pornographic books. In a volume by Pierre Louys all the girls are young and their figures perfect; there's no hiccoughing or bad breath, no fatigue or boredom, no sudden recollections of unpaid bills or business letters unanswered, to interrupt the raptures. Art gives you the sensation, the thought, the feeling quite pure – chemically pure,

I mean,' he had added with a laugh, 'not morally.'

'But *Epipsychidion* isn't pornography,' Walter had objected.

'No, but it's equally pure from the chemist's point of view. How does that sonnet of Shakespeare's go?

> My mistress' eyes are nothing like the sun;
> Coral is far more red than her lips' red:
> If snow be white, why then her breasts are dun;
> If hairs be wires, black wires grow on her head.
> I have seen roses damask'd, red and white,
> But no such roses see I in her cheeks;
> And in some perfumes is there more delight
> Than in the breath that from my mistress reeks.

And so on. He'd taken the poets too literally and was reacting. Le him be a warning to you.'

Philip had been right, of course. Those months in the cottage hadn't been at all like *Epipsychidion* or *La Maison du Berger*. What with the well and the walk to the village. ... But even if there hadn't been the well and the walk, even if he had had Marjorie unadulterated, would it have been any better? It might even have been worse. Marjorie unadulterated might have been worse than Marjorie tempered by irrelevancies.

That refinement of hers, for example, that rather cold virtuousness, so bloodless and spiritual – from a distance and theoretically he admired. But in practice and close at hand? It was with that virtue, that refined, cultured, bloodless spirituality that he had fallen in love – with that and with her unhappiness; for Carling was unspeakable. Pity made him a knight errant. Love, he had then believed (for he was only twenty-two at the time, ardently pure, with the adolescent purity of sexual desires turned inside out, just down from Oxford and stuffed with poetry and the lucubrations of philosophers and mystics), love was talk, love was spiritual communion and companionship. That was real love. The sexual business was only an irrelevancy, unavoidable, because unfortunately human beings had bodies, but to be kept as far as possible in the background. Ardently pure with the ardour of young desires taught artificially to burn on the side of the angels, he had admired that refined and quiet purity which, in Marjorie, was the product of a natural coldness, a congenitally low vitality.

'You're so good,' he had said. 'It seems to come to you so easily. I wish I could be good, like you.'

14

It was the equivalent, but he did not realize it, of wishing himself half dead. Under the shy, diffident, sensitive skin of him, he was ardently alive. It was indeed hard for him to be good, as Marjorie was good. But he tried. And meanwhile, he admired her goodness and purity. And he was touched – at least until it bored and exasperated him – by her devotion to him, he was flattered by her admiration.

Walking now towards Chalk Farm station he suddenly remembered that story his father used to tell about an Italian chauffeur he had once talked to about love. (The old man had a genius for getting people to talk; all sorts of people, even servants, even workmen. Walter envied him the talent.) Some women, according to the chauffeur, are like wardrobes. *Sono come cassettoni.* How richly old Bidlake used to tell the anecdote! They may be as lovely as you like; but what's the point of a lovely wardrobe in your arms? What on earth's the point? (And Marjorie, Walter reflected, wasn't even really good looking.) 'Give me,' said the chauffeur, 'the other kind, even if they're ugly. My girl,' he had confided, 'is the other kind. *È un frullino, proprio un frullino* – a regular egg-whisk.' And the old man would twinkle like a jovial, wicked old satyr behind his monocle. Stiff wardrobes or lively egg-whisks? Walter had to admit that his preferences were the same as the chauffeur's. At any rate, he knew by personal experience that (whenever 'real' love was being tempered by the sexual irrelevancies) he didn't much like the wardrobe kind of woman. At a distance, theoretically, purity and goodness and refined spirituality were admirable. But in practice and close to they were less appealing. And from someone who does not appeal to one, even devotion, even the flattery of admiration are unbearable. Confusedly and simultaneously he hated Marjorie for her patient, martyred coldness; he accused himself of swinish sensuality. His love for Lucy was mad and shameful, but Marjorie was bloodless and half dead. He was at once justified and without excuse. But more without excuse, all the same; more without excuse. They were low, those sensual feelings; they were ignoble. Egg-whisk and chest of drawers – could anything be more base and ignoble than such a classification? In imagination he heard his father's rich and fleshy laugh. Horrible! Walter's whole conscious life had been orientated in opposition to his father, in opposition to the old man's jolly, careless sensuality. Consciously he had always been on the side of his mother, on the side of purity, refinement, the spirit. But his blood was at least half his father's. And now two years of Marjorie had made him consciously dislike cold virtue. He consciously disliked it, even though at the same time he was still ashamed of his dislike, ashamed of what he regarded as his beastly sensual desires, ashamed of his love for Lucy. But oh, if only Marjorie would leave him in peace! If only she'd refrain from clamouring for a return to the unwelcome love she persisted in forcing on him! If only she'd stop being so dreadfully devoted! He could give her friendship – for he liked her, genuinely; she was so good and kind, so loyal and devoted. He'd be glad of her friendship in return. But love – that was suffocating. And when, imagining she was fighting the other woman with her own weapons, she did violence to her own virtuous coldness and tried to win him back by the ardour of her caresses – oh, it was terrible, really terrible.

And then, he went on to reflect, she was really rather a bore with her heavy, insensitive earnestness. Really rather stupid in spite of her culture – because of it perhaps. The culture was genuine all right; she had read the books, she remembered them. But did she understand them? *Could* she understand them? The remarks with which she broke her long, long silences, the cultured, earnest remarks – how heavy they were, how humourless and without understanding! She was wise to be so silent; silence is as full of potential wisdom and wit as the unhewn marble of great sculpture. The silent bear no witness against themselves. Marjorie knew how to listen well and sympathetically. And when she did break silence, half her utterances were quotations. For Marjorie had a retentive memory and had formed the habit of learning the great thoughts and the purple passages by heart. It had taken Walter some time to discover the heavy, pathetically uncomprehending stupidity that underlay the silence and the quotations. And when he discovered, it was too late.

He thought of Carling. A drunkard *and* religious. Always chattering away about chasubles and saints and the Immaculate Conception, and at the same time a nasty drunken pervert. If the man hadn't been quite so detestably disgusting, if he hadn't made Marjorie quite so wretched – what then? Walter imagined his freedom. He wouldn't have pitied, he wouldn't have loved. He remembered Marjorie's red and swollen eyes after one of those disgusting scenes with Carling. The dirty brute!

'And what about me?' he suddenly thought.

He knew that the moment the door had shut behind him, Marjorie had started to cry. Carling at least had the excuse of whisky. Forgive them, for they know not what they do. He himself was never anything but sober. At this moment, he knew, she was crying.

'I ought to go back,' he said to himself. But instead, he quickened his pace till he was almost running down the street. It was a flight from his conscience and at the same time a hastening towards his desire.

'I ought to go back, I ought.'

He hurried on, hating her because he had made her so unhappy.

A man looking into a tobacconist's window suddenly stepped backwards as he was passing. Walter violently collided with him.

'Sorry,' he said automatically, and hurried on without looking round.

'Where yer going?' the man shouted after him angrily. 'Wotcher think you're doing? Being a bloody Derby winner?'

Two loitering street boys whooped with ferociously derisive mirth.

'You in yer top 'at,' the man pursued contemptuously, hating the uniformed gentleman.

The right thing would have been to turn round and give the fellow back better than he gave. His father would have punctured him with a word. But for Walter there was only flight. He dreaded these encounters, he was frightened of the lower classes. The noise of the man's abuse faded in his ears.

Odious! He shuddered. His thoughts returned to Marjorie.

'Why can't she be reasonable?' he said to himself. 'Just reasonable. If only at least she had something to do, something to keep her occupied.'

She had too much time to think, that was the trouble with Marjorie. Too much time to think about him. Though after all it was his fault; it was he who had robbed her of her occupation and made her focus her mind exclusively on himself. She had taken a partnership in a decorator's shop when he first knew her; one of those lady-like. artistic, amateurish decorating establishments in Kensington. Lampshades and the companionship of the young women who painted them and above all devotion to Mrs Cole, the senior partner, were Marjorie's compensations for a wretched marriage. She had created a little world of her own, apart from Carling; a feminine world, with something of the girl's school about it, where she could talk about clothes and shops, and listen to gossip, and indulge in what schoolgirls call a 'pash' for an elder woman, and imagine in the intervals that she was doing part of the world's work and helping on the cause of Art.

17

Walter had persuaded her to give it all up. Not without difficulty, however. For her happiness in being devoted to Mrs Cole, in having a sentimental 'pash' for her, was almost a compensation for her misery with Carling. But Carling turned out to be more than Mrs Cole could compensate for. Walter offered what the lady perhaps could not, and certainly did not wish to, provide – a place of refuge, protection, financial support. Besides, Walter was a man, and a man ought, by tradition, to be loved, even when, as Walter had finally concluded about Marjorie, one doesn't really like men and is only naturally attuned to the company of women. (The effect of literature again! He remembered Philip Quarles's comments on the disastrous influence which art can exercise on life.) Yes, he was a man; but 'different', as she had never tired of telling him, from ordinary men. He had accepted his 'difference' as a flattering distinction, then. But was it? He wondered. Anyhow, 'different' she had then found him and so was able to get the best of both worlds – a man who yet wasn't a man. Charmed by Walter's persuasions, driven by Carling's brutalities, she had consented to abandon the shop and with it Mrs Cole, whom Walter detested as a bullying, slave-driving, blood-sucking embodiment of female will.

'You're too good to be an amateur upholsterer,' he had flattered her out of the depths of a then genuine belief in her intellectual capacities.

She should help him in some unspecified way with his literary work, she should write herself. Under his influence she had taken to writing essays and short stories. But they were obviously no good. From having been encouraging, he became reticent; he said no more about her efforts. In a little while Marjorie abandoned the unnatural and futile occupation. She had nothing after that but Walter. He became the reason of her existence, the foundation on which her whole life was established. The foundation was moving away from under her.

'If only,' thought Walter, 'she'd leave me in peace!'

He turned into the Underground station. At the entrance a man was selling the evening papers. SOCIALIST ROBBERY SCHEME. FIRST READING. The words glared out from the placard. Glad of an excuse to distract his mind Walter bought a paper. The Liberal-Labour Government's Bill for the nationalization of the mines had passed its first reading by the usual majority. Walter read the news with pleasure. His political opinions were advanced. Not so the opinions of the proprietor of the evening paper. The language of the leading article was savagely violent.

'The ruffians,' thought Walter as he read it. The article evoked in him a stimulating enthusiasm for all that it assailed, a delightful hatred for Capitalists and Reactionaries. The barriers of his individuality were momentarily thrown down, the personal complexities were abolished. Possessed by the joy of political battle, he overflowed his boundaries, he became, so to speak, larger than himself – larger and simpler.

'The ruffians,' he repeated, thinking of the oppressors, the monopolizers.

At Camden Town station a wizened little man with a red handkerchief round his neck took the seat next to his. The stink of the old man's pipe was so suffocating, that Walter looked up the car to see if there were not another vacant seat. There was, as it happened; but on second thoughts, he decided not to move. To retire from the stink would seem too offensively pointed, might occasion comment from the stinker. The acrid smoke rasped his throat; he coughed.

'One should be loyal to one's tastes and instincts,' Philip Quarles used to say. 'What's the good of a philosophy with a major premiss that isn't the rationalization of your feelings? If you've never had a religious experience, it's folly to believe in God. You might as well believe in the excellence of oysters, when you can't eat them without being sick.'

A whiff of stale sweat came up with the nicotine fumes to Walter's nostrils. 'The Socialists call it Nationalization,' he read in his paper; 'but the rest of us have a shorter and homelier name for what they propose to do. That name is Theft.' But at least it was theft from thieves and for the benefit of their victims. The little old man leaned forward and spat, cautiously and perpendicularly, between his feet. With the heel of his boot he spread the gob over the floor. Walter looked away; he wished that he could personally like the oppressed and personally hate the rich oppressors. One should be loyal to one's tastes and instincts. But one's tastes and instincts were accidents. There were eternal principles. But if the axiomatic principles didn't happen to be your personal major premiss …?

And suddenly he was nine years old and walking with his mother in the fields near Gattenden. Each of them carried a bunch of cowslips. They must have been up to Batt's Corner; it was the only place where cowslips grew in the neighbourhood.

'We'll stop for a minute and see poor Wetherington,' his mother said. 'He's very ill.' She knocked at a cottage door.

Wetherington had been the under-gardener at the Hall; but for the past month he had not been working. Walter remembered him as a pale, thin man with a cough, not at all communicative. He was not much interested in Wetherington. A woman opened the door. 'Good afternoon, Mrs Wetherington.' They were shown in.

Wetherington was lying in bed propped up with pillows. His face was terrible. A pair of enormous, large-pupilled eyes stared out of cavernous sockets. Stretched over the starting bones, the skin was white and clammy with sweat. But almost more appalling even than the face was the neck, the unbelievably thin neck. And from the sleeves of his nightshirt projected two knobbed sticks, his arms, with a pair of immense skeleton hands fastened to the end of them, like rakes at the end of their slender hafts. And then the smell in that sick-room! The windows were tightly shut, a fire burned in the little grate. The air was hot and heavy with a horrible odour of stale sick breath and the exhalations of a sick body – an old inveterate smell that seemed to have grown sickeningly sweetish with long ripening in the pent-up heat. A new, fresh smell, however pungently disgusting, would have been less horrible. It was the inveterateness, the sweet decaying over-ripeness of this sick-room smell that made it so peculiarly unbearable. Walter shuddered even now to think of it. He lit a cigarette to disinfect his memory. He had been brought up on baths and open windows. The first time that, as a child, he was taken to church, the stuffiness, the odour of humanity made him sick; he had to be hurried out. His mother did not take him to church again. Perhaps we're brought up too wholesomely and aseptically, he thought. An education that results in one's feeling sick in the company of one's fellow-men, one's brothers – can it be good? He would have liked to love them. But love does not flourish in an atmosphere that nauseates the lover with an uncontrollable disgust.

In Wetherington's sick-room even pity found it hard to flourish. He sat there, while his mother talked to the dying man and his wife, gazing, reluctant but compelled by the fascination of horror, at the ghastly skeleton in the bed and breathing through his bunch of cowslips the warm and sickening air. Even through the fresh delicious scent of the cowslips he could smell the inveterate odours of the sick-room. He felt almost no pity, only horror, fear, and disgust. And even when Mrs Wetherington began to cry, turning her face away so that the sick man should not see her tears, he felt not pitiful so much as uncomfortable, embarrassed. The spectacle of her grief only made him more urgently long to escape, to get out of that horrible room into the pure enormous air and the sunshine.

He felt ashamed of these emotions as he remembered them. But that was how he had felt, how he still felt. 'One should be loyal to one's instincts.' No, not to all, not to the bad ones; one should resist these. But they were not so easily overcome. The old man in the next seat relit his pipe. He remembered that he had held every breath for as long as he possibly could, so as not to have to draw in and smell the tainted air too often. A deep breath through the cowslips; then he counted forty before he let it out again and inhaled another. The old man once more leaned forward and spat. 'The idea that nationalization will increase the prosperity of the workers is entirely fallacious. During the past years the tax-payer has learned to his cost the meaning of bureaucratic control. If the workers imagine ...' He shut his eyes and saw the sick-room. When the time came to say good-bye, he had shaken the skeleton hand. It lay there, unmoving, on the bed-clothes; he slipped his fingers underneath those dead and bony ones, lifted the hand a moment and let it fall again.

It was cold and wettish to the touch. Turning away, he surreptitiously wiped his palm on his coat. He let out his long-contained breath with an explosive sigh and inhaled another lungful of the sickening air. It was the last he had to take; his mother was already moving towards the door. Her little Pekingese frisked round her, barking.

'Be quiet, T'ang!' she said in her clear, beautiful voice. She was perhaps the only person in England, he now reflected, who regularly pronounced the apostrophe in T'ang.

They walked home by the footpath across the fields. Fantastic and improbable as a little Chinese dragon, T'ang ran on ahead of them bounding lightly over what were to him enormous obstacles. His feathery tail fluttered in the wind. Sometimes, when the grass was very long he sat up on his little fat rump as though he were begging for sugar, and looked out with his round bulgy eyes over the tussocks, aking his bearings.

Under the bright dappled sky Walter had felt like a reprieved prisoner. He ran, he shouted. His mother walked slowly, without speaking. Every now and then she halted for a moment and shut her eyes. It was a habit she had, when she felt pensive or perplexed. She was often perplexed, Walter reflected, smiling tenderly to himself. Poor Wetherington must have perplexed her a great deal. He remembered how often she had halted on their way home.

'Do hurry up, mother,' he had shouted impatiently. 'We shall be late for tea.'

Cook had baked scones for tea and there was yesterday's plum cake and a newly opened pot of Tiptree's cherry jam.

'One should be loyal to one's tastes and instincts.' But an accident of birth had determined them for him. Justice was eternal; charity and brotherly love were beautiful in spite of the old man's pipe and Wetherington's sick-room. Beautiful precisely because of such things. The train slowed down. Leicester Square. He stepped out on to the platform and made his way towards the lifts. But the personal major premiss, he was thinking, is hard to deny; and the major premiss that isn't personal is hard, however excellent, to believe in. Honour, fidelity – these were good things. But the personal major premiss of his present philosophy was that Lucy Tantamount was the most beautiful, the most desirable. ...

'All tickets, please!'

The debate threatened to start again. Deliberately he stifled it, the liftman slammed the gates. The lift ascended. In the street he hailed a taxi.

'Tantamount House, Pall Mall.'

Chapter Two

THREE Italian ghosts unobtrusively haunt the eastern end of Pall Mall. The wealth of newly industrialized England and the enthusiasm, the architectural genius, of Charles Barry called them up out of the past and their native sunshine. Under the encrusting grime of the Reform Club the eye of faith recognizes something agreeably reminiscent of the Farnese Palace. A few yards further down the street, Sir Charles's recollections of the house that Raphael designed for the Pandolfini loom up through the filmy London air – the Travellers' Club. And between them, austerely classical, grim like a prison and black with soot, rises a smaller (but still enormous) version of the Cancelleria. It is Tantamount House.

Barry designed it in 1839. A hundred workmen laboured for a year or two. And the third marquess paid the bills. They were heavy; but the suburbs of Leeds and Sheffield had begun to spread over the land which his ancestors had stolen from the monasteries three hundred years before. 'The Catholic Church, instructed by the Holy Spirit, has from the sacred writings and the ancient traditions of the Fathers, taught that there is a Purgatory and that the souls there detained are helped by the suffrages of the faithful, but principally by the acceptable sacrifice of the altar.' Rich men with uneasy consciences had left their land to the monks that their souls might be helped through Purgatory by a perpetual performance of the acceptable sacrifice of the altar. But Henry VIII had lusted after a young woman and desired a son; and because Pope Clement VII was in the power of Henry's first wife's daughter's cousin, he would not grant him a divorce. The monasteries were in consequence suppressed. An army of beggars, of paupers, of the infirm died miserably of hunger. But the Tantamounts acquired some scores of square miles of ploughland, forest, and pasture. A few years later, under Edward VI, they stole the property of two disestablished grammar schools; children remained uneducated that the Tantamounts might be rich. They farmed their land scientifically with a view to the highest profit. Their contemporaries regarded them as 'men that live as though there were no God at all, men that would have all in their own hands, men that would leave nothing to others, men that be never satisfied.' From the pulpit of St Paul's, Lever accused them of having 'offended God, and brought a common wealth into a common ruin.' The Tantamounts were unperturbed. The land was theirs, the money came in regularly.

The corn was sown, grew, and was harvested, again and again. The beasts were born, fattened, and went to the slaughter. The ploughmen, the shepherds, the cow-herds laboured from before dawn till sunset, year after year, until they died. Their children took their places. Tantamount succeeded Tantamount. Elizabeth made them barons; they became viscounts under Charles II, earls under William and Mary, marquesses under George II. They married heiress after heiress – ten square miles of Nottinghamshire, fifty thousand pounds, two streets in Bloomsbury, half a brewery, a bank, a plantation and six hundred slaves in Jamaica. Meanwhile, obscure men were devising machines which made things more rapidly than they could be made by hand. Villages were transformed into towns, towns into great cities. On what had been the Tantamounts' pasture and ploughland, houses and factories were built. Under the grass of their meadows half-naked men hewed at the black and shining coal face. The laden trucks were hauled by little boys and women. From Peru the droppings of ten thousand generations of sea-gulls were brought in ships to enrich their fields. The corn grew thicker; the new mouths were fed. And year by year the Tantamounts grew richer and richer and the souls of the Black Prince's pious contemporaries continued, no doubt, to writhe, unaided as they were by any acceptable sacrifice of the altar, in the unquenchable fires of Purgatory. The money that might, if suitably applied, have shortened their term among the flames served, among other things, to call into existence a model of the Papal Chancellery in Pall Mall.

The interior of Tantamount House is as nobly Roman as its façade. Round a central quadrangle run two tiers of open arcades with an attic, lit by small square windows, above. But instead of being left open to the sky, the quadrangle is covered by a glass roof, which converts it into an immense hall rising the whole height of the building. With its arcades and gallery it makes a very noble room – but too large, too public, too much like a swimming bath or a roller-skating rink to be much lived in. To-night, however, it was justifying its existence. Lady Edward Tantamount was giving one of her musical parties. The floor was crowded with seated guests and in the hollow architectural space above them the music intricately pulsed.

'What a pantomime!' said old John Bidlake to his hostess. 'My dear Hilda, you really must look.'

24

'Sh-sh!' Lady Edward protested behind her feather fan. 'You mustn't interrupt the music. Besides I *am* looking.'

Her whisper was colonial and the r's of 'interrupt' were rolled far back in the throat; for Lady Edward came from Montreal and her mother had been a Frenchwoman. In 1897 the British Association met in Canada. Lord Edward Tantamount read a much-admired paper to the Biological Section. 'One of the coming men,' the professors had called him. But for those who weren't professors, a Tantamount and a millionaire might be regarded as already having arrived. Hilda Sutton was most decidedly of that opinion. Lord Edward was the guest, during his stay in Montreal, of Hilda's father. She took her opportunity. The British Association went home; but Lord Edward remained in Canada.

'Believe me,' Hilda had once confided to a friend, 'I never took so much interest in osmosis before or since.'

The interest in osmosis roused Lord Edward's attention. He became aware of a fact which he had not previously noticed; that Hilda was exceedingly pretty. Hilda also knew her woman's business. Her task was not difficult. At forty Lord Edward was in all but intellect a kind of child. In the laboratory, at his desk, he was as old as science itself. But his feelings, his intuitions, his instincts were those of a little boy. Unexercised, the greater part of his spiritual being had never developed. He was a kind of child, but with his childish habits ingrained by forty years of living. Hilda helped him over his paralysing twelve-year-old shynesses, and whenever terror prevented him from making the necessary advances, came half or even all the way to meet him. His ardours were boyish – at once violent and timid, desperate and dumb. Hilda talked for two and was discreetly bold. Discreetly – for Lord Edward's notions of how young girls should behave were mainly derived from the *Pickwick Papers*. Boldness undisguised would have alarmed him, would have driven him away. Hilda kept up all the appearance of Dickensian young-girlishness, but contrived at the same time to make all the advances, create all the opportunities and lead the conversation into all the properly amorous channels. She had her reward. In the spring of 1898 she was Lady Edward Tantamount.

'But I assure you,' she had once said to John Bidlake, quite angrily – for he had been making fun of poor Edward, 'I'm genuinely fond of him, genuinely.'

'In your own way, no doubt,' mocked Bidlake. 'In your own way.

But you must admit it's a good thing it isn't everybody's way. Just look at yourself in that mirror.'

She looked and saw the reflection of her naked body lying, half sunk in deep cushions, on a divan.

'Beast!' she said. 'But it doesn't make any difference to my being fond of him.'

'Oh, not to your particular way of being fond, I'm sure.' He laughed. 'But I repeat that it's perhaps a good thing that –'

She put her hand over his mouth. That was a quarter of a century ago. Hilda had been married five years and was thirty. Lucy was a child of four. John Bidlake was forty-seven, at the height of his powers and reputation as a painter; handsome, huge, exuberant, careless; a great laugher, a great worker, a great eater, drinker, and taker of virginities.

'Painting's a branch of sensuality,' he retorted to those who reproved him for his way of life. 'Nobody can paint a nude who hasn't learnt the human body by heart with his hands and his lips and his own body. I take my art seriously. I'm unremitting in my preliminary studies.' And the skin would tighten in laughing wrinkles round his monocle, his eyes would twinkle like a genial satyr's.

To Hilda, John Bidlake brought the revelation of her own body, her physical potentialities. Lord Edward was only a kind of child, a fossil boy preserved in the frame of a very large middle-aged man. Intellectually, in the laboratory, he understood the phenomena of sex. But in practice and emotionally he was a child, a fossil mid-Victorian child, preserved intact, with all the natural childish timidities and all the taboos acquired from the two beloved and very virtuous maiden aunts, who had taken the place of his dead mother, all the amazing principles and prejudices sucked in with the humours of Mr Pickwick and Micawber. He loved his young wife, but loved her as a fossil child of the sixties might love – timidly and very apologetically; apologizing for his ardours, apologizing for his body, apologizing for hers. Not in so many words, of course; for the fossil child was dumb with shyness; but by a silent ignoring, a silent pretending that the bodies weren't really involved in the ardours, which anyhow didn't really exist. His love was one long tacit apology for itself; and being nothing more than an apology was therefore quite inexcusable. Love must justify itself by its results in intimacy of mind and body, in warmth, in tender contact, in pleasure. If it has to be justified from outside, it is thereby proved a thing without justification. John Bidlake made no apologies for the kind of love he had to offer. So far as it went, it entirely justified itself. A healthy sensualist, he made his love straightforwardly, naturally, with the good animal gusto of a child of nature.

'Don't expect me to talk about the stars and madonna lilies and the cosmos,' he said. 'They're not my line. I don't believe in them. I believe in –' And his language became what a mysterious convention has decreed to be unprintable.

It was a love without pretensions, but warm, natural, and, being natural, good so far as it went – a decent, good-humoured, happy sensuality. To Hilda, who had never known anything but a fossil child's reticent apology for love, it was a revelation. Things which had been dead in her came alive. She discovered herself, rapturously. But not too rapturously. She never lost her head. If she had lost her head, she might have lost Tantamount House and the Tantamount millions and the Tantamount title as well. She had no intention of losing these things. So she kept her head, coolly and deliberately; kept it high and secure above the tumultuous raptures, like a rock above the waves. She enjoyed herself, but never to the detriment of her social position. She could look on at her own enjoyment; her cool head, her will to retain her social position remained apart from and above the turmoil. John Bidlake approved the way she made the best of both worlds.

'Thank God, Hilda,' he had often said, 'you're a sensible woman.'

Women who believed the world well lost for love were apt to be a terrible nuisance, as he knew only too well by personal experience. He liked women; love was an indispensable enjoyment. But nobody was worth involving oneself in tiresome complications for, nothing was worth messing up one's life for. With the women who hadn't been sensible and had taken love too seriously, John Bidlake had been ruthlessly cruel. It was the battle of 'all for love' against 'anything for a quiet life.' John Bidlake always won. Fighting for his quiet life, he drew the line at no sort of frightfulness.

Hilda Tantamount was as much attached to the quiet life as John himself. Their affair had lasted, pleasantly enough, for a space of years and slowly faded out of existence. They had been good lovers, they remained good friends – conspirators, even, people called them, mischievous conspirators leagued together to amuse themselves at the world's expense. They were laughing now. Or rather old John, who hated music, was laughing alone. Lady Edward was trying to preserve the decorums.

'You simply must be quiet,' she whispered.

'But you're not realizing how incredibly comic it is,' Bidlake insisted.

'Sh-sh.'

'But I'm *whispering*.' This continual shushing annoyed him.

'Like a lion.'

'I can't help that,' he answered crossly. When he took the trouble to whisper, he assumed that his voice was inaudible to all but the person to whom his remarks were addressed. He did not like to be told that what he chose to assume as true was not true. 'Lion, indeed!' he muttered indignantly. But his face suddenly brightened again. 'Look!' he said. 'Here's another late arrival. What's the betting she'll do the same as all the others?'

'Sh-sh,' Lady Edward repeated.

But John Bidlake paid no attention to her. He was looking in the direction of the door, where the latest of the late-comers was still standing, torn between the desire to disappear unobtrusively into the silent crowd and the social duty of making her arrival known to her hostess. She looked about her in embarrassment. Lady Edward hailed her over the heads of the intervening crowd with a wave of her long feather and a smile. The late arrival smiled back, blew a kiss, laid a finger to her lips, pointed to an empty chair at the other side of the room, threw out both hands in a little gesture that was meant to express apologies for being late and despairing regret at being unable in the circumstances to come and speak to Lady Edward, then shrugging up her shoulders and shrinking into herself so as to occupy the smallest possible amount of space, tiptoed with extraordinary precautions down the gangway towards the vacant seat.

Bidlake was in ecstasies of merriment. He had echoed the poor lady's every gesture as she made it. Her blown kiss he had returned with extravagant interest, and when she laid a finger to her lips, he had covered his mouth with a whole hand. He had repeated her gesture of regret, grotesquely magnifying it until it expressed a ludicrous despair. And when she tiptoed away, he began to count on his fingers, to make the gestures that, in Naples, avert the evil eye, and to tap his forehead. He turned to Lady Edward in triumph.

'I told you so,' he whispered, and his whole face was wrinkled with suppressed laughter. 'It's like being in a deaf and dumb asylum.

Or talking to pygmies in Central Africa.' He opened his mouth and pointed into it with a stretched forefinger; he went through the motions of drinking from a glass. 'Me hungly,' he said, 'me velly velly thirsty.'

Lady Edward flapped her ostrich at him.

Meanwhile the music played on – Bach's Suite in B minor, for flute and strings. Young Tolley conducted with his usual inimitable grace, bending in swan-like undulations from the loins, and tracing luscious arabesques on the air with his waving arms, as though he were dancing to the music. A dozen anonymous fiddlers and cellists scraped at his bidding. And the great Pongileoni glueily kissed his flute. He blew across the mouth hole and a cylindrical air column vibrated; Bach's meditations filled the Roman quadrangle. In the opening *largo* John Sebastian had, with the help of Pongileoni's snout and the air column, made a statement: There are grand things in the world, noble things; there are men born kingly; there are real conquerors, intrinsic lords of the earth. But of an earth that is, oh! complex and multitudinous, he had gone on to reflect in the fugal allegro. You seem to have found the truth; clear, definite, unmistakable, it is announced by the violins; you have it, you triumphantly hold it. But it slips out of your grasp to present itself in a new aspect among the cellos and yet again in terms of Pongileoni's vibrating air column. The parts live their separate lives; they touch, their paths cross, they combine for a moment to create a seemingly final and perfected harmony, only to break apart again. Each is always alone and separate and individual. 'I am I,' asserts the violin; 'the world revolves round me.' 'Round me,' calls the cello. 'Round me,' the flute insists. And all are equally right and equally wrong; and none of them will listen to the others.

In the human fugue there are eighteen hundred million parts. The resultant noise means something perhaps to the statistician, nothing to the artist. It is only by considering one or two parts at a time that the artist can understand anything. Here, for example, is one particular part; and John Sebastian puts the case. The Rondeau begins, exquisitely and simply melodious, almost a folk-song. It is a young girl singing to herself of love, in solitude, tenderly mournful. A young girl singing among the hills, with the clouds drifting overhead. But solitary as one of the floating clouds, a poet had been listening to her song. The thoughts that it provoked in him are the Sarabande that follows the Rondeau. His is a slow and lovely meditation on the beauty (in spite of squalor and stupidity), the profound goodness (in spite of all the evil), the oneness (in spite of such bewildering diversity) of the world. It is a beauty, a goodness, a unity that no intellectual research can discover, that analysis dispels, but of whose reality the spirit is from time to time suddenly and overwhelmingly convinced. A girl singing to herself under the clouds suffices to create the certitude. Even a fine morning is enough. Is it illusion or the revelation of profoundest truth? Who knows? Pongileoni blew, the fiddlers drew their rosined horse-hair across the stretched intestines of lambs; through the long Sarabande the poet slowly meditated his lovely and consoling certitude.

'This music is beginning to get rather tedious,' John Bidlake whispered to his hostess. 'Is it going to last much longer?'

Old Bidlake had no taste or talent for music, and he had the frankness to say so. He could afford to be frank. When one can paint as well as John Bidlake, why should one pretend to like music, when in fact one doesn't? He looked over the seated audience and smiled.

'They look as though they were in church,' he said.

Lady Edward raised her fan protestingly.

'Who's that little woman in black,' he went on, 'rolling her eyes and swaying her body like St Teresa in an ecstasy?'

'Fanny Logan,' Lady Edward whispered back. 'But do keep quiet.'

'People talk of the tribute vice pays to virtue,' John Bidlake went on, incorrigibly. 'But everything's permitted nowadays – there's no more need of moral hypocrisy. There's only intellectual hypocrisy now. The tribute philistinism pays to art, what? Just look at them all paying it – in pious grimaces and religious silence!'

'You can be thankful they pay *you* in guineas,' said Lady Edward. 'And now I absolutely insist that you should hold your tongue.'

Bidlake made a gesture of mock terror and put his hand over his mouth. Tolley voluptuously waved his arms; Pongileoni blew, the fiddlers scraped. And Bach, the poet, meditated of truth and beauty.

Fanny Logan felt the tears coming into her eyes. She was easily moved, especially by music; and when she felt an emotion, she did not try to repress it, but abandoned herself whole-heartedly to it. How beautiful this music was, how sad, and yet how comforting! She felt it within her, as a current of exquisite feeling, running smoothly but irresistibly through all the labyrinthine intricacies of her being. Even her body shook and swayed in time with the pulse and undulation of the melody. She thought of her husband; the memory of him came to her on the current of the music, of darling, darling Eric, dead now almost two years; dead, and still so young. The tears came faster. She wiped them away. The music was infinitely sad; and yet it consoled. It admitted everything, so to speak – poor Eric's dying before his time, the pain of his illness, his reluctance to go – it admitted everything. It expressed the whole sadness of the world, and from the depths of that sadness it was able to affirm – deliberately, quietly, without protesting too much – that everything was in some way right, acceptable. It included the sadness within some vaster, more comprehensive happiness. The tears kept welling up into Mrs Logan's eyes; but they were somehow happy tears, in spite of her sadness. She would have liked to tell Polly, her daughter, what she was feeling. But Polly was sitting in another row. Mrs Logan could see the back of her head, two rows further forward, and her slim little neck with the pearls that darling Eric had given her on her eighteenth birthday, only a few months before he died. And suddenly, as though she had felt that her mother was looking at her, as though she understood what she was feeling, Polly turned round and gave her a quick smile. Mrs Logan's sad and musical happiness was complete.

Her mother's were not the only eyes that looked in Polly's direction. Advantageously placed behind and to one side of her, Hugo Brockle admiringly studied her profile. How lovely she was! He was wondering whether he would have the courage to tell her that they had played together in Kensington Gardens when they were children. He would come up to her when the music was over and boldly say: 'We were introduced in our perambulators, you know.' Or, if he wanted to be more unconventionally witty, 'You're the person who hit me on the head with a battledore.'

Looking restlessly round the room, John Bidlake had suddenly caught sight of Mary Betterton. Yes, Mary Betterton – that monster! He put his hand under his chair, he touched wood. Whenever John Bidlake saw something unpleasant, he always felt safer if he could touch wood. He didn't believe in God, of course; he liked to tell disobliging stories about the clergy. But wood, wood – there was something about wood. … And to think that he had been in love with her, wildly, twenty, twenty-two, he dared not think how many years ago. How fat, how old and hideous! His hand crept down again to the chair leg. He averted his eyes and tried to think of something that wasn't Mary Betterton. But the memories of the time when Mary had been young imposed themselves upon him. He still used to ride then. The image of himself on a black horse, of Mary on a bay, rose up before him. They had often gone riding in those days. It was the time he was painting the third and best of his groups of 'Bathers'. What a picture, by God! Mary was already a little too plump for some tastes, even then. Not for his; he had never objected to plumpness. These women nowadays, wanting to look like drain-pipes. ... He looked at her again for a moment and shuddered. He hated her for being so repulsive, for having once been so charming. And he was the best part of twenty years her senior.

Chapter Three

Two flights up, between the *piano nobile* and the servants' quarters under the roof, Lord Edward Tantamount was busy in his laboratory.

The younger Tantamounts were generally military. But the heir being a cripple, Lord Edward's father had destined him for the political career, which the eldest sons had always traditionally begun in the Commons and continued majestically in the Lords. Hardly had Lord Edward come of age, when he was given a constituency to nurse. He nursed it dutifully. But oh, how he hated public speaking! And when one met a potential voter, what on earth was one to say? And he couldn't even remember the main items in the Conservative party programme, much less feel enthusiastic about them. Decidedly, politics were not his line.

'But what *are* you interested in?' his father had asked. And the trouble was that Lord Edward didn't know. Going to concerts was about the only thing he thoroughly enjoyed. But obviously, one couldn't spend one's life going to concerts. The fourth marquess could not conceal his anger and disappointment. 'The boy's an imbecile,' he said, and Lord Edward himself was inclined to agree. He was good for nothing, a failure; the world had no place for him There were times when he thought of suicide.

'If only he'd sow a few wild oats!' his father had complained. But the young man was, if possible, even less interested in debauchery than in politics. 'And he's not even a sportsman,' the accusation continued. It was true. The massacre of birds, even in the company of the Prince of Wales, left Lord Edward quite unmoved, except perhaps by a faint disgust. He preferred to sit at home and read, vaguely, desultorily, a little of everything. But even reading seemed to him unsatisfactory. The best that could be said of it was that it kept his mind from brooding and killed time. But what was the good of that? Killing time with a book was not intrinsically much better than killing pheasants and time with a gun. He might go on reading like this for the rest of his days; but it would never help him to achieve anything.

On the afternoon of April 18th, 1887, he was sitting in the library at Tantamount House, wondering whether life was worth living and whether drowning were preferable, as a mode of dying, to shooting. It was the day that *The Times* had published the forged letter, supposed to be Parnell's, condoning the Phœnix Park murders. The fourth marquess had been in a state of apoplectic agitation ever since breakfast. At the clubs men talked of nothing else. 'I suppose it's very important,' Lord Edward kept saying to himself. But he found it impossible to take much interest either in Parnellism or in crime. After listening for a little to what people were saying at the club, he went home in despair. The library door was open; he entered and dropped into a chair, feeling utterly exhausted as though he had come in from a thirty-mile walk. 'I must be an idiot,' he assured himself, when he thought of other people's political enthusiasms and his own indifference. He was too modest to attribute the idiocy to the other people. 'I'm hopeless, hopeless.' He groaned aloud, and in the learned silence of the vast library the sound was appalling. Death; the end of everything; the river; the revolver. ... Time passed. Even about death, Lord Edward found, he could not think consecutively and attentively. Even death was a bore. The current *Quarterly* lay on the table beside him. Perhaps it would bore him less than death was doing. He picked it up, opened it casually and found himself reading a paragraph in the middle of an article about someone called Claude Bernard. He had never previously heard of Claude Bernard. A Frenchman, he supposed. And what, he wondered, was the glycogenic function of the liver? Some scientific business, evidently. His eyes skimmed over the page. There were inverted commas; it was a quotation from Claude Bernard's own writings.

'The living being does not form an exception to the great natural harmony which makes things adapt themselves to one another; it breaks no concord; it is neither in contradiction to, nor struggling against, general cosmic forces. Far from that, it is a member of the universal concert of things, and the life of the animal, for example, is only a fragment of the total life of the universe.'

He read the words, idly first, then more carefully, then several times with a strained attention. 'The life of the animal is only a fragment of the total life of the universe.' Then what about suicide? A fragment of the universe would be destroying itself? No, not destroying; it couldn't destroy itself even if it tried. It would be changing its mode of existence. Changing. ... Bits of animals and plants became human beings. What was one day a sheep's hind leg and leaves of spinach was the next part of the hand that wrote, the brain that conceived the slow movement of the Jupiter Symphony. And another day had come when thirty-six years of pleasures, pains, hungers loves, thoughts, music, together with infinite unrealized potentialities of melody and harmony had manured an unknown corner of a Viennese cemetery, to be transformed into grass and dandelions, which in their turn had been transformed into sheep, whose hind legs had in their turn been transformed into other musicians, whose bodies in their turn ... It was all obvious, but to Lord Edward an apocalypse. Suddenly and for the first time he realized his solidarity with the world. The realization was extraordinarily exciting; he rose from his chair and began to walk agitatedly up and down the room. His thoughts were confused, but the muddle was bright and violent, not dim, not foggily languid as at ordinary times. 'Perhaps when I was at Vienna last year, I actually consumed a piece of Mozart's substance. It might have been in a Wiener Schnitzel, or a sausage, or even a glass of beer. Communion, physical communion. And that wonderful performance of *The Magic Flute* – another sort of communion, or perhaps the same, really. Transubstantiation, cannibalism, chemistry. It comes down to chemistry in the end, of course. Legs of mutton and spinach ... all chemistry. Hydrogen, oxygen ... What are the other things? God, how infuriating, how infuriating not to know! All those years at Eton. Latin verses. What the devil was the good? *En! distenta ferunt perpingues ubera vaccae.* Why didn't they teach me anything sensible? 'A member of the universal concert of things.' It's all like music; harmonies and counterpoint and modulations. But you've got to be trained to listen. Chinese music ... we can't make head or tail of it. The universal concert – that's Chinese music for me, thanks to Eton. Glycogenic function of the liver ... it might be in Bantu, so far as I'm concerned. What a humiliation! But I can learn, I will learn, I *will* ...'

Lord Edward was filled with an extraordinary exultation; he had never felt so happy in his life before.

That evening he told his father that he was not going to stand for Parliament. Still agitated by the morning's revelations of Parnellism, the old gentleman was furious. Lord Edward was entirely unmoved; his mind was made up. The next day he advertised for a tutor. In the spring of the following year he was in Berlin working under Du Bois Reymond.

Forty years had passed since then. The studies of osmosis, which had indirectly given him a wife, had also given him a reputation. His work on assimilation and growth was celebrated. But what he regarded as the real task of his life – the great theoretical treatise on physical biology – was still unfinished. 'The life of the animal is only a fragment of the total life of the universe.' Claude Bernard's words had been his life-long theme as well as his original inspiration. The book on which he had been working all these years was but an elaboration, a quantitative and mathematical illustration of them.

Upstairs in the laboratory the day's work had just begun. Lord Edward preferred to work at night. He found the daylight hours disagreeably noisy. Breakfasting at half-past one, he would walk for an hour or two in the afternoon and return to read or write till lunchtime at eight. At nine or half-past he would do some practical work with his assistant, and when that was over they would sit down to work on the great book or to discussion of its problems. At one, Lord Edward had his supper, and at about four or five he would go to bed.

Diminished and in fragments the B minor Suite came floating up from the great hall to the ears of the two men in the laboratory. They were too busy to realize that they were hearing it.

'Forceps,' said Lord Edward to his assistant. He had a very deep voice, indistinct and without, so to speak, a clearly defined contour. 'A furry voice,' his daughter Lucy had called it, when she was a child.

Illidge handed him the fine bright instrument. Lord Edward made a deep noise that signified thanks and turned back with the forceps to the anaesthetized newt that lay stretched out on the diminutive operating table. Illidge watched him critically, and approved. The Old Man was doing the job extraordinarily well. Illidge was always astonished by Lord Edward's skill. You would never have expected a huge, lumbering creature like the Old Man to be so exquisitely neat. His big hands could do the finest work; it was a pleasure to watch them.

'There!' said Lord Edward at last and straightened himself up as far as his rheumatically bent back would allow him. 'I think that's all right, don't you?'

Illidge nodded. 'Perfectly all right,' he said in an accent that had certainly not been formed in any of the ancient and expensive seats of learning. It hinted of Lancashire origins. He was a small man, with a boyish-looking freckled face and red hair.

The newt began to wake up. Illidge put it away in a place of safety. The animal had no tail; it had lost that eight days ago, and to-night the little bud of regenerated tissue which would normally have grown into a new tail had been removed and grafted on to the stump of its amputated right foreleg. Transplanted to its new position, would the bud turn into a foreleg, or continue incongruously to grow as a tail? Their first experiment had been with a tail-bud only just formed; it had duly turned into a leg. In the next, they had given the bud time to grow to a considerable size before they transplanted it; it had proved too far committed to tailhood to be able to adapt itself to the new conditions; they had manufactured a monster with a tail where an arm should have been. To-night they were experimenting on a bud of intermediate age.

Lord Edward took a pipe out of his pocket and began to fill it, looking meditatively meanwhile at the newt. 'Interesting to see what happens this time,' he said in his profound indistinct voice. 'I should think we must be just about on the border line between ...' He left the sentence unfinished: it was always difficult for him to find the words to express his meaning. 'The bud will have a difficult choice.'

'To be or not to be,' said Illidge facetiously, and started to laugh; but seeing that Lord Edward showed no signs of having been amused, he checked himself. Almost put his foot in it again. He felt annoyed with himself and also, unreasonably, with the Old Man.

Lord Edward filled his pipe. 'Tail becomes leg,' he said meditatively. 'What's the mechanism? Chemical peculiarities in the neighbouring ...? It can't obviously be the blood. Or do you suppose it has something to do with the electric tension? It does vary, of course, in different parts of the body. Though why we don't all just vaguely proliferate like cancers ... Growing in a definite shape is very unlikely, when you come to think of it. Very mysterious and ...' His voice trailed off into a deep and husky murmur.

Illidge listened disapprovingly. When the Old Man started off like this about the major and fundamental problems of biology, you never knew where he'd be getting to. Why, as likely as not he'd begin talking about God. It really made one blush. He was determined to prevent anything so discreditable happening this time. 'The next step with these newts,' he said in his most briskly practical tone, 'is to tinker with the nervous system and see whether that has any influence on the grafts. Suppose, for example, we excised a piece of the spine ...'

But Lord Edward was not listening to his assistant. He had taken his pipe out of his mouth, he had lifted his head and at the same time slightly cocked it on one side. He was frowning, as though making an effort to seize and remember something. He raised his hand in a gesture that commanded silence; Illidge interrupted himself in the middle of his sentence and also listened. A pattern of melody faintly traced itself upon the silence.

'Bach?' said Lord Edward in a whisper.

Pongileoni's blowing and the scraping of the anonymous fiddlers had shaken the air in the great hall, had set the glass of the windows looking on to it vibrating; and this in turn had shaken the air in Lord Edward's apartment on the further side. The shaking air rattled Lord Edward's *membrana tympani*; the interlocked *malleus*, *incus* and stirrup bones were set in motion so as to agitate the membrane of the oval window and raise an infinitesimal storm in the fluid of the labyrinth. The hairy endings of the auditory nerve shuddered like weeds in a rough sea; a vast number of obscure miracles were performed in the brain, and Lord Edward ecstatically whispered 'Bach!' He smiled with pleasure, his eyes lit up. The young girl was singing to herself in solitude under the floating clouds. And then the cloud-solitary philosopher began poetically to meditate. 'We must really go downstairs and listen,' said Lord Edward. He got up. 'Come,' he said. 'Work can wait. One doesn't hear this sort of thing every night.'

'But what about clothes,' said Illidge doubtfully. 'I can't come down like this.' He looked down at himself. It had been a cheap suit at the best of times. Age had not improved it.

'Oh, that doesn't matter.' A dog with the smell of rabbits in his nostrils could hardly have shown a more indecent eagerness than Lord Edward at the sound of Pongileoni's flute. He took his assistant's arm and hurried him out of the door, and along the corridor towards the stairs. 'It's just a little party,' he went on. 'I seem to remember my wife having said … Quite informal. And besides,' he added, inventing new excuses to justify the violence of his musical appetite, 'we can just slip in without … Nobody will notice.'

Illidge had his doubts. 'I'm afraid it's not a very small party,' he began; he had seen the motors arriving.

'Never mind, never mind,' interrupted Lord Edward, lusting irrepressibly for Bach.

Illidge abandoned himself. He would look like a horrible fool, he reflected, in his shiny blue serge suit. But perhaps, on second thoughts, it was better to appear in shiny blue – straight from the laboratory, after all, and under the protection of the master of the house (himself in a tweed jacket), than in that old and, as he had perceived during previous excursions into Lady Edward's luscious world, deplorably shoddy and ill-made evening suit of his It was better to be totally different from the rich and smart – a visitor from another intellectual planet – than a fourth-rate and snobbish imitator. Dressed in blue, one might be stared at as an oddity; in badly cut black (like a waiter) one was contemptuously ignored, one was despised for trying without success to be what one obviously wasn't.

Illidge braced himself to play the part of the Martian visitor with firmness, even assertively.

Their entrance was even more embarrassingly conspicuous than Illidge had anticipated. The great staircase at Tantamount House comes down from the first floor in two branches which join, like a pair of equal rivers, to precipitate themselves in a single architectural cataract of Verona marble into the hall. It debouches under the arcades, in the centre of one of the sides of the covered quadrangle, opposite the vestibule and the front door. Coming in from the street, one looks across the hall and sees through the central arch of the opposite arcade the wide stairs and shining balustrades climbing up to a landing on which a Venus by Canova, the pride of the third marquess's collection, stands pedestalled in an alcove, screening with a modest but coquettish gesture of her two hands, or rather failing to screen, her marble charms. It was at the foot of this triumphal slope of marble that Lady Edward had posted the orchestra; her guests were seated in serried rows confronting it. When Illidge and Lord Edward turned the corner in front of Canova's Venus, tiptoeing, as they approached the music and the listening crowd, with steps ever more laboriously conspiratorial, they found themselves suddenly at the focus of a hundred pairs of eyes. A gust of curiosity stirred the assembled guests. The apparition from a world so different from theirs of this huge bent old man, pipe-smoking and tweed-jacketed, seemed strangely portentous. He had a certain air of the skeleton in the cupboard – broken loose; or of one of those monsters which haunt the palaces of only the best and most aristocratic families. The Beastie of Glamis, the Minotaur itself could hardly have aroused more interest than did Lord Edward. Lorgnons were raised, there was a general craning to left and right, as people tried to look round the well-fed obstacles in front of them. Becoming suddenly aware of so many inquisitive glances, Lord Edward took fright. A consciousness of social sin possessed him; he took his pipe out of his mouth and put it away, still smoking, into the pocket of his jacket. He halted irresolutely. Flight or advance? He turned this way and that, pivoting his whole bent body from the hips with a curious swinging motion, like the slow ponderous balancing of a camel's neck. For a moment he wanted to retreat. But love of Bach was stronger than his terrors. He was the bear whom the smell of molasses constrains in spite of all his fears to visit the hunters' camp; the lover who is ready to face an armed and outraged husband and the divorce court for the sake of an hour in his mistress's arms. He went forward, tiptoeing down the stairs more conspiratorially than ever – Guy Fawkes discovered, but yet irrationally hoping that he might escape notice by acting as though the Gunpowder Plot were still unrolling itself according to plan. Illidge followed him. His face had gone very red with the embarrassment of the first moment; but in spite of this embarrassment, or rather because of it, he came downstairs after Lord Edward with a kind of swagger, one hand in his pocket, a smile on his lips. He turned his eyes coolly this way and that over the crowd. The expression on his face was one of contemptuous amusement. Too busy being the Martian to look where he was going, Illidge suddenly missed his footing on this unfamiliarly regal staircase with its inordinate treads and dwarfishly low risers. His foot slipped, he staggered wildly on the brink of a fall, waving his arms, to come to rest, however, still miraculously on his feet, some two or three steps lower down. He resumed his descent with such dignity as he could muster up. He felt exceedingly angry, he hated Lady Edward's guests one and all, without exception.

Chapter Four

PONGILEONI surpassed himself in the final Badinerie. Euclidean axioms made holiday with the formulae of elementary statics. Arithmetic held a wild saturnalian kermesse; algebra cut capers. The music came to an end in an orgy of mathematical merry-making. There was applause. Tolley bowed, with all his usual grace; Pongileoni bowed, even the anonymous fiddlers bowed. The audience pushed back its chairs and got up. Torrents of pent-up chatter broke loose.

'Wasn't the Old Man too *mar*-vellously funny?' Polly Logan had found a friend.

'And the little carroty man with him.'

'Like Mutt and Jeff.'

'I thought I should die of laughing,' said Norah.

'Such an old magician!' Polly spoke in a thrilling whisper, leaning forward and opening her eyes very wide, as though to express in dramatic pantomime as well as words the mysteriousness of the magical old man. 'A wizard.'

'But what *does* he do up there?'

'Cuts up toads and salamanders and all that,' Polly answered.

'Eye of newt and toe of frog,
Wool of bat and tongue of dog ...'

She recited with gusto, intoxicated by the words. 'And he takes guinea-pigs and makes them breed with serpents. Can you imagine it – a cross between a cobra and a guinea-pig?'

'Ugh!' the other shuddered. 'But why did he ever marry her, if that's the only sort of thing he's interested in? That's what I always wonder.'

'Why did *she* marry him?' Polly's voice dropped again to a stage whisper. She liked to make everything sound exciting – as exciting as she still felt everything to be. She was only twenty. 'There were very good reasons for *that*.'

'Yes, I suppose so.'

'And she was a Canadian, remember, which made the reasons even more cogent.'

'One wonders how Lucy ever ...'

'Sh-sh.'

The other looked round. 'Wasn't Pongileoni splendid,' she exclaimed very loudly, and with altogether too much presence of mind.

'Too wonderful!' Polly bawled back, as though she were on the stage at Drury Lane. 'Ah, there's Lady Edward.' They were both enormously surprised and delighted. 'We were just saying how *mar*-vellous Pongileoni's playing was.'

'Were you?' said Lady Edward smiling and looking from one to the other. She had a deep rich voice and spoke slowly, as though everything she said were very serious and important. 'That was *very* nice of you.' The 'r' was most emphatically rolled. 'He's an Italian,' she added, and her face was now quite grave and unsmiling. 'Which makes it even more wonderful.' And she passed on, leaving the two young girls haggardly looking into one another's blushing face.

Lady Edward was a small, thin woman, with an elegance of figure that, in a low-cut dress, was visibly beginning to run to bones and angles, as were also the aquiline good looks of a rather long and narrow face. A French mother and perhaps, in these later days, the hairdresser's art accounted for the jetty blackness of her hair. Her skin was whitely opaque. Under arched black eyebrows her eyes had that boldness and insistence of regard which is the characteristic of all very dark eyes set in a pale face. To this generic boldness Lady Edward added a certain candid impertinence of fixed gaze and bright ingenuous expression that was entirely her own. They were the eyes of a child, '*mais d'un enfant terrible*,' as John Bidlake had warned a French colleague whom he had taken to see her. The French colleague had occasion to make the discovery on his own account. At the luncheon table he found himself sitting next to the critic who had written of his pictures that they were the work either of an imbecile or of a practical joker. Wide-eyed and innocent, Lady Edward had started a discussion on art.... John Bidlake was furious. He drew her aside when the meal was over and gave her a piece of his mind.

'Damn it all,' he said, 'the man's my friend. I bring him to see you. And this is how you treat him. It's a bit thick.'

Lady Edward's bright black eyes had never been more candid, nor her voice more disarmingly French-Canadian (for she could modify her accent at will, making it more or less colonial according as it suited her to be the simple-hearted child of the North American steppe or the English aristocrat). 'But what's too thick?' she asked. 'What *have* I done this time?'

'None of your comedy with me,' said Bidlake.

'But it isn't a comedy. I've no idea what's thick. No idea.'

Bidlake explained about the critic. 'You knew as well as I do,' he said. 'And now I come to think of it, we were talking about his article only last week.'

Lady Edward frowned, as though trying to recapture a vanished memory. 'So we were!' she cried at last, and looked at him with an expression of horror and repentance. 'Too awful! But you know what a hopeless memory I have.'

'You have the best memory of any person I know,' said Bidlake.

'But I *always* forget,' she protested.

'Only what you know you ought to remember. It's a damned sight too regular to be accidental. You deliberately remember to forget.'

'What nonsense!' cried Lady Edward.

'If you had a bad memory,' Bidlake went on, 'you might occasionally forget that husbands oughtn't to be asked to meet the notorious lovers of their wives; you might sometimes forget that anarchists and leader writers in the *Morning Post* aren't likely to be the best friends, and that pious Catholics don't much enjoy listening to blasphemy from professional atheists. You might occasionally forget, if your memory were bad. But, I assure you, it needs a first-class memory to forget every time. A first-class memory and a first-class love of mischief.'

For the first time since the conversation had begun Lady Edward relaxed her ingenuous seriousness. She laughed. 'You're too absurd, my dear John.'

Talking, Bidlake had recovered his good humour; he echoed her laughter. 'Mind you,' he said, 'I don't in the least object to your playing practical jokes on other people. I enjoy it. But I do draw the line at having them played on me.'

'I'll do my best to remember next time,' she said meekly and looked at him with an ingenuousness that was so impertinent, that he had to laugh.

That had been many years before; she had kept her word and played no more tricks on him. But with other people, she was just as embarrassingly innocent and forgetful as ever. Throughout the world in which she moved her exploits were proverbial. People laughed. But there were too many victims; she was feared, she was not liked. But her parties were always thronged; her cook, her wine merchant and caterer were of the first class. Much was forgiven her for her husband's wealth. Besides, the company at Tantamount House was always variously and often eccentrically distinguished.

People accepted her invitations and took their revenge by speaking ill of her behind her back. They called her, among other things, a snob and a lion hunter. But a snob, they had to admit to her defenders, who laughed at the pomps and grandeurs for which she lived. A hunter who collected lions in order that she might bait them. Where a middle-class Englishwoman would have been serious and abject, Lady Edward was mockingly irreverent. She hailed from the New World; for her the traditional hierarchies were a joke – but a picturesque joke and one worth living for.

'She might have been the heroine of that anecdote,' old Bidlake had once remarked of her, 'that anecdote about the American and the two English peers. You remember? He got into conversation with two Englishmen in the train, liked them very much, wanted to renew the acquaintance later and asked their names. 'My name,' says one of them, 'is the Duke of Hampshire and this is my friend the Master of Ballantrae.' 'Glad to meet you,' says the American. 'Allow me to present my son Jesus Christ.' That's Hilda all over. And yet her whole life consists precisely in asking and being asked out by the people whose titles seem to her so comic. Queer.' He shook his head. 'Very queer indeed.'

Turning away from the two discomfited young girls, Lady Edward was almost run down by a very tall and burly man, who was hurrying with dangerous speed across the crowded room.

'Sorry,' he said without looking down to see who it was he had almost knocked over. His eyes were following the movements of somebody at the other end of the room; he was only aware of a smallish obstacle, presumably human, since all the obstacles in the neighbourhood were human. He checked himself in mid career and took a step to the side, so as to get round the obstacle. But the obstacle was not of the kind one circumvents as easily as that.

Lady Edward reached out and caught him by the sleeve. 'Webley!' Pretending not to have felt the hand on his sleeve, not to have heard the calling of his name, Everard Webley still moved on; he had no wish and no leisure to talk to Lady Edward. But Lady Edward would not be shaken off; she suffered herself to be dragged along, still tugging, at his side.

'Webley!' she repeated. 'Stop! Woa!' And her imitation of a country carter was so loud and so realistically rustic that Webley was compelled to listen, for fear of attracting the laughing attention of his fellow guests.

He looked down at her. 'Oh, it's you,' he said gruffly. 'Sorry I hadn't noticed.' The annoyance, expressed in his frown and his ill-mannered words, was partly genuine, partly assumed. Many people, he had found, are frightened of anger; he cultivated his natural ferocity. It kept people at a distance, saved him from being bothered.

'Goodness!' exclaimed Lady Edward with an expression of terror that was frankly a caricature.

'Did you want anything?' he demanded in the tone in which he might have addressed an importunate beggar in the street.

'You *do* look cross.'

'If that was all you wanted to say to me, I think I might as well ...'

Lady Edward, meanwhile, had been examining him critically out of her candidly impertinent eyes.

'You know,' she said, interrupting him in the middle of his sentence, as though unable to delay for a moment longer the announcement of her great and sudden discovery, 'you ought to play the part of Captain Hook in *Peter Pan.* Yes, really. You have the ideal face for a pirate king. Hasn't he, Mr Babbage?' She caught at Illidge as he was passing, disconsolately alien, through the crowd of strangers.

'Good evening,' he said. The cordiality of Lady Edward's smile did not entirely make up for the insult of his unremembered name.

'Webley, this is Mr Babbage, who helps my husband with his work.' Webley nodded a distant acknowledgement of Illidge's existence. 'But don't you think he's like a pirate king, Mr Babbage?' Lady Edward went on. 'Look at him now.'

Illidge uncomfortably laughed. 'Not that I've seen many pirate kings,' he said.

'But of course,' Lady Edward cried out, 'I'd forgotten; he *is* a pirate king. In real life. Aren't you, Webley?'

Everard Webley laughed. 'Oh, certainly, certainly.'

'Because, you see,' Lady Edward explained, turning confidentially to Illidge, 'this is Mr *Everard* Webley. The head of the British Freemen. You know those men in the green uniforms? Like the male chorus at a musical comedy.'

Illidge smiled maliciously and nodded. So this, he was thinking, was Everard Webley. The founder and the head of the Brotherhood of British Freemen – the B.B.F.'s, the 'B — y, b — ing, f — s,' as their enemies called them. Inevitably; for, as the extremely well-informed correspondent of the *Figaro* once remarked in an article devoted to the Freemen, 'les initiales B.B.F. ont, pour le public anglais, une signification plutôt péjorative.' Webley had not thought of that, when he gave his Freemen their name. It pleased Illidge to reflect that he must be made to think of it very often now.

'If you've finished being funny,' said Everard, 'I'll take my leave.'

Tinpot Mussolini, Illidge was thinking. Looks his part, too. (He had a special personal hatred of anyone who was tall and handsome, or who looked in any way distinguished. He himself was small and had the appearance of a very intelligent street Arab, grown up.) Great lout!

'But you're not offended by anything I said, are you?' Lady Edward asked with a great show of anxiety and contrition.

Illidge remembered a cartoon in the *Daily Herald*. 'The British Freemen,' Webley had had the insolence to say, 'exist to keep the world safe for intelligence.' The cartoon showed Webley and half a dozen of his uniformed bandits kicking and bludgeoning a workman to death. Behind them a top-hatted company-director looked on approvingly. Across his monstrous belly sprawled the word: INTELLIGENCE.

'Not offended, Webley?' Lady Edward repeated.

'Not in the least. I'm only rather busy. You see,' he explained in his silkiest voice, 'I have things to do. I work, if you know what that means.'

Illidge wished that the hit had been scored by someone else. The dirty ruffian! He himself was a communist.

Webley left them. Lady Edward watched him ploughing his way through the crowd. 'Like a steam engine,' she said. 'What energy! But so touchy. These politicians – worse than actresses. Such vanity! And dear Webley hasn't got much sense of humour. He wants to be treated as though he were his own colossal statue, erected by an admiring and grateful nation.' (The r's roared like lions.) 'Post-humously, if you see what I mean. As a great historical character. I can never remember, when I see him, that he's really Alexander the Great. I always make the mistake of thinking it's just Webley.'

Illidge laughed. He found himself positively liking Lady Edward. She had the right feelings about things. She seemed even to be on the right side, politically.

'Not but what his Freemen aren't a very good thing,' Lady Edward went on. Illidge's sympathy began to wane as suddenly as it had shot up. 'Don't you think so, Mr Babbage?'

He made a little grimace. 'Well ...' he began.

'By the way,' said Lady Edward, cutting short what would have been an admirably sarcastic comment on Webley's Freemen, 'you must really be careful coming down those stairs. They're *terribly* slippery.'

Illidge blushed. 'Not at all,' he muttered and blushed still more deeply – a beetroot to the roots of his carrot-coloured hair – as he realized the imbecility of what he had said. His sympathy declined still further.

'Well, rather slippery all the same,' Lady Edward politely insisted, with an emphatic rolling in the throat. 'What were you working at with Edward this evening?' she went on. 'It always interests me *so* much.'

Illidge smiled. 'Well, if you really want to know,' he said, 'we were working at the regeneration of lost parts in newts.' Among the newts he felt more at ease; a little of his liking for Lady Edward returned.

'Newts? Those things that swim?' Illidge nodded. 'But how do they lose their parts?'

'Well, in the laboratory,' he explained, 'they lose them because we cut them off.'

'And they grow again?'

'They grow again.'

'Dear me,' said Lady Edward. 'I never knew that. How fascinating these things are. Do tell me some more.'

She wasn't so bad after all. He began to explain. Warming to his subject, he warmed also to Lady Edward. He had just reached the crucial, the important and significant point in the proceedings – the conversion of the transplanted tail-bud into a leg – when Lady Edward, whose eyes had been wandering, laid her hand on his arm.

'Come with me,' she said, 'and I'll introduce you to General Knoyle. Such an amusing old man – if only unintentionally sometimes.'

Illidge's exposition froze suddenly in his throat. He realized that she had not taken the slightest interest in what he had been saying, had not even troubled to pay the least attention. Detesting her, he followed in resentful silence.

General Knoyle was talking with another military-looking gentleman. His voice was martial and asthmatic. ' "My dear fellow," I said to him' (they heard him as they approached), ' "my dear fellow, don't enter the horse now. It would be a crime," I said. "It would be sheer

47

madness. Scratch him," I said, "scratch him." And he scratched him.'

Lady Edward made her presence known. The two military gentlemen were overwhelmingly polite; they had enjoyed their evening *immensely*.

'I chose the Bach specially for you, General Knoyle,' said Lady Edward with something of the charming confusion of a young girl confessing an amorous foible.

'Well – er – really, that was very kind of you.' General Knoyle's confusion was genuine; he did not know what to do with the musical present she had made him.

'I hesitated,' Lady Edward went on in the same significantly intimate tone, 'between Handel's *Water Music* and the B minor Suite with Pongileoni. Then I remembered *you* and decided on the Bach.' Her eyes took in the signs of embarrassment on the General's ruddy face.

'That was very kind of you,' he protested. 'Not that I can pretend to understand much about music. But I know what I like, I know what I like.' The phrase seemed to give him confidence. He cleared his throat and started again. 'What I always say is …'

'And now,' Lady Edward concluded triumphantly, 'I want to introduce Mr Babbage, who helps Edward with his work and who is a real expert on newts. Mr Babbage, this is General Knoyle and this is Colonel Pilchard.' She gave a last smile and was gone.

'Well, I'm damned!' exclaimed the General, and the Colonel said she was a holy terror.

'One of the holiest,' Illidge feelingly agreed.

The two military gentlemen looked at him for a moment and decided that from one so obviously beyond the pale the comment was an impertinence. Good Catholics may have their little jokes about the saints and the habits of the clergy; but they are outraged by the same little jokes on the lips of infidels. The General made no verbal comment and the Colonel contented himself with looking his disapproval. But the way in which they turned to one another and continued their interrupted discussion of race-horses, as though they were alone, was so intentionally offensive, that Illidge wanted to kick them.

*

Lucy, my child!'

'Uncle John!' Lucy Tantamount turned round and smiled at her adopted uncle. She was of middle height and slim, like her mother,

48

with short black hair, oiled to complete blackness and brushed back from her forehead. Naturally pale, she wore no rouge. Only her thin lips were painted and there was a little blue round the eyes. A black dress emphasized the whiteness of her arms and shoulders. It wa more than two years now since Henry Tantamount had died – for Lucy had married her second cousin. But she still mourned in her dress, at any rate by artificial light. Black suited her so well. 'How are you?' she added, thinking as she spoke the words that he was beginning to look very old.

'Perishing,' said John Bidlake. He took her arm familiarly, grasping it just above the elbow with a big, blue-veined hand. 'Give me an excuse for going to have supper. I'm ravenously hungry.'

'But I'm not.'

'No matter,' said old Bidlake. 'My need is greater than thine, as Sir Philip Sidney so justly remarked.'

'But I don't want to eat.' She objected to being domineered, to following instead of leading. But Uncle John was too much for her.

'I'll do all the eating,' he declared. 'Enough for two.' And jovially laughing, he continued to lead her along towards the dining-room.

Lucy abandoned the struggle. They edged their way through the crowd. Greenish-yellow and freckled, the orchid in John Bidlake's button-hole resembled the face of a yawning serpent. His monocle glittered in his eye.

'Who's that old man with Lucy?' Polly Logan inquired as they passed.

'That's old Bidlake.'

'Bidlake? The man who … who painted the pictures?' Polly spoke hesitatingly, in the tone of one who is conscious of a hole in her education and is afraid of making a ridiculous mistake. 'Do you mean *that* Bidlake?' Her companion nodded. She felt enormously relieved. 'Well I never,' she went on, raising her eyebrows and opening her eyes very wide. 'I always thought he was an Old Master. But he must be about a hundred by this time, isn't he?'

'I should think he must be.' Norah was also under twenty.

'I must say,' Polly handsomely admitted, 'he doesn't look it. He's still quite a beau, or a buck, or a Champagne Charlie, or whatever people were in his young days.'

'He's had about fifteen wives,' said Norah.

It was at this moment that Hugo Brockle found the courage to present himself. 'You don't remember me. We were introduced in our perambulators.' How idiotic it sounded! He felt himself blushing all over.

The third and finest of John Bidlake's 'Bathers' hung over the mantelpiece in the dining-room of Tantamount House. It was a gay and joyous picture, very light in tone, the colouring very pure and brilliant. Eight plump and pearly bathers grouped themselves in the water and on the banks of a stream so as to form with their moving bodies and limbs a kind of garland (completed above by the foliage of a tree) round the central point of the canvas. Through this wreath of nacreous flesh (and even their faces were just smiling flesh, not a trace of spirit to distract you from the contemplation of the lovely forms and their relations) the eye travelled on towards a pale bright landscape of softly swelling downland and clouds.

Plate in hand and munching caviar sandwiches, old Bidlake stood with his companion, contemplating his own work. An emotion of mingled elation and sadness possessed him.

'It's good,' he said, 'it's enormously good. Look at the way it's composed. Perfect balance, and yet there's no suggestion of repetition or artificial arrangement.' The other thoughts and feelings which the picture had evoked in his mind he left unexpressed. They were too many and too confused to be easily put into words. Too melancholy above all; he did not care to dwell on them. He stretched out a finger and touched the sideboard; it was mahogany, genuine wood. 'Look at the figure on the right with the arms up.' He went on with his technical exposition in order that he might keep down, might drive away the uninvited thoughts. 'See how it compensates for the big stooping one there on the left. Like a long lever lifting a heavy weight.' But the figure with the arms up was Jenny Smith, the loveliest model he had ever had. Incarnation of beauty, incarnation of stupidity and vulgarity. A goddess as long as she was naked, kept her mouth shut, or had it kept shut for her with kisses; but oh, when she opened it, when she put on her clothes, her frightful hats! He remembered the time he had taken her to Paris with him. He had to send her back after a week. 'You ought to be muzzled, Jenny,' he told her, and Jenny cried. 'It was a mistake going to Paris,' he went on. 'Too much sun in Paris, too many artificial lights. Next time, we'll go to Spitsbergen. In winter. The nights are six months long up there.' That had made her cry still more loudly. The girl had treasures of sensuality as well as of beauty. Afterwards she took to drink and decayed, came round begging and drank up the charity. And finally what was left of her died. But the real Jenny remained here in the picture with her arms up and the pectoral muscles lifting her little breasts. What remained of John Bidlake, the John Bidlake of five and twenty years ago, was there in the picture too. Another John Bidlake still existed to contemplate his own ghost. Soon even he would have disappeared. And in any case, was he the real Bidlake, any more than the sodden and bloated woman who died had been the real Jenny? Real Jenny lived among the pearly bathers. And real Bidlake, their creator, existed by implication in his creatures.

'It's good,' he said again, when he had finished his exposition, and his tone was mournful; his face as he looked at his picture was sad. 'But after all,' he added, after a little pause and with a sudden explosion of voluntary laughter, 'after all, everything I do is good; damn good even.' It was a bidding of defiance to the stupid critics who had seen a falling off in his later paintings; it was a challenge to his own past, to time and old age, to the real John Bidlake who had painted real Jenny and kissed her into silence.

'Of course it's good,' said Lucy, and wondered why the old man's painting had fallen off so much of late. This last exhibition – it was deplorable. He himself, after all, had remained so young, comparatively speaking. Though of course, she reflected, as she looked at him, he had certainly aged a good deal during the last few months.

'Of course,' he repeated. 'That's the right spirit.'

'Though I must confess,' Lucy added, to change the subject, 'I always find your bathers rather an insult.'

'An insult?'

'Speaking as a woman, I mean. Do you really find us so profoundly silly as you paint us?'

'Yes, do you?' another voice inquired. 'Do you *really*?' It was an intense, emphatic voice, and the words came out in gushes, explosively, as though they were being forced through a narrow aperture under emotional pressure.

Lucy and John Bidlake turned and saw Mrs Betterton, massive in dove grey, with arms, old Bidlake reflected, like thighs, and hair that was, in relation to the fleshy cheeks and chins, ridiculously short, curly and auburn. Her nose, which had tilted up so charmingly in the days when he had ridden the black horse and she the bay, was now preposterous, an absurd irrelevance in the middle-aged face. Real Bidlake had ridden with her, just before he had painted these bathers. She had talked about art with a naïve, schoolgirlish earnestness which he had found laughable and charming. He had cured her, he remembered, of a passion for Burne-Jones, but never, alas, of her prejudice in favour of virtue. It was with all the old earnestness and a certain significant sentimentality as of one who remembers old times and would like to exchange reminiscences as well as general ideas, that she now addressed him. Bidlake had to pretend that he was pleased to see her after all these years. It was extraordinary, he reflected as he took her hand, how completely he had succeeded in avoiding her; he could not remember having spoken to her more than three or four times in all the quarter of a century which had turned Mary Betterton into a *memento mori*.

'Dear Mrs Betterton!' he exclaimed. 'This is delightful.' But he disguised his repugnance very badly. And when she addressed him by his Christian name – 'Now, John,' she said, 'you must give us an answer to our question,' and she laid her hand on Lucy's arm, so as to associate her in the demand – old Bidlake was positively indignant. Familiarity from a *memento mori* – it was intolerable. He'd give her a lesson. The question, it happened, was well chosen for his purposes; it fairly invited the retort discourteous. Mary Betterton had intellectual pretensions, was tremendously keen on the soul. Remembering this, old Bidlake asserted that he had never known a woman who had anything worth having beyond a pair of legs and a figure. Some of them, he added, significantly, lacked even those indispensables. True, many of them had interesting faces; but that meant nothing. Bloodhounds, he pointed out, have the air of learned judges, oxen when they chew the cud seem to meditate the problems of metaphysics, the mantis looks as though it were praying; but these appearances are entirely deceptive. It was the same with women. He had preferred to paint his bathers unmasked as well as naked, to give them faces that were merely extensions of their charming bodies and not deceptive symbols of a non-existent spirituality. It seemed to him more realistic, truer to the fundamental facts. He felt his good humour returning as he talked, and, as it came back, his dislike for Mary Betterton seemed to wane. When one is in high spirits, *memento mori*'s cease to remind.

'John, you're incorrigible,' said Mrs Betterton, indulgently. She turned to Lucy, smiling. 'But he doesn't mean a word he says.'

'I should have thought, on the contrary, that he meant it all,' objected Lucy. 'I've noticed that men who like women very much are the ones who express the greatest contempt for them.'

Old Bidlake laughed.

'Because they're the ones who know women most intimately.'

'Or perhaps because they resent our power over them.'

'But I assure you,' Mrs Betterton insisted, 'he doesn't mean it. I knew him before you were born, my dear.'

The gaiety went out of John Bidlake's face. The *memento mori* grinned for him again behind Mary Betterton's flabby mask.

'Perhaps he was different then,' said Lucy. 'He's been infected by the cynicism of the younger generation, I suppose. We're dangerous company, Uncle John. You ought to be careful.'

She had started one of Mrs Betterton's favourite hares. That lady dashed off in serious pursuit. 'It's the upbringing,' she explained. 'Children are brought up so stupidly nowadays. No wonder they're cynical.' She proceeded eloquently. Children were given too much, too early. They were satiated with amusements, inured to all the pleasures from the cradle. 'I never saw the inside of a theatre till I was eighteen,' she declared, with pride.

'My poor dear lady!'

'I began going when I was six,' said Lucy.

'And dances,' Mrs Betterton continued. 'The hunt ball – what an excitement! Because it only happened once a year.' She quoted Shakespeare.

> 'Therefore are feasts so solemn and so rare,
> Since seldom coming, in the long year set,
> Like stones of worth they thinly placed are. . . .

They're a row of pearls nowadays.'

'And false ones at that,' said Lucy.

Mrs Betterton was triumphant. 'False ones – you see? But for us they were genuine, because they were rare. We didn't "blunt the fine point of seldom pleasure" by daily wear. Nowadays young people are bored and world-weary before they come of age. A pleasure too often repeated produces numbness; it's no more felt as a pleasure.'

'And what's your remedy?' inquired John Bidlake. 'If a member of the congregation may be permitted to ask questions,' he added ironically.

'Naughty!' cried Mrs Betterton with an appalling playfulness. Then, becoming serious, 'The remedy,' she went on, 'is fewer diversions.'

'But I don't want them fewer,' objected John Bidlake.

'In that case,' said Lucy, 'they must be stronger – progressively.

'Progressively?' Mrs Betterton repeated. 'But where would that sort of progress end?'

'In bull fighting?' suggested John Bidlake. 'Or gladiatorial shows? Or public executions, perhaps? Or the amusements of the Marquis de Sade? Where?'

Lucy shrugged her shoulders. 'Who knows?'

*

Hugo Brockle and Polly were already quarrelling.

'I think it's detestable,' Polly was saying – and her face was flushed with anger, 'to make war on the poor.'

'But the Freemen don't make war on the poor.'

'They do.'

'They don't,' said Hugo. 'Read Webley's speeches.'

'I only read about his actions.'

'But they're in accordance with his words.'

'They are not.'

'They are. All he's opposed to is dictatorship of a class.'

'Of the poor class.'

'Of any class,' Hugo earnestly insisted. 'That's his whole point. The classes must be equally strong. A strong working class clamouring for high wages keeps the professional middle class active.'

'Like fleas on a dog,' suggested Polly and laughed with a return towards good humour. When a ludicrous thought occurred to her she could never prevent herself from giving utterance to it, even when she was supposed to be serious, or, as in this case, in a rage.

'They've jolly well got to be inventive and progressive,' Hugo continued, struggling with the difficulties of lucid exposition. 'Otherwise they wouldn't be able to pay the workers what they demand and make a profit for themselves. And at the same time a strong and intelligent middle class is good for the workers, because they get good leadership and good organization. Which means better wages and peace and happiness.'

'Amen,' said Polly.

'So the dictatorship of one class is nonsense,' continued Hugo. 'Webley wants to keep all the classes and strengthen them. He wants them to live in a condition of tension, so that the state is balanced by each pulling as hard as it can its own way. Scientists say that the different organs of the body are like that. They live in a state –' he hesitated, he blushed – 'of hostile symbiosis.'

'Golly!'

'I'm sorry,' Hugo apologized.

'All the same,' said Polly, 'he doesn't want to allow men to strike.'

'Because strikes are stupid.'

'He's against democracy.'

'Because it allows such awful people to get power. He wants the best to rule.'

'Himself, for example,' said Polly sarcastically.

'Well, why not? If you knew what a wonderful chap he was.' Hugo became enthusiastic. He had been acting as one of Webley's aides-de-camp for the last three months. 'I never met anyone like him,' he said.

Polly listened to his outpourings with a smile. She felt old and superior. At school she herself had felt and talked like that about the domestic economy mistress. All the same, she liked him for being so loyal.

Chapter Five

A JUNGLE of innumerable trees and dangling creepers – it was in this form that parties always presented themselves to Walter Bidlake's imagination. A jungle of noise; and he was lost in the jungle, he was trying to clear a path for himself through its tangled luxuriance. The people were the roots of the trees and their voices were the stems and waving branches and festooned lianas – yes, and the parrots and the chattering monkeys as well.

The trees reached up to the ceiling and from the ceiling they were bent back again, like mangroves, towards the floor. But in this particular room, Walter reflected, in this queer combination of a Roman courtyard and the Palm House at Kew, the growths of sound shooting up, uninterrupted, through the height of three floors, would have gathered enough momentum to break clean through the flimsy glass roof that separated them from the outer night. He pictured them going up and up, like the magic beanstalk of the Giant Killer, into the sky. Up and up, loaded with orchids and bright cockatoos, up through the perennial mist of London, into the clear moonlight beyond the smoke. He fancied them waving up there in the moonlight, the last thin aerial twigs of noise. That loud laugh, for example, that exploding guffaw from the fat man on the left – it would mount and mount, diminishing as it rose, till it no more than delicately tinkled up there under the moon. And all these voices (what were they saying? ' ... made an excellent speech ... '; ' ... no idea how comfortable those rubber reducing belts are till you've tried them ... '; ' ... such a bore ... '; ' ... eloped with the chauffeur ...'), all these voices – how exquisite and tiny they'd be up there! But meanwhile down here, in the jungle ... Oh, loud, stupid, vulgar, fatuous.

Looking over the heads of the people who surrounded him, he saw Frank Illidge, alone, leaning against a pillar. His attitude, his smile were Byronic, at once world-weary and contemptuous; he glanced about him with a languid amusement, as though he were watching the drolleries of a group of monkeys. Unfortunately, Walter reflected, as he made his way through the crowd towards him, poor Illidge hadn't the right physique for being Byronically superior. Satirical romantics should be long, slow-moving, graceful and handsome. Illidge was small, alert, and jerky. And what a comic face! Like a street Arab's, with its upturned nose and wide slit of a mouth; a very intelligent, sharp-witted street Arab's face, but not exactly one to be languidly contemptuous with. Besides, who can be superior with freckles? Illidge's complexion was sandy with them. Protectively coloured, the sandy-brown eyes, the sandy-orange eyebrows and lashes disappeared, at a little distance, into the skin, as a lion dissolves into the desert. From across a room his face seemed featureless and unregarding, like the face of a statue carved out of a block of sandstone. Poor Illidge! The Byronic part made him look rather ridiculous.

'Hullo,' said Walter, as he got within speaking distance. The two young men shook hands. 'How's science?' What a silly question! thought Walter as he pronounced the words.

Illidge shrugged his shoulders. 'Less fashionable than the arts, to judge by this party.' He looked round him. 'I've seen half the writing and painting section of *Who's Who* this evening. The place fairly stinks of art.'

'Isn't that rather a comfort for science?' said Walter. 'The arts don't enjoy being fashionable.'

'Oh, don't they! Why are you here, then?'

'Why indeed?' Walter parried the question with a laugh. He looked round, wondering where Lucy could have gone. He had not caught sight of her since the music stopped.

'You've come to do your tricks and have your head patted,' said Illidge, trying to get a little of his own back; the memory of that slip on the stairs, of Lady Edward's lack of interest in newts, of the military gentlemen's insolence, still rankled. 'Just look at that girl there with the frizzy dark hair, in cloth of silver. The one like a little white negress. What about her, for example? It'd be pleasant to have one's head patted by that sort of thing – eh?'

'Well, would it?'

Illidge laughed. 'You take the high philosophical line, do you? But, my dear chap, admit it's all humbug. I take it myself, so I ought to know. To tell you the honest truth, I envy you art-mongers your success. It makes me really furious when I see some silly, half-witted little writer ...'

'Like me, for example.'

'No, you're a cut above most of them,' conceded Illidge. 'But when I see some wretched little scribbler with a tenth of my intelligence, making money and being cooed over, while I'm disregarded, I do get furious sometimes.'

'You ought to regard it as a compliment. If they coo over us, it's because they can understand, more or less, what we're after. They can't understand you; you're above them. Their neglect is a compliment to your mind.'

'Perhaps; but it's a damned insult to my body.' Illidge was painfully conscious of his appearance. He knew that he was ugly and looked undistinguished. And knowing, he liked to remind himself of the unpleasant fact, like a man with an aching tooth, who is for ever fingering the source of his pain, just to make sure it is still painful. 'If I looked like that enormous lout, Webley, they wouldn't neglect me, even if my mind were like Newton's. The fact is,' he said, giving the aching tooth a good tug this time, 'I look like an anarchist. You're lucky, you know. You look like a gentleman, or at least like an artist. You've no idea what a nuisance it is to look like an intellectual of the lower classes.' The tooth was responding excruciatingly; he pulled at it the harder. 'It's not merely that the women neglect you – *these* women, at any rate. That's bad enough. But the police refuse to neglect you; they take a horrid inquisitive interest. Would you believe it, I've been twice arrested, simply because I look like the sort of man who makes infernal machines.'

'It's a good story,' said Walter sceptically.

'But true, I swear. Once it was in this country. Near Chesterfield. They were having a coal strike. I happened to be looking on at a fight between strikers and blacklegs. The police didn't like my face and grabbed me. It took me hours to get out of their clutches. The other time was in Italy. Somebody had just been trying to blow up Mussolini, I believe. Anyhow, a gang of black-shirted bravoes made me get out of the train at Genoa and searched me from top to toe. Intolerable! Simply because of my subversive face.'

'Which corresponds, after all, to your ideas.'

'Yes, but a face isn't evidence, a face isn't a crime. Well, yes,' he added parenthetically, 'perhaps some faces *are* crimes. Do you know General Knoyle?' Walter nodded. 'His is a capital offence. Nothing short of hanging would do for a man like that. God! how I'd like to kill them all!' Had he not slipped on the stairs and been snubbed by a stupid man-butcher? 'How I loathe the rich! Loathe them! Don't you think they're horrible?'

'More horrible than the poor?' The recollection of Wetherington's sick-room made him almost at once feel rather ashamed of the question.

'Yes, yes. There's something peculiarly base and ignoble and diseased about the rich. Money breeds a kind of gangrened insensitiveness. It's inevitable. Jesus understood. That bit about the camel and the needle's eye is a mere statement of fact. And remember that other bit about loving your neighbours. You'll be thinking I'm a Christian at this rate,' he added with parenthetic apology. 'But honour where honour is due. The man had sense; he saw what was what. Neighbourliness is the touchstone that shows up the rich. The rich haven't got any neighbours.'

'But, damn it, they're not anchorites.'

'But they have no neighbours in the sense that the poor have neighbours. When my mother had to go out, Mrs Cradock from next door on the right kept an eye on us children. And my mother did the same for Mrs Cradock when it was her turn to go out. And when somebody had broken a leg, or lost his job, people helped with money and food. And how well I remember, as a little boy, being sent running round the village after the nurse, because young Mrs Foster from next door on the left had suddenly been taken with birth pains before she expected! When you live on less than four pounds a week, you've damned well got to behave like a Christian and love your neighbour. To begin with, you can't get away from him; he's practically in your back-yard. There can be no refined and philosophical ignoring of his existence. You must either hate or love; and on the whole you'd better make a shift to love, because you may need his help in emergencies and he may need yours – so urgently, very often, that there can be no question of refusing to give it. And since you *must* give, since, if you're a human being, you can't help giving, it's better to make an effort to like the person you've anyhow got to give to.'

Walter nodded. 'Obviously.'

'But you rich,' the other went on, 'you have no real neighbours. You never perform a neighbourly action or expect your neighbours to do you a kindness in return. It's unnecessary. You can pay people to look after you. You can hire servants to simulate kindness for three pounds a month and board. Mrs Cradock from next door doesn't have to keep an eye on your babies when you go out. You have nurses and governesses doing it for money. No, you're generally not even aware of your neighbours. You live at a distance from them. Each of you is boxed up in his own secret house. There may be tragedies going on behind the shutters; but the people next door don't know anything about it.'

'Thank God!' ejaculated Walter.

'Thank him by all means. Privacy's a great luxury. Very pleasant, I agree. But you pay for luxuries. People aren't moved by misfortunes they don't know about. Ignorance is insensitive bliss. In a poor street misfortune can't be hidden. Life's too public. People have their neighbourly feeling kept in constant training. But the rich never have a chance of being neighbourly to their equals. The best they can do is to feel mawkish about the sufferings of their inferiors, which they can never begin to understand, and to be patronizingly kind. Horrible! And that's when they're doing their best. When they're at their worst, they're like this.' He indicated the crowded room. 'They're Lady Edward – the lowest hell! They're that daughter of hers. ...' He made a grimace, he shrugged his shoulders.

Walter listened with a strained and agonized attention.

'Damned, destroyed, irrevocably corrupted,' Illidge went on like a denouncing prophet. He had only once spoken to Lucy Tantamount, casually, for a moment. She had seemed hardly to notice that he was there.

It was true, Walter was thinking. She was all that people enviously or disapprovingly called her, and yet the most exquisite and marvellous of beings. Knowing all, he could listen to anything that might be said about her. And the more atrocious the words the more desperately he loved her. *Credo quia absurdum. Amo quia turpe, quia indignum.* ...

'What a putrefaction!' Illidge continued grandiloquently. 'The consummate flower of this charming civilization of ours – that's what she is. A refined and perfumed imitation of a savage or an animal. The logical conclusion, so far as most people are concerned, of having money and leisure.'

Walter listened, his eyes shut, thinking of Lucy. 'A perfumed imitation of a savage or an animal.' The words were true and an excruciation; but he loved her all the more because of the torment and because of the odious truth.

'Well,' said Illidge in a changed voice, 'I must go and see if the Old Man wants to go on working to-night. We don't generally knock off before half-past one or two. It's rather pleasant living upside down like this. Sleeping till lunch-time, starting work after tea. Very pleasant, really.' He held out his hand. 'So long.'

'We must dine together one evening,' said Walter without much conviction.

Illidge nodded. 'Let's fix it up one of these days,' he said and was gone.

Walter edged his way through the crowd, searching.

*

Everard Webley had got Lord Edward into a corner and was trying to persuade him to support the British Freemen.

'But I'm not interested in politics,' the Old Man huskily protested. 'I'm not interested in politics. ...' Obstinately, mulishly, he repeated the phrase, whatever Webley might say.

Webley was eloquent. Men of good will, men with a stake in the country ought to combine to resist the forces of destruction. It was not only property that was menaced, not only the material interests of a class; it was the English tradition, it was personal initiative, it was intelligence, it was all natural distinction of any kind. The Freemen were banded to resist the dictatorship of the stupid; they were armed to protect individuality from the mass man, the mob; they were fighting for the recognition of natural superiority in every sphere. The enemies were many and busy.

But forewarned was forearmed; when you saw the bandits approaching, you formed up in battle order and drew your swords. (Webley had a weakness for swords; he wore one when the Freemen paraded, his speeches were full of them, his house bristled with panoplies.) Organization, discipline, force were necessary. The battle could no longer be fought constitutionally. Parliamentary methods were quite adequate when the two parties agreed about fundamentals and disagreed only about trifling details. But where fundamental principles were at stake, you couldn't allow politics to go on being treated as a Parliamentary game. You had to resort to direct action or the threat of it.

'I was five years in Parliament,' said Webley. 'Long enough to convince myself that there's nothing to be done in these days by Parliamentarism. You might as well try to talk a fire out. England can only be saved by direct action. When it's saved we can begin to think about Parliament again. (Something very unlike the present ridiculous collection of mob-elected rich men it'll have to be.) Meanwhile, there's nothing for it but to prepare for fighting. And preparing for fighting, we may conquer peacefully. It's the only hope. Believe me, Lord Edward, it's the only hope.'

Harassed, like a bear in a pit set upon by dogs, Lord Edward turned uneasily this way and that, pivoting his bent body from the loins. 'But I'm not interested in pol ...' He was too agitated to be able to finish the word.

'But even if you're not interested in politics,' Webley persuasively continued, 'you must be interested in your fortune, your position, the future of your family. Remember, all those things will go down in the general destruction.'

'Yes, but ... No. ...' Lord Edward was growing desperate. 'I ... I'm not interested in money.'

Once, years before, the head of the firm of solicitors to whom he left the entire management of his affairs had called, in spite of Lord Edward's express injunction that he was never to be troubled with matters of business, to consult his client about a matter of investments. There were some eighty thousand pounds to be disposed of. Lord Edward was dragged from the fundamental equations of the statics of living systems. When he learned the frivolous cause of the interruption, the ordinarily mild Old Man became unrecognizably angry. Mr Figgis, whose voice was loud and whose manner confident, had been used, in previous interviews, to having things all his own way. Lord Edward's fury astonished and appalled him. It was as though, in his rage, the Old Man had suddenly thrown back atavistically to the feudal past, had remembered that he was a Tantamount, talking to a hired servant. He had given orders; they had been disobeyed and his privacy unjustifiably disturbed. It was insufferable. If this sort of thing should ever happen again, he would transfer his affairs to another solicitor. And with that he wished Mr Figgis a very good afternoon.

'I'm not interested in money,' he now repeated.

Illidge, who had approached and was hovering in the neighbourhood, waiting for an opportunity to address the Old Man, overheard the remark and exploded with inward laughter. 'These rich!' he thought. 'These bloody rich!' They were all the same.

'But if not for your own sake,' Webley insisted, attacking from another quarter, 'for the sake of civilization, of progress.'

Lord Edward started at the word. It touched a trigger, it released a flood of energy. 'Progress!' he echoed, and the tone of misery and embarrassment was exchanged for one of confidence. 'Progress! You politicians are always talking about it. As though it were going to last. Indefinitely. More motors, more babies, more food, more advertising, more money, more everything, for ever. You ought to

62

take a few lessons in my subject. Physical biology. Progress, indeed! What do you propose to do about phosphorus, for example?' His question was a personal accusation.

'But all this is entirely beside the point,' said Webley impatiently.

'On the contrary,' retorted Lord Edward, 'it's the only point.' His voice had become loud and severe. He spoke with a much more than ordinary degree of coherence. Phosphorus had made a new man of him; he felt very strongly about phosphorus and, feeling strongly, he was strong. The worried bear had become the worrier. 'With your intensive agriculture,' he went on, 'you're simply draining the soil of phosphorus. More than half of one per cent a year. Going clean out of circulation. And then the way you throw away hundreds of thousands of tons of phosphorus pentoxide in your sewage! Pouring it into the sea. And you call that progress. Your modern sewage systems!' His tone was witheringly scornful. 'You ought to be putting it back where it came from. On the land.' Lord Edward shook an admonitory finger and frowned. 'On the land, I tell you.'

'But all this has nothing to do with me,' protested Webley.

'Then it ought to,' Lord Edward answered sternly. 'That's the trouble with you politicians. You don't even think of the important things. Talking about progress and votes and Bolshevism and every year allowing a million tons of phosphorus pentoxide to run away into the sea. It's idiotic, it's criminal, it's … it's fiddling while Rome is burning.' He saw Webley opening his mouth to speak and made haste to anticipate what he imagined was going to be his objection. 'No doubt,' he said, 'you think you can make good the loss with phosphate rocks. But what'll you do when the deposits are exhausted?' He poked Everard in the shirt front. 'What then? Only two hundred years and they'll be finished. You think we're being progressive because we're living on our capital. Phosphates, coal, petroleum, nitre – squander them all. That's your policy. And meanwhile you go round trying to make our flesh creep with talk about revolutions.'

'But damn it all,' said Webley, half angry, half amused, 'your phosphorus can wait. This other danger's imminent. Do you *want* a political and social revolution?'

'Will it reduce the population and check production?' asked Lord Edward.

'Of course.'

'Then certainly I want a revolution.' The Old Man thought in terms of geology and was not afraid of logical conclusions. 'Certainly.' Illidge could hardly contain his laughter.

'Well, if that's your view ...' began Webley; but Lord Edward interrupted him.

'The only result of your progress,' he said, 'will be that in a few generations there'll be a real revolution – a natural, cosmic revolution. You're upsetting the equilibrium. And in the end, nature will restore it. And the process will be very uncomfortable for you. Your decline will be as quick as your rise. Quicker, because you'll be bankrupt, you'll have squandered your capital. It takes a rich man a little time to realize all his resources. But when they've all been realized, it takes him almost no time to starve.'

Webley shrugged his shoulders. 'Dotty old lunatic!' he said to himself, and aloud, 'Parallel straight lines never meet, Lord Edward. So I'll bid you good-night.' He took his leave.

A minute later the Old Man and his assistant were making their way up the triumphal staircase to their world apart.

'What a relief!' said Lord Edward, as he opened the door of his laboratory. Voluptuously, he sniffed the faint smell of the absolute alcohol in which the specimens were pickled. 'These parties! One's thankful to get back to science. Still, the music was really ...' His admiration was inarticulate.

Illidge shrugged his shoulders. 'Parties, music, science – alternative entertainments for the leisured. You pays your money and you takes your choice. The essential is to have the money to pay.' He laughed disagreeably.

Illidge resented the virtues of the rich much more than their vices. Gluttony, sloth, sensuality, and all the less comely products of leisure and an independent income could be forgiven, precisely because they were discreditable. But disinterestedness, spirituality, incorruptibility, refinement of feeling, and exquisiteness of taste – these were commonly regarded as qualities to be admired; that was why he so specially disliked them. For these virtues, according to Illidge, were as fatally the product of wealth as were chronic guzzling and breakfast at eleven.

'These bourgeois,' he complained, 'they go about handing one another bouquets for being so disinterested – that is to say, for having enough to live on without being compelled to work or be preoccupied about money. Then there's another bouquet for being able to afford to refuse a tip. And another for having enough money to buy the apparatus of cultured refinement. And yet another for having the time to spare for art and reading and elaborate long-drawn love-making. Why can't they be frank and say outright what they're all the time implying – that the root of all their virtue is a five per cent gilt-edged security?'

The amused affection which he felt for Lord Edward was tempered by a chronic annoyance at the thought that all the Old Man's intellectual and moral virtues, all his endearing eccentricities and absurdities were only made possible by the really scandalous state of his bank balance. And this latent disapproval became acute whenever he heard Lord Edward being praised, admired, or even laughed at by others. Laughter, liking and admiration were permitted to *him*, because he understood and could forgive. Other people did not even realize that there was anything to forgive. Illidge was always quick to inform them.

'If the Old Man wasn't the descendant of monastery-robbers,' he would say to the praisers or admirers, 'he'd be in the workhouse or the loony asylum.'

And yet he was genuinely fond of the Old Man, he genuinely admired his talents and his character. The world, however, might be excused for not realizing the fact. 'Unpleasant' was the ordinary comment on Lord Edward's assistant.

But being unpleasant to and about the rich, besides a pleasure, was also, in Illidge's eyes, a sacred duty. He owed it to his class, to society at large, to the future, to the cause of justice. Even the Old Man himself was not spared. He had only to breathe a word in favour of the soul (for Lord Edward had what his assistant could only regard is a shameful and adulterous passion for idealistic metaphysics); Illidge would at once leap out at him with a sneer about capitalist philosophy and bourgeois religion. An expression of distaste for hard-headed business men, of indifference to material interests, of sympathy for the poor, would bring an immediate reference, more or less veiled, but always sarcastic, to the Tantamount millions. There were days (and owing to the slip on the stairs and that snub from the General, this day was one of them) when even a reference to pure science elicited its ironic comment. Illidge was an enthusiastic biologist; but as a class-conscious citizen he had to admit that pure science, like good taste and boredom, perversity and platonic love, is a product of wealth and leisure. He was not afraid of being logical and deriding even his own idol.

'Money to pay,' he repeated. 'That's the essential.'

The Old Man looked rather guiltily at his assistant. These implied reproofs made him feel uncomfortable. He tried to change the subject. 'What about our tadpoles?' he asked. 'The asymmetrical ones.' They had a brood of tadpoles hatched from eggs that had been kept abnormally warm on one side and abnormally cold on the other. He moved towards the glass tank in which they were kept. Illidge followed.

'Asymmetrical tadpoles!' he repeated. 'Asymmetrical tadpoles! What a refinement! Almost as good as playing Bach on the flute or having a palate for wine.' He thought of his brother Tom, who had weak lungs and worked a broaching machine in a motor factory at Manchester. He remembered washing days and the pink crinkled skin of his mother's water-sodden hands. 'Asymmetrical tadpoles!' he said once more and laughed.

*

'Strange,' said Mrs Betterton, 'strange that a great artist should be such a cynic.' In Burlap's company she preferred to believe that John Bidlake had meant what he said. Burlap on cynicism was uplifting and Mrs Betterton liked to be uplifted. Uplifting too on greatness, not to mention art. 'For you must admit,' she added, 'he *is* a great artist.'

Burlap nodded slowly. He did not look directly at Mrs Betterton, but kept his eyes averted and downcast as though he were addressing some little personage invisible to everyone but himself, standing to one side of her – his private daemon, perhaps; an emanation from himself, a little *doppelgänger*. He was a man of middle height with stoop and a rather slouching gait. His hair was dark, thick and curly, with a natural tonsure as big as a medal showing pink on the crown of his head. His grey eyes were very deeply set, his nose and chin pronounced but well shaped, his mouth full-lipped and rather wide. A mixture, according to old Bidlake, who was a caricaturist in words as well as with the pencil, of a movie villain and St Anthony of Padua by a painter of the baroque, of a card-sharping Lothario and a rapturous devotee.

'Yes, a great artist,' he agreed, 'but not one of the greatest.' He spoke slowly, ruminatively, as though he were talking to himself. All his conversation was a dialogue with himself or that little *doppelgänger* which stood invisibly to one side of the people he was supposed to be talking to; Burlap was unceasingly and exclusively self-conscious. 'Not one of the greatest,' he repeated slowly. As it happened, he had just been writing an article about the subject-matter of art for next week's number of the *Literary World*. 'Precisely because of that cynicism.' Should he quote himself? he wondered.

'How true that is!' Mrs Betterton's applause exploded perhaps a little prematurely; her enthusiasm was always on the boil. She clasped her hands together. '*How true!*' She looked at Burlap's averted face and thought it so spiritual, so beautiful in its way.

'How can a cynic be a great artist?' Burlap went on, having decided that he'd spout his own article at her and take the risk of her recognizing it in print next Thursday. And even if she did recognize it, that wouldn't efface the personal impression he'd made by spouting it. 'Though why you want to make an impression,' a mocking devil had put in, 'unless it's because she's rich and useful, goodness knows!' The devil was pitchforked back to where he came from. 'One has responsibilities,' an angel hastily explained. 'The lamp mustn't be hidden under a bushel. One must let it shine, especially on people of good-will.' Mrs Betterton was on the side of the angels; her loyalty should be confirmed. 'A great artist,' he went on aloud, 'is a man who synthesizes all experience. The cynic sets out by denying half the facts – the fact of the soul, the fact of ideals, the fact of God. And yet we're aware of spiritual facts just as directly and indubitably as we're aware of physical facts.'

'Of course, of course!' exclaimed Mrs Betterton.

'It's absurd to deny either class of facts.' 'Absurd to deny me,' said the demon, poking out his head into Burlap's consciousness.

'Absurd!'

'The cynic confines himself to only half the world of possible experience. Less than half. For there are more spiritual than bodily experiences.'

'Infinitely more!'

'He may handle his limited subject-matter very well. Bidlake, I grant you, does. Extraordinarily well. He has all the sheer ability of the most consummate artists. Or had, at any rate.'

'Had,' Mrs Betterton sighed. 'When I first knew him.' The implication was that it was her influence that had made him paint so well.

'But he's always applied his powers to something small. What he synthesizes in his art was limited, comparatively unimportant.'

'That's what I always told him,' said Mrs Betterton, reinterpreting those youthful arguments about Pre-Raphaelitism in a new and, for her own reputation, favourable light. 'Consider Burne-Jones, I used to say.' The memory of John Bidlake's huge and Rabelaisian laughter reverberated in her ears. 'Not that Burne-Jones was a particularly good painter,' she hastened to add. ('He painted,' John Bidlake had said – and how shocked she had been, how deeply offended! – 'as though he had never seen a pair of buttocks in the whole of his life.') 'But his subjects were noble. If you had *his* dreams, I used to tell John Bidlake, if you had *his* ideals, you'd be a *really* great artist.'

Burlap nodded, smiling his agreement. Yes, she's on the side of the angels, he was thinking; she needs encouraging. One has a responsibility. The demon winked. There was something in his smile, Mrs Betterton reflected, that reminded one of a Leonardo or a Sodoma – something mysterious, subtle, inward.

'Though, mind you,' he said regurgitating his article slowly, phrase by phrase, 'the subject doesn't make the work of art. Whittier and Longfellow were fairly stuffed with Great Thoughts. But what they wrote was very small poetry.'

'How true!'

'The only generalization one can risk is that the greatest works of art have had great subjects; and that works with small subjects, however accomplished, are never so good as ...'

'There's Walter,' said Mrs Betterton, interrupting him. 'Wandering like an unlaid ghost. Walter!'

At the sound of his name, Walter turned. The Betterton – good Lord! And Burlap! He assumed a smile. But Mrs B. and his colleague on the *Literary World* were among the last people he wanted at this moment to see.

'We were just discussing greatness in art,' Mrs Betterton explained. 'Mr Burlap was saying such *profound* things.'

She began to reproduce the profundities for Walter's benefit.

He meanwhile was wondering why Burlap's manner towards him had been so cold, so distant, shut, even hostile. That was the trouble with Burlap. You never knew where you stood with him. Either he loved you, or he hated. Life with him was a series of scenes — scenes of hostility or, even more trying in Walter's estimation, scenes of affection. One way or the other, the emotion was always flowing. There were hardly any intervals of comfortably slack water. The tide was always running. Why was it running now towards hostility?

Mrs Betterton went on with her exposition of the profundities. To Walter they sounded curiously like certain paragraphs in that article of Burlap's, the proof of which he had only that morning been correcting for the printers. Reproduced – explosion after enthusiastic explosion – from Burlap's spoken reproduction, the article did sound rather ridiculous. A light dawned. Could *that* be the reason? He looked at Burlap. His face was stony.

'I'm afraid I must go,' said Burlap abruptly, when Mrs Betterton paused.

'But no,' she protested. 'But why?'

He made an effort and smiled his Sodoma smile. 'The world is too much with us,' he quoted mysteriously. He liked saying mysterious things, dropping them surprisingly into the middle of the conversation.

'But you're not enough with us,' flattered Mrs Betterton.

'It's the crowd,' he explained. 'After a time, I get into a panic. I feel they're crushing my soul to death. I should begin to scream if I stayed.' He took his leave.

'Such a wonderful man!' Mrs Betterton exclaimed before he was well out of earshot. 'It must be wonderful for you to work with him.'

'He's a very good editor,' said Walter.

'But I was thinking of his *personality*. How shall I say? The spiritual *quality* of the man.'

Walter nodded and said, 'Yes,' rather vaguely. The spiritual quality of Burlap was just the thing he wasn't very enthusiastic about.

'In an age like ours,' Mrs Betterton continued, 'he's an oasis in the desert of stupid frivolity and cynicism.'

'Some of his ideas are first rate,' Walter cautiously agreed.

He wondered how soon he could decently make his escape.

*

'There's Walter,' said Lady Edward.

'Walter who?' asked Bidlake. Borne by the social currents, they had drifted together again.

'Your Walter.'

'Oh, mine.' He was not much interested, but he followed the direction of her glance. 'What a weed!' he said. He disliked his children for growing up; growing, they pushed him backwards, year after year, backwards towards the gulf and the darkness. There was Walter; it was only yesterday he was born. And yet the fellow must be five-and-twenty, if he was a day.

'Poor Walter; he doesn't look at all well.'

'Looks as though he had worms,' said Bidlake ferociously.

'How's that deplorable affair of his going?' she asked.

Bidlake shrugged his shoulders. 'As usual, I suppose.'

'I never met the woman.'

'I did. She's awful.'

'What, vulgar?'

'No, no. I wish she were,' protested Bidlake. 'She's refined, terribly refined. And she speaks like this.' He spoke into a drawling falsetto that was meant to be an imitation of Marjorie's voice. 'Like a sweet little innocent girlie. And so serious, such a highbrow.' He interrupted the imitation with his own deep laugh. 'Do you know what she said to me once? I may mention that she always talks to me about Art. Art with a capital A. She said': (his voice went up again to the babyish falsetto) ' "I think there's a place for Fra Angelico *and* Rubens." ' He laughed again, homerically. 'What an imbecile! And she has a nose that's at least three inches too long.'

*

Marjorie had opened the box in which she kept her private papers. All Walter's letters. She untied the ribbon and looked them over one by one. 'Dear Mrs Carling, I enclose under separate cover that volume of Keats's Letters I mentioned to-day. Please do not trouble to return it. I have another copy, which I shall re-read for the pleasure of accompanying you, even at a distance, through the same spiritual adventure.'

That was the first of them. She read it through and recaptured in memory something of the pleased surprise which that passage about the spiritual adventure had originally evoked in her. In conversation he had always seemed to shrink from the direct and personal approach, he was painfully shy. She hadn't expected him to write like that. Later, when he had written to her often, she became accustomed to his peculiarities. She took it for granted that he should be bolder with the pen than face to face. All his love – all of it, at any rate, that was articulate and all of it that, in the days of his courtship, was in the least ardent – was in his letters. The arrangement suited Marjorie perfectly. She would have liked to go on indefinitely making cultured and verbally burning love by post. She liked the idea of love; what she did not like was lovers, except at a distance and in imagination. A correspondence course of passion was, for her, the perfect and ideal relationship with a man. Better still were personal relationships with women; for women had all the good qualities of men at a distance, with the added advantage of being actually there. They could be in the room with you and yet demand no more than a man at the other end of a system of post-offices. With his face-to-face shyness and his postal freedom and ardour, Walter had seemed in Marjorie's eyes to combine the best points of both sexes. And then he was so deeply, so flatteringly interested in everything she did and thought and felt. Poor Marjorie was not much used to having people interested in her.

'Sphinx,' she read in the third of his letters. (He had called her that because of her enigmatic silences. Carling, for the same reason, had called her Turnip or Dumb-Bell.) 'Sphinx, why do you hide yourself inside such a shell of silence? One would think you were ashamed of your goodness and sweetness and intelligence. But they pop their heads out all the same and in spite of you.'

The tears came into her eyes. He had been so kind to her, so tender and gentle. And now ...

'Love,' she read dimly, through the tears, in the next letter, 'love can transform physical into spiritual desire; it has the magic power to turn the body into pure soul. ...'

Yes, he had had those desires too. Even he. All men had, she supposed. Rather dreadful. She shuddered, remembering Carling, remembering even Walter with something of the same horror. Yes, even Walter, though he *had* been so gentle and considerate. Walter had understood what she felt. That made it all the more extraordinary that he should be behaving as he was behaving now. It was as though he had suddenly become somebody else, become a kind of wild animal, with the animal's cruelty as well as the animal's lusts.

'How can he be so cruel?' she wondered. 'How *can* he, deliberately? Walter?' Her Walter, the real Walter, was so gentle and understanding and considerate, so wonderfully unselfish and good. It was for that goodness and gentleness that she had loved him, in spite of his being a man and having 'those' desires; her devotion was to that tender, unselfish, considerate Walter, whom she had got to know and appreciate after they had begun to live together. She had loved even the weak and unadmirable manifestations of his considerateness; had loved him even when he let himself be overcharged by cabmen and porters, when he gave handfuls of silver to tramps with obviously untrue stories about jobs at the other end of the country and no money to pay the fare. He was too sensitively quick to see the other person's point of view. In his anxiety to be just to others he was often prepared to be unjust to himself. He was always ready to sacrifice his own rights rather than run any risk of infringing the rights of others. It was a considerateness, Marjorie realized, that had become a weakness, that was on the point of turning into a vice; a considerateness, moreover, that was due to his timidity, his squeamish and fastidious shrinking from every conflict, even very disagreeable contact. All the same, she loved him for it, loved him even when it led him to treat her with something less than justice. For having come to regard her as a being on the hither side of the boundary between himself and the rest of the world, he had sometimes in his excessive considerateness for the rights of others, sacrificed not only his own rights, but also hers. How often, for example, she had told him that he was being underpaid for his work on the *Literary World*! She thought of the latest of their conversations on what was to him the most odious of topics.

'Burlap's sweating you, Walter,' she had said.

'The paper's very hard up.' He always had excuses for the shortcomings of other people towards himself.

'But why should you let yourself be swindled?'

'I'm not being swindled.' There was a note of exasperation in his voice, the exasperation of a man who knows he is in the wrong. 'And even if I were, I prefer being swindled to haggling for my pound of flesh. After all, it's my business.'

'And mine!' She held up the account book on which she had been busy when the conversation began. 'If you knew the price of vegetables!'

He had flushed up and left the room without answering. The conversation, the case were typical of many others. Walter had never been deliberately unkind to her, only by mistake, out of excessive consideration for other people and while he was being unkind to himself. She had never resented these injustices. They proved how closely he associated her with himself. But now, now there was nothing accidental about his unkindness. The gentle considerate

Walter had disappeared and somebody else – somebody ruthless and full of hate – was deliberately making her suffer.

*

Lady Edward laughed. 'One wonders what he saw in her, if she's so deplorable as you make out.'

'What does one ever see in anyone?' John Bidlake spoke in a melancholy tone. Quite suddenly he had begun to feel rather ill. An oppression in the stomach, a feeling of sickness, a tendency to hiccough. It often happened now. Just after eating. Bicarbonate didn't seem to do much good. 'In these matters,' he added, 'we're all equally insane.'

'Thanks!' said Lady Edward, laughing.

Making an essay to be gallant, 'Present company excepted,' he said with a smile and a little bow. He stifled another hiccough. How miserable he was feeling! 'Do you mind if I sit down?' he asked. 'All this standing about …' He dropped heavily into a chair.

Lady Edward looked at him with a certain solicitude, but said nothing. She knew how much he hated all references to age, or illness, or physical weakness.

'It must have been that caviar,' he was thinking. 'That beastly caviar.' He violently hated caviar. Every sturgeon in the Black Sea was his personal enemy.

'Poor Walter!' said Lady Edward, taking up the conversation where it had been dropped. 'And he has such a talent.'

John Bidlake snorted contemptuously.

Lady Edward perceived that she had said the wrong thing – by mistake, genuinely by mistake, this time. She changed the subject.

'And Elinor?' she asked. 'When's your Elinor coming home? Elinor and Quarles?'

'Leaving Bombay to-morrow,' John Bidlake answered telegraphically. He was too busy thinking of the caviar and his visceral sensations to be more responsive.

Chapter Six

DE Indians drank deir liberalism at your fountains,' said Mr Sita Ram, quoting from one of his own speeches in the Legislative Assembly. He pointed an accusing finger at Philip Quarles. The drops of sweat pursued one another down his brown and pouchy cheeks; he seemed to be weeping for Mother India. One drop had been hanging, an iridescent jewel in the lamplight, at the end of his nose. It flashed and trembled while he spoke, as if responsive to patriotic sentiments. There came a moment when the sentiments were too much for it. At the word 'fountain,' it gave a last violent shudder and fell among the broken morsels of fish on Mr Sita Ram's plate.

'Burke and Bacon,' Mr Sita Ram went on sonorously, 'Milton and Macaulay ...'

'Oh, look!' Elinor Quarles's voice was shrill with alarm. She got up so suddenly that her chair fell over backwards. Mr Sita Ram turned towards her.

'What's de matter?' he asked in a tone of annoyance. It is vexatious to be interrupted in the middle of a peroration.

Elinor pointed. A very large grey toad was laboriously hopping across the veranda. In the silence its movements were audible – a soft thudding, as though a damp sponge were being repeatedly dropped.

'De toad can do no harm,' said Mr Sita Ram, who was accustomed to the tropical fauna.

Elinor looked beseechingly at her husband. The glance that he returned was one of disapproval.

'Really, my darling,' he protested. He himself had a strong dislike for squashy animals. But he knew how to conceal his disgust, stoically. It was the same with the food. There had been (the right, the fully expressive word now occurred to him) a certain toad-like quality about the fish. But he had managed, none the less, to eat it. Elinor had left hers, after the first mouthful, untouched.

'Perhaps you wouldn't mind driving it away,' she whispered. Her face expressed her inward agony. 'You know how much I detest them.'

Her husband laughed and, apologizing to Mr Sita Ram, got up, very tall and slim, and limped across the veranda. With the toe of his clumsy surgical boot he manoeuvred the animal to the edge of the platform. It flopped down heavily into the garden below. Looking out, he caught a glimpse of the sea shining between the palm stems. The moon was up and the tufted foliage stood out black against the sky. Not a leaf stirred. It was enormously hot and seemed to be growing hotter as the night advanced. Heat under the sun was not so bad; one expected it. But this stifling darkness ... Philip mopped his face and went back to his seat at the table.

'You were saying, Mr Sita Ram?'

But Mr Sita Ram's first fine careless rapture had evaporated. 'I was re-reading some of de works of Morley to-day,' he announced.

'Golly!' said Philip Quarles, who liked on occasion, very deliberately, to bring out a piece of schoolboy slang. It made such an effect in the middle of a serious conversation.

But Mr Sita Ram could hardly be expected to catch the full significance of that 'Golly.' 'What a tinker!' he pursued. 'What a great tinker! And de style is so chaste.'

'I suppose it is.'

'Dere are some good phrases,' Mr Sita Ram went on. 'I wrote dem down.' He searched his pockets, but failed to discover his note-book. 'Never mind,' he said. 'But dey were good phrases. Sometimes one reads a whole book widout finding a single phrase one can remember or quote. What's de good of such a book, I ask you?'

'What indeed?'

Four or five untidy servants came out of the house and changed the plates. A dish of dubious rissoles made its appearance. Elinor glanced despairingly at her husband, then turned to Mr Sita Ram to assure him that she never ate meat. Himself stoically eating, Philip approved her wisdom. They drank sweet champagne that was nearly as warm as tea. The rissoles were succeeded by sweetmeats – large, pale balls (much fingered, one felt sure, long and lovingly rolled between the palms) of some equivocal substance, at once slimy and gritty, and tasting hauntingly through their sweetness of mutton fat.

Under the influence of the champagne, Mr Sita Ram recovered his eloquence. His latest oration re-uttered itself.

'Dere is one law for de English,' he said, 'and anoder for de Indians, one for de oppressors and anoder for de oppressed. De word justice has eider disappeared from your vocab'lary, or else it has changed its meaning.'

'I'm inclined to think that it has changed its meaning,' said Philip.

Mr Sita Ram paid no attention. He was filled with a sacred indignation, the more violent for being so hopelessly impotent. 'Consider de case,' he went on (and his voice trembled out of his control), 'of de unfortunate station-master of Bhowanipore.'

But Philip refused to consider it. He was thinking of the way in which the word justice changes its meaning. Justice for India had meant one thing before he visited the country. It meant something very different now, when he was on the point of leaving it.

The station-master of Bhowanipore, it appeared, had had a spotless record and nine children.

'But why don't you teach them birth control, Mr Sita Ram?' Elinor had asked. These descriptions of enormous families always made her wince. She remembered what she had suffered when little Phil was born. And after all, she had had chloroform and two nurses and Sir Claude Aglet. Whereas the wife of the station-master of Bhowanipore ... She had heard accounts of Indian midwives. She shuddered. 'Isn't it the only hope for India?'

Mr Sita Ram, however, thought that the only hope was universal suffrage and self-government. He went on with the station-master's history. The man had passed all his examinations with credit; his qualifications were the highest possible. And yet he had been passed over for promotion no less than four times. Four times, and always in favour of Europeans or Eurasians. Mr Sita Ram's blood boiled when he thought of the five thousand years of Indian civilization, Indian spirituality, Indian moral superiority, cynically trampled, in the person of the station-master of Bhowanipore, under English feet. ...

'Is dat justice, I ask?' He banged the table.

Who knows? Philip wondered. Perhaps it is.

Elinor was still thinking of the nine children. To obtain a quick delivery, the midwives, she had heard, stamp on their patients. And, instead of ergot, they use a paste made of cow-dung and powdered glass.

'Do you call dat justice?' Mr Sita Ram repeated.

Realizing that he was expected to make some response, Philip shook his head and said, 'No.'

'You ought to write about it,' said Mr Sita Ram, 'you ought to show de scandal up.'

Philip excused himself; he was only a writer of novels, not a politician, not a journalist. 'Do you know old Daulat Singh?' he added with apparent irrelevance. 'The one who lives at Ajmere?'

'I have met de man,' said Mr Sita Ram, in a tone that made it quite clear that he didn't like Daulat Singh, or perhaps (more probably, thought Philip) hadn't been liked or approved by him.

'A fine man, I thought,' said Philip. For men like Daulat Singh justice would have to mean something very different from what it meant for Mr Sita Ram or the station-master of Bhowanipore. He remembered the noble old face, the bright eyes, the restrained passion of his words. If only he could have refrained from chewing *pan*. ...

The time came for them to go. At last. They said good-bye with an almost excessive cordiality, climbed into the waiting car and were driven away. The ground beneath the palm trees of Joohoo was littered with a mintage of shining silver, splashed with puddles of mercury. They rolled through a continuous flickering of light and dark – the cinema film of twenty years ago – until, emerging from under the palm trees, they found themselves in the full glare of the enormous moon.

'Three-formed Hecate,' he thought, blinking at the round brilliance. 'But what about Sita Ram and Daulat Singh and the station-master, what about old appalling India, what about justice and liberty, what about progress and the future? The fact is, I don't care. Not a pin. It's disgraceful. But I don't. And the forms of Hecate aren't three. They're a thousand, they're millions. The tides. The Nemorensian goddess, the Tifatinian. Varying directly as the product of the masses and inversely as the square of the distances. A florin at arm's length, but as big as the Russian Empire. Bigger than India. What a comfort it will be to be back in Europe again! And to think there was a time when I read books about yoga and did breathing exercises and tried to persuade myself that I didn't really exist! What a fool! It was the result of talking with that idiot Burlap. But luckily people don't leave much trace on me. They make an impression easily, like a ship in water. But the water closes up again. I wonder what this Italian ship will be like to-morrow? The Lloyd Triestino boats are always supposed to be good. "Luckily," I said; but oughtn't one to be ashamed of one's indifference? That parable of the sower. The seed that fell in shallow ground. And yet, obviously, it's no use pretending to be what one isn't. One sees the results of that in Burlap. What a comedian! But he takes in a lot of people. Including himself, I suppose. I don't believe there's such a thing as a conscious hypocrite, except for special occasions. You can't keep it up all the time. All the same, it would be good to know what it's like to believe in something to the point of being prepared to kill people or get

77

yourself killed. It would be an experience. ...'

Elinor had lifted her face towards the same bright disc. Moon, full moon. ... And instantly she had changed her position in space and time. She dropped her eyes and turned towards her husband; she took his hand and leaned tenderly against him.

'Do you remember those evenings?' she asked. 'In the garden, at Gattenden. Do you remember, Phil?'

Elinor's words came to his ears from a great distance and from a world in which, for the moment, he felt no interest. He roused himself with reluctance. 'Which evenings?' he asked, speaking across gulfs, and in the rather flat and colourless voice of one who answers an importunate telephone.

At the sound of that telephone voice Elinor quickly drew away from him. To press yourself against someone who turns out simply not to be there is not only disappointing; it is also rather humiliating. Which evenings, indeed!

'Why don't you love me any more?' she asked despairingly. As if she could have been talking about any other evenings than those of that wonderful summer they had spent, just after their marriage, at her mother's house. 'You don't even take any interest in me now – less than you would in a piece of furniture, much less than in a book.'

'But, Elinor, what *are* you talking about?' Philip put more astonishment into his voice than he really felt. After the first moment, when he had had time to come to the surface, so to speak, from the depths of his reverie, he had understood what she meant, he had connected this Indian moon with that which had shone, eight years ago, on the Hertfordshire garden. He might have said so, of course. It would have made things easier. But he was annoyed at having been interrupted, he didn't like to be reproached, and the temptation to score a debater's point against his wife was strong. 'I ask a simple question,' he went on, 'merely wanting to know what you mean. And you retort by complaining that I don't love you. I fail to see the logical connexion.'

'But you know quite well what I was talking about,' said Elinor. 'And besides, it *is* true – you don't love me any more.'

'I do, as it happens,' said Philip and, still skirmishing (albeit, vainly as he knew) in the realm of dialectic, went on like a little Socrates with his cross-examination. 'But what I really want to know is how we ever got to this point from the place where we started. We began with evenings and now ...'

But Elinor was more interested in love than in logic. 'Oh, I know you don't want to say you don't love me,' she interrupted. 'Not in so many words. You don't want to hurt my feelings. But it would really hurt them less if you did so straight out, instead of just avoiding the whole question, as you do now. Because this avoiding is really just as much of an admission as a bald statement. And it hurts more because it lasts longer, because there's suspense and uncertainty and repetition of pain. So long as the words haven't been definitely spoken, there's always just a chance that they mayn't have been tacitly implied. Always a chance, even when one *knows* that they have been implied. There's still room for hope. And where there's hope there's disappointment. It isn't really kinder to evade the question, Phil; it's crueller.'

'But I don't evade the question,' he retorted. 'Why should I, seeing that I do love you?'

'Yes, but how? How do you love me? Not in the way you used to, at the beginning. Or perhaps you've forgotten. You didn't even remember the time when we were first married.'

'But my dear child,' Philip protested, 'do be accurate. You just said "those evenings" and expected me to guess which.'

'Of course I expected,' said Elinor. 'You ought to have known. You would have known, if you took any interest. That's what I complain of. You care so little now that the time when you did care means nothing to you. Do you think *I* can forget those evenings?'

She remembered the garden with its invisible and perfumed flowers, the huge black Wellingtonia on the lawn, the rising moon, and the two stone griffins at either end of the low terrace wall, where they had sat together. She remembered what he had said and his kisses, the touch of his hands. She remembered everything – remembered with the minute precision of one who loves to explore and reconstruct the past, of one who is for ever turning over and affectionately verifying each precious detail of recollected happiness.

'It's all simply faded out of your mind,' she added, mournfully reproachful. For her, those evenings were still more real, more actual than much of her contemporary living.

'But of course I remember,' said Philip impatiently. 'Only one can't readjust one's mind instantaneously. At the moment, when you spoke, I happened to be thinking of something else; that was all.'

Elinor sighed. 'I wish I had something else to think about,' she said. 'That's the trouble; I haven't. Why should I love you so much?

Why? It isn't fair. You're protected by an intellect and a talent. You have your work to retire into, your ideas to shield you. But I have nothing – no defence against my feelings, no alternative to you. And it's I who need the defence and the alternative. For I'm the one who really cares. You've got nothing to be protected from. You don't care. No, it isn't fair, it isn't fair.'

And after all, she was thinking, it had always been like this. He hadn't ever really loved her, even at the beginning. Not profoundly and entirely, not with abandonment. For even at the beginning he had evaded her demands, he had refused to give himself completely to her. On her side she had offered everything, everything. And he had taken, but without return. His soul, the intimacies of his being, he had always withheld. Always, even from the first, even when he had loved her most. She had been happy then – but only because she had not known better than to be happy, because she had not realized, in her inexperience, that love could be different and better. She took a perverse pleasure in the retrospective disparagement of her felicity, in laying waste her memories. The moon, the dark and perfumed garden, the huge black tree and its velvet shadow on the lawn. ... She denied them, she rejected the happiness which they symbolized in her memory.

Philip Quarles, meanwhile, said nothing. There was nothing, really, to say. He put his arm round her and drew her towards him; he kissed her forehead and her fluttering eyelids; they were wet with tears.

The sordid suburbs of Bombay slid past them – factories and little huts and huge tenements, ghastly and bone-white under the moon. Brown, thin-legged pedestrians appeared for a moment in the glare of the headlights, like truths apprehended intuitively and with immediate certainty, only to disappear again almost instantly into the void of outer darkness. Here and there, by the roadside, the light of a fire mysteriously hinted at dark limbs and faces. The inhabitants of a world of thought starrily remote from theirs peered at them, as the car flashed past, from creaking bullock carts.

'My darling,' he kept repeating, 'my darling ...'

Elinor permitted herself to be comforted. 'You love me a little?' 'So much.'

She actually laughed, rather sobbingly, it is true; but still, it was a laugh. 'You do your best to be nice to me.' And after all, she thought, those days at Gattenden had really been blissful. They were hers, she had had them; they couldn't be denied. 'You make such efforts. It's sweet of you.'

'It's silly to talk like that,' he protested. 'You know I love you.'

'Yes, I know you do.' She smiled and stroked his cheek. 'When you have time and then by wireless across the Atlantic.'

'No, that isn't true.' But secretly he knew that it was. All his life long he had walked in a solitude, in a private void, into which nobody, not his mother, not his friends, not his lovers had ever been permitted to enter. Even when he held her thus, pressed close to him, it was by wireless, as she had said, and across an Atlantic that he communicated with her.

'It isn't true,' she echoed, tenderly mocking. 'But, my poor old Phil, you couldn't even take in a child. You don't know how to lie convincingly. You're too honest. That's one of the reasons why I love you. If you knew how transparent you were!'

Philip was silent. These discussions of personal relations always made him uncomfortable. They threatened his solitude – that solitude which, with a part of his mind, he deplored (for he felt himself cut off from much he would have liked to experience), but in which alone, nevertheless, his spirit could live in comfort, in which alone he felt himself free. At ordinary times he took this inward solitude for granted, as one accepts the atmosphere in which one lives. But when it was menaced, he became only too painfully aware of its importance to him; he fought for it, as a choking man fights for air. But it was a fight without violence, a negative battle of retirement and defence. He entrenched himself now in silence, in that calm, remote, frigid silence, which he was sure that Elinor would not attempt, knowing the hopelessness of the venture, to break through. He was right; Elinor glanced at him for an instant, and then, turning away, looked out at the moonlit landscape. Their parallel silences flowed on through time, unmeeting.

They were driven on through the Indian darkness. Almost cool against their faces, the moving air smelt now of tropical flowers, now of sewage, or curry, or burning cow-dung.

'And yet,' said Elinor suddenly, unable any longer to contain her resentful thoughts, 'you couldn't do without me. Where would you be, if I left you, if I went to somebody who was prepared to give me something in return for what I give? Where would you be?'

The question dropped into the silence. Philip made no answer. But where *would* he be? He too wondered. For in the ordinary daily world of human contacts he was curiously like a foreigner, uneasily not at home among his fellows, finding it difficult or impossible to enter into communication with any but those who could speak his native intellectual language of ideas. Emotionally, he was a foreigner. Elinor was his interpreter, his dragoman. Like her father, Elinor Bidlake had been born with a gift of intuitive understanding and social ease. She was quickly at home with anybody. She knew, instinctively, as well as old John himself, just what to say to every type of person – to every type except, perhaps, her husband's. It is difficult to know what to say to someone who does not say anything in return, who answers the personal word with the impersonal, the particular and feeling word with an intellectual generalization. Still, being in love with him, she persisted in her efforts to lure him into direct contact; and though the process was rather discouraging – like singing to deaf-mutes or declaiming poetry to an empty hall – she went on giving him her intimacies of thought and feeling. There were occasions when, making a great effort, he did his best, in exchange, to admit her into his own personal privacies. But whether it was that the habit of secrecy had made it impossible for him to give utterance to his inward feelings, or whether the very capacity to feel had actually been atrophied by consistent silence and repression, Elinor found these rare intimacies disappointing. The holy of holies into which he so painfully ushered her was almost as naked and empty as that which astonished the Roman invaders, when they violated the temple of Jerusalem. Still, she was grateful to Philip for his good intentions in at least wanting to admit her to his emotional intimacy, even though there mightn't be much of an emotional life to be intimate with. A kind of Pyrrhonian indifference, tempered by a consistent gentleness and kindness, as well as by the more violent intermittences of physical passion – this was the state of being which nature and second nature had made normal for him. Elinor's reason told her that this was so; but her feelings would not accept in practice what she was sure of in theory. What was living and sensitive and irrational in her was hurt by his indifference, as though it were a personal coldness directed only against herself. And yet, whatever she might feel, Elinor knew all the time that his indifference wasn't personal, that he was like that with everybody, that he loved her as much as it was possible for him to love, that his love for her hadn't diminished, because it had never really been greater – more passionate once perhaps, but never more emotionally rich in intimacies and self-giving, even at its most passionate, than it was now. But all the same her feelings were outraged; he oughtn't to be like this. He oughtn't to be; but there, he was. After an outburst, she would settle down and try to love him as reasonably as she could, making the best of his kindness, his rather detached and separate passion, his occasional and laborious essays at emotional intimacy, and finally his intelligence – that quick, comprehensive, ubiquitous intelligence that could understand everything, including the emotions it could not feel and the instincts it took care not to be moved by.

Once, when he had been telling her about Koehler's book on the apes, 'You're like a monkey on the superman side of humanity,' she said. 'Almost human, like those poor chimpanzees. The only difference is that *they're* trying to think up with their feelings and instincts, and *you're* trying to feel down with your intellect. Almost human. Trembling on the verge, my poor Phil.'

He understood everything so perfectly. That was why it was such fun being his dragoman and interpreting other people for him. (It was less amusing when one had to interpret oneself.) All that the intelligence could seize upon he seized. She reported her intercourse with the natives of the realm of emotion and he understood at once, he generalized her experience for her, he related it with other experiences, classified it, found analogies and parallels. From single and individual it became in his hands part of a system. She was astonished to find that she and her friends had been, all unconsciously, substantiating a theory, or exemplifying some interesting generalization. Her functions as dragoman were not confined to mere scouting and reporting. She acted also directly as personal interpreter between Philip and any third party he might wish to get into touch with, creating the atmosphere in which alone the exchange of personalities is possible, preserving the conversation from intellectual desiccation. Left to himself Philip would never have been able to establish personal contact or preserve it when once established. But when Elinor was there to make and keep the contact for him, he could understand, he could sympathize, with his intelligence, in a way which Elinor assured him was all but human. In his subsequent generalizations from the experience she had made possible for him he became once more undisguisedly the overman.

Yes, it was fun to serve as dragoman to such an exceptionally intelligent tourist in the realm of feeling. But it was more than fun; it was also, in Elinor's eyes, a duty. There was his writing to consider.

'Ah, if you were a little less of an overman, Phil,' she used to say, 'what good novels you'd write!'

Rather ruefully he agreed with her. He was intelligent enough to know his own defects. Elinor did her best to supply them – gave him first-hand information about the habits of the natives, acted as go-between when he wanted to come into personal contact with one of them. Not only for her own sake, but for the sake of the novelist he might be, she wished he could break his habit of impersonality and learn to live with the intuitions and feelings and instincts as well as with the intellect. Heroically, she had even encouraged him in his velleities of passion for other women. It might do him good to have a few affairs. So anxious was she to do him good as a novelist, that on more than one occasion, seeing him look admiringly at some young woman or other, she had gone out of her way to establish for him the personal contact which he would never have been able to establish for himself. It was risky, of course. He might really fall in love; he might forget to be intellectual and become a reformed character, but for some other woman's benefit. Elinor took the risk, partly because she thought that his writing ought to come before everything else, even her own happiness, and partly because she was secretly convinced that there was in reality no risk at all, that he would never lose his head so wholly as to want to run off with another woman. The cure by affairs, if it worked at all, would be gentle in its action; and if it did work, she was sure she would know how to profit by its good effects on him. Anyhow, it hadn't worked so far. Philip's infidelities amounted to very little and had had no appreciable effect on him. He remained depressingly, even maddeningly the same – intelligent to the point of being almost human, remotely kind, separately passionate and sensual, impersonally sweet. Maddening. Why did she go on loving him? She wondered. One might almost as well go on loving a book-case. One day she would really leave him. There was such a thing as being too unselfish and devoted. One should think of one's own happiness sometimes. To be loved for a change, instead of having to do all the loving oneself; to receive instead of perpetually giving. ... Yes, one day she really would leave him. She had herself to think about. Besides, it would be a punishment for Phil. A punishment – for she was sure that, if she left him, he would be genuinely unhappy, in his way, as much as it lay in him to be unhappy. And perhaps the unhappiness might achieve the miracle she had been longing and working for all these years; perhaps it would sensitize him, personalize him. Perhaps it might be the making of him as a writer. Perhaps it was even her duty to make him unhappy, the most sacred of her duties. ...

The sight of a dog running across the road just in front of the car aroused her from her reverie. How suddenly, how startlingly it had dashed into the narrow universe of the headlamps! It existed for a fraction of a second, desperately running, and was gone again into the darkness on the other side of the luminous world. Another dog was suddenly in its place, pursuing.

'Oh!' cried Elinor. 'It'll be ...' The headlights swerved and swung straight again, there was a padded jolt, as though one of the wheels had passed over a stone; but the stone yelped. ' ... run over,' she concluded.

'It *has* been run over.'

The Indian chauffeur looked round at them, grinning. They could see the flash of his teeth. 'Dog!' he said. He was proud of his English.

'Poor beast!' Elinor shuddered.

'It was his fault,' said Philip. 'He wasn't looking. That's what comes of running after the females of one's species.'

There was a silence. It was Philip who broke it.

'Morality'd be very queer,' he reflected aloud, 'if we loved seasonally, not all the year round. Moral and immoral would change from one month to another. Primitive societies are apt to be more seasonal than cultivated ones. Even in Sicily there are twice as many births in January as in August. Which proves conclusively that in the spring the young man's fancy ... But nowhere *only* in the spring. There's nothing human quite analogous to heat in mares or she-dogs. Except,' he added, 'except perhaps in the moral sphere. A bad reputation in a woman allures like the signs of heat in a bitch. Ill-fame announces accessibility. Absence of heat is the animal's equivalent of the chaste woman's habits and principles. ...'

Elinor listened with interest and at the same time a kind of horror. Even the squashing of a wretched animal was enough to set that quick untiring intelligence to work. A poor starved pariah dog had its back broken under the wheels and the incident evoked from Philip a selection from the vital statistics of Sicily, a speculation about the relativity of morals, a brilliant psychological generalization. It was amusing, it was unexpected, it was wonderfully interesting; but oh! she almost wanted to scream.

Chapter Seven

Mrs Betterton had been shaken off, his father and Lady Edward distantly waved to and avoided; Walter was free to continue his search. And at last he found what he was looking for. Lucy Tantamount had just emerged from the dining-room and was standing under the arcades, glancing in indecision this way and that. Against the mourning of her dress the skin was luminously white. A bunch of gardenias was pinned to her bodice. She raised a hand to touch her smooth black hair, and the emerald of her ring shot a green signal to him across the room. Critically, with a kind of cold intellectual hatred, Walter looked at her and wondered why he loved. Why? There was no reason, no justification. All the reasons were against his loving her.

Suddenly she moved, she walked out of sight. Walter followed. Passing the entrance to the dining-room, he noticed Burlap, no longer the anchorite, drinking champagne and being talked to by the Comtesse d'Exergillod. Gosh! thought Walter, remembering his own experiences with Molly d'Exergillod. 'But Burlap probably adores her. He would ... He ...' But there she was again, talking – damnation! – with General Knoyle. Walter hung about at a little distance, waiting impatiently for an opportunity to address her.

'Caught at last,' said the General patting her hand. 'Been looking for you the whole evening.'

Half satyr, half uncle, he had an old man's weakness for Lucy. 'Charming little girl!' he would assure all those who wanted to hear. 'Charming little figure! Such eyes!' For the most part he preferred them rather younger. 'Nothing like youth!' he was fond of saying. His life-long prejudice against America and Americans had been transformed into enthusiastic admiration ever since, at the age of sixty-five, he had visited California and seen the flappers of Hollywood and the bathing beauties on the Pacific beaches. Lucy was nearly thirty; but the General had known her for years; he continued to regard her as hardly more than the young girl of his first memories. For him, she was still about seventeen. He patted her hand again. 'We'll have a good talk,' he said.

'That will be fun,' said Lucy with sarcastic politeness.

From his post of observation Walter looked on. The General had been handsome once. Corseted, his tall figure still preserved its military bearing. The gallant and the guardsman, he smiled; he fingered his white moustache. The next moment he was the playful, protective and confidential old uncle. Faintly smiling, Lucy looked at him out of her pale grey eyes with a detached and unmerciful amusement. Walter studied her. She was not even particularly good looking. So why, why? He wanted reasons, he wanted justification. Why? The question persistently reverberated. There was no answer. He had just fallen in love with her – that was all; insanely, the first time he set eyes on her.

Turning her head, Lucy caught sight of him. She beckoned and called his name. He pretended to be surprised and delightfully astonished.

'I hope you've not forgotten our appointment,' he said.

'Do I ever forget? Except occasionally on purpose,' she qualified with a little laugh. She turned to the General. 'Walter and I are going to see your stepson this evening,' she announced in the tone and with the smile which one employs when one talks to people about those who are dear to them. But between Spandrell and his stepfather the quarrel, she knew very well, was mortal. Lucy had inherited all her mother's fondness for the deliberate social blunder and with it a touch of her father's detached scientific curiosity. She enjoyed experimenting, not with frogs and guinea-pigs, but with human beings. You did unexpected things to people, you put them in curious situations and waited to see what would happen. It was the method of Darwin and Pasteur.

What happened in this case was that General Knoyle's face became extremely red. 'I haven't seen him for some time,' he said stiffly.

'Good,' she said to herself. 'He's reacting.'

'But he's *such* good company,' she said aloud.

The General grew redder and frowned. What he hadn't done for that boy! And how ungratefully the boy had responded, how abominably he had behaved! Getting himself kicked out of every job the General had wangled him into. A waster, an idler; drinking and drabbing; making his mother miserable, sponging on her, disgracing the family name. And the insolence of the fellow, the things he had ventured to say the last time they had met and, as usual, had a scene together! The General was never likely to forget being called 'an impotent old fumbler.'

'And so intelligent,' Lucy was saying. With an inward smile she remembered Spandrell's summary of his stepfather's career. 'Superannuated from Harrow,' it began, 'passed out from Sandhurst at the bottom of the list, he had a most distinguished career in the Army, rising during the War to a high post in the Military Intelligence Department.' The way he rolled out this anticipated obituary was really magnificent. He was *The Times* made audible. And then his remarks on Military Intelligence in general! 'If you look up "Intelligence" in the new volumes of the *Encyclopaedia Britannica*,' he had said, 'you'll find it classified under the following three heads: Intelligence, Human; Intelligence, Animal; Intelligence, Military. My stepfather's a perfect specimen of Intelligence, Military.'

'So intelligent,' Lucy repeated.

'Some people think so, I know,' said General Knoyle very stiffly. 'But personally ...' He cleared his throat with violence. That was *his* personal opinion.

A moment later, still rigid, still angrily dignified, he took his leave. He felt that Lucy had offended him. Even her youth and her bare shoulders did not compensate him for those laudatory references to Maurice Spandrell. Insolent, bad-blooded young cub! His existence was the General's standing grievance against his wife. A woman had no right to have a son like that, no right. Poor Mrs Knoyle had often atoned to her second husband for the offences of her son. She was there, she could be punished, she was too weak to resist. The exasperated General visited the sins of the child on his parent.

Lucy glanced after the retreating figure, then turned to Walter. 'I can't risk that sort of thing happening again,' she said. 'It would be bad enough even if he didn't smell so unpleasant. Shall we go away?'

Walter desired nothing better. 'But what about your mother and the social duties?' he asked.

She shrugged her shoulders. 'After all, mother can look after her own bear garden.'

'Bear garden's the word,' said Walter, feeling suddenly hopeful. 'Let's sneak away to some place where it's quiet.'

'My poor Walter!' Her eyes were derisive. 'I never knew anybody with such a mania for quietness as you. But I don't *want* to be quiet.'

His hope evaporated, leaving a feeble little bitterness, an ineffective anger. 'Why not stay here then?' he asked, with an attempt at sarcasm. 'Isn't it noisy enough?'

'Ah, but noisy with the wrong sort of noise,' she explained. 'There's nothing I hate more than the noise of cultured, respectable, eminent people, like these creatures.' She waved her hand comprehensively. The words evoked, for Walter, the memory of hideous evenings passed with Lucy in the company of the disreputable and uncultured – tipsy at that. Lady Edward's guests were bad enough. But the others were surely worse. How could she tolerate them?

Lucy seemed to divine his thoughts. Smiling, she laid a hand reassuringly on his arm. 'Cheer up!' she said. 'I'm not taking you into low company this time. There's Spandrell ...'

'Spandrell,' he repeated and made a grimace.

'And if Spandrell isn't classy enough for you, we shall probably find Mark Rampion and his wife, if we don't arrive too late.'

At the name of the painter and writer, Walter nodded approvingly.

'No, I don't mind listening to Rampion's noise,' he said. And then, making an effort to overcome the timidity which always silenced him when the moment came to give words to his feelings, 'but I'd much rather,' he added, jocularly, so as to temper the boldness of his words, 'I'd much rather listen to *your* noise, in private.'

Lucy smiled, but said nothing. He flinched away in a kind of terror from her eyes. They looked at him calmly, coldly, as though they had seen everything before and were not much interested – only faintly amused, very faintly and coolly amused.

'All right,' he said, 'let's go.' His tone was resigned and wretched.

'We must do a creep,' she said. 'Furtive's the word. No good being caught and headed back.'

But they did not escape entirely unobserved. They were approaching the door when there was a rustle and a sound of hurrying steps behind them. A voice called Lucy's name. They turned round and saw Mrs Knoyle, the General's wife. She laid a hand on Lucy's arm.

'I've just heard that you're going to see Maurice this evening,' she said, but did not explain that the General had told her so only because he wanted to relieve his feelings by saying something disagreeable to somebody who couldn't resent the rudeness. 'Give him a message from me, will you?' She leaned forward appealingly. 'Will you?' There was something pathetically young and helpless about her manner, something very young and soft even about her middle-aged looks. To Lucy, who might have been her daughter, she appealed as though to someone older and stronger than herself. 'Please.'

'But of course,' said Lucy.

Mrs Knoyle smiled gratefully. 'Tell him I'll come to see him to-morrow afternoon,' she said.

'To-morrow afternoon.'

'Between four and half-past. And don't mention it to anyone else, she added after a moment of embarrassed hesitation.

'Of course I won't.'

'I'm so grateful to you,' said Mrs Knoyle, and with a sudden shy impulsiveness she leaned forward and kissed her. 'Good night, my dear.' She slipped away into the crowd.

'One would think,' said Lucy, as they crossed the vestibule, 'that it was an appointment with her lover she was making, not her son.'

Two footmen let them out, obsequiously automatic. Closing the door, one winked to the other significantly. For an instant, the machines revealed themselves disquietingly as human beings.

Walter gave the address of Sbisa's restaurant to the taxi driver and stepped into the enclosed darkness of the cab. Lucy had already settled into her corner.

Meanwhile, in the dining-room, Molly d'Exergillod was still talking. She prided herself on her conversation. Conversation was in the family. Her mother had been one of the celebrated Miss Geoghegans of Dublin. Her father was that Mr Justice Brabant, so well known for his table talk and his witticisms from the bench. Moreover she had married into conversation. D'Exergillod had been a disciple of Robert de Montesquiou and had won the distinction of being mentioned in *Sodome et Gomorrhe* by Marcel Proust. Molly would have had to be a talker by marriage, if she had not already been one by birth. Nature and environment had conspired to make her a professional athlete of the tongue. Like all conscientious professionals, she was not content to be merely talented. She was industrious, she worked hard to develop her native powers. Malicious friends said that she could be heard practising her paradoxes in bed, before she got up in the morning. She herself admitted that she kept diaries in which she recorded, as well as the complicated history of her own feelings and sensations, every trope and anecdote and witticism that caught her fancy. Did she refresh her memory with a glance at these chronicles each time she dressed to go out to dinner? The same friends who had heard her practising in bed had also found her, like an examinee the night before his ordeal, laboriously mugging up Jean Cocteau's epigrams about art and Mr Birrell's after-dinner stories and W. B. Yeats's anecdotes about George Moore and what Charlie Chaplin had said to and of her last time she was in Hollywood. Like all professional talkers Molly was very economical with her wit and wisdom. There are not enough *bons mots* in existence to provide any industrious conversationalist with a new stock for every social occasion.

Though extensive, Molly's repertory was, like that of other more celebrated talkers, limited. A good housewife, she knew how to hash up the conversational remains of last night's dinner to furnish out this morning's lunch. Monday's funeral baked meats did service for Tuesday's wedding.

To Denis Burlap she was at this moment serving up the talk that had already been listened to with such appreciation by Lady Benger's lunch party, by the week-enders at Gobley, by Tommy Fitton, who was one of her young men, and Vladimir Pavloff, who was another, by the American Ambassador and Baron Benito Cohen. The talk turned on Molly's favourite topic.

'Do you know what Jean said about me?' she was saying (Jean was her husband). 'Do you?' she repeated insistently, for she had a curious habit of demanding answers to merely rhetorical questions. She leaned towards Burlap, offering dark eyes, teeth, a décolleté.

Burlap duly replied that he didn't know.

'He said that I wasn't quite human. More like an elemental than a woman. A sort of fairy. Do you think it's a compliment or an insult?'

'That depends on one's tastes,' said Burlap, making his face look arch and subtle as though he had said something rather daring, witty and at the same time profound.

'But I don't feel that it's even true,' Molly went on. 'I don't strike myself as at all elemental or fairy-like. I've always considered myself a perfectly simple, straightforward child of nature. A sort of peasant, really.' At this point in Molly's performance all her other auditors had burst into laughing protestation. Baron Benito Cohen had vehemently declared that she was 'one of Nature'th Roman Empreththeth.'

Burlap's reaction was unexpectedly different from that of the others. He wagged his head, he smiled with a far-away, whimsical sort of expression. 'Yes,' he said, 'I think that's true. A child of nature, *malgré tout*. You wear disguises, but the simple genuine person shows through.'

Molly was delighted by what she felt was the highest compliment Burlap could pay her. She had been equally delighted by the others' denials of her peasanthood. Denial had been *their* highest compliment. The flattering intention, the interest in her personality were the things that mattered. About the actual opinions of her admirers she cared little.

Burlap, meanwhile, was developing Rousseau's antithesis between the Man and the Citizen. She cut him short and brought the conversation back to the original theme.

'Human beings and fairies – I think it's a very good classification, don't you?' She leaned forward with offered face and bosom, intimately. 'Don't you?' she repeated the rhetorical question.

'Perhaps.' Burlap was annoyed at having been interrupted.

'The ordinary human – yes, let's admit it – all too human being on the one hand. And the elemental on the other. The one so attached and involved and sentimental – I'm terribly sentimental, I may say.' ('About ath thentimental ath the Thirenth in the Odyththey,' had been Baron Benito's classical comment.) 'The other, the elemental, quite free and apart from things, like a cat; coming and going – and going just as light-heartedly as it came; charming, but never charmed; making other people feel, but never really feeling itself. Oh, I envy them their free airiness.'

'You might as well envy a balloon,' said Burlap, gravely. He was always on the side of the heart.

'But they have such fun.'

'They haven't got enough feelings to have fun with. That's what I should have thought.'

'Enough to have fun,' she qualified; 'but perhaps not enough to be happy. Certainly not enough to be unhappy. That's where they're so enviable. Particularly if they're intelligent. Take Philip Quarles, for example. There's a fairy if ever there was one.' She launched into her regular description of Philip. 'Zoologist of fiction,' 'learnedly elfish,' 'a scientific Puck' were a few of her phrases. But the best of them had slipped her memory. Desperately she hunted it, but it eluded her. Her Theophrastian portrait had to go out into the world robbed this time of its most brilliantly effective passage, and a little marred as a whole by Molly's consciousness of the loss and her desperate efforts, as she poured forth, to make it good. 'Whereas his wife,' she concluded, rather painfully aware that Burlap had not smiled as frequently as he should have done, 'is quite the opposite of a fairy. Neither elfish, nor learned, nor particularly intelligent.' Molly smiled rather patronizingly. 'A man like Philip must find her a little inadequate sometimes, to say the least.' The smile persisted, a smile now of self-satisfaction. Philip had had a *faible* for her, still had. He wrote such amusing letters, almost as amusing as her own. ('*Quand je veux briller dans le monde*,' Molly was fond of quoting her husband's compliments, '*je cite des phrases de tes lettres*.') Poor Elinor! 'A little bit of a bore sometimes,' Molly went on. 'But mind you, a most charming creature. I've known her since we were children together. Charming, but not exactly a Hypatia.' Too much of a fool even to realize that Philip was bound to be attracted by a woman of his own mental stature, a woman he could talk to on equal terms. Too much of a fool to notice, when she had brought them together, how thrilled he had been. Too much of a fool to be jealous. Molly had felt the absence of jealousy as a bit of an insult. Not that she ever gave *real* cause for jealousy. She didn't sleep with husbands; she only talked to them. Still, they *did* do a lot of talking; there was no doubt of that. And wives *had* been jealous. Elinor's ingenuous confidingness had piqued her into being more than ordinarily gracious to Philip. But he had started to go round the world before much conversation had taken place. The talk, she anticipated, would be agreeably renewed on his return. Poor Elinor, she thought pityingly. Her feelings might have been a little less Christian, if she had realized that poor Elinor had noticed the admiring look in Philip's eye even before Molly had noticed it herself, and, noticing, had conscientiously proceeded to act the part of dragoman and go-between. Not that she had much hope or fear that Molly would achieve the transforming miracle. One does not fall very desperately in love with a loud speaker, however pretty, however firmly plump (for Philip's tastes were rather old-fashioned), however attractively callipygous. Her only hope was that the passions aroused by the plumpness and prettiness would be so very inadequately satisfied by the talking (for talk was all, according to report, that Molly ever conceded) that poor Philip would be reduced to a state of rage and misery most conducive to good writing.

'But of course,' Molly went on, 'intelligence ought never to marry intelligence. That's why Jean is always threatening to divorce me. He says I'm too stimulating. "*Tu ne m'ennuies pas assez*," he says; and that what he needs is *une femme sédative*. And I believe he's really right. Philip Quarles has been wise. Imagine an intelligent fairy of a man like Philip married to an equally fairyish intelligent woman – Lucy Tantamount, for example. It would be a disaster, don't you think?'

'Lucy'd be rather a disaster for any man, wouldn't she, fairy or no fairy?'

'No, I must say, I like Lucy.' Molly turned to her inner storehouse of Theophrastian phrases. 'I like the way she floats through life instead of trudging. I like the way she flits from flower to flower –

which is perhaps a rather too botanical and poetical description of Bentley and Jim Conklin and poor Reggie Tantamount and Maurice Spandrell and Tom Trivet and Poniatovsky and that young Frenchman who writes plays, what *is* his name? and the various others one has forgotten or never heard about.' Burlap smiled; they all smiled at this passage. 'Anyhow, she flits. Doing a good deal of damage to the flowers, I must admit.' Burlap smiled again. 'But getting nothing but fun out of it herself. I must say, I rather envy her. I wish I were a fairy and could float.'

'She has much more reason to envy you,' said Burlap, looking deep, subtle and Christian once more, and wagging his head.

'Envy me for being unhappy?'

'Who's unhappy?' asked Lady Edward breaking in on them at this moment. 'Good evening, Mr Burlap,' she went on without waiting for an answer. Burlap told her how much he had enjoyed the music.

'We were just talking about Lucy,' said Molly d'Exergillod, interrupting him. 'Agreeing that she was like a fairy. So light and detached.'

'Fairy!' repeated Lady Edward, emphatically rolling the 'r' far back in her throat. 'She's like a leprechaun. You've no idea, Mr Burlap, how hard it is to bring up a leprechaun.' Lady Edward shook her head. 'She used really to frighten me sometimes.'

'Did she?' said Molly. 'But I should have thought you were a bit of a fairy yourself, Lady Edward.'

'A bit,' Lady Edward admitted. 'But never to the point of being a leprechaun.'

*

'Well?' said Lucy, as Walter sat down beside her in the cab. She seemed to be uttering a kind of challenge. 'Well?'

The cab started. He lifted her hand and kissed it. It was his answer to her challenge. 'I love you. That's all.'

'Do you, Walter?' She turned towards him and, taking his face between her two hands, looked at him intently in the half-darkness. Do you?' she repeated; and as she spoke, she shook her head slowly and smiled. Then, leaning forward, she kissed him on the mouth. Walter put his arms round her; but she disengaged herself from the embrace. 'No, no,' she protested and dropped back into her corner. 'No.'

He obeyed her and drew away. There was a silence. Her perfume was of gardenias; sweet and tropical, the perfumed symbol of her being enveloped him. 'I ought to have insisted,' he was thinking. 'Brutally. Kissed her again and again. Compelled her to love me. Why didn't I? Why?' He didn't know. Nor why she had kissed him, unless it was just provocatively, to make him desire her more violently, to make him more hopelessly her slave. Nor why, knowing this, he still loved her. Why, why? he kept repeating to himself. And echoing his thoughts out loud her voice suddenly spoke.

'Why do you love me?' she asked from her corner.

He opened his eyes. They were passing a street lamp. Through the window of the moving cab the light of it fell on her face. It stood out for a moment palely against the darkness, then dropped back into invisibility – a pale mask that had seen everything before and whose expression was one of amused detachment and a hard, rather weary languor. 'I was just wondering,' Walter answered. 'And wishing I didn't.'

'I might say the same, you know. You're not particularly amusing when you're like this.'

How tiresome, she reflected, these men who imagined that nobody had ever been in love before! All the same, she liked him. He was attractive. No, 'attractive' wasn't the word. Attractive, as a possible lover, was just what he wasn't. 'Appealing' was more like it. An appealing lover? It wasn't exactly her style. But she liked him. There was something very *nice* about him. Besides, he was clever, he could be a pleasant companion. And tiresome as it was, his love-sickness did at least make him very faithful. That, for Lucy, was important. She was afraid of loneliness and needed her cavalier servants in constant attendance. Walter attended with a dog-like fidelity. But why did he look so like a *whipped* dog sometimes? So abject. What a fool! She felt suddenly annoyed by his abjection.

'Well, Walter,' she said mockingly, laying her hand on his, 'why don't you talk to me?'

He did not reply.

'Or is mum the word?' Her fingers brushed electrically along the back of his hand and closed round his wrist. 'Where's your pulse?' she asked after a moment. 'I can't feel it anywhere.' She groped over the soft skin for the throbbing of the artery. He felt the touch of her finger tips, light and thrilling and rather cold against his wrist. 'I don't believe you've got a pulse,' she said. 'I believe your blood stagnates.

The tone of her voice was contemptuous. What a fool! she was thinking. What an abject fool! 'Just stagnates,' she repeated and suddenly, with sudden malice, she drove her sharp file-pointed nails into his flesh. Walter cried out in surprise and pain. 'You deserved it,' she said and laughed in his face.

He seized her by the shoulders and began to kiss her, savagely. Anger had quickened his desire; his kisses were a vengeance. Lucy shut her eyes and abandoned herself unresistingly, limply. Little premonitions of pleasure shot with a kind of panic flutter, like fluttering moths, through her skin. And suddenly sharp fingers seemed to pluck, *pizzicato*, at the fiddle-strings of her nerves; Walter could feel her whole body starting involuntarily within his arms, starting as though it had been suddenly hurt. Kissing her, he found himself wondering if she had expected him to react in this way to her provocation, if she had hoped he would. He took her slender neck in his two hands. His thumbs were on her wind-pipe. He pressed gently. 'One day,' he said between his clenched teeth, 'I shall strangle you.'

Lucy only laughed. He bent forward and kissed her laughing mouth. The touch of his lips against her own sent a thin, sharp sensation that was almost pain running unbearably through her. The panic moth-wings fluttered over her body. She hadn't expected such fierce and savage ardours from Walter. She was agreeably surprised.

The taxi turned into Soho Square, slowed down, came to a halt. They had arrived. Walter let fall his hands and drew away from her.

She opened her eyes and looked at him. 'Well?' she asked challengingly, for the second time that evening. There was a moment's silence.

'Lucy,' he said, 'let's go somewhere else. Not here; not this horrible place. Somewhere where we can be alone.' His voice trembled, his eyes were imploring. The fierceness had gone out of his desire; it had become abject again, dog-like. 'Let's tell the man to drive on,' he begged.

She smiled and shook her head. Why did he implore, like that? Why was he so abject? The fool, the whipped dog!

'Please, *please!*' he begged. But he should have commanded. He should simply have ordered the man to drive on, and taken her in his arms again.

'Impossible,' said Lucy and stepped out of the cab. If he behaved like a whipped dog, he could be treated like one.

Walter followed her, abject and miserable.

Sbisa himself received them on the threshold. He bowed, he waved his fat white hands, and his expanding smile raised a succession of waves in the flesh of his enormous cheeks. When Lucy arrived, the consumption of champagne tended to rise. She was an honoured guest.

'Mr Spandrell here?' she asked. 'And Mr and Mrs Rampion?'

'Oo yez, oo yez,' old Sbisa repeated with Neapolitan, almost oriental emphasis. The implication was that they were not only there, but that if it had been in his power, he would have provided two of each of them for her benefit. 'And you? Quaite well, quaite well, I hope? Sooch lobster we have to-night, sooch lobster …' Still talking, he ushered them into the restaurant.

Chapter Eight

'WHAT I complain of,' said Mark Rampion, 'is the horrible unwholesome tameness of our world.'

Mary Rampion laughed whole-heartedly from the depths of her lungs. It was a laugh one could not hear without wishing to laugh oneself. 'You wouldn't say that,' she said, 'if you'd been your wife instead of you. Tame? I could tell you something about tameness.

There was certainly nothing very tame about Mark Rampion's appearance. His profile was steep, with a hooked fierce nose like a cutting instrument and a pointed chin. The eyes were blue and piercing, and the very fine hair, a little on the reddish side of golden, fluttered up at every moment, every breath of wind, like wisps of blown flame.

'Well, you're not exactly a sheep either,' said Rampion. 'But two people aren't the world. I was talking about the world, not us. It's tame, I say. Like one of those horrible big gelded cats.'

'Did you find the War so tame?' asked Spandrell, speaking from the half-darkness outside the little world of pink-tinged lamplight in which their table stood. He sat leaning backwards, his chair tilted on its hind legs against the wall.

'Even the War,' said Rampion. 'It was a domesticated outrage. People didn't go and fight because their blood was up. They went because they were told to; they went because they were good citizens. 'Man is a fighting animal,' as your stepfather is so fond of saying in his speeches. But what I complain of is that he's a domestic animal.'

'And getting more domestic every day,' said Mary Rampion, who shared her husband's opinions – or perhaps it would be truer to say, shared most of his feelings and, consciously or unconsciously, borrowed his opinions when she wanted to express them. 'It's factories, it's Christianity, it's science, it's respectability, it's our education,' she explained. 'They weigh on the modern soul. They suck the life out of it. They ...'

'Oh, for God's sake shut up!' said Rampion.

'But isn't that what you say?'

'What I say is what *I* say. It becomes quite different when you say it.'

The expression of irritation which had appeared on Mary Rampion's face cleared away. She laughed. 'Ah, well,' she said good-humouredly, 'ratiocination was never my strongest point. But you might be a little more polite about it in public.'

'I don't suffer fools gladly.'

'You'll suffer one very painfully, if you're not careful,' she menaced laughingly.

'If you'd like to throw a plate at him,' said Spandrell, pushing one over to her as he spoke, 'don't mind me.'

Mary thanked him. 'It would do him good,' she said. 'He gets so bumptious.'

'And it would do you no harm,' retorted Rampion, 'if I gave you a black eye in return.'

'You just try. I'll take you on with one hand tied behind my back.'

They all burst out laughing.

'I put my money on Mary,' said Spandrell, tilting back his chair. Smiling with a pleasure which he would have found it hard to explain, he looked from one to the other – from the thin, fierce, indomitable little man to the big golden woman. Each separately was good; but together, as a couple, they were better still. Without realizing it, he had quite suddenly begun to feel happy.

'We'll have it out one of these days,' said Rampion and laid his hand for a moment on hers. It was a delicate hand, sensitive and expressive. An aristocrat's hand if ever there was one, thought Spandrell. And hers, so blunt and strong and honest, was a peasant's. And yet by birth it was Rampion who was the peasant and she the aristocrat. Which only showed what nonsense the genealogists talked.

'Ten rounds,' Rampion went on. 'No gloves.' He turned to Spandrell.

'You ought to get married, you know,' he said.

Spandrell's happiness suddenly collapsed. It was as though he had come with a jolt to his senses. He felt almost angry with himself. What business had *he* to go and sentimentalize over a happy couple?

'I can't box,' he answered; and Rampion detected a bitterness in his jocularity, an inward hardening.

'No, seriously,' he said, trying to make out the expression on the other's face. But Spandrell's head was in the shadow, and the light of the interposed lamp on the table between them dazzled him.

'Yes, seriously,' echoed Mary. 'You ought. You'd be a changed man.'

Spandrell uttered a brief and snorting laugh, and letting his chair fall back on its four legs, leaned forward across the table. Pushing aside his coffee cup and his half-emptied liqueur glass, he planted his elbows on the table and his chin in his hands. His face came into the light of the rosy lamp. Like a gargoyle, Mary thought, a gargoyle in a pink boudoir. There was one on Notre Dame in just that attitude, leaning forward with his demon's face between his claws. Only the gargoyle was a comic devil, so extravagantly diabolical that you couldn't take his devilishness very seriously. Spandrell was a real person, not a caricature; that was why his face was so much more sinister and tragical. It was a gaunt face. Cheekbone and jaw showed in hard outline through the tight skin. The grey eyes were deeply set. In the cadaverous mask only the mouth was fleshy – a wide mouth, with lips that stood out from the skin like two thick weals.

'When he smiles,' Lucy Tantamount had once said of him, 'it's like an appendicitis operation with ironical corners.' The red scar was sensual, but firm at the same time and determined, as was the round chin below. There were lines round the eyes and at the corners of his lips. The thick brown hair had begun to retreat from the forehead.

'He might be fifty, to look at him,' Mary Rampion was thinking. 'And yet, what is his age?' She made calculations and decided that he couldn't be more than thirty-two or thirty-three. Just the right age for settling down.

'A changed man,' she repeated.

'But I don't particularly want to be changed.'

Mark Rampion nodded. 'Yes, that's the trouble with you, Spandrell. You like stewing in your disgusting suppurating juice. You don't want to be made healthy. You enjoy your unwholesomeness. You're rather proud of it, even.'

'Marriage would be the cure,' persisted Mary, indefatigably enthusiastic in the cause of the sacrament to which she herself owed all her life and happiness.

'Unless, of course, it merely destroyed the wife,' said Rampion. 'He might infect her with his own gangrene.'

Spandrell threw back his head and laughed profoundly, but, as was his custom, almost inaudibly, a muted explosion. 'Admirable!' he said. 'Admirable! The first really good argument in favour of matrimony I ever heard. Almost thou persuadest me, Rampion. I've never actually carried it as far as marriage.'

'Carried what?' asked Rampion, frowning a little. He disliked the other's rather melodramatically cynical way of talking. So damned pleased with his naughtinesses! Like a stupid child, really.

'The process of infection. I'd always stopped this side of the registry office. But I'll cross the threshold next time.' He drank some more brandy. 'I'm like Socrates,' he went on. 'I'm divinely appointed to corrupt the youth, the female youth more particularly. I have a mission to educate them in the way they shouldn't go.' He threw back his head to emit that voiceless laugh of his. Rampion looked at him distastefully. So theatrical. It was as though the man were over-acting in order to convince himself he was there at all.

'But if you only knew what marriage could mean,' Mary earnestly put in. 'If you only knew …'

'But, my dear woman, of course he knows,' Rampion interrupted with impatience.

'We've been married more than fifteen years now,' she went on, the missionary spirit strong within her. 'And I assure you …'

'I wouldn't waste my breath, if I were you.'

Mary glanced enquiringly at her husband. Wherever human relationships were concerned, she had an absolute trust in Rampion's judgement. Through those labyrinths he threaded his way with a sure tact which she could only envy, not imitate. 'He can smell people's souls,' she used to say of him. She herself had but an indifferent nose for souls. Wisely then, she allowed herself to be guided by him. She glanced at him. Rampion was staring into his coffee cup. His forehead was puckered into a frown; he had evidently spoken in earnest. 'Oh, very well,' she said and lit another cigarette.

Spandrell looked from one to the other almost triumphantly. 'I have a regular technique with the young ones,' he went on in the same too cynical manner. Mary shut her eyes and thought of the time when she and Rampion had been young.

Chapter Nine

'WHAT a blotch!' said the young Mary, as they topped the crest of the hill and looked down into the valley. Stanton-in-Teesdale lay below them, black with its slate roofs and its sooty chimneys and its smoke. The moors rose up and rolled away beyond it, bare as far as the eye could reach. The sun shone, the clouds trailed enormous shadows. 'Our poor view! It oughtn't to be allowed. It really oughtn't.'

'Every prospect pleases and only man is vile,' quoted her brother George.

The other young man was more practically minded. 'If one could plant a battery here,' he suggested, 'and drop a few hundred rounds onto the place ...'

'It would be a good thing,' said Mary emphatically. 'A really good thing.'

Her approval filled the military young man with happiness. He was desperately in love. 'Heavy howitzers,' he added, trying to improve on his suggestion. But George interrupted him.

'Who the devil is that?' he asked.

The others looked round in the direction he was pointing. A stranger was walking up the hill towards them.

'No idea,' said Mary, looking at him.

The stranger approached. He was a young man in the early twenties, hook-nosed, with blue eyes and silky pale hair that blew about in the wind – for he wore no hat. He had on a Norfolk jacket, ill cut and of cheap material, and a pair of baggy grey flannel trousers. His tie was red; he walked without a stick.

'Looks as if he wanted to talk to us,' said George.

And indeed, the young man was coming straight towards them. He walked rapidly and with an air of determination, as though he were on some very important business.

'What an extraordinary face!' thought Mary, as he approached. 'But how ill he looks! So thin, so pale.' But his eyes forbade her to feel pity. They were bright with power.

He came to a halt in front of them drawing up his thin body very rigidly, as though he were on parade. There was defiance in the attitude, an earnest defiance in the expression of his face. He looked at them fixedly with his bright eyes, turning from one to the other.

'Good afternoon,' he said. It was costing him an enormous effort to speak. But speak he must, just because of that insolent unawareness in their blank rich faces.

Mary answered for the others. 'Good afternoon.'

'I'm trespassing here,' said the stranger. 'Do you mind?' The seriousness of his defiance deepened. He looked at them sombrely. The young men were examining him from the other side of the bars, from a long way off, from the vantage ground of another class. They had noticed his clothes. There was hostility and contempt in their eyes. There was also a kind of fear. 'I'm a trespasser,' he repeated. His voice was rather shrill, but musical. His accent was of the country.

'One of the local cads,' George had been thinking.

'A trespasser.' It would have been much easier, much pleasanter to sneak out unobserved. That was why he had to affront them.

There was a silence. The military man turned away. He dissociated himself from the whole unpleasant business. It had nothing to do with him, after all. The park belonged to Mary's father. He was only a guest. 'I've gotta motta: Always merry and bright,' he hummed to himself, as he looked out over the black town in the valley.

It was George who broke the silence. 'Do we mind?' he said, repeating the stranger's words. His face had gone very red.

'How absurd he looks!' thought Mary, as she glanced at him. 'Like a bull calf. A blushing bull calf.'

'Do we mind?' Damned insolent little bounder! George was working up a righteous indignation. 'I should just think we do mind. And I'll trouble you to …'

Mary broke out into laughter. 'We don't mind at all,' she said. 'Not in the least.'

Her brother's face became even redder. 'What do you mean, Mary?' he asked furiously. ('Always merry and bright,' hummed the military man, more starrily detached than ever.) 'The place is private.'

'But we don't mind a bit,' she said, not looking at her brother, but at the stranger. 'Not a bit, when people come and are frank about it, like you.' She smiled at him; but the young man's face remained as proudly serious as ever. Looking into those serious bright eyes, she too suddenly became serious. It was no joke, she saw all at once, no joke. Grave issues were involved, important issues. But why grave and in what way important she did not know. She was only obscurely and profoundly aware that it was no joke. 'Good-bye,' she said in an altered voice, and held out her hand.

The stranger hesitated for a second, then took it. 'Good-bye,' he said. 'I'll get out of the park as quick as I can.' And turning round, he walked rapidly away.

'What the devil!' George began, turning angrily on his sister.

'Oh, hold your tongue!' she answered impatiently.

'Shaking hands with the fellow,' he went on protesting.

'A bit of a pleb, wasn't he?' put in the military friend.

She looked from one to the other without speaking and walked away. What louts they were! The two young men followed.

'I wish to God Mary would learn how to behave herself properly,' said George, still fuming.

The military young man made deprecating noises. He was in love with her; but he had to admit that she *was* rather embarrassingly unconventional sometimes. It was her only defect.

'Shaking that bounder's hand!' George went on grumbling.

That was their first meeting. Mary then was twenty-two and Mark Rampion a year younger. He had finished his second year at Sheffield University and was back at Stanton for the summer vacation. His mother lived in one of a row of cottages near the station. She had a little pension – her husband had been a postman – and made a few extra shillings by sewing. Mark was a scholarship boy. His younger and less talented brothers were already at work.

'A very remarkable young man,' the Rector insisted more than once in the course of his sketch of Mark Rampion's career, some few days later.

The occasion was a church bazaar and charitable garden party at the Rectory. Some of the Sunday School children had acted a little play in the open air. The dramatist was Mark Rampion.

'Quite unassisted,' the Rector assured the assembled gentry. 'And what's more, the lad can draw. They're a little eccentric perhaps, his pictures, a little … ah …' he hesitated.

'Weird,' suggested his daughter, with an upper middle-class smile, proud of her incomprehension.

'But full of talent,' the Rector continued. 'The boy's a real cygnet of Tees,' he added with a self-conscious, almost guilty laugh. He had a weakness for literary allusions. The gentry smiled perfunctorily.

The prodigy was introduced. Mary recognized the trespasser.

'I've met you before,' she said.

'Poaching your view.'

'You're welcome to it.' The words made him smile, a little ironically it seemed to her. She blushed, fearful lest she had said something that might have sounded rather patronizing. 'But I suppose you'd go on poaching whether you were welcome or not,' she added with a nervous little laugh.

He said nothing, but nodded, still smiling.

Mary's father stepped in with congratulations. His praises went trampling over the delicate little play like a herd of elephants. Mary writhed. It was all wrong, hopelessly wrong. She could feel that. But the trouble, as she realized, was that she couldn't have said anything better herself. The ironic smile still lingered about his lips. 'What fools he must think us all!' she said to herself.

And now it was her mother's turn. 'Jolly good' was replaced by 'too charming.' Which was just as bad, just as hopelessly beside the point.

When Mrs Felpham asked him to tea, Rampion wanted to refuse the invitation – but to refuse it without being boorish or offensive. After all, she meant well enough, poor woman. She was only rather ludicrous. The village Maecenas, in petticoats, patronizing art to the extent of two cups of tea and a slice of plum cake. The rôle was a comic one. While he was hesitating, Mary joined in the invitation.

'Do come,' she insisted. And her eyes, her smile expressed a kind of rueful amusement and an apology. She saw the absurdity of the situation. 'But I can't do anything about it,' she seemed to say. 'Nothing at all. Except apologize.

'I should like to come very much,' he said, turning back to Mrs Felpham.

The appointed day came. His tie as red as ever, Rampion presented himself. The men were out fishing; he was received by Mary and her mother. Mrs Felpham tried to rise to the occasion. The village Shakespeare, it was obvious, must be interested in the drama.

'Don't you love Barrie's plays?' she asked. 'I'm so fond of them.' She talked on; Rampion made no comment. It was only later, when Mrs Felpham had given him up as a bad job and had commissioned Mary to show him round the garden, that he opened his lips.

'I'm afraid your mother thought me very rude,' he said, as they walked along the smooth flagged paths between the roses.

'Of course not,' Mary protested with an excessive heartiness.

Rampion laughed. 'Thank you,' he said. 'But of course she did. Because I *was* rude. I was rude in order that I shouldn't be ruder. Better say nothing than say what I thought about Barrie.'

'Don't you like his plays?'

'Do I like them? I?' He stopped and looked at her. The blood rushed up into her cheeks; what had she said? 'You can ask that here.' He waved his hand at the flowers, the little pool with the fountain, the high terrace, with the stonecrops and the aubretias growing from between the stones, the grey, severe Georgian house beyond. 'But come down with me into Stanton and ask me there. We're sitting on the hard reality down there, not with an air cushion between us and the facts. You must have an assured five pounds a week at least, before you can begin to enjoy Barrie. If you're sitting on the bare facts, he's an insult.'

There was a silence. They walked up and down among the roses – those roses which Mary was feeling that she ought to disclaim, to apologize for. But a disclaimer, an apology would be an offence. A big retriever puppy came frisking clumsily along the path towards them. She called its name; the beast stood up on its hind legs and pawed at her.

'I think I like animals better than people,' she said, as she protected herself from its ponderous playfulness.

'Well, at least they're genuine, they don't live on air cushions like the sort of people you have to do with,' said Rampion, bringing out the obscure relevance of her remark to what had been said before. Mary was amazed and delighted by the way he understood.

'I'd like to know more of your sort of people,' she said; 'genuine people, people without air cushions.'

'Well, don't imagine I'm going to do the Cook's guide for you,' he answered ironically. 'We're not a Zoo, you know; we're not natives in quaint costume, or anything of that sort. If you want to go slumming, apply to the Rector.'

She flushed very red. 'You know I wasn't meaning that,' she protested.

'Are you sure?' he asked her. 'When one's rich, it's difficult not to mean that. A person like you simply can't imagine what it is not to be rich. Like a fish. How can a fish imagine what life out of the water is like?'

'But can't one discover, if one tries?'

'There's a great gulf,' he answered.

'It can be crossed.'

'Yes, I suppose it can be crossed.' But his tone was dubious.

They walked and talked among the roses for a few minutes longer;

then Rampion looked at his watch and said he must be going.

'But you'll come again?'

'Would there be much point in my coming again?' he asked. 'It's rather like interplanetary visiting, isn't it?'

'I hadn't felt it like that,' she answered, and added, after a little pause, 'I suppose you find us all very stupid, don't you?' She looked at him. He had raised his eyebrows, he was about to protest. She wouldn't allow him to be merely polite. 'Because, you know, we *are* stupid. Terribly stupid.' She laughed, rather ruefully. With people of her own kind stupidity was rather a virtue than a defect. To be too intelligent was to risk not being a gentleman. Intelligence wasn't altogether safe. Rampion had made her wonder whether there weren't better things than gentlemanly safety. In his presence she didn't feel at all proud of being stupid.

Rampion smiled at her. He liked her frankness. There was something genuine about her. She hadn't been spoilt – not yet, at any rate.

'I believe you're an *agent provocateur*,' he bantered, 'trying to tempt me to say rude and subversive things about my betters. But as a matter of fact, my opinions aren't a bit rude. You people aren't stupider than anyone else. Not naturally stupider. You're victims of your way of living. It's put a shell round you and blinkers over your eyes. By nature a tortoise may be no stupider than a bird. But you must admit that its way of living doesn't exactly encourage intelligence.'

They met again several times in the course of that summer. Most often they walked together over the moors. 'Like a force of nature,' he thought as he watched her with bent head tunnelling her way through the damp wind. A great physical force. Such energy, such strength and health – it was magnificent. Rampion himself had been a delicate child, constantly ailing. He admired the physical qualities he did not himself possess. Mary was a sort of beserker Diana of the moors. He told her as much one day. She liked the compliment.

'*Was für ein Atavismus!* That was what my old German governess always used to say about me. She was right, I think. I *am* a bit of an Atavismus.'

Rampion laughed. 'It sounds ridiculous in German. But it isn't at all absurd in itself. An atavismus – that's what we all ought to be. Atavismuses with all modern conveniences. Intelligent primitives. Big game with a soul.'

It was a wet cold summer. On the morning of the day fixed for their next meeting, Mary received a letter from him. 'Dear Miss Felpham,' she read, and this first sight of his handwriting gave her a strange pleasure. 'I've idiotically gone and caught a chill. Will you be more forgiving than I am – for I can't tell you how inexpressibly disgusted and angry I am with myself – and excuse me for putting you off till to-day week?'

He looked pale and thin, when she next saw him, and was still troubled by a cough. When she enquired about his health, he cut her short almost with anger. 'I'm quite all right,' he said sharply, and changed the subject.

'I've been re-reading Blake,' he said. And he began to speak about the *Marriage of Heaven and Hell*.

'Blake was civilized,' he insisted, '*civilized*. Civilization is harmony and completeness. Reason, feeling, instinct, the life of the body – Blake managed to include and harmonize everything. Barbarism is being lopsided. You can be a barbarian of the intellect as well as of the body. A barbarian of the soul and the feelings as well as of sensuality. Christianity made us barbarians of the soul, and now science is making us barbarians of the intellect. Blake was the last civilized man.'

He spoke of the Greeks and those naked sunburnt Etruscans in the sepulchral wall paintings. 'You've seen the originals?' he said. 'My word, I envy you.'

Mary felt terribly ashamed. She had seen the painted tombs at Tarquinia; but how little she remembered of them! They had just been curious old works of art like all those other innumerable old works of art she had dutifully seen in company with her mother on their Italian journey the year before. They had really been wasted on her. Whereas if he could have afforded to go to Italy …

'*They* were civilized,' he was saying, 'they knew how to live harmoniously and completely, with their whole being.' He spoke with a kind of passion, as though he were angry – with the world, with himself, perhaps. 'We're all barbarians,' he began; but was interrupted by a violent fit of coughing. Mary waited for the paroxysm to subside. She felt anxious and at the same time embarrassed and ashamed, as one feels when one has come upon a man off his guard and displaying a weakness which at ordinary times he is at pains to conceal. She wondered whether she ought to say something sympathetic about the cough, or pretend that she hadn't noticed it. He solved her problem by referring to it himself.

'Talk of barbarism,' he said, when the fit was over. He spoke in a tone of disgust, his smile was wry and angry. 'Have you ever heard anything more barbarous than that cough? A cough like that wouldn't be allowed in a civilized society.'

Mary proffered solicitude and advice. He laughed impatiently.

'My mother's very words,' he said. 'Word for word. You women are all the same. Clucking like hens after their chickens.'

'But think how miserable you'd be if we didn't cluck!'

A few days later – with some misgivings – he took her to see his mother. The misgivings were groundless; Mary and Mrs Rampion seemed to find no difficulties in making spiritual contact. Mrs Rampion was a woman of about fifty, still handsome and with an expression on her face of calm dignity and resignation. Her speech was slow and quiet. Only once did Mary see her manner change and that was when, Mark being out of the room preparing the tea, she began to talk about her son.

'What do you think of him?' she asked, leaning forward towards her guest with a sudden brightening of the eyes.

'What do I think?' Mary laughed. 'I'm not impertinent enough to set up as a judge of my betters. But he's obviously somebody, somebody that matters.'

Mrs Rampion nodded, smiling with pleasure. 'He's somebody,' she repeated. 'That's what I've always said.' Her face became grave. 'If only he were stronger! If I could only have afforded to bring him up better. He was always delicate. He ought to have been brought up more carefully than I could do. No, not more carefully. I was as careful as I could be. More comfortably, more healthily. But there, I couldn't afford it.' She shook her head. 'There you are.' She gave a little sigh and, leaning back in her chair, sat there in silence, with folded arms, looking at the floor.

Mary made no comment; she did not know what to say. Once more she felt ashamed, miserable and ashamed.

'What did you think of my mother?' Rampion asked later, when he was escorting her home.

'I liked her,' Mary answered. 'Very much indeed. Even though she did make me feel so small and petty and bad. Which is another way of saying that I admired her, and liked her because of my admiration.'

Rampion nodded. 'She *is* admirable,' he said. 'She's courageous and strong and enduring. But she's too resigned.'

'But I thought that was one of the wonderful things about her.'

'She has no right to be resigned,' he answered, frowning. 'No right. When you've had a life like hers, you oughtn't to be resigned. You ought to be rebellious. It's this damned religion. Did I tell you she was religious?'

'No; but I guessed it, when I saw her,' Mary answered.

'She's a barbarian of the soul,' he went on. 'All soul and future. No present, no past, no body, no intellect. Only the soul and the future and in the meantime resignation. Could anything be more barbarous? She ought to rebel.'

'I should leave her as she is,' said Mary. 'She'll be happier. And you can rebel enough for two.'

Rampion laughed. 'I'll rebel enough for millions,' he said.

At the end of the summer Rampion returned to Sheffield, and a little later the Felphams moved southwards to their London house. It was Mary who wrote the first letter. She had expected to hear from him; but he did not write. Not that there was any good reason why he should. But somehow she had expected that he would write; she was disappointed when he did not. The weeks passed. In the end she wrote to ask him the name of a book about which he had spoken in one of their conversations. The pretext was flimsy; but it served. He answered; she thanked him; the correspondence became an established fact.

At Christmas Rampion came up to London; he had had some things accepted by the newspapers and was unprecedentedly rich – he had ten pounds to do what he liked with. He did not let Mary know of his proximity till the day before his departure.

'But why didn't you tell me before?' she asked reproachfully, when she heard how many days he had already been in London.

'I didn't want to inflict myself on you,' he answered.

'But you knew I should have been delighted.'

'You have your own friends.' *Rich* friends, the ironical smile implied.

'But aren't you one of my friends?' she asked, ignoring the implication.

'Thank you for saying so.'

'Thank you for being so,' she answered without affectation or coquetry.

He was moved by the frankness of her avowal, the genuineness and simplicity of her sentiment. He knew, of course, that she liked and admired him; but to know and to be told are different things.

'I'm sorry, then, I didn't write to you before,' he said, and then regretted his words. For they were hypocritical. The real reason why he had kept away from her was not a fear of being badly received; it was pride. He could not afford to take her out; he did not want to accept anything.

They spent the afternoon together and were unreasonably, disproportionately happy.

'If only you'd told me before,' she repeated when it was time for her to go. 'I wouldn't have made this tiresome engagement for the evening.'

'You'll enjoy it,' he assured her with a return of that ironical tone in which all his references to her life as a member of the monied class were made. The expression of happiness faded from his face. He felt suddenly rather resentful at having been so happy in her company. It was stupid to feel like that. What was the point of being happy on opposite sides of a gulf? 'You'll enjoy it,' he repeated, more bitterly 'Good food and wine, distinguished people, witty conversation, the theatre afterwards. Isn't it the ideal evening?' His tone was savagely contemptuous.

She looked at him with sad, pained eyes, wondering why he should suddenly have started thus to lay waste retrospectively to their afternoon. 'I don't know why you talk like that,' she said. 'Do you know yourself?'

The question reverberated in his mind long after they had parted. 'Do you know yourself?' Of course he knew. But he also knew that there was a gulf.

They met again at Stanton in Easter week. In the interval they had exchanged many letters, and Mary had received a proposal of marriage from the military friend who had wanted to obliterate Stanton with howitzers. To the surprise and somewhat to the distress of her relations, she refused him.

'He's such a nice boy,' her mother had insisted.

'I know. But one simply can't take him seriously, can one?'

'Why not?'

'And then,' Mary continued, 'he doesn't really exist. He isn't completely there. Just a lump: nothing more. One can't marry someone who isn't there.' She thought of Rampion's violently living face; it seemed to burn, it seemed to be sharp and glowing. 'One can't marry a ghost, even when it's tangible and lumpy – particularly when it's lumpy.' She burst out laughing.

'I don't know what you're talking about,' said Mrs Felpham with dignity.

'But *I* do,' Mary answered. '*I* do. And after all, that's what chiefly matters in the circumstances.'

Walking with Rampion on the moors, she told him of the laying of this too, too solid military phantom. He made no comment. There was a long silence. Mary felt disappointed and at the same time ashamed of her disappointment. 'I believe,' she said to herself, 'I believe I was trying to get him to propose to me.'

The days passed; Rampion was silent and gloomy. When she asked him the reason, he talked unhappily about his future prospects. At the end of the summer, he would have finished his university course; it would be time to think of a career. The only career that seemed to be immediately open – for he could not afford to wait – was teaching.

'Teaching,' he repeated with emphatic horror, 'teaching! Does it surprise you that I should feel depressed?' But his misery had other causes besides the prospect of having to teach. 'Would she laugh at me, if I asked her?' he was wondering. He didn't think she would. But if she wasn't going to refuse, was it fair on his part to ask? Was it fair to let her in for the kind of life she would have to lead with him? Or perhaps she had money of her own; and in that case his own honour would be involved.

'Do you see me as a pedagogue?' he asked aloud. The pedagogue was his scapegoat.

'But why should you be a pedagogue, when you can write and draw? You can live on your wits.'

'But can I? At least pedagogy's safe.'

'What do you want to be safe for?' she asked, almost contemptuously.

Rampion laughed. 'You wouldn't ask if you'd had to live on a weekly wage, subject to a week's notice. Nothing like money for promoting courage and self-confidence.'

'Well then, to that extent money's a good thing. Courage and self-confidence are virtues.'

They walked on for a long time in silence. 'Well, well,' said Rampion at last, looking at her, 'you've brought it on yourself.' He made an attempt at laughter. 'Courage and self-confidence are virtues; you said so yourself. I'm only trying to live up to your moral standards. Courage and self-confidence! I'm going to tell you that I love you.' There was another long silence. He waited; his heart was beating as though with fear.

'Well?' he questioned at last. Mary turned towards him and, taking his hand, lifted it to her lips.

Before and after their marraige Rampion had many occasions of admiring those wealth-fostered virtues. It was she who made him give up all thought of teaching and trust exclusively to his wits for a career. She had confidence for both.

'I'm not going to marry a schoolmaster,' she insisted. And she didn't; she married a dramatist who had never had a play performed, except at the Stanton-in-Teesdale church bazaar, a painter who had never sold a picture.

'We shall starve,' he prophesied. The spectre of hunger haunted him; he had seen it too often to be able to ignore its existence.

'Nonsense,' said Mary, strong in the knowledge that people didn't starve. Nobody that she knew had ever been hungry. 'Nonsense.' She had her way in the end.

What made Rampion the more reluctant to take the unsafe course was the fact that it could only be taken at Mary's expense.

'I can't live on you,' he said. 'I can't take your money.'

'But you're not taking my money,' she insisted, 'you're simply an investment. I'm putting up capital in the hope of getting a good return. You shall live on me for a year or two, so that I may live on you for the rest of my life. It's business; it's positively sharp practice.'

He had to laugh.

'And in any case,' she continued, 'you won't live very long on me. Eight hundred pounds won't last for ever.'

He agreed at last to borrow her eight hundred pounds at the current rate of interest. He did it reluctantly, feeling that he was somehow betraying his own people. To start life with eight hundred pounds – it was too easy, it was a shirking of difficulties, a taking of unfair advantages. If it had not been for that sense of responsibility which he felt towards his own talents, he would have refused the money and either desperately risked the career of literature without a penny, or gone the safe and pedagogical way. When at last he consented to take the money, he made it a condition that she should never accept anything from her relations. Mary agreed.

'Not that they'll be very anxious to give me anything,' she added with a laugh.

She was right. Her father's horror at the misalliance was as profound as she had expected. Mary was in no danger, so far as he was concerned, of becoming rich.

They were married in August and immediately went abroad. They took the train as far as Dijon and from there began to walk southeast, towards Italy. Rampion had never been out of England before. The strangeness of France was symbolical to him of the new life he had just begun, the new liberty he had acquired. And Mary herself was no less symbolically novel than the country through which they travelled. She had not only self-confidence, but a recklessness which was altogether strange and extraordinary in his eyes. Little incidents impressed him. There was that occasion, for example, when she left her spare pair of shoes behind in the farm where they had spent the night. It was only late in the afternoon that she discovered her loss. Rampion suggested that they should walk back and reclaim them. She would not hear of it.

'They're gone,' she said. 'It's no use bothering. Let the boots bury their boots.' He got quite angry with her. 'Remember you're not rich any more,' he insisted. 'You can't afford to throw away a good pair of shoes. We shan't be able to buy a new pair till we get home.' They had taken a small sum with them for their journey and had vowed that in no circumstances would they spend more. 'Not till we get home,' he repeated.

'I know, I know,' she answered impatiently. 'I shall learn to walk barefoot.'

And she did.

'I was born to be a tramp,' she declared one evening when they were lying on hay in a barn. 'I can't tell you how I enjoy not being respectable. It's the Atavismus coming out. You bother too much, Mark. Consider the lilies of the field.'

'And yet,' Rampion meditated, 'Jesus was a poor man. Tomorrow's bread and boots must have mattered a great deal in his family. How was it that he could talk about the future like a millionaire?'

'Because he was one of nature's dukes,' she answered. 'That's why. He was born with the title; he felt he had a divine right, like a king. Millionaires who make their money are always thinking about money; they're terribly preoccupied about to-morrow. Jesus had the real ducal feeling that he could never be let down. None of your titled financiers or soap boilers. A genuine aristocrat. And besides, he was

114

an artist, he was a genius. He had more important things to think about than bread and boots and to-morrow.' She was silent for a little and then added, as an afterthought: 'And what's more, he wasn't respectable. He didn't care about appearances. They have their reward. But I don't mind if we do look like scarecrows.'

'You've paid yourself a nice lot of compliments,' said Rampion. But he meditated her words and her spontaneous, natural, untroubled way of living. He envied her her Atavismus.

It was not merely tramping that Mary liked. She got almost as much enjoyment out of the more prosaic settled life they led, when they returned to England. 'Marie-Antoinette at the Trianon,' was what Rampion called her, when he saw her cooking the dinner; she did it with such child-like enthusiasm.

'Think carefully,' he had warned her before they married. 'You're going to be poor. *Really* poor; not poor on a thousand a year like your impecunious friends. There'll be no servants. You'll have to cook and mend and do house-work. You won't find it pleasant.'

Mary only laughed. '*You'll* be the one who won't find it pleasant,' she answered, 'at any rate until I've learnt to cook.'

She had never so much as fried an egg when she married him.

Strangely enough that child-like, Marie-Antoinette-ish enthusiasm for doing things – for cooking on a real range, using a real carpet sweeper, a real sewing machine – survived the first novel and exciting months. She went on enjoying herself.

'I could never go back to being a perfect lady,' she used to say. 'It would bore me to death. Goodness knows, house-work and managing and looking after the children can be boring and exasperating enough. But being quite out of touch with all the ordinary facts of existence, living in a different planet from the world of daily, physical reality – that's much worse.'

Rampion was of the same opinion. He refused to make art and thought excuses for living a life of abstraction. In the intervals of painting and writing he helped Mary with the housework.

'You don't expect flowers to grow in nice clean vacuums.' That was his argument. 'They need mould and clay and dung. So does art.'

For Rampion, there was also a kind of moral compulsion to live the life of the poor. Even when he was making quite a reasonable income, they kept only one maid and continued to do a great part of the housework themselves. It was a case, with him, of *noblesse oblige* –

or rather *roture oblige*. To live like the rich, in a comfortable abstraction from material cares would be, he felt, a kind of betrayal of his class, his own people. If he sat still and paid servants to work for him, he would somehow be insulting his mother's memory, he would be posthumously telling her that he was too good to lead the life she had led.

There were occasions when he hated this moral compulsion, because he felt that it was compelling him to do foolish and ridiculous things; and hating, he would try to rebel against it. How absurdly shocked he had been, for example, by Mary's habit of lying in bed of a morning. When she felt lazy, she didn't get up; and there was an end of it. The first time it happened, Rampion was really distressed.

'But you can't stay in bed all the morning,' he protested.

'Why not?'

'Why not? But because you *can't*.'

'But I *can*,' said Mary calmly. 'And I *do*.'

It shocked him. Unreasonably, as he perceived when he tried to analyse his feelings. But all the same, he *was* shocked. He was shocked because he had always got up early himself, because all his people had had to get up early. It shocked him that one should lie in bed while other people were up and working. To get up late was somehow to add insult to injury. And yet, obviously, getting up early oneself, unnecessarily, did nothing to help those who *had* to get up early. Getting up, when one wasn't compelled to get up, was just a tribute of respect, like taking off one's hat in a church. And at the same time it was an act of propitiation, a sacrificial appeasement of the conscience.

'One oughtn't to feel like that,' he reflected. 'Imagine a Greek feeling like that!'

It was unimaginable. And yet the fact remained that, however much he might disapprove of the feeling, he did in fact feel like that.

'Mary's healthier than I am,' he thought; and he remembered those lines of Walt Whitman about the animals. 'They do not sweat and whine about their condition. They do not lie awake in the dark and weep for their sins.' Mary was like that and it was good. To be a perfect animal *and* a perfect human – that was the ideal. All the same, he was shocked when she didn't get up in the morning. He tried not to be; but he was shocked. Rebelling, he would sometimes lie in bed himself till noon, on principle. It was a duty not to be a barbarian of the conscience. But it was a very long time before he could genuinely enjoy his laziness.

Slug-abed habits were not the only things in Mary that distressed him. During those first months of their marriage he was often, secretly and against his own principles, shocked by her. Mary soon learnt to recognize the signs of his unexpressed disapproval and made a point, when she saw that she had shocked him, of shocking him yet more profoundly. The operation, she thought, did him nothing but good.

'You're such an absurd old puritan,' she told him.

The taunt annoyed him, because he knew it was well founded. By birth, to some extent, and yet more by training, he *was* half a puritan. His father had died when he was only a child and he had been brought up exclusively by a virtuous and religious mother who had done her best to abolish, to make him deny the existence of all the instinctive and physical components of his being. Growing up, he had revolted against her teaching, but with the mind only, not in practice. The conception of life against which he had rebelled was a part of him; he was at war against himself. Theoretically, he approved of Mary's easy aristocratic tolerance of behaviour which his mother had taught him was horribly sinful; he admired her unaffected enjoyment of food and wine and kisses, of dancing and singing, fairs and theatres and every kind of jollification. And yet, whenever, in those early days, she began to talk in her calm matter-of-fact way of what he had only heard of, portentously, as fornication and adultery, he felt a shock, not in his reason (for that, after a moment's reflection, approved), but in some deeper layer of his being. And the same part of him obscurely suffered from her great and whole-heartedly expressed capacity for pleasure and amusement, from her easy laughter, her excellent appetite, her unaffected sensuality. It took him a long time to unlearn the puritanism of his childhood. There were moments when his love for his mother turned almost to hatred.

'She had no right to bring me up like that,' he said. 'Like a Japanese gardener deliberately stunting a tree. No right.'

And yet he was glad that he had not been born a noble savage, like Mary. He was glad that circumstances had compelled him laboriously to learn his noble savagery. Later, when they had been married several years and had achieved an intimacy impossible in those first months of novelties, shocks, and surprises, he was able to talk to her about these matters.

'Living comes to you too easily,' he tried to explain. 'You live by instinct. You know what to do quite naturally, like an insect when it comes out of the pupa. It's too simple, too simple.' He shook his head. 'You haven't earned your knowledge; you've never realized the alternatives.'

'In other words,' said Mary, 'I'm a fool.'

'No, a woman.'

'Which is your polite way of saying the same thing. But I'd like to know,' she went on with an irrelevance that was only apparent, 'where you'd be without me. I'd like to know what you'd be doing if you'd never met me.' She moved from stage to stage of an emotionally coherent argument.

'I'd be where I am and be doing exactly what I'm doing now.' He didn't mean it, of course; for he knew, better than anyone, how much he owed to her, how much he had learnt from her example and precept. But it amused him to annoy her.

'You know that's not true,' Mary was indignant.

'It *is* true.'

'It's a lie. And to prove it,' she added, 'I've a very good mind to go away with the children and leave you for a few months to stew in your own juice. I'd like to see how you get on without me.'

'I should get on perfectly well,' he assured her with exasperating calmness.

Mary flushed; she was beginning to be genuinely annoyed. 'Very well then,' she answered, 'I'll really go. This time I really will.' She had made the threat before; they quarrelled a good deal, for both were quick-tempered.

'Do,' said Rampion. 'But remember that two can play at that going-away game. When you go away from me, I go away from you.'

'We'll see how you get on without me,' she continued menacingly.

'And you?' he asked.

'What about me?'

'Do you imagine you can get on any better without me than I can get on without you?'

They looked at one another for a little time in silence and then, simultaneously, burst out laughing.

Chapter Ten

A REGULAR technique,' Spandrell repeated. 'One chooses them unhappy, or dissatisfied, or wanting to go on the stage, or trying to write for the magazines and being rejected and consequently thinking they're *âmes incomprises*.' He was boastfully generalizing from the case of poor little Harriet Watkins. If he had just baldly recounted his affair with Harriet, it wouldn't have sounded such a very grand exploit. Harriet was such a pathetic, helpless little creature; anybody could have done her down. But generalized like this, as though her case was only one of hundreds, told in a language of the cookery book ('one chooses them unhappy' – it was one of Mrs Beeton's recipes), the history sounded, he thought, most cynically impressive. 'And one starts by being very, very kind, and so wise, and perfectly pure, an elder brother, in fact. And they think one's really wonderful, because, of course, they've never met anybody who wasn't just a city man, with city ideas and city ambitions. Simply wonderful, because one knows all about art and has met all the celebrities and doesn't think exclusively about money and in terms of the morning paper. And they're a little in awe of one too,' he added remembering little Harriet's expression of scared admiration; 'one's so unrespectable and yet so high-class, so at ease and at home among the great works and the great men, so wicked but so extraordinarily good, so learned, so well travelled, so brilliantly cosmopolitan and West-End (have you ever heard a suburban talking of the West-End?), like that gentleman with the order of the Golden Fleece in the advertisements for De Reszke cigarettes. Yes, they're in awe of one; but at the same time they adore. One's so understanding, one knows so much about life in general and their souls in particular, and one isn't a bit flirtatious or saucy like ordinary men, not a bit. They feel they could trust one absolutely; and so they can, for the first weeks. One has to get them used to the trap; quite tame and trusting, trained not to shy at an occasional brotherly pat on the back or an occasional chaste uncle-ish kiss on the forehead. And meanwhile one coaxes out their little confidences, one makes them talk about love, one talks about it oneself in a man-to-man sort of way, as though they were one's own age and as sadly disillusioned and bitterly knowing as oneself – which they find terribly shocking (though of course they don't say so), but oh, so thrilling, so enormously flattering. They simply love you for that. Well then, finally, when the moment seems ripe and they're thoroughly domesticated and no more frightened, one stages the dénouement. Tea in one's rooms – one's got them thoroughly used to coming with absolute impunity to one's rooms – and they're going to go out to dinner with one, so that there's no hurry. The twilight deepens, one talks disillusionedly and yet feelingly about the amorous mysteries, one produces cocktails – very strong – and goes on talking so that they ingurgitate them absent-mindedly without reflection. And sitting on the floor at their feet, one begins very gently stroking their ankles in an entirely platonic way, still talking about amorous philosophy, as though one were quite unconscious of what one's hand were doing. If that's not resented and the cocktails have done their work, the rest shouldn't be difficult. So at least I've always found.' Spandrell helped himself to more brandy and drank. 'But it's then, when they've become one's mistress that the fun really begins. It's then one deploys all one's Socratic talents. One develops their little temperaments, one domesticates them – still so wisely and sweetly and patiently – to every outrage of sensuality. It can be done, you know; the more easily, the more innocent they are. They can be brought in perfect ingenuousness to the most astonishing pitch of depravity.'

'I've no doubt they can,' said Mary indignantly. 'But what's the point of doing it?'

'It's an amusement,' said Spandrell with theatrical cynicism. 'It passes the time and relieves the tedium.'

'And above all,' Mark Rampion went on, without looking up from his coffee cup, 'above all it's a vengeance. It's a way of getting one's own back on women, it's a way of punishing them for being women and so attractive, it's a way of expressing one's hatred of them and of what they represent, it's a way of expressing one's hatred of oneself. The trouble with you, Spandrell,' he went on, suddenly and accusingly raising his bright pale eyes to the other's face, 'is that you really hate yourself. You hate the very source of your life, its ultimate basis – for there's no denying it, sex *is* fundamental. And you hate it, *hate* it.'

'Me?' It was a novel accusation. Spandrell was accustomed to hearing himself blamed for his excessive love of women and the sensual pleasures.

'Not only you. All these people.' With a jerk of his head he indicated the other diners. 'And all the respectable ones too. Practically everyone. It's the disease of modern man. I call it Jesus's disease on the analogy of Bright's disease. Or rather Jesus's and Newton's disease; for the scientists are as much responsible as the Christians. So are the big business men, for that matter. It's Jesus's and Newton's and Henry Ford's disease. Between them, the three have pretty well killed us. Ripped the life out of our bodies and stuffed us with hatred.'

Rampion was full of his subject. He had been busy all day on a drawing that symbolically illustrated it. Jesus, in the loin-cloth of the execution morning, and an overalled surgeon were represented, scalpel in hand, one on either side of an operating table, on which, foreshortened, the soles of his feet presented to the spectator, lay crucified a half-dissected man. From the horrible wound in his belly escaped a coil of entrails which, falling to the earth, mingled with those of the gashed and bleeding woman lying in the foreground, to be transformed by an allegorical metamorphosis into a whole people of living snakes. In the background receded a landscape of hills, dotted with black collieries and chimneys. On one side of the picture, behind the figure of Jesus, two angels – the spiritual product of the vivisectors' mutilations – were trying to rise on their outspread wings. Vainly, for their feet were entangled in the coils of the serpents. For all their efforts, they could not leave the earth.

'Jesus and the scientists are vivisecting us,' he went on, thinking of his picture. 'Hacking our bodies to bits.'

'But after all, why not?' objected Spandrell. 'Perhaps they're meant to be vivisected. The fact of shame is significant. We feel spontaneously ashamed of the body and its activities. That's a sign of the body's absolute and natural inferiority.'

'Absolutely and natural rubbish!' said Rampion indignantly. 'Shame isn't spontaneous, to begin with. It's artificial, it's acquired. You can make people ashamed of anything. Agonizingly ashamed of wearing brown boots with a black coat, or speaking with the wrong sort of accent, or having a drop at the end of their noses. Of absolutely anything, including the body and its functions. But that particular shame's just as artificial as any other. The Christians invented it, just as the tailors in Savile Row invented the shame of wearing brown boots with a black coat. There was precious little of it before Christian times. Look at the Greeks, the Etruscans.'

The antique names transported Mary back to the moors above Stanton. He was just the same. Stronger now, that was all. How ill he had looked that day! She had felt ashamed of being healthy and rich. Had she loved him then as much as she loved him now?

Spandrell had lifted a long and bony hand. 'I know, I know. Noble and nude and antique. But I believe they're entirely a modern invention, those Swedish-drill pagans of ours. We trot them out whenever we want to bait the Christians. But did they ever exist? I have my doubts.'

'But look at their art,' put in Mary, thinking of the paintings at Tarquinia. She had seen them a second time with Mark – really seen them on that occasion.

'Yes, and look at ours,' retorted Spandrell. 'When the Royal Academy sculpture room is dug up three thousand years hence, they'll say that twentieth-century Londoners wore fig-leaves, suckled their babies in public and embraced one another in the parks, stark naked.'

'I only wish they did,' said Rampion.

'But they don't. And then – leaving this question of shame on one side for the moment – what about asceticism as the preliminary condition of the mystical experience?'

Rampion brought his hands together with a clap and, leaning back in his chair, turned up his eyes. 'Oh, my sacred aunt!' he said. 'So it's come to that, has it? Mystical experience and asceticism. The fornicator's hatred of life in a new form.'

'But seriously …' the other began.

'No, seriously, have you read Anatole France's *Thaïs*?'

Spandrell shook his head.

'Read it,' said Rampion. 'Read it. It's elementary, of course. A boy's book. But one mustn't grow up without having read all the boys' books. Read it and then come and talk to me again about asceticism and mystical experiences.'

'I'll read it,' said Spandrell. 'Meanwhile, all I wanted to say is that there are certain states of consciousness known to ascetics that are unknown to people who aren't ascetics.'

'No doubt. And if you treat your body in the way nature meant you to, as an equal, you attain to states of consciousness unknown to the vivisecting ascetics.'

'But the states of the vivisectors are better than the states of the indulgers.'

'In other words, lunatics are better than sane men. Which I deny. The sane, harmonious, Greek man gets as much as he can of both sets of states. He's not such a fool as to want to kill part of himself. He strikes a balance. It isn't easy of course; it's even damnably difficult. The forces to be reconciled are intrinsically hostile. The conscious soul resents the activities of the unconscious, physical, instinctive part of the total being. The life of the one is the other's death and vice versa. But the sane man at least tries to strike a balance. The Christians, who weren't sane, told people that they'd got to throw half of themselves in the waste-paper basket. And now the scientists and business men come and tell us that we must throw away half of what the Christians left us. But I don't want to be three-quarters dead. I prefer to be alive, entirely alive. It's time there was a revolt in favour of life and wholeness.'

'But from your point of view,' said Spandrell, 'I should have thought this epoch needed no reforming. It's the golden age of guzzling, sport, and promiscuous love-making.'

'But if you knew what a puritan Mark really was!' Mary Rampion laughed. 'What a regular old puritan!'

'Not a puritan,' said her husband. 'Merely sane. You're like everyone else,' he went on, addressing himself to Spandrell. 'You seem to imagine that the cold, modern, civilized lasciviousness is the same as the healthy – what shall I call it? – phallism (that gives the religious quality of the old way of life; you've read the *Acharnians*?), phallism, then, of the ancients.'

Spandrell groaned and shook his head. 'Spare us the Swedish exercisers.'

'But it *isn't* the same,' the other went on. 'It's just Christianity turned inside out. The ascetic contempt for the body expressed in a different way. Contempt and hatred. That was what I was saying just now. You hate yourselves, you hate life. Your only alternatives are promiscuity or asceticism. Two forms of death. Why, the Christians themselves understood phallism a great deal better than this godless generation. What's that phrase in the marriage service? "With my body I thee worship." Worshipping with the body – that's the genuine phallism. And if you imagine it has anything to do with the unimpassioned civilized promiscuity of our advanced young people, you're very much mistaken indeed.'

'Oh, I'm quite ready to admit the deathliness of our civilized entertainments,' Spandrell answered. 'There's a certain smell,' he went on speaking in snatches between sucks at the half-smoked cigar he was trying to relight, 'of cheap scent ... and stale unwashedness ... I often think … the atmosphere of hell … must be composed of it.' He threw the match away. 'But the other alternative – there's surely no death about that. No death in Jesus or St Francis, for example.'

'In spots,' said Rampion. 'They were dead in spots. Very much alive in others, I quite agree. But they simply left half of existence out of account. No, no, they won't do. It's time people stopped talking about them. I'm tired of Jesus and Francis, terribly tired of them.'

'Well then, the poets,' said Spandrell. 'You can't say that Shelley's a corpse.'

'Shelley?' exclaimed Rampion. 'Don't talk to me of Shelley.' He shook his head emphatically. 'No, no. There's something very dreadful about Shelley. Not human, not a man. A mixture between a fairy and a white slug.'

'Come, come,' Spandrell protested.

'Oh, exquisite and all that. But what a bloodless kind of slime inside! No blood, no real bones and bowels. Only pulp and a white juice. And oh, that dreadful lie in the soul! The way he was always pretending for the benefit of himself and everybody else that the world wasn't really the world, but either heaven or hell. And that going to bed with women wasn't really going to bed with them, but just two angels holding hands. Ugh! Think of his treatment of women – shocking, really shocking. The women loved it of course – for a little. It made them feel so spiritual – that is, until it made them feel like committing suicide. *So* spiritual. And all the time he was just a young schoolboy with a sensual itch like anybody else's, but persuading himself and other people that he was Dante and Beatrice rolled into one, only much more so. Dreadful, dreadful! The only excuse is that, I suppose, he couldn't help it. He wasn't born a man; he was only a kind of fairy slug with the sexual appetites of a schoolboy. And then, think of that awful incapacity to call a spade a spade. He always had to pretend it was an angel's harp or a platonic imagination. Do you remember the *Ode to the Skylark*? "Hail to thee, blithe spirit! Bird thou never wert!"' Rampion recited with a ludicrous parody of an elocutionist's 'expression.' 'Just pretending, just lying to himself, as usual. The lark couldn't be allowed to be a mere bird, with blood and feathers and a nest and an appetite for caterpillars. Oh no! That wasn't nearly poetical enough, that was much too coarse. It had to be a disembodied spirit. Bloodless, boneless. A kind of ethereal flying slug. It was only to be expected. Shelley was a kind of flying slug himself; and, after all, nobody can really write about anything except himself. If you're a slug, you must write about slugs, even though your subject is supposed to be a skylark. But I wish to God,' Rampion added, with a sudden burst of comically extravagant fury, 'I wish to God the bird had had as much sense as those sparrows in the book of Tobit and dropped a good large mess in his eye. It would have served him damned well right for saying it wasn't a bird. Blithe spirit, indeed! Blithe spirit!'

Chapter Eleven

In Lucy's neighbourhood life always tended to become exceedingly public. The more the merrier was her principle; or if 'merrier' were too strong a word, at least the noisier, the more tumultuously distracting. Within five minutes of her arrival, the corner in which Spandrell and the Rampions had been sitting all evening in the privacy of quiet conversation was invaded and in a twinkling overrun by a loud and alcoholic party from the inner room. Cuthbert Arkwright was the noisiest and the most drunken – on principle and for the love of art as well as for that of alcohol. He had an idea that by bawling and behaving offensively, he was defending art against the Philistines. Tipsy, he felt himself arrayed on the side of the angels, of Baudelaire, of Edgar Allan Poe, of De Quincey, against the dull unspiritual mob. And if he boasted of his fornications, it was because respectable people had thought Blake a madman, because Bowdler had edited Shakespeare, and the author of *Madame Bovary* had been prosecuted, because when one asked for the Earl of Rochester's *Sodom* at the Bodleian, the librarians wouldn't give it unless one had a certificate that one was engaged on *bona fide* literary research. He made his living, and in the process convinced himself that he was serving the arts, by printing limited and expensive editions of the more scabrous specimens of the native and foreign literatures. Blond, beef-red, with green and bulging eyes, his large face shining, he approached vociferating greetings. Willie Weaver jauntily followed, a little man perpetually smiling, spectacles astride his long nose, bubbling with good humour and an inexhaustible verbiage. Behind him, his twin in height and also spectacled, but grey, dim, shrunken, and silent, came Peter Slipe.

'They look like the advertisement of a patent medicine,' said Spandrell as they approached. 'Slipe's the patient before, Weaver's the same after one bottle, and Cuthbert Arkwright illustrates the appalling results of taking the complete cure.'

Lucy was still laughing at the joke when Cuthbert took her hand. 'Lucy!' he shouted. 'My angel! But why in heaven's name do you always write in pencil! I simply cannot read what you write. It's a mere chance that I'm here to-night.'

So she'd written to tell him to meet her here, thought Walter. That vulgar, stupid lout.

Willie Weaver was shaking hands with Mary Rampion and Mark. 'I had no idea I was to meet the great,' he said. 'Not to mention the fair.' He bowed towards Mary, who broke into loud and masculine laughter. Willie Weaver was rather pleased than offended. 'Positively the Mermaid Tavern!' he went on.

'Still busy with the bric-à-brac?' asked Spandrell, leaning across the table to address Peter Slipe, who had taken the seat next to Walter's. Peter was an Assyriologist employed at the British Museum.

'But why in pencil, why in pencil?' Cuthbert was roaring.

'I get my fingers so dirty when I use a pen.'

'I'll kiss the ink away,' protested Cuthbert, and bending over the hand he was still holding, he began to kiss the thin fingers.

Lucy laughed. 'I think I'd rather buy a stylo,' she said.

Walter looked on in misery. Was it possible? A gross and odious clown like that?

'Ungrateful!' said Cuthbert. 'But I simply must talk to Rampion.'

And turning away, he gave Rampion a clap on the shoulder and simultaneously waved his other hand at Mary.

'What an agape!' Willie Weaver simmered on, like a tea kettle. The spout was now turned towards Lucy. 'What a symposium! What a –' he hesitated for a moment in search of the right, the truly staggering phrase – 'what Athenian enlargements! What a more than Platonic orgy!'

'What *is* an Athenian enlargement?' asked Lucy.

Willie sat down and began to explain. 'Enlargements, I mean, by contrast with our bourgeois and Pecksniffian smuggeries ...'

'Why don't you give me something of yours to print?' Cuthbert was persuasively inquiring.

Rampion looked at him with distaste. 'Do you think I'm ambitious of having my books sold in the rubber shops?'

'They'd be in good company,' said Spandrell. '*The Works of Aristotle* ...' Cuthbert roared in protest.

'Compare an eminent Victorian with an eminent Periclean,' said Willie Weaver. He smiled, he was happy and eloquent.

On Peter Slipe the burgundy had acted as a depressant, not a stimulant. The wine had only enhanced his native dimness and melancholy.

'What about Beatrice?' he said to Walter, 'Beatrice Gilray?' he hiccoughed and tried to pretend that he had coughed. 'I suppose you see her often, now that she works on the *Literary World.*'

Walter saw her three times a week and always found her well.

'Give her my love, when you see her next,' said Slipe.

'The stertorous borborygms of the dyspeptic Carlyle!' declaimed Willie Weaver, and beamed through his spectacles. The *mot*, he flattered himself, could hardly have been more exquisitely *juste*. He gave the little cough which was his invariable comment on the best of his phrases. 'I would laugh, I would applaud,' the little cough might be interpreted; 'but modesty forbids.'

'Stertorous what?' asked Lucy. 'Do remember that I've never been educated.'

'Warbling your native woodnotes wild!' said Willie. 'May I help myself to some of that noble brandy? The blushful Hippocrene.'

'She treated me badly, extremely badly.' Peter Slipe was plaintive. 'But I don't want her to think that I bear her any grudge.'

Willie Weaver smacked his lips over the brandy. 'Solid joys and liquid pleasures none but Zion's children know,' he misquoted and repeated his little cough of self-satisfaction.

'The trouble with Cuthbert,' Spandrell was saying, 'is that he's never quite learnt to distinguish art from pornography.'

'Of course,' continued Peter Slipe, 'she had a perfect right to do what she liked with her own house. But to turn me out at such short notice.'

At another time Walter would have been delighted to listen to poor little Slipe's version of that curious story. But with Lucy on his other hand, he found it difficult to take much interest.

'But I sometimes wonder if the Victorians didn't have more fun than we did,' she was saying. 'The more prohibitions, the greater the fun. If you want to see people drinking with real enjoyment, you must go to America. Victorian England was dry in every department. For example, there was a nineteenth amendment about love. They must have made it as enthusiastically as the Americans drink whiskey. I don't know that I really believe in Athenian enlargements – that is, if we're one of them.'

'You prefer Pecksniff to Alcibiades,' Willie Weaver concluded.

Lucy shrugged her shoulders. 'I've had no experience of Pecksniff.'

'I don't know,' Peter Slipe was saying, 'whether you've ever been pecked by a goose.'

'Been what?' asked Walter, recalling his attention.

'Been pecked by a goose.

'Never, that I can remember.'

'It's a hard, dry sensation.' Slipe jabbed the air with a tobacco-stained forefinger. 'Beatrice is like that. She pecks; she enjoys pecking. But she can be very kind at the same time. She insists on being kind in *her* way, and she pecks if you don't like it. Pecking's part of the kindness; so I always found. I never objected. But why should she have turned me out of the house as though I were a criminal? And rooms are so difficult to find now. I had to stay in a boarding house for three weeks. The food …' He shuddered.

Walter could not help smiling.

'She must have been in a great hurry to instal Burlap in your place.'

'But why in such a hurry as all that?'

'When it's a case of off with the old love and on with the new …'

'But what has love to do with it?' asked Slipe. 'In Beatrice's case.'

'A great deal,' Willie Weaver broke in. 'Everything. These superannuated virgins – always the most passionate.'

'But she's never had a love affair in her life.'

'Hence the violence,' concluded Willie triumphantly. 'Beatrice has a nigger sitting on the safety valve. And my wife assures me that her underclothes are positively Phrynean. That's most sinister.'

'Perhaps she likes being well dressed,' suggested Lucy.

Willie Weaver shook his head. The hypothesis was too simple.

'That woman's unconscious as a black hole.' Willie hesitated a moment. 'Full of batrachian grapplings in the dark,' he concluded and modestly coughed to commemorate his achievement.

*

Beatrice Gilray was mending a pink silk camisole. She was thirty-five, but seemed younger, or rather seemed ageless. Her skin was clear and fresh. From shallow and unwrinkled orbits the eyes looked out, shining. In a sharp, determined way her face was not unhandsome, but with something intrinsically rather comic about the shape and tilt of the nose, something slightly absurd about the bright beadiness of the eyes, the pouting mouth and round defiant chin. But one laughed with as well as at her; for the set of her lips was humorous and the expression of her round astonished eyes was mocking and mischievously inquisitive.

She stitched away. The clock ticked. The moving instant which, according to Sir Isaac Newton, separates the infinite past from the infinite future advanced inexorably through the dimension of time. Or, if Aristotle was right, a little more of the possible was every instant made real; the present stood still and drew into itself the future, as a man might suck for ever at an unending piece of macaroni. Every now and then Beatrice actualized a potential yawn. In a basket by the fireplace a black she-cat lay on her side purring and suckling four blind and parti-coloured kittens. The walls of the room were primrose yellow. On the top shelf of the bookcase the dust was thickening on the text-books of Assyriology which she had bought when Peter Slipe was the tenant of her upper floor. A volume of Pascal's *Thoughts*, with pencil annotations by Burlap, lay open on the table. The clock continued to tick.

Suddenly the front door banged. Beatrice put down her pink silk camisole and sprang to her feet.

'Don't forget that you must drink your hot milk, Denis,' she said, looking out into the hall. Her voice was clear, sharp, and commanding.

Burlap hung up his coat and came to the door. 'You oughtn't to have sat up for me,' he said, with tender reproachfulness, giving her one of his grave and subtle Sodoma smiles.

'I had some work I simply had to get finished,' Beatrice lied.

'Well, it was most awfully sweet of you.' These pretty colloquialisms, with which Burlap liked to pepper his conversation, had for sensitive ears a most curious ring. 'He talks slang,' Mark Rampion once said, 'as though he were a foreigner with a perfect command of English – but a foreigner's command. I don't know if you've ever heard an Indian calling anyone a "jolly good sport." Burlap's slang reminds me of that.'

For Beatrice, however, that 'awfully sweet' sounded entirely natural and un-alien. She flushed with a young-girlishly timid pleasure. But, 'Come in and shut the door,' she rapped out commandingly. Over that soft young timidity the outer shell was horny; there was a part of her being that pecked and was efficient. 'Sit down there,' she ordered; and while she was briskly busy over the milk-jug, the saucepan, the gas-ring, she asked him if he had enjoyed the party.

Burlap shook his head. '*Fascinatio nugacitatis*,' he said. '*Fascinatio nugacitatis*.' He had been ruminating the fascination of nugacity all the way from Piccadilly Circus.

Beatrice did not understand Latin; but she could see from his face that the words connoted disapproval. 'Parties are rather a waste of time, aren't they?' she said.

Burlap nodded. 'A waste of time,' he echoed in his slow ruminant's voice, keeping his blank preoccupied eyes fixed on the invisible daemon standing a little to Beatrice's left. 'One's forty, one has lived more than half one's life, the world is marvellous and mysterious. And yet one spends four hours chattering about nothing at Tantamount House. Why should triviality be so fascinating? Or is there something else besides the triviality that draws one? Is it some vague fantastic hope that one may meet the messianic person one's always been looking for, or hear the revealing word?' Burlap wagged his head as he spoke with a curious loose motion, as though the muscles of his neck were going limp. Beatrice was so familiar with the motion that she saw nothing strange in it any more. Waiting for the milk to boil, she listened admiringly, she watched him with a serious church-going face. A man whose excursions into the drawing-rooms of the rich were episodes in a lifelong spiritual quest might justifiably be regarded as the equivalent of Sunday morning church.

'All the same,' Burlap added, glancing up at her with a sudden mischievous, guttersnipish grin, most startlingly unlike the Sodoma smile of a moment before, 'the champagne and the caviar were really marvellous.' It was the demon that had suddenly interrupted the angel at his philosophic ruminations. Burlap had allowed him to speak out loud. Why not? It amused him to be baffling. He looked at Beatrice.

Beatrice was duly baffled. 'I'm sure they were,' she said, readjusting her church-going face to make it harmonize with the grin. She laughed rather nervously and turned away to pour out the milk into a cup. 'Here's your milk,' she rapped out, taking refuge from her bafflement in officious command. 'Mind you drink it while it's hot.'

There was a long silence. Burlap sipped slowly at his steaming milk and, seated on a pouf in front of the empty fireplace, Beatrice waited, rather breathlessly, she hardly knew for what.

'You look like little Miss Muffett sitting on her tuffet,' said Burlap at last.

Beatrice smiled. 'Luckily there's no big spider.'

'Thanks for the compliment, if it is one.'

'Yes it is,' said Beatrice. That was the really delightful thing about Denis, she reflected; he was so trustworthy. Other men were liable to pounce on you and try to paw you about and kiss you. Dreadful that was, quite dreadful. Beatrice had never really got over the shock she received as a young girl, when her Aunt Maggie's brother-in-law, whom she had always looked up to as an uncle, had started pawing her about in a hansom. The incident so scared and disgusted her that when Tom Field, whom she really did like, asked her to marry him, she refused, just because he was a man, like that horrible Uncle Ben, and because she was so terrified of being made love to, she had such a panic fear of being touched. She was over thirty now and had never allowed anyone to touch her. The soft quivering little girl underneath the business-like shell of her had often fallen in love. But the terror of being pawed about, of being even touched, had always been stronger than the love. At the first sign of danger, she had desperately pecked, she had hardened her shell, she had fled. Arrived in safety, the terrified little girl had drawn a long breath. Thank Heaven! But a little sigh of disappointment was always included in the big sigh of relief. She wished she hadn't been frightened, she wished that the happy relationship that had existed before the pawing could have gone on for ever, indefinitely. Sometimes she was angry with herself; more often she thought there was something fundamentally wrong with love, something fundamentally dreadful about men. That was the wonderful thing about Denis Burlap; he was so reassuringly not a pouncer or a pawer. Beatrice could adore him without a qualm.

'Susan used to sit on poufs, like little Miss Muffett,' Burlap resumed after a pause. His voice was melancholy. He had spent the last minutes in ruminating the theme of his dead wife. It was nearly two years now since Susan had been carried off in the influenza epidemic. Nearly two years; but the pain, he assured himself, had not diminished, the sense of loss had remained as overwhelmingly as ever. Susan, Susan, Susan — he had repeated the name to himself over and over again. He would never see her any more, even if he lived for a million years. A million years, a million years. Gulfs opened all round the words. 'Or on the floor,' he went on, reconstructing her image as vividly as he could. 'I think she liked sitting on the floor best. Like a child.' A child, a child, he repeated to himself. So young.

Beatrice sat in silence, looking into the empty grate. To have looked at Burlap, she felt, would have been indiscreet, indecent almost. Poor fellow! When she turned towards him at last, she saw that there were tears on his cheeks. The sight filled her with a sudden passion of maternal pity. 'Like a child,' he had said. But he was like a child himself. Like a poor unhappy child. Leaning forward she drew her fingers caressingly along the back of his limply hanging hand.

*

'Batrachian grapplings!' Lucy repeated and laughed. 'That was a stroke of genius, Willie.'

'All my strokes are strokes of genius,' said Willie modestly. He acted himself; he was Willie Weaver in the celebrated rôle of Willie Weaver. He exploited artistically that love of eloquence, that passion for the rotund and reverberating phrase with which, more than three centuries too late, he had been born. In Shakespeare's youth he would have been a literary celebrity. Among his contemporaries, Willie's euphuisms only raised a laugh. But he enjoyed applause, even when it was derisive. Moreover, the laughter was never malicious; for Willie Weaver was so good-natured and obliging that everybody liked him. It was to a hilariously approving audience that he played his part; and, feeling the approval through the hilarity, he played it for all it was worth. 'All my strokes are strokes of genius.' The remark was admirably in character. And perhaps true? Willie jested, but with a secret belief. 'And mark my words,' he added, 'one of these days the batrachians will erump, they'll break out.'

'But why batrachians?' asked Slipe. 'Anything less like a batrachian than Beatrice ...'

'And why should they break out?' put in Spandrell.

'Frogs don't peck.' But Slipe's thin voice was drowned by Mary Rampion's.

'Because things do break out,' she cried. 'They do.'

'Moral,' Cuthbert concluded: 'don't shut anything up. I never do.'

'But perhaps the fun consists in breaking out,' Lucy speculated.

'Perverse and paradoxical prohibitionist!'

'But obviously,' Rampion was saying, 'you get revolutions occurring inside as well as outside. It's poor against rich in the state. In the individual, it's the oppressed body and instincts against the intellect. The intellect's been exalted as the spiritual upper classes; the spiritual lower classes rebel.'

'Hear, hear!' shouted Cuthbert, and banged the table.

Rampion frowned. He felt Cuthbert's approbation as a personal insult.

'I'm a counter-revolutionary,' said Spandrell. 'Put the spiritual lower classes in their place.'

'Except in your own case, eh?' said Cuthbert grinning.

'Mayn't one theorize?'

'People have been forcibly putting them in their place for centuries,' said Rampion; 'and look at the result. *You*, among other things.' He looked at Spandrell, who threw back his head and noiselessly laughed. 'Look at the result,' he repeated. 'Inward personal revolution and consequent outward and social revolution.'

'Come, come,' said Willie Weaver. 'You talk as though the thermidorian tumbrils were already rumbling. England still stands very much where it did.'

'But what do you know of England and Englishmen?' Rampion retorted. 'You've never been out of London or your class. Go to the North.'

'God forbid!' Willie piously interjected.

'Go to the coal and iron country. Talk a little with the steel workers. It isn't revolution for a cause. It's revolution as an end in itself. Smashing for smashing's sake.'

'Rather sympathetic it sounds,' said Lucy.

'It's terrifying. It simply isn't human. Their humanity has all been squeezed out of them by civilized living, squeezed out by the weight of coal and iron. It won't be a rebellion of men. It'll be a revolution of elementals, monsters, pre-human monsters. And you just shut your eyes and pretend everything's too perfect.'

*

'Think of the disproportion,' Lord Edward was saying, as he smoked his pipe. 'It's positively ...' His voice failed. 'Take coal, for example. Man's using a hundred and ten times as much as he used in 1800. But population's only two and a half times what it was. With other animals ... Surely quite different. Consumption's proportionate to numbers.'

Illidge objected. 'But if animals can get more than they actually require to subsist, they take it, don't they? If there's been a battle or a plague, the hyenas and vultures take advantage of the abundance to overeat. Isn't it the same with us? Forests died in great quantities some millions of years ago. Man has unearthed their corpses, finds he can use them and is giving himself the luxury of a real good guzzle while the carrion lasts. When the supplies are exhausted, he'll go back to short rations, as the hyenas do in the intervals between wars and epidemics.' Illidge spoke with gusto. Talking about human beings as though they were indistinguishable from maggots filled him with a peculiar satisfaction. 'A coal-field's discovered; oil's struck. Towns spring up, railways are built, ships come and go. To a long-lived observer on the moon, the swarming and crawling must look like the pullulation of ants and flies round a dead dog. Chilean nitre, Mexican oil, Tunisian phosphates – at every discovery another scurrying of insects. One can imagine the comments of the lunar astronomers. "These creatures have a remarkable and perhaps unique tropism towards fossilized carrion." '

*

'Like ostriches,' said Mary Rampion. 'You live like ostriches.'

'And not about revolutions only,' said Spandrell, while Willie Weaver was heard to put in something about 'strouthocamelian philosophies.' 'About all the important things that happen to be disagreeable. There was a time when people didn't go about pretending that death and sin didn't exist. "*Au détour d'un sentier une charogne infâme,*" ' he quoted. 'Baudelaire was the last poet of the Middle Ages as well as the first modern. "*Et pourtant,*" ' he went on, looking with a smile to Lucy and raising his glass.

> ' Et pourtant vous serez semblable à cette ordure,
>   A cette horrible infection,
> Étoile de mes yeux, soleil de ma nature,
>   Vous, mon ange et ma passion!
>
> Alors, ô ma beauté, dites à la vermine
>   Qui vous mangera de baisers …'

'My dear Spandrell!' Lucy held up her hand protestingly.

'Really too necrophilous!' said Willie Weaver.

'Always the same hatred of life,' Rampion was thinking. 'Different kinds of death – the only alternatives.' He looked observantly into Spandrell's face.

*

'And when you come to think of it,' Illidge was saying, 'the time it took to form the coal measures divided by the length of a human life isn't so hugely different from the life of a sequoia divided by a generation of decay bacteria.'

*

Cuthbert looked at his watch. 'But good God!' he shouted. 'It's twenty-five to one.' He jumped up. 'And I promised we'd put in an appearance at Widdicombe's party. Peter, Willie! Quick march.'

'But you can't go,' protested Lucy. 'Not so absurdly early.'

'The call of duty,' Willie Weaver explained. 'Stern Daughter of the Voice of God.' He uttered his little cough of self-approbation.

'But it's ridiculous, it's not permissible.' She looked from one to another with a kind of angry anxiety. The dread of solitude was chronic with her. And it was always possible, if one sat up another five minutes, that something really amusing might happen. Besides, it was insufferable that people should do things she didn't want them to do.

'And we too, I'm afraid,' said Mary Rampion rising.

Thank heaven, thought Walter. He hoped that Spandrell would follow the general example.

'But this is impossible!' cried Lucy. 'Rampion, I simply cannot allow it.'

Mark Rampion only laughed. These professional sirens! he thought. She left him entirely cold, she repelled him. In desperation Lucy even appealed to the woman of the party.

'Mrs Rampion, you *must* stay. Five minutes more. Only five minutes,' she coaxed.

In vain. The waiter opened the side door. Furtively they slipped out into the darkness.

'Why *will* they insist on going?' asked Lucy, plaintively.

'Why will *we* insist on staying?' echoed Spandrell. Walter's heart sank; that meant the man didn't intend to go. 'Surely, that's much more incomprehensible.'

Utterly incomprehensible! On Walter the heat and alcohol were having their usual effects. He was feeling ill as well as miserable. What was the point of sitting on, hopelessly, in this poisonous air? Why not go home at once. Marjorie would be pleased.

'You, at least, are faithful, Walter.' Lucy gave him a smile. He decided to postpone his departure. There was a silence.

*

Cuthbert and his companions had taken a cab. Refusing all invitations, the Rampions had preferred to walk.

136

'Thank heaven!' said Mary as the taxi drove away. 'That dreadful Arkwright!'

'Ah, but that woman's worse,' said Rampion. 'She gives me the creeps. That poor silly little Bidlake boy. Like a rabbit in front of a weasel.'

'That's male trade unionism. I rather like her for making you men squirm a bit. Serves you right.'

'You might as well like cobras.' Rampion's zoology was wholly symbolical.

'But if it's a matter of creeps, what about Spandrell? He's like a gargoyle, a demon.'

'He's like a silly schoolboy,' said Rampion emphatically. 'He's never grown up. Can't you see that? He's a permanent adolescent. Bothering his head about all the things that preoccupy adolescents. Not being able to live, because he's too busy thinking about death and God and truth and mysticism and all the rest of it; too busy thinking about sins and trying to commit them and being disappointed because he's not succeeding. It's deplorable. The man's a sort of Peter Pan – much worse even than Barrie's disgusting little abortion, because he's got stuck at a sillier age. He's Peter Pan à la Dostoevsky-cum-de Musset-cum-the-Nineties-cum-Bunyan-cum-Byron and the Marquis de Sade. Really deplorable. The more so as he's potentially a very decent human being.'

Mary laughed. 'I suppose I shall have to take your word for it.'

*

'By the way,' said Lucy, turning to Spandrell. 'I had a message from your mother.' She gave it. Spandrell nodded, but made no comment.

'And the General?' he enquired as soon as she had finished speaking. He wanted no more said about his mother.

'Oh, the General!' Lucy made a grimace. 'I had at least half an hour of Military Intelligence this evening. Really, he oughtn't to be allowed. What about a Society for the Prevention of Generals?'

'I'm an honorary and original member.'

'Or why not for the Prevention of the Old, while one was about it?' Lucy went on. 'The old really aren't possible. Except your father, Walter. He's perfect. Really perfect. The only possible old man.'

'One of the few completely *im*possible, if you only knew.' Among the Bidlakes of Walter's generation the impossibility of old John was almost axiomatic. 'You wouldn't find him quite so perfect if you'd been his wife or his daughter.' As he uttered the words, Walter suddenly remembered Marjorie. The blood rushed to his cheeks.

'Oh, of course, if you will go and choose him as a husband or a father,' said Lucy, 'what can you expect? He's a possible old man just because he's been such an impossible husband and father. Most old people have had the life crushed out of them by their responsibilities. Your father never allowed himself to be squashed. He's had wives and children and all the rest. But he's always lived as though he were a boy on the spree. Not very pleasant for the wives and children, I grant. But how delightful for the rest of us!'

'I suppose so,' said Walter. He had always thought of himself as so utterly unlike his father. But he was acting just as his father had acted.

'Think of him unfilially.'

'I'll try.' How should he think of himself?

'Do, and you'll see that I'm right. One of the few possible old men. Compare him with the others.' She shook her head. 'It's no good; you can't have any dealings with them.'

Spandrell laughed. 'You speak of the old as though they were Kaffirs or Eskimos.'

'Well, isn't that just about what they are? Hearts of gold, and all that. And wonderfully intelligent – in their way, and all things considered. But they don't happen to belong to our civilization. They're aliens. I shall always remember the time I went to tea with some Arab ladies in Tunis. So kind they were, so hospitable. But they *would* make me eat such uneatable cakes, and they talked French so badly, and there was nothing whatever to say to them, and they were so horrified by my short skirts and my lack of children. Old people always remind me of an Arab tea party. Do you suppose we shall be an Arab tea party when we're old?'

'Yes, and probably a death's head into the bargain,' said Spandrell. 'It's a question of thickening arteries.'

'But what makes the old such an Arab tea party is their ideas. I simply cannot believe that thick arteries will ever make me believe in God and morals and all the rest of it. I came out of the chrysalis during the War, when the bottom had been knocked out of everything. I don't see how our grandchildren could possibly knock it out any more thoroughly than it was knocked then. So where would the misunderstanding come in?'

'They might have put the bottom in again,' suggested Spandrell. She was silent for a moment. 'I never thought of that.'

'Or else you might have put it in yourself. Putting the bottom in again is one of the traditional occupations of the aged.'

*

The clock struck one and, like the cuckoo released by the bell, Simmons popped into the library, carrying a tray. Simmons was middle-aged and had that statesman-like dignity of demeanour which the necessity of holding the tongue and keeping the temper, of never speaking one's real mind and preserving appearances tends always to produce in diplomats, royal personages, high government officials and butlers. Noiselessly, he laid the table for two, and, announcing that his lordship's supper was served, retired. The day had been Wednesday; two grilled mutton chops were revealed when Lord Edward lifted the silver cover. Mondays, Wednesdays, and Fridays were chop days. On Tuesdays and Thursdays there was steak with chips. On Saturdays as a treat, Simmons prepared a mixed grill. On Sundays he went out; Lord Edward had to be content with cold ham and tongue, and a salad.

'Curious,' said Lord Edward, as he handed Illidge his chop, 'curious that the sheep population doesn't rise. Not at the same rate as the human population. One would have expected ... seeing that the symbiosis is such a close ...' He chewed in silence.

'Mutton must be going out of fashion,' said Illidge. 'Like God,' he added provocatively, 'and the immortal soul.' Lord Edward was not to be baited. 'Not to mention the Victorian novelists,' Illidge went on. He had slipped on the stairs; and the only literature Lord Edward ever read was Dickens and Thackeray. But the Old Man calmly masticated. 'And innocent young girls.' Lord Edward took a scientific interest in the sexual activities of axolotls and chickens, guinea-pigs and frogs; but any reference to the corresponding activities of humans made him painfully uncomfortable. 'And purity,' Illidge continued, looking sharply into the Old Man's face, 'and virginities, and ...' He was interrupted and Lord Edward saved from persecution by the ringing of the telephone bell.

'I'll deal with it,' said Illidge jumping up from his place.

He put the receiver to his ear. 'Hullo!'

'Edward, is that you?' said a deep voice, not unlike Lord Edward's own. 'This is me. Edward, I've just this moment discovered a most extraordinary mathematical proof of the existence of God, or rather of ...'

139

'But this isn't Lord Edward,' shouted Illidge. 'Wait. I'll ask him to come.' He turned back to the Old Man. 'It's Lord Gattenden,' he said. 'He's just discovered a new proof of the existence of God.' He did not smile, his tone was grave. Gravity in the circumstances was the wildest derision. The statement made fun of itself. Laughing comment made it less, not more, ridiculous. Marvellous old imbecile! Illidge felt himself revenged for all the evening's humiliations. 'A mathematical proof,' he added, more seriously than ever.

'Oh dear!' exclaimed Lord Edward, as though something deplorable had happened. Telephoning always made him nervous. He hurried to the instrument. 'Charles, is that …'

'Ah, Edward,' cried the disembodied voice of the head of the family from forty miles away at Gattenden. 'Such a really remarkable discovery. I wanted your opinion on it. About God. You know the formula, m over nought equals infinity, m being any positive number? Well, why not reduce the equation to a simpler form by multiplying both sides by nought? In which case you have m equals infinity times nought. That is to say that a positive number is the product of zero and infinity. Doesn't that demonstrate the creation of the universe by an infinite power out of nothing? Doesn't it?' The diaphragm of the telephone receiver was infected by Lord Gattenden's excitement, forty miles away. It talked with breathless speed; its questions were earnest and insistent. 'Doesn't it, Edward?' All his life the fifth marquess had been looking for the absolute. It was the only sort of hunting possible to a cripple. For fifty years he had trundled in his wheeled chair at the heels of the elusive quarry. Could it be that he had now caught it, so easily, and in such an unlikely place as an elementary school-book on the theory of limits? It was something that justified excitement. 'What's your opinion, Edward?'

'Well,' began Lord Edward, and at the other end of the electrified wire, forty miles away, his brother knew, from the tone in which that single word was spoken, that it was no good. The Absolute's tail was still unsalted.

*

'Talking about elders,' said Lucy, 'did I ever tell either of you that really marvellous story about my father?'

'Which story?'

'The one about the conservatories.' The mere thought of the story made her smile.

140

'No, I never remember hearing about the conservatories,' said Spandrell, and Walter shook his head.

'It was during the War,' Lucy began. 'I was getting on for eighteen, I suppose. Just launched. And by the way, somebody did almost literally break a bottle of champagne over me. Parties were rather feverish in those days, if you remember.'

Spandrell nodded and, though as a matter of fact he had been at school during the War, Walter also nodded, knowingly.

'One day,' Lucy continued, 'I got a message: Would I go upstairs and see his Lordship? It was unprecedented. I was rather alarmed. You know how the old imagine one lives. And how upset they are when they discover they've been wrong. The usual Arab tea party.' She laughed and, for Walter, her laughter laid waste to all the years before he had known her. To elaborate the history of their young and innocent loves had been one of his standing consolations. She had laughed; and now not even fancy could take pleasure in that comforting romance.

Spandrell nodded. 'So you went upstairs, feeling as though you were climbing a scaffold ...'

'And found my father in his library, pretending to read. My arrival really terrified him. Poor man! I never saw anyone so horribly embarrassed and distressed. You can imagine how his terrors increased mine. Such strong feelings must surely have an adequate cause. What could it be? Meanwhile, he suffered agonies. If his sense of duty hadn't been so strong, I believe he would have told me to go away again at once. You should have seen his face!' The comic memories were too much for her. She laughed.

His elbow on the table, his head in his hand, Walter stared into his wine-glass. The bright little bubbles came rushing to the surface one by one, purposively, as though determined at all costs to be free and happy. He did not dare to raise his eyes. The sight of Lucy's laughter-distorted face, he was afraid, might make him do something stupid – cry aloud, or burst into tears.

'Poor man!' repeated Lucy, and the words came out on a puff of explosive mirth. 'He could hardly speak for terror.' Suddenly changing her tone, she mimicked Lord Edward's deep blurred voice bidding her sit down, telling her (stammeringly and with painful hesitations) that he had something to talk to her about. The mimicry was admirable. Lord Edward's embarrassed phantom was sitting at their table.

'Admirable!' Spandrell applauded. And even Walter had to laugh; but the depths of his unhappiness remained undisturbed.

'It must have taken him a good five minutes,' Lucy went on, 'to screw himself up to the talking point. I was in an agony, as you can imagine. But guess what it was he wanted to say.'

'What?'

'Guess.' And all at once Lucy began to laugh again, uncontrollably. She covered her face with her hands, her whole body shook, as though she were passionately weeping. 'It's too good,' she gasped, dropping her hands and leaning back in her chair. Her face still worked with laughter; there were tears on her cheeks. 'Too good.' She opened the little beaded bag that lay on the table in front of her and taking out a handkerchief, began to wipe her eyes. A gust of perfume came out with the handkerchief, reinforcing those faint memories of gardenias that surrounded her, that moved with her wherever she went like a second ghostly personality. Walter looked up; the strong gardenia perfume was in his nostrils; he was breathing what was for him the very essence of her being, the symbol of her power, of his own insane desires. He looked at her with a kind of terror.

'He told me,' Lucy went on, still laughing spasmodically, still dabbing at her eyes, 'he told me that he had heard that I sometimes allowed young men to kiss me at dances, in conservatories. Conservatories!' she repeated. 'What a wonderful touch! So marvellously in period. The eighties. The old Prince of Wales. Zola's novels. Conservatories! Poor dear man! He said he hoped I wouldn't let it happen again. My mother'd be so dreadfully distressed if she knew. Oh dear, oh dear!' She drew a deep breath. The laughter finally died down.

Walter looked at her and breathed her perfume, breathed his own desires and the terrible power of her attraction. And it seemed to him that he was seeing her for the first time. Now for the first time – with the half-emptied glass in front of her, the bottle, the dirty ash-tray; now, as she leaned back in her chair, exhausted with laughter, and wiping the tears of laughter from her eyes.

'Conservatories,' Spandrell was repeating. 'Conservatories. Yes, that's very good. That's very good indeed.'

'Marvellous,' said Lucy. 'The old are really marvellous. But hardly possible, you must admit. Except, of course, Walter's father.'

*

John Bidlake climbed slowly up the stairs. He was very tired. 'These awful parties,' he was thinking. He turned on the light in his bedroom. Over the mantelpiece one of Degas's realistically unlovely women sat in her round tin bath trying to scrub her back. On the opposite wall a little girl by Renoir played the piano between a landscape of his own and one of Walter Sickert's visions of Dieppe. Above the bed hung two caricatures of himself by Max Beerbohm and another by Rouveyre. There was a decanter of brandy on the table, with a siphon and glass. Two letters were propped conspicuously against the edge of the tray. He opened them. The first contained press cuttings about his latest show. The *Daily Mail* called him 'the veteran of British Art' and assured its readers that 'his hand has lost nothing of its cunning.' He crumpled up the cutting and threw it angrily into the fireplace. The next was from one of the superior weeklies. The tone was almost contemptuous. He was judged by his own earlier performance and condemned. 'It is difficult to believe that works so cheap and flashy – ineffectively flashy, at that – as those collected in the present exhibition should have been produced by the painter of the Tate Gallery 'Haymakers' and the still more magnificent 'Bathers', now at Tantamount House. In these empty and trivial pictures we look in vain for those qualities of harmonious balance, of rhythmic calligraphy, of three-dimensional plasticity which …' What a rigmarole! What tripe! He threw the whole bunch of cuttings after the first. But his contempt for the critics could not completely neutralize the effects of their criticism. 'Veteran of British Art' – it was the equivalent of 'poor old Bidlake.' And when they complimented him on his hand having lost none of its cunning, they were patronizingly assuring him that he still painted wonderfully well for an old dotard in his second childhood. The only difference between the hostile and the favourable critic was that one said brutally in so many words what the other implied in his patronizing compliment. He almost wished that he had never painted those Bathers.

He opened the other envelope. It contained a letter from his daughter Elinor. It was dated from Lahore:

The bazaars are the genuine article – maggoty. What with the pullulations and the smells, it is like burrowing through a cheese. From the artist's point of view, the distressing thing about all this oriental business is that it's exactly like that painting of Eastern scenes they did in France in the middle of last century. You know the stuff, smooth and shiny, like those pictures that used to be printed on tea canisters. When you're here, you see that the style is necessary. The brown skin makes the faces uniform and the sweat puts a polish on the skin. One would have to paint with a surface at least as slick as an Ingres.

He read on with pleasure. The girl always had something amusing to say in her letters. She saw things with the right sort of eye. But suddenly he frowned.

Yesterday, who should come to see us but John Bidlake Junior. We had imagined him in Waziristan; but he was down here on leave. I hadn't seen him since I was a little girl. You can imagine my surprise when an enormous military gentleman with a grey moustache stalked in and called me by my Christian name. He had never seen Phil, of course. We killed such fatted calves as this hotel can offer in honour of the prodigal brother.

John Bidlake leaned back in his chair and closed his eyes. The enormous military man with the grey moustache was his son. Young John was fifty. Fifty. There had been a time when fifty seemed a Methusalem age. 'If Manet hadn't died prematurely ...' He remembered the words of his old teacher at the art school in Paris. 'But did Manet die so young?' The old man had shaken his head. (Old? John Bidlake reflected. He had seemed very old then. But probably he wasn't more than sixty.) 'Manet was only fifty-one,' the teacher had answered. He had found it difficult to restrain his laughter. And now his own son was the age of Manet when Manet died. An enormous military gentleman with a grey moustache. And his brother was dead and buried at the other side of the world, in California. Cancer of the intestine. Elinor had met his son at Santa Barbara – a young man with a rich young wife, evading the Prohibition laws to the tune of a bottle of gin a day between them.

John Bidlake thought of his first wife, the mother of the military gentleman and the Californian who had died of cancer of the intestine. He was only twenty-two when he married for the first time. Rose was not yet twenty. They loved one another frantically, with a tigerish passion. They quarrelled too, quarrelled rather enjoyably at first, when the quarrels could be made up in effusions of sensuality as violent as the furies they assuaged. But the charm began to wear off when the children arrived, two of them within twenty-five months. There was not enough money to keep the brats at a distance, to hire professionals to do the tiresome and dirty work. John Bidlake's paternity was no sinecure. His studio became a nursery. Very soon, the results of passion – the yelling and the wetted diapers, the broken sleep, the smells – disgusted him of passion. Moreover, the object of

144

his passion was no longer the same. After the babies were born, Rose began to put on fat. Her face became heavy; her body swelled and sagged. The quarrels, now, were not so easily made up. At the same time, they were more frequent; paternity got on John Bidlake's nerves. His art provided him with a pretext for going to Paris. He went for a fortnight and stayed away four months. The quarrels began again on his return. Rose now frankly disgusted him. His models offered him facile consolations; he had a more serious love affair with a married woman who had come to him to have her portrait painted. Life at home was a dreariness tempered by scenes. After a particularly violent scene Rose packed up and went to live with her parents. She took the children with her; John Bidlake was only too delighted to be rid of them. The elder of the squalling diaper-wetters was now an enormous military gentleman with a grey moustache. And the other was dead of cancer of the intestine. He had not seen either of them since they were boys of five-and-twenty. The sons had stuck to their mother. She too was dead, had been in the grave these fifteen years.

Once bitten, twice shy. After his divorce John Bidlake had promised himself that he would never marry again. But when one falls desperately in love with a virtuous young woman of good family, what can one do? He had married, and those two brief years with Isabel had been the most extraordinary, the most beautiful, the happiest of all his life. And then she had died in childbirth, pointlessly. He did his best never to think of her. The recollection was too painful. Between her remembered image and the moment of remembering, the abysses of time and separation were vaster than any other gulf between the present and the past. And by comparison with the past which he had shared with Isabel every present seemed dim; and her death was a horrible reminder of the future. He never spoke of her, and all that might remind him of her – her letters, her books, the furniture of her room – he destroyed or sold. He wished to ignore all but here and now, to be as though he had only just entered the world and were destined to be eternal. But his memory survived, even though he never deliberately made use of it; and though the things which had been Isabel's were destroyed, he could not guard against chance reminders. Chance had found many gaps in his defences this evening. The widest breach was opened by this letter of Elinor's. Sunk in his armchair, John Bidlake sat for a long time, unmoving.

*

Polly Logan sat in front of the looking-glass. As she drew the comb through her hair there was a fine small crackling of electric sparks.

'Little sparks, like a tiny battle, tiny, tiny ghosts shooting. Tiny battle, tiny ghost of a battle-rattle.'

Polly pronounced the words in a sonorous monotone, as though she were reciting to an audience. She lingered lovingly over them, rolling the r's, hissing on the s's, humming like a bee on the m's, drawing out the long vowels and making them round and pure. 'Ghost rattle of ghost rifles, in-fin-it-es-imal ghost cannonade.' Lovely words! It gave her a peculiar satisfaction to be able to roll them out, to listen with an appreciative, a positively gluttonous ear, to the rumble of the syllables as they were absorbed into the silence. Polly had always liked talking to herself. It was a childish habit which she would not give up. 'But if it amuses me,' she protested, when people laughed at her for it, 'why shouldn't I? It does nobody any harm.'

She refused to let herself be laughed out of the habit.

'Electric, electric,' she went on, dropping her voice, and speaking in a dramatic whisper. 'Electrical musketry, metrical biscuitry. Ow!' The comb had caught in a tangle. She leaned forward to see more clearly in the glass what she was doing. The reflected face approached. 'Ma chère,' exclaimed Polly in another tone, 'tu as l'air fatigué. Tu es vieille. You ought to be ashamed of yourself. At your age. Tz, tz!' She clicked her tongue disapprovingly against her teeth and shook her head. 'This won't do, this won't do. Still, you looked all right to-night. "My dear, how sweet you look in white!"' She imitated Mrs Betterton's emphatic voice. 'Same to you and many of them. Do you think I shall look like an elephant when I'm sixty? Still, I suppose one ought to be grateful even for an elephant's compliments. "Count your blessings, count them one by one,"' she chanted softly, '"And it will surprise you what the Lord has done." Oh, heavens, heavens!' She put down her comb, she violently shuddered and covered her face with her hands. 'Heavens!' She felt the blood rushing up into her cheeks. 'The *gaffe*! The enormous and ghastly floater!' She had thought suddenly of Lady Edward. Of course she had overheard. 'How could I have risked saying that about her being a Canadian?' Polly moaned, overwhelmed with retrospective shame and embarrassment. 'That's what comes of wanting to say something clever at any cost. And then think of wasting attempted cleverness on Norah!

Norah! Oh Lord, oh Lord!' She jumped up and, pulling her dressing-gown round her as she went, hurried down the corridor to her mother's room. Mrs Logan was already in bed and had turned out the light. Polly opened the door and stepped into darkness.

'Mother,' she called, 'mother!' Her tone was urgent and agonized.

'What is it?' Mrs Logan answered anxiously out of the dark. She sat up and fumbled for the electric switch by the bed. 'What is it?' The light went on with a click. 'What is it, my darling?'

Polly threw herself down on the bed and hid her face against her mother's knees. 'Oh, mother, if you knew what a *terrible* floater I made with Lady Edward! If you *knew*! I forgot to tell you.'

Mrs Logan was almost angry that her anxiety had been for nothing. When one has put forth all one's strength to raise what seems an enormous weight, it is annoying to find that the dumb-bell is made of cardboard and could have been lifted between two fingers. 'Was it necessary to come and wake me up out of my first sleep to tell me?' she asked crossly.

Polly looked up at her mother. 'I'm sorry, mother,' she said repentantly. 'But if you knew what an *awful* floater it was!'

Mrs Logan could not help laughing.

'I couldn't have gone to sleep if I hadn't told you,' Polly went on.

'And I mayn't go to sleep until you have.' Mrs Logan tried to be severe and sarcastic. But her eyes, her smile betrayed her.

Polly took her mother's hand and kissed it. 'I knew you wouldn't mind,' she said.

'I do mind. Very much.'

'It's no good trying to bluff *me*,' said Polly. 'But now I *must* tell you about the floater.'

Mrs Logan heaved the parody of a sigh of resignation and, pretending to be overwhelmed with sleepiness, closed her eyes. Polly talked. It was after half past two before she went back to her room. They had discussed, not only the floater and Lady Edward, but the whole party, and everyone who was there. Or rather Polly had discussed and Mrs Logan had listened, had laughed and laughingly protested when her daughter's comments became too exuberantly high-spirited.

'But Polly, Polly,' she had said, 'you really mustn't say that people look like elephants.'

'But Mrs Betterton *does* look like an elephant,' Polly had replied. 'It's the truth.' And in her dramatic stage whisper she had added, rising from fancy to still more preposterous fancy: 'Even her nose is like a trunk.'

'But she's got a short nose.'

Polly's whisper had become more gruesome. 'An amputated trunk. They bit it off when she was a baby. Like puppies' tails.'

Chapter Twelve

F OR valued clients, Sbisa never closed his restaurant. They could sit there, in spite of the law, and consume intoxicating poisons as far into the small hours as they liked. An extra waiter came on at midnight to attend to the valued clients who wished to break the law. Old Sbisa saw to it that their value, to him, was very high. Alcohol was cheaper at the Ritz than at Sbisa's.

It was about half past one – 'only half past one,' Lucy complained – when she and Walter and Spandrell left the restaurant.

'Still young,' was Spandrell's comment on the night. 'Young and rather insipid. Nights are like human beings – never interesting till they're grown up. Round about midnight they reach puberty. At a little after one they come of age. Their prime is from two to half-past. An hour later they're growing rather desperate, like those man-eating women and waning middle-aged men who hop around twice as violently as they ever did in the hope of persuading themselves that they're not old. After four they're in full decay. And their death is horrible. Really horrible at sunrise, when the bottles are empty and people look like corpses and desire's exhausted itself into disgust. I have rather a weakness for the death-bed scenes, I must confess,' Spandrell added.

'I'm sure you have,' said Lucy.

'And it's only in the light of ends that you can judge beginnings and middles. The night has just come of age. It remains to be seen how it will die. Till then, we can't judge it.'

Walter knew how it would die for him – in the midst of Marjorie's tears and his own complicated misery and exasperation, in an explosion of self-hatred and hatred for the woman to whom he had been cruel. He knew, but would not admit his knowledge; nor that it was already half past one and that Marjorie would be awake and anxiously wondering why he hadn't returned.

At five to one Walter had looked at his watch and declared that he must go. What was the good of staying? Spandrell was immovable. There was no prospect of his having a moment alone with Lucy. He lacked even that justification for making Marjorie suffer. He was torturing her, not that he might be happy, but that he might feel bored, ill, exasperated, impatiently wretched.

'I must really go,' he had said, standing up.

But Lucy had protested, cajoled, commanded. In the end he sat down again. That had been more than half an hour ago and now they were out in Soho Square, and the evening, according to Lucy and Spandrell, had hardly begun.

'I think it's time,' Spandrell had said to Lucy, 'that you saw what revolutionary communist looked like.'

Lucy demanded nothing better.

'I belong to a sort of club,' Spandrell explained. He offered to take them in with him.

'There'll still be a few enemies of society on view, I expect,' he went on, as they stepped out into the refreshing darkness. 'Good fellows mostly. But absurdly childish. Some of them seem genuinely to believe that a revolution would make people happier. It's charming, it's positively touching.' He uttered his noiseless laugh. 'But I'm an aesthete in these matters. Dynamite for dynamite's sake.'

'But what's the point of dynamite, if you don't believe in Utopia?' asked Lucy.

'The point? But haven't you eyes?'

Lucy looked round her. 'I see nothing particularly frightful.'

'They have eyes and see not.' He halted, took her arm with one hand and with the other pointed round the square. 'The deserted pickle factory, transformed into a dance hall; the lying-in hospital; Sbisa's; the publishers of *Who's Who*. And once,' he added, 'the Duke of Monmouth's palace. You can imagine the ghosts:

> Whether inspired by some diviner lust,
> His father got him with a keener gust ...

And so forth. You know the portrait of him after the execution, lying on a bed, with the sheet up to his chin, so that you can't see the place where the neck was cut through? By Kneller. Or was it Lely? Monmouth and pickles, lying-in and *Who's Who*, and dancing and Sbisa's champagne – think of them a little, think of them.'

'I'm thinking of them,' said Lucy. 'Hard.'

'And do you still ask what the point of dynamite is?'

They walked on. At the door of a little house in St Giles's Spandrell called a halt. 'Wait a moment,' he said, beckoning the others back into the darkness. He rang. The door opened at once. There was a brief parleying in the shadows; then Spandrell turned and called to his companions. They followed him into a dark hall up a flight of stairs and into a brightly-lighted room on the first floor. Two men were standing near the fireplace, a turbaned Indian and a little man with red hair. At the sound of footsteps they turned round. The red-haired man was Illidge.

'Spandrell? Bidlake?' he raised his invisibly sandy eyebrows in astonishment. And what's that woman doing here? he wondered.

Lucy came forward with outstretched hand. 'We're old acquaintances,' she said with a smile of friendly recognition.

Illidge, who was preparing to make his face look coldly hostile found himself smiling back at her.

*

A taxi turned into the street, suddenly and startlingly breaking the silence. Marjorie sat up in bed, listening. The hum of the engine grew louder and louder. It was Walter's taxi; this time she felt sure of it, she knew. Nearer it came and nearer. At the bottom of the little hill on the right of the house, the driver changed down to a lower gear; the engine hummed more shrilly, like an angry wasp. Nearer and nearer. She was possessed by an anxiety that was of the body as well as of the mind. She felt breathless, her heart beat strongly and irregularly – beat, beat, beat and then it seemed to fail; the expected beat did not make itself felt; it was as though a trap-door had been opened beneath her into the void; she knew the terror of emptiness, of falling, falling – and the next retarded beat was the impact of her body against solid earth. Nearer, nearer. She almost dreaded, though she had so unhappily longed for, his return. She dreaded the emotions she would feel at the sight of him; the tears she would shed, the reproaches she would find herself uttering, in spite of herself. And what would he say and do, what would be his thoughts? She was afraid of imagining. Nearer; the sound was just below her windows; it retreated, it diminished. And she had been so certain that it was Walter's taxi. She lay down again. If only she could have slept. But that physical anxiety of her body would not allow her. The blood thumped in her ears. Her skin was hot and dry. Her eyes ached. She lay quite still, on her back, her arms crossed on her breast, like a dead woman laid out for burial. Sleep, sleep, she whispered to herself; she imagined herself relaxed, smoothed out, asleep. But suddenly, a malicious hand seemed to pluck at her taut nerves. A violent tic contracted the muscles of her limbs; she started as though with terror. And the physical reaction of fear evoked an emotion of terror in her mind, quickening and intensifying the anxiety of unhappiness which, all the time, had underlain her conscious efforts to achieve tranquillity. 'Sleep, sleep, relax' –

it was useless to go on trying to be calm, to forget, to sleep. She allowed her misery to come to the surface of her mind. 'Why should he want to make me so unhappy?' She turned her head. The luminous hands of the clock on the little table beside her bed marked a quarter to three. A quarter to three – and he knew she could never get to sleep before he came in. 'He knows I'm ill,' she said aloud. 'Doesn't he care?'

A new thought suddenly occurred to her. 'Perhaps he wants me to die.' To die, not to be, not to see his face any more, to leave him with that other woman. The tears came into her eyes. Perhaps he was deliberately trying to kill her. It was not in spite of her being ill that he treated her like this; it was because she suffered so much, it was precisely because she was ill. He was cruel with a purpose. He hoped, he intended that she should die; die and leave him in peace with that other woman. She pressed her face against the pillow and sobbed. Never see him again, never any more. Darkness, loneliness, death, for ever. For ever and ever. And on top of everything, it was all so unfair. Was it her fault that she couldn't afford to dress well?

'If I could afford to buy the clothes she buys.' Chanel, Lanvin, – the pages of *Vogue* floated before her eyes – Molyneux, Groult. ... At one of those cheap-smart shops where cocottes buy their clothes, off Shaftesbury Avenue, there was a model for sixteen guineas. 'He likes her because she's attractive. But if I had the money ...' It wasn't fair. He was making her pay for not being well off. She had to suffer because he didn't earn enough to buy her good clothes.

And then there was the baby. He was making her pay for that. His child. He was bored with her, because she was always tired and ill; he didn't like her any more. That was the greatest injustice of all.

A cell had multiplied itself and become a worm, the worm had become a fish, the fish was turning into the foetus of a mammal. Marjorie felt sick and tired. Fifteen years hence a boy would be confirmed. Enormous in his robes, like a full-rigged ship, the Bishop would say: 'Do ye here in the presence of God, and of this congregation, renew the solemn promise and vow that was made in your name at your Baptism?' And the ex-fish would answer with passionate conviction: 'I do.'

For the thousandth time she wished she were not pregnant. Walter might not succeed in killing her now. But perhaps it would happen in any case, when the child was born. The doctor had said it would be difficult for her to have a baby. The pelvis was narrow.

Death re-appeared before her, a great pit at her feet.

A sound made her start violently. The outside door of the flat was being furtively opened. The hinges squeaked. There were muffled footsteps. Another squeak, the hardly perceptible click of the spring latch being carefully let back into place, then more footsteps. Another click and simultaneously the light showed yellow under the door that separated her room from his. Did he mean to go to bed without coming to bid her good-night? She lay quite still, quiveringly awake, her eyes wide open, listening to the noises that came from the other room and to the quick terrified beating of her own heart.

Walter sat on the bed unlacing his shoes. He was wondering why he had not come home three hours before, why he had ever gone out at all. He hated a crowd; alcohol disagreed with him and the twice-breathed air, the smell, the smoke of restaurants acted on him like a depressing poison. He had suffered to no purpose; except for those painful exasperating moments in the taxi, he had not been alone with Lucy the whole evening. The hours he had spent with her had been hours of boredom and impatience – endlessly long, minute after minute of torture. And the torture of desire and jealousy had been reinforced by the torture of self-conscious guilt. Every minute they lingered at Sbisa's, every minute among the revolutionaries, was a minute that retarded the consummation of his desire and that, increasing Marjorie's unhappiness, increased at the same time his own remorse and shame. It was after three when finally they left the club. Would she dismiss Spandrell and let him drive her home? He looked at her; his eyes were eloquent. He willed, he commanded.

'There'll be sandwiches and drinks at my house,' said Lucy, when they were in the street.

'That's very welcome news,' said Spandrell.

'Come along, Walter darling.' She took his hand, she pressed it affectionately.

Walter shook his head. 'I must go home.' If misery could kill, he would have died there in the street.

'But you can't desert us now,' she protested. 'Now that you've got thus far, you really must see it through. Come along.' She tugged at his hand.

'No, no.' But what she said was true. He could hardly make Marjorie any more wretched than he had certainly done already. If she weren't there, he thought, if she were to die – a miscarriage, blood poisoning ...

Spandrell looked at his watch. 'Half past three. The death rattle has almost started.' Walter listened in horror; was the man reading his thoughts? '*Munie des conforts de notre sainte religion.* Your place is at the bedside, Walter. You can't go and leave the night to die like a dog in a ditch.'

Like a dog in a ditch. The words were terrible, they condemned him. 'I *must* go.' He was firm, three hours too late. He walked away. In Oxford Street he found a taxi. Hoping, he knew vainly, to come home unobserved, he paid off the cab at Chalk Farm station and walked the last furlong to the door of the house in which he and Marjorie occupied the two upper floors. He had crept upstairs, he had opened the door with the precautions of a murderer. No sound from Marjorie's room. He undressed, he washed as though he were performing a dangerous operation. He turned out the light and got into bed. The darkness was utterly silent. He was safe.

'Walter!'

It was with the feelings of a condemned criminal when the warders come to wake him on the morning of his execution that he answered, putting an imitation of astonishment into his voice: 'Are you awake, Marjorie?' He got up and walked, as though from the condemned cell to the scaffold, into her room.

'Do you want to make me die, Walter?'

Like a dog in a ditch, alone. He made as if to take her in his arms, Marjorie pushed him away. Her misery had momentarily turned to anger, her love to a kind of hatred and resentment. 'Don't be a hypocrite on top of everything else,' she said. 'Why can't you tell me frankly that you hate me, that you'd like to get rid of me, that you'd be glad if I died? Why can't you be honest and tell me?'

'But why should I tell you what isn't true?' he protested.

'Are you going to tell me that you love me, then?' she asked sarcastically.

He almost believed it while he said so; and besides it was true, in a way.

'But I do, I do. This other thing's a kind of madness. I don't want to. I can't help it. If you knew how wretched I felt, what an unspeakable brute.' All that he had ever suffered from thwarted desire, from remorse and shame and self-hatred seemed to be crystallized by his words into a single agony. He suffered and he pitied his own sufferings. 'If you knew, Marjorie.' And suddenly something in his body seemed to break. An invisible hand took him by the throat, his eyes

154

were blinded with tears and a power within him that was not himself shook his whole frame and wrenched from him, against his will, a muffled and hardly human cry.

At the sound of this dreadful sobbing in the darkness beside her, Marjorie's anger suddenly fell. She only knew that he was unhappy, that she loved him. She even felt remorse for her anger, for the bitter words she had spoken.

'Walter. My darling.' She stretched out her hands, she drew him down towards her. He lay there like a child in the consolation of her embrace.

*

'Do you enjoy tormenting him?' Spandrell enquired, as they walked towards Charing Cross Road.

'Tormenting whom?' said Lucy. 'Walter? But I don't.'

'But you don't let him sleep with you?' said Spandrell. Lucy shook her head. 'And then you say you don't torment him! Poor wretch!'

'But why should I have him, if I don't want to?'

'Why indeed? Meanwhile, however, keeping him dangling's mere torture.'

'But I like him,' said Lucy. 'He's such good company. Too young, of course; but really rather perfect. And I assure you, I don't torment him. He torments himself.'

Spandrell delayed his laughter long enough to whistle for the taxi he had seen at the end of the street. The cab wheeled round and came to a halt in front of them. He was still silently laughing when they climbed in. 'Still, he only get what's due to him,' Spandrell went on from his dark corner. 'He's the real type of murderee.'

'Murderee?'

'It takes two to make a murder. There are born victims, born to have their throats cut, as the cutthroats are born to be hanged. You can see it in their faces. There's a victim type as well as a criminal type. Walter's the obvious victim; he fairly invites maltreatment.'

'Poor Walter!'

'And it's one's duty,' Spandrell went on, 'to see that he gets it.'

'Why not to see that he doesn't get it, poor lamb?'

'One should always be on the side of destiny. Walter's manifestly born to catch it. It's one's duty to give his fate a helping hand. Which I'm glad to see you're already doing.'

'But I tell you, I'm not. Have you a light?' Spandrell struck a match. The cigarette between her thin lips, she leaned forward to drink the flame. He had seen her leaning like this, with the same swift, graceful and ravenous movement, leaning towards him to drink his kisses. And the face that approached him now was focused and intent on the flame, as he had seen it focused and intent upon the inner illumination of approaching pleasure. There are many thoughts and feelings, but only a few gestures; and the mask has only half a dozen grimaces to express a thousand meanings. She drew back; Spandrell threw the match out of the window. The red cigarette brightened and faded in the darkness.

'Do you remember that curious time of ours in Paris?' he asked, still thinking of her intent and eager face. Once, three years before, he had been her lover for perhaps a month.

Lucy nodded. 'I remember it as rather perfect, while it lasted. But you were horribly fickle.'

'In other words I didn't make as much of an outcry as you hoped I would, when you went off with Tom Trivet.'

'That's a lie!' Lucy was indignant. 'You'd begun to fade away long before I even dreamt of Tom.'

'Well, have it your own way. As a matter of fact you weren't enough of a murderee for my taste.' There was nothing of the victim about Lucy; not much even, he had often reflected, of the ordinary woman. She could pursue her pleasure as a man pursues his, remorselessly, single-mindedly, without allowing her thoughts and feelings to be in the least involved. Spandrell didn't like to be used and exploited for someone else's entertainment. He wanted to be the user. But with Lucy there was no possibility of slave-holding. 'I'm like you,' he added. 'I need victims.'

'The implication being that I'm one of the criminals?'

'I thought we'd agreed to that long ago, my dear Lucy.'

'I've never agreed to anything in my life,' she protested, 'and never will. Not for more than half an hour at a time, at any rate.'

'It was in Paris, do you remember? At the *Chaumière*. There was a young man painting his lips at the next table.'

'Wearing a platinum and diamond bracelet.' She nodded, smiling. 'And you called me an angel, or something.'

'A bad angel,' he qualified, 'a born bad angel.'

'For an intelligent man, Maurice, you talk a lot of drivel. Do you genuinely believe that some things are right and some wrong?'

Spandrell took her hand and kissed it. 'Dear Lucy,' he said, 'you're magnificent. And you must never bury your talents. Well done, thou good and faithful succubus!' He kissed her hand again. 'Go on doing your duty as you've already done it. That's all heaven asks of you.'

'I merely try to amuse myself.' The cab drew up in front of her little house in Bruton Street. 'God knows,' she added, as she stepped out, 'without much success. Here, I've got money.' She handed the driver a ten-shilling note. Lucy insisted, when she was with men, on doing as much of the paying as possible. Paying, she was independent, she could call her own tune. 'And nobody gives me much help,' she went on, as she fumbled with her latchkey. 'You're all so astonishingly dull.'

In the dining-room a rich still-life of bottles, fruits, and sandwiches was awaiting them. Round the polished flanks of the vacuum flask their reflections walked fantastically in a non-Euclidean universe. Professor Dewar had liquefied hydrogen in order that Lucy's soup might be kept hot for her into the small hours. Over the sideboard hung one of John Bidlake's paintings of the theatre. A curve of the gallery, a slope of faces, a corner of the bright proscenium.

'How good that is!' said Spandrell, shading his eyes to see it more clearly.

Lucy made no comment. She was looking at herself in an old grey-glassed mirror.

'What shall I do when I'm old?' she suddenly asked.

'Why not die?' suggested Spandrell with his mouth full of bread and Strasbourg goose liver.

'I think I'll take to science, like the Old Man. Isn't there such a thing as human zoology? I'd get a bit tired of frogs. Talking of frogs,' she added, 'I rather liked that little carroty man – what's his name? – Illidge. How he does hate us for being rich!'

'Don't lump me in with the rich. If you knew ...' Spandrell shook his head. 'Let's hope she'll bring some cash when she comes tomorrow,' he was thinking, remembering the message Lucy had brought from his mother. He had written that the case was urgent.

'I like people who can hate,' Lucy went on.

'Illidge knows how to. He's fairly stuffed with theories and bile and envy. He longs to blow you all up.'

'Then why doesn't he? Why don't you? Isn't that what your club's there for?'

Spandrell shrugged his shoulders. 'There's a slight difference between theory and practice, you know. And when one's a militant

157

communist and a scientific materialist and an admirer of the Russian Revolution, the theory's uncommonly queer. You should hear our young friend talking about murder! Political murder is what especially interests him, of course; but he doesn't make much distinction between the different branches of the profession. One kind, according to him, is as harmless and morally indifferent as another. Our vanity makes us exaggerate the importance of human life; the individual is nothing; Nature cares only for the species. And so on and so forth. Queer,' Spandrell commented parenthetically, 'how old-fashioned and even primitive the latest manifestations of art and politics generally are! Young Illidge talks like a mixture of Lord Tennyson in *In Memoriam* and a Mexican Indian, or a Malay trying to make up his mind to run amok. Justifying the most primitive, savage, animal indifference to life and individuality by means of obsolete scientific arguments. Very queer indeed.'

'But why should the science be obsolete?' asked Lucy. 'Seeing that he's a scientist himself ...'

'But also a communist. Which means he's committed to nineteenth-century materialism. You can't be a true communist without being a mechanist. You've got to believe that the only fundamental realities are space, time and mass, and that all the rest is nonsense, mere illusion and mostly bourgeois illusion at that. Poor Illidge! He's sadly worried by Einstein and Eddington. And how he hates Henri Poincaré! How furious he gets with old Mach! They're undermining his simple faith. They're telling him that the laws of nature are useful conventions of strictly human manufacture and that space and time and mass themselves, the whole universe of Newton and his successors, are simply our own invention. The idea's as inexpressibly shocking and painful to him as the idea of the non-existence of Jesus would be to a Christian. He's a scientist, but his principles make him fight against any scientific theory that's less than fifty years old. It's exquisitely comic.'

'I'm sure it is,' said Lucy, yawning. 'That is, if you happen to be interested in theories, which I'm not.'

'But I am,' retorted Spandrell; 'so I don't apologize. But if you prefer it, I can give you examples of his practical inconsistencies. I discovered not long ago, quite accidentally, that Illidge has the most touching sense of family loyalty. He keeps his mother, he pays for his younger brother's education, he gave his sister fifty pounds when she married.'

'What's wrong in that?'

'Wrong? But it's disgustingly bourgeois! Theoretically he sees no distinction between his mother and any other aged female. He knows that, in a properly organized society, she'd be put into the lethal chamber, because of her arthritis. In spite of which he sends her I don't know how much a week to enable her to drag on a useless existence. I twitted him about it the other day. He blushed and was terribly upset, as though he'd been caught cheating at cards. So, to restore his prestige, he had to change the subject and begin talking about political murder and its advantages with the most wonderfully calm, detached, scientific ferocity. I only laughed at him. "One of these days," I threatened, "I'll take you at your word and invite you to a man-shooting party." And what's more, I will.'

'Unless you just go on chattering, like everybody else.'

'Unless,' Spandrell agreed, 'I just go on chattering.'

'Let me know if you ever stop chattering and do something. It might be lively.'

'Deathly, if anything.'

'But the deathly sort of liveliness is the most lively, really.' Lucy frowned. 'I'm so sick of the ordinary conventional kinds of liveliness. Youth at the prow and pleasure at the helm. You know. It's silly, it's monotonous. Energy seems to have so few ways of manifesting itself nowadays. It was different in the past, I believe.'

'There was violence as well as love-making. Is that what you mean?'

'That's it.' She nodded. 'The liveliness wasn't so exclusively ... so exclusively bitchy, to put it bluntly.'

'They broke the sixth commandment too. There are too many policemen nowadays.'

'Many too many. They don't allow you to stir an eyelid. One ought to have had all the experiences.'

'But if none of them are either right or wrong – which is what you seem to feel – what's the point?'

'The point? But they might be amusing, they might be exciting.'

'They could never be very exciting if you didn't feel they were wrong.' Time and habit had taken the wrongness out of almost all the acts he had once thought sinful. He performed them as unenthusiastically as he would have performed the act of catching the morning train to the city. 'Some people,' he went on meditatively, trying to formulate the vague obscurities of his own feelings, 'some people can only realize goodness by offending against it.' But when the old offences have ceased to be felt as offences, what then? The argument pursued itself internally. The only solution seemed to be to commit new and progressively more serious offences, to have all the experiences, as Lucy would say in her jargon. 'One way of knowing God,' he concluded slowly, 'is to deny Him.'

'My good Maurice!' Lucy protested.

'I'll stop.' He laughed. 'But really, if it's a case of "my good Maurice"' (he imitated her tone), 'if you're equally unaware of goodness and offence against goodness, what *is* the point of having the sort of experiences the police interfere with?'

Lucy shrugged her shoulders. 'Curiosity. One's bored.'

'Alas, one is.' He laughed again. 'All the same, I do think the cobbler should stick to his last.'

'But what *is* my last?'

Spandrell grinned. 'Modesty,' he began, 'forbids ...'

Chapter Thirteen

WALTER travelled down to Fleet Street feeling not exactly happy, but at least calm – calm with the knowledge that everything was now settled. Yes, everything had been settled; everything – for in the course of last night's emotional upheaval, everything had come to the surface. To begin with, he was never going to see Lucy again; that was definitely decided and promised, for his own good as well as for Marjorie's. Next he was going to spend all his evenings with Marjorie. And finally he was going to ask Burlap for more money. Everything was settled. The very weather seemed to know it. It was a day of white insistent mist, so intrinsically calm that all the noises of London seemed an irrelevance. The traffic roared and hurried, but somehow without touching the essential stillness and silence of the day. Everything was settled; the world was starting afresh – not very exultantly, perhaps, not at all brilliantly, but with resignation, with a determined calm that nothing could disturb.

Remembering the incident of the previous evening, Walter had expected to be coldly received at the office. But on the contrary, Burlap was in one of his most genial moods. He too remembered last night and was anxious that Walter should forget it. He called Walter 'old man' and squeezed his arm affectionately, looking up at him from his chair with those eyes that expressed nothing, but were just holes into the darkness inside his skull. His mouth, meanwhile, charmingly and subtly smiled. Walter returned the 'old man' and the smile, but with a painful consciousness of insincerity. Burlap always had that effect on him; in his presence, Walter never felt quite honest or genuine. It was a most uncomfortable sensation. With Burlap he was always, in some obscure fashion, a liar and a comedian. And at the same time all that he said, even when he was speaking his innermost convictions, became a sort of falsehood.

'I liked your article on Rimbaud,' Burlap declared, still pressing Walter's arm, still smiling up at him from his tilted swivel chair.

'I'm glad,' said Walter, feeling uncomfortably that the remark wasn't really addressed to him, but to some part of Burlap's own mind which had whispered, 'You ought to say something nice about his article,' and was having its demands duly satisfied by another part of Burlap's mind.

'What a man!' exclaimed Burlap. 'That was someone who believed in Life, if you like!'

Ever since Burlap had taken over the editorship, the leaders of the *Literary World* had almost weekly proclaimed the necessity of believing in Life. Burlap's belief in Life was one of the things Walter found most disturbing. What did the words mean? Even now he hadn't the faintest idea. Burlap had never explained. You had to understand intuitively; if you didn't, you were as good as damned. Walter supposed that he was among the damned. He was never likely to forget his first interview with his future chief. 'I hear you're in want of an assistant editor,' he had shyly begun. Burlap nodded. 'Yes, I am.' And after an enormous and horrible silence, he suddenly looked up with his blank eyes and asked: 'Do you believe in Life?' Walter blushed to the roots of his hair and said, Yes. It was the only possible answer. There was another desert of speechlessness and then Burlap looked up again. 'Are you a virgin?' he inquired. Walter blushed yet more violently, hesitated and at last shook his head. It was only later that he discovered, from one of Burlap's own articles, that the man had been modelling his behaviour on that of Tolstoy – 'going straight to the great simple fundamental things,' as Burlap himself described the old Salvationist's soulful impertinences.

'Yes, Rimbaud certainly believed in Life,' Walter acquiesced feebly, feeling while he spoke the words as he felt when he had to write a formal letter of condolence. Talking about believing in Life was as bad as talking about grieving with you in your great bereavement.

'He believed in it so much,' Burlap went on, dropping his eyes (to Walter's great relief) and nodding as he ruminatively pronounced the words, 'so profoundly that he was prepared to give it up. That's how I interpret his abandonment of literature – as a deliberate sacrifice.' (He uses the big words too easily, thought Walter.) 'He that would save his life must lose it.' (Oh, oh!) 'To be the finest poet of your generation and, knowing it, to give up poetry – that's losing your life to save it. That's really believing in life. His faith was so strong, that he was prepared to lose his life, in the certainty of gaining a new and better one.' (Much too easily! Walter was filled with embarrassment.) 'A life of mystical contemplation and intuition. Ah, if only one knew what he did and thought in Africa, if only one knew!'

'He smuggled guns for the Emperor Menelik,' Walter had the courage to reply. 'And to judge from his letters, he seems to have thought chiefly about making enough money to settle down. He carried forty thousand francs in his belt. A stone and a half of gold round his loins.' Talking of gold, he was thinking, I really ought to speak to him about my screw.

But at the mention of Menelik's rifles and the forty thousand francs, Burlap smiled with an expression of Christian forgiveness. 'But do you *really* imagine,' he asked, 'that gun-running and money were what occupied his mind in the desert? The author of *Les Illuminations*?'

Walter blushed, as though he had been guilty of some nasty solecism. 'Those are the only facts we know,' he said self-excusingly.

'But there is an insight that sees deeper than the mere facts.' 'Deeper insight' was Burlap's pet name for his own opinion. 'He was realizing the new life, he was gaining the Kingdom of Heaven.'

'It's a hypothesis,' said Walter, wishing uncomfortably that Burlap had never read the New Testament.

'For me,' retorted Burlap, 'it's a certainty. An absolute certainty.' He spoke very emphatically, he wagged his head with violence. 'A complete and absolute certainty,' he repeated, hypnotizing himself by the reiteration of the phrase into a fictitious passion of conviction. 'Complete and absolute.' He was silent; but within, he continued to lash himself into mystical fury. He thought of Rimbaud until he himself was Rimbaud. And then suddenly his devil popped out its grinning face and whispered, 'A stone and a half of gold round his loins.' Burlap exorcized the creature by changing the subject. 'Have you seen the new books for review?' he said, pointing to a double pile of volumes on the corner of the table. 'Yards of contemporary literature.' He became humorously exasperated. 'Why can't authors stop? It's a disease. It's a bloody flux, like what the poor lady suffered from in the Bible, if you remember.'

What Walter chiefly remembered was the fact that the joke was Philip Quarles's.

Burlap got up and began to look through the books. 'Pity the poor reviewer!' he said with a sigh.

The poor reviewer – wasn't that the cue for his little speech about salary? Walter nerved himself, focused his will. 'I was wondering,' he began.

But Burlap had almost simultaneously begun on his own account. 'I'll get Beatrice to come in,' he said and pressed the bell-push three times. 'Sorry. What were you saying?'

'Nothing.' The demand would have to be postponed. It couldn't be made in public, particularly when the public was Beatrice. Damn Beatrice! he thought unjustly. What business had she to do subediting and Shorter Notices for nothing? Just because she had a private income and adored Burlap.

Walter had once complained to her, jokingly, of his miserable six pounds a week.

'But the *World*'s worth making sacrifices for,' she rapped out. 'After all, one has a responsibility towards people; one *ought* to do something for them.' Echoed in her clear rapping voice, Burlap's Christian sentiments sounded, Walter thought, particularly odd. 'The *World* does do something; one ought to help.'

The obvious retort was that his own private income was very small and that he wasn't in love with Burlap. He didn't make it, however, but suffered himself to be pecked. Damn her, all the same!

Beatrice entered, a neat, plumply well-made little figure, very erect and business-like. 'Morning, Walter,' she said, and every word she uttered was like a sharp little rap with an ivory mallet over the knuckles. She examined him with her bright, rather protuberant brown eyes. 'You look tired,' she went on. 'Worn out, as though you'd been on the tiles last night.' Peck after peck. 'Were you?'

Walter blushed. 'I slept badly,' he mumbled and engrossed himself in a book.

They sorted out the volumes of the various reviewers. A little heap for the scientific expert, another for the accredited metaphysician, a whole mass for the fiction specialist. The largest pile was of Tripe. Tripe wasn't reviewed, or only got a Shorter Notice.

'Here's a book about Polynesia for you, Walter,' said Burlap generously. 'And a new anthology of French verse. No, on second thoughts, I think *I'll* do that.' On second thoughts he generally did keep the most interesting books for himself.

'*The Life of St Francis re-told for the Children by Bella Jukes.* Theology or tripe?' asked Beatrice.

'Tripe,' said Walter, looking over her shoulder.

'But I'd rather like an excuse to do a little article on St Francis,' said Burlap. In the intervals of editing, he was engaged on a full-length study of the Saint. 'St Francis and the Modern Psyche,' it was to be called. He took the little book from Beatrice and let the pages flick past under his thumb. 'Tripe-ish' he admitted. 'But what an extraordinary man! Extraordinary!' He began to hypnotize himself, to lash himself up into the Franciscan mood.

'Extraordinary!' Beatrice rapped out, her eyes fixed on Burlap.

Walter looked at her curiously. Her ideas and her pecking goose-billed manner seemed to belong to two different people, between whom the only perceptible link was Burlap. Was there any inward, organic connexion?

'What a devastating integrity!' Burlap went on, self-intoxicated. He shook his head and, sighing, sobered himself sufficiently to proceed with the morning's business.

When the opportunity came for Walter to talk (with what diffidence, what a squeamish reluctance!) about his salary, Burlap was wonderfully sympathetic.

'I know, old man,' he said, laying his hand on the other's shoulder with a gesture that disturbingly reminded Walter of the time when, as a schoolboy, he had played Antonio in *The Merchant of Venice* and the detestable Porter Major, disguised as Bassanio, had been coached to register friendship. 'I know what being hard up is.' His little laugh gave it to be understood that he was a Franciscan specialist in poverty, but was too modest to insist upon the fact. 'I know, old man.' And he really almost believed that he wasn't half owner and salaried editor of the *World*, that he hadn't a penny invested, that he had been living on two pounds a week for years. 'I wish we could afford to pay you three times as much as we do. You're worth it, old man.' He gave Walter's shoulder a little pat.

Walter made a vague mumbling sound of depreciation. That little pat, he was thinking, was the signal for him to begin:

> I am a tainted wether of the flock,
> Meetest for slaughter.

'I wish for your sake,' Burlap continued, 'for mine too,' he added, putting himself with a rueful little laugh in the same financial boat as Walter, 'that the paper did make more money. If you wrote worse, it might.' The compliment was graceful. Burlap emphasized it with another friendly pat and a smile. But the eyes expressed nothing. Meeting them for an instant, Walter had the strange impression that they were not looking at him at all, that they were not looking at anything. 'The paper's too good. It's largely your fault. One cannot serve God and mammon.'

'Of course not,' Walter agreed; but he felt again that the big words had come too easily.

'I wish one could.' Burlap spoke like a jocular St Francis pretending to make fun of his own principles.

Walter joined mirthlessly in the laughter. He was wishing that he had never mentioned the word 'salary.'

'I'll go and talk to Mr Chivers,' said Burlap. Mr Chivers was the business manager. Burlap made use of him, as the Roman statesman made use of oracles and augurs, to promote his own policy. His unpopular decisions could always be attributed to Mr Chivers; and when he made a popular one, it was invariably made in the teeth of the business manager's soulless tyranny. Mr Chivers was a most convenient fiction. 'I'll go this morning.'

'Don't bother,' said Walter.

'If it's humanly possible to scrape up anything more for you ...'

'No, please.' Walter was positively begging not to be given more. 'I know the difficulties. Don't think I want ...'

'But we're sweating you, Walter, positively sweating you.' The more Walter protested, the more generous Burlap became. 'Don't think I'm not aware of it. I've been worrying about it for a long time.'

His magnanimity was infectious. Walter was determined not to take any more money, quite determined, even though he was sure the paper could afford to give it. 'Really, Burlap,' he almost begged, 'I'd much rather you left things as they are.' And then suddenly he thought of Marjorie. How unfairly he was treating her! Sacrificing her comfort to his. Because he found haggling distasteful, because he hated fighting on the one hand and accepting favours on the other, poor Marjorie would have to go without new clothes and a second maid.

But Burlap waved his objections aside. He insisted on being generous. 'I'll go and talk to Chivers at once. I think I can persuade him to let you have another twenty-five a year.'

Twenty-five. That was ten shillings a week. Nothing. Marjorie had said that he ought to stand out for at least another hundred. 'Thank you,' he said and despised himself for saying it.

'It's ridiculously little, I'm afraid. Quite ridiculously.'

That's what I ought to have said, thought Walter.

'One feels quite ashamed of offering it. But what can one do?' 'One' could obviously do nothing, for the good reason that 'one' was impersonal and didn't exist.

Walter mumbled something about being grateful. He felt humiliated and blamed Marjorie for it.

When Walter worked at the office, which was only three days a week, he sat with Beatrice. Burlap, in editorial isolation, sat alone.

It was the day of Shorter Notices. Between them, on the table, stood the stacks of Tripe. They helped themselves. It was a Literary Feast – a feast of offal. Bad novels and worthless verses, imbecile systems of philosophy and platitudinous moralizings, insignificant biographies, boring books of travel, pietism so nauseating and children's books so vulgar and so silly that to read them was to feel ashamed for the whole human race – the pile was high, and every week it grew higher. The ant-like industry of Beatrice, Walter's quick discernment and facility were utterly inadequate to stem the rising flood. They settled down to their work 'like vultures,' said Walter, 'in the Towers of Silence.' What he wrote this morning was peculiarly pungent.

On paper Walter was all he failed to be in life. His reviews were epigrammatically ruthless. Poor earnest spinsters, when they read what he had written of their heartfelt poems about God and Passion and the Beauties of Nature, were cut to the quick by his brutal contempt. The big-game shooters who had so much enjoyed their African trip would wonder how the account of anything so interesting could be called tedious. The young novelists who had modelled their styles and their epical conceptions on those of the best authors, who had daringly uncovered the secrets of their most intimate and sexual life, were hurt, were amazed, were indignant to learn that their writing was stilted, their construction non-existent, their psychology unreal, their drama stagy and melodramatic. A bad book is as much of a labour to write as a good one; it comes as sincerely from the author's soul. But the bad author's soul being, artistically at any rate, of inferior quality, its sincerities will be, if not always intrinsically uninteresting, at any rate uninterestingly expressed, and the labour expended on the expression will be wasted. Nature is monstrously unjust. There is no substitute for talent. Industry and all the virtues are of no avail. Immersed in his Tripe, Walter ferociously commented on lack of talent. Conscious of their industry, sincerity and good artistic intentions, the authors of the Tripe felt themselves outrageously and unfairly treated.

Beatrice's methods of criticism were simple; she tried in every case to say what she imagined Burlap would say. In practice what happened was that she praised all books in which Life and its problems were taken, as she thought, seriously, and condemned all those in which they were not. She would have ranked Bailey's *Festus* higher than *Candide*, unless of course Burlap or some other authoritative person had previously told her that it was her duty to prefer

Candide. As she was never permitted to criticize anything but Tripe, her lack of all critical insight was of little importance.

They worked, they went out to lunch, they returned and set to work again. Eleven new books had arrived in the interval.

'I feel,' said Walter, 'as the Bombay vultures must feel when there's been an epidemic among the Parsees.'

Bombay and the Parsees reminded him of his sister Elinor. She and Philip would be sailing to-day. He was glad they were coming home. They were almost the only people he could talk to intimately about his affairs. He would be able to discuss his problems with them. It would be a comfort, an alleviation of his responsibility. And then suddenly he remembered that everything was settled, that there were no more problems. No more. And then the telephone bell rang. He lifted the receiver, he hallooed into the mouthpiece.

'Is that you, Walter darling?' The voice was Lucy's.

His heart sank; he knew what was going to happen.

'I've just woken up,' she explained. 'I'm all alone.'

She wanted him to come to tea. He refused. After tea, then.

'I can't,' he persisted.

'Nonsense! Of course you can.'

'Impossible.'

'But why?'

'Work.'

'But not after six. I insist.'

After all, he thought, perhaps it would be better to see her and explain what he had decided.

'I'll never forgive you if you don't come.'

'All right,' he said, 'I'll make an effort. I'll come if I possibly can.'

'What a flirt you are!' Beatrice mocked, as he hung up the receiver. 'Saying no for the fun of being persuaded!'

And when, at a few minutes after five, he left the office on the pretext that he must get to the London Library before closing time, she sent ironical good wishes after him. '*Bon amusement!*' were her last words.

*

In the editorial room Burlap was dictating letters to his secretary. 'Yours etcetera,' he concluded and picked up another batch of papers. 'Dear Miss Saville,' he began, after glancing at them for a moment. 'No,' he corrected himself. 'Dear Miss Romola Saville. Thank you for your note and for the enclosed manuscripts.' He paused and, leaning back in his chair, closed his eyes in brief reflection. 'It is not my custom,' he went on at last in a soft remote voice, 'it is not my custom to write personal letters to unknown contributors.' He re-opened his eyes, to meet the dark bright glance of his secretary from across the table. The expression in Miss Cobbett's eyes was sarcastic; the faintest little smile almost imperceptibly twitched the corners of her mouth. Burlap was annoyed; but he concealed his feelings and continued to stare straight in front of him as though Miss Cobbett were not there at all and he were looking absent-mindedly at a piece of furniture. Miss Cobbett looked back at her note-book.

'How contemptible!' she said to herself. 'How unspeakably vulgar!'

Miss Cobbett was a small woman, black-haired, darkly downy at the corners of her upper lip, with brown eyes disproportionately large for her thin, rather sickly little face. Sombre and passionate eyes in which there was, almost permanently, an expression of reproach that could flash up into sudden anger or, as at this moment, derision. She had a right to look reproachfully on the world. Fate had treated her badly. Very badly indeed. Born and brought up in the midst of a reasonable prosperity, her father's death had left her, from one day to another, desperately poor. She got engaged to Harry Markham. Life promised to begin again. Then came the War. Harry joined up and was killed. His death condemned her to shorthand and typing for the rest of her natural existence. Harry was the only man who had ever loved her, who had been prepared to take the risk of loving her. Other men found her too disquietingly violent and impassioned and serious. She took things terribly seriously. Young men felt uncomfortable and silly in her company. They revenged themselves by laughing at her for having no 'sense of humour,' for being a pedant and, as time went on, for being an old maid who was longing for a man. They said she looked like a witch. She had often been in love, passionately, with a hopeless violence. The men had either not noticed; or, if they noticed, had fled precipitately, or had mocked, or, what was almost worse, had been patronizingly kind as though to a poor misguided creature who might be a nuisance but who ought, none the less, to be treated with charity. Ethel Cobbett had every right to look reproachful.

She had met Burlap because, as a girl, in the prosperous days, she had been at school with Susan Paley, who had afterwards become

Burlap's wife. When Susan died and Burlap exploited the grief he felt, or at any rate loudly said he felt, in a more than usually painful series of those always painfully personal articles which were the secret of his success as a journalist (for the great public has a chronic and cannibalistic appetite for personalities), Ethel wrote him a letter of condolence, accompanying it with a long account of Susan as a girl. A moved and moving answer came back by return of post. 'Thank you, thank you for your memories of what I have always felt to be the *realest* Susan, the little girl who survived so beautifully and purely in the woman, to the very end; the lovely child that in spite of chronology she always was, underneath and parallel with the physical Susan living in time. In her heart of hearts, I am sure, she never quite believed in her chronological adult self; she could never quite get it out of her head that she was a little girl playing at being grown up.' And so it went on – pages of a rather hysterical lyricism about the dead child-woman. He incorporated a good deal of the substance of the letter in his next week's article. 'Of such is the Kingdom of Heaven' was its title. A day or two later he travelled down to Birmingham to have a personal interview with this woman who had known the realest Susan when she was chronologically as well as spiritually a child. The impression each made upon the other was favourable. For Ethel, living bitterly and reproachfully between her dismal lodgings and the hateful insurance office where she was a clerk, the arrival first of his letter and now of Burlap himself had been great and wonderful events. A real writer, a man with a mind and a soul. In the state into which he had then worked himself Burlap would have liked any woman who could talk to him about Susan's childhood and into whose warm maternal compassion, a child himself, he could luxuriously sink as into a feather bed. Ethel Cobbett was not only sympathetic and a friend of Susan's; she had intelligence, was earnestly cultured and an admirer. The first impressions were good.

Burlap wept and was abject. He agonized himself with the thought that he could never, never ask Susan's forgiveness for all the unkindness he had ever done her, for all the cruel words he had spoken. He confessed in an agony of contrition that he had once been unfaithful to her. He recounted their quarrels. And now she was dead; he would never be able to ask her pardon. Never, never. Ethel was moved. Nobody, she reflected, would care like that when she was dead. But being cared for when one is dead is less satisfactory then being cared for when one is alive. These agonies which Burlap, by a process of intense concentration on the idea of his loss and grief, had succeeded in churning up within himself were in no way proportionate or even related to his feelings for the living Susan. For every Jesuit novice Loyola prescribed a course of solitary meditation on the passion of Christ; a few days of this exercise, accompanied by fasting, were generally enough to produce in the novice's mind a vivid, mystical and personal realization of the Saviour's real existence and sufferings. Burlap employed the same process; but instead of thinking about Jesus, or even about Susan, he thought of himself, his own agonies, his own loneliness, his own remorses. And duly, at the end of some few days of incessant spiritual masturbation, he had been rewarded by a mystical realization of his own unique and incomparable piteousness. He saw himself in an apocalyptic vision as a man of sorrows. (The language of the New Testament was constantly on Burlap's lips and under his pen. 'To each of us,' he wrote, 'is given a Calvary proportionate to his or her powers of endurance and capabilities of self-perfection.' He spoke familiarly of agonies in the garden and cups.) The vision rent his heart; he was overwhelmed with self-pity. But with the sorrows of this Christ-like Burlap poor Susan had really very little to do. His love for the living Susan had been as much self-induced and self-intensified as his grief at her death. He had loved, not Susan, but the mental image of Susan and the idea of love, fixedly concentrated on, in the best Jesuitical manner, until they became hallucinatingly real. His ardours for this phantom, and the love of love, the passion for passion which he had managed to squeeze out of his inner consciousness, conquered Susan, who imagined that they had some connexion with herself. What pleased her most about his feelings was their 'pure' unmasculine quality. His ardours were those of a child for its mother (a rather incestuous child, it is true; but how tactfully and delicately the little Oedipus!); his love was at once babyish and maternal; his passion was a kind of passive snuggling. Frail, squeamish, less than fully alive and therefore less than adult, permanently under-aged, she adored him as a superior and almost holy lover. Burlap in return adored his private phantom, adored his beautifully Christian conception of matrimony, adored his own adorable husbandliness. His periodical articles in praise of marriage were lyrical. He was, however, frequently unfaithful; but he had such a pure, childlike, and platonic way of going to bed with women, that neither they nor he ever considered that the process really counted as going to bed. His life with Susan was a succession of scenes in every variety of emotional key. He would chew and chew on some grievance until he had poisoned himself into a passion of anger or jealousy. Or else he would pore over his own shortcomings and grow abjectly repentant, or roll at her feet in an ecstasy of incestuous adoration for the imaginary mother-baby of a wife with whom he had chosen to identify the corporeal Susan. And then sometimes, very disquietingly for poor Susan, he would suddenly interrupt his emotions with an oddly cynical little laugh and would become for a while somebody entirely different, somebody like the Jolly Miller in the song. 'I care for nobody, no, not I, and nobody cares for me.' 'One's devil' was how he described those moods, when he had worked himself back again into emotional spirituality; and he would quote the Ancient Mariner's words about the wicked whisper that had turned his heart as dry as dust. 'One's devil' – or was it, perhaps the genuine, fundamental Burlap, grown tired of trying to be somebody else and of churning up emotions he did not spontaneously feel, taking a brief holiday?

Susan died; but the prolonged and passionate grief which he felt on that occasion could have been worked up, if Burlap had chosen to imagine her dead and himself desolate and lonely, almost equally well during her lifetime. Ethel was touched by the intensity of his feelings, or rather by the loudness and insistence of their expression. Burlap seemed to be quite broken down, physically and spiritually, by his grief. Her heart bled for him. Encouraged by her sympathy, he plunged into an orgy of regrets, whose vanity made them exasperatingly poignant, of repentances, excruciating for being too late, of unnecessary confessions and self-abasements. Feelings are not separate entities that can be stimulated in isolation from the rest of the mind. When a man is emotionally exalted in one direction, he is liable to become emotionally exalted in others. Burlap's grief made him noble and generous; his self-pity made it easy to feel Christian about other people. 'You're unhappy, too,' he said to Ethel. 'I can see it.' She admitted it; told him how much she hated her work, hated the place, hated the people; told him her wretched history. Burlap churned up his sympathy. 'But what do my little miseries matter in comparison with yours,' she protested, remembering the violence of his outcry. Burlap talked about the freemasonry of suffering and then, dazzled by the vision of his own generous self, proceeded to offer Miss Cobbett a secretarial job on the staff of the *Literary World.*

Infinitely preferable as London and the *Literary World* seemed to the Insurance office and Birmingham, Ethel hesitated. The insurance job was dull, but it was safe, permanent, pensioned. In another and yet more explosive burst of generous feeling Burlap guaranteed her all the permanence she wanted. He felt warm with goodness.

Miss Cobbett allowed herself to be persuaded. She came. If Burlap had hoped to slide by gradual stages and almost imperceptibly into Ethel's bed, he was disappointed. A broken-hearted child in need of consolation, he would have liked to lure his consoler, ever so spiritually and platonically, into a gentle and delicious incest. But to Ethel Cobbett the idea was unthinkable; it never entered her head. She was a woman of principles, as passionate and violent in her moral loyalties as in her love. She had taken Burlap's grief seriously and literally. When they had agreed, with tears, to found a kind of private cult for poor Susan, to raise and keep perpetually illumined and adorned an inward altar to her memory, Ethel had imagined that they were meaning what they were saying. She meant it in any case. It never occurred to her that Burlap did not. His subsequent behaviour had astonished and shocked her. Was this the man, she asked herself as she watched him living his life of disguised and platonic and slimily spiritual promiscuities, was this the man who had vowed to keep the candles for ever burning in front of poor little Susan's altar? She looked, she spoke her disapproval. Burlap cursed himself for his foolishness in having lured her away from the insurance office, his double-dyed idiocy in promising her permanence of tenure. If only she'd go of her own accord! He tried to make her life a misery for her by treating her with a cold, superior impersonality, as though she were just a machine for taking down letters and copying articles. But Ethel Cobbett grimly stuck to her job, had stuck to it for eighteen months now and showed no signs of giving notice. It was intolerable; it couldn't go on. But how should he put an end to it? Of course, he wasn't *legally* bound to keep her for ever. He had never put down anything in black and white. If the worst came to the worst ...

Stonily ignoring the look in Ethel Cobbett's eyes, the almost imperceptible smile of irony, Burlap went on with his dictation. One doesn't deign to notice machines; one uses them. But still, this sort of thing simply could not go on.

'It is not my custom to write personal letters to unknown contributors,' he repeated in a firm, determined tone. 'But I cannot refrain from telling you – no, no – from thanking you for the great pleasure your poems have given me. The lyrical freshness of your work, its passionate sincerity, its untamed and almost savage brilliance have come as a surprise and a refreshment to me. An editor must read through such quantities of bad literature, that he is almost pathetically grateful to those who – no; say: to the rare and precious spirits who offer him gold instead of the customary dross. Thank you for the gift of …' he looked again at the papers, 'of "Love in the Greenwood" and "Passion Flowers." Thank you for their bright and turbulent verbal surface. Thank you also for the sensitiveness … no, the quivering sensibility, the experience of suffering, the ardent spirituality which a deeper insight detects beneath that surface. I am having both poems set up at once and hope to print them early next month.

'Meanwhile, if you ever happen to be passing in the neighbourhood of Fleet Street, I should esteem it a great honour to hear from you personally some account of your poetical projects. The literary aspirant, even of talent, is often balked by material difficulties which the professional man of letters knows how to circumvent. I have always regarded it as one of my greatest privileges and duties as a critic and editor to make smooth the way for literary talent. This must be my excuse for writing to you at such length. Believe me, yours very truly.'

He looked again at the typewritten poems and read a line or two. 'Real talent,' he said to himself several times, 'real talent.' But 'one's devil' was thinking that the girl was remarkably outspoken, must have a temperament, seemed to know a thing or two. He dropped the papers into the basket on his right hand and picked up another letter from the basket on his left.

'To the Reverend James Hitchcock,' he dictated. 'The Vicarage, Tuttleford, Wilts. Dear Sir, I regret very much that I am unable to use your long and very interesting article on the relation between agglutinative languages and agglutinative chimera-forms in symbolic art. Exigencies of space …'

*

Pink in her dressing-gown like the tulips in the vases, Lucy lay propped on her elbow, reading. The couch was grey, the walls were hung with grey silk, the carpet was rose-coloured. In its gilded cage even the parrot was pink and grey. The door opened.

'Walter, darling! At last!' She threw down her book.

'Already. If you knew all the things I ought to be doing instead of being here.' ('Do you promise?' Marjorie had asked. And he had answered, 'I promise.' But this last visit of explanation didn't count.)

The divan was wide. Lucy moved her feet towards the wall, making place for him to sit down. One of her red Turkish slippers fell.

'That tiresome manicure woman,' she said, raising the bare foot a few inches so that it came into her line of sight. 'She will put that horrible red stuff on my toe nails. They look like wounds.'

Walter did not speak. His heart was violently beating. Like the warmth of a body transposed into another sensuous key, the scent of her gardenias enveloped him. There are hot perfumes and cold, stifling and fresh. Lucy's gardenias seemed to fill his throat and lungs with a tropical and sultry sweetness. On the grey silk of the couch, her foot was flower-like and pale, like the pale fleshy buds of lotus flowers. The feet of Indian goddesses walking among their lotuses are themselves flowers. Time flowed in silence, but not to waste, as at ordinary moments. It was as though it flowed, pumped beat after beat by Walter's anxious heart, into some enclosed reservoir of experience to mount and mount behind the dam until at last, suddenly ... Walter suddenly reached out and took her bare foot in his hand. Under the pressure of those silently accumulated seconds, the dam had broken. It was a long foot, long and narrow. His fingers closed round it. He bent down and kissed the instep.

'But my dear Walter!' She laughed. 'You're becoming quite oriental.'

Walter said nothing, but kneeling on the ground beside the couch, he leaned over her. The face that bent to kiss her was set in a kind of desperate madness. The hands that touched her trembled. She shook her head, she shielded her face with her hand.

'No, no.'

'But why not?'

'It wouldn't do,' she said.

'Why not?'

'It would complicate things too much for you, to begin with.'

'No, it wouldn't,' said Walter. There were no complications. Marjorie had ceased to exist.

'Besides,' Lucy went on, 'you seem to forget me. I don't want to.'

But his lips were soft, his hands touched slightly. The moth-winged premonitions of pleasure came flutteringly to life under his kisses and caresses. She shut her eyes. His caresses were like a drug, at once intoxicant and opiate. She had only to relax her will; the drug would possess her utterly. She would cease to be herself. She would become nothing but a skin of fluttering pleasure enclosing a void, a warm abysmal darkness.

'Lucy!' Her eyelids fluttered and shuddered under his lips. His hand was on her breast. 'My sweetheart.' She lay quite still, her eyes still closed.

A sudden and piercing shriek made both of them start, broad awake, out of their timelessness. It was as though a murder had been committed within a few feet of them, but on someone who found the process of being slaughtered rather a joke, as well as painful.

Lucy burst out laughing. 'It's Polly.'

Both turned towards the cage. His head cocked a little on one side, the bird was examining them out of one black and circular eye. And while they looked, a shutter of parchment skin passed like a temporary cataract across the bright expressionless regard and was withdrawn. The jocular martyr's dying shriek was once again repeated.

'You'll have to cover his cage with the cloth,' said Lucy.

Walter turned back towards her, and angrily began to kiss her. The parrot yelled again. Lucy's laughter redoubled.

'It's no good,' she gasped. 'He won't stop till you cover him.'

The bird confirmed what she had said with another scream of mirthful agony. Feeling furious, outraged, and a fool, Walter got up from his knees and crossed the room. At his approach the bird began to dance excitedly on its perch; its crest rose, the feathers of its head and neck stood apart from one another like the scales of a ripened fir-cone. 'Good-morning,' it said in a guttural ventriloquial voice 'good-morning, Auntie, good-morning, Auntie, good-morning, Auntie. ...' Walter unfolded the pink brocade that lay on the table near the cage and extinguished the creature. A last 'Good morning, Auntie' came out from under the cloth. Then there was silence.

'He likes his little joke,' said Lucy, as the parrot disappeared. She had lighted a cigarette.

Walter strode back across the room and without saying anything took the cigarette from between her fingers and threw it into the fireplace. Lucy raised her eyebrows, but he gave her no time to speak. Kneeling down again beside her, he began to kiss her, angrily.

'Walter,' she protested. 'No! What's come over you?' She tried to disengage herself, but he was surprisingly strong. 'You're like a wild beast.' His desire was dumb and savage. 'Walter! I insist.' Struck by an absurd idea, she suddenly laughed. 'If you knew how

176

like the movies you were! A great huge grinning close-up.'

But ridicule was as unavailing as protest. And did she really desire it to be anything but unavailing? Why shouldn't she abandon herself? It was only rather humiliating to be carried away, to be compelled instead of to choose. Her pride, her will resisted him, resisted her own desire. But after all, why not? The drug was potent and delicious. Why not? She shut her eyes. But as she was hesitating, circumstances suddenly decided for her. There was a knock at the door. Lucy opened her eyes again. 'I'm going to say come in,' she whispered.

He scrambled to his feet and, as he did so, heard the knock repeated.

'Come in!'

The door opened. 'Mr Illidge to see you, madam,' said the maid.

Walter was standing by the window, as though profoundly interested in the delivery van drawn up in front of the opposite house.

'Show him up,' said Lucy.

He turned round as the door closed behind the maid. His face was very pale, his lips were trembling.

'I quite forgot,' she explained. 'I asked him last night; this morning rather.'

He averted his face and without saying a word crossed the room, opened the door and was gone.

'Walter!' she called after him, 'Walter!' But he did not return.

On the stairs he met Illidge ascending behind the maid.

Walter responded to his greetings with a vague salute and hurried past. He could not trust himself to speak.

'Our friend Bidlake seemed to be in a great hurry,' said Illidge, when the preliminary greetings were over. He felt exultantly certain that he had driven the other fellow away.

She observed the triumph on his face. Like a little ginger cock, she was thinking. 'He'd forgotten something,' she vaguely explained.

'Not himself, I hope,' he questioned waggishly. And when she laughed, more at the fatuous masculinity of his expression than at his joke, he swelled with self-confidence and satisfaction. This social business was as easy as playing skittles. Feeling entirely at his ease, he stretched his legs, he looked round the room. Its richly sober elegance impressed him at once as the right thing. He sniffed the perfumed air appreciatively.

'What's under that mysterious red cloth there?' he asked, pointing at the mobled cage.

'That's a cockatoo,' Lucy answered. 'A cock-a-doodle-doo,' she emended, breaking out into a sudden disquieting and inexplicable laughter.

There are confessable agonies, sufferings of which one can positively be proud. Of bereavement, of parting, of the sense of sin and the fear of death the poets have eloquently spoken. They command the world's sympathy. But there are also discreditable anguishes, no less excruciating than the others, but of which the sufferer dare not, cannot speak. The anguish of thwarted desire, for example. That was the anguish which Walter carried with him into the street. It was pain, anger, disappointment, shame, misery all in one. He felt as though his soul were dying in torture. And yet the cause was unavowable, low, even ludicrous. Suppose a friend were now to meet him and to ask why he looked so unhappy.

'I was making love to a woman when I was interrupted, first by the screaming of a cockatoo, then by the arrival of a visitor.'

The comment would be enormous and derisive laughter. His confession would have been a smoking-room joke. And yet he could not be suffering more if he had lost his mother.

He wandered for an hour through the streets, in Regents Park. The light gradually faded out of the white and misty afternoon; he became calmer. It was a lesson, he thought, a punishment; he had broken his promise. For his own good as well as for Marjorie's, never again. He looked at his watch and seeing that it was after seven, turned homewards. He arrived at the house tired and determinedly repentant. Marjorie was sewing; the lamplight was bright on her thin fatigued face. She too was wearing a dressing-gown. It was mauve and hideous; he had always thought her taste bad. The flat was pervaded with a smell of cooking. He hated kitchen smells, but that was yet another reason why he should be faithful. It was a question of honour and duty. It was not because he preferred gardenia to cabbage that he had a right to make Marjorie suffer.

'You're late,' she said.

'There was a lot to do,' Walter explained. 'And I walked home.' That at least was true. 'How are you feeling?' He laid his hand on her shoulder and bent down. Dropping her sewing, Marjorie threw her hands round his neck. What a happiness, she was thinking, to have him again! Hers once more. What a comfort! But even as she pressed herself against him, she realized that she was once more betrayed. She broke away from him.

'Walter, how could you?'

The blood rushed to his face; but he tried to keep up the pretence. 'How could I what?' he asked.

'You've been to see that woman again.'

'But what *are* you talking about?' He knew it was useless; but he went on pretending all the same.

'It's no use lying.' She got up so suddenly that her work basket overturned and scattered its contents on the floor. Unheeding, she walked across the room. 'Go away!' she cried, when he tried to follow her. Walter shrugged his shoulders and obeyed. 'How could you?' she went on. 'Coming home reeking of her perfume.' So it was the gardenias. What a fool he was not to have foreseen. ... 'After all you said last night. How could you?'

'But if you'd let me explain,' he protested in the tone of a victim — an exasperated victim.

'Explain why you lied,' she said bitterly. 'Explain why you broke your promise.'

Her contemptuous anger evoked an answering anger in Walter. 'Merely explain,' he said with hard and dangerous politeness. What a bore she was with her scenes and jealousies! What an intolerable, infuriating *bore*!

'Merely go on lying,' she mocked.

Again he shrugged his shoulders. 'If you like to put it like that,' he said politely.

'Just a despicable liar — that's what you are.' And turning away from him, she covered her face with her hands and began to cry.

Walter was not touched. The sight of her heaving shoulders just exasperated and bored him. He looked at her with a cold and weary anger.

'Go away,' she cried through her tears, 'go away.' She did not want him to be there, triumphing over her, while she cried. 'Go away.'

'Do you really want me to go?' he asked with the same cool, aggravating politeness.

'Yes, go, go.'

'Very well,' he said and opening the door, he went.

At Camden Town he took a cab and was at Bruton Street just in time to find Lucy on the point of going out to dinner.

'You're coming out with me,' he announced very calmly.

'Alas!'

'Yes, you are.'

She looked at him curiously and he looked back at her, with steady eyes, smiling, with a queer look of amused triumph and invincible obstinate power, which she had never seen on his face before. 'All right,' she said at last and, ringing for the maid, 'Telephone to Lady Sturlett, will you,' she ordered, 'and say I'm sorry, but I've got a very bad headache and can't come to-night.' The maid retired. 'Well, are you grateful now?'

'I'm beginning to be,' he answered.

'Beginning?' She assumed indignation. 'I like your damned impertinence.'

'I know you do,' said Walter, laughing. And she did. That night Lucy became his mistress.

*

It was between three and four in the afternoon. Spandrell had only just got out of bed. He was still unshaved; over his pyjamas he wore a dressing-gown of rough brown cloth, like a monk's cassock. (The monastic note was studied; he liked to remind himself of the ascetics. He liked, rather childishly, to play the part of the anchorite of diabolism.) He had filled the kettle and was waiting for it to boil on the gas ring. It seemed to be taking an unconscionably long time about it. His mouth was dry and haunted by a taste like the fumes of heated brass. The brandy was having its usual effects.

'Like as the hart desireth the water brooks,' he said to himself, 'so longeth my soul ... With a morning-after thirst. If only Grace could be bottled like Perrier water.'

He walked to the window. Outside a radius of fifty yards everything in the universe had been abolished by the white mist. But how insistently that lamp-post thrust itself up in front of the next house on the right, how significantly! The world had been destroyed and only the lamp-post, like Noah, preserved from the universal cataclysm. And he had never even noticed there was a lamp-post there; it simply hadn't existed until this moment. And now it was the only thing that existed. Spandrell looked at it with a fixed and breathless attention. This lamp-post alone in the mist – hadn't he seen something like it before? This queer sensation of being with the sole survivor of the Deluge was somehow familiar. Staring at the lamp-post, he tried to remember. Or rather he breathlessly didn't try; he held back his will and his conscious thoughts, as a policeman might hold back the crowd round a woman who had fainted in the street; he held back his consciousness to give the stunned memory a place to stretch itself, to breathe, to come to life. Staring at the lamp-post, Spandrell waited, agonized and patient, like a man who feels he is just going to sneeze, tremulously awaiting the anticipated paroxysm; waited for the long-dead memory to revive. And suddenly it sprang up, broad awake, out of its catalepsy and, with a sense of enormous relief, Spandrell saw himself walking up the steep hard-trodden snow of the road leading from Cortina towards the pass of Falzarego. A cold white cloud had descended on to the valley. There were no more mountains. The fantastic coral pinnacles of the Dolomites had been abolished. There were no more heights and depths. The world was only fifty paces wide, white snow on the ground, white cloud around and above. And every now and then, against the whiteness appeared some dark shape of house or telegraph pole, of tree or man or sledge, portentous in its isolation and uniqueness, each one a solitary survivor from the general wreck. It was uncanny, but how thrillingly new and how beautiful in a strange way! The walk was an adventure; he felt excited and a kind of anxiety intensified his happiness till he could hardly bear it.

'But look at that little chalet on the left,' he cried to his mother. 'That wasn't here when I came up last. I swear it wasn't here.'

He knew the road perfectly, he had been up and down it a hundred times and never seen that little chalet. And now it loomed up almost appallingly, the only dark and definite thing in a vague world of whiteness.

'Yes, I've never noticed it, either,' said his mother. 'Which only shows,' she added with that note of tenderness which always came into her voice when she mentioned her dead husband, 'how right your father was. Mistrust all evidence, he used to say, even your own.'

He took her hand and they walked on together in silence, pulling their sledges after them.

Spandrell turned away from the window. The kettle was boiling. He filled the tea-pot, poured himself out a cup and drank. Symbolically enough, his thirst remained unassuaged. He went on sipping, meditatively, remembering and analysing those quite incredible felicities of his boyhood. Winters among the Dolomites. Springs in Tuscany or Provence or Bavaria, summers by the Mediterranean or in Savoy. After his father's death and before he went to school, they lived almost continuously abroad – it was cheaper. And almost all his holidays from school were spent out of England. From seven to fifteen, he had moved from one European beauty spot to another, appreciating their beauty, what was more – genuinely, a precocious Childe Harold. England seemed a little tame afterwards. He thought of another day in winter. Not misty, this time, but brilliant; the sun hot in a cloudless sky; the coral precipices of the Dolomites shining pink and orange and white above the woods and the snow slopes. They were sliding down on skis through the bare larchwoods. Streaked with tree-shadows, the snow was like an immense white and blue tiger-skin beneath their feet. The sunlight was orange among the leafless twigs, sea-green in the hanging beards of moss. The powdery snow sizzled under their skis, the air was at once warm and eager. And when he emerged from the woods the great rolling slopes lay before him like the contour of a wonderful body, and the virgin snow was a smooth skin, delicately grained in the low afternoon sunlight, and twinkling with diamonds and spangles. He had gone ahead. At the outskirts of the wood he halted to wait for his mother. Looking back he watched her coming through the trees. A strong tall figure, still young and agile, the young face puckered into a smile. Down she came towards him, and she was the most beautiful and at the same time the most homely and comforting and familiar of beings.

'Well!' she said, laughing, as she drew up beside him.

'Well!' He looked at her and then at the snow and the tree-shadows and the great bare rocks and the blue sky, then back again at his mother. And all at once he was filled with an intense, inexplicable happiness.

'I shall never be so happy as this again,' he said to himself, when they set off once more. 'Never again, even though I live to be a hundred.' He was only fifteen at the time, but that was how he felt and thought.

And his words had been prophetic. That was the last of his happinesses. Afterwards ... No, no. He preferred not to think of afterwards. Not at the moment. He poured himself out another cup of tea.

A bell rang startlingly. He went to the door of the flat and opened it. It was his mother.

'You?' Then he suddenly remembered that Lucy had said something.

'Didn't you get my message?' Mrs Knoyle asked anxiously.

'Yes. But I'd clean forgotten.'

182

'But I thought you needed …' she began. She was afraid she might have intruded; his face was so unwelcoming.

The corners of his mouth ironically twitched. 'I do need,' he said. He was chronically penniless.

They passed into the other room. The windows, Mrs Knoyle observed at a glance, were foggy with grime. On shelf and mantel the dust lay thick. Sooty cobwebs dangled from the ceiling. She had tried to get Maurice's permission to send a woman to clean up two or three times a week. But, 'None of your slumming,' he had said. 'I prefer to wallow. Filth's my natural element. Besides, I haven't a distinguished military position to keep up.' He laughed, noiselessly, showing his big strong teeth. That was for her. She never dared to repeat her offer. But the room really did need cleaning.

'Would you like some tea?' he asked. 'It's ready. I'm just having breakfast,' he added, purposely drawing attention to the irregularity of his way of life.

She refused, without venturing any comment on the unusual breakfast hour. Spandrell was rather disappointed that he had not succeeded in drawing her. There was a long silence.

From time to time Mrs Knoyle glanced almost surreptitiously at her son. He was staring fixedly into the empty fireplace. He looked old, she thought, and rather ill and dreadfully uncared for. She tried to recognize the child, the big schoolboy he had been in those far-off times when they were happy, just the two of them together. She remembered how distressed he used to be when she didn't wear what he thought were the right clothes, when she wasn't smart or failed to look her best. He was as jealously proud of her as she was of him. But the responsibility of his upbringing weighed on her heavily. The future had always frightened her; she had always been afraid of taking decisions; she had no trust in her own powers. Besides, after her husband's death, there wasn't much money; and she had no head for affairs, no talent for management. How to afford to send him to the university, how to get him started in life? The questions tormented her. She lay awake at night, wondering what she ought to do. Life terrified her. She had a child's capacity for happiness, but also a child's fears, a child's inefficiency. When existence was a holiday, none could be more rapturously happy; but when there was business to be done, plans to be made, decisions taken, she was simply lost and terrified. And to make matters worse, after Maurice went to school she was very lonely. He was with her only in the holidays. For nine months out of the twelve she was alone, with nobody to love but her old dachshund. And at last even he failed her – fell ill, poor old beast, and had to be put out of his misery. It was shortly after poor old Fritz's death that she first met Major Knoyle, as he then was.

'You say you brought that money?' Spandrell asked, breaking the long silence.

Mrs Knoyle flushed. 'Yes, it's here,' she said and opened her bag. The moment to speak had come. It was her duty to admonish, and the wad of bank notes gave her the right, the power. But the duty was odious and she had no wish to use her power. She raised her eyes and looked at him imploringly. 'Maurice,' she begged, 'why can't you be reasonable? It's such a madness, such a folly.'

Spandrell raised his eyebrows. 'What's a madness?' he asked, pretending not to know what she was talking about.

Embarrassed at being thus compelled to specify her vague reproaches, Mrs Knoyle blushed. 'You know what I mean,' she said. 'This way of living. It's bad and stupid. And such a waste, such a suicide. Besides, you're not happy; I can see that.'

'Mayn't I even be unhappy, if I want to?' he asked ironically.

'But do you want to make me unhappy too?' she asked. 'Because if you do, you succeed, Maurice, you succeed. You make me terribly unhappy.' The tears came into her eyes. She felt in her bag for a handkerchief.

Spandrell got up from his chair and began to walk up and down the room. 'You didn't think much of my happiness in the past,' he said.

His mother did not answer, but went on noiselessly crying.

'When you married that man,' he went on, 'did you think of my happiness?'

'You know I thought it would be for the best,' she answered brokenly. She had explained it so often; she couldn't begin again. 'You know it,' she repeated.

'I only know what I felt and said at the time,' he answered. 'You didn't listen to me, and now you tell me you wanted to make me happy.'

'But you were so unreasonable,' she protested. 'If you had given me any reasons ...'

'Reasons,' he repeated slowly. 'Did you honestly expect a boy of fifteen to tell his mother the reasons why he didn't want her to share her bed with a stranger?'

He was thinking of that book which had circulated surreptitiously among the boys of his house at school. Disgusted and ashamed, but irresistibly fascinated, he had read it at night, by the light of an electric torch, under the bed-clothes. *A Girls' School in Paris* it was called, innocuously enough; but the contents were pure pornography. The sexual exploits of the military were pindarically exalted. A little later his mother wrote to him that she was going to marry Major Knoyle.

'It's no good, mother,' he said aloud. 'Hadn't we better talk about something else?'

Mrs Knoyle drew her breath sharply and with determination, gave her eyes a final wipe and put away the handkerchief. 'I'm sorry,' she said. 'It was stupid of me. Perhaps I'd better go.'

Secretly she hoped that he would protest, would beg her to stay. But he said nothing.

'Here's the money,' she added.

He took the folded bank-notes and stuffed them into the pocket of his dressing-gown. 'I'm sorry I had to ask you for it,' he said. 'I was in a hole. I'll try not to get into it again.'

He looked at her for a moment, smiling, and suddenly, through the worn mask, she seemed to see him as he was in boyhood. Tenderness like a soft warmth expanded within her, soft but irresistible. It would not be contained. She laid her hands on his shoulders.

'Good-bye, my darling boy,' she said, and Spandrell recognized in her voice that note which used to come into it when she talked to him of his dead father. She leaned forward to kiss him. Averting his face, he passively suffered her lips to touch his cheek.

Chapter Fourteen

MISS FULKES rotated the terrestrial globe until the crimson triangle of India was opposite their eyes.

'That's Bombay,' she said, pointing with her pencil. 'That's where Daddy and Mummy took the ship. Bombay is a big town in India,' she went on instructively. 'All this is India.'

'Why is India red?' asked little Phil.

'I told you before. Try to remember.'

'Because it's English?' Phil remembered, of course; but the explanation had seemed inadequate. He had hoped for a better one this time.

'There, you see, you can remember if you try,' said Miss Fulkes, scoring a small triumph.'

'But why should English things be red?'

'Because red is England's colour. Look, here's little England.' She spun the globe. 'Red too.'

'We live in England, don't we?' Phil looked out of the window. The lawn with its Wellingtonia, the clot-polled elms looked back at him.

'Yes, we live just about here,' and Miss Fulkes poked the red island in the stomach.

'But it's green, where we live,' said Phil. 'Not red.'

Miss Fulkes tried to explain, as she had done so many times before, just precisely what a map was.

In the garden Mrs Bidlake walked among her flowers, weeding and meditating. Her walking-stick had a little pronged spud at the end of it; she could weed without bending. The weeds in the flowerbeds were young and fragile; they yielded without a struggle to the spud. But the dandelions and plantains on the lawn were more formidable enemies. The dandelions' roots were like long tapering white serpents. The plantains, when she tried to pull them up, desperately clawed the earth.

It was the season of tulips. Duc van Thol and Keizers Kroon, Proserpine, and Thomas Moore stood at attention in all the beds, glossy in the light. Atoms in the sun vibrated and their trembling filled all space. Eyes felt the pulses as light; the tulip atoms absorbed or reverberated the accorded movements, creating colours for whose sake the burgesses of seventeenth-century Haarlem were prepared to part with hoarded guilders. Red tulips and yellow, white, and parti-coloured, smooth or feathery – Mrs Bidlake looked at them, happily. They were like those gay and brilliant young men, she reflected, in Pinturicchio's frescoes at Siena. She halted so as to be able to shut her eyes and think more thoroughly of Pinturicchio. Mrs Bidlake could only think really well when she had her eyes shut. Her face tilted a little upwards towards the sky, her heavy, wax-white eyelids closed against the light, she stood remembering, confusedly thinking. Pinturicchio, Siena, the solemn huge cathedral – the Tuscan Middle Ages marched past her in a rich and confused pageant. ... She had been brought up on Ruskin. Watts had painted her portrait as a child. Rebelling against the Pre-Raphaelites, she had thrilled with an ad-miration that was quickened, at first, by a sense of sacrilege, over the Impressionists. It was because she loved art she had married John Bidlake. Liking his pictures, she had imagined, when the painter of 'The Haymakers' had paid his court to her, that she adored the man. He was twenty years her senior; his reputation as a husband was bad; her family objected strenuously. She did not care. John Bidlake was embodied Art. His was a sacred function and through his function he appealed to all her vague, but ardent, idealism.

John Bidlake's reasons for desiring to marry yet again were un-romantic. Travelling in Provence he had caught typhoid. ('That's what comes of drinking water,' he used to say afterwards. 'If only I'd stuck to Burgundy and cognac!') After a month in hospital at Avi-gnon he returned to England, a thin and tottering convalescent. Three weeks later influenza, followed by pneumonia, brought him again to death's door. He recovered slowly. The doctor congratulated him on having recovered at all. 'Do you call this recovering?' grumbled John Bidlake. 'I feel as though about three-quarters of me were dead and buried.' Accustomed to being well, he was terrified of illness. He saw himself living miserably, a lonely invalid. Marriage would be an alleviation. He decided to marry. The girl must be good-looking – that went without saying. But serious, not flighty; devoted, a stay-at-home.

In Janet Paston he found all that he had been looking for. She had a face like a saint's; she was serious almost to excess; her adoration for himself was flattering.

They were married, and if John Bidlake had remained the invalid he had imagined himself doomed to be, the marriage might have been a success. Her devotion would have made up for her incompetence as a nurse; his helplessness would have rendered her indispensable to his happiness. But health returned. Six months after his marriage John Bidlake was entirely his old self. The old self began to behave in the old way. Mrs Bidlake took refuge from unhappiness in an endless imaginative meditation, which even her two children were hardly able to interrupt.

It had lasted now for a quarter of a century. A tall imposing lady of fifty all in white, with a white veil hanging from her hat, she stood among the tulips, her eyes shut, thinking of Pinturicchio and the Middle Ages, and time flowing and flowing, and God immobile on the eternal bank.

A shrill barking precipitated her out of her high eternity. She opened her eyes, reluctantly, and looked round. The small and silky parody of an extreme-oriental monster, her little Pekingese was barking at the kitchen cat. Frisking this way and that round the circumference of a circle whose radius was proportionate to his terror of the arched and spitting tabby, he yapped hysterically. His tail waved like a plume in the wind, his eyes goggled out of his black face.

'T'ang!' Mrs Bidlake called. 'T'ang!' All her Pekingese for the last thirty years had had dynastic names. T'ang the First had flourished before her children were born. It was with T'ang the Second that she and Walter had visited the dying Wetherington. The kitchen cat was now spitting at T'ang the Third. In the intervals, little Mings and Sungs had lived, grown decrepit and, in the lethal chamber, gone the way of all pets. 'T'ang, come here.' Even in this emergency Mrs Bidlake was careful to pronounce the apostrophe. Or rather she was not careful to pronounce it; she pronounced it by cultured instinct, because, being what nature and education had made her, she simply could not pronounce the word without the apostrophe even when the fur was threatening to fly.

The little dog obeyed at last. The cat ceased to spit, its fur lay down on its back, it walked away majestically. Mrs Bidlake went on with her weeding and her vague, unending meditation among the flowers. God, Pinturicchio, dandelions, eternity, the sky, the clouds, the early Venetians, dandelions. ...

Upstairs in the schoolroom lessons were over. At least they were over as far as little Phil was concerned; for he was doing what he liked best in the world, drawing. Miss Fulkes, it is true, called the process 'Art' and 'Imagination Training,' and allotted half an hour to it every morning, from twelve to half-past. But for little Phil it was just fun.

He sat bent over his paper, the tip of his tongue between his teeth, his face intent and serious, drawing, drawing with a kind of inspired violence. Wielding a pencil that seemed disproportionately large, his little brown hand indefatigably laboured. At once rigid and wavering, the lines of the childish composition traced themselves out on the paper.

Miss Fulkes sat by the window, looking out at the sunny garden, but not consciously seeing it. What she saw was behind the eyes, in a fanciful universe. She saw herself – herself in that lovely Lanvin frock that had been illustrated last month in *Vogue*, with pearls, dancing at Ciro's, which looked (for she had never been at Ciro's) curiously like the Hammersmith Palais de Danse, where she had been. 'How lovely she looks!' all the people were saying. She walked swayingly, like that actress she had seen at the London Pavilion – what was her name? She held out her white hand; it was young Lord Wonersh who kissed it, Lord Wonersh, who looked like Shelley and lived like Byron and owned half Oxford Street and had come to the house last February with old Mr Bidlake and had perhaps spoken to her twice. And then, all at once, she saw herself riding in the Park. And a couple of seconds later she was on a yacht in the Mediterranean. And then in a motor car. Lord Wonersh had just taken his seat beside her, when the noise of T'ang's shrill barking startlingly roused her to consciousness of the lawn, the gay tulips, the Wellingtonia and, on the other side, the schoolroom. Miss Fulkes felt guilty, she had been neglecting her charge.

'Well, Phil,' she asked turning round briskly to her pupil, 'what are you drawing?'

'Mr Stokes and Albert pulling the mow-lawner,' Phil answered, without looking up from his paper.

'Lawn-mower,' Miss Fulkes corrected.

'Lawn-mower,' Phil dutifully repeated.

'You never get your compound words right,' Miss Fulkes continued. 'Mow-lawner, hopgrasser, crack-nutter – it's a sort of mental defect, like mirror-writing, I suppose.' Miss Fulkes had taken a course in educational psychology. 'You must really try to correct it, Phil,' she added, earnestly. After so long and flagrant a dereliction of duty (at Ciro's, on horseback, in the limousine with Lord Wonersh) Miss Fulkes felt it incumbent upon her to be particularly solicitous, scientifically so: she was a very conscientious young woman. 'Will you try?' she insisted.

189

'Yes, Miss Fulkes,' the child answered. He had no idea what she wanted him to try to do. But it would keep her quiet if he said yes. He was busy on a particularly difficult bit of his drawing.

Miss Fulkes sighed and looked out of the window again. This time she consciously perceived what her eyes saw. Mrs Bidlake wandered among the tulips, dressed flowingly in white, with a white veil hanging from her hat, a sort of Pre-Raphaelitic ghost. Every now and then she paused and looked at the sky. Old Mr Stokes, the gardener, passed carrying a rake; the tips of his white beard fluttered gently in the breeze. The village clock struck the half-hour. The garden, the trees, the fields, the wooded hills in the distance were always the same. Miss Fulkes felt all at once so hopelessly sad that she could have cried.

'Do mow-lawners, I mean lawn-mowers, have wheels?' asked little Phil, looking up with a frown of effort and perplexity wrinkling his forehead. 'I can't remember.'

'Yes. Or let me think ...' Miss Fulkes also frowned; 'no. They have rollers.'

'Rollers!' cried Phil. 'That's it.' He attacked his drawing again with fury.

Always the same. There seemed to be no escape, no prospect of freedom. 'If I had a thousand pounds,' thought Miss Fulkes, 'a thousand pounds. A thousand pounds.' The words were magical. 'A thousand pounds.'

'There!' cried Phil. 'Come and look.' He held up his paper. Miss Fulkes got up and crossed to the table. 'What a lovely drawing!' she said.

'That's all the little bits of grass flying up,' said Phil, pointing to a cloud of dots and dashes in the middle of his picture. He was particularly proud of the grass.

'I see,' said Miss Fulkes.

'And look how hard Albert is pulling!' It was true; Albert was pulling like mad. And old Mr Stokes, recognizable by the four parallel pencil strokes issuing from his chin, pushed as energetically at the other end of the machine.

For a child of his age, little Phil had an observant eye, and a strange talent for rendering on paper what he had seen – not realistically, of course, but in terms of expressive symbols. Albert and Mr Stokes were, for all their scratchy uncertainty of outline, violently alive.

'Albert's left leg is rather funny, isn't it?' said Miss Fulkes. 'Rather long and thin and ...' She checked herself, remembering what old Mr Bidlake had said. 'On no account is the child to be taught how to draw, in the art-school sense of the word. On no account. I don't want him to be ruined.'

Phil snatched the paper from her. 'No, it isn't,' he said angrily. His pride was hurt, he hated criticism, refused ever to be in the wrong.

'Perhaps it isn't really,' Miss Fulkes made haste to be soothing. 'Perhaps I made a mistake.' Phil smiled again. 'Though why a child,' Miss Fulkes was thinking, 'shouldn't be told when he's drawn a leg that's impossibly long and thin and waggly, I really don't understand.' Still, old Mr Bidlake ought to know. A man in his position, with his reputation, a great painter – she had often heard him called a great painter, read it in newspaper articles, even in books. Miss Fulkes had a profound respect for the Great. Shakespeare, Milton, Michelangelo ...' Yes, Mr Bidlake, the Great John Bidlake, ought to know best. She had been wrong in mentioning that left leg.

'It's after half past twelve,' she went on in a brisk efficient voice. 'Time for you to lie down.' Little Phil always lay down for half an hour before lunch.

'No!' Phil tossed his head, scowled ferociously and made a furious gesture with his clenched fists.

'Yes,' said Miss Fulkes calmly. 'And don't make those silly faces.' She knew, by experience, that the child was not really angry; he was just making a demonstration, in order to assert himself and in the vague hope, perhaps, that he might frighten his adversary into yielding – as Chinese soldiers are said to put on devils' masks and to utter fearful yells when they approach the enemy, in the hope of inspiring terror.

'Why should I?' Phil's tone was already much calmer.

'Because you must.'

The child got up obediently. When the mask and the yelling fail to take effect, the Chinese soldier, being a man of sense and not at all anxious to get hurt, surrenders.

'I'll come and draw the curtains for you,' said Miss Fulkes.

Together, they walked down the passage to Phil's bedroom. The child took off his shoes and lay down. Miss Fulkes drew the folds of orange cretonne across the windows.

'Not too dark,' said Phil, watching her movements through the richly coloured twilight.

'You rest better when it's dark.'

'But I'm frightened,' protested Phil.

'You're not frightened in the least. Besides, it isn't really dark at all.' Miss Fulkes moved towards the door.

'Miss Fulkes!' She paid no attention. 'Miss Fulkes!'

On the threshold Miss Fulkes turned round. 'If you go on shouting,' she said severely, 'I shall be very angry. Do you understand?' She turned and went out, shutting the door behind her.

'Miss Fulkes!' he continued to call, but in a whisper, under his breath. 'Miss Fulkes! Miss Fulkes!' She mustn't hear him, of course; for then she would really be cross. At the same time he wasn't going to obey tamely and without a protest. Whispering her name he rebelled, he asserted his personality, but in complete safety.

Sitting in her own room, Miss Fulkes was reading – to improve her mind. The book was *The Wealth of Nations*. Adam Smith, she knew, was Great. His book was one of those that one ought to have read. The best that has been thought or said. Her family was poor, but cultured. We needs must love the highest when we see it. But when the highest takes the form of a chapter beginning, 'As it is the power of exchanging that gives occasion to the division of labour, so the extent of this division must always be limited by the extent of that power, or in other words, by the extent of the market,' then, really, it is difficult to love it as ardently as one ought to do. 'When the market is very small, no person can have any encouragement to dedicate himself entirely to one employment, for want of the opportunity to exchange all that surplus part of the produce of his own labour, which is over and above his own consumption, for such parts of the produce of other men's labour as he has occasion for.'

Miss Fulkes read the sentence through; but before she had come to the end of it, she had forgotten what the beginning was about. She began again; … 'for want of the opportunity to exchange all that surplus … (I could take the sleeves out of my brown dress, she was thinking; because it's only under the arms that it's begun to go, and wear it for the skirt only with a jumper over it) … over and above his own consumption for such parts … (an orange jumper perhaps).' She tried a third time, reading the words out aloud. 'When the market is very small …' A vision of the cattle market at Oxford floated before her inward eye; it was quite a large market. 'No person can have any encouragement to dedicate himself …' What was it all about? Miss Fulkes suddenly rebelled against her own conscientiousness. She hated the highest when she saw it. Getting up, she put *The Wealth of Nations* back on the shelf. It was a row of very high books – 'my treasures,' she called them. Wordsworth, Longfellow, and Tennyson bound in squashy leather and looking, with their rounded corners and Gothic titles, like so many Bibles. *Sartor Resartus*, also Emerson's *Essays*. Marcus Aurelius in one of those limp leathery artistic little editions that one gives, at Christmas, and in sheer despair, to those to whom one can think of nothing more suitable to give. Macaulay's *History*. Thomas à Kempis, Mrs Browning. Miss Fulkes did not select any of them. She put her hand behind the best that has been thought or said and withdrew from its secret place a copy of *The Mystery of the Castlemaine Emeralds*. A ribbon marked her place. She opened and began to read. 'Lady Kitty turned on the lights and walked in. A cry of horror broke from her lips, a sudden faintness almost overcame her. In the middle of the room lay the body of a man in faultless evening dress. The face was almost unrecognizably mangled; there was a red gash in the white shirt front. The rich Turkey carpet was darkly soaked with blood ...' Miss Fulkes read on, avidly. The thunder of the gong brought her back with a start from the world of emeralds and murder. She sprang up. 'I ought to have kept an eye on the time,' she thought, feeling guilty. 'We shall be late.' Pushing *The Mystery of the Castlemaine Emeralds* back into its place behind the best that has been thought or said, she hurried along to the night nursery. Little Phil had to be washed and brushed.

*

There was no breeze except the wind of the ship's own speed; and that was like a blast from the engine-room. Stretched in their chairs Philip and Elinor watched the gradual diminution against the sky of a jagged island of bare red rock. From the deck above came the sound of people playing shuffle-board. Walking on principle or for an appetite, their fellow passengers passed and repassed with the predictable regularity of comets.

'The way people take exercise,' said Elinor in a tone positively of resentment; it made her hot to look at them. 'Even in the Red Sea.'

'It explains the British Empire,' he said.

There was a silence. Burnt brown, burnt scarlet, the young men on leave passed laughing, four to a girl. Sun-dried and curry-pickled veterans of the East strolled by with acrimonious words, about the Reforms and the cost of Indian living, upon their lips. Two female missionaries padded past in a rarely broken silence. The French globe-trotters reacted to the oppressively imperial atmosphere by

G

talking very loud. The Indian students slapped one another on the back like stage subalterns in the days of *Charley's Aunt*; and the slang they talked would have seemed old-fashioned in a preparatory school.

Time flowed. The island vanished; the air was if possible hotter.

'I'm worried about Walter,' said Elinor, who had been ruminating the contents of that last batch of letters she had received just before leaving Bombay.

'He's a fool,' Philip answered. 'After committing one stupidity with that Carling female, he ought to have had the sense not to start again with Lucy.'

'Of course he ought,' said Elinor irritably. 'But the point is that he hasn't had the sense. It's a question of thinking of a remedy.'

'Well, it's no good thinking about it five thousand miles away.'

'I'm afraid he may suddenly rush off and leave poor Marjorie in the lurch. With a baby on the way, too. She's a dreary woman. But he mustn't be allowed to treat her like that.'

'No,' Philip agreed. There was a pause. The sparse procession of exercise-lovers marched past. 'I've been thinking,' he went on reflectively, 'that it would make an excellent subject.'

'What?'

'This business of Walter's.'

'You don't propose to exploit poor Walter as copy?' Elinor was indignant. 'No really, I won't have it. Botanizing on his grave – or at any rate his heart.'

'But of course not!' Philip protested.

'*Mais je vous assure*,' one of the Frenchwomen was shouting so loud that he had to abandon the attempt to continue, '*aux Galeries Lafayette les camisoles en flanelle pour enfant ne coutent que ...*'

'*Camisoles en flanelle*,' repeated Philip. 'Phew!'

'But seriously, Phil ...'

'But, my dear, I never intended to use more than the situation. The young man who tries to make his life rhyme with his idealizing books and imagines he's having a great spiritual love, only to discover that he's got hold of a bore whom he really doesn't like at all.'

'Poor Marjorie! But why can't she keep her face better powdered? And those artistic beads and earrings she always wears ...'

'And who then goes down like a ninepin,' Philip continued, 'at the mere sight of a Siren. It's the situation that appealed to me. Not the individuals. After all, there are plenty of other nice young men besides Walter. And Marjorie isn't the only bore. Nor Lucy the only man-eater.'

'Well, if it's only the situation,' Elinor grudgingly allowed.

'And besides,' he went on, 'it isn't written and probably never will be. So there's nothing to get upset about, I assure you.'

All right. I won't say anything more till I see the book.'

There was another pause.

' ... such a wonderful time at Gulmerg last summer,' the young lady was saying to her four attentive cavaliers. 'There was golf, and dancing every evening, and ...'

'And in any case,' Philip began again in a meditative tone, 'the situation would only be a kind of ...'

'Mais je lui ai dit, les hommes sont comme ça. Une jeune fille bien élevée doit ...'

' ... a kind of excuse,' bawled Philip. 'It's like trying to talk in the parrot-house at the Zoo,' he added with parenthetic irritation. 'A kind of excuse, as I was saying, for a new way of looking at things that I want to experiment with.'

'I wish you'd begin by looking at me in a new way,' said Elinor with a little laugh. 'A more human way.'

'But seriously, Elinor ...'

'Seriously,' she mocked. 'Being human isn't serious. Only being clever.'

'Oh, well,' he shrugged his shoulders, 'if you don't want to listen, I'll shut up.'

'No, no, Phil. Please.' She laid her hand on his. 'Please.'

'I don't want to bore you.' He was huffy and dignified.

'I'm sorry, Phil. But you do look so comic when you're more in sorrow than in anger. Do you remember those camels at Bikaner – what an extraordinarily superior expression? But do go on!'

'This year,' one female missionary was saying to the other, as they passed by, 'the Bishop of Kuala Lumpur ordained six Chinese deacons and two Malays. And the Bishop of British North Borneo ...' The quiet voices faded into inaudibility...

Philip forgot his dignity and burst out laughing. 'Perhaps he ordained some Orang-utans.'

'But do you remember the wife of the Bishop of Thursday Island?' asked Elinor. 'The woman we met on that awful Australian ship with the cockroaches.'

'The one who would eat pickles at breakfast?'

'Pickled onions at that,' she qualified with a shudder. 'But what about your new way of looking at things? We seem to have wandered rather a long way from that.'

'Well, as a matter of fact,' said Philip, 'we haven't. All these *camisoles en flanelle* and pickled onions and bishops of cannibal islands are really quite to the point. Because the essence of the new way of looking is multiplicity. Multiplicity of eyes and multiplicity of aspects seen. For instance, one person interprets events in terms of bishops; another in terms of the price of flannel camisoles; another, like that young lady from Gulmerg,' he nodded after the retreating group, 'thinks of it in terms of good times. And then there's the biologist, the chemist, the physicist, the historian. Each sees, professionally, a different aspect of the event, a different layer of reality. What I want to do is to look with all those eyes at once. With religious eyes, scientific eyes, economic eyes, *homme moyen sensuel* eyes ...'

'Loving eyes too.'

He smiled at her and stroked her hand. 'The result ...' he hesitated.

'Yes, what would the result be?' she asked.

'Queer,' he answered. 'A very queer picture indeed.'

'Rather too queer, I should have thought.'

'But it can't be too queer,' said Philip. 'However queer the picture is, it can never be half so odd as the original reality. We take it all for granted; but the moment you start thinking, it becomes queer. And the more you think, the queerer it grows. That's what I want to get in this book – the astonishingness of the most obvious things. Really any plot or situation would do. Because everything's implicit in anything. The whole book could be written about a walk from Piccadilly Circus to Charing Cross. Or you and I sitting here on an enormous ship in the Red Sea. Really, nothing could be queerer than that. When you reflect on the evolutionary processes, the human patience and genius, the social organization, that have made it possible for us to be here, with stokers having heat apoplexy for our benefit and steam turbines doing five thousand revolutions a minute, and the sea being blue, and the rays of light not flowing round obstacles, so that there's a shadow, and the sun all the time providing us with energy to live and think – when you think of all this and a million other things, you must see that nothing could well be queerer and that no picture can be queer enough to do justice to the facts.'

'All the same,' said Elinor, after a long silence, 'I wish one day you'd write a simple straightforward story about a young man and a young woman who fall in love and get married and have difficulties, but get over them, and finally settle down.'

'Or why not a detective novel?' He laughed. But if, he reflected, he didn't write that kind of story, perhaps it was because he couldn't. In art there are simplicities more difficult than the most serried complications. He could manage the complications as well as anyone. But when it came to the simplicities, he lacked the talent – that talent which is of the heart, no less than of the head, of the feelings, the sympathies, the intuitions, no less than of the analytical understanding. The heart, the heart, he said to himself. 'Perceive ye not, neither understand? have ye your heart yet hardened?' No heart, no understanding.

' ... a terrible flirt!' cried one of the four cavaliers, as the party rounded the corner into hearing.

'I am not!' the young lady indignantly retorted.

'You are!' they all shouted together. It was courtship by chorus and by teasing.

'It's a lie!' But, one could hear, the ticklish impeachment really delighted her.

Like dogs, he thought. But the heart, the heart ... The heart was Burlap's speciality. 'You'll never write a good book,' he had said oracularly, 'unless you write from the heart.' It was true; Philip knew it. But was Burlap the man to say so, Burlap whose books were so heartfelt that they looked as though they had come from the stomach, after an emetic? If he went in for the grand simplicities, the results would be no less repulsive. Better to cultivate his own particular garden for all it was worth. Better to remain rigidly and loyally oneself. Oneself? But this question of identity was precisely one of Philip's chronic problems. It was so easy for him to be almost anybody, theoretically and with his intelligence. He had such a power of assimilation, that he was often in danger of being unable to distinguish the assimilator from the assimilated, of not knowing among the multiplicity of his rôles who was the actor. The amoeba, when it finds a prey, flows round it, incorporates it and oozes on. There was something amoeboid about Philip Quarles's mind. It was like a sea of spiritual protoplasm, capable of flowing in all directions, of engulfing every object in its path, of trickling into every crevice, of filling every mould and, having engulfed, having filled, of flowing on towards other obstacles, other receptacles, leaving the first empty and dry. At different times in his life and even at the same moment he had filled the most various moulds. He had been a cynic and also a mystic, a humanitarian and also a contemptuous misanthrope; he had tried to live the life of detached and stoical reason and another time he had aspired to the unreasonableness of natural and uncivilized existence. The choice of moulds depended at any given moment on the books he was reading, the people he was associating with. Burlap, for example, had redirected the flow of his mind into those mystical channels which it had not filled since he discovered Boehme in his undergraduate days. Then he had seen through Burlap and flowed out again, ready however at any time to let himself trickle back once more, whenever the circumstances seemed to require it. He was trickling back at this moment, the mould was heart-shaped. Where was the self to which he could be loyal?

The female missionaries passed in silence. Looking over Elinor's shoulder he saw that she was reading the *Arabian Nights* in Mardrus's translation. Burtt's *Metaphysical Foundations of Modern Science* lay on his knees; he picked it up and began looking for his place. Or wasn't there a self at all? he was wondering. No, no, that was untenable, that contradicted immediate experience. He looked over the top of his book at the enormous blue glare of the sea. The essential character of the self consisted precisely in that liquid and undeformable ubiquity; in that capacity to espouse all contours and yet remain unfixed in any form, to take, and with an equal facility efface, impressions. To such moulds as his spirit might from time to time occupy, to such hard and burning obstacles as it might flow round, submerge, and, itself cold, penetrate to the fiery heart of, no permanent loyalty was owing. The moulds were emptied as easily as they had been filled, the obstacles were passed by. But the essential liquidness that flowed where it would, the cool indifferent flux of intellectual curiosity – that persisted and to that his loyalty was due. If there was any single way of life he could lastingly believe in, it was that mixture of pyrrhonism and stoicism which had struck him, an enquiring schoolboy among the philosophers, as the height of human wisdom and into whose mould of sceptical indifference he had poured his unimpassioned adolescence. Against the pyrrhonian suspense of judgement and the stoical imperturbability he had often rebelled. But had the rebellion ever been really serious? Pascal had made him a Catholic – but only so long as the volume of *Pensées* was open before him. There were moments when, in the company of Carlyle or Whitman or bouncing Browning, he had believed in strenuousness for strenuousness' sake. And then there was Mark Rampion. After a few hours in Mark Rampion's company he really believed in noble savagery; he felt convinced that the proudly conscious intellect ought to humble itself a little and admit the claims of the heart, aye and the bowels, the loins, the bones and skin and muscles, to a fair share of life. The heart again! Burlap had been right, even though he was a charlatan, a sort of swindling thimble-rigger of the emotions. The heart! But always, whatever he might do, he knew quite well in the secret depths of his being that he wasn't a Catholic, or a strenuous liver, or a mystic, or a noble savage. And though he sometimes nostalgically wished he were one or other of these beings, or all of them at once, he was always secretly glad to be none of them and at liberty, even though his liberty was in a strange paradoxical way a handicap and a confinement to his spirit.

'That simple story of yours,' he said aloud; 'it wouldn't do.'

Elinor looked up from the *Arabian Nights*. 'Which simple story?'

'That one you wanted me to write.'

'Oh, *that!*' She laughed. 'You've been brooding over it a long time.'

'It wouldn't give me my opportunity,' he explained. 'It would have to be solid and deep. Whereas I'm wide; wide and liquid. It wouldn't be in my line.'

'I could have told you that the first day I met you,' said Elinor, and returned to Scheherazade.

'All the same,' Philip was thinking, 'Mark Rampion's right. In practice, too; which makes it so much more impressive. In his art and his living, as well as in his theories. Not like Burlap.' He thought with disgust of Burlap's emetic leaders in the *World*. Like a spiritual channel crossing. And such a nasty, slimy sort of life. But Rampion was the proof his own theories. 'If I could capture something of his secret!' Philip sighed to himself. 'I'll go and see him the moment I get home.'

Chapter Fifteen

During the weeks which followed their final scene, Walter and Marjorie lived in relations of a peculiar and unpleasant falsity. They were very considerate to one another, very courteous, and whenever they were left together alone they made a great deal of polite unintimate conversation. The name of Lucy Tantamount was never mentioned and no reference whatsoever was made to Walter's almost nightly absences. There was a tacit agreement to pretend that nothing had happened and that all was for the best in the best of all possible worlds.

In the first outburst of anger Marjorie had actually begun to pack her clothes. She would leave at once, that very night, before he came back. She would show him that there was a limit to the outrages and insults she would put up with. Coming home reeking of that woman's scent! It was disgusting. He seemed to imagine that she was so abjectly devoted to him and materially so dependent on him, that he could go on insulting her without any fear of provoking her to open revolt. She had made a mistake not to put her foot down before. She oughtn't to have allowed herself to be touched by his misery the previous night. But better late than never. This time it was final. She had her self-respect to consider. She pulled out her trunks from the box-room and began to pack.

But where was she going? What was she going to do? What should she live on? The questions asked themselves more and more insistently with every minute. The only relation she had was a married sister, who was poor and had a disapproving husband. Mrs Cole had quarrelled with her. There were no other friends who could or would support her. She had been trained to no profession, she had no particular gifts. Besides, she was going to have a baby; she would never find a job. And after all and in spite of everything she was very fond of Walter, she loved him, she didn't know how she would be able to do without him. And he had loved her, did still love her a little, she was sure. And perhaps this madness would die down of its own accord; or perhaps she would be able to bring him round again gradually. And in any case it was better not to act precipitately. In the end she unpacked her clothes again and dragged the trunks back to the box room. Next day she started to play her comedy of pretence and deliberately feigned ignorance.

On his side Walter was only too happy to play the part assigned to him in the comedy. To say nothing, to act as though nothing particular had happened, suited him perfectly. The evaporation of his anger, the slaking of his desire had reduced him from momentary strength and ruthlessness to his normal condition of gentle, conscience-stricken timidity. Upon the fibres of the spirit bodily fatigue has a softening effect. He came back from Lucy feeling guiltily that he had done Marjorie a great wrong and looking forward with dread to the outcry she was sure to raise. But she was asleep when he crept to his room. Or at any rate she pretended to be, she didn't call him. And next day it was only the more than ordinarily courteous and formal manner of her greeting that so much as hinted at any untowardness. Enormously relieved, Walter requited portentous silence with silence and politely trivial courtesy with a courtesy that, in his case, was more than merely formal, that came from the heart, that was a genuine attempt (so uneasy was his conscience) to be of service, to make solicitous and affectionate amends for past offences, to beg forgiveness in advance for the offences he had no intention of not committing in the future.

That there had been no outcry, no reproaches, only a polite ignoring silence, was a great relief. But as the days passed, Walter began to find the falsity of their relationship more and more distressing. The comedy got on his nerves, the silence was accusatory. He became more and more polite, solicitous, affectionate; but though he genuinely did like her, though he genuinely desired to make her happy, his nightly visits to Lucy made even his genuine affection for Marjorie seem a lie and his real solicitude had the air of an hypocrisy, even to himself, so long as he persisted in doing, in the intervals of his kindness, precisely those things which he knew must make her unhappy. 'But if only,' he said to himself, with impotent complaining anger, 'if only she'd be content with what I can give her and stop distressing herself about what I can't.' (For it was obvious, in spite of the comedy of silence and courtesy, that she was distressing herself. Her thin, haggard face was alone sufficient to belie the studied indifference of her manner.) 'What I can give her is so much. What I can't give is so unimportant. At any rate for her,' he added; for he had no intention of cancelling his unimportant engagement with Lucy that evening.

> Enjoy'd no sooner but despised straight;
> Past reason hunted; and no sooner had,
> Past reason hated.

Literature, as usual, had been misleading. So far from making him hate and despise, having and enjoying had only made him long for more having and enjoying. True, he was still rather ashamed of his longing. He wanted it to be justified by something higher – by love. ('After all,' he argued, 'there's nothing impossible or unnatural in being in love with two women at the same time. Genuinely in love.') He accompanied his ardours with all the delicate and charming tenderness of his rather weak and still adolescent nature. He treated Lucy, not as the hard, ruthless amusement-hunter he had so clearly recognized her as being before he became her lover, but as an ideally gracious and sensitive being, to be adored as well as desired, a sort of combined child, mother, and mistress, whom one should maternally protect and be maternally protected by, as well as virilely and yes! faunishly make love to. Sensuality and sentiment, desire and tenderness are as often friends as they are enemies. There are some people who no sooner enjoy, but they despise what they have enjoyed. But there are others in whom the enjoyment is associated with kindliness and affection. Walter's desire to justify his longings by love was only, on final analysis, the articulately moral expression of his natural tendency to associate the act of sexual enjoyment with a feeling of tenderness, at once chivalrously protective and childishly self-abased. In him sensuality produced tenderness; and conversely, where there was no sensuality, tenderness remained undeveloped. His relations with Marjorie were too sexless and platonic to be fully tender. It was as a hard, angrily cynical sensualist that Walter had conquered Lucy. But put into action, his sensuality sentimentalized him. The Walter who had held Lucy naked in his arms was different from the Walter who had only desired to do so; and this new Walter required, in sheer self-preservation, to believe that Lucy felt no less tenderly under the influence of his caresses that he did himself. Tenderness can only live in an atmosphere of tenderness. To have gone on believing, as the old Walter had believed, that she was hard, selfish, incapable of warm feeling would have killed the soft tenderness of the new Walter. It was essential for him to believe her tender. He did his best to deceive himself. Every movement of languor and abandonment was eagerly interpreted by him as a symptom of inner softening, of trustfulness and surrender. Every loving word – and Lucy was fashionably free with her 'darlings' and 'angels' and 'beloveds,' her rapturous or complimentary phrases – was treasured as a word come straight from the depths of the heart. To these marks of an imaginary softness and warmth of feeling he responded with a grateful redoubling of his own tenderness; and this redoubled tenderness was doubly anxious to find an answering tenderness in Lucy. Love produced a desire to be loved. Desire to be loved begot a strained precarious belief that he was loved. The belief that he was loved strengthened his love. And so, self-intensified, the circular process began again.

Lucy was touched by his adoring tenderness, touched and surprised. She had had him because she was bored, because his lips were soft and his hands knew how to caress and because, at the last moment, she had been amused and delighted by his sudden conversion from abjectness to conquering impertinence. What a queer evening it had been! Walter sitting opposite to her at dinner with that hard look on his face, as though he were terribly angry and wanted to grind his teeth; but being very amusing, telling the most malicious stories about everybody, producing the most fantastic and grotesque pieces of historical information, the most astonishing quotations from odd books. When dinner was over, 'We'll go back to your house,' he said. But Lucy wanted to go and see Nellie Wallace's turn at the Victoria Palace and then drop in at the Embassy for some food and a little dancing, and then perhaps drive round to Cuthbert Arkwright's on the chance that ... Not that she had any real and active desire to go to the music hall, or dance, or listen to Cuthbert's conversation. She only wanted to assert her will against Walter's. She only wanted to dominate, to be the leader and make him do what she wanted, not what he wanted. But Walter was not to be shaken. He said nothing, merely smiled. And when the taxi came to the restaurant door, he gave the address in Bruton Street.

'But this is a rape,' she protested.

Walter laughed. 'Not yet,' he answered. 'But it's going to be.'

And in the grey and rose-coloured sitting-room it almost was. Lucy provoked and submitted to all the violences of sensuality. But what she had not expected to provoke was the adoring and passionate tenderness which succeeded those first violences. The hard look of anger faded from his face and it was as though a protection had been stripped from him and he were left bare, in the quivering, vulnerable nakedness of adoring love. His caresses were like the soothing of pain or terror, like the appeasements of anger, like delicate propitiations. His words were sometimes like whispered and fragmentary prayers to a god, sometimes words of whispered comfort to a sick child. Lucy was surprised, touched, almost put to shame by this passion of tenderness.

'No, I'm not like that, not like that,' she protested in answer to his whispered adorations. She could not accept such love on false pretences. But his soft lips, brushing her skin, his lightly drawn finger tips were soothing and caressing her into tenderness, were magically transforming her into the gentle, loving, warm-hearted object of his adoration, were electrically charging her with all those qualities his whispers had attributed to her and the possession of which she had denied.

She drew his head on to her breast, she ran her fingers through his hair. 'Darling Walter,' she whispered, 'darling Walter.' There was a long silence, a warm still happiness. And then suddenly, just because this silent happiness was so deep and perfect and therefore, in her eyes, intrinsically rather absurd and even rather dangerous in its flawless impersonality, rather menacing to her conscious will, 'Have you gone to sleep, Walter?' she asked and tweaked his ear.

In the days that followed Walter desperately did his best to credit her with the emotions he himself experienced. But Lucy did not make it easy for him. She did not want to feel that deep tenderness which is a surrender of the will, a breaking down of personal separateness. She wanted to be herself, Lucy Tantamount, in full command of the situation, enjoying herself consciously to the last limit, ruthlessly having her fun; free, not only financially and legally, but emotionally too – emotionally free to have him or not to have him. To drop him as she had taken him, at any moment, whenever she liked. She had no wish to surrender herself. And that tenderness of his – why, it was touching, no doubt, and flattering and rather charming in itself, but a little absurd and, in its anxious demand for a response from her side, really rather tiresome. She would let herself go a little way towards surrender, would suffer herself to be charged by his caresses with some of his tenderness; only to suddenly draw herself back from him into a teasing, provocative detachment. And Walter would be woken from his dream of love into a reality of what Lucy called 'fun,' into the cold daylight of sharply conscious, laughingly deliberate sensuality. She left him unjustified, his guiltiness unpalliated.

'Do you love me?' he asked her one night. He knew she didn't. But perversely he wanted to have his knowledge confirmed, made explicit.

'I think you're a darling,' said Lucy. She smiled up at him. But Walter's eyes remained unansweringly sombre and despairing.

'But do you *love* me?' he insisted. Propped on his elbow, he hung over her almost menacingly. Lucy was lying on her back, her hands clasped under her head, her flat breasts lifted by the pull of the stretched muscles. He looked down at her; under his fingers was the curved elastic warmth of the body he had so completely and utterly possessed. But the owner of the body smiled up at him through half-closed eyelids, remote and unattained. 'Do you *love* me?'

'You're enchanting.' Something like mockery shone between the dark lashes.

'But that isn't an answer to my question. Do you love me?'

Lucy shrugged up her shoulders and made a little grimace. 'Love?' she repeated. 'It's rather a big word, isn't it?' Disengaging one of her hands from under her head she raised it to give a little tug to the lock of brown hair that had fallen across Walter's forehead. 'Your hair's too long,' she said.

'Then why did you have me?' Walter insisted.

'If you knew how absurd you looked with your solemn face and your hair in your eyes!' She laughed. 'Like a constipated sheep-dog.'

Walter brushed back the drooping lock. 'I want to be answered,' he went on obstinately. 'Why did you have me?'

'Why? Because it amused me. Because I wanted to. Isn't that fairly obvious?'

'Without loving?'

'Why must you always bring in love?' she asked impatiently.

'Why?' he repeated. 'But how can you leave it out?'

'But if I can have what I want without it, why should I put it in? And besides, one doesn't put it in. It happens to one. How rarely! Or perhaps it never happens; I don't know. Anyhow, what's one to do in the intervals?' She took him again by the forelock and pulled his face down towards her own. 'In the intervals, Walter darling, there's you.'

His mouth was within an inch or two of hers. He stiffened his neck and would not let himself be pulled down any further. 'Not to mention all the others,' he said.

Lucy tugged harder at his hair. 'Idiot!' she said, frowning. 'Instead of being grateful for what you've got.'

'But what *have* I got?' Her body curved away, silky and warm, under his hand; but he was looking into her mocking eyes. 'What *have* I got?'

Lucy still frowned. 'Why don't you kiss me?' she demanded, as though she were delivering an ultimatum. Walter did not answer, did not stir. 'Oh, very well.' She pushed him away. 'Two can play at that game.'

Repelled, Walter anxiously bent down to kiss her. Her voice had been hard with menace; he was terrified of losing her. 'I'm a fool,' he said.

'You are.' Lucy averted her face.

'I'm sorry.'

But she would not make peace. 'No, no,' she said, and when, with a hand under her cheek, he tried to turn her face back towards his kisses, she made a quick fierce movement and bit him in the ball of the thumb. Full of hatred and desire, he took her by force.

'Still bothering about love?' she asked at last, breaking the silence of that languid convalescence which succeeds the fever of accomplished desires.

Reluctantly, almost with pain, Walter roused himself to answer. Her question in that deep silence was like the spurt of a match in the darkness of the night. The night is limitless, enormous, pricked with stars. The match is struck and all the stars are instantly abolished; there are no more distances and profundities. The universe is reduced to a little luminous cave scooped out of the solid blackness, crowded with brightly lit faces, with hands and bodies and the near familiar objects of common life. In that deep night of silence Walter had been happy. Convalescent after the fever, he held her in his arms, hating no more, but filled with a drowsy tenderness. His spirit seemed to float in the warm serenity between being and annihilation. She stirred within his arms, she spoke, and that marvellous unearthly serenity wavered and broke like a smooth reflecting surface of water suddenly disturbed.

'I wasn't bothering about anything.' He opened his eyes to find her looking at him, amused and curious. Walter frowned. 'Why do you stare at me?' he asked.

'I didn't know it was prohibited.'

'Have you been looking at me like that all this time?' The idea was strangely unpleasant to him.

'For hours,' Lucy answered. 'But admiringly, I assure you. I thought you looked really charming. Quite a sleeping beauty.' She was smiling, mockingly; but she spoke the truth. Aesthetically, with a connoisseur's appreciation, she had really been admiring him as he lay there, pale, with closed eyes and as though dead, at her side.

Walter was not mollified by the flattery. 'I don't like you to exult over me,' he said, still frowning.

'Exult?'

'As though you'd killed me.'

'What an incorrigible romantic!' She laughed. But it was true, all the same. He *had* looked dead; and death, in these circumstances, had something slightly ridiculous and humiliating about it. Herself alive, wakefully and consciously alive, she had studied his beautiful deadness. Admiringly, but with amused detachment, she had looked at this pale exquisite creature which she had used for her delight and which was now dead. 'What a fool!' she had thought. And 'Why do people make themselves miserable, instead of taking the fun that comes to them?' She had expressed her thoughts in the mocking question which recalled Walter from his eternity. Bothering about love – what a fool!

'All the same,' insisted Walter, 'you were exulting.'

'Romantic, romantic!' she jeered. 'You think in such an absurdly unmodern way about everything. Killing and exulting over corpses and love and all the rest of it. It's absurd. You might as well walk about in a stock and a swallow-tail coat. Try to be a little more up to date.'

'I prefer to be human.'

'Living modernly's living quickly,' she went on. 'You can't cart a waggon-load of ideals and romanticisms about with you these days. When you travel by aeroplane, you must leave your heavy baggage behind. The good old-fashioned soul was all right when people lived slowly. But it's too ponderous nowadays. There's no room for it in the aeroplane.'

'Not even for a heart?' asked Walter. 'I don't so much care about the soul.' He had cared a great deal about the soul once. But now that his life no more consisted in reading the philosophers, he was somehow less interested in it. 'But the heart,' he added, 'the heart …'

Lucy shook her head. 'Perhaps it's a pity,' she admitted. 'But you can't get something for nothing. If you like speed, if you want to cover the ground, you can't have luggage. The thing is to know what you want and to be ready to pay for it. I know exactly what I want;

so I sacrifice the luggage. If you choose to travel in a furniture van, you may. But don't expect me to come along with you, my sweet Walter. And don't expect me to take your grand piano in my two-seater monoplane.'

There was a long silence. Walter shut his eyes. He wished he were dead. The touch of Lucy's hand on his face made him start. He felt her taking his lower lip between her thumb and forefinger. She pinched it gently.

'You have the most delicious mouth,' she said.

Chapter Sixteen

THE Rampions lived in Chelsea. Their house consisted of one large studio with three or four little rooms tacked on to it. A very nice little place, in its rather ramshackle way, Burlap reflected, as he rang the bell that Saturday afternoon. And Rampion had bought it for nothing, literally for nothing, just before the War. No post-War rents for him. A sheer gift of a hundred and fifty a year. Lucky devil, thought Burlap, forgetting for the moment that he himself was living rent-free at Beatrice's, and only remembering that he had just spent twenty-four and ninepence on a luncheon for himself and Molly d'Exergillod.

Mary Rampion opened the door. 'Mark's expecting you in the studio,' she said when salutations had been exchanged. Though why on earth, she was inwardly wondering, why on earth he goes on being friendly with this creature passes all comprehension. She herself detested Burlap. 'He's a sort of vulture,' she had said to her husband after the journalist's previous visit. 'No, not a vulture, because vultures only eat carrion. He's a parasite that feeds on living hosts, and always the choicest he can find. He has a nose for the choicest; I'll grant him that. A spiritual leech, that's what he is. Why do you let him suck your blood?'

'Why shouldn't he suck?' retorted Mark. 'He doesn't do me any harm, and he amuses me.'

'I believe he tickles your vanity,' said Mary. 'It's flattering to have parasites. It's a compliment to the quality of your blood.'

'And besides,' Rampion went on, 'he has something in him.'

'Of course he has something in him,' Mary answered. 'He has your blood in him, among other things. And the blood of all the other people he feeds on.'

'Now, don't exaggerate, don't be romantic.' Rampion objected to all hyperboles that weren't his own.

'Well, all I can say is that I don't like parasites.' Mary spoke with finality. 'And next time he comes I shall try sprinkling a little Keating's powder on him, just to see what happens. So there.'

However, the next time had arrived, and here she was opening the door for him and telling him to find his own way to the studio, as if he were a welcome guest. Even in atavistic Mary the force of polite habit was stronger than her desire to sprinkle Keating's.

Burlap's thoughts, as he found his own way to the studio, were still of financial matters. The memory of what he had paid for lunch continued to rankle.

'Not only does Rampion pay no rent,' he was thinking; 'he has hardly any expenses. Living as they do with only one servant, doing most of the housework themselves, having no car, they really must spend ridiculously little. True, they have two children to educate.' But Burlap managed by a kind of mental conjuring trick, at which he was extremely adept, to make the two children disappear out of his field of consciousness. 'And yet Rampion must make quite a lot. He sells his pictures and drawings very decently. And he has a regular market for anything he chooses to write. What does he do with all his money?' Burlap wondered rather resentfully, as he knocked at the studio door. 'Does he hoard it up? Or what?'

'Come in,' called Rampion's voice from the other side of the door. Burlap adjusted his face to a smile and opened.

'Ah, it's you,' said Rampion. 'Can't shake hands at the moment, I'm afraid.' He was cleaning his brushes. 'How are you?'

Burlap shook his head and said that he needed a holiday but couldn't afford to take it. He walked round the studio looking reverentially at the paintings. St Francis would hardly have approved of most of them. But what life, what energy, what imagination! Life, after all, was the important thing. 'I believe in life.' That was the first article of one's creed.

'What's the title of this?' he asked, coming to a halt in front of the canvas on the easel.

Wiping his hands as he came, Rampion crossed the room and stood beside him. 'That?' he said. 'Well, "*Love*," I suppose, is what *you*'d call it.' He laughed; he had worked well that afternoon and was in the best of humours. 'But less refined and soulful people might prefer something less printable.' Grinning, he suggested a few of the less printable alternatives. Burlap's smile was rather sickly. 'I don't know if you can think of any others,' Rampion concluded maliciously. When Burlap was in the neighbourhood it amused him, and at the same time he felt it positively a duty, to be shocking.

It was a smallish painting, in oils. Low down in the left-hand corner of the canvas, set in a kind of recess between a foreground of dark rocks and tree trunks and a background of precipitous crags, and arched over by a mass of foliage, two figures, a man and a woman, lay embraced. Two naked bodies, the woman's white, the man's a red brown. These two bodies were the source of the whole illumination of the picture. The rocks and tree trunks in the foreground were silhouetted against the light that issued from them. The precipice behind them was golden with the same light. It touched the lower surface of the leaves above, throwing shadows up into a thickening darkness of greenery. It streamed out of the recess in which they lay, diagonally into and across the picture, illuminating and, one felt, creating by its radiance an astounding flora of gigantic roses and zinnias and tulips, with horses and leopards and little antelopes coming and going between the huge flowers, and beyond, a green landscape deepening, plane after plane, into blue, with a glimpse of the sea between the hills and over it the shapes of huge, heroic clouds in the blue sky.

'It's fine,' said Burlap slowly, wagging his head over the picture.

'But I can see you hate it.' Mark Rampion grinned with a kind of triumph.

'But why do you say that?' the other protested with a martyred and gentle sadness.

'Because it happens to be true. The thing's not gentle-Jesusish enough for you. Love, *physical* love, as the source of light and life and beauty – Oh, no, no, no! That's much too coarse and carnal; it's quite deplorably straightforward.'

'But do you take me for Mrs Grundy?'

'Not Mrs Grundy, no.' Rampion's high spirits bubbled over in mockery. 'Say St Francis. By the way, how's your Life of him progressing? I hope you've got a good juicy description of his licking the lepers.' Burlap made a gesture of protest. Rampion grinned. 'As a matter of fact even St Francis is a little too grown up for you. Children don't lick lepers. Only sexually perverted adolescents do that. St Hugh of Lincoln, that's who you are, Burlap. He was a child, you know, a pure sweet chee-yild. Such a dear snuggly-wuggly, lovey-dovey little chap. So wide-eyed and reverent towards the women, as though they were all madonnas. Coming to be petted and have his pains kissed away and be told about poor Jesus – even to have a swig of milk if there happened to be any going.'

'Really! Burlap protested.

'Yes, really,' Rampion mimicked. He liked baiting the fellow, making him look like a forgiving Christian martyr. Serve him right for coming in that beloved-disciple attitude and being so disgustingly reverential and admiring.

'Toddling wide-eyed little St Hugh. Toddling up to the women so reverently, as though they were all madonnas. But putting his dear little hand under their skirts all the same. Coming to pray, but staying to share madonnina's bed.' Rampion knew a good deal about Burlap's amorous affairs and had guessed more. 'Dear little St Hugh! How prettily he toddles to the bedroom, and what a darling babyish way he has of snuggling down between the sheets! This sort of thing is much too gross and unspiritual for our little Hughie.' He threw back his head and laughed.

'Go on, go on,' said Burlap. 'Don't mind me.' And at the sight of his martyred, spiritual smile, Rampion laughed yet louder.

'Oh, dear, oh dear!' he gasped. 'Next time you come, I'll have a copy of Ary Scheffer's "St Monica and St Augustine" for you. That ought to make you really happy. Would you like to see some of my drawings?' he asked in another tone. Burlap nodded. 'They're grotesques mostly. Caricatures. Rather ribald, I warn you. But if you *will* come to look at my work, you must expect what you get.'

He opened a portfolio that was lying on the table.

'Why do you imagine I don't like your work?' asked Burlap. 'After all, you're a believer in life and so am I. We have our differences; but on most matters our point of view's the same.'

Rampion looked up at him. 'Oh, I'm sure it is, I know it is,' he said, and grinned.

'Well, if you know it's the same,' said Burlap, whose averted eyes had not seen the grin on the other's face, 'why do you imagine I'll disapprove of your drawings?'

'Why indeed?' the other mocked.

'Seeing that the point of view's the same ...'

'It's obvious that the people looking at the view from the same point must be identical.' Rampion grinned again. 'Q.E.D.' He turned away again to take out one of the drawings. 'This is what I call "Fossils of the Past and Fossils of the Future."' He handed Burlap the drawing. It was in ink touched with coloured washes, extraordinarily brilliant and lively. Curving in a magnificently sweeping S, a grotesque procession of monsters marched diagonally down and across the paper. Dinosaurs, pterodactyls, titanotheriums, diplodocuses, ichthyosauruses walked, swam or flew at the tail of the procession; the van was composed of human monsters, huge-headed

212

creatures, without limbs or bodies, creeping slug-like on vaguely slimy extensions of chin and neck. The faces were mostly those of eminent contemporaries. Among the crowd Burlap recognized J. J. Thomson and Lord Edward Tantamount, Bernard Shaw, attended by eunuchs and spinsters, and Sir Oliver Lodge, attended by a sheeted and turnip-headed ghost and a walking cathode tube, Sir Alfred Mond and the head of John D. Rockefeller carried on a charger by a Baptist clergyman, Dr Frank Crane and Mrs Eddy wearing haloes, and many others.

'The lizards died of having too much body and too little head,' said Rampion in explanation. 'So at least the scientists are never tired of telling us. Physical size is a handicap after a certain point. But what about mental size? These fools seem to forget that they're just as top heavy and clumsy and disproportioned as any diplodocus. Sacrificing physical life and affective life to mental life. What do they imagine's going to happen?'

Burlap nodded his agreement. 'That's what I've always asked. Man can't live without a heart.'

'Not to mention bowels and skin and bones and flesh,' said Rampion. 'They're just marching towards extinction. And a damned good thing too. Only the trouble is that they're marching the rest of the world along with them. Blast their eyes! I must say, I resent being condemned to extinction because these imbeciles of scientists and moralists and spiritualists and technicians and literary and political uplifters and all the rest of them haven't the sense to see that man must live as a man, not as a monster of conscious braininess and soulfulness. Grr! I'd like to kill the lot of them.' He put the drawing back into the portfolio and extracted another. 'Here are two Outlines of History, the one on the left according to H. G. Wells, the one on the right according to me. ...'

Burlap looked, smiled, laughed outright. 'Excellent!' he said. The drawing on the left was composed on the lines of a simple crescendo. A very small monkey was succeeded by a very slightly larger pithecanthropus, which was succeeded in in its turn by a slightly larger Neanderthal man. Paleolithic man, neolithic man, bronze-age Egyptian and Babylonian man, iron-age Greek and Roman man – the figures slowly increased in size. By the time Galileo and Newton had appeared on the scene, humanity had grown to quite respectable dimensions. The crescendo continued uninterrupted through Watt and Stephenson, Faraday and Darwin, Bessemer and Edison, Rockefeller and Wanamaker, to come to a contemporary consummation in the figures of Mr H. G. Wells himself and Sir Alfred Mond. Nor was the future neglected. Through the radiant mist of prophecy the forms of Wells and Mond, growing larger and larger at every repetition, wound away in a triumphant spiral clean off the paper, towards Utopian infinity. The drawing on the right had a less optimistic composition of peaks and declines. The small monkey very soon blossomed into a good-sized bronze-age man, who gave place to a very large Greek and a scarcely smaller Etruscan. The Romans grew smaller again. The monks of the Thebaid were hardly distinguishable from the primeval little monkeys. There followed a number of good-sized Florentines, English, French. They were succeeded by revolting monsters labelled Calvin and Knox, Baxter, and Wesley. The stature of the representative men declined. The Victorians had begun to be dwarfish and misshapen. Their twentieth-century successors were abortions. Through the mists of the future one could see a diminishing company of little gargoyles and foetuses with heads too large for their squelchy bodies, the tails of apes and the faces of our most eminent contemporaries, all biting and scratching and disembowelling one another with that methodical and systematic energy which belongs only to the very highly civilized.

'I'd like to have one or two of these for the *World*,' said Burlap, when they had looked through the contents of the portfolio. 'We don't generally reproduce drawings. We're frankly missionaries, not an art for art concern. But these things of yours are parables as well as pictures. I must say,' he added, 'I envy you your power of saying things so immediately and economically. It would take me hundreds and thousands of words to say the same things less vividly in an essay.'

Rampion nodded. 'That's why I've almost given up writing for the moment. Writing's not much good for saying what I find I want to say now. And what a comfort to escape from words! Words, words, words, they shut one off from the universe. Three-quarters of the time one's never in contact with things, only with the beastly words that stand for them. And often not even with those – only with some poet's damned metaphorical rigmarole about a thing. "Nor what soft incense hangs upon the bough," for example. Or "every fall soothing the raven wing of darkness till it smiled." Or even "then will I visit with a roving kiss the vale of lilies and the bower of bliss."' He looked at Burlap with a grin. 'Even the bower of bliss is turned into a metaphorical abstraction. Vale of lilies, indeed! Oh, these words! I'm thankful to have escaped from them. It's like getting out of a prison – oh, a very elegant fantastic sort of prison, full of frescoes and tapestries and what not. But one prefers the genuine country outside. Painting, I find, puts you in real touch with it. I can say what I want to say.'

'Well, all I can do,' said Burlap, 'is to provide an audience to listen to what you've got to say.'

'Poor devils!' laughed Rampion.

'But I think they *ought* to listen. One has a responsibility. That's why I'd like to publish some of your drawings in the *World*. I feel it's really a duty.'

'Oh, if it's a question of the categorical imperative,' Rampion laughed again, 'why then of course you must. Take what you like. The more shocking the drawings you publish, the better I shall be pleased.'

Burlap shook his head. 'We must begin mildly,' he said. He didn't believe in Life to the point of taking any risks with the circulation.

'Mildly, mildly,' the other mockingly repeated. 'You're all the same, all you newspaper men. No jolts. Safety first. Painless literature. No prejudices extracted or ideas hammered in except under an anaesthetic. Readers kept permanently in a state of twilight sleep. You're hopeless, all of you.'

'Hopeless,' repeated Burlap penitently, 'I know. But, alas, one simply must compromise a little with the world, the flesh and the devil.'

'I don't mind your doing that,' Rampion answered. 'What I resent is the disgusting way you compromise with heaven, respectability and Jehovah. Still, I suppose in the circumstances you can't help it. Take what you want.'

Burlap made his selection. 'I'll take these,' he said at last, holding up three of the least polemical and scandalous of the drawings. 'Is that all right?'

Rampion glanced at them. 'If you'd waited another week,' he grumbled, 'I'd have had that copy of Ary Scheffer ready for you.'

'I'm afraid,' said Burlap with that wistfully spiritual expression which always came over his face when he began to speak about money, 'I'm afraid I shan't be able to pay much for them.'

'Ah well, I'm used to it,' Rampion shrugged his shoulders. Burlap was glad he took it like that. And after all, he reflected, it was true.

Rampion wasn't used to being paid much. And with his way of living he did not need much. No car, no servants ...

'One wishes one could,' he said aloud, drifting away into impersonality. 'But the paper ...' He shook his head. 'Trying to persuade people to love the highest when they see it doesn't pay. One might manage four guineas a drawing.'

Rampion laughed. 'Not exactly princely. But take them. Take them for nothing if you like.'

'No, no,' protested Burlap. 'I wouldn't do that. The *World* doesn't live on charity. It pays for what it uses – not much, alas, but something, it pays something. I make a point of that,' he went on, wagging his head, 'even if I have to pay out of my own pocket. It's a question of principle. Absolutely of principle,' he insisted, contemplating with a thrill of justifiable satisfaction the upright and self-sacrificing Denis Burlap who paid contributors out of his own pocket and in whose existence he was beginning, as he talked, almost genuinely to believe. He talked on, and with every word the outlines of this beautifully poor but honest Burlap became clearer before his inward eyes; and at the same time the *World* crept closer and closer to the brink of insolvency, while the bill for lunch grew momently larger and larger, and his income correspondingly decreased. Rampion eyed him curiously. What the devil is he lashing himself up into a fury about this time? he wondered. A possible explanation suddenly occurred to him. When Burlap next paused for breath, he nodded sympathetically.

'What you need is a capitalist,' he said. 'If I had a few hundreds or thousands to spare, I'd put them into the *World*. But alas, I haven't. Not sixpence,' he concluded, almost triumphantly, and the sympathetic expression turned suddenly into a grin.

*

That evening Burlap addressed himself to the question of Franciscan poverty. 'Bare-footed through the Umbrian hills she goes, the Lady Poverty.' It was thus that he began his chapter. His prose, in moments of exaltation, was apt to turn into blank verse. ... 'Her feet are set on the white dusty roads that seem, to one who gazes from the walls of the little cities, taut-stretched white ribbons in the plain below ...'

There followed references to the gnarled olive trees, the vineyards, the terraced fields, 'the great white oxen with their curving horns,' the little asses patiently carrying their burdens up the stony paths, the blue mountains, the hill towns in the distance, each like a little New Jerusalem in a picture book, the classical waters of Clitumnus and the yet more classical waters of Trasimene. 'That was a land,' continued Burlap, 'and that a time when poverty was a practical, workable ideal. The land supplied all the needs of those who lived on it; there was little functional specialization; every peasant was, to a great extent, his own manufacturer as well as his own butcher, baker, greengrocer and vintner. It was a society in which money was still comparatively unimportant. The majority lived in an almost money-less condition. They dealt directly in things – household stuff of their own making and the kindly fruits of the earth – and so had no need of the precious metals which buy things. St Francis's ideal of poverty was practicable then, because it held up for admiration a way of life not so enormously unlike the actual way of his humbler contemporaries. He was inviting the leisured and the functionally specialized members of society – those who were living mainly in terms of money – to live as their inferiors were living, in terms of things. How different is the state of things to-day!' Burlap relapsed once more into blank verse, moved this time by indignation, not by lyrical tenderness. 'We are all specialists, living in terms only of money, not of real things, inhabiting remote abstractions, not the actual world of growth and making.' He rumbled on a little about 'the great machines that having been man's slaves are now his masters,' about standardization, about industrial and commercial life and its withering effect on the human soul (for which last he borrowed a few of Rampion's favourite phrases). Money, he concluded, was the root of the whole evil; the fatal necessity under which man now labours of living in terms of money, not of real things. 'To modern eyes St Francis's ideal appears fantastic, utterly insane. The Lady Poverty has been degraded by modern circumstances into the semblance of a sack-aproned, leaky-booted charwoman ... No one in his senses would dream of following her. To idealize so repulsive a Dulcinea one would have to be madder than Don Quixote himself. Within our modern society the Franciscan idea is unworkable. We have made poverty detestable. But this does not mean that we can just neglect St Francis as a dreamer of mad dreams. No, on the contrary, the insanity is ours, not his. He is the doctor in the asylum. To the lunatics the doctor seems the only madman. When we recover our senses, we shall see that the doctor has been all the time the only healthy man.

As things are at present the Franciscan ideal is unworkable. The moral of that is that things must be altered, radically. Our aim must be to create a new society in which Lady Poverty shall be, not a draggled charwoman, but a lovely form of light and graciousness and beauty. Oh Poverty, Poverty, beautiful Lady Poverty! ...'

Beatrice came in to say that supper was on the table.

'Two eggs,' she commanded, rapping out her solicitude. 'Two, I insist. They were made especially for you.'

'You treat me like the prodigal son,' said Burlap. 'Or the fatted calf while it was being fattened.' He wagged his head, he smiled a Sodoma smile and helped himself to the second egg.

'I want to ask your advice about some gramophone shares I've got,' said Beatrice. 'They've been rising so violently.'

'Gramophones!' said Burlap. 'Ah ...' He advised.

Chapter Seventeen

IT had been raining for days. To Spandrell it seemed as though the fungi and the mildew were sprouting even in his soul. He lay in bed, or sat in his dismal room, or leaned against the counter in a public house, feeling the slimy growth within him, watching it with his inward eyes.

'But if only you'd do something,' his mother had so often implored. 'Anything.'

And all his friends had said the same thing, had gone on saying it or years.

But he was damned if he'd do anything. Work, the gospel of work, the sanctity of work, *laborare est orare* – all that tripe and nonsense. 'Work!' he once broke out contemptuously against the reasonable expostulations of Philip Quarles, 'work's no more respectable than alcohol, and it serves exactly the same purpose: it just distracts the mind, makes a man forget himself. Work's simply a drug, that's all. It's humiliating that men shouldn't be able to live without drugs, soberly; it's humiliating that they shouldn't have the courage to see the world and themselves as they really are. They must intoxicate themselves with work. It's stupid. The gospel of work's just a gospel of stupidity and funk. Work may be prayer; but it's also hiding one's head in the sand, it's also making such a din and a dust that a man can't hear himself speak or see his own hand before his face. It's hiding yourself from yourself. No wonder the Samuel Smileses and the big business men are such enthusiasts for work. Work gives them the comforting illusion of existing, even of being important. If they stopped working, they'd realize that they simply weren't there at all, most of them. Just holes in the air, that's all. Holes with perhaps a rather nasty smell in them. Most Smilesian souls must smell rather nasty, I should think. No wonder they daren't stop working. They might find out what they really are, or rather *aren't*. It's a risk they haven't the courage to take.'

'And what has your courage permitted *you* to find out about yourself?' asked Philip Quarles.

Spandrell grinned rather melodramatically. 'It needed some courage,' he said, 'to go on looking at what I discovered. If I hadn't been such a brave man, I'd have taken to work or morphia long ago.'

Spandrell dramatized himself a little, made his conduct appear

219

rather more rational and romantic than it really was. If he did nothing, it was out of habitual laziness as well as on perverse and topsy-turvy moral principle. The sloth, indeed, had preceded the principle and was its root. Spandrell would never have discovered that work was a pernicious opiate, if he had not had an invincible sloth to find a reason and a justification for. But that it did require some courage on his part to do nothing was true; for he was idle in spite of the ravages of a chronic boredom that could become, at moments like the present, almost unbearably acute. But the habit of idleness was so deeply ingrained that to break it would have demanded more courage than to bear the agonies of boredom to which it gave rise. Pride had reinforced his native laziness – the pride of an able man who is not quite able enough, of an admirer of great achievements who realizes that he lacks the talent to do original work and who will not humiliate himself by what he knows will be an unsuccessful attempt to create, or by stooping, however successfully, to some easier task.

'It's all very well you talking about work,' he had said to Philip. 'But *you* can do something, *I* can't. What do you want me to do? Bank clerking? Commercial travelling?'

'There are other professions,' said Philip. 'And since you've got some money, there's all scholarship, all natural history …'

'Oh, you want me to be an ant collector, do you? Or a writer of theses on the use of soap among the Angevins. A dear old Uncle Toby with a hobby to ride. But I tell you, I don't want to be an Uncle Toby. If I'm no real good, I prefer to be just frankly no good. I don't want to disguise myself as a man of learning. I don't want to be the representative of a hobby. I want to be what nature made me – no good.'

Ever since his mother's second marriage Spandrell had always perversely made the worst of things, chosen the worst course, deliberately encouraged his own worst tendencies. It was with debauchery that he distracted his endless leisures. He was taking his revenge on her, on himself also for having been so foolishly happy and good. He was spiting her, spiting himself, spiting God. He hoped there was a hell for him to go to and regretted his inability to believe in its existence. Still, hell or no hell, it was satisfactory, it was even exciting in those early days to know that one was doing something bad and wrong. But there is in debauchery something so intrinsically dull, something so absolutely and hopelessly dismal, that it is only the rarest beings, gifted with much less than the usual amount of intelligence and much more than the usual intensity of appetite, who can go on actively enjoying a regular course of vice or continue actively to believe in its wickedness. Most habitual debauchees are debauchees not because they enjoy debauchery, but because they are uncomfortable when deprived of it. Habit converts luxurious enjoyments into dull and daily necessities. The man who has formed a habit of women or gin, of opium-smoking or flagellation, finds it as difficult to live without his vice as to live without bread and water, even though the actual practice of the vice may have become in itself as unexciting as eating a crust or drinking a glass from the kitchen tap. Habit is as fatal to a sense of wrongdoing as to active enjoyment. After a few years the converted or sceptical Jew, the Westernized Hindu, can eat their pork and beef with an equanimity which to their still believing brothers seems brutally cynical. It is the same with the habitual debauchee. Actions which at first seemed thrilling in their intrinsic wickedness become after a certain number of repetitions morally neutral. A little disgusting, perhaps; for the practice of most vices is followed by depressing physiological reactions; but no longer wicked, because so ordinary. It is difficult for a routine to seem wicked.

Robbed gradually by habit both of his active enjoyment and of his active sense of wrong-doing (which had always been a part of his pleasure), Spandrell had turned with a kind of desperation to the refinements of vice. But the refinements of vice do not produce corresponding refinements of feeling. The contrary is in fact true; the more refined in its far-fetched extravagance, the more uncommon and abnormal the vice, the more dully and hopelessly unemotional does the practice of it become. Imagination may exert itself in devising the most improbable variations on the normal sexual theme; but the emotional product of all the varieties of orgy is always the same – a dull sense of humiliation and abasement. There are many people, it is true (and they are generally the most intellectually civilized, refined and sophisticated), who have a hankering after lowness and eagerly pursue their own abasement in the midst of multiple orgies, masochistic prostitutions, casual and almost bestial couplings with strangers, sexual association with gross and uneducated individuals of a lower class. Excessive intellectual and aesthetic refinement is liable to be bought rather dearly at the expense of some strange emotional degeneration, and the perfectly civilized Chinaman with his love of art and his love of cruelty is suffering from another form of the same disease which gives the perfectly civilized modern aesthete his taste for guardsmen and apaches, for humiliating promiscuities and violences. 'High brows, low loins,' was how Rampion had once summed up in Spandrell's hearing. 'The higher the one, the lower the other.' Spandrell, for his part, did not enjoy humiliation. The emotional results of all the possible refinements of vice seemed to him dully uniform. Divorced from all significant emotion, whether approving or remorseful, the mere sensations of physical excitement and pleasure were insipid. The corruption of youth was the only form of debauchery that now gave him any active emotion. Inspired, as Rampion had divined, by that curious vengeful hatred of sex, which had resulted from the shock of his mother's second marriage supervening, in an uneasy moment of adolescence, on the normal upper middle-class training in refinement and gentlemanly repression, he could still feel a peculiar satisfaction in inflicting what he regarded as the humiliation of sensual pleasure on the innocent sisters of those too much loved and therefore detested women who had been for him the personification of the detested instinct. Mediaevally hating, he took his revenge, not (like the ascetics and puritans) by mortifying the hated flesh of women, but by teaching it an indulgence which he himself regarded as evil, by luring and caressing it on to more and more complete and triumphant rebellion against the conscious soul. And the final stage of his revenge consisted in the gradual insinuation into the mind of his victim of the fundamental wrongness and baseness of the raptures he himself had taught her to feel. Poor little Harriet was the only innocent on whom, so far, he had been able to carry out the whole of his programme. With her predecessors he had never gone so far and she had had no successors. Seduced in the manner he had described to the Rampions, Harriet had adored him and imagined herself adored. And she was almost right; for Spandrell did genuinely care for her, even while he was deliberately making her his victim. The violation of his own feelings as well as of hers gave an added spice of perversity to the proceedings. Patiently, with the tact and gentleness and understanding of the most delicate, most exquisitely sympathetic lover, he allayed her virgin fears and gradually melted the coldness of her youth, thawed down the barriers raised by her education – only, however, to impose on her inexperience the ingenuous acceptance of the most fantastic lubricities. To see her accepting these as ordinary marks of affection was already, for the reversed ascetic in Spandrell, an admirable revenge on her for being a woman. But it was not enough; he began to simulate scruples, to shrink with an air of distress from her ardours or, if he accepted them, to accept them passively as though he were being outraged and violated. Harriet became suddenly anxious and distressed, felt ashamed, as a sensitive person always feels whose ardours meet with no response; and suddenly, at the same time, she found herself a little grotesque, like an actor who has been performing with a group of companions and who, deserted, suddenly realizes he is alone on the stage – grotesque and even a little disgusting. Didn't he love her any more? But so much, he answered. Then why? Precisely because of the depth of his love; and he began to talk about the soul. The body was like a wild beast that devoured the soul, annihilated the consciousness, abolished the real you and me. And as though by accident, somebody, that very evening, had sent him a mysterious parcel, which when he opened, as he now did, turned out to contain a portfolio full of pornographic French etchings, in which poor Harriet saw with a growing sense of horror and disgust all the actions she had so innocently and warm-heartedly accepted as love, represented in cold and lucid outlines and made to look so hideous, so low, so bottomlessly vulgar that but to glance was to hate and despise the whole human race. For some days Spandrell skilfully rubbed the horror in; and then, when she was thoroughly penetrated with the sense of guilt and creeping with self-disgust, cynically and violently renewed his now obscene love-making. In the end she had left him, hating him, hating herself. That was three months ago. Spandrell had made no attempt to have her back or to renew the experiment on another victim. It wasn't worth the effort; nothing was worth the effort. He contented himself with talking about the excitements of diabolism, while in practice he remained sunk apathetically in the dismal routine of brandy and hired love. The talk momentarily excited him; but when it was over he fell back again yet deeper into boredom and despondency. There were times when he felt as though he were becoming inwardly paralysed, with a gradual numbing of the very soul. It was a paralysis which it was within his power, by making an effort of the will, to cure. But he could not, even would not, make the effort.

'But if you're bored by it, if you hate it,' Philip Quarles had interrogated, focussing on Spandrell his bright intelligent curiosity, 'why the devil do you go on with the life?' It was nearly a year since the question had been asked; the paralysis had not then crept so deep into Spandrell's soul. But even in those days Philip had found his case very puzzling. And since the man was prepared to talk about himself without demanding any personalities in return, since he didn't seem to mind being an object of scientific curiosity and was boastful rather than reticent about his weaknesses, Philip had taken the opportunity of cross-examining him. 'I can't see why,' he insisted.

Spandrell shrugged his shoulders. 'Because I'm committed to it. Because in some way it's my destiny. Because that's what life finally is – hateful and boring; that's what human beings are, when they're left to themselves – hateful and boring again. Because, once one's damned, one ought to damn oneself doubly. Because ... yes, because I really like hating and being bored.'

He liked it. The rain fell and fell; the mushrooms sprouted in his very heart and he deliberately cultivated them. He could have gone to see his friends; but he preferred to be bored and alone. The concert season was in full swing, there was opera at Covent Garden, all the theatres were open; but Spandrell only read the advertisements – the *Eroica* at the Queen's Hall, Schnabel playing Op. 106 at the Wigmore, *Don Giovanni* at Covent Garden, Little Tich at the Alhambra, *Othello* at the Old Vic, Charlie Chaplin at Marble Arch – read them very carefully and stayed at home. There was a pile of music on the piano, his shelves were full of books, all the London Library was at his disposal; Spandrell read nothing but magazines and the illustrated weeklies and the morning and evening papers. The rain went sliding incessantly down the dirty glass of the windows; Spandrell turned the enormous crackling pages of *The Times*. 'The Duke of York,' he read, having eaten his way, like a dung beetle's maggot in its native element, through Births, Deaths, and the Agony Column, through Servants and Real Estate, through Legal Reports, through Imperial and Foreign News, through Parliament, through the morning's history, through the five leading articles, through Letters to the Editor, as far as Court and Personal and the little clerical essay on *The Bible in Bad Weather*, 'the Duke of York will be presented with the Honorary Freedom of the Gold and Silver Wire Drawers' Company on Monday next. His Royal Highness will take luncheon with the Master and Wardens of the Company after the presentation.' Pascal and Blake were within reach, on the bookshelf. But 'Lady Augusta Crippen has left England on the *Berengaria*. She will travel across America to visit her brother-in-law and sister, the Governor-General of South Melanesia and Lady Ethelberta Todhunter.' Spandrell laughed, and the laughter was a liberation, was a source of energy. He got up; he put on his mackintosh and went out. 'The Governor-General of South Melanesia and Lady Ethelberta Todhunter.' Still smiling, he turned into the public-house round the corner. It was early; there was only one other drinker in the bar.

'But why should two people stay together and be unhappy?' the barmaid was saying. 'Why? When they can get a divorce and be happy?'

'Because marriage is a sacrament,' replied the stranger.

'Sacrament yourself!' the barmaid retorted contemptuously. Catching sight of Spandrell, she nodded and smiled. He was a regular customer.

Double brandy,' he ordered, and leaning against the bar examined the stranger. He had a face like a choir-boy's – but a choir-boy suddenly overwhelmed by middle age; chubby, prettily doll-like, but withered. The mouth was horribly small, a little slit in a rosebud. The cherub's cheeks had begun to sag and were grey, like the chin, with a day's beard.

'Because,' the stranger went on – and Spandrell noticed that he was never still, but must always be smiling, frowning, lifting eyebrows, cocking his head on one side or another, writhing his body in a perpetual ecstasy of self-consciousness, 'because a man shall cleave unto his wife and they shall be one flesh. One flesh,' he repeated and accompanied the words by a more than ordinary writhe of the body and a titter. He caught Spandrell's eye, blushed, and to keep himself in countenance, hastily emptied his glass.

'What do *you* think, Mr Spandrell?' asked the barmaid as she turned to reach for the brandy bottle.

'Of what? Of being one flesh?' The barmaid nodded. 'H'm. As a matter of fact, I was just envying the Governor-General of South Melanesia and Lady Ethelberta Todhunter for being so unequivocally two fleshes. If you were called the Governor-General of South Melanesia,' he went on, addressing himself to the withered choir-boy, 'and your wife was Lady Ethelberta Todhunter, do you imagine you'd be one flesh?' The stranger wriggled like a worm on a hook. 'Obviously not. It would be shocking if you were.'

The stranger ordered another whiskey. 'But joking apart,' he said, 'the sacrament of marriage ...'

'But why should two people be unhappy?' persisted the barmaid. 'When it isn't necessary?'

'Why *shouldn't* they be unhappy?' Spandrell inquired. 'Perhaps it's what they're here for. How do you know that the earth isn't some other planet's hell?'

A positivist, the barmaid laughed. 'What rot!'

'But the Anglicans don't regard it as a sacrament,' Spandrell continued.

The choir-boy writhed indignantly. 'Do you take me for an Anglican?'

The working day was over; the bar began to fill up with men in quest of spiritual relaxation. Beer flowed, spirits were measured out in little noggins, preciously. In stout, in bitter, in whiskey they bought the equivalents of foreign travel and mystical ecstasy, of poetry and a week-end with Cleopatra, of big-game hunting and music. The choir-boy ordered another drink.

'What an age we live in!' he said, shaking his head. 'Barbarous. Such abysmal ignorance of the most rudimentary religious truths.'

'Not to mention hygienic truths,' said Spandrell. 'These damp clothes! And not a window.' He pulled out his handkerchief and held it to his nose.

The choir-boy shuddered and held up his hands. 'But what a handkerchief!' he exclaimed, 'what a horror!'

Spandrell held it out for inspection. 'It seems to me a very nice handkerchief,' he said. It was a silk bandana, red with bold patterns in black and pink. 'Extremely expensive, I may add.'

'But the colour, my dear sir. The colour!'

'I like it.'

'But not at this season of the year. Not between Easter and Whitsun. Impossible! The liturgical colour is white.' He pulled out his own handkerchief. It was snowy. 'And my socks.' He lifted a foot.

'I wondered why you looked as though you were going to play tennis.'

'White, white,' said the choir-boy. 'It's prescribed. Between Easter and Pentecost the chasuble must be predominantly white. Not to mention the fact that to-day's the feast of St Natalia the Virgin. And white's the colour for all virgins who aren't also martyrs.'

'I should have thought they were all martyrs,' said Spandrell. 'That is, if they've been virgins long enough.'

The swing-door opened and shut, opened and shut. Outside was loneliness and the damp twilight; within, the happiness of being many, of being close and in contact. The choir-boy began to talk of little St Hugh of Lincoln and St Piran of Perranzabuloe, the patron saint of Cornish tin-miners. He drank another whiskey and confided to Spandrell that he was writing the lives of the English saints, in verse.

'Another wet Derby,' prophesied a group of pessimists at the bar, and were happy because they could prophesy in company and with fine weather in their bellies and beery sunshine in their souls. The wet clothes steamed more suffocatingly than ever, – a steam of felicity; the sound of talk and laughter was deafening. Into Spandrell's face the withered choir-boy breathed alcohol and poetry.

> 'To and fro, to and fro,
> Piran of Perranzabuloe,'

he intoned. Four whiskeys had almost cured him of writhing and grimacing. He had lost his self-consciousness. The onlooker who was conscious of the self had gone to sleep. A few more whiskeys and there would be no more self to be conscious of.

> 'Walked weightless,'

he continued,

> 'Walked weightless on the heaving seas
> Among the Cassiterides.'

That was Piran's chief miracle,' he explained; 'walking from Land's End to the Scilly Islands.'

'Pretty nearly the world's record, I should think,' said Spandrell.

The other shook his head. 'There was an Irish saint who walked to Wales. But I can't remember his name. Miss!' he called. 'Here! Another whiskey, please.'

'I must say,' said Spandrell, 'you seem to make the best of both worlds. Six whiskeys ...'

'Only five,' the choir-boy protested. 'This is only the fifth.'

'Five whiskeys, then, and the liturgical colours. Not to mention St Piran of Perranzabuloe. Do you really believe in that walk to the Scillies?'

'Absolutely.'

'And here's for young Sacramento,' said the barmaid, pushing his glass across the counter.

The choir-boy shook his head as he paid. 'Blasphemies all round,' he said. 'Every word another wound in the Sacred Heart.' He drank. 'Another bleeding, agonizing wound.'

'What fun you have with your Sacred Heart!'

'Fun!' said the choir-boy indignantly.

'Staggering from the bar to the altar rails. And from the confessional to the bawdy house. It's the ideal life. Never a dull moment. I envy you.'

'Mock on, mock on!' He spoke like a dying martyr. 'And if you knew what a tragedy my life has been, you wouldn't say you envied me.'

The swing-door opened and shut, opened and shut. God-thirsty from the spiritual deserts of the workshop and the office, men came, as to a temple. Bottled and barrelled by Clyde and Liffey, by Thames, Douro, and Trent, the mysterious divinity revealed itself to them. For the Brahmins who pressed and drank the soma, its name was Indra; for the hemp-eating yogis, Siva. The gods of Mexico inhabited the peyotl. The Persian Sufis discovered Allah in the wine of Shiraz, the shamans of the Samoyedes ate toadstools and were filled with the spirit of Num.

'Another whiskey, Miss,' said the choir-boy, and turning back to Spandrell almost wept over his misfortunes. He had loved, he had married – sacramentally; he insisted on that. He had been happy. They had both been happy.

Spandrell raised his eyebrows. 'Did she like the smell of whiskey?'

The other shook his head sadly. 'I had my faults,' he admitted. 'I was weak. This accursed drink! Accursed!' And in a sudden enthusiasm for temperance he poured his whiskey on the floor. 'There!' he said triumphantly.

'Very noble!' said Spandrell. He beckoned to the barmaid. 'Another whiskey for this gentleman.'

The choir-boy protested, but without much warmth. He sighed. 'It was always my besetting sin,' he said. 'But I was always sorry afterwards. Genuinely repentant.'

'I'm sure you were. Never a dull moment.'

'If she'd stood by me, I might have cured myself.'

'A pure woman's help, what?' said Spandrell.

'Exactly,' the other nodded. 'That's exactly it. But she left me. Ran off. Or rather, not ran. She was lured. She wouldn't have done it on her own. It was that horrible little snake in the grass. That little ...' He ran through the sergeant-major's brief vocabulary. 'I'd wring his neck if he were here,' the choir-boy went on. The Lord of Battles had been in his fifth whiskey. 'Dirty little swine!' he banged the counter. 'You know the man who painted those pictures in the Tate; Bidlake? Well, it was that chap's son. Walter Bidlake.'

Spandrell raised his eyebrows, but made no comment. The choir-boy talked on.

At Sbisa's, Walter was dining with Lucy Tantamount.

'Why don't you come to Paris too?' Lucy was saying.

Walter shook his head. 'I've got to work.'

'I find it's really impossible to stay in one place more than a couple of months at a time. One gets so stale and wilted, so unutterably bored. The moment I step into the aeroplane at Croydon I feel as though I had been born again – like the Salvation Army.'

'And how long does the new life last?'

Lucy shrugged her shoulders. 'As long as the old one. But fortunately there's an almost unlimited supply of aeroplanes. I'm all for Progress.'

The swing-doors of the temple of the unknown god closed behind them. Spandrell and his companion stepped out into the cold and rainy darkness.

'Oof!' said the choir-boy, shivering, and turned up the collar of his raincoat. 'It's like jumping into a swimming-bath.'

'It's like reading Haeckel after Fénelon. You Christians live in such a jolly little public-house of a universe.'

They walked a few yards down the street.

'Look here,' said Spandrell, 'do you think you can get home on foot? Because you don't look as though you could.'

Leaning against a lamp-post the choir-boy shook his head.

'We'll wait for a cab.'

They waited. The rain fell. Spandrell looked at the other man with a cold distaste. The creature had amused him, while they had been in the pub, had served as a distraction. Now, suddenly, he was merely repulsive.

'Aren't you afraid of going to hell?' he asked. 'They'll make you drink burning whiskey there. A perpetual Christmas pudding in your belly. If you could see yourself! The revolting spectacle ...'

The choir-boy's sixth whiskey had been full of contrition. 'I know, I know,' he groaned. 'I'm disgusting. I'm contemptible. But if you knew how I'd struggled and striven and ...'

'There's a cab.' Spandrell gave a shout.

'How I'd prayed,' the choir-boy continued.

'Where do you live?'

'Forty-one Ossian Gardens. I've wrestled ...'

The cab drew up in front of them. Spandrell opened the door.

'Get in, you sot,' he said, and gave the other a push. 'Forty-one Ossian Gardens,' he said to the driver. The choir-boy, meanwhile, had crawled into his seat. Spandrell followed. 'Disgusting slug!'

'Go on, go on. I deserve it. You have every right to despise me.'

'I know,' said Spandrell. 'But if you think I'm going to do you the pleasure of telling you so any more, you're much mistaken.' He leaned back in his corner and shut his eyes. All his appalling weariness and disgust had suddenly returned. 'God,' he said to himself. 'God, God, God.' And like a grotesque derisive echo of his thoughts, the choir-boy prayed aloud. 'God have mercy upon me,' the maudlin voice repeated. Spandrell burst out laughing.

Leaving the drunkard on his front doorstep, Spandrell went back to the cab. He remembered suddenly that he had not dined. 'Sbisa's Restaurant,' he told the driver. 'God, God,' he repeated in the darkness. But the night was a vacuum.

'There's Spandrell,' cried Lucy, interrupting her companion in the middle of a sentence. She raised her arm and waved.

'Lucy!' Spandrell took her hand and kissed it. He sat down at their table. 'It'll interest you to hear, Walter, that I've just been doing a good Samaritan to your victim.'

'My victim?'

'Your cuckold. Carling; isn't that his name?' Walter blushed in an agony. 'He wears his horns without any difference. Quite traditionally.' He looked at Walter and was glad to see the signs of distress on his face. 'I found him drowning his sorrows,' he went on maliciously. 'In whiskey. The grand romantic remedy.' It was a relief to be able to take some revenge for his miseries.

Chapter Eighteen

At Port Said they went ashore. The flank of the ship was an iron precipice. At its foot the launch heaved on a dirty and slowly wallowing sea; between its gunwale and the end of the ship's ladder a little chasm alternately shrank and expanded. For a sound pair of legs the leap would have been nothing. But Philip hesitated. To jump with his game leg foremost might mean to collapse under the impact of arrival; and if he trusted to the game leg to propel him, he had a good chance of falling ignominiously short. He was delivered from his predicament by the military gentleman who had preceded him in the leap.

'Here, take my hand,' he called, noticing Philip's hesitation and its cause.

'Thanks so much,' said Philip when he was safely in the launch.

'Awkward, this sort of thing,' said the other. 'Particularly if one's short of a leg, what?'

'Very.'

'Damaged in the War?'

Philip shook his head. 'Accident when I was a boy,' he explained telegraphically, and the blood mounted to his cheeks. 'There's my wife,' he mumbled, glad of an excuse to get away. Elinor jumped, steadied herself against him; they picked their way to seats at the other end of the launch.

'Why didn't you let me go first and help you over?' she asked.

'I was all right,' he answered curtly and in a tone that decided her to say no more. She wondered what was the matter. Something to do with his lameness? Why was he so queer about it?

Philip himself would have found it hard to explain what there was in the military gentleman's question to distress him. After all there was nothing in the least discreditable in having been run over by a cart. And to have been rejected as totally unfit for military service was not in the least unpatriotic. And yet, quite unreasonably, the question had disturbed him, as all such questions, as any too overt reference to his lameness, unless deliberately prepared for by himself, invariably did.

Discussing him with Elinor, 'Philip was the last person,' his mother had once said, 'the very last person such an accident ought to have happened to. He was born far away, if you know what I mean. It was always too easy for him to dispense with people. He was too fond of shutting himself up inside his own private silence. But he

231

might have learned to come out more, if that horrible accident hadn't happened. It raised an artificial barrier between him and the rest of the world. It meant no games, to begin with; and no games meant fewer contacts with other boys, more solitude, more leisure for books. And then (poor Phil!) it meant fresh causes for shyness. A sense of inferiority. Children can be so horribly ruthless; they used to laugh at him sometimes at school. And later, when girls began to matter, how I wish he'd been able to go to dances and tennis parties! But he couldn't waltz or play. And of course he didn't want to go as an onlooker and an outsider. His poor smashed leg began by keeping him at a physical distance from girls of his own age. And it kept him at a psychological distance, too. For I believe he was always afraid (secretly, of course, and without admitting it) that they might laugh at him, as some of the boys did; and he didn't want to run the risk of being rejected in favour of someone who wasn't handicapped as he was. Not that he'd ever have taken very much interest in girls,' Mrs Quarles had added.

And Elinor had laughed. 'I shouldn't imagine so.'

'But he wouldn't have got into such a habit of deliberately avoiding them. He wouldn't have so systematically retired from all personal contacts – and not with girls only; with men, too. Intellectual contacts – those are the only ones he admits.'

'It's as though he only felt safe among ideas,' Elinor had said.

'Because he can hold his own there; because he can be certain of superiority. He's got into the habit of feeling afraid and suspicious outside that intellectual world. He needn't have. And I've always tried to reassure him and tempt him out; but he won't let himself be tempted, he creeps back into his shell.' And after a silence, 'It's had only one good result,' she had added, 'the accident, I mean. It saved him from going to the War, from being killed, probably. Like his brother.'

The launch began to move towards the shore. From being an impending wall of black iron, the liner, as they receded, became a great ship, seen in its entirety. Fixed motionless between the sea and the blue glare of the sky, it looked like the advertisement of tropical cruises in the window of a Cockspur Street shipping office.

'It was an impertinence to ask,' Philip was thinking. 'What business was it of his whether I'd been damaged in the War? How they go on gloating over their War, those professional soldiers! Well, I can be thankful I kept out of the bloody business. Poor Geoffrey!' He thought of his dead brother.

'And yet,' Mrs Quarles had concluded after a pause, 'in a certain sense I wish he had gone to the War. Oh, not for fire-eating patriotic reasons. But because, if one could have guaranteed that he wouldn't have been killed or mangled, it would have been so good for him – violently good, perhaps; painfully good; but still good. It might have smashed his shell for him and set him free from his own prison. Emotionally free; for his intellect's free enough already. Too free, perhaps, for my old-fashioned taste.' And she had smiled rather sadly. 'Free to come and go in the human world, instead of being boxed up in that indifference of his.'

'But isn't the indifference natural to him?' Elinor had objected.

'Partly. But in part it's a habit. If he could break the habit, he'd be so much happier. And I think he knows it, but can't break it himself. If it could be broken for him … But the War was the last chance. And circumstances didn't allow it to be taken.'

'Thank heaven!'

'Well, perhaps you're right.'

The launch had arrived; they stepped ashore. The heat was terrific, the pavements glared, the air was full of dust. With much display or teeth, much flashing of black and liquid eyes, much choreographic gesticulation, an olive-coloured gentleman in a tarboosh tried to sell them carpets. Elinor was for driving him away. But, 'Don't waste energy,' said Philip. 'Too hot. Passive resistance, and pretend not to understand.'

They walked on like martyrs across an arena; and like a hungry lion, the gentleman in the tarboosh frisked round them. If not carpets, then artificial pearls. No pearls? Then genuine Havana cigars at three-halfpence each. Or a celluloid comb. Or imitation amber. Or almost genuine gold bangles. Philip continued to shake his head.

'Nice corals. Nice scarabs – real old.' That winning smile was beginning to look like a snarl.

Elinor had seen the drapery shop she was looking for; they crossed the street and entered.

'Saved!' she said. 'He daren't follow. I had such a horrible fear that he might suddenly begin to bite. Poor wretch, though. I think we ought to buy something.' She turned and addressed herself to the assistant behind the counter.

'Meanwhile,' said Philip, foreseeing that Elinor's shopping would be interminably tedious, 'I'll go and get a few cigarettes.'

He stepped out into the glare. The man in the tarboosh was waiting. He pounced, he caught Philip by the sleeve. Desperately, he played his last trump.

'Nice post-cards,' he whispered confidentially and produced an envelope from his breast-pocket. 'Hot stuff. Only ten shillings.'

Philip stared uncomprehending. 'No English,' he said and limped away along the street. The man in the tarboosh hurried at his side.

'Très curieuses,' he said. 'Très amusantes. Mœurs arabes. Pour passer le temps à bord. Soixante francs seulement.' He saw no answering light of comprehension. 'Molto artistiche,' he suggested in Italian. 'Proprio curiose. Cinquanta franchi.' He peered in desperation into Philip's face; it was a blank. 'Hübsch,' he went on, 'sehr geschlechtlich. Zehn mark.' Not a muscle moved. 'Muy hermosas, muy agraciadas, mucho indecorosas.' He tried again. 'Skon bref kort. Liderlig fotografi bild. Nakna jungfrun. Verklig smutsig.' Philip was evidently no Scandinavian. Was he a Slav? 'Sprosny obraz,' the man wheedled. It was no good. Perhaps Portuguese would do it. 'Photographía deshonesta,' he began.

Philip burst out laughing. 'Here,' he said, and gave him half a crown. 'You deserve it.'

'Did you discover what you wanted?' asked Elinor when he returned.

He nodded. 'And I also discovered the only possible basis for the League of Nations. The one common interest. Our toothy friend offered me indecent postcards in seventeen languages. He's wasting himself at Port Said. He ought to be at Geneva.'

*

'Two ladies to see you, sir,' said the office boy.

'Two?' Burlap raised his dark eyebrows. 'Two?' The office boy insisted. 'Well, show them up.' The boy retired. Burlap was annoyed. He was expecting Romola Saville, the Romola Saville who had written,

> Already old in passion, I have known
> All the world's lovers since the world began;
> Have held in Leda's arms the immortal Swan;
> And felt fair Paris take me as his own.

And she was coming with a duenna. It wasn't like her. *Two* ladies…

The two doors of his sanctum opened simultaneously. Ethel Cobbett appeared at one holding a bunch of galley proofs. By the other entered the two ladies. Standing on the threshold Ethel looked at them. One of them was tall and remarkably thin. Almost equally tall, the other was portly. Neither of them was any longer young. The thin lady seemed a withered and virgin forty-three or four. The portly one was perhaps a little older, but had preserved a full-blown and widowed freshness. The thin one was sallow, with sharp bony features, nondescript brown hair and grey eyes, and was dressed rather fashionably, not in the style of Paris, but in the more youthful and jaunty mode of Hollywood, in pale grey and pink. The other lady was very blonde, with blue eyes, and long dangling earrings and lapis lazuli beads to match. Her style of dressing was more matronly and European than the other's, and numbers of not very precious ornaments were suspended here and there all over her person and tinkled a little as she walked.

The two ladies advanced across the room. Burlap pretended to be so deeply immersed in composition that he had not heard the opening of the door. It was only when the ladies had come to within a few feet of his table that he looked up from the paper on which he had been furiously scribbling – with what a start of amazement, what an expression of apologetic embarrassment! He sprang to his feet.

'I'm so sorry. Forgive ... I hadn't noticed. One gets so deeply absorbed.' The n's and m's had turned to d's and b's. He had a cold. 'So idvolved id ode's work.'

He came round the table to meet them, smiling his subtlest and most spiritual Sodoma smile. But, 'Oh God!' he was inwardly exclaiming. 'What appalling females!'

'And which,' he went on aloud, smiling from one to the other, 'which, may I venture to ask, is Miss Saville?'

'Neither of us,' said the portly lady in a rather deep voice, but playfully and with a smile.

'Or both, if you like,' said the other. Her voice was high and metallic and she spoke sharply, in little spurts, and with an extraordinary and vertiginous rapidity. 'Both *and* neither.'

And the two ladies burst into simultaneous laughter. Burlap looked and listened with a sinking heart. What had he let himself in for? They were formidable. He blew his nose; he coughed. They were making his cold worse.

'The fact is,' said the portly lady, cocking her head rather archly on one side and affecting the slightest lisp, 'the fact ith ...'

But the thin one interrupted her. 'The fact is,' she said, pouring out her words so fast that it was extraordinary that she should have been able to articulate them at all, 'that we're a partnership, a combination, almost a conspiracy.' She uttered her sharp shrill laugh.

'Yeth, a conthpirathy,' said the portly one lisping from sheer playfulness.

'We're the two parts of Romola Saville's dual personality.'

'I being the Dr Jekyll,' put in the portly one, and both laughed yet once more.

'A conspiracy,' thought Burlap with a growing sense of horror. 'I should think it was!'

'Dr Jekyll, *alias* Ruth Goffer. May I introduce you to Mrs Goffer?'

'While I do the same for Mr Hyde, *alias* Miss Hignett?'

'While together we introduce ourselves as the Romola Saville whose poor poems you said such very kind things about.'

Burlap shook hands with the two ladies and said something about his pleasure at beeting the authors of work he had so much adbired. 'But how shall I ever get rid of them?' he wondered. So much energy, such an exuberance of force and will! Getting rid of them would be no joke. He shuddered inwardly. 'They're like steam engines,' he decided. And they'd pester him to go on printing their beastly verses. Their obscene verses – for that's what they were, in the light of these women's age and energy and personal appearance – just obscene. 'The bitches!' he said to himself, feeling resentfully that they'd got something out of him on false pretences, that they'd taken advantage of his innocence and swindled him. It was at this moment that he caught sight of Miss Cobbett. She held up her bundle of proofs inquiringly. He shook his head. 'Later,' he said to her, with a dignified and editorial expression. Miss Cobbett turned away, but not before he had remarked the look of derisive triumph on her face. Damn the woman! It was intolerable.

'We were so thrilled and delighted by your kind letter,' said the stouter of the ladies.

Burlap smiled Franciscanly. 'One's glad to be able to do something for literature.'

'So *few* take any interest.'

'Yes, so few,' echoed Miss Hignett. And speaking with the rapidity of one who tries to say 'Peter Piper picked a peck of pickled pepper' in the shortest possible time and with the fewest possible mistakes, she poured out their history and their grievances. It appeared that they had been living together at Wimbledon and conspiring to be Romola Saville for upwards of six years now, and that only on nine

236

occasions in all that time had any of their works been printed. But they hadn't lost courage. Their day, they knew, would come. They had gone on writing. They had written a great deal. Perhaps Mr Burlap would be interested to see the plays they had written? And Miss Hignett opened a despatch case and laid four thick wads of typescript on the table. Historical plays they were, in blank verse. And the titles were 'Fredegond,' 'The Bastard of Normandy,' 'Semiramis,' and 'Gilles de Retz.'

They went at last, taking with them Burlap's promise to read their plays, to print a sonnet sequence, to come to lunch at Wimbledon. Burlap sighed; then recomposing his face to stoniness and superiority, rang for Miss Cobbett.

'You've got the proofs?' he asked distantly and without looking at her.

She handed them to him. 'I've telephoned to say they must hurry up with the rest.'

'Good.'

There was a silence. It was Miss Cobbett who broke it, and though he did not deign to look up at her, Burlap could tell from the tone of her voice that she was smiling.

'Your Romola Saville,' she said; 'that was a bit of a shock, wasn't it?'

Miss Cobbett's loyalty to Susan's memory was the intenser for being forced and deliberate. She had been in love with Burlap herself. Her loyalty to Susan and to that platonic spirituality which was Burlap's amorous speciality (she believed, at first, that he meant what he so constantly and beautifully said) was exercised by a continual struggle against love, and grew strong in the process. Burlap, who was experienced in these matters, had soon realized, from the quality of her response to his first platonic advances, that there was, in the vulgar language which even his devil hardly ever used, 'nothing doing.' Persisting, he would only damage his own high spiritual reputation. In spite of the fact that the girl was in love with him, or even in a certain sense because of it (for, loving, she realized how dangerously easy it would be to betray the cause of Susan and pure spirit and, realizing the danger, braced herself against it), she would never, he saw, permit his passage, however gradual, from spirituality to a carnality however refined. And since he himself was not in love with her, since she had aroused in him only the vague adolescent itch of desire which almost any personable woman could satisfy, it cost

237

him little to be wise and retire. Retirement, he calculated, would enhance her admiration for his spirituality, would quicken her love. It is always useful, as Burlap had found in the past, to have employees who are in love with one. They work much harder and ask much less than those who are not in love. For a little everything went according to plan. Miss Cobbett did the work of three secretaries and an office boy, and at the same time worshipped. But there were incidents. Burlap was too much interested in female contributors. Some women he had actually been to bed with came and confided in Miss Cobbett. Her faith was shaken. Her righteous indignation at what she regarded as Burlap's treachery to Susan and his ideals, his deliberate hypocrisy, was inflamed by personal feelings. He had betrayed her too. She was angry and resentful. Anger and resentment intensified her ideal loyalty. It was only in terms of loyalty to Susan and the spirit that she could express her jealousy.

The last straw was Beatrice Gilray. The cup of Miss Cobbett's bitterness overflowed when Beatrice was installed at the office – in the editorial department, what was more, actually doing some of the writing for the paper. Miss Cobbett comforted herself a little by the thought that the writing was only Shorter Notices, which were quite unimportant. But still, she was bitterly resentful. She was much better educated than that fool of a Beatrice, much more intelligent too. It was just because Beatrice had money that she was allowed to write. Beatrice had put a thousand pounds into the paper. She worked for nothing – and worked, what was more, like mad; just as Miss Cobbett herself had worked, at the beginning. Now, Miss Cobbett did as little as she could. She stood on her rights, never arrived a minute early, never stayed a minute past her allotted time. She did no more than she was paid to do. Burlap was annoyed, resentful, distressed; he would either have to do more work himself or employ another secretary. And then, providentially, Beatrice turned up. She took over all the sub-editing which Miss Cobbett now had no time to do. To compensate her for the sub-editing and the thousand pounds he allowed her to do a little writing. She didn't know how to write, of course; but that didn't matter. Nobody ever read the Shorter Notices.

When Burlap went to live in Beatrice Gilray's house, Miss Cobbett's cup overflowed again. In the first moment of anger she was rash enough to give Beatrice a solemn warning against her tenant. But her disinterested solicitude for Beatrice's reputation and virginity was too manifestly and uncontrollably tinged with spite against

Burlap. The only effect of her admonition was to exasperate Beatrice into sharp retort.

'She's really insufferable,' Beatrice complained to Burlap afterwards, without, however, detailing all the reasons she had for finding the woman insufferable.

Burlap looked Christ-like. 'She's difficult,' he admitted. 'But one's sorry for her. She's had a hard life.'

'I don't see that a hard life excuses anybody from behaving properly,' she rapped out.

'But one has to make allowances,' said Burlap, wagging his head.

'If I were you,' said Beatrice, 'I wouldn't have her in the place; I'd send her away.'

'No, I couldn't do that,' Burlap answered, speaking slowly and ruminatively, as though the whole discussion were taking place inside himself. 'Not in the circumstances.' He smiled a Sodoma smile, subtle, spiritual and sweet; once more he wagged his dark, romantic head. 'The circumstances are rather peculiar.' He went on vaguely, never quite definitely explaining what the rather peculiar circumstances were, and with a kind of diffidence, as though he were reluctant to sing his own praises. Beatrice was left to gather that he had taken and was keeping Miss Cobbett out of charity. She was filled with a mixed feeling of admiration and pity – admiration for his goodness and pity for his helplessness in an ungrateful world.

'All the same,' she said, and she looked fierce, her words were like sharp little mallet taps, 'I don't see why you should let yourself be bullied. *I* wouldn't let myself be treated like that.'

From that time forward she took every opportunity of snubbing Miss Cobbett and being rude. Miss Cobbett snapped, snubbed, and was sarcastic in return. In the offices of the *Literary World* the war was open. Remotely, but not quite impartially, like a god with a prejudice in favour of virtue – virtue being represented in the present case by Beatrice – Burlap hovered mediatingly above the battle.

The episode of Romola Saville gave Miss Cobbett an opportunity for being malicious.

'Did you see those two terrifying poetesses?' she inquired of Beatrice, with a deceptive air of friendliness, the next morning.

Beatrice glanced at her sharply. What was the woman up to? 'Which poetesses?' she asked suspiciously.

'Those two formidable middle-aged ladies the editor asked to come and see him under the impression that they were one young one.' She laughed. 'Romola Saville. That's how the poems were signed. It sounded so romantic. And the poems were quite romantic too. But the two authoresses! Oh, my goodness. When I saw the editor in their clutches I really felt quite sorry for him. But after all, he did bring it on himself. If he will write to his lady contributors. ...'

That evening Beatrice renewed her complaints about Miss Cobbett. The woman was not only tiresome and impertinent; one could put up with that if she did her job properly; she was lazy. Running a paper was a business like any other. One couldn't afford to do business on a basis of sentimentality. Vaguely, diffidently, Burlap talked again about the peculiar circumstances of the case. Beatrice retorted. There was an argument.

'There's such a thing as being too kind,' Beatrice sharply concluded.

'Is there?' said Burlap; and his smile was so beautifully and wistfully Franciscan, that Beatrice felt herself inwardly melting into tenderness.

'Yes, there is,' she rapped out, feeling more hard and hostile towards Miss Cobbett as she felt more softly and maternally protective towards Burlap. Her tenderness was lined, so to speak, with indignation. When she didn't want to show her softness, she turned her feelings inside out and was angry. 'Poor Denis,' she thought, underneath her indignation. 'He really needs somebody to look after him. He's too good.' She spoke aloud. 'And you've got a shocking cough,' she said reproachfully with an irrelevance that was only apparent. Being too good, having nobody to look after one and having a cough – the ideas were logically connected. 'What you need,' she went on in the same sharp commanding tones, 'is a good rubbing with camphorated oil and a wad of Thermogene.' She spoke the words almost menacingly, as though she were threatening him with a good beating and a month on bread and water. Her solicitude expressed itself that way; but how tremulously soft it was underneath the surface!

Burlap was only too happy to let her carry out her tender threat. At half-past ten he was lying in bed with an extra hot-water bottle. He had drunk a glass of hot milk and honey and was now sucking a soothing lozenge. It was a pity, he was thinking, that she wasn't younger. Still, she was really amazingly youthful for her age. Her face, her figure – more like twenty-five than thirty-five. He wondered how she'd behave when finally she'd been coaxed past her terrors. There was something very strange about these childish terrors in a

240

grown woman. Half of her was arrested at the age when Uncle Ben had made his premature experiment. Burlap's devil grinned at the recollection of her account of the incident.

There was a tap at the door and Beatrice entered carrying the camphorated oil and the Thermogene.

'Here's the executioner,' said Burlap, laughing. 'Let me die like a man.' He undid his pyjama jacket. His chest was white and well-covered; the contour of the ribs only faintly showed through the flesh. Between the paps a streak of dark curly hair followed the line of the breastbone. 'Do your worst,' he bantered on. 'I'm ready.' His smile was playfully tender.

Beatrice uncorked the bottle and poured a little of the aromatic oil into the palm of her right hand. 'Take the bottle,' she commanded, 'and put it down.' He did as he was told. 'Now,' she said, when he was stretched out again unmoving; and she began to rub.

Her hand slid back and forth over his chest, back and forth, vigorously, efficiently. And when the right was tired, she began again with the left, back and forth, back and forth.

'You're like a little steam engine,' said Burlap with his playfully tender smile.

'I feel like one,' she answered. But it wasn't true. She felt like almost anything but a steam engine. She had had to overcome a kind of horror before she could touch that white, full-fleshed chest of his. Not that it was ugly or repulsive. On the contrary, it was rather beautiful in its smooth whiteness and fleshy strength. Fine, like the torso of a statue. Yes, a statue. Only the statue had dark little curls along the breastbone and a little brown mole that fluttered up and down with the pulsing skin over the heart. The statue lived; that was the disquieting thing. The white naked breast was beautiful; but it was almost repulsively alive. To touch it … She shuddered inwardly with a little spasm of horror, and was angry with herself for having felt so stupidly. Quickly she had stretched out her hand and begun to rub. Her palm slid easily over the lubricated skin. The warmth of his body was against her hand. Through the skin she could feel the hardness of the bones. There was a bristle of roughness against her fingers as they touched the hairs along the breastbone, and the little paps were firm and elastic. She shuddered again, but there was something agreeable in the feeling of horror and the overcoming of it; there was a strange pleasure in the creeping of alarm and repulsion that travelled through her body. She went on rubbing, a steam engine only in the vigour and regularity of her movements, but, within, how quiveringly and self-dividedly alive!

Burlap lay with his eyes shut, faintly smiling with the pleasure of abandonment and self-surrender. He was feeling, luxuriously, like a child, helpless; he was in her hands, like a child who is its mother's property and plaything, no longer his own master. Her hands were cold on his chest; his flesh was passive and abandoned, like so much clay, under those strong cold hands.

'Tired?' he asked, when she paused to change hands for the third time. He opened his eyes to look at her. She shook her head. 'I'm as much bother as a sick child.'

'No bother at all.'

But Burlap insisted on being sorry for her and apologetic for himself. 'Poor Beatrice!' he said. 'All you have to do for me! I'm quite ashamed.'

Beatrice only smiled. Her first shudderings of unreasonable repulsion had passed off. She felt extraordinarily happy.

'There!' she said at last. 'Now for the Thermogene.' She opened the cardboard box and unfolded the orange wool. 'The problem is how to stick it on to your chest. I'd thought of keeping it in place with a bandage. Two or three turns right round the body. What do you think?'

'I don't think anything,' said Burlap who was still enjoying the luxury of infantility. 'I'm utterly in your hands.'

'Well, then, sit up,' she commanded. He sat up. 'Hold the wool on to your chest while I pass the bandage round.' To bring the bandage round his body she had to lean very close to him, almost embracing him; her hands met for a moment behind his back, as she unwound the bandage. Burlap dropped his head forward and his forehead rested against her breast. The forehead of a tired child on the soft breast of its mother.

'Hold the end a moment while I get a safety-pin.'

Burlap lifted his forehead and drew back. Rather flushed, but still very business-like and efficient, Beatrice was detaching one from a little card of assorted safety-pins.

'Now comes the really difficult moment,' she said, laughing. 'You won't mind if I run the pin into your flesh.'

'No, I won't mind,' said Burlap, and it was true; he wouldn't have minded. He'd have been rather pleased if she had hurt him. But she

242

didn't. The bandage was pinned into position with quite professional neatness.

'There!'

'What do you want me to do now?' asked Burlap, greedy to obey.

'Lie down.'

He lay down. She did up the buttons of his pyjama jacket. 'Now you must go to sleep as quickly as you can.' She pulled the bed-clothes up to his chin and tucked them in. Then she laughed. 'You look like a little boy.'

'Aren't you going to kiss me good-night?'

The colour came into Beatrice's cheeks. She bent down and kissed him on the forehead. 'Good-night,' she said. And suddenly she wanted to take him in her arms, to press his head against her breast and stroke his hair. But she only laid her hand for a moment against his cheek, then hurried out of the room.

Chapter Nineteen

LITTLE PHIL was lying on his bed. The room was in an orange twilight. A thin needle of sunshine came probing in between the drawn curtains. Phil was more than usually restless.

'What's the time?' he shouted at last, though he had shouted before and been told to keep quiet.

'Not time for you to get up,' Miss Fulkes called back from across the passage. Her voice came muffled, for she was half-way into her blue frock, her head involved in silken darkness, her arms struggling blindly to find the entrance to their respective sleeves. Phil's parents were arriving to-day; they would be at Gattenden for lunch. Miss Fulkes's blue best was imperatively called for.

'But what's the *time*?' the child shouted back angrily. 'On your watch, I mean.'

Miss Fulkes's head came through into the light. 'Twenty to one,' she called back. 'You must be quiet.'

'Why isn't it one?'

'Because it isn't. Now I shan't answer you any more. And if you shout again I shall tell your mother how naughty you've been.'

'Naughty!' Phil retorted, putting a tearful fury into his voice – but so softly, that Miss Fulkes hardly heard him. 'I hate you!' He didn't, of course. But he had made his protest; honour was saved.

Miss Fulkes went on with her toilet. She felt agitated, afraid, painfully excited. What would they think of Phil – *her* Phil, the Phil she had made? 'I hope he'll be good,' she thought. 'I hope he'll be good.' He could be an angel, so enchanting when he chose. And when he wasn't an angel, there was always a reason; but one had to know him, one had to understand him in order to see the reason. Probably they wouldn't be able to see the reason. They had been away so long; they might have forgotten what he was like. And in any case they couldn't know what he was like now, what he had grown into during these last months. She alone knew *that* Phil. Knew him and loved him – so much, so much. She alone. And one day she would have to leave him. She had no rights over him, no claim to him; she only loved him. They could take him away from her whenever they wanted. The image of herself in the glass wavered and was lost in a rainbow fog and suddenly the tears overflowed on to her cheeks.

The train was punctual, the car in attendance. Philip and Elinor climbed in.

'Isn't it wonderful to be here?' Elinor took her husband's hand. Her eyes shone. 'But, good Lord,' she added, in a tone of horror and without waiting for his answer, 'they're building a lot of new houses on the hill there. How dare they?'

Philip looked. 'Rather garden city, isn't it?' he said. 'It's a pity the English love the country so much,' he added. 'They're killing it with kindness.'

'But how lovely it still is, all the same. Aren't you tremendously excited?'

'Excited?' he questioned, cautiously. 'Well ...'

'Aren't you even pleased that you're going to see your son again?'

'Of course.'

'Of course!' Elinor repeated the words derisively. 'And in *that* tone of voice. I never thought there was any 'of course' about it; but now the time has come, I've never been so excited in my life.'

There was a silence; the car drove on windingly, down the lanes. The road mounted; they climbed through beechwoods to a wooded plateau. At the end of a long green vista the most colossal monument of Tantamount grandeur, the palace of the Marquess of Gattenden, basked far off in the sun. The flag flew; his lordship was in residence. 'We must go and call on the old madman one day,' said Philip. The fallow deer browsed in the park.

'Why does one ever travel?' said Elinor, as she looked at them.

Miss Fulkes and little Phil were waiting on the steps. 'I believe I hear the car,' said Miss Fulkes. Her rather lumpy face was very pale; her heart was beating with more than ordinary force. 'No,' she added, after a moment of intent listening. What she had heard was only the sound of her own anxiety.

Little Phil moved about uncomfortably, conscious only of a violent desire to 'go somewhere.' Anticipation had lodged a hedgehog in his entrails.

'Aren't you *happy*?' asked Miss Fulkes, with assumed enthusiasm, self-sacrificingly determined that the child should show himself wild with joy to see his parents again. 'Aren't you *tremendously* excited?' But they could take him away from her if they wanted to, take him away and never let her see him again.

'Yes,' little Phil replied rather vaguely. He was preoccupied exclusively with the approach of visceral events.

Miss Fulkes was disappointed by the flatness of his tone. She looked at him inquiringly. 'Phil?' She had noticed his uneasy Charleston. The child nodded. She took his hand and hurried him into the house.

A minute later Philip and Elinor drove up to a deserted porch. Elinor couldn't help feeling disappointed. She had so clearly visualized the scene—Phil on the steps frantically waving—she had so plainly, in anticipation, heard his shouting. And the steps were a blank.

'Nobody to meet us,' she said, and her tone was mournful.

'You could hardly expect them to hang about, waiting,' Philip replied. He hated anything in the nature of a fuss. For him, the perfect homecoming would have been in a cloak of invisibility. This was a good second best.

They got out of the car. The front door was open. They entered. In the silent, empty hall three and a half centuries of life had gone to sleep. The sunlight stared through flat-arched windows. The panelling had been painted pale green in the eighteenth century. All ancient oak and high-lights, the staircase climbed up, out of sight, towards the higher floors. A smell of pot-pourri faintly haunted the air; it was as though one apprehended the serene old silence through another sense.

Elinor looked round her, she took a deep breath, she drew her finger-tips along the polished walnut wood of a table, with the knuckle of a bent forefinger she rapped the round Venetian bowl that stood on it; the glassy bell-note lingered sweetly on the perfumed silence.

'Like the Sleeping Beauty,' she said. But even as she spoke the words, the spell was broken. Suddenly, as though the ringing glass had called the house back to life, there was sound and movement. Somewhere upstairs a door opened, through the sanitary noise of rushing water came the sound of Phil's piercing young voice; small feet thudded along the carpet of the corridor, clattered like little hoofs on the naked oak of the stairs. At the same moment a door on the ground floor flew open and the enormous form of Dobbs, the parlourmaid, hastened into the hall.

'Why, Miss Elinor, I never heard you ...'

Little Phil rounded the last turn of the staircase. At the sight of his parents he gave a shout, he quickened his pace; he almost slid from step to step.

'Not so fast, not so fast!' his mother called anxiously and ran towards him.

246

'Not so fast!' echoed Miss Fulkes hurrying down the stairs behind. And suddenly, from the morning-room, which had a door leading out into the garden, Mrs Bidlake appeared, white and silent and with floating veils, like an imposing phantom. In a little basket she carried a bunch of cut tulips; her gardening scissors dangled at the end of a yellow ribbon. T'ang the Third followed her, barking. There was a confusion of embracing and handshaking. Mrs Bidlake's greetings had the majesty of ritual, the solemn grace of an ancient and sacred dance. Miss Fulkes writhed with shyness and excitement, stood first on one leg and then on the other, went into the attitudes of fashion-plates and mannequins and from time to time piercingly laughed. When she shook hands with Philip, she writhed so violently that she almost lost her balance.

'Poor creature!' Elinor had time to think between the answering and asking of questions. 'How urgently she needs marrying! Much worse than when we left.'

'But how he's grown!,' she said aloud. 'And how he's changed!' She held the child at arm's length with the gesture of a connoisseur who stands back to examine a picture. 'He used to be the image of Phil. But now ...' She shook her head. Now the broad face had lengthened, the short straight nose (the comical 'cat's nose' which in Philip's face she had always laughed at and so much loved) had grown finer and faintly aquiline, the hair had darkened. 'Now he's exactly like Walter. Don't you think so?' Mrs Bidlake remotely nodded. 'Except when he laughs,' she added. 'His laugh's pure Phil.'

'What have you brought me?' asked little Phil almost anxiously. When people went away and came back again, they always brought him something. 'Where's my present?'

'What a question!' Miss Fulkes protested, blushing with vicarious shame, and writhing.

But Elinor and Philip only laughed.

'He's Walter when he's serious,' said Elinor.

'Or you.' Philip looked from one to the other.

'The first minute your father and mother arrive!' Miss Fulkes continued her reproaches.

'Naughty!' the child retorted and threw back his head with a little movement of anger and pride.

Elinor, who had been looking at him, almost laughed aloud. That sudden lifting of the chin – why it was the parody of old Mr Quarles's gesture of superiority. For a moment the child was her father-in-

law, her absurd deplorable father-in-law, caricatured and in minia-
ture. It was comic, but at the same time it was somehow no joke. She
wanted to laugh, but she was oppressed by a sudden realization of the
mysteries and complexities of life, the terrible inscrutabilities of the
future. Here was her child – but he was also Philip, he was also herself, he was also Walter, her father, her mother; and now, with that
upward tilting of the chin, he had suddenly revealed himself as the
deplorable Mr Quarles. And he might be hundreds of other people
too. Might be? He certainly was. He was aunts and cousins she hardly
ever saw; grandfathers and great-uncles she had only known as a
child and utterly forgotten; ancestors who had died long ago, back
to the beginning of things. A whole population of strangers inhabited
and shaped that little body, lived in that mind and controlled its
wishes, dictated its thoughts and would go on dictating and control-
ling. Phil, little Phil – the name was an abstraction, a title arbitrarily
given, like 'France' or 'England,' to a collection, never long the
same, of many individuals, who were born, lived and died within
him, as the inhabitants of a country appear and disappear, but keep
alive in their passage the identity of the nation to which they belong.
She looked at the child with a kind of terror. What a responsibility!

'I call that cupboard love,' Miss Fulkes was still going on. 'And
you mustn't say "naughty" to me like that.'

Elinor gave a little sigh, shook herself out of her reverie and, picking up the child in her arms, pressed him against her. 'Never mind,'
she said, half to the reproving Miss Fulkes, half to her own apprehensive self. 'Never mind.' She kissed him.

Philip was looking at his watch. 'Perhaps we ought to go and wash
and brush up a bit before lunch,' he said. He had the sentiment of
punctuality.

'But first,' said Elinor, to whom it seemed that meals were made
for man, not man for meals, 'first we simply *must* run into the kitchen
and say how-do-you-do to Mrs Inman. It would be unforgivable if
we didn't. Come.' Still carrying the child, she led the way through
the dining-room. The smell of roast duck grew stronger and stronger
as they advanced.

Fretted a little by his consciousness of unpunctuality, and a little
uneasy at having to risk himself, even with Elinor for dragoman, in
the kitchen among the servants, Philip reluctantly followed her.

At luncheon, little Phil celebrated the occasion by behaving atrociously.

'The excitement has been too much for him,' poor Miss Fulkes kept repeating, trying to excuse the child and indirectly to justify herself. She would have liked to cry. 'You'll see when he's got used to your being here, Mrs Quarles,' she said, turning to Elinor, 'you'll see; he can be such an angel. It's the excitement.'

She had come to love the child so much that his triumphs and humiliations, his virtues and his crimes made her exult or mourn, feel self-satisfaction or shame, as if they had been her own. Besides there was her professional pride. She had been alone responsible for him all these months, teaching him the social virtues and why the triangle of India is painted crimson on the map; she had made him, had moulded him. And now, when this object of tenderest love, this product of her skill and patience, screamed at table, spat out mouthfuls of half-masticated food and spilt the water, Miss Fulkes not only blushed with agonizing shame, as though it were she who had screamed, had spat, had spilled, but experienced at the same time all the humiliation of the conjurer whose long-prepared trick fails to come off in public, the inventor of the ideal flying machine which simply refuses to leave the ground.

'After all,' said Elinor, consolingly, 'it's only to be expected.' She felt genuinely sorry for the poor girl. She looked at the child. He was crying – and she had expected (how unreasonably!) that it would be quite different now, that she would find him entirely rational and grown up. Her heart sank. She loved him, but children were terrible, terrible. And he was still a child. 'Now, Phil,' she said severely, 'you must eat. No more nonsense.'

The child howled louder. He would have liked to behave well, but he did not know how to stop behaving badly. He had voluntarily worked up this mood of rebellious misery within himself; but now the emotion was his master and stronger than his will. It was impossible for him, even though he desired it, to return by the way he had come. Besides he had always rather disliked roast duck; and having now, for five minutes, thought of roast duck with concentrated disgust and horror, he loathed it. The sight, the smell, the taste of it really and genuinely made him sick.

Mrs Bidlake meanwhile preserved her metaphysical calm. Her soul swam on steadily, like a great ship through a choppy sea; or perhaps it was more like a balloon, drifting high above the waters in the serene and windless world of fancy. She had been talking to Philip about Buddhism (Mrs Bidlake had a special weakness for Buddhism). At the first screams, she had not even turned round to see what was the matter, contenting herself with raising her voice so as to make it audible above the tumult. The yelling was renewed, was continued. Mrs Bidlake was silent and shut her eyes. A cross-legged Buddha, serene and golden, appeared against the red background of her closed lids; she saw the yellow-robed priests around him, each in the attitude of the god and plunged in ecstatic meditation.

'Maya,' she said with a sigh, as though to herself, 'maya – the eternal illusion.' She opened her eyes again. 'It *is* rather tough,' she added, addressing herself to Elinor and Miss Fulkes who were desperately trying to make the child eat.

Little Phil seized the excuse which she had thus gratuitously given him. 'It's tough,' he shouted tearfully, pushing away the fork on which Miss Fulkes, her hand trembling with the excess of painful emotions, was offering him a shred of roast duck and half a new potato.

Mrs Bidlake shut her eyes again for a moment; then turned to Philip and went on discussing the Eight-Fold Way.

*

That evening Philip wrote at some length in the notebook, in which he recorded, pell mell, thoughts and events, conversations, things heard and seen. 'The kitchen in the old house,' was how he headed the page. 'You can render it easily enough. The Tudor casements reflected in the bottoms of the copper pots. The huge black range with its polished steel trimmings and the fire peeping out through the half-opened porthole in the top. The mignonette in the window boxes. The cat, an enormous ginger eunuch, dozing in its basket by the dresser. The kitchen table so worn with time and constant scrubbing that the graining stands out above the softer wood – as though an engraver had prepared a wood-block of some gigantic fingerprint. The beams in the low ceiling. The brown beechwood chairs. The raw pastry in process of rolling. The smell of cookery. The leaning column of yellow sunlight full of motes. And finally old Mrs Inman, the cook, small, frail, indomitable, the authoress of how many thousand meals! Work that up a little, and you'd have your picture. But I want something more. A sketch of the kitchen in time as well as space, a hint of its significance in the general human cosmos. I write one sentence. 'Summer after summer, from the time when Shakespeare was a boy till now, ten generations of cooks have employed infra-red radiations to break up the protein molecules of spitted ducklings; ("thou wast not born for death, immortal bird," etc.).' One sentence, and I am already involved in history, art and all the sciences. The whole story of the universe is implicit in any part of it. The meditative eye can look through any single object and see, as through a window, the entire cosmos. Make the smell of roast duck in an old kitchen diaphanous and you will have a glimpse of everything, from the spiral nebulae to Mozart's music and the stigmata of St Francis of Assisi. The artistic problem is to produce diaphanousness in spots, selecting the spots so as to reveal only the most humanly significant of distant vistas behind the near familiar object. But in all cases, the things seen at the end of the vista must be strange enough to make the familiar seem fantastically mysterious. Question; can this be achieved without pedantry, and without spinning out the work interminably? It needs a great deal of thinking about.

Meanwhile, how charming the kitchen is! How sympathetic its inhabitants. Mrs Inman has been in the house as long as Elinor. A miracle of aged beauty. And how serene, how aristocratically commanding! When one has been monarch of all one surveys for thirty years, one looks the royal part, even when all one surveys is only the kitchen. And then there is Dobbs, the parlourmaid. Dobbs has only been in the house since a little before the War. An invention of Rabelais. Six feet high and proportionately thick. And the enormous body houses Gargantua's spirit. What broad humours, what a relish for life, what anecdotes, what facile and enormous laughter! Dobbs's laughter is almost terrifying. And on a shelf of the pantry dresser I noticed, when we went to pay our respects, a green bottle, half full of pills – but pills like good-sized marbles, such as one blows down the throats of horses from a rubber hose. What Homeric indigestions they imply!

The kitchen is good; but so is the drawing-room. We came in from our afternoon walk to find the vicar and his wife talking Art over the tea-cups. Yes, Art. For it was their first call since their visit to the Academy.

It is an annual affair. Every year on the day following Ascension Day they take the 8.52 to town and pay the tribute that even Religion owes to Art – Established Religion and Established Art. They scour every corner of Burlington House annotating the catalogue as they go round, humorously, wherever humour is admissible – for Mr Truby (who looks rather like Noah in a child's ark) is one of those facetious churchmen who crack jokes in order to show that, in spite of the black coat and the reversed collar, they are 'human,' 'good chaps,' etc.

Plumply pretty Mrs Truby is less uproariously waggish than her husband, but is none the less what upper middle-class readers of *Punch* would call a 'thoroughly cheery soul,' up to any amount of innocent fun and full of quaint remarks. I looked on and listened, fascinated, while Elinor drew them out about the parish and the Academy, feeling like Fabre among the coleoptera. Every now and then some word of the conversation would cross the spiritual abysses separating Elinor's mother from her surroundings, would penetrate her reverie and set up a curious reaction. Oracularly, disconcertingly, with a seriousness that was almost appalling in the midst of the Truby waggeries, she would speak out of another world. And outside, meanwhile, the garden is green and flowery. Old Stokes the gardener has a beard and looks like Father Time. The sky is pale blue. There is a noise of birds. The place is good. How good, one must have circumnavigated the globe to discover. Why not stay? Take root? But roots are chains. I have a terror of losing my freedom. Free, without ties, unpossessed by any possessions, free to do as one will, to go at a moment's notice wherever the fancy may suggest – it is good. But so is this place. Might it not be better? To gain freedom one sacrifices something – the house. Mrs Inman, Dobbs, facetious Truby from the parsonage, the tulips in the garden, and all that these things and people signify. One sacrifices something – for a greater gain in knowledge, in understanding, in intensified living? I sometimes wonder?

*

Lord Edward and his brother were taking the air in Gattenden Park. Lord Edward took it walking. The fifth Marquess took it in a bath chair drawn by a large grey donkey. He was a cripple. 'Which luckily doesn't prevent the mind from running,' he was fond of saying. It had been running, mazily, hither and thither all his life. Meanwhile, the grey ass only walked, very slowly. Before the two brothers and behind stretched Gattenden Broad Walk. A mile in front of them at the end of the straight vista stood a model of Trajan's column in Portland stone with a bronze statue of the first Marquess on the top and an inscription in large letters round the pedestal setting forth his claims to fame. He had been, among other things, Viceroy of Ireland and the Father of Scientific Agriculture. At the other end of the Broad

Walk, a mile behind the brothers, rose the fantastic towers and pin-nacles of Gattenden Castle, built for the second Marquess by James Wyatt in the most extravagant style of Strawberry Hill Gothic, and looking more mediaeval than anything that the real chronological Middle Ages had ever dreamt of. The Marquess lived permanently at Gattenden. Not that he particularly liked the house or the sur-rounding scenery. He was hardly aware of them. When he wasn't reading, he was thinking about what he had read; the world of appearances, as he liked, platonically, to call visible and tangible reality, did not interest him. This lack of interest was his revenge on the universe for having made him a cripple. He inhabited Gattenden, because it was only at Gattenden that he could safely go for drives in his bath chair. Pall Mall is no place for grey donkeys and paralytic old gentlemen who read and meditate as they drive. He had made over Tantamount House to his brother and continued to drive his ass through the beechwoods of Gattenden Park.

The ass had halted to browse at the wayside. The fifth Marquess and his brother were having an argument about God. Time passed. They were still talking about God when, half an hour later, Philip and Elinor, who had been taking their afternoon walk in the Park, emerged from the beechwood and unexpectedly came upon the Marquess's bath chair.

'Poor old creatures!' was Philip's comment when they were once more out of earshot. 'What else have they got to talk about? Too old to want to talk about love – too old and much too good. Too rich to talk about money. Too highbrow to talk about people and too hermit-like to know any people to talk about. Too shy to talk about themselves, too blankly inexperienced to talk about life or even literature. What is there left for the poor old wretches to talk about? Nothing – only God.'

'And at the present rate of progress,' said Elinor, 'you'll be exactly like them ten years from now.'

Chapter Twenty

Of Philip Quarles's father old John Bidlake used to say that he was like one of those baroque Italian churches with sham façades. High, impressive, bristling with classical orders, broken pedimenta and statuary, the façade seems to belong to a great cathedral. But look more closely and you discover that it is only a screen. Behind the enormous and elaborate front there crouches a wretched little temple of brick and rubble and scabby plaster. And warming to his simile, John Bidlake would describe the unshaven priest gabbling the office, the snotty little acolyte in his unwashed surplice, the congregation of goitrous peasant women and their brats, the cretin begging at the door, the tin crowns on the images, the dirt on the floor, the stale smell of generations of pious humanity.

'Why is it,' he concluded, forgetting that he was making an uncomplimentary comment on his own successes, 'that women always needs must love the lowest when they see it – or rather him? Curious. Particularly in this case. One would have given Rachel Quarles too much sense to be taken in by such a vacuum.'

Other people had thought so too, had also wondered why. Rachel Quarles seemed so incomparably too good for her husband. But one does not marry a set of virtues and talents; one marries an individual human being. The Sidney Quarles who had proposed to Rachel was a young man whom anyone might have fallen in love with and even believed in – anyone; and Rachel was only eighteen and particularly inexperienced. He too was young (youth is in itself a virtue), young and good-looking. Broad-shouldered and proportionately tall, portly now to the verge of stoutness, Sidney Quarles was still an imposing figure. At twenty-three the big body had been athletic, the greyish hair which now surrounded a pink and polished tonsure had then been golden-brown and had covered the whole of his scalp with a waving luxuriance. The large, high-coloured, fleshy face had been fresher, firmer, less moon-like. The forehead, even before baldness had set in, had seemed intellectual in its smooth height. Nor did Sidney Quarles's conversation belie the circumstantial evidence offered by his brow. He talked well, albeit perhaps with a little too much arrogance and self-satisfaction for every taste. Moreover, he had at that time a reputation; he had just come down from the university in something that was almost a blaze of academic and debating-society glory. On the virgin expanses of his future sanguine friends painted the brightest visions. At the time when Rachel first knew him, these prophecies had a positively reasonable air. And in any case, reasonably or unreasonably, she loved him. They were married when she was only nineteen.

From his father Sidney had inherited a handsome fortune. The business (old Mr Quarles was in sugar) was a going concern. The estate in Essex paid its way. The town house was in Portman Square, the country house at Chamford was commodious and Georgian. Sidney's ambitions were political. After an apprenticeship in local government, he would go into Parliament. Hard work, speeches at once sound and brilliant would mark him out as the coming man. He would be offered an assistant under-secretaryship, there would be rapid promotions. He might expect (so at least it had seemed five-and-thirty years ago) to realize the most extravagant ambitions.

But Sidney, as old Bidlake had said, was only a façade, an impressive appearance, a voice, a superficial cleverness and nothing more. Behind the handsome front lived the genuine Sidney, feeble, lacking all tenacity of purpose in important matters, though obstinate where trifles were concerned, easily fired with enthusiasm and still more easily bored. Even the cleverness turned out to be no more than the kind of cleverness which enables brilliant schoolboys to write Ovidian Latin verses or humorous parodies of Herodotus. Brought to the test, this sixth-form ability proved to be as impotent in the purely intellectual as in the practical sphere. For when, by a course of neglect tempered by feverish speculation and mismanagement, he had half ruined his father's business (Rachel made him sell out completely before it was too late), when his political prospects had been completely ruined by years of alternating indolence and undisciplined activity, he decided that his real vocation was to be a publicist. In the first flush of this new conviction, he actually contrived to finish a book about the principles of government. Shallow and vague, commonplace with an ordinariness made emphatic by the pretensions of an ornate style that coruscated with verbal epigrams, the book met with a deserved neglect, which Sidney Quarles attributed to the machinations of political enemies. He trusted to posterity for his due.

Ever since the publication of that first book, Mr Quarles had been writing, or at least had been supposed to be writing, another, much larger and more important, about democracy. The largeness and the importance justified an almost indefinite delay in its completion. He had already been at work on it for more than seven years and as yet, he would say to anyone who asked him about the progress of the book (shaking his head as he spoke with the expression of a man who bears an almost intolerable burden), as yet he had not even finished collecting the materials.

'It's a labour of Hercules,' he would say with an air at once martyred and fatuously arrogant. He had a way when he spoke to you of tilting his face upwards and shooting his words into the air, as though he were a howitzer, looking at you meanwhile, if he condescended to look at you at all, along his nose and from under half-shut eyelids. His voice was resonant and full of those baa-ings with which the very Oxonian are accustomed to enrich the English language. 'Really' in Sidney's mouth was always 'ryahly,' 'mere' was 'myah.' It was as though a flock of sheep had broken loose in his vocabulary. 'A labour of Hercules.' The words were accompanied by a sigh. 'Ryahly fyahful.'

If the questioner were sufficiently sympathetic, he would take him into his study and show him (or preferably her) the enormous apparatus of card indices and steel filing-cabinets which he had accumulated round his very professional-looking roll-top desk. As time passed and the book showed no signs of getting itself written, Mr Quarles had collected more and more of these impressive objects. They were the visible proofs of his labour, they symbolized the terrific difficulty of his task. He possessed no less than three typewriters. The portable Corona accompanied him wherever he went, in case he should at any time feel inspired when on his travels. Occasionally, when he felt the need of being particularly impressive, he took the Hammond, a rather larger machine, on which the letters were carried, not on separate arms, but on a detachable band of metal clipped to a revolving drum, so that it was possible to change the type at will and write in Greek or Arabic, mathematical symbols or Russian, according to the needs of the moment; Mr Quarles had a large collection of these alternative types which, of course, he never used, but of which he felt very proud, as though each of them represented a separate talent or accomplishment of his own. Finally there was the third and latest of the typewriters, a very large and very expensive office instrument, which was not only a typewriter, but also a calculating machine. So useful, Mr Quarles would explain, for compiling statistics for his great book and for doing the accounts of the estate. And he would point with special pride to the little electric motor attached to the machine; you made a connexion with the wall plug and the motor did everything for you – everything, that is to say, except actually compose your book. You had only to touch the keys, *so* (and Mr Quarles would give a demonstration); the electricity provided the force to bring the type into contact with the paper. All muscular effort was eliminated. You could go on typing for eighteen hours at a stretch – and Mr Quarles gave it to be understood that it was a common thing for him to spend eighteen hours at his desk (like Balzac, or Sir Isaac Newton) – you could go on, indeed, almost indefinitely without experiencing the slightest fatigue, at any rate in the fingers. An American invention. Very ingenious.

Mr Quarles had bought his calculating typewriter at the moment when, for all practical purposes, he had ceased to have anything to do with the management of the estate. For Rachel had left him the estate. Not that he ran it any better than the business which she had persuaded him, only just in time, to abandon. But the absence of profit did not matter, the loss, when there actually was a loss, was inconsiderable. The estate, Rachel Quarles had hoped, would keep her husband healthily occupied. For that it was worth paying something. But the price that had to be paid in these post-War years of depression was very high; and as Sidney occupied himself less and less with the routine of management, the price rose alarmingly, while the object for which it was being paid – healthy occupation for Sidney – was not achieved. Occasionally, it is true, Sidney would get an idea into his head and suddenly plunge into an orgy of what he called 'estate improvements.' On one occasion after reading a book about American efficiency, he bought a large outfit of costly machinery, only to discover that the estate was not large enough to justify the expenditure; he could not give his machines enough to do. Later, he built a jam factory; it had never paid. Their lack of success made him rapidly lose interest in his 'improvements.' Hard work and constant attention might conceivably have made them profitable in time; meanwhile, however, owing to Sidney's neglect, the improvement had resulted in a dead loss. Decidedly, the price was too high, and it was being paid for nothing. Mrs Quarles decided that it was time to get the estate out of Sidney's hands. With her usual tact – for after more than thirty years of marriage she knew her husband only too well – she persuaded him that he would have more time for his great work if he left the tiresome business of estate management to others. She and the bailiff were good enough for that. There was no sense in wasting talents that might be better, more suitably employed, on such mechanical labour. Sidney was easily persuaded. The estate bored him; it had hurt his vanity by being so malevolently unsuccessful in spite of his improvements. At the same time, he realized that to give up all connexion with it would be an acknowledgement of failure and a tribute – yet another – to his wife's inherent superiority. He agreed to devote less time to the details of management, but promised, or threatened, in a god-like way, that he would continue to keep an eye on it, would supervise it distantly, but none the less effectively in the intervals of his literary labours. It was now that, to justify himself, to magnify his importance, he bought the calculating typewriter. It symbolized the enormous complexity of the literary work to which he was now mainly to devote himself; and it proved at the same time that he had not completely abandoned all interest in practical affairs. For the calculating machine was to deal not only with statistics (in what way Mr Quarles was wise enough never precisely to specify), but also with the accounts under which, it was implied, poor Rachel and the bailiff would infallibly succumb without his higher aid.

Sidney did not, of course, acknowledge his wife's superiority. But the obscure realization and resentment of it, the desire to prove that, in spite of everything, he was really just as good as she, or indeed much better, conditioned his whole life. It was this resentment, this desire to assert his domestic superiority that had made him cling so long to his unsuccessful political career. Left to himself, he would probably have abandoned political life at the first discovery of its difficulties and tediousness; his indolence was stronger than his ambition. But a reluctance to admit failure and the personal inferiority which failure would have implied, kept him (for ever desperately sanguine of his prospects) from resigning his parliamentary seat. With the exasperating spectacle of Rachel's quiet efficiency perpetually before his eyes, he could not admit himself defeated. What Rachel did, she did well; people loved and admired her. It was to rival and outdo her, in the eyes of the world and in his own, that he clung to politics, that he plunged into the erratic activities which had distinguished his parliamentary career. Disdaining to be the mere slave of his party and desirous of personal distinction, he had championed with enthusiasm, only to desert again with disgust, a succession of Causes. The abolition of capital punishment, anti-vivisection, prison reform, the amelioration of labour conditions in West Africa had called forth, each in its turn, his fieriest eloquence and a brief outburst of energy. He had visions of himself as a conquering reformer bringing victory by his mere presence to whatever cause he chose to take up. But the walls of Jericho never collapsed at the sound of his trumpet, and he was not the man to undertake laborious sieges. Hangings, operations on dogs and frogs, solitary convicts and maltreated Negroes – one after another, all lost their charm for him. And Rachel continued to be efficient, continued to be loved and admired.

Meanwhile, her direct encouragement had always supplemented that indirect stimulus to ambition which she had provided, all unintentionally, by the mere fact of being herself and Sidney's wife. At first she genuinely believed in him; she encouraged her hero. A few years sufficed to change faith in his ultimate success into a pious hope. When the hope was gone she encouraged him for diplomatic reasons – because failure in politics cost less than failure in the City. For Sidney's mismanagement of the business was threatening to be ruinous. She dared not tell him so, dared not advise him to sell out; to have done so would have been to provoke him to cling more tenaciously than ever to the business. By throwing doubts on his capacity she would only have spurred him on to new and more dangerous speculations. To hostile criticism Sidney reacted with a violent and obstinate contrariness. Made wise by experience Rachel Quarles averted the danger by redoubling her encouragement of his political ambitions. She magnified the importance of his parliamentary activities. What good, what noble work he was doing! And what a pity that the care of the business should take up so much of the time and energies that might be better employed! Sidney responded at once and with a secret and unrealized gratitude. The routine of business bored him; he was becoming alarmed by his speculative failures. He welcomed the excuse for divesting himself of his responsibilities, which Rachel had so diplomatically offered. He sold out before it was too late and reinvested the money in securities which might be trusted to look after themselves. His income was in this way reduced by about a third; but in any case it was now secure – that was what Rachel chiefly cared about. Sidney went about hinting at the great financial sacrifices he had made in order that he might devote all his time to the poor convicts. (Later it was the poor Negroes; but the sacrifices remained the same.)

When finally, tired of being a political nonentity and outraged by what he regarded as the injustice of his party chiefs, Sidney resigned his seat, Mrs Quarles made no objection. There was no business now for her husband to ruin, and the estate in those times of agricultural prosperity that immediately followed the Armistice was still profitable. Sidney explained that he was too good for practical politics; they degraded a man of worth, their dirt came off. He had decided (for his consciousness of Rachel's superiority would not let him rest) to devote himself to something more important than 'myah' politics, something worthier of his powers. To be the philosopher of politics was better than to be a politician. He actually finished and published a first instalment of his political philosophy. The prolonged effort of writing blunted his enthusiasm for philosophical authorship; the poor success of the book disgusted him completely. But Rachel was still efficient and beloved. In self-defence he announced his intention of producing the largest and most comprehensive work on democracy that had ever been written. Rachel might be very active on committees, do good works, be loved by the villagers, have friends and correspondents galore; but, after all, what was that compared with writing the largest book on democracy? The only trouble was that the book did not get written. When Rachel showed herself too efficient, when people liked her too much, Mr Quarles bought another card-index, or a new and more ingenious kind of loose-leaf notebook, or a fountain-pen with a particularly large ink capacity – a fountain-pen, he explained, that could write six thousand words without requiring to be refilled. The retort was perhaps inadequate. But it seemed to Sidney Quarles good enough.

Philip and Elinor spent a couple of days with Mrs Bidlake at Gattenden. Then it was the turn of Philip's parents. They arrived at Chamford to find that Mr Quarles had just bought a dictaphone. Sidney did not allow his son to remain for long in ignorance of his triumph. The dictaphone was his greatest achievement since the calculating typewriter.

'I've just made an acquisition,' he said in his rich voice, shooting the words up over Philip's head. 'Something that will interest you, as a writer.' He led the way to his study.

Philip followed him. He had expected to be overwhelmed with questions about the East and the tropics. Instead of which his father had only perfunctorily inquired if the voyage had been good, and had gone on, almost before Philip could answer, to speak about his own affairs. For the first moment Philip had been surprised and even a little nettled. But the moon, he reflected, seems larger than Sirius, because it is nearer. The voyage, *his* voyage, was to him a moon, to his father the smallest of little stars.

'Here,' said Mr Quarles, and raised the cover. The dictaphone was revealed. 'Wonderful invention!' He spoke with profound self-satisfaction. It was the sudden rising, in all its refulgence, of *his* moon. He explained the workings of the machine. Then, tilting up his face, 'It's so useful,' he said, 'when an idyah occurs to you. You put it into wahds at once. Talk to yourself; the machine remembahs. I have it brought up to my bedroom every night. Such valuable idyahs come to one when one's in bed, don't you find? Without a dictaphone they would get lost.'

'And what do you do when you've got to the end of one of these phonograph records?' Philip inquired.

'Send it to my secretarah to be typed.'

Philip raised his eyebrows. 'You've got a secretary now?'

Mr Quarles nodded importantly. 'Only a half-time one, so far,' he said, addressing the cornice of the opposite wall. 'You've no idyah what a lot I have to do. What with the book, and the estate, and letters, and accounts and … and … things,' he concluded rather lamely. He sighed, he shook the martyr's head. 'You're lucky, my dyah boy,' he went on. 'You have no distractions. You can give your whole time to writing. I wish I could give all mine. But I have the estate and all the rest. Trivial – but the business must be done.' He sighed again. 'I envy you your freedom.'

Philip laughed. 'I almost envy myself sometimes. But the dictaphone will be a great help.'

'Oh, it will,' said Mr Quarles. 'Undoubtedlah.'

'How's the book going?'

'Slowly,' his father replied, 'but surely. I think I have most of my materials now.'

'Well, that's something.'

'You novelists,' said Mr Quarles patronizingly, 'you're fortunate. You can just sit down and write. No preliminarah labour necessarah. Nothing like this.' He pointed to the filing cabinets and the card-index boxes. They were the proofs of his superiority, as well as of the enormous difficulties against which he had to struggle. Philip's books might be successful. But after all, what was a novel? An hour's entertainment, that was all; to be picked up and thrown aside again, carelessly. Whereas the largest book on democracy … And anyone could write a novel. It was just a question of living and then proceeding to record the fact. To compose the largest book on democracy one had to take notes, collect materials from innumerable sources, buy filing cabinets and typewriters, portable, polyglottic, calculating; one needed a card-index and loose-leaf notebooks and a fountain-pen that could write six thousand words without having to be refilled; one required a dictaphone and a half-time secretary who would shortly have to become a whole-time one. 'Nothing like this,' he insisted.

'Oh, no,' said Philip, who had been wandering round the room examining the literary apparatus. 'Nothing like this.' He picked up some newspaper clippings that were lying under a paper weight on the lid of the unopened Corona. 'Puzzles?' he asked, holding up the irregularly chequered diagrams. 'I didn't know you'd become a crossword fiend.'

Mr Quarles took the clippings from his son and put them away in a drawer. He was annoyed that Philip should have seen them. The crosswords spoiled the effect of the dictaphone. 'Childish things,' he said with a little laugh. 'But they're a distraction when the mind is tired. I like to amuse myself with them occasionalah.' In reality Mr Quarles spent almost the whole of his mornings on crosswords. They exactly suited his type of intelligence. He was one of the most expert puzzle-solvers of his epoch.

In the drawing-room, meanwhile, Mrs Quarles was talking with her daughter-in-law. She was a small and active woman, grey-haired but preserving unblurred and hardly distorted the pure outlines of regular and well-moulded features. The expression of the face was at once vivacious and sensitive. It was a delicate energy, a strong but quiveringly responsive life, that shone in incessant variations of brilliance and shade of colour from her expressive grey-blue eyes. Her lips responded hardly less closely and constantly to her thoughts and feelings than did her eyes, and were grave or firm, smiled or were melancholy through an almost infinitesimally chromatic scale of emotional expression.

'And little Phil?' she said, inquiring after her grandchild.

'Radiant.'

'Darling little man!' The warmth of Mrs Quarles's affection enriched her voice and was visible as a light in her eyes. 'You must have felt miserable, leaving him for such a long time.'

Elinor gave an almost imperceptible shrug of the shoulders. 'Well, I knew that Miss Fulkes and mother between them would look after him much better than I could do.' She laughed and shook her head. 'I don't believe nature ever meant me to have children. Either I'm impatient with them, or else I spoil them. Little Phil's a pet, of course; but I know that a family would have driven me crazy.'

Mrs Quarles's expression changed. 'But wasn't it wonderful to see him again after all those months?' The tone of the question was almost anxious. She hoped that Elinor would answer it with the enthusiastic affirmative which would have been natural in the circumstances to herself. But at the same time she was haunted by a fear lest the strange girl might answer (with the frankness which was so admirable a quality in her, but which was also so disquieting, in its revelation of unfamiliar and to Rachel incomprehensible states of soul) that she hadn't been in the least pleased to see her child again. Elinor's first words came to her as a relief.

'Yes, it was wonderful,' she said, but robbed the phrase of its full effect by adding, 'I didn't imagine I *could* be so glad to see him again. But it was really a wild excitement.'

There was a silence. 'A queer girl,' Mrs Quarles was thinking; and her face reflected something of that bewilderment which she always felt in Elinor's presence. She did her best to love her daughter-in-law; and up to a point she succeeded. Elinor had many excellent qualities. But something seemed to be lacking in her, something without which no human being could be entirely sympathetic to Rachel Quarles. It was as though she had been born without certain natural instincts. Not to have expected to feel happy when she saw her baby again – that was strange enough. But what Rachel found almost stranger was Elinor's calm and casual admission of the fact. She herself would have blushed to make such an admission, even if it had been the truth. It would have seemed to her something shameful – a kind of blasphemy, a denial of what was holy. To Rachel the reverence for holy things came naturally. It was Elinor's lack of this reverence, her inability even to realize that holy things *were* holy, which made it impossible for Mrs Quarles to love her daughter-in-law as much as she would have liked.

On her side Elinor admired, respected, and genuinely liked her husband's mother. For her, the chronic difficulty was to establish effectual contact with a person whose ruling ideas and motives seemed to her so oddly incomprehensible and even so absurd. Mrs Quarles was unobtrusively but ardently religious and lived to the best of her ability in accordance with her beliefs. Elinor admired, but felt that it was all rather absurd and superfluous. Her education had been orthodox. But she never remembered a time, even in her child-hood, when she seriously believed what people told her about the other world and its inhabitants. The other world bored her; she was interested only in this. Confirmation had evoked in her no more en-thusiasm than a visit to the theatre, indeed considerably less. Her adolescence had passed without the trace of a religious crisis.

'It all seems to me just nonsense,' she would say when the matter was discussed in her presence. And there was no affectation in her words, they were not uttered provocatively. She simply stated a fact of her personal history. Religion and, along with religion, all trans-cendental morality, all metaphysical speculation seemed to her non-sensical in precisely the same way as the smell of Gorgonzola seemed to her disgusting. There was no getting behind the immediate experi-ence. Often, on occasions like this, she wished there were. She would have liked to cross the abyss which separated her from Mrs Quarles. As it was, she felt a certain uneasiness when she was with her mother-in-law; she hesitated in her presence to express her feelings or to say what she thought. For she had found, only too often, that the frank utterance of what seemed to her perfectly natural sentiments and reasonable opinions, was apt to distress her mother-in-law, to strike her as strange and shocking. It had happened again now, as she could see from the expression which showed itself for an instant on Mrs Quarles's mobile and sensitive face. What had it been this time? Conscious of no offence, Elinor could only wonder. In future, she decided, she would volunteer nothing of her own; she would just agree with what was said.

As it happened, however, the next topic of conversation to be broached was one in which Elinor was too deeply interested to be able to keep her new-made resolution. Moreover it was one on which, as she knew by experience, she could speak freely without risk of unintentional offence. For where Philip was concerned, Elinor's feelings and opinions seemed to Mrs Quarles entirely appropriate.

'And big Philip?' she now asked.

'You see how well he looks,' Elinor answered for his health, though she knew that the question had not concerned his bodily well-being. It was with a certain dread that she looked forward to the conversation that impended. At the same time, however, she was glad to have an opportunity of discussing that which so constantly and distressingly occupied her thoughts.

'Yes, yes, I can see that,' said Mrs Quarles. 'But what I really meant was: how is he in himself? How is he with you?'

There was a silence. Elinor frowned slightly and looked at the floor. 'Remote,' she said at last.

Mrs Quarles sighed. 'He was always that,' she said. 'Always remote.'

He too, it seemed to her, was lacking in something – in the desire and the capacity to give himself, to go out and meet his fellows, even those who loved him, even those he loved. Geoffrey had been so different. At the memory of her dead son Mrs Quarles felt her whole being invaded by a poignant sadness. If anyone had suggested that she had loved him more than she loved Philip, she would have protested. Her own feelings, she felt sure, had been initially the same. But Geoffrey had permitted himself to be loved more fully, more intimately than his brother. If only Philip had allowed her to love him more! But there had always been barriers between them, barriers of his erecting. Geoffrey had come out to meet her, had given that he might receive. But Philip had always been reluctant and parsimonious. He had always shut doors when she approached, always locked up his mind lest she should catch a glimpse of his secrets. She had never known what he really felt and thought. 'Even as a little boy,' she said aloud.

'And now he has his work,' said Elinor after a pause. 'Which makes it worse. It's like a castle on the top of a mountain, his work. He shuts himself up in it and he's impregnable.'

Mrs Quarles smiled sadly. 'Impregnable.' It was the right word. Even as a little boy he had been impregnable. 'Perhaps in the end he'll surrender of his own accord.'

'To me?' said Elinor. 'Or to someone else? It wouldn't be much satisfaction if it was to somebody else, would it? Though when I'm feeling unselfish,' she added, 'I wish he'd surrender to anyone – *anyone*, for his own good.'

Elinor's words set Mrs Quarles thinking of her husband – not resentfully, though he had done wrong, though he had hurt her, but pityingly, rather, and solicitously. For she could never feel that it was entirely his fault. It was his misfortune.

Elinor sighed. 'I can't really expect to receive his surrender,' she said. 'When one has become a habit, one can't very well suddenly turn into an overwhelming revelation.'

Mrs Quarles shook her head. In recent years Sidney's overwhelming revelations had come from such unexpectedly humble sources.

The little kitchen-maid, the gamekeeper's daughter. How could he, she wondered for the thousandth time, how *could* he? It was incomprehensible.

'If at least,' she said almost in a whisper, 'you had God as a companion.' God had always been her comfort, God and the doing of God's will. She could never understand how people could get through life without Him. 'If only you could find God.'

Elinor's smile was sarcastic. Remarks of this sort annoyed her by being so ridiculously beside the point. 'It might be simpler,' she began, but checked herself after the first words. She had meant to say that it might be simpler perhaps to find a man. But she remembered her resolution and was silent.

'What were you saying?'

Elinor shook her head. 'Nothing.'

*

Fortunately for Mr Quarles the British Museum had no Essex branch. It was only in London that he could make researches and collect the documents necessary for his book. The house in Portman Square was let (Mr Quarles blamed the income tax, but his own speculations in sugar were mainly responsible); and it was in a modest little flat in Bloomsbury ('convenientlah nyah the Museum') that he now camped whenever the claims of scholarship brought him to town.

During the last few weeks the claims had been more than usually peremptory. His visits to London had been frequent and prolonged. After the second of these visits Mrs Quarles had wondered, sadly, whether Sidney had found another woman. And when, on his return from a third journey and, a few days later, on the eve of a fourth, he began to groan ostentatiously over the vast complexity of the history of democracy among the Ancient Indians, Rachel felt convinced that the woman had been found. She knew Sidney well enough to be certain that, if he had really been reading about the Ancient Indians, he would never have troubled to talk about them over the dinner-table – not at such length, in any case, nor so insistently. Sidney talked for the same reason as the hunted sepia squirts ink, to conceal his movements. Behind the ink-cloud of the Ancient Indians he hoped to go jaunting up to town unobserved. Poor Sidney! He thought himself so Machiavellian. But his ink was transparent, his cunning like a child's.

'Couldn't you get the books sent down from the London Library?' Mrs Quarles rather pointedly asked.

Sidney shook his head. 'They're the sort of books,' he said importantly, 'that are only in the Museum.'

Rachel sighed and could only hope that the woman could be trusted to look after herself well enough to keep out of serious trouble and not so well as to want to make mischief.

'I think I shall run up to town with you to-morrow,' he announced on the morning before Philip and Elinor took their leave.

'Again?' asked Mrs Quarles.

'There's a point about those wretched Indians,' he explained, 'that I ryahly must clyahr up. I think I may find it in Pramathanatha Banerjea's book ... Or it may be dealt with by Radakhumud Mookerji.' He rolled out the names impressively, professionally. 'It's about local government in Maurya times. So democratic, you know, in spite of the central despotism. For example ...'

Through the ink-cloud Mrs Quarles caught glimpses of a female figure.

Breakfast over, Sidney retired to his study and addressed himself to the morning's crossword. A kind of onion, six letters. Anticipations of the morrow distracted him; he could not fix his attention. Her breasts, he was thinking, her smooth white back ... What about 'chive'? No good; only five letters. Walking over to the book-shelf he took out his Bible; its thin pages rustled under his fingers. 'Thy navel is like a round goblet that wanteth not liquor, thy belly is like an heap of wheat set about with lilies. Thy two breasts are like young roes that are twins.' Solomon spoke for him, with what rich thunders! 'The joints of thy thighs are like jewels, the work of the hands of a cunning workman.' He read the words out loud. Gladys had a perfect figure. 'Like a round goblet that wanteth not liquor.' These orientals knew what passion was. Miscalling libidinousness 'passion', Mr Quarles regarded himself as a very passionate man. 'Thy belly is like an heap of wheat.' Passion is respectable, is actually respected by the law in some countries. For the poets it is even sacred. He agreed with the poets. But 'like young roes' was an odd, inadequate simile. Gladys was plump without being fat, firmly resilient. Roes, on the contrary ... As a man of great passions, Sidney could regard himself as positively a noble and heroic figure. 'A garden enclosed is my sister, my spouse; a spring shut up, a fountain sealed. The plants are an orchard of pomegranates, with pleasant fruits; camphire with spikenard; spikenard and saffron, calamus and cinnamon, with all trees of frankincense; myrrh ...' But, of course, the word was 'garlic'! Six letters. A kind of onion. 'Myrrh and aloes, with all the chief spices.'

Their train next morning was nearly twenty minutes late. 'Scandalous,' Mr Quarles kept repeating, as he looked at his watch, 'disgraceful.'

'You're in a great hurry to be at your Indians,' said Philip, smiling from his corner.

His father frowned and talked about something else. At Liverpool Street they parted, Sidney in one taxi, Philip and Elinor in a second. Sidney reached his flat only just in time. He was still engaged in washing the grime of the journey from his large, flesh-padded hands, when the bell rang. He made haste to rinse and dry himself, then, adjusting his face, he stepped into the hall and opened. It was Gladys. He received her with a kind of condescending regality, his chin tilted, his chest thrown back, his waistcoat projecting, but smiling down at her (Gladys called herself 'petite') and graciously twinkling through half-shut eyelids. It was an impudent, vulgar, snubby little face that smiled back at him. But it was not her face that had brought Mr Quarles to London, it was not the individual Gladys Helmsley; it was the merely generic aspect of the woman, her 'figah,' as Sidney would have euphemistically put it.

'You're very punctual, my dyah,' he said, holding out his hand.

Gladys was rather taken aback by the coolness of his greeting. After what had happened last time, she had expected something tenderer.

'Am I!' she said, for lack of anything better to say; and since human beings have only a limited number of noises and grimaces with which to express the multiplicity of their emotions, she laughed as though she had been amused by something, when in fact she was only surprised and disquieted. It was on the tip of her tongue to ask him, provocative-petulantly, why he didn't kiss her, whether he was tired of her – *already*. But she decided to wait.

'Almost too punctual,' Sidney went on. 'My train was scandalouslah late. Scandalouslah!' He radiated indignation.

'Fancy!' said Gladys. The refinement that hung around her speech, like a too genteel disguise, dropped away from time to time, leaving individual words and phrases nakedly cockney.

'Ryahly disgraceful!' said Sidney. 'Trains have no business to be

268

late. I shall write to the Traffic Superintendent at Liverpool Street. I'm not sure,' he added, still more importantly, 'that I shan't write to *The Times* as well.'

Gladys was impressed. Mr Quarles had intended that she should be. Apart from all merely sensual satisfactions, the greatest charm of his sexual holidays resided in the fact that they were shared with impressible companions. Sidney liked them, not only young, but of a lower class, and poor. To feel himself unequivocally superior and genuinely admired was for Sidney a luxury almost as great as an embracement. His escapades were holidays not only from chastity, but also from that sense of inferiority which, at home, in parliament, at the office, had always inveterately haunted him. In relation to young women of the lower classes he was a great man, as well as a 'passionate' one.

Gladys, on her side, was impressed by his thunderings. But she was also amused. Impressed, because she belonged to the world of poor and patient wage-slaves, who accept the unpleasantnesses of social life as so many natural phenomena, uncontrollable by human agency and recalcitrant to human desires. But Sidney was one of the Olympian rich; the rich refuse to accept unpleasantness; they write letters to *The Times* about it, they pull wires, use influence, lodge formal complaints with an always friendly and obsequious police. To Gladys it was wonderful – wonderful, but also very funny. There was such a lot of loud haw-haw and lahdy-da about the whole performance. It was so like the parody of itself on the music-hall stage. She admired, she realized very accurately the economic and social causes of Sidney's behaviour (it was that realization which had made her so promptly his mistress). But she also laughed. She lacked reverence.

Mr Quarles opened the sitting-room door to let her pass.

'Ta,' said Gladys and walked in.

He followed. On the nape of her neck, her dark cropped hair ended in a little triangle that pointed downwards along the spine. She was wearing a thin green dress. Through the fine stuff he could see, just below her shoulders, the line where the underclothes gave place to bare skin. A belt of black shiny leather was fastened in a slant very low on her hips. At every stride it rose and fell on her left hip with a rhythmical regularity. Her stockings were the colour of sunburnt flesh. Brought up in an epoch when ladies apparently rolled along on wheels, Mr Quarles was peculiarly susceptible to calves, found

269

modern fashions a treat and could never quite get over the belief that the young women who adopted them had deliberately made themselves indecent for his benefit and because they wanted him to become their lover. His eyes followed the curves of the lustrous sunburn. But what fascinated him most to-day was the black leather belt flicking up and down over the left haunch, with the regularity of a piece of machinery, every time she moved her leg. In that rise and fall the whole unindividualized species, the entire sex semaphored their appeal.

Gladys halted and turned towards him with a smile, expectantly coquettish. But Mr Quarles made no responding gesture.

'I've got the Corona hyah,' he said. 'Perhaps we had better begin at once.'

For the second time Gladys was surprised, thought of making a comment, and again said nothing, but sat down in silence before the typewriter.

Mr Quarles put on his tortoiseshell-rimmed pince-nez and opened his despatch case. He had found a mistress, but he did not see why that should entail the loss of a typist, for whose services, after all, he paid.

'Perhaps,' he said, looking up at her over the top of his pince-nez, 'we'd better begin with those letters to the Traffic Superintendent and *The Times*.' Gladys adjusted the paper, typed the date. Mr Quarles cleared his throat and dictated. There were some good phrases, he flattered himself, in the letters. 'Inexcusable slackness entailing the waste of time otherwise valuable than that of drowsy railway bureaucrats' – that, for example, was excellent. And so (for the benefit of *The Times*) was 'the pampered social parasites of a protected industry.'

'That'll teach the dogs,' he said with satisfaction, as he read the letters through. 'That'll make them squirm.' He looked to Gladys for applause, and was not entirely satisfied with the smile on that impertinent face. 'Pity old Lord Hagworm's not alive,' he added, calling up strong allies. 'I'd have written to him. He was a director of the company.' But the last of the Hagworms had died in 1912. And Gladys continued to be more amused than admiring.

Mr Quarles dictated a dozen more letters, the answers to a correspondence which he had allowed to accumulate for several days before coming to London, so that the total might seem more important and also that he might get his full money's worth out of Gladys's secretaryship.

'Thank goodness,' he said, when the last of the letters was answered. 'You've no idyah,' he went on (and the great thinker had come to reinforce the landed gentleman), 'you've no idyah how exasperating these trivial little things can be, when you've got something more syahrious and important to think about.'

'I suppose they must be,' said Gladys, thinking how funny he was.

'Take down,' commanded Mr Quarles, to whom a *pensée* had suddenly occurred. He leaned back in his chair and, closing his eyes, pursued the elusive phrase.

Gladys waited, her fingers poised above the keyboard. She looked at the watch on her wrist. Ten past twelve. It would be lunch-time soon. A new watch – that would be the first thing she'd make him give her. The one she had was such a cheap, nasty-looking watch; and it kept such bad time.

'Note for the volume of Reflections,' said Mr Quarles, without opening his eyes. The keys briefly rattled. 'The ivory pinnacles of thought' – he repeated the words inwardly. They made a satisfying reverberation along the corridors of his mind. The phrase was caught. He sat up briskly and opened his eyes – to become aware that the lisle-thread top of one of Gladys's sunburnt stockings was visible, from where he was sitting, to a considerable distance above the knee.

'All my life,' he dictated, his eyes fixed on the lisle thread, 'I have suffered from the irrelevant – no, say "importunate" – interruptions of the wahld's trivialitah, full stop. Some thinkers comma I know comma are able to ignore these interruptions comma to give them a fleeting but sufficient attention and return with a serene mind to higher things full stop.'

There was silence. Above the lisle thread, Mr Quarles was thinking, was the skin – soft, curving tightly over the firm curved flesh. To caress and, caressing, to feel the finger-tips silkily caressed; to squeeze a handful of elastic flesh. Even to bite. Like a round goblet, like a heap of wheat.

Suddenly conscious of the direction of his glances, Gladys pulled down her skirt.

'Where was I?' asked Mr Quarles.

'Higher things with a serene mind,' Gladys answered, reading from the page in front of her.

'H'm.' He rubbed his nose. 'For me comma alas comma this serenitah has always been impossible semi-colon; my nahvous sensibilitah is too great full stop. Dragged down from the ivorah pinnacles of thought' (he rolled out the phrase with relish) 'into the common dust comma, I am exasperated comma, I lose my peace of mind and am unable to climb again into my tower.'

He rose and began to walk restlessly about the room.

'That's always been my trouble,' he said. 'Too much sensibilitah. A syahrious thinker ought to have no temperament, no nerves. He has no business to be passionate.'

The skin, he was thinking, the firm elastic flesh. He halted behind her chair. The little triangle of cropped hair pointed down along her spine. He put his hands on her shoulders and bent over her.

Gladys looked up, smiling impertinently, with triumph. 'Well?' she asked.

Mr Quarles bent lower and kissed her neck. She giggled.

'How you tickle!'

His hands explored her, sliding along her arms, pressing her body – the body of the species, of the entire sex. The individual Gladys continued to giggle.

'Naughty!' she said, and made a pretence of pushing his hands away. 'Naughty!'

Chapter Twenty-one

'A MONTH ago,' said Elinor, as their taxi drove out of Liverpool Street Station, 'we were in Udaipur.'

'It certainly seems improbable,' said Philip, agreeing with the implications of her remark.

'These ten months of travel have been like an hour in a cinema. There's the Bank. I begin to doubt whether I've ever been away.' She sighed. 'It's rather a dreadful feeling.'

'Is it?' said Philip. 'I suppose I'm used to it. I never do feel that anything has really happened before this morning.' He craned his neck out of the window. 'Why people should bother about the Taj Maha when there's St Paul's to look at, I can't imagine. What a marvel!'

'That wonderful black and white of the stone.'

'As though it were an engraving. Doubly a work of art. Not merely architecture, but an etching of architecture.' He leaned back. 'I often doubt whether I ever had a childhood,' he went on, returning to the previous conversation.

'That's because you never think of it. Lots of my childhood is more real to me than Ludgate Hill here. But then I constantly think of it.'

'That's true,' said Philip. 'I don't often try to remember. Hardly ever, in fact. I always seem to have too much to do and think about.'

'You have no natural piety,' said Elinor. 'I wish you had.'

They drove along the Strand. The two little churches protested against Australia House, in vain. In the courtyard of King's College a group of young men and women sat in the sun waiting for the Professor of Pastoral Theology. At the pit door of the Gaiety there was already a queue; the placards advertised the four hundredth performance of 'The Girl from Biarritz.' Next door to the Savoy, Philip noticed, you could still buy a pair of boots for twelve-and-six. In Trafalgar Square the fountains were playing, Sir Edwin Landseer's lions mildly glared, the lover of Lady Hamilton stood perched among the clouds, like St Simeon the Stylite. And behind the grim colonnade of the National Gallery Uccello's horsemen timelessly fought and Rubens raped his Sabines, Venus looked into her mirror and in the midst of Piero's choiring angels Jesus was born into a magically lovely world.

The cab turned down Whitehall.

'I like to think of all the bureaucrats.'

'I don't,' said Elinor.

'Scribbling away,' he went on, 'scribbling from morning till night in order that we may live in freedom and comfort. Scribble, scribble – the result is the British Empire. What a comfort,' he added, 'to live in a world where one can delegate everything tiresome, from governing to making sausages, to somebody else.'

At the Gate of the Horse Guards the mounted sentries looked as though they were stuffed. Near the Cenotaph a middle-aged lady was standing with raised eyes, murmuring a prayer over the Kodak with which she proposed to take a snapshot of the souls of the nine hundred thousand dead. A Sikh with a black beard and a pale mauve turban emerged from Grindley's as they passed. The time, according to Big Ben, was twenty-seven minutes past eleven. In the library of the House of Lords was there a dozing marquess? A charabanc disgorged Americans at the door of Westminster Abbey. Looking back through the little porthole in the hood they were able to see that the hospital was still urgently in need of funds.

John Bidlake's house was in Grosvenor Road, overlooking the river.

'Pimlico,' said Philip meditatively, as they approached the house. He laughed. 'Do you remember that absurd song your father used always to quote?'

' "To Pimlico Then let us go," ' Elinor chanted.

' "One verse omitted here." You mustn't forget that.' They both laughed, remembering John Bidlake's comments.

' "One verse omitted here." It's omitted in all the anthologies. I've never been able to discover what happened when they'd got to Pimlico. It's kept me wondering for years, feverishly. Nothing like Bowdlerism for heating the imagination.'

'Pimlico,' Philip repeated. Old Bidlake, he was thinking, had made of Pimlico a sort of Rabelaisian Olympus. He liked the phrase. But 'Gargantuan' would be better for public use than 'Rabelaisian.' For those who had never read him, Rabelais connoted nothing but smut. Gargantuan Olympus, then. They had at least heard rumours that Gargantua was large.

But the John Bidlake they found sitting by the stove in his studio was not at all Olympian, seemed less instead of more than life size. He suffered himself to be kissed by his daughter, limply shook hands with Philip.

'Good to see you again,' he said. But there was no resonance in his voice; the undertone of jovial thunders and jovial laughters was absent. He spoke without gusto. His eyes were without lustre, and bloodshot. He looked thin and grey.

'How are you, father?' Elinor was surprised and distressed. She had never seen her father like this before.

'Not well,' he answered, shaking his head, 'not well. Something wrong with my insides.' The old lion suddenly and recognizably roared. 'Making us go through life with a barrow-full of tripes! I've always resented God's practical jokes.' The roar became plaintive. 'I don't know what's happening to mine now. Something very unpleasant.' It degenerated almost into a whine. 'I feel wretched.' Lengthily, the old man described his symptoms.

'Have you seen a doctor?' Elinor asked, when he had finished.

He shook his head. 'Don't believe in them. They never do one any good.' The truth was that he had a superstitious terror of doctors. Birds of evil omen – he hated to see them in the house.

'But you really ought.' She tried to persuade him.

'All right,' he said at last consented grumblingly. 'Let the quacks come.' But secretly he was rather relieved. He had been wanting to see the doctor for some time now; but his superstition had been stronger hitherto than his desire. The ill-omened medicine man was now to come, but not on his invitation; on Elinor's. The responsibility was not his; not on him, therefore, would fall the bad luck. Old Bidlake's private religion was obscurely complicated.

They began to talk of other things. Now that he knew he could consult a doctor in safety, John Bidlake felt better and more cheerful.

'I'm worried about him,' said Elinor, as they drove away.

Philip nodded. 'Being seventy-three's no joke. He's begun to look his age.'

What a head! he was thinking. He wished he could paint. Literature couldn't render it. One could describe it, of course, down to the last wrinkle. But where would one be then? Nowhere. Descriptions are slow. A face is instantaneously perceived. A word, a single phrase – that was what one needed. 'The glory that was Greece, grown old.' That, for example, would give you something of the man. Only of course it wouldn't do. Quotations have something facetiously pedantic about them. 'A statue in parchment' would be better. 'The parchment statue of what had once been Achilles was sitting, crumpled, near the stove.' That was getting nearer the mark. No long-winded description. But for anyone who had ever seen a cast of the Disco-bolos, handled a vellum-bound book, heard of Achilles, John Bidlake was in that sentence visible. And for those who had never seen a Greek statue or read about Achilles in a book with a crinkly sheep-skin cover? Well, presumably they could go to the devil.

'All the same,' he thought, 'it's too literary. Too much culture.'

Elinor broke the silence. 'I wonder how I shall find Everard, now that he's become such a great man.' With her mind's eye she saw the keen face, the huge but agile body. Swiftness and violence. And he was in love with her. Did she like the man? Or did she detest him?

'I wonder if he's started pinching people's ears, like Napoleon?' Philip laughed. 'Anyhow, it's only a matter of time.'

'All the same,' said Elinor, 'I like him.' Philip's mockery had answered her question for her.

'So do I. But mayn't I laugh at what I like?'

'You certainly laugh at me. Is that because you like me?'

He took her hand and kissed it. 'I adore you, and I never laugh at you. I take you perfectly seriously.'

Elinor looked at him, unsmiling. 'You make me desperate some-times. What would you do, if I went off with another man? Would you care two pins?'

'I should be perfectly wretched.'

Would you?' She looked at him. Philip was smiling; he was a thousand miles away. 'I've a good mind to make the experiment,' she added, frowning. 'But *would* you be wretched? I'd like to be certain before I began.'

'And who'd be your fellow experimenter?'

'Ah, that's the trouble. Most other men are so impossible.'

'What a compliment!'

'But you're impossible too, Phil. The most impossible of them all, really. And the worst of it is I love you, in spite of it. And you know it. Yes, and exploit it too.' The cab drew up at the kerb. She reached for her umbrella. 'But you be careful,' she went on, as she rose to her feet. 'I'm not indefinitely exploitable. I won't go on giving something for nothing for ever. One of these days I shall start looking for some-body else.' She stepped out on to the pavement.

'Why not try Everard,' he chaffed, looking out at her through the window of the cab.

'Perhaps I shall,' she answered. 'I know Everard would ask nothing better.'

Philip laughed and blew her a kiss. 'Tell the man to drive to the Club,' he said.

Everard kept her waiting nearly ten minutes. When she had finished re-powdering her face, Elinor wandered inquisitively about the room. The flowers were abominably arranged. And that cabinet full of old swords and daggers and inlaid pistols was hideous, like a thing in a museum; a monstrosity, but at the same time rather touchingly absurd. Everard had such a schoolboyish ambition to ride about on a horse and chop people's heads off; the cabinet gave him away. So did that glass-topped table with the trayful of coins and medals under the crystal lid. How proudly he had shown her his treasures! There was the Macedonian tetradrachm, with the head of Alexander the Great in the guise of Hercules; the sestertius of 44 B.C. with the formidable profile of Caesar, and next to it Edward III.'s rose noble stamped with the ship that symbolized the beginning of England's power at sea. And there, on Pisanello's medal, was Sigismondo Malatesta, most beautiful of ruffians; and there was Queen Elizabeth in her ruff and Napoleon with laurels in his hair, and the Duke of Wellington. She smiled at them affectionately; they were old friends. The satisfactory thing about Everard, she reflected, was that you always knew where you were with him. He was always so definitely himself; he lived up to character. She opened the piano and played a couple of chords; out of tune, as usual. On the little table near the fireplace was a volume of Everard's latest Speeches and Addresses. She picked it up, she turned over the pages. 'The policy of the British Freemen,' she read, 'may be summarized as Socialism without Political Democracy, combined with Nationalism without insularity.' That sounded excellent. But if he had written 'political democracy without socialism combined with insularity without nationalism' she would probably have admired just as sincerely. These abstractions! she shook her head and sighed. 'I must be a fool,' she thought. But really they meant nothing to her. They were quite empty. Words, nothing more. She turned a page. 'The party system works well enough in cases where the parties are merely two groups of rival oligarchs, belonging to the same class and having fundamentally the same interests and ideals, competing with one another for power. But when parties become identified with classes and develop strict party principles, the system becomes an insanity. Because I sit on one side of the house and you sit on the other, I am compelled to believe in individualism to the exclusion of all state interference, you are compelled to believe in state interference to the exclusion of all individualism; I am compelled to believe in nationalism, even in economic nationalism (which is an imbecility), and you are compelled to believe in internationalism, even political internationalism, (which is no less of an imbecility); I am compelled to believe in the dictatorship of the rich (to the exclusion of the intelligent), you are compelled to believe in the dictatorship of the poor (also to the exclusion of the intelligent). All this for the simple and politically irrelevant reason that I am on the Right and you are on the Left. In our parliaments the claims of topography are stronger than those of sense. Such are the blessings of the modern party system. It is the aim of the British Freemen to abolish that system, along with the corrupt and inefficient parliamentarism which is its corollary.' That sounded all right, she thought; but she wondered, nevertheless, why people should bother about this sort of thing. Instead of just living. But apparently, if one were a man, one found just living dull. She re-opened the book in the middle. 'Every English liberty has been paid for by a new slavery. The destruction of feudalism strengthened the Crown. At the Reformation, we disposed of Papal infallibility, but we saddled ourselves with the divine right of kings. Cromwell smashed the divine right of kings, but imposed the tyranny of the landowners and the middle classes. The tyranny of the landowners and the middle classes is rapidly being destroyed, in order that we may have the dictatorship of the proletariat. A new infallibility, not of the Pope, but of the majority, has been propounded – an infallibility which we are compelled by law to believe in. The British Freemen are pledged to a new reformation and a new political revolution. We shall dispose of the dictatorship of the proletariat as our fathers disposed of the divine right of kings. We shall deny majority infallibility as they denied papal infallibility. The British Freemen stand for ...' Elinor had some difficulty in turning the page. Stand for what? she wondered. For the dictatorship of Everard and the infallibility of Webley? She blew at the recalcitrant pages; they fluttered apart. ' ... for justice and liberty. Their policy is that the best men shall rule, whatever their origin. Careers, in a word, must be fully open to talents. That is justice. They demand that every problem shall be dealt with on its own merits, intelligently, without reference to traditional party prejudices or the worthless opinion of stupid majorities. That is liberty. Those who imagine that liberty is synonymous with universal suffrage ...' A door banged;

a loud voice resounded in the hall. There was a rush of feet on the stairs; the house shook. The door of the drawing-room burst open, as though a bomb had exploded on the outside. Everard Webley came in on a burst of loud apology and welcome.

'How can I excuse myself?' he cried, as he took her hands. 'But if you knew what a whirl I live in! How marvellous it is to see you again! Not changed at all. As lovely as ever.' He looked intently into her face. The same serene pale eyes, the same full and melancholy lips. 'And looking so wonderfully well!'

She smiled back at him. His eyes were a very dark brown; from a little distance they seemed all pupil. Fine eyes, but rather disquieting, she found, in their intent, bright, watchful fixity. She looked into them a moment, then turned away. 'You too,' she said. 'Just the same. But then I don't know why we should be different.' She glanced back into his face and found him still intently looking at her. 'Ten months and travelling in the tropics don't turn one into somebody else.'

Everard laughed. 'Thank heaven for that!' he said. 'Let's come down to lunch.'

'And Philip?' he asked, when the fish had been served. 'Is he also the same as ever?'

'A little more so, if possible.'

Everard nodded. 'A little more so. Quite. One would expect it. Seeing blackamoors walking about without trousers must have made him still more sceptical about the eternal verities than he was.'

Elinor smiled, but at the same time was a little offended by his mockery. 'And what's been the effect on you of seeing so many Englishmen walking about in pea-green uniforms?' she retorted.

Everard laughed. 'Strengthened my belief in the eternal verities, of course.'

'Of which you're one?'

He nodded. 'Of which, naturally, I'm one.' They looked at one another, smiling. It was Elinor again who first averted her eyes.

'Thanks for telling me.' She kept up the note of irony. 'I mightn't have guessed by myself.' There was a little silence.

'Don't imagine,' he said at last in a tone that was no more bantering, but serious, 'that you can make me lose my temper by telling me that I've got a swelled head.' He spoke softly; but you were conscious of huge reserves of power. 'Other people might succeed perhaps. But then one doesn't like to be bothered by the lower animals. One squashes them. But with fellow humans one discusses things rationally.'

'I'm most relieved to hear it,' laughed Elinor.

'You think I've got a swelled head,' he went on. 'And I suppose it's true in a way. But the trouble is, I know it's justified – experimentally. Modesty's harmful if it's false. Milton said that "nothing profits more than self-esteem grounded on just and right." I know that mine is grounded on just and right. I know, I'm absolutely convinced that I can do what I want to do. What's the good of denying the knowledge? I'm going to be master, I'm going to impose my will. I have the determination and the courage. Very soon I shall have the organized strength. And then I shall take control. I know it; why should I pretend that I don't?' He leaned back in his chair and there was a long silence.

'It's absurd,' Elinor was thinking, 'it's ridiculous to talk like that.' It was the protest of her critical intellect against her feelings. For her feelings had been strangely moved. His words, the tone of his voice – so soft, yet with such vibrating latencies of power and passion divinable beneath its softness – had carried her away. When he had said, 'I'm going to be master,' it was as though she had taken a gulp of mulled wine – such a warmth had suddenly tingled through her whole body. 'It's ridiculous,' she inwardly repeated, trying to avenge herself on him for his easy conquest, trying to punish the traitors within her own soul who had so easily surrendered. But what had been done could not wholly be undone. The words might be ridiculous; but the fact remained that, while he was uttering them, she had thrilled with sudden admiration, with excitement, with a strange desire to exult and laugh aloud.

The servant changed the plates. They talked of indifferent matters – of her travels, of doings in London while she had been away, of common friends. The coffee was brought, they lit their cigarettes; there was a silence. How would it be broken? Elinor wondered apprehensively. Or rather did not wonder; for she knew and it was this prophetic knowledge that made her apprehensive. Perhaps she could forestall him by breaking the silence herself. Perhaps, if she rattled on, she could keep the conversation insignificant till it was time for her to go. But there seemed suddenly to be nothing to say. She felt as though paralysed by the approach of the inevitable event. She could only sit and wait. And at last the inevitable duly happened.

'Do you remember,' he said slowly, without looking up, 'what I told you before you went away?'

'I thought we'd agreed not to talk about it again.'

He threw back his head with a little laugh. 'Well, you thought wrong.' He looked at her and saw in her eyes an expression of distress and anxiety, an appeal for mercy. But Everard was merciless. He planted his elbows on the table and leaned towards her. She dropped her eyes.

'You said I hadn't changed to look at,' he said in his soft voice with its latencies of violence. 'Well, my mind hasn't changed either. It's still the same, Elinor, still the same as it was when you went away. I love you just as much, Elinor. No, I love you more.' Her hand lay limp on the table in front of her. He stretched out one of his and took it. 'Elinor,' he whispered.

She shook her head, without looking at him.

Softly and passionately he talked on. 'You don't know what love can be,' he said. 'You don't know what I can give you. Love that's desperate and mad, like a forlorn hope. And at the same time tender, like a mother's love for a sick child. Love that's violent and gentle, violent like a crime and as gentle as sleep.'

'Words,' Elinor was thinking, 'absurd melodramatic words.' But they moved her, as his boasting had moved her. 'Please, Everard,' she said aloud, 'no more.' She didn't want to be moved. With an effort she held her glance steady while she looked into his face, into those bright and searching eyes. She essayed a laugh, she shook her head. 'Because it's impossible, and you know it.'

'All I know,' he said slowly, 'is that you're afraid. Afraid of coming to life. Because you've been half dead all these years. You haven't had a chance to come fully alive. And you know I can give it you. And you're afraid, you're afraid.'

'What nonsense!' she said. It was just ranting and melodrama.

'And perhaps you're right, in a way,' he went on. 'Being alive, really alive, isn't entirely a joke. It's dangerous. But by God,' he added, and the latent violence in his soft voice suddenly broke out into ringing actuality, 'it's exciting.'

'If you knew what a fright you gave me!' she said. 'Shouting like that!' But it was not only a fright she had had. Her nerves and her very flesh still crept and quivered with the obscure and violent exultations which his voice had evoked in her. 'It's ridiculous,' she assured herself. But it was as though she had heard the voice directly

281

with her body. The echoes of it seemed to vibrate at her very mid-riff. 'Ridiculous,' she repeated. And then what was this love he talked about so thrillingly? Just an occasional brief violence in the intervals of business. He despised women, resented them because they wasted a man's time and energy. She had often heard him say that he had no time for love-making. His advances were almost an insult – the propositions one makes to a woman of the streets.

'Do be reasonable, Everard,' she said.

Everard withdrew his hand from hers and, with a laugh, leaned back in his chair. 'Very well,' he answered. 'For to-day.'

'For every day.' She felt profoundly relieved. 'Besides,' she added, quoting a phrase of his, with a little ironical smile, 'you're not a member of the leisured class. You've got more important things to do than make love.'

Everard looked at her for a little in silence and his face was grave with a kind of lowering thoughtfulness. More important things to do? It was true, of course. He was angry with himself for wanting so much to have her. Angry with Elinor for keeping him unsatisfied. 'Shall we talk about Shakespeare?' he asked sarcastically. 'Or the musical glasses?'

*

The fare was three-and-six. Philip gave the driver two half-crowns and climbed the steps of the club's pillared portico pursued by the sound of thanks. He made a habit of overtipping. It was not out of ostentation or because he had asked, or meant to ask, special services. (Indeed, few men could have demanded less of their servants than did Philip, could have been more patient to put up with bad service, and more willing to excuse remissness.) His overtipping was the practical expression of a kind of remorseful and apologetic contempt. 'My poor devil!' the superfluous gratuity seemed to imply, 'I'm sorry to be your superior.' And perhaps also there was a shilling's worth of apology for his very considerateness as an employer. For if he was unexacting in his demands, that was due as much to a dread and dis-like of unnecessary human contacts as to consideration and kindness. From those who served him Philip demanded little, for the good reason that he wanted to have as little as possible to do with them. Their presence disturbed him. He did not like to have his privacy intruded upon by alien personalities. To be compelled to speak with them, to have to establish a direct contact – not of intelligences, but of wills, feelings, intuitions – with these intruders was always disagreeable to him. He avoided it as much as he could; and when contact was necessary, he did his best to dehumanize the relation. Philip's generosity was in part a compensation for his inhuman kindness towards its recipients. It was conscience money.

The doors stood open; he entered. The hall was vast, dim, pillared, and cool. Sir Francis Chantrey's allegorical marble group of Science and Virtue subduing the Passions writhed with classical decorum in a niche on the stairs. He hung up his hat and went to the smoking-room to look at the papers and await the arrival of his guests. Spandrell was the first to arrive.

'Tell me,' said Philip, as soon as the greetings were over and the vermouth ordered, 'tell me quickly, before he comes, what about my absurd young brother-in-law. What's happening with him and Lucy Tantamount?'

Spandrell shrugged his shoulders. 'What *does* usually happen on these occasions? And in any case, is this the place and time to go into details?' He indicated the other occupants of the smoking-room. A cabinet minister, two judges, and a bishop were within earshot.

Philip laughed. 'But I only wanted to know how serious the affair really was, how long it's likely to last ...'

'Very serious as far as Walter's concerned. As for duration – who knows? But Lucy's going abroad very soon.'

'Thank heaven for small mercies! Ah, here you are!' It was Walter. 'And there's Illidge.' He waved his hand. The newcomers refused an aperitive. 'Let's come and eat at once, then,' said Philip.

The dining-room at Philip's club was enormous. A double row of stucco Corinthian pillars supported a gilded ceiling. From the pale chocolate-brown walls, the portraits of distinguished members, now deceased, glared down. Curtains of claret-coloured velvet were looped up at either side of the six windows, a claret-coloured carpet muffled the floor and in their claret-coloured liveries the waiters darted about almost invisibly, like leaf-insects in a forest.

'I always like this room,' said Spandrell as they entered. 'It's like a scene for Belshazzar's feast.'

'But a very Anglican Belshazzar,' Walter qualified.

'Gosh!' exclaimed Illidge, who had been looking round. 'This is the sort of thing that really does make me feel pleb-ish.'

Philip laughed, rather uncomfortably. Changing the subject, he pointed out the protectively coloured waiters. They proved the

283

Darwinian hypothesis. 'Survival of the fittest,' he said as they sat down at their appointed table. 'The men in other colours must have been killed off by infuriated members.' One of the claret-coloured survivors brought the fish. They began to eat.

'It's curious,' said Illidge, pursuing the train of thought suggested by his first impressions of the room, 'it's really extraordinary that I should be here at all. Sitting with you, at any rate, as a guest. For there wouldn't have been anything so very surprising about my being here in one of these wine-coloured coats. That at least would have been in harmony with what the parsons would call "my station in life."' He uttered a brief resentful laugh. 'But to be sitting with you – that's really almost incredible. And it's all due to the fact that a Manchester shopkeeper had a son with tendencies to scrofula. If Reggie Wright had been normally healthy, I'd probably be cobbling shoes in Lancashire. But luckily Reggie had tubercle bacilli in his lymph-system. The doctors prescribed a country life. His father took a cottage in our village for his wife and child, and Reggie went to the village school. But his father was ambitious for Reggie. (What a disgusting little rat he was!)' Illidge remarked parenthetically. 'Wanted him to go to Manchester Grammar School, later on. With a scholarship. Paid our schoolmaster to give him special coaching. I was a bright boy; the master liked me. While he was coaching Reggie, he thought he might as well coach me. Gratis, what's more. Wouldn't let my mother pay a penny. Not that she could have done so very easily, poor woman. The time came, and it was I who got the scholarship. Reggie failed.' Illidge laughed. 'Miserable scrofulous little squit! But I'm eternally grateful to him and the busy bacilli in his glands. But for them I'd be carrying on my uncle's cobbling business in a Lancashire village. And that's the sort of thing one's life hinges on – some absolutely absurd, million-to-one chance. An irrelevance, and your life's altered.'

'Not an irrelevance,' objected Spandrell. 'Your scholarship wasn't irrelevant; it was very much to the point, it was in harmony with you. Otherwise you wouldn't have won it, you wouldn't be here. I doubt if anything is really irrelevant. Everything that happens is intrinsically like the man it happens to.'

'That's a bit oracular, isn't it?' Philip objected. 'Perceiving events, men distort them – put it like that – so that what happens seems to be like themselves.'

Spandrell shrugged his shoulders. 'There may be that sort of distortion. But I believe that events come ready-made to fit the people they happen to.'

'What rot!' said Illidge, disgustedly.

Philip dissented more politely. 'But many people can be influenced by the same event in entirely different and characteristic ways.'

'I know,' Spandrell answered. 'But in some indescribable way the event's modified, qualitatively modified, so as to suit the character of each person involved in it. It's a great mystery and a paradox.'

'Not to say an absurdity and impossible,' put in Illidge.

'Absurd, then, and impossible,' Spandrell agreed. 'But all the same, I believe that's how it happens. Why should things be logically explainable?'

'Yes, why indeed?' Walter echoed.

'Still,' said Philip, 'your providence that makes the same event qualitatively different for different people – isn't that a bit thick?'

'No thicker than our being here at all. No thicker than all this.' With a wave of his hand he indicated the Belshazzaresque dining-room, the eaters, the plum-coloured waiters and the Perpetual Secretary of the British Academy, who happened at that moment to be entering the room with the Professor of Poetry at the University of Cambridge.

But Philip was argumentatively persistent. 'But assuming, as the scientists do, that the simplest hypothesis is the best – though I could never for the life of me see what justification, beyond human ineptitude, they had for doing so ...'

'Hear, hear.'

'What justification?' repeated Illidge. 'Only the justification of observed fact, that's all. It happens to be found experimentally that nature does do things in the simplest way.'

'Or else,' said Spandrell, 'that human beings understand only the simplest explanations. In practice, you couldn't distinguish between those alternatives.'

'But if a thing has a simple, natural explanation, it can't at the same time have a complicated supernatural one.'

'Why not?' asked Spandrell. 'You mayn't be able to understand or measure the supernatural forces behind the superficially natural ones (whatever the difference between natural and supernatural may be). But that doesn't prove they're not there. You're simply raising your stupidity to the rank of a general law.'

Philip took the opportunity to continue his argument. 'But assuming, all the same,' he broke in before Illidge could speak again, 'that the simpler explanation is likely to be the truer – aren't the facts more simply explained by saying it's the individual, with his history and character, who distorts the event into his own likeness? We can see individuals, but we can't see providence; we have to postulate it. Isn't it best, if we can do without it, to omit the superfluous postulate?'

'But *is* it superfluous?' said Spandrell. '*Can* you cover the facts without it? I have my doubts. What about the malleable sort of people – and we're all more or less malleable, we're all more or less made as well as born? What about the people whose characters aren't given but are formed, inexorably, by a series of events all of one type? A run of luck, if you like to call it that, or a run of bad luck; a run of purity or a run of impurity; a run of fine heroic chances or a run of ignoble drab ones. After the run has gone on long enough (and it's astounding the way such runs persist), the character will be formed; and then, if you like to explain it that way, you can say that it's the individual who distorts all that happens to him into his own likeness. But before he had a definite character to distort events into the likeness of – what then? Who decided the sort of things that should happen to him then?'

'Who decides whether a penny shall come down heads or tails?' asked Illidge contemptuously.

'But why bring in pennies?' Spandrell retorted. 'Why bring in pennies, when we're talking about human beings? Consider yourself. Do you *feel* like a penny when things happen to you?'

'It doesn't matter how I feel. Feelings have nothing to do with objective facts.'

'But sensations have. Science is the rationalization of sense-perceptions. Why should one class of psychological intuitions be credited with scientific value and all others denied it? A direct intuition of providential action is just as likely to be a bit of information about objective facts as a direct intuition of blueness and hardness. And when things happen to one, one doesn't feel like a penny. One feels that events are significant; that they've been arranged. Particularly when they occur in series. Tails a hundred times in succession, shall we say?'

'Give us the credit of coming down heads,' said Philip laughing. 'We're the intelligentsia, remember.'

Spandrell frowned; he felt the frivolity as an irrelevance. The sub-

286

ject for him was a serious one. 'When I think of myself,' he said, 'I feel sure that everything that has happened to me was somehow engineered in advance. As a young boy I had a foretaste of what I might have grown up to be, but for events. Something entirely different from this actual Me.'

'A little angel, what?' said Illidge.

Spandrell ignored the interruption. 'But from the time that I was fifteen onwards, things began happening to me which were prophetically like what I am now.' He was silent.

'And so you grew a tail and hoofs instead of a halo and a pair of wings. A sad story. Has it ever struck you,' Illidge went on, turning towards Walter, 'you who are an expert on art, or at least ought to be – has it ever struck you that the paintings of angels are entirely incorrect and unscientific?' Walter shook his head. 'A seventy-kilogram man, if he developed wings, would have to develop colossal muscles to work them. And big flying muscles would mean a correspondingly large sternum, like a bird's. A ten-stone angel, if he wanted to fly as well as a duck, would have to have a breast-bone projecting at least four or five feet. Tell your father that, next time he wants to paint a picture of the Annunciation. All the existing Gabriels are really shockingly improbable.'

Spandrell, meanwhile, was thinking of those raptures among the mountains, those delicacies of feeling, those scruples and sensitivenesses and remorses of his boyhood; and how they were all – the repentance for a bad action no less than the piercing delight at the spectacle of a flower or a landscape – in some way bound up with his sentiment for his mother, somehow rooted and implied in it. He remembered that *Girls' School in Paris*, those erotic readings by flashlight under the sheets. The book had been written in the age when long black stockings and long black gloves had been the height of pornographic fashion, when 'kissing a man without a moustache was like eating an egg without salt.' The seductive and priapic major's moustaches had been long, curly, and waxed. What shame he had felt and what remorse! Struggled how hard, and prayed how earnestly for strength! And the god to whom he had prayed wore the likeness of his mother. To resist temptation was to be worthy of her. Succumbing, he betrayed her, he denied God. He had began to triumph. And then, one morning, out of the blue, came the news that she was going to marry Major Knoyle. Major Knoyle's moustaches were also curly.

'Augustine and the Calvinists were right,' he said aloud, breaking in on the discussion of Seraphim's breast-bones.

'Still harping?' said Illidge.

'God means to save some people and damn others.'

'Or rather he might do so if (a) he existed, (b) there were such a thing as salvation, and (c) ...'

'When I think of the War,' Spandrell went on, interrupting him, what it might have been for me and what in fact it was ...' He shrugged his shoulders. 'Yes, Augustine was right.'

'Well, I must say,' said Philip, 'I've always been very grateful to Augustine, or whoever else it may have been, for giving me a game leg. It prevented me from being a hero; but it also preserved me from becoming a corpse.'

Spandrell looked at him; the corners of his wide mouth ironically twitched. 'Your accident guaranteed you a quiet detached life. In other words, the event was like you. Just as the War, so far as I was concerned, was exactly like me. I'd been up at Oxford a year, when it began,' he went on.

'The dear old College, what?' said Illidge, who could never hear the name of one of the more ancient and expensive seats of learning mentioned without making some derisive comment.

'Three lively terms and two still more lively vacs – discovering alcohol and poker and the difference between women in the flesh and women in the pubescent imagination. Such an apocalypse, the first real woman!' he added parenthetically. 'And at the same time, such a revolting disappointment! So flat, in a way, after the superheated fancy and the pornographic book.'

'Which is a tribute to art,' said Philip. 'As I've so often pointed out.' He smiled at Walter, who blushed, remembering what his brother-in-law had said about the dangers of trying to make love after high poetic models. 'We're brought up topsy-turvy,' Philip went on. 'Art before life; *Romeo and Juliet* and filthy stories before marriage or its equivalents. Hence all young modern literature is disillusioned. Inevitably. In the good old days poets began by losing their virginity; and then, with a complete knowledge of the real thing and just where and how it was unpoetical, deliberately set to work to idealize and beautify it. We start with the poetical and proceed to the unpoetical. If boys and girls lost their virginities as early as they did in Shakespeare's day, there'd be a revival of the Elizabethan love lyric.'

'You may be right,' said Spandrell. 'All I know is that, when I discovered the reality, I found it disappointing – but attractive, all the same. Perhaps so attractive just because it was so disappointing. The heart's a curious sort of manure-heap; dung calls to dung, and the great charm of vice consists in its stupidity and sordidness. It attracts because it's so repellent. But repellent it always remains. And I remember when the War came, how exultantly glad I was to have a chance of getting out of the muck and doing something decent, for a change.'

'For King and Country!' mocked Illidge.

'Poor Rupert Brooke! One smiles now at that thing of his about honour having come back into the world again. Events have made it seem a bit comical.'

'It was a bad joke even when it was written,' said Illidge.

'No, no. At the time it was exactly what I felt myself.'

'Of course you did. Because you were what Brooke was – a spoilt and blasé member of the leisured class. You needed a new thrill, that was all. The War and that famous "honour" of yours provided it.'

Spandrell shrugged his shoulders. 'Explain it like that if you want. All I say is that in August 1914 I wanted to do something noble. I'd even have been quite pleased to get killed.'

' "Rather death than dishonour," what?'

'Yes, quite literally,' said Spandrell. 'For I can assure you that all the melodramas are perfectly realistic. There are certain occasions when people do say that sort of thing. The only defect of melodrama is that it leads you to believe that they say it all the time. They don't, unfortunately. But "rather death than dishonour" was exactly what I was thinking in August 1914. If the alternative to death was the stupid kind of life I'd been leading. I wanted to get killed.'

'There speaks the gentleman of leisure again,' said Illidge.

'And then, just because I'd been brought up a good deal abroad and knew three foreign languages, because I had a mother who was too fond of me and a stepfather with military influence, I was transferred willy-nilly into the Intelligence. God was really bent on damning me.'

'He was very kindly trying to save your life,' said Philip.

'But I didn't want it saved. Not unless I could do something decent with it, something heroic for preference, or at least difficult and risky. Instead of which they put me on to liaison work and then to hunting spies. Of all the sordid and ignoble businesses ...'

'But after all the trenches weren't so very romantic.'

'No, but they were dangerous. Sitting in a trench, you needed courage and endurance. A spy catcher was perfectly safe and didn't have to display any of the nobler virtues; while as to his opportunities for vice ... Those towns behind the lines, and Paris, and the ports – whores and alcohol were their chief products.'

'But after all,' said Philip, 'those are avoidable evils.' Naturally cold, he found it easy to be reasonable.

'Not avoidable by me,' Spandrell answered. 'Particularly in those circumstances. I'd wanted to do something decent, and I'd been prevented. So it became a kind of point of honour to do the opposite of what I'd desired. A point of honour – can you understand that?'

Philip shook his head. 'A little too subtle for me.'

'But just imagine yourself in the presence of a man you respect and like and admire more than you've ever admired and liked anyone before.'

Philip nodded. But in point of fact, he reflected, he had never deeply and whole-heartedly admired anyone. Theoretically, yes; but never in practice, never to the point of wanting to make himself a disciple, a follower. He had adopted other people's opinions, even their modes of life – but always with the underlying conviction that they weren't really his, that he could and certainly would abandon them as easily as he had taken them up. And whenever there had seemed any risk of his being carried away, he had deliberately resisted, had fought or fled for his liberty.

'You're overcome with your feeling for him,' Spandrell continued. 'And you go towards him with outstretched hands, offering your friendship and devotion. His only response is to put his hands in his pockets and turn away. What would you do then?'

Philip laughed. 'I should have to consult Vogue's *Book of Etiquette*.'

'You'd knock him down. At least that's what I would do. It would be a point of honour. And the more you'd admired, the more violent the knock and the longer the subsequent dance on his carcass. That's why the whores and the alcohol weren't avoidable. On the contrary, it became a point of honour never to avoid them. That life in France was like the life I'd been leading before the War – only much nastier and stupider, and utterly unrelieved by any redeeming feature. And after a year of it, I was desperately wangling to cling to my dishonour and avoid death. Augustine was right, I tell you; we're damned or saved in advance. The things that happen are a providential conspiracy.'

'Providential balderdash!' said Illidge; but in the silence that followed he thought again how extraordinary it was, how almost infinitely improbable that he should be sitting there, drinking claret, with the Perpetual Secretary of the British Academy two tables away and the second oldest Judge of the High Court just behind him. Twenty years before the odds against his being there under the gilded ceiling had been at the rate of several hundreds or thousands of millions to one. But there, all the same, he was. He took another draught of claret.

And Philip, meanwhile, was remembering that immense black horse, kicking, plunging, teeth bared and ears laid back; and how it suddenly started forward, dragging the carter along with it; and the rumble of the wheels; and, 'Aie!' his own scream; and how he shrank back against the steep bank, how he tried to climb, slipped, fell; and the appalling rush and trampling of the giant; and 'Aie, aie!' the huge shape between him and the sun, the great hoofs and suddenly an annihilating pain.

And through the same silence Walter was thinking of that afternoon when, for the first time, he entered Lucy Tantamount's drawing-room. 'Everything that happens is intrinsically like the man it happens to.'

*

'But what's her secret?' Marjorie asked. 'Why should he have gone mad about her? Because he has gone mad. Literally.'

'Isn't it rather an obvious secret?' said Elinor. What she found queer was not that Walter should have lost his head about Lucy, but that he should ever have seen anything attractive in poor Marjorie. 'After all,' she continued, 'Lucy's very amusing and alive. And besides,' she added, remembering Philip's exasperating comments on the dog they had run over at Bombay, 'she has a bad reputation.'

'But is that attractive? A bad reputation?' The tea-pot hung suspended over the cup as she asked.

'Of course. It means that the woman who enjoys it is accessible. No sugar, thanks.'

'But surely,' said Marjorie, handing her the cup, 'men don't want to share their mistress with other lovers.'

'Perhaps not. But the fact that a woman has had other lovers gives a man hope. "Where others have succeeded, I can succeed." That's the man's argument. And at the same time a bad reputation makes him immediately think of the woman in terms of love-making. It gives a twist to his imaginations about her. When you met Lola Montes, her reputation made you automatically think of bedrooms. You didn't think of bedrooms when you met Florence Nightingale. Only sick-rooms. Which are rather different,' Elinor concluded.

There was a silence. It was horrid of her, Elinor was thinking, not to feel more sympathetic. But there it was; she didn't. She reminded herself of the abominable life the poor woman had had—first with her husband, and now with Walter. Really abominable. But those dreadful, dangling, sham jade earrings! And the voice, the earnest manner...

Marjorie looked up. 'But is it possible that men can be so easily taken in? By such a cheap bait? Men like Walter. Like *Walter*,' she insisted. 'Can men like that be such ... such ...'

'Pigs?' suggested Elinor. 'Apparently they can. It seems odd, certainly.' Perhaps it would be better, she reflected, if Philip were rather more of a pig and less of a hermit crab. Pigs are human – all too much so, perhaps; but still human. Whereas hermit crabs are doing their best to be molluscs.

Marjorie shook her head and sighed. 'It's extraordinary,' she said with a conviction that struck Elinor as rather ludicrous. 'What sort of an opinion can she have of herself?' she wondered. But Marjorie's good opinion was not for herself so much as for virtue. She had been brought up to believe in the ugliness of vice and the animal part of human nature, the beauty of virtue and the spirit. And cold by nature, she had the cold woman's utter incomprehension of sensuality. That Walter should suddenly cease to be the Walter she had known and behave 'like a pig,' as Elinor rather crudely put it, was to her really extraordinary, quite apart from any personal considerations of her own attractiveness.

'And then you must remember,' Elinor said aloud, 'Lucy has another advantage where men like Walter are concerned. She's one of those women who have the temperament of a man. Men can get pleasure out of casual encounters. Most women can't; they've got to be in love, more or less. They've got to be emotionally involved. All but a few of them. Lucy's one of the few. She has the masculine detachment. She can separate her appetite from the rest of her soul.'

'What a horror!' Marjorie shuddered.

Elinor observed the shudder and was annoyed by it into contradiction.

'Do you think so? It seems to me sometimes rather an enviable talent.' She laughed and Marjorie was duly shocked by her cynicism. 'For a boy with Walter's shyness and timidity,' she went on, 'there's something very exciting about that kind of bold temperament. It's the opposite of his. Reckless, without scruple, wilful, unconscientious. I can so well understand its going to his head.' She thought of Everard Webley. 'Force is always attractive,' she added. 'Particularly if one lacks it oneself, as Walter does. Lucy's obviously a force. You may not like that kind of force.' She herself didn't much like Webley's energetic ambition. 'But you can't help admiring the force in itself. It's like Niagara. Fine, even though you mayn't want to be standing underneath. May I take another piece of bread and butter?' She helped herself. Out of politeness Marjorie also took another slice. 'Delicious brown bread,' Elinor commented and wondered how Walter could have lived with anyone who crooked the little finger of the hand that held the tea-cup and who took such horribly small bites from a slice of bread and then chewed only with the front teeth, like a guinea-pig – as though the process of eating were an indelicate and rather disgusting affair.

'But what do you think I ought to do?' Marjorie brought herself finally to ask.

Elinor shrugged her shoulders. 'What *can* you do, but hope he'll get what he wants and soon be sick of it.'

It was obvious; but Marjorie thought her rather unfeeling, hard, and cruel to have said it.

*

In London the Quarleses sketchily inhabited what had once been the last of a row of stables in a Belgravian mews. You passed under an archway. A cliff of cream-coloured stucco rose sheer on your left – windowless, for the Belgravians had declined to be aware of the squalid domesticity of their dependants. On the right stretched the low line of stables with the single storey of living rooms above, tenanted now by enormous Daimlers and the families of their chauffeurs. The mews ended in a wall, over the top of which you could see the waving plane-trees of Belgravian gardens. The Quarleses' doorstep lay in the shadow of this wall. Set between the gardens and the sparsely inhabited mews, the little house was very quiet. The coming and going of limousines and the occasional yelling of a child were the only disturbances.

'But fortunately,' Philip had remarked, 'the rich can afford to buy silent cars. And there's something about internal combustion engines that makes for birth control. Who ever heard of a chauffeur with eight children?' Coach-house and horse-boxes had been knocked together in the reconstruction of the stable, into a single spacious living-room. Two screens hinted at a division. Behind the screen on the right, as you entered, was the drawing-room end of the apartment – chairs and a sofa grouped around the fireplace. The screen on the left concealed the dining-table and the entrance to a tiny kitchen. A little staircase slanted up across one of the walls, leading to the bedrooms. Yellow cretonnes mimicked the sunshine that never shone through the northward-looking windows. There were many books. Old Bidlake's portrait of Elinor as a young girl hung over the mantelpiece.

Philip was lying on the sofa, book in hand. 'Very remarkable,' he read, 'is Mr Tate Regan's account of pigmy parasitic males in three species of Cerativid Angler-fishes. In the Arctic *Ceratias holbolli* a female about eight inches in length carried on her ventral surface two males of about two-and-a-half inches. The snout and chin region of the dwarf male was permanently attached to a papilla of the female's skin, and the blood-vessels of the two were confluent. The male is without teeth; the mouth is useless; the alimentary canal is degenerate. In *Photocarynus spiniceps* the female, about two-and-a-half inches in length, bore a male under half an inch long on the top of her head in front of her right eye. In *Edriolychnus schmidti* the dimensions were about the same as in the last case, and the female carried the pigmy male upside down on the inner surface of her gill-cover.'

Philip put down the book and feeling in his breast pocket pulled out his pocket diary and his fountain-pen. 'Female Angler-fishes,' he wrote, 'carry dwarf parasitic males attached to their bodies. Draw the obvious comparison, when my Walter rushes after his Lucy. What about a scene at an aquarium? They go in with a scientific friend who shows them the female Anglers and their husbands. The twilight, the fishes – perfect background.' He was just putting his diary away, when another thought occurred to him. He re-opened it. 'Make it the aquarium at Monaco and describe Monte Carlo and the whole Riviera in terms of deep-sea monstrosity.' He lit a cigarette and went on with his book.

There was a rap at the door. He got up and opened; it was Elinor. 'What an afternoon!' She dropped into a chair.

'Well, what news of Marjorie?' he asked.

'No *news*,' she sighed, as she took off her hat. 'The poor creature's as dreary as ever. But I'm very sorry for her.'

'What did you advise her to do?'

'Nothing. What else could she do? And Walter?' she asked in her turn. 'Did you get a chance to be the heavy father?'

'The middle-weight father, shall we say. I persuaded him to come down to Chamford with Marjorie.'

'Did you? That was a real triumph.'

'Not quite such a triumph as you think. I had no enemy to fight with. Lucy's going to Paris next Saturday.'

'Let's hope she'll stay there. Poor Walter!'

'Yes, poor Walter. But I must tell you about Angler-fishes.' He told her. 'One of these days,' he concluded, 'I shall really have to write a modern Bestiary. Such moral lessons! But tell me, how was Everard? I quite forgot you'd seen him.'

'You would have forgotten,' she answered scornfully.

'Would I? I don't know why.'

'No, you wouldn't.'

'I'm crushed,' said Philip with a mock humility. There was a silence.

'Everard's in love with me,' said Elinor at last without looking at her husband and in the flattest, most matter-of-fact of voices.

'Is that news?' asked Philip. 'I thought he was an old admirer.'

'But it's serious,' Elinor went on. 'Very serious.' She waited anxiously for his comment. It came, after a little pause.

'That must be less amusing.'

Less amusing! Couldn't he understand? After all, he wasn't a fool. Or perhaps he did understand and was only pretending not to; perhaps he was secretly glad about Everard. Or was it just indifference that made him blind? Nobody understands what he does not feel. Philip couldn't understand her because he didn't feel as she felt. He was confident in the belief that other people were as reasonably lukewarm as he was himself. 'But I like him,' she said aloud in a last desperate attempt to provoke him into at least a semblance of caring. If only he'd show himself jealous, or sad, or angry, how happy she'd be, how grateful! 'Very much,' she went on. 'There's something very attractive about him. That passionateness of his, that violence. …'

Philip laughed. 'Quite the irresistible cave-man, in fact.'

Elinor rose with a little sigh, picked up her hat and bag, and bending over her husband's chair, kissed him on the forehead, as though she were saying good-bye; then turned away and still without a word went upstairs to her bedroom.

Philip picked up his abandoned book. '*Bonellia viridis*,' he read, 'is a green worm, not uncommon in the Mediterranean. The female has a body about the size of a prune, bearing a string-like, terminally bifid, very contractile proboscis, which may be two feet long. But the male is microscopic and lives in what may be called the reproductive duct (modified nephridium) of the female. It has no mouth and depends on what it absorbs parasitically through its ciliated surfaces. ...'

Philip once more put down the book. He was wondering whether he oughtn't to go upstairs and say something to Elinor. He was sure she'd never really care for Everard. But perhaps he oughtn't to take it so much for granted. She had seemed rather upset. Perhaps she had expected him to say something – how much he cared for her, how wretched he'd be, how angry, if she were to stop caring for him. But these precisely were the almost unsayable things. In the end he decided not to go upstairs. He'd wait and see, he'd put it off to another time. He went on reading about *Bonellia viridis*.

Chapter Twenty-two

To-DAY, at Lucy Tantamount's, I was the victim of a very odd association of ideas. Lucy, as usual, was the French tricolor; blue round the eyes, a scarlet mouth and the rest dead white against a background of shiny metal-black hair. I made some sort of a joke. She laughed, opening her mouth – and her tongue and gums were so much paler than the paint on her lips that they seemed (it gave me a queer creepy shock of astonished horror) quite bloodless and white by contrast. And then, without transition, I was standing in front of those sacred crocodiles in the palace gardens at Jaipur, and the Indian guide was throwing them bits of meat, and the inside of the animals' mouths was almost white, as though the mouths were lined with a slightly glacé cream-coloured kid. And that's how one's mind naturally works. And one has intellectual pretensions! Well, well. But what a windfall for my novel! I shall begin the book with it. My Walterish hero makes his Lucyish siren laugh and immediately (to his horror; but he goes on longing for her, with an added touch of perversity, all the same and perhaps all the more) sees those disgusting crocodiles he had been looking at in India a month before. In this way I strike the note of strangeness and fantasticality at once. Everything's incredible, if you can skin off the crust of obviousness our habits put on it. Every object and event contains within itself an infinity of depths within depths. Nothing's in the least like what it seems – or rather it's like several million other things at the same time. All India rushes like a cinema film through his head while she's laughing and showing – she the beloved, longed-for, lusted-after, beautiful one – those gruesomely bloodless crocodile's gums and palate.

*

The musicalization of fiction. Not in the symbolist way, by subordinating sense to sound. (*Pleuvent les bleus baisers des astres taciturnes.* Mere glossolalia). But on a large scale, in the construction. Meditate on Beethoven. The changes of moods, the abrupt transitions. (Majesty alternating with a joke, for example, in the first movement of the B flat major quartet. Comedy suddenly hinting at prodigious and tragic solemnities in the scherzo of the C sharp minor quartet.)

More interesting still the modulations, not merely from one key to another, but from mood to mood. A theme is stated, then developed, pushed out of shape, imperceptibly deformed, until, though still recognizably the same, it has become quite different. In sets of variations the process is carried a step further. Those incredible Diabelli variations, for example. The whole range of thought and feeling, yet all in organic relation to a ridiculous little waltz tune. Get this into a novel. How? The abrupt transitions are easy enough. All you need is a sufficiency of characters and parallel, contrapuntal plots. While Jones is murdering a wife, Smith is wheeling the perambulator in the park. You alternate the themes. More interesting, the modulations and variations are also more difficult. A novelist modulates by re-duplicating situations and characters. He shows several people falling in love, or dying, or praying in different ways – dissimilars solving the same problem. Or, *vice versa*, similar people confronted with dis-similar problems. In this way you can modulate through all the aspects of your theme, you can write variations in any number of different moods. Another way: The novelist can assume the god-like creative privilege and simply elect to consider the events of the story in their various aspects – emotional, scientific, economic, religious, metaphysical, etc. He will modulate from one to the other – as from the aesthetic to the physico-chemical aspect of things, from the religi-ous to the physiological or financial. But perhaps this is a too tyran-nical imposition of the author's will. Some people would think so. But need the author be so retiring? I think we're a bit too squeamish about these personal appearances nowadays.

*

Put a novelist into the novel. He justifies aesthetic generalizations, which may be interesting – at least to me. He also justifies experi-ment. Specimens of his work may illustrate other possible or impos-sible ways of telling a story. And if you have him telling parts of the same story as you are, you can make a variation on the theme. But why draw the line at one novelist inside your novel? Why not a second inside his? And a third inside the novel of the second? And so on to infinity, like those advertisements of Quaker Oats where there's a quaker holding a box of oats, on which is a picture of another quaker holding another box of oats, on which etc., etc. At about the tenth remove you might have a novelist telling your story in algebraic symbols or in terms of variations in blood-pressure,

298

pulse, secretion of ductless glands and reaction times.

*

Novel of ideas. The character of each personage must be implied, as far as possible, in the ideas of which he is the mouthpiece. In so far as theories are rationalizations of sentiments, instincts, dispositions of soul, this is feasible. The chief defect of the novel of ideas is that you must write about people who have ideas to express – which excludes all but about ·01 per cent of the human race. Hence the real, the congenital novelists don't write such books. But then I never pretended to be a congenital novelist.

*

The great defect of the novel of ideas is that it's a made-up affair. Necessarily; for people who can reel off neatly formulated notions aren't quite real; they're slightly monstrous. Living with monsters becomes rather tiresome in the long run.

*

The instinct of acquisitiveness has more perverts, I believe, than the instinct of sex. At any rate, people seem to me odder about money than about even their amours. Such amazing meannesses as one's always coming across, particularly among the rich! Such fantastic extravagances too. Both qualities, often, in the same person. And then the hoarders, the grubbers, the people who are entirely and almost unceasingly preoccupied with money. Nobody's unceasingly preoccupied with sex in the same way – I suppose because there's a physiological satisfaction possible in sexual matters, while there's none where money's concerned. When the body's satiated, the mind stops thinking about food or women. But the hunger for money and possessions is an almost purely mental thing. There's no physical satisfaction possible. That would account for the excesses and perversities of acquisitiveness. Our bodies almost compel the sexual instinct to behave in a normal fashion. Perversions must be violent before they overrule the normal physiological tendencies. But where acquisitiveness is concerned, there's no regulating body, no lump of too too solid flesh to be pushed out of the grooves of physiological habit. The slightest tendency to perversion is at once made manifest. But perhaps the word 'perversion' is meaningless in this context.

For perversion implies the existence of a norm from which it departs. What is the norm of acquisitiveness? One guesses vaguely at some golden mean; but is it in fact the true statistical norm? I should imagine myself rather 'under-acquisitivized'; less interested in money and possessions in general than the average. Illidge would say it's entirely due to having been brought up in an atmosphere of easy money. It may be partly true. But not entirely, I think. Consider the many people born rich who are preoccupied with nothing but money making. No, my under-acquisitiveness is hereditary as well as acquired. In any case I find myself uninterested in possessions and rather unsympathetic with, and without understanding of, those who are. No predominantly acquisitive character has appeared in any of my stories. It is a defect; for acquisitives are obviously very common in real life. But I doubt if I could make such a character interesting – not being interested myself in the acquisitive passion. Balzac could; circumstances and heredity had made him passionately interested in money. But when one finds a thing boring, one's apt to be boring about it.

Chapter Twenty-three

THE writing table was under the window. Dimmed by the smoky air of Sheffield, a shaft of yellow, viscous-looking sunlight lit up a corner of the table and a patch of red and flowered carpet. Everard Webley was writing a letter. His pen rushed over the paper. Whatever he did was done with rapidity and decision.

'Dearest Elinor,' he wrote. '*De profundis clamavi*, from the depths of this repulsive hotel bedroom and the even lower depths of this political tour of the North, I call to you.' (He wrote his I's as though they were pillars – a strong straight shaft and two little transverse strokes at top and bottom for capital and base. The crosses on his t's were firm and uncompromising.) 'But I don't suppose you listen. I've always felt such sympathy for the savages who give their gods a good beating when they don't answer prayers or respond to sacrifices. England expects that every god this day will do his duty. And if he doesn't – well, so much the worse for him; he'll get a taste of the cat-o'-nine-tails. The modern worship of a remote Ineffable, whose acts one doesn't criticize, seems to me very unsatisfactory. What's the good of making a contract with somebody who can break it at will and against whom one has no redress? Women have gone the same way as the gods. They mayn't be questioned. You're not allowed to compel them to do their duty by their worshippers or fulfil their part in the natural contract between the sexes. I write, I implore. But, like the new-fangled god of modern philosophies and broad theologies, you don't listen. And one's not allowed to take reprisals; it's bad form to beat the defaulting god. It isn't done. All the same, I warn you: one of these days I'll try the good old methods. I'll do a slight Rape of the Sabines and then where will your ineffable remote superiority be? How I hate you really for compelling me to love you so much! It's such a damnable injustice – getting so much passion and longing out of me and giving nothing in return. And you not here to receive the punishment you deserve! I have to take a vicarious revenge on the ruffians who disturb my meetings. I had a terrific battle last night. Howls, booing, organized singing of the International. But I fought them down. Literally at one moment. I had to give one of the ringleaders a black eye. Poor devil! He was only paying for your misdeeds. He was your scapegoat. For it was really you I was fighting. If it hadn't been for you I wouldn't have been half so savage. I probably wouldn't have won. So indirectly I owe you my victory. For which I'm duly grateful. But another time there won't be any Communists to vent my rage on. The next fight will be against the real enemy – against you. So be careful, my dear. I'll try to stop short of black eyes; but in the heat of the moment one never knows. But seriously, Elinor, seriously. Why are you so cold and aloof and dead? Why do you shut yourself off from me? I think of you so incessantly, so insistently. The thought of you is always there. It lies hidden, a latency, in the most unlikely things and places, ready at the command of some chance association to jump out at me from its ambush. Haunting, like a guilty conscience. If I …'

There was a knock at the door. It was Hugo Brockle who came in. Everard looked at his watch, then at Hugo. The expression on his face was menacing. 'Why are you so late?' he asked in a terrifyingly quiet voice.

Hugo blushed. 'I hadn't realized the time.' It was only too true. He had been lunching with the Upwiches, twenty miles away across the moors. Polly Logan was staying with them. After lunch old Upwich and the others had gone to play a round of golf on the private links in the park. Polly, providentially, didn't play. He had taken her for a walk through the woods along the river. How should he have realized the time? 'I'm sorry,' he added.

'I should hope you were,' said Everard and the latent violence broke out from under his quietness. 'I tell you to be back at five and it's now a quarter past six. When you're with me on British Freeman business you're under military discipline. My orders are to be obeyed, do you understand? Do you understand?' he insisted.

Sheepishly Hugo nodded. 'Yes.'

'And now go away and see that all the arrangements for this evening's meeting have been properly made. And mind, this sort of thing mustn't happen again. You won't get off so lightly next time.'

Hugo shut the door after him. All the anger instantly vanished from Everard's face. He believed in frightening his subordinates from time to time. Anger, he always found, was an excellent weapon so long as you didn't let yourself be mastered by it. He never did. Poor Hugo! he smiled to himself and went on with his letter. Ten minutes later Hugo came in to say that dinner was ready. The meeting was at eight; they had to eat very early.

*

'But it's so silly, all this political squabbling,' said Rampion, his voice shrill with exasperation, 'so utterly silly. Bolsheviks and Fascists, Radicals and Conservatives, Communists and British Freemen – what the devil are they all fighting about? I'll tell you. They're fighting to decide whether we shall go to hell by communist express train or capitalist racing motor car, by individualist bus or collectivist tram running on the rails of state control. The destination's the same in every case. They're all of them bound for hell, all headed for the same psychological impasse and the social collapse that results from psychological collapse. The only point of difference between them is: How shall we get there? It's simply impossible for a man of sense to be interested in such disputes. For the man of sense the important thing is hell, not the means of transport to be employed in getting there. The question for the man of sense is: Do we or do we not want to go to hell? And his answer is: No, we don't. And if that's his answer, then he won't have anything to do with any of the politicians. Because they all want to land us in hell. All, without exception. Lenin *and* Mussolini, MacDonald *and* Baldwin. All equally anxious to take us to hell and only squabbling about the means of taking us.'

'Some of them may take us a little more slowly than others,' suggested Philip.

Rampion shrugged his shoulders. 'But so very little more slowly that it wouldn't make any appreciable difference. They all believe in industrialism in one form or another, they all believe in Americanization. Think of the Bolshevist ideal. America but much more so. America with government departments taking the place of trusts and state officials instead of rich men. And then the ideal of the rest of Europe. The same thing, only with the rich men preserved. Machinery and government officials there. Machinery and Alfred Mond or Henry Ford here. The machinery to take us to hell; the rich or the officials to drive it. You think one set may drive more cautiously than the other? Perhaps you're right. But I can't see that there's anything to choose between them. They're all equally in a hurry. In the name of science, progress, and human happiness! Amen and step on the gas.'

Philip nodded. 'They do step on it all right,' he said. 'They get a move on. Progress. But as you say, it's probably in the direction of the bottomless pit.'

'And the only thing the reformers can find to talk about is the shape, colour, and steering arrangements of the vehicle. Can't the imbeciles see that it's the direction that matters, that we're entirely on the wrong road and ought to go back – preferably on foot, without the stinking machine?'

'You may be right,' said Philip. 'But the trouble is that, given our existing world, you can't go back, you can't scrap the machine. That is, you can't do it unless you're prepared to kill off about half the human race. Industrialism made possible the doubling of the world's population in a hundred years. If you want to get rid of industrialism, you've got to get back to where you started. That's to say, you've got to slaughter half the existing number of men and women. Which might, *sub specie aeternitatis* or merely *historiae*, be an excellent thing. But hardly a matter of practical politics.'

'Not at the moment,' Rampion agreed. 'But the next war and the next revolution will make it only too practical.'

'Possibly. But one shouldn't count on wars and revolutions. Because, if you count on them happening, they certainly will happen.'

'They'll happen,' said Rampion, 'whether you count on them or not. Industrial progress means over-production, means the need for getting new markets, means international rivalry, means war. And mechanical progress means more specialization and standardization of work, means more ready-made and unindividual amusements, means diminution of initiative and creativeness, means more intellectualism and the progressive atrophy of all the vital and fundamental things in human nature, means increased boredom and restlessness, means finally a kind of individual madness that can only result in social revolution. Count on them or not, wars and revolutions are inevitable, if things are allowed to go on as they are at present.'

'So the problem will solve itself,' said Philip.

'Only by destroying itself. When humanity's destroyed, obviously there'll be no more problem. But it seems a poor sort of solution. I believe there may be another, even within the framework of the present system. A temporary one while the system's being modified in the direction of a permanent solution. The root of the evil's in the individual psychology; so it's there, in the individual psychology, that you'd have to begin. The first step would be to make people live dualistically, in two compartments. In one compartment as industrialized workers, in the other as human beings. As idiots and machines for eight hours out of every twenty-four and real human beings for the rest.'

'Don't they do that already?'

304

'Of course they don't. They live as idiots and machines all the time, at work and in their leisure. Like idiots and machines, but imagining they're living like civilized humans, even like gods. The first thing to do is to make them admit that they are idiots and machines during working hours. "Our civilization being what it is," this is what you'll have to say to them, "you've got to spend eight hours out of every twenty-four as a mixture between an imbecile and a sewing machine. It's very disagreeable, I know. It's humiliating and disgusting. But there you are. You've got to do it; otherwise the whole fabric of our world will fall to bits and we'll all starve. Do the job, then, idiotically and mechanically; and spend your leisure hours in being a real complete man or woman, as the case may be. Don't mix the two lives together; keep the bulkheads watertight between them. The genuine human life in your leisure hours is the real thing. The other's just a dirty job that's got to be done. And never forget that it *is* dirty and, except in so far as it keeps you fed and society intact, utterly unimportant, utterly irrelevant to the real human life. Don't be deceived by the canting rogues who talk of the sanctity of labour and the Christian Service that business men do their fellows. It's all lies. Your work's just a nasty, dirty job, made unfortunately necessary by the folly of your ancestors. They piled up a mountain of garbage and you've got to go on digging it away, for fear it might stink you to death, dig for dear life, while cursing the memory of the maniacs who made all the dirty work for you to do. But don't try to cheer yourself up by pretending the nasty mechanical job is a noble one. It isn't; and the only result of saying and believing that it is, will be to lower your humanity to the level of the dirty work. If you believe in business as Service and the sanctity of labour, you'll merely turn yourself into a mechanical idiot for twenty-four hours out of the twenty-four. Admit it's dirty, hold your nose and do it for eight hours and then concentrate on being a real human being in your leisure. A real complete human being. Not a newspaper reader, not a jazzer, not a radio fan. The industrialists who purvey standardized ready-made amusements to the masses are doing their best to make you as much of a mechanical imbecile in your leisure as in your hours of work. But don't let them. Make the effort of being human." That's what you've got to say to people; that's the lesson you've got to teach the young. You've got to persuade everybody that all this grand industrial civilization is just a bad smell and that the real, significant life can only be lived apart from it. It'll be a very long time before decent living and industrial smell can be reconciled. Perhaps, indeed, they're irreconcilable. It remains to be seen. In the meantime, at any rate, we must shovel the garbage and bear the smell stoically, and in the intervals try to lead the real human life.'

'It's a good programme,' said Philip. 'But I don't see you winning many votes on it at the next election.'

'That's the trouble.' Rampion frowned. 'One would have them all against one. For the only thing they're all agreed on – Tories, Liberals, Socialists, Bolsheviks – is the intrinsic excellence of the industrial stink and the necessity of standardizing and specializing every trace of genuine manhood or womanhood out of the human race. And we're expected to take an interest in politics. Well, well.' He shook his head. 'Let's think about something pleasanter. Look, I want to show you this picture.' He crossed the studio and pulled out one from a stack of canvases leaning against the wall. 'There,' he said when he had set it up on an easel. Seated on the crest of a grassy bank, where she formed the apex of the pyramidal composition, a naked woman was suckling a child. Below and in front of her to the left crouched a man, his bare back turned to the spectator, and in the corresponding position on the right stood a little boy. The crouching man was playing with a couple of tiny leopard cubs that occupied the centre of the picture, a little below the seated mother's feet; the little boy looked on. Close behind the woman and filling almost the whole of the upper part of the picture, stood a cow, its head slightly averted, ruminating. The woman's head and shoulders stood out pale against its dun flank.

'It's a picture I like particularly,' said Rampion after a little silence. 'The flesh is good. Don't you think. Has a bloom to it, a living quality. By God, how marvellously your father-in-law could paint flesh in the open air! Amazing! Nobody's done it better. Not even Renoir. I wish I had his gifts. But this is all right, you know,' he went on, turning back to the picture. 'Quite good, really. And there are other qualities. I feel I've managed to get the living relationship of the figures to each other and the rest of the world. The cow, for example. It's turned away, it's unaware of the human scene. But somehow you feel it's happily in touch with the humans in some milky, cud-chewing, bovine way. And the humans are in touch with it. And also in touch with the leopards, but in a quite different way – a way corresponding to the quick leopardy way the cubs are in touch with them. Yes, I like it.'

'So do I,' said Philip. 'It's something to put over against the industrial stink.' He laughed. 'You ought to paint a companion picture of life in the civilized world. The woman in a mackintosh, leaning against a giant Bovril bottle and feeding her baby with Glaxo. The bank covered with asphalt. The man dressed in a five-guinea suit for fifty shillings, squatting down to play with a wireless set. And the little boy, pimpled and with rickets, looking interestedly on.'

'And the whole thing painted in the cubist manner,' said Rampion; 'so as to make quite sure that there should be no life in it whatever. Nothing like modern art for sterilizing the life out of things. Carbolic acid isn't in it.'

Chapter Twenty-four

LOCAL government among the Indians under the Maurya emperors continued, week after week, to necessitate Mr Quarles's attendance at the British Museum for at least two full days in every seven.

'I had no idyah,' he explained, 'that there was so much available matyahrial.'

Gladys, meanwhile, was discovering that she had made a mistake. The good time which she had looked forward to enjoying under Mr Quarles's protection was no better than the good time she might have enjoyed with 'boys' hardly richer than herself. Mr Quarles, it seemed, was not prepared to pay for the luxury of feeling superior. He wanted to be a great man, but for very little money. His excuse for the cheap restaurant and the cheap seats at the theatre was always the necessity of secrecy. It would never do for him to be seen by an acquaintance in Gladys's company; and since his acquaintances belonged to the world which is carried, replete, from the Berkeley to the stalls of the Gaiety, Mr Quarles and Gladys ate at a Corner House and looked at the play remotely from the Upper Circle. Such was the official explanation of the very unprincely quality of Sidney's treats. The real explanation was not the need for secrecy, but Sidney's native reluctance to part with hard cash. For though large sums meant little to him, small ones meant a great deal. When it was a matter of 'improving the estate,' he would light-heartedly sign away hundreds, even thousands of pounds. But when it was a question of parting with two or three half-crowns to give his mistress a better seat at the play or a more palatable meal, a bunch of flowers or a box of chocolates, he became at once the most economical of men. His avarice was at the root of a certain curious puritanism, which tinged his opinions about almost all pleasures and amusements other than the strictly sexual. Dining with a seduced work-girl in the cheap obscurity of a Soho eating-hell, he would (with all the passion of a Milton reproving the sons of Belial, all the earnestness of a Wordsworth advocating low living and high thinking) denounce the hoggish guzzlers at the Carlton, the gluttons at the Ritz, who in the midst of London's serried miseries would carelessly spend a farm labourer's monthly wage on a *tête-à-tête* dinner. Thus his inexpensive preferences in the matter of restaurants and theatre seats were made to assume a high moral as well as a merely diplomatic character. Seduced by an ageing libertine,

Mr Quarles's mistresses were surprised to find themselves dining with a Hebrew prophet, and taking their amusements with a disciple of Cato or of Calvin.

'One would think you were a blessed saint to hear you talk,' said Gladys sarcastically, when he had paused for breath in the midst of one of his Corner House denunciations of the extravagant and greedy. 'You!' Her laughter was mockingly savage.

Mr Quarles was disconcerted. He was used to being listened to respectfully, as an Olympian. Gladys's tone was ribald and rebellious; he didn't like it; it even alarmed him.

He raised his chin with dignity and fired a dropping shot of rebuke upon her head. 'It isn't a question of myah personalities,' he pronounced. 'It's a question of general principles.'

'I can't see any difference,' retorted Gladys, abolishing at one stroke all the solemn pretensions of all the philosophers and moralists, all the religious leaders and reformers and Utopia-makers from the beginning of human time.

What exasperated Gladys most was the fact that even in the world of the Maison Lyons and cheap seats, Mr Quarles did not abandon his Olympian pretensions and his Olympian manners. His indignation, when one evening there was a crowd on the stairs leading to the Upper Circle, was loud and righteous. 'A ryahl scandal!' he called it.

'One would think you'd taken the royal box,' said Gladys sarcastically.

And when, at a tea-shop, he complained that the one-and-fourpenny slice of salmon tasted as though it had come from British Columbia rather than from Scotland, she advised him to write to *The Times* about it. The discovery tickled her fancy and, after that, she was always ironically telling him to write to *The Times*. Did he complain, a noble and disillusioned philosopher, of the shallowness of politicians and the sordid triviality of political life, Gladys bade him write to *The Times*. He was eloquent about iniquitous Mrs Grundy and English illiberality; let him write to *The Times*. It was a ryahl scandal that neither Sir Edward Grey nor Lloyd George should have been able to speak French; *The Times* again was indicated. Mr Quarles was hurt and outraged. Nothing like this had ever happened before. In the company of his other mistresses the consciousness of his superiority had been a serene happiness. They had worshipped and admired; he had felt himself a god. And during the first days Gladys too had seemed a worshipper. But coming to pray, she had stayed to mock. His spiritual happiness was ruined. If it had not been for the bodily solace which the species in her provided, Mr Quarles would have quickly exhausted the subject of local self-government under the Mauryas and stayed at home. But there was in Gladys a more than usually large admixture of undifferentiated species. It was too much for Mr Quarles. The derisive individual in her pained and repelled him; but the attraction of what was generic, of the whole feminine species, the entire sex, was stronger than that individual repulsion. In spite of her mockery, Mr Quarles returned. The claims of the Indians became increasingly peremptory.

Realizing her power, Gladys began to withhold what he desired. Perhaps he could be blackmailed into the generosity which it was not in his nature to display spontaneously. Returning from a very inexpensive evening at Lyons' and the pictures, she pushed him angrily away when, in the taxi, he attempted the usual endearments.

'Can't you leave me in peace?' she snapped. And a moment later, 'Tell the driver to go to my place first and drop me.'

'But, my dyah child!' Mr Quarles protested. Hadn't she promised to come back with him?

'I've changed my mind. Tell the driver.'

The thought that, after three days of fervid anticipation, he would have to pass the evening in solitude was agonizing. 'But, Gladys, my darling …'

'Tell the driver.'

'But it's ryahly too cruel; you're *too* unkind.'

'Better write to *The Times* about it,' was all her answer. 'I'll tell the driver myself.'

After a night of insomnia and suffering Mr Quarles went out as soon as the shops were open and bought a fourteen-guinea wrist watch.

*

The advertisement was for a dentifrice. But as the picture represented two fox-trotting young people showing their teeth at one another in an amorous and pearly smile and as the word began with a D, little Phil unhesitatingly read 'dancing.'

His father laughed. 'You old humbug!' he said. 'I thought you said you could read.'

'But they *are* dancing,' the child protested.

'Yes, but that isn't what the word says. Try again.' He pointed.

Little Phil glanced again at the impossible word and took a long look at the picture. But the fox-trotting couple gave him no help. 'Dynamo,' he said at last in desperation. It was the only other word beginning with a D that he could think of at the moment.

'Or why not dinosaurus, while you're about it?' mocked his father. 'Or dolicocephalous? Or dicotyledon?' Little Phil was deeply offended; he could not bear to be laughed at. 'Try again. Try to *read* it this time. Don't guess.'

Little Phil turned his head away. 'It bores me,' he said. His vanity made him reluctant to attempt what he could not achieve successfully. Miss Fulkes, who believed in teaching by rational persuasion and with the reasoned consent of the taught (she was still very young), had lectured him on his own psychology, in the hope that, once he had realized his defects, he would mend them. 'You've got the wrong sort of pride,' she had told him. 'You're not ashamed of being a dunce and not knowing things. But you *are* ashamed of making mistakes. You'd rather not do a thing at all than do it badly. That's quite wrong.' Little Phil would nod his head and say 'Yes, Miss Fulkes' in the most rational and understanding way imaginable. But he continued to prefer doing things not at all to doing them with difficulty and badly. 'It bores me,' he repeated. 'But would you like me to make you a drawing?' he suggested, turning back to his father with a captivating smile. He was always ready to draw; he drew well.

'No thanks. I'd like you to read,' said Philip.

'But it bores me.'

'Never mind. You must try.'

'But I don't want to try.'

'But *I* want you to. Try.'

Little Phil burst into tears. Tears, he knew, were an irresistible weapon. And, sure enough, they proved their value yet once more.

Elinor looked up from where she was sitting, dissociated, book in hand, at the other end of the room. 'Don't make him cry,' she called. 'It's so bad for him.'

Philip shrugged his shoulders. 'If you imagine that's the way to educate a child …' he said with a bitterness that the occasion did not justify, a bitterness gradually accumulated during the past weeks of silence and distant hostility, of self-questioning and ineffective self-reproach, and finding now an almost irrelevant expression.

'I don't imagine anything,' said Elinor in a cold hard voice. 'I only know that I don't want him to cry.' Little Phil redoubled his noise. She called him to her and took him on to her knee.

'But seeing that he has the misfortune to be an only child, one really ought to make the effort not to spoil him.'

Elinor pressed her cheek against the boy's hair. 'Seeing that he is an only child,' she said, 'I don't see why he shouldn't be treated as one.'

'You're hopeless,' said Philip. 'It's high time we settled down, so that the boy can have a chance of being brought up rationally.'

'And who's going to do the rational upbringing?' asked Elinor. 'You?' She laughed sarcastically. 'At the end of a week you'd be so bored that you'd either commit suicide or take the first aeroplane to Paris and not come back for six months.'

'Naughty father!' put in the child.

Philip was offended, the more so as he was secretly aware that what she said was true. The ideal of a rustic domesticity, filled with small duties and casual human contacts, was one that, for him, precariously verged on absurdity. And though the idea of supervising little Phil's upbringing was interesting, he knew that the practice would be intolerably tedious. He remembered his own father's spasmodic essays at education. He'd be just the same. Which was precisely why Elinor had no business to say so.

'I'm not quite so childishly frivolous as you seem to imagine,' he said with dignity and bottled anger.

'On the contrary,' she answered, 'you're too adultly serious. You couldn't manage a child because you're not enough of a child yourself. You're like one of those dreadfully grown-up creatures in Shaw's *Methuselah*.'

'Naughty father!' repeated little Phil exasperatingly, like a parrot with only one phrase.

Philip's first impulse was to seize the child out of his mother's arms, smack him for his impertinence, drive him from the room and then turn on Elinor and violently 'have things out' with her. But a habit of gentlemanly self-control and a dread of scenes made him keep his temper. Instead of healthily breaking out he made an effort of will and more than ever tightly shut himself in. Preserving his dignity and his unexpressed grievance, he got up and walked through the French window into the garden. Elinor watched his departure. Her impulse was to run after him, take him by the hand and make peace. But she too checked herself. Philip limped away out of sight. The child continued to whimper. Elinor gave him a little shake.

'Stop, Phil,' she said almost angrily. 'That's enough now. Stop at once.'

*

The two doctors were examining what to an untrained eye might have seemed the photograph of a typhoon in the Gulf of Siam, of an explosion of black smoke in the midst of clouds, or merely of an ink stain.

'Particularly clear,' said the young radiographer. 'Look.' He pointed at the smoke cloud. 'There's a most obvious new growth there, at the pylorus.' He glanced with a certain inquiring deference at his distinguished colleague.

Sir Herbert nodded. 'Obvious,' he repeated. He had an oracular manner; what he said, you felt, was always and necessarily true.

'It couldn't very well be large. Not with the symptoms so far recorded. There's been no vomiting yet.'

'No vomiting?' exclaimed the radiographer with an almost excessive display of interest and astonishment. 'That would explain the smallness.'

'The obstruction's only slight.'

'It would certainly be worth opening up the abdomen for exploration purposes.'

Sir Herbert made a little pouting grimace and dubiously shook his head. 'One has to think of the patient's age.'

'Quite,' the radiographer made haste to agree.

'He's older than he seems.'

'Yes, yes. He certainly doesn't look his age.'

'Well, I must be going,' said Sir Herbert.

The young radiographer darted to the door, handed him his hat and gloves, personally escorted him to the attendant Daimler. Returning to his desk he glanced again at the black-blotched, grey-cloudy photograph.

'A really remarkably successful exposure,' he said to himself with satisfaction and, turning the picture over, he wrote a few words in pencil on the back.

'J. Bidlake, Esq. Stomach after barium meal. New growth at pylorus, small but v. clear. Photographed. ...' He looked up at his calendar for the date, recorded it and put the photograph away in his file for future reference.

*

The old manservant announced the visitor and retired, closing the door of the studio behind him.

'Well, John,' said Lady Edward, advancing across the room. 'How are you? I heard you'd been seedy. Nothing serious, I hope.'

John Bidlake did not even get up to receive her. From the depth of the arm-chair in which he had spent the day meditating in terror the themes of disease and death, he held out a hand.

'But, my poor John!' exclaimed Lady Edward sitting down beside him. 'You look very low and wretched. What is it?'

John Bidlake shook his head. 'God knows,' he said. He had guessed, of course, from Sir Herbert's vaguely professional words about 'slight obstructions in the neighbourhood of the pylorus,' he *knew* what was the matter. Hadn't his son Maurice died of the same thing five years ago, in California? He knew; but he would not speak his knowledge. Uttered, the worst was more frightful, more irrevocable. Besides, one should never formulate one's knowledge of coming evil; for then fate would have, so to speak, a model on which to shape events. There was always a kind of impossible chance that, if one didn't put one's foreboding of evil into words, the evil wouldn't happen. The mysteries of John Bidlake's personal religion were quite as obscure and paradoxical as any of those in the 'theolatrous' orthodoxies which he liked to deride.

'But haven't you seen a doctor?' Lady Edward's tone was accusatory; she knew her friend's strange prejudice against doctors.

'Of course I have,' he answered irritably, knowing that she knew. 'Do you take me for a fool? But they're all charlatans. I went to one with a knighthood. But do you suppose he knew anything more than the others? He just told me in quick jargon what I'd told him in plain words; that I'd got something wrong with my innards. Stupid rogue!' His hatred of Sir Herbert and all doctors had momentarily revived him.

'But he must have told you something,' Lady Edward insisted.

The words brought him back to the thought of that 'slight obstruction in the neighbourhood of the pylorus,' of disease and pain and the creeping approach of death. He relapsed into his old misery and terror. 'Nothing of significance,' he muttered, averting his face.

'Then perhaps it's nothing really serious,' Lady Edward comfortingly suggested.

'No, no!' To the old man her light-hearted hopefulness seemed an outrage. He would not put himself into the power of fate by formulating the horrible truth. But at the same time he wanted to be treated as though the truth had been formulated. Treated with a grave commiseration. 'It's bad. It's very bad,' he insisted.

He was thinking of death; death in the form of a new life growing and growing in his belly, like an embryo in a womb. The one thing fresh and active in his old body, the one thing exuberantly and increasingly alive was death.

All round, on the walls of the studio, hung fragmentary records of John Bidlake's life. Two little landscapes painted in the Pincian Gardens in the days when Rome had only just ceased to be the Pope's – a view of belfries and cupolas seen through a gap in the ilex trees, a pair of statues silhouetted against the sky. Next to them a satyr's face, snubby and bearded – the portrait of Verlaine. A London street scene, full of hansoms and top hats and lifted skirts. Three sketches of the plump, bright-coloured Mary Betterton of thirty years ago. And Jenny, loveliest of models, lying naked on a long chair, with a window behind her, white clouds beyond, a bowl of roses on the window-sill and a great blue Persian cat stretched like a couchant lion, on Jenny's white belly, dozing, its paws between her round and shallow breasts.

Lady Edward brightly changed the subject. 'Lucy's just flown off to Paris again,' she began.

Chapter Twenty-five

THE air was rough, I forgot the *Quies* for my ears and was in a Hell of Noise for 2½ hours. Feeling very tired and consequently, sweet Walter, rather sentimental and *sola sola*. Why aren't you here to console me for the unbearable sadness of this lovely evening outside my window? The Louvre, the river, the green glass sky, the sunlight and those velvet shadows – they make me feel like bursting into tears. And not the scenery only. My arms in the sleeves of my dressing-gown, my hand writing, even my bare toes, now that I've dropped my slippers – terrible, terrible. And as for my face in the glass, and my shoulders, and the orange roses and the Chinese goldfish to match, and the Dufy curtains and all the rest – yes, *all*, because everything's equally beautiful and extraordinary, even the things that are dull and ugly – they're too much to be borne. Too much. I can't stand it and what's more, I won't. Interval of 5 minutes. That's why I've telephoned to René Tallemant to come and have a cocktail and take me out somewhere amusing, malgré my headache. I simply won't let myself be bullied by the universe. Do you know René? Rather a divine little man. But I wish it were you, all the same. Must go and put on a few clothes. A toi. LUCY.

Your letter was tiresome. Such yammering. And it isn't flattering to be called a poison in the blood. It's the equivalent of being called a stomach-ache. If you can't write more sensibly, don't write at all. Quant à moi, je m'amuse. Pas follement. But sufficiently, sufficiently. Theatres; mostly bad; but I like them; I'm still childish enough to feel involved in the imbecile plots. And buying clothes; such ravishments! I simply adored myself in Lanvin's looking-glasses. Looking at pictures, on the other hand, is an overrated sport. Not dancing, though. There'd be some point, if life were always like dancing with a professional. But it ain't. And if it were, I dare say one would long to walk. In the evenings a little pub-crawling in Mont Parnasse through hordes of Americans, Poles, Esthonians, Rumanians, Finns, Letts, Lapps, Wends, etcetera, and all of them (God help us!) artists. Shall we found a league for the suppression of art? Paris makes me long to. Also I wish one met a few more heterosexuals for a change. I don't really like ni les tapettes ni les gousses. And since Proust and Gide made them fashionable one sees nothing else

316

n this tiresome town. All my English respectability breaks out!
Yours, L.

This time your letter was much better. (My only poem, and an accident at that. Rather good, all the same.) If only everybody would realize that being miserable or jolly about love is chiefly a matter of fashion. Being poetically miserable is an old fashion, and besides, the rhymes don't justify it in English. Cuore-dolore-amore; you can't escape it in Italian. Nor in German; herz must feel schmerz and liebe is inevitably full of triebe. But in English, no. There's no pain connected with English loves; only gloves and turtle doves. And the only things that, by the laws of poetry, can go straight to Englishmen's hearts are tarts and amorous arts. And I assure you, a man's much better occupied when he's thinking about those subjects than when he's telling himself how wretched he is, how jealous, how cruelly wronged and all the nonsensical rest of it. I wish that idiot René would understand this. But unfortunately cœur rhymes with douleur, and he's French. He's becoming almost as much of a bore as you were, my poor Walter. But I hope you're now a reformed character. I like you. L.

Suffering from a cold and intense boredom, only momentarily relieved by your letter. Paris is really terribly dreary. I have a good mind to fly away somewhere else, only I don't know where. Eileen came to see me to-day. She wants to leave Tim, because he will insist on her lying naked in bed while he sets fire to newspapers over her and lets the hot ashes fall on her body. Poor Tim! It seems unkind to deprive him of his simple pleasures. But Eileen's so nervous of being grilled. She was furious with me for laughing and not being more sympathetic. I took it all as a joke. Which it is. A very mild one, however. For really, like the Queen, we are not amused. How I hate you for not being here to entertain me! One can forgive anything except absence. Unpardonably absent Walter, goodbye. I have an *envie* for you to-night, for your hands and your mouth. And you? Do you remember? L.

So Philip Quarles is going to settle in the country and be a mixture of Mrs Gaskell and Knud Hamsun. Well, well. ... But it's good that somebody should have illusions. At any rate he can't be more bored

317

in his village than I am here. What straits one's reduced to! Last nigh
I went with Tim and Eileen, who seems to be reconciled to the fire
work displays, to one of those places where you pay a hundred franc
for the privilege of looking on at orgies (in masks – the one amusin
feature) and if you want to, participating in them. Dim religiou
lights, little cubicles, divans, a great deal of what the French cal
amour promiscuously going on. Odd and grotesque, but terribl
dreary and all so very *medical*. A sort of cross between very stupi
clowns and an operating theatre. Tim and Eileen wanted me to stay
I told them I'd rather pay a visit to the Morgue, and left them there
I hope they amused themselves. But what a *bore*, what a hopeles
unmitigated *bore*! I always thought Heliogabalus was such a ver
sophisticated young person. But now I've seen what amused him
I realize that he must have had a mind like a baby's, really infantile
I have the misfortune to be rather grown up about some things
I've a notion of going to Madrid next week. It'll be terrifically ho
of course. But I love the heat. I blossom in ovens. (Rather a signi
ficant imitation of my particular immortality, perhaps?) Why don'
you come with me? Seriously, I mean. You could surely get away
Murder Burlap and come and be a tripper *à la* Maurice Barrè
Du sang, de la volupté et de la mort. I feel rather bloodthirsty a
the moment. Spain would suit me. Meanwhile, I'll make inquirie
about the bull-fighting season. The ring makes you sick; even m
bloodthirstiness won't run to disembowelled cab-horses. But th
spectators are marvellous. Twenty thousand simultaneous sadisti
frissons. Really remarkable. You simply must come, my swee
Walter. Say yes. I insist. LUCY.

QUAI VOLTAIRE

It was too sweet of you, Walter darling, to do the impossible to com
to Spain. I wish, for once, you hadn't taken my momentary *env*
quite so seriously. Madrid's off – for the present, at any rate. If *i*
should come on again, I'll let you know at once. Meanwhile, Paris
Hastily. L.

Chapter Twenty-six

Found Rampion gloomy and exasperated, I don't know what about, and consequently pessimistic – lyrically and violently so. 'I give the present dispensation ten years,' he said, after cataloguing the horrors of the modern world. 'After that the most appalling and sanguinary bust up that's ever been.' And he prophesied class wars, wars between the continents, the final catastrophic crumbling of our already dreadfully unsteady society. 'Not a pleasant look-out for our children,' I said. 'We've at least had our thirty years or so. They'll only grow up to see the Last Judgement.' 'We oughtn't to have brought them into the world,' he answered. I mentioned those Melanesians that Rivers wrote about, who simply refused to breed any more after the white people had robbed them of their religion and their traditional civilization. 'The same thing's been happening in the West,' I said, 'but more slowly. No sudden race suicide, but gradual diminution of births. Gradual, because with us the poison of modern civilization has infected men so slowly. The thing has been going on for a long time; but we're only just beginning to realize that we're being poisoned. That's why we've only just begun to stop begetting children. The Melanesians had their souls suddenly murdered, so they couldn't help realizing what was being done to them. That's why they decided, almost from one day to another, that they wouldn't bother to keep the race alive any longer.' 'The poison isn't slow any more. It works faster and faster.' 'Like arsenic – the effects are cumulative. After a certain moment you begin to gallop towards death.' 'Breeding would have slowed down much more completely if people had realized. Well, well; our brats will have to look out for themselves now they're here.' 'And meanwhile,' I said, 'one's got to go on behaving as if our world were going on for ever – teaching them good manners and Latin grammar and all the rest. What do you do about yours?' 'If I could have my way, I wouldn't teach them anything. Just turn them loose in the country, on a farm, and tell them to amuse themselves. And if they couldn't amuse themselves, I'd give them rat poison.' 'Rather Utopian as an educational programme, isn't it?' 'I know. They've got to be scholars and gentlemen, damn them! Twenty years ago, I'd have objected to the gentility. I'd have brought them up as peasants. But the working classes are just as bad as the others nowadays. Just rather bad imitations of the bourgeoisie, a little worse than the original in some ways. So it's as gentlemen my boys are being brought up after all. *And* scholars. What an imbecility!' He complained to me that both his children have a passion for machinery – motor cars, trains, aeroplanes, radios. 'It's an infection, like smallpox. The love of death's in the air. They breathe it and get infected. I try to persuade them to like something else. But they won't have it. Machinery's the only thing for them. They're infected with the love of death. It's as though the young were absolutely determined to bring the world to an end – mechanize it first into madness, then into sheer murder. Well, let them if they want to, the stupid little devils! But it's humiliating, it's horribly humiliating that human beings should have made such a devilish mess of things. Life could have been so beautiful, if they'd cared to make it so. Yes, and it *was* beautiful once, I believe. Now it's just an insanity; it's just death violently galvanized, twitching about and making a hellish hullabaloo to persuade itself that it isn't really death, but the most exuberant sort of life. Think of New York, for example; think of Berlin! God! Well, let them go to hell if they want to. I don't care.' But the trouble is that he does care.

*

Since reading Alverdes and Wheeler I have quite decided that my novelist must be an amateur zoologist. Or, better still, a professional zoologist who is writing a novel in his spare time. His approach will be strictly biological. He will be constantly passing from the termitary to the drawing-room and the factory, and back again. He will illustrate human vices by those of the ants, which neglect their young for the sake of the intoxicating liquor exuded by the parasites that invade their nests. His hero and heroine will spend their honeymoon by a lake, where the grebes and ducks illustrate all the aspects of courtship and matrimony. Observing the habitual and almost sacred 'pecking order' which prevails among the hens in his poultry yard – hen A pecking hen B, but not being pecked by it, hen B pecking hen C and so forth – the politician will meditate on the Catholic hierarchy and Fascism. The mass of intricately copulating snakes will remind the libertine of his orgies. (I can visualize quite a good scene with a kind of Spandrell drawing the moral, to an innocent and idealistic young woman, of a serpents' petting party.) Nationalism and the middle classes' religious love of property will be illustrated by the male warbler's passionate and ferocious defence of his chosen territory. And so on. Something queer and quite amusing could be made out of this.

*

One of the hardest things to remember is that a man's merit in one sphere is no guarantee of his merit in another. Newton's mathematics don't prove his theology. Faraday was right about electricity, but not about Sandemanianism. Plato wrote marvellously well, and that's why people still go on believing in his pernicious philosophy. Tolstoy was an excellent novelist; but that's no reason for regarding his ideas about morality as anything but detestable, or for feeling anything but contempt for his aesthetics, his sociology, and his religion. In the case of scientists and philosophers this ineptitude outside their own line of business isn't surprising. Indeed, it's almost inevitable. For it's obvious that excessive development of the purely mental functions leads to atrophy of all the rest. Hence the notorious infantility of professors and the ludicrous simplicity of the solutions they offer for the problems of life. The same is true of the specialists in spirituality. The profound silliness of saintly people; their childishness. But in an artist there's less specialization, less one-sided development; consequently the artist ought to be sounder right through than the lop-sided man of science; he oughtn't to have the blind spots and the imbecilities of the philosophers and saints. That's why a man like Tolstoy is so specially unforgivable. Instinctively you trust him more than you would trust an intellectual or a spiritual specialist. And there he goes perverting all his deepest instincts and being just as idiotic and pernicious as St Francis of Assisi, or as Kant the moralist (oh, those categorical imperatives! and then the fact that the only thing the old gentleman felt at all deeply about was crystallized fruit!), or Newton the theologian. It puts one on one's guard, even against those one thinks are probably in the right. Such as Rampion, for example. An extraordinary artist. But right in his views about the world? Alas, it doesn't follow from the excellence of his painting and writing. But two things give me confidence in his opinions about the problems of living. The first is that he himself lives in a more satisfactory way than anyone I know. He lives more satisfactorily, because he lives more realistically than other people. Rampion, it seems to me, takes into account all the facts (whereas other people hide from them, or try to pretend that the ones they find unpleasant don't or shouldn't exist), and then proceeds to make his way of living fit the facts, and doesn't try to compel the facts to fit in with a preconceived idea of the right way of living (like these imbecile Christians and intellectuals and moralists and efficient business men). The second thing which gives me confidence in his judgement is that so many of his opinions agree with mine, which, apart from all questions of vanity, is a good sign, because we start from such distant points, from opposite poles in fact. Opinions on which two opponents agree (for that's what essentially, and to start with, we are: opponents) have a fair chance of being right. The chief difference between us, alas, is that his opinions are lived and mine, in the main, only thought. Like him, I mistrust intellectualism, but intellectually I disbelieve in the adequacy of any scientific or philosophical theory, any abstract moral principle, but on scientific, philosophical, and abstract-moral grounds. The problem for me is to transform a detached intellectual scepticism into a way of harmonious all-round living.

The course of every intellectual, if he pursues his journey long and unflinchingly enough, ends in the obvious, from which the non-intellectuals have never stirred. The theme was developed by Burlap in one of those squelchy emetic articles of his. And there's a good deal of truth in it, in spite of Burlap. (Here we are, back again among the personalities. The thoroughly contemptible man may have valuable opinions, just as the in some ways admirable man can have detestable opinions. And I suppose, parenthetically, that I belong to the first class – though not so completely, I hope, as Burlap and in a differen way.) Many intellectuals, of course, don't get far enough to reach the obvious again. They remain stuck in a pathetic belief in rationalism and the absolute supremacy of mental values and the entirely conscious will. You've got to go further than the nineteenth-century fellows, for example; as far at least as Protagoras and Pyrrho, before you get back to the obvious in which the non-intellectuals have always remained. And one must hasten to make it clear that these non-intellectuals aren't the modern canaille who read the picture papers and listen-in and jazz and are preoccupied with making money and having the awful modern 'good time.' No, no; one isn't paying a compliment to the hard-headed business man or the low-brow. For, in spite of their stupidity and tastelessness and vulgarity and infantility (or rather because of all these defects), they aren't the non-intellectuals I'm talking about. They take the main intellectualist axiom for granted – that there's an intrinsic superiority in mental, conscious, voluntary life over physical, intuitive, instinctive, emotional life.

The whole of modern civilization is based on the idea that the specialized function which gives a man his place in society is more important than the whole man, or rather *is* the whole man, all the rest being irrelevant or even (since the physical, intuitive, instinctive, and emotional part of man doesn't contribute appreciably to making money or getting on in an industrialized world) positively harmful and detestable. The low-brow of our modern industrialized society has all the defects of the intellectual and none of his redeeming qualities. The non-intellectuals I'm thinking of are very different beings. One might still find a few of them in Italy (though Fascism has probably turned them all into bad imitations of Americans and Prussians by this time); a few perhaps in Spain, in Greece, in Provence. Not elsewhere in modern Europe. There were probably quite a lot of them three thousand years ago. But the combined efforts of Plato and Aristotle, Jesus, Newton, and big business have turned their descendants into the modern bourgeoisie and proletariat. The obvious that the intellectual gets back to, if he goes far enough, isn't of course the same as the obvious of the non-intellectuals. For their obvious is life itself and his recovered obvious is only the idea of that life. Not many can put flesh and blood on the idea and turn it into reality. The intellectuals who, like Rampion, don't have to return to the obvious, but have always believed in it and lived it, while at the same time leading the life of the spirit, are rarer still.

Being with Rampion rather depresses me; for he makes me see what a great gulf separates the knowledge of the obvious from the actual living of it. And oh, the difficulties of crossing that gulf! I perceive now that the real charm of the intellectual life – the life devoted to erudition, to scientific research, to philosophy, to aesthetics, to criticism – is its easiness. It's the substitution of simple intellectual schemata for the complexities of reality; of still and formal death for the bewildering movements of life. It's incomparably easier to know a lot, say, about the history of art and to have profound ideas about metaphysics and sociology, than to know personally and intuitively a lot about one's fellows and to have satisfactory relations with one's friends and lovers, one's wife and children. Living's much more difficult than Sanskrit or chemistry or economics. The intellectual life is child's play; which is why intellectuals tend to become children – and then imbeciles and finally, as the political and industrial history of the last few centuries clearly demonstrates, homicidal lunatics and wild beasts. The repressed functions don't die; they

323

deteriorate, they fester, they revert to primitiveness. But meanwhile it's much easier to be an intellectual child or lunatic or beast than a harmonious adult man. That's why (among other reasons) there's such a demand for higher education. The rush to books and universities is like the rush to the public-house. People want to drown their realization of the difficulties of living properly in this grotesque contemporary world, they want to forget their own deplorable inefficiency as artists in life. Some drown their sorrows in alcohol, but still more drown them in books and artistic dilettantism; some try to forget themselves in fornication, dancing, movies, listening-in, others in lectures and scientific hobbies. The books and lectures are better sorrow-drowners than drink and fornication; they leave no headache, none of that despairing *post coitum triste* feeling. Till quite recently, I must confess, I took learning and philosophy and science – all the activities that are magniloquently lumped under the title of 'The Search for Truth' – very seriously. I regarded the Search for Truth as the highest of human tasks and the Searchers as the noblest of men. But in the last year or so I have begun to see that this famous Search for Truth is just an amusement, a distraction like any other, a rather refined and elaborate substitute for genuine living; and that Truth-Searchers become just as silly, infantile, and corrupt in their way as the boozers, the pure aesthetes, the business men, the Good-Timers in theirs. I also perceived that the pursuit of Truth is just a polite name for the intellectual's favourite pastime of substituting simple and therefore false abstractions for the living complexities of reality. But seeking Truth is much easier than learning the art of integral living (in which, of course, Truth-Seeking will take its due and proportionate place along with the other amusements, like skittles and mountain-climbing). Which explains, though it doesn't justify, my continued and excessive indulgence in the vices of informative reading and abstract generalization. Shall I ever have the strength of mind to break myself of these indolent habits of intellectualism and devote my energies to the more serious and difficult task of living integrally? And even if I did try to break these habits, shouldn't I find that heredity was at the bottom of them and that I was congenitally incapable of living wholly and harmoniously?

Chapter Twenty-seven

JOHN BIDLAKE and his third wife had never definitely or officially parted company. They simply didn't see one another very often, that was all. The arrangement suited John very well. He hated everything in the nature of a fuss, and he was the enemy of every definite and irrevocable contract. Any arrangement that bound him down, that imposed responsibilities and kept him in mind of duties, was intolerable to him. 'God knows what I should have done,' he used to say, 'if I'd had to go to an office every day, or get work done by a certain date. I think I should have run amok after a few months of it.' Of marriage he had always consistently disapproved. Unfortunately, however, he could not have all the women he wanted without marriage. He had had to enter into no less than three of what he called, in Ciceronian language, 'those inopportune and obscene compacts.' The idea of divorce or an official separation was hardly less disagreeable to him than that of marriage; it was too definite, it committed you. Why not leave things to settle themselves, instead of trying to give an arbitrary shape to them? The ideal was to live, emotionally and socially speaking, from hand to mouth – without plans, without a status, in good company of one's own daily choosing, not the choosing of others or of some dead self. 'Sleeping around' – that was how he had heard a young American girl describe the amorous side of the ideal life, as lived in Hollywood. Its other aspects might be lumped under the head of 'waking around.' The unideal life, the life which John Bidlake had always refused to lead, was that which consisted of waking and sleeping not 'around,' but definitely here or there, day after day, according to a fixed foreseeable schedule that only death, or at the least the act of God or the king's enemies, could alter.

With his third wife John Bidlake's relations were, and had been for years, most satisfyingly indefinite. They did not live together, but they were not separated. They rarely communicated, but they had never quarrelled. John had been sleeping and waking 'around' for upwards of twenty years, and yet they met, whenever they *did* meet, on friendly terms; and if ever he desired to refresh his memories of the landscape of the northern Chilterns, his arrival at Gattenden was accepted without comment, as though it were the most natural thing in the world. The arrangement entirely suited John Bidlake; and, to do him justice, he was grateful to his wife for making it possible. He refrained, however, from expressing his gratitude; for to have done so would have been to comment on the arrangement; and a comment would have brought a touch of destructive definition into a situation whose fragile excellence consisted precisely in its virgin and beautifully unsullied vagueness. Few women, as her husband gratefully recognized, would have been willing or even able to preserve the indefiniteness of the situation so chronically inviolate as Janet Bidlake. Another wife would have demanded explanations, would have wanted to know where she stood, would have offered the irrevocable choice of peace or war, life in common or separation. But Mrs Bidlake had permitted her husband to fade out of their married life without a quarrel, with hardly a word. And his brief spasmodic re-entries were accepted by her with as little comment. She had been from childhood more at home in the fictitious world of her invention than in the real. As a little girl she had had an imaginary sister who lived in the signal-box by the level crossing. Between the ages of ten and thirteen, her inability to distinguish between the testimony of her senses and that of her fancy had often resulted in her being punished for lying. Pictures and books gave a new turn to her imagining, which became less personal and more classically artistic, literary, and speculative. From sixteen onwards she was an inhabitant of the country of art and letters and was little more than a reluctant stranger in mere England. It was because she had imagined John Bidlake a spiritual compatriot that she had fallen in love with him – artistically, poetically in love – and consented to become his wife. Her parents, who considered him only as a fellow-subject of the Queen and attached more importance, in the circumstances, to his career as a husband than as an artist, did their best to dissuade her. But Janet was of age and had the obstinacy of those who can simply retire from the plane on which the argument is taking place, leaving the opponent to waste his energy on a mere untenanted body. She ended by doing what she wanted. When she discovered, as she discovered only too soon, that there was very little connexion between the admirable artist she had loved and the husband she had married, Janet Bidlake was restrained by a very natural pride from complaining. She had no wish to give her relations the pleasure of saying, 'I told you so.' John slept and woke 'around,' faded more and more completely out of conjugality. She held her peace and herself retired for consolation into those regions of artistic and literary fancy, where she was native and felt most at home. A private income, supplemented by the irregular and fluctuating contributions which John Bidlake made whenever he remembered or felt he could afford to support a wife and family, allowed her to make a habit of this foreign travel of the imagination. Elinor was born a year after their marriage. Four years later an ulcerated stomach brought John Bidlake home, a temporarily reformed character, to be nursed. Walter was the result of his still domestic convalescence. The ulcers healed, John Bidlake faded away again. Nurses and governesses looked after the children. Mrs Bidlake superintended their upbringing dimly and as though from a distance. From time to time she swooped across the border dividing her private country from the world of common fact; and her interferences with the quotidian order of things had always a certain disconcerting and almost supernatural quality. Incalculable things were liable to happen whenever she descended, a being from another plane and judging events by other standards than those of the common world, into the midst of the children's educational routine. Once, for example, she dismissed a governess because she had heard her playing Dan Leno's song about the Wasp and the Hard-boiled Egg on the schoolroom piano. She was a good girl, taught well and supported a paralytic father. But great artistic principles were at stake. Elinor's musical taste might be irretrievably ruined (incidentally Elinor resembled her father in detesting music); and the fact that she was very fond of Miss Dempster made the danger of contamination even greater. Mrs Bidlake was firm. 'The Wasp and the Hard-boiled Egg' could not be permitted. Miss Dempster was sent away. When he heard the news, her old father had another stroke and was picked up blind in one eye and unable to speak. But Mrs Bidlake's returns from imaginative travel were generally less serious in their results. When she interfered with the practical business of her children's upbringing, it was usually only to insist that they should read classical authors usually considered incomprehensible or unsuitable for the very young. Children, it was her theory, should be brought up only with the very best in the way of philosophy and the arts. Elinor had had *Hamlet* read to her when she was three, her picture-books were reproductions of Giotto and Rubens. She had been taught French out of *Candide*, had been given *Tristram Shandy* and Bishop Berkeley's *Theory of Vision* when she was seven, Spinoza's *Ethics*, Goya's etchings and, as a German text-book, *Also sprach Zarathustra* when she was nine. The result of this premature introduction to the best philosophy was to produce in Elinor that slightly amused contempt for the grand abstractions and high-faluting idealisms, which had come to be so characteristic of her. Brought up at the same time on the unexpurgated classics, she had acquired in childhood a complete theoretical knowledge of all those matters which it is thought least suitable for the young to know. This knowledge had reinforced rather than tempered the coldness and practical incuriosity about all amorous matters which were natural to her; and she had grown up in a state of well-informed and super-ficially cynical innocence, like one of those Shakespearean heroines, whose scientific and Rabelaisian speech accompanies actions of the most delicately virtuous refinement. Mrs Bidlake was a little dis-tressed by Elinor's irreverent attitude towards her cherished fancies; but, wise in her way, she did not comment, did not try to reform, only ignored and retired, as she had ignored her husband's shortcomings, had retired from the realization of them into the happier realms of art and imagination. There can be no cancellation of accomplished facts; but for practical purposes a conspiracy of silence is almost as effective as cancellation. Unmentioned, what is can become as though it were not. When John Bidlake arrived at Gattenden, a sick man made sicker by dejection, terror, and an all-absorbing self-pity, Mrs Bidlake passed over in silence the fact, upon which she might so easily have commented: that he only came to her when he needed a nurse. His room was made ready, he settled in. It was as though he had never been away. In the privacy of the kitchen the housemaids grumbled a little at the extra work, while Mrs Inman sighed and Dobbs was massively and Anglicanly indignant over old Mr Bidlake's treatment of his wife. At the same time all felt a kind of gloating pity for the old man. His disease and its symptoms were talked of in lowered voices, religiously. Aloud, the servants might grumble and disapprove. But secretly they were all rather pleased. John Bidlake's arrival broke the daily monotony, and the fact that he was going to die made them all feel somehow more important. To the domesticities of Gattenden his approaching death gave a new significance. That future event was the sun round which the souls of the household now meaningfully and almost stealthily revolved. They might grumble and disapprove, but they looked after him solicitously. In an obscure way they were grateful to him. Dying, he was quickening their life.

Chapter Twenty-eight

WITH Molly d'Exergillod everything had to be articulate, formulated, expressed. The whole of experience was, for her, only the raw material out of which an active mind could manufacture words. Ironstone was of no use to man until he learnt to smelt it and hammer out the pure metal into tools and swords. For Molly, the raw facts of living, the sensations, the feelings, the thoughts and recollections, were as uninteresting in themselves as so many lumps of rock. They were of value only when they had been transformed by conversational art and industry into elegant words and well-shaped phrases. She loved a sunset because she could say of it: 'It's like a mixture of Bengal lights, Mendelssohn, soot, and strawberries and cream'; or of spring flowers: 'They make you feel as you feel when you're convalescent after influenza. Don't you think so?' And leaning intimately she would press the rhetorical question. 'Don't you think so?' What she liked about a view of distant mountains in a thunderstorm was that it was so like El Greco's landscapes of Toledo. As for love, why, the whole charm of love, in Molly's eyes, was its almost infinite capacity for being turned into phrases. You could talk about it for ever.

She was talking about it now to Philip Quarles – had been talking about it for the last hour; analysing herself, recounting her experiences, questioning him about his past and his feelings. Reluctantly and with difficulty (for he hated talking about himself and did it very badly) he answered her.

'Don't you think,' she was saying, 'that the most exciting thing about being in love is the discoveries it enables you to make about yourself?'

Philip duly thought so.

'I'd no idea how motherly I really was, before I married Jean. I'm so preoccupied now when he gets his feet wet.'

'I'd be very worried if you got your feet wet,' said Philip essaying a gallantry. Too stupid! he thought. He was not very good at gallantries. He wished he wasn't so much attracted by Molly's rather creamy and florid beauty. He wouldn't be here making a fool of himself if she were ugly.

'Too sweet of you,' said Molly. 'Tell me,' she added, leaning towards him with offered face and bosom, 'why do you like me?'

'Isn't it fairly obvious why?'

Molly smiled. 'Do you know why Jean says I'm the only woman he could ever fall in love with?'

'No,' said Philip, thinking that she was really superb in her Junonian way.

'Because,' Molly went on, 'according to him, I'm the only woman who isn't what Baudelaire calls *le contraire du dandy*. You remember that fragment in *Mon Cœur Mis à Nu*? "La femme a faim et elle veut manger; soif, et elle veut boire. La femme est *naturelle*, c'est-à-dire abominable. Aussi est-elle ..." '

Philip interrupted her. 'You've left out a sentence,' he said, laughing. 'Soif, et elle veut boire. And then: Elle est en rut, et elle veut être ... They don't print the word in Crépet's edition; but I'll supply it if you like.'

'No, thanks,' said Molly, rather put out by the interruption. It had spoilt the easy unfolding of a well-tried conversational gambit. She wasn't accustomed to people being so well up in French literature as Philip. 'The word's irrelevant.'

'Is it?' Philip raised his eyebrows. 'I wonder.'

'Aussi est-elle toujours vulgaire,' Molly went on, hurrying back to the point at which she had been interrupted, 'c'est-à-dire le contraire du dandy. Jean says I'm the only female dandy. What do you think?'

'I'm afraid he's right.'

'Why "afraid"?'

'I don't know that I like dandies much. Particularly female ones. A woman who uses the shapeliness of her breasts to compel you to admire her mind – a good character, he reflected, for his novel. But trying in private life, very trying indeed. 'I prefer them natural,' he added.

'But what's the point of being natural unless you have enough art to do it well and enough consciousness to know how natural you're being?' Molly was pleased with her question. A little polishing and it would be epigrammatically perfect. 'There's no point in being in love with a person unless you know exactly what you feel and can express it.'

'I can see a great deal of point,' said Philip. 'One doesn't have to be a botanist or a still-life painter to enjoy flowers. And equally, my dear Molly, one doesn't have to be Sigmund Freud or Shakespeare to enjoy you.' And sliding suddenly nearer to her along the sofa, he took her in his arms and kissed her.

'But what *are* you thinking about?' she cried in pained astonishment.

'I'm not thinking about anything,' he answered rather angrily from the other end of the arm with which she had pushed him away from her. 'Not thinking; only wanting.' He felt humiliated, made a fool of. 'But I'd forgotten you were a nun.'

'I'm nothing of the kind,' she protested. 'I'm merely civilized. All this pouncing and clawing – it's really too savage.' She readjusted a water-waved lock of hair, and began to talk about platonic relationships as aids to spiritual growth. The more platonic the relations between an amorous man and woman, the more intense in them the life of the conscious mind.

'What the body loses, the soul gains. Wasn't it Paul Bourget who pointed that out in his *Psychologie contemporaine*? A bad novelist,' she added, finding it necessary to apologize for quoting from so very old-fashioned and disreputed an author; 'but good as an essayist, I always find. Wasn't it Paul Bourget?' she repeated.

'I should think it must have been Paul Bourget,' said Philip wearily.

'The energy which wanted to expend itself in physical passion is diverted and turns the mills of the soul.' ('Turn the mills of the soul' was perhaps a shade too romantic, Victorian, Meredithian, she felt as she pronounced the words.) 'The body's dammed and canalized,' she emended, 'and made to drive the spiritual dynamos. The thwarted unconscious finds vent in making consciousness more intense.'

'But does one want one's consciousness intensified?' asked Philip, looking angrily at the rather luscious figure at the other end of the sofa. 'I'm getting a bit tired of consciousness, to tell you the truth.' He admired her body, but the only contact she would permit was with her much less interesting and beautiful mind. He wanted kisses, but all he got was analytical anecdotes and philosophic epigrams. 'Thoroughly tired,' he repeated. It was no wonder.

Molly only laughed. 'Don't start pretending you're a paleolithic cave-man,' she said. 'It doesn't suit you. Tired of consciousness, indeed! *You!* Why, if you're tired of consciousness, you must be tired of yourself.'

'Which is exactly what I am,' said Philip. 'You've made me tired of myself. Sick to death.' Still irritated, he rose to take his leave.

'Is that an insult?' she asked, looking up at him. 'Why have I made you tired of yourself?'

Philip shook his head. 'I can't explain. I've given up explaining.' He held out his hand. Still looking inquiringly into his face, Molly took it. 'If you weren't one of the vestal virgins of civilization,' he went on, 'you'd understand without any explaining. Or rather, there wouldn't be any explaining to do. Because you wouldn't have made me feel tired of myself. And let me add, Molly, that if you were really and consistently civilized, you'd take steps to make yourself less desirable. Desirability's barbarous. It's as savage as pouncing and clawing. You ought to look like George Eliot. Good-bye.' And giving her hand a final shake, he limped out of the room. In the street he gradually recovered his temper. He even began to smile to himself. For it was a joke. The spectacle of a biter being bitten is always funny, even when the bitten biter happens to be oneself. Conscious and civilized, he had been defeated by someone even more civilized than himself. The justice was poetic. But what a warning! Parodies and caricatures are the most penetrating of criticisms. In Molly he perceived a kind of Max Beerbohm version of himself. The spectacle was alarming. Having smiled, he became pensive.

'I must be pretty awful,' he thought.

Sitting on a chair in the Park, he considered his shortcomings. He had considered them before, often. But he had never done anything about them. He knew in advance that he wouldn't do anything about them this time. Poor Elinor! That rigmarole of Molly's about platonic relations and Paul Bourget gave him a notion of what she had to put up with. He decided to tell her of his adventure with Molly – comically, for it was always easier to talk unseriously – and then go on to talk about themselves. Yes, that was what he'd do. He ought to have spoken before. Elinor had been so strangely and unnaturally silent of late, so far away. He had been anxious, had wanted to speak, had felt he ought to have spoken. But about what? The ridiculous episode with Molly provided him with an opening gambit.

'I saw Molly d'Exergillod this afternoon,' he began, when he saw Elinor. But the tone of her 'Did you?' was so coldly uninterested, that he went no further. There was a silence. Elinor went on with her reading. He glanced at her surreptitiously over the top of his book. Her pale face wore an expression of calm remoteness. He felt a renewal of that uneasy anxiety which had come upon him so often during the last few weeks.

'Why don't you ever talk now?' he screwed up the courage to ask her that evening after dinner.

Elinor looked up at him from her book. 'Don't I ever talk?' she said, ironically smiling. 'Well, I suppose there's nothing of any particular interest to say.'

Philip recognized one of the answers he was in the habit of making to her reproaches, and was abashed into silence. And yet it was unfair of her to retort it upon him. For in his case it was true: there really wasn't anything of interest to say. By dint of being secretive about them, he had almost abolished his intimate feelings. Very little seemed to go on in the unintellectual part of his mind – very little, at any rate, that wasn't either trivial or rather discreditable. Whereas Elinor always had a mass of things to say. Things that said themselves, that came out of their own accord from the depths of her being. Philip would have liked to explain this to her; but somehow it was difficult, he couldn't.

'All the same,' he brought himself to say, after a pause, 'you used to talk much more. It's only in these last days ...'

'I suppose I'm rather tired of talking, that's all.'

'But why should you be tired?'

'Mayn't one be tired sometimes?' She uttered a rather resentful little laugh. 'You seem to be permanently tired.'

Philip looked at her with a kind of anxiety. His eyes seemed to implore. But she wouldn't allow herself to be touched. She had allowed herself to be touched too often. He had exploited her love, systematically underpaid her and, whenever she threatened rebellion, had turned suddenly rather pathetic and helpless, appealing to her better feelings. This time she was going to be hard. He might look as imploring and anxious as he liked, but she wouldn't take any notice. It only served him right. All the same she felt rather guilty. And yet it was his own fault. Why couldn't he love her actively, articulately, outright? When she gave him her love, he took it for granted, he accepted it passively as his right. And when she stopped giving it, he looked dumbly anxious and imploring. But as for saying anything, as for doing anything ...

The seconds passed. Elinor waited, pretending to read. If only he'd speak or move! She longed for an excuse to love him again. As for Everard – why, Everard simply didn't count. To the deep instinctive core of her being he really didn't matter, and if Philip would only take the trouble to love her a little, he wouldn't matter any more even to the conscious part of her that was trying to love him – to love him on principle, so to speak, to love him deliberately, of set purpose. But the seconds passed in silence. And at last, with a little sigh (for he too would have liked to say something, to do something; only it was impossible, because the something said or done would have to be personal), Philip picked up his book and, in the interests of the zoological novelist in his novel, went on reading about the possessive instinct in birds. Reading again. He wasn't going to say anything after all. Oh, very well; if he wanted her to become Everard's mistress, then he'd have only himself to blame. She tried to shrug her shoulders and feel truculently. But the threat, she inwardly felt, was directed against herself rather than against Philip. It was she, not he, who was being condemned. Condemned to be Everard's mistress.

Taking a lover had seemed to Elinor, theoretically and in advance, a matter of no great difficulty. Morally wrong she did not think it. All the fuss that Christians and the heroines of novels managed to make about it! It was incomprehensible. 'If people want to go to bed with one another,' she would say, 'why can't they do it quite simply and straightforwardly, without tormenting themselves and everyone else within range?' Nor had she any fear of the social consequences of taking a lover. The people who, if they knew, would object, were precisely the people she herself had always objected to. By refusing to meet her, they would be doing her a favour. As for Phil, he would have deserved it. He had had it in his power to prevent any such thing happening. Why couldn't he have come nearer, given a little more of himself? She had begged for love; but what he had given her was a remote impersonal benevolence. Mere warmth, that was all she wanted; mere humanity. It was not much to ask. And she had warned him so often of what would happen if he didn't give it.

Didn't he understand? Or was it that he simply didn't care? Perhaps it wouldn't hurt him at all; the punishment wouldn't punish. That would be humiliating. But after all, she would go on to remind herself, whenever she had arrived (yet once more) at this point in her inward argument, after all it wasn't only or mainly to punish Philip, it wasn't primarily to teach him humanity by pain and jealousy, that she was going to take a lover. It was in the interest of her own happiness. (She would try to forget how very wretched the pursuit of her own happiness made her.) Her own independent happiness. She had grown accustomed to think and act too exclusively in relation to Philip. Even when she planned to take a lover, it was still of him that she thought. Which was absurd, absurd.

But these self-reminders of her right, her intention to be independently happy, had to be constantly repeated. Her natural and habitual mode of thinking even about a possible lover was still in terms of her husband – of his conversion, or his punishment. It was only by an effort, deliberately, that she could remember to forget him.

But anyhow, for whatever reasons she might do it, to take a lover had seemed, in advance, a matter of no great psychological difficulty. Particularly if the lover were to be Everard Webley. For she liked Everard, very much; she admired him; she felt herself strangely moved and thrilled by the power that seemed to radiate out of him. And yet, when it came to the point of physical contact with the man, what extraordinary difficulties at once arose! She liked to be with him, she liked his letters, she could imagine, when he did not touch her, that she was in love with him. But when, at their second meeting after her return, Everard took her in his arms and kissed her, she was seized with a kind of horror, she felt herself turning cold and stony in his embrace. It was the same horror, the same coldness as she had felt, nearly a year before, when he had first tried to kiss her. The same, in spite of the fact she had prepared herself in the interval to feel differently, had accustomed her conscious mind to the idea of taking him as a lover. That horror, that wincing coldness were the spontaneous reactions of the instinctive and habitual part of her being. It was only her mind that had decided to accept. Her feelings, her body, all the habits of her instinctive self were in rebellion. What her intellect found harmless, her stiffened and shrinking body passionately disapproved. The spirit was a libertine, but the flesh and its affections were chaste.

'Please, Everard,' she begged, 'please.'

He let her go. 'Why do you hate me?'

'But I don't, Everard.'

'I only give you the creeps, that's all!' he said with a savage derision. Hurt, he took a pleasure in opening his own wound. 'I merely disgust you.'

'But how can you say such a thing?' She felt wretched and ashamed of her shrinking; but the sense of repulsion still persisted.

'Because it happens to be true.'

'No, it isn't.' At the words Everard stretched out his hands again. She shook her head. 'But you mustn't touch me,' she begged. 'Not now. It would spoil everything. I can't explain why. I don't know why. But not now. Not yet,' she added, implicitly promising but meanwhile avoiding.

The implication of a promise revived his importunity. Elinor was half sorry that she had pronounced the words, half glad that she had, to this extent, committed herself. She was relieved to have escaped from the immediate menace of his bodily contact, and at the same time angry with herself for having shrunk from him. Her body and her instincts had rebelled against her will. Her implied promise was the will's reprisal against the traitors within her. It made the amends which, she felt, she owed to Everard. 'Not yet.' But when? When? Any time, her will replied, any time you like. It was easy to promise, but oh, how hard to fulfil! Elinor sighed. If only Philip would let her love him! But he did not speak, he did not act, he just went on reading. Silently he condemned her to unfaithfulness.

Chapter Twenty-nine

THE scene was Hyde Park; the day, a Saturday in June.

Dressed in green and wearing a sword, Everard Webley was addressing a thousand British Freemen from the back of his white horse, Bucephalus. With a military precision which would have done credit to the Guards, the Freemen had formed up on the Embankment at Blackfriars, had marched with music and symbolic standards to Charing Cross, up Northumberland Avenue, through Trafalgar Square and Cambridge Circus to the Tottenham Court Road and thence along the whole length of Oxford Street to the Marble Arch. At the entrance to the Park they had met an Anti-Vivisection procession and there had been some slight confusion – a mingling of ranks, a musical discord, as the bands collided, of 'The British Grenadiers' and 'My Faith looks up to Thee, Thou Lamb of Calvary,' an entangling of banners, 'Protect our Doggies' with 'Britons never shall be slaves,' 'Socialism is Tyranny' with 'Doctors or Devils?' But the admirable discipline of the Freemen had prevented the confusion from becoming serious, and after a short delay the thousand had entered the Park, marched past their leader and finally formed themselves into three sides of a hollow square, with Everard and his staff at the centre of the fourth side. The trumpets had sounded a fanfare and the thousand had sung the four verses of Everard's rather Kiplingesque 'Song of the Freemen.' When the singing was done Everard began his speech.

'British Freemen!' he said, 'comrades!' and at the sound of that strong effortless voice there was a silence even among the spectators who had idly collected to watch the proceedings. Carrying a power not intrinsically theirs, a power that belonged to the speaker, not to what he spoke, his words fell one by one, thrillingly audible, into the attentive hush they had created. He began by praising the Freemen's discipline. 'Discipline,' he said, 'voluntarily accepted discipline is the first condition of freedom, the first virtue of Freemen. Free and disciplined Spartans held the Persian hordes at bay. Free and disciplined Macedonians conquered half the world. It is for us free and disciplined Englishmen to deliver our country from the slaves who have enslaved it. Three hundred fought at Thermopylae against tens of thousands. The odds we face are not so desperate. Your battalion is only one of more than sixty, a single thousand among the sixty thousand Freemen of England. The numbers daily increase. Twenty, fifty, sometimes a hundred recruits join us every day. The army grows, the green army of Freemen.

'The British Freemen are uniformed in green. Theirs is the livery of Robin Hood and Little John, the livery of outlaws. For outlaws they are in this stupid democratic world. Outlaws proud of their outlawry. The law of the democratic world is quantity. We outlaws believe in quality. For the democratic politicians, the voice of the greatest number is the voice of God; their law is the law that pleases the mob. Outside the pale of mob-made law, we desire the rule of the best, not the most numerous. Stupider than their liberal grandfathers, the democrats of to-day would discourage individual enterprise and, by nationalizing industry and land, invest the state with tyrannical powers such as it has never possessed, except perhaps in India in the time of the Moguls. We outlaws are freemen. We believe in the value of individual liberty. We would encourage individual enterprise; for we believe that, co-ordinated and controlled in the interests of society as a whole, individual enterprise produces the best economic and moral results. The law of the democratic world is human standardization, is the reduction of all humanity to the lowest common measure. Its religion is the worship of the average man. We outlaws believe in diversity, in aristocracy, in the natural hierarchy. We would remove every removable handicap and give every man his chance, in order that the best may rise to the position for which nature has qualified them. In a word, we believe in justice. And we revere, not the ordinary, but the extraordinary man. I could go on almost indefinitely with this list of the points on which we British Freemen are in radical disagreement with the democratic governors of what once was free and merry England. But I have said enough to show that there can be no peace between them and us. Their white is our black, their political good is our evil, their earthly paradise is our hell. Voluntary outlaws, we repudiate their rule, we wear the green livery of the forest. And we bide our time, we bide our time. For our time is coming and we do not propose to remain outlaws for ever. The time is coming when the laws will be of our making and the forest will be the place for those who now hold power. Two years ago our band was insignificant. To-day it is an army. An army of outlaws. Yet a little while, my comrades, and it will be the army of those who make the laws, not of those who break them. Yes, of those who break them. For before we can become the makers of good laws,

we must be the breakers of bad laws. We must have the courage of
our outlawry. British Freemen, fellow outlaws, when the time comes,
will you have that courage?'

From the green-coated ranks rose an enormous shout.

'When I give the word, will you follow?'

'We will, we will,' the green thousand repeated.

'Even if laws must be broken?'

There was another burst of affirmative cheering. When it died
down and as Everard Webley was opening his mouth to continue, a
voice shouted, 'Down with Webley! Down with the rich man's
militia! Down with the Bloody B ...' But before the voice could
enunciate the whole hated parody of their name, half a dozen of the
nearest British Freemen had thrown themselves upon its owner.

Everard Webley rose in his stirrups. 'Keep your ranks,' he called
peremptorily. 'How dare you leave the ranks?'

There was a scurrying of officers to the scene of confusion, an
angry shouting of orders. The over-zealous Freemen slunk back to
their places. Holding a bloody handkerchief to his nose and escorted
by two policemen, their enemy marched away. He had lost his hat.
The dishevelled hair blazed red in the sunlight. It was Illidge.

Everard Webley turned to the officer commanding the company
whose men had broken their ranks. 'Insubordination,' he began; and
his voice was cold and hard, not loud, but dangerously penetrating,
'insubordination is the worst ...'

Illidge removed his handkerchief from his nose and shouted in a
shrill falsetto, 'Oh, you naughty boys!'

There was a guffaw from the spectators. Everard ignored the interruption and having concluded his rebuke, went on with his speech.
Commanding and yet persuasive, passionate, but controlled and
musical, his voice thrilled out; and in a moment the shattered silence
was reconstructed round his words, the dissipated attention was once
more focussed and concentrated. There had been a rebellion; he had
made another conquest.

*

Spandrell waited without impatience. Illidge's tardiness gave him the
opportunity to drink an extra cocktail or two. He was at his third
and feeling already much better and more cheerful, when the restaurant door swung open and in walked Illidge, very militant and defiant,
with an air of truculently parading his blackened eye.

'Drunk and disorderly?' questioned Spandrell at the sight of the bruise. 'Or did you meet an outraged husband? Or have words with a lady?'

Illidge sat down and recounted his adventure, boastfully and with embellishments. He had been, according to his own account, a mixture of Horatius defending the bridge and St Stephen under the shower of stones.

'The ruffians!' said Spandrell sympathetically. But his eyes shone with malicious laughter. The misfortunes of his friends were an unfailing source of amusement to him, and this of Illidge's was a particularly entertaining disaster.

'But at least I spoilt the best effect in Webley's disgusting oration,' Illidge went on in the same self-congratulating tone.

'It might have been slightly more satisfactory if you'd spoilt his face for him.'

Illidge was stung by the note of mockery in Spandrell's words. 'Spoiling his face wouldn't be enough,' he said with ferocity, scowling as he spoke. 'The man ought to be exterminated. He's a public danger, he and his gang of bravoes.' He broke into profanity.

Spandrell only laughed. 'It's easy to yammer,' he said. 'Why not do something for a change? A little direct action in Webley's own style.'

The other shrugged his shoulders apologetically. 'We're not well enough organized.'

'I shouldn't have thought it needed much organization to knock a man on the head. No, the real trouble is that you're not courageous enough.'

Illidge blushed. 'That's a lie!'

'Not well enough organized!' Spandrell went on contemptuously. 'At least you're modern in your excuses. The great god organization. Even art and love will soon be bowing down like everything else. Why are your verses so bad? Because the poetry industry isn't well enough organized. And the impotent lover will excuse himself in the same way and assure the indignant lady that, next time, she'll find his organization perfect. No, no, my dear Illidge, it won't do, you know; it won't do.'

'You're being very funny, no doubt,' said Illidge, still pink with anger. 'But you're talking rot. You can't compare poetry and politics. A political party's a lot of men who've got to be disciplined and held together. A poet's one man.'

'But so's a murderer, isn't he?' Spandrell's tone, his smile were

340

still sarcastic. Illidge felt the blood running up again into his face like the warmth of a suddenly flaring inward fire. He hated Spandrell for his power of humiliating him, for making him feel small, a fool and ashamed. He had come in feeling important and heroic, flushed with satisfaction. And now, with a few slow sneering words, Spandrell had turned his self-satisfaction to an angry shame. There was a silence; they ate their soup without speaking. When his plate was empty, 'One man,' said Spandrell meditatively, leaning back in his chair. 'With all one man's responsibility. A thousand men have no responsibility. That's why organization's such a wonderful comfort. A member of a political party feels himself as safe as the member of a church. The party may order civil war, rape, massacre; he does what he's told cheerfully, because the responsibility isn't his. It's the leader's. And the leader is the rare man, like Webley. The man with courage.'

'Or cowardice, in his case,' said Illidge. 'Webley's the bourgeois rabbit terrified into ferocity.'

'Is he?' asked Spandrell raising his eyebrows derisively. 'Well, you may be right. But anyhow, he's rather different from the ordinary rabbit. The ordinary rabbit isn't scared into ferocity. He's scared into abject inactivity or abject activity in obedience to somebody else's orders. Never into activity on his own account, for which he has to take the responsibility. When it's a question of murder, for example, you don't find the ordinary rabbits exactly eager, do you? They wait to be organized. The responsibility's too great for the little individual. He's scared.'

'Well, obviously nobody wants to be hanged.'

'He'd be scared even if there wasn't any hanging.'

'You're not going to trot out the categorical imperative again, are you?' It was Illidge's turn to be sarcastic.

'It trots itself out. Even in your case. When it came to the point, you'd never dare do anything about Webley, unless you had an organization to relieve you of all responsibility. You simply wouldn't dare,' he repeated, with a kind of mocking challenge. He looked at Illidge intently between half-closed eyelids, and through the whole of Illidge's rather rhetorical speech about the scotching of snakes, the shooting of tigers, the squashing of bugs, he studied his victim's flushed and angry face. How comic the man was when he tried to be heroic! Illidge stormed on, uncomfortably conscious that his phrases were too big and sounded hollow. But emphasis and still more emphasis, as the smile grew more contemptuous, seemed to be the

341

only possible retort to Spandrell's maddeningly quiet derision – more and still more, however false the rhetoric might sound. Like a man who stops shouting because he is afraid his voice may break, he was suddenly silent. Spandrell slowly nodded.

'All right,' he said mysteriously. 'All right.'

*

'It's absurd,' Elinor kept assuring herself. 'It's childish. Childish and absurd.'

It was an irrelevance. Everard was no different because he had sat on a white horse, because he had commanded and been acclaimed by a cheering crowd. He was no better because she had seen him at the head of one of his battalions. It was absurd, it was childish to have been so moved. But moved she had been; the fact remained. What an excitement when he had appeared, riding, at the head of his men! A quickening of the heart and a swelling. And what an anxiety in the seconds of silence before he began to speak! A real terror. He might stammer and hesitate; he might say something stupid or vulgar; he might be long-winded and a bore; he might be a mountebank. And then, when the voice spoke, unstrained, but vibrant and penetrating, when the speech began to unroll itself in words that were passionate and stirring, but never theatrical, in phrases rich, but brief and incis- ive – then what an exultation, what pride! But when that man made his interruption, she had felt, together with a passion of indignation against the interrupter, a renewal of her anxiety, her terror lest he might fail, might be publicly humiliated and put to shame. But he had sat unmoved, he had uttered his stern rebuke, he had made a pregnant and breathless silence and then, at last, continued his speech, as though nothing had happened. Elinor's anxiety had given place to an extraordinary happiness. The speech came to an end; there was a burst of cheering and Elinor had felt enormously proud and elated and at the same time embarrassed, as though the cheering had been in part directed towards herself; and she had laughed aloud, she did not know why, and the blood had rushed up into her cheeks and she had turned away in confusion, not daring to look at him; and then, for no reason, she had begun to cry.

Absurd and childish, she now assured herself. But there, the absurd and childish thing had happened; there was no undoing it.

*

In the *Sunday Pictorial*, a snapshot of Everard Webley with his mouth open – a black hole in the middle of a straining face – bawling. 'Mr E. W., the founder and chief of the B.B.F., addressed a battalion of British Freemen in Hyde Park on Saturday.' And that was all that remained of the event, that gargoylish symbol of demagogy. A mouth opened to bray. What a horror!

And yet the event was genuinely impressive. And E.'s bawling sounded quite nobly, at the time. And he looked monumental on his white horse. Selecting a separate instant out of what had been a continuity, the camera turned him into a cautionary scarecrow. Unfair? Or was the camera's vision the true one and mine the false? For after all, the impressive continuity must have been made up of such appalling instants as the camera recorded. Can the whole be something quite different from its parts? In the physical world, yes. Taken as a whole a body and brain are radically different from their component electrons. But what about the moral world? Can a collection of low values make up a single high value? Everard's photo poses a genuine problem. Millions of monstrous instants making up a splendid half-hour.

Not that I was without my doubts of the splendidness at the time. E. talked a lot about Thermopylae and the Spartans. But my resistance was even more heroic. Leonidas had three hundred companions. I defended my spiritual Thermopylae single-handed against E. and his Freemen. They impressed me; but I resisted. The drill, to begin with, was superb. I watched, enchanted. As usual. How does one explain the fascination of the military spectacle? Explain it away, by preference. I wondered all the time I was watching.

A squad is merely ten men and emotionally neutral. The heart only begins to beat at the sight of a company. The evolutions of a battalion are intoxicating. And a brigade is already an army with banners – which is the equivalent, as we know from the Song of Songs, of being in love. The thrill is proportional to the numbers. Given the fact that one is only two yards high, two feet wide and solitary, a cathedral is necessarily more impressive than a cottage and a mile of marching men is grander than a dozen loafers at a street corner. But that's not all. A regiment's more impressive than a crowd. The army with banners is equivalent to love only when it's perfectly drilled. Stones in the form of a building are finer than stones in a heap. Drill and uniforms impose an architecture on the crowd. An army's beautiful.

But that's not all; it panders to lower instincts than the aesthetic. The spectacle of human beings reduced to automatism satisfies the lust for power. Looking at mechanized slaves, one fancies oneself a master. So I thought, as I admired the evolutions of Everard's Freemen. And by taking the admiration to bits, I preserved myself from being overwhelmed by it. Divide and rule. I did the same with the music and afterwards with Everard's speech.

What a great stage manager was lost in Everard! Nothing could have been more impressive than (breaking the studiously prolonged silence) that fanfare of trumpets and then, solemnly, the massive harmonies of a thousand voices singing 'The Song of the Freemen.' The trumpets were prodigious – like the overture to the Last Judgement. (Why should upper partials be so soul-shaking?) And when the trumpet overture was done, the thousand voices burst out with that almost supernatural sound which choral singing always has. Enormous, like the voice of Jehovah. Reinhardt himself couldn't have done the trick more effectually. I felt as though there were a hole where my diaphragm should be; a kind of anxious tingling ran over my skin, the tears were very nearly at the surface of my eyes. I did the Leonidas turn again and reflected how bad the music was, what ridiculous rant the words.

The Last Trump, the voice of God – and then it was Everard's turn to speak. And one wasn't let down. How well he did it! His voice took you in the solar plexus, like those upper partials on the trumpets. Moving and convincing, even though you knew that what he said was vague and more or less meaningless. I analysed the tricks. They were the usual ones. The most effective was the employment of inspiring words with two or more meanings. 'Liberty,' for example. The liberty in the title and programme of the British Freemen is the liberty to buy and sell and own property with a minimum of government interference. (A pretty large minimum, parenthetically; but let that pass.) Everard bawls out the word in his solar-plexus-punching voice: 'we are fighting for *liberty*; we are going to *free* the country,' etcetera. The hearer immediately visualizes himself sitting in shirtsleeves with a bottle and a complaisant wench and no laws, no code of good manners, no wife, no policeman, no parson to forbid. Liberty! Naturally it arouses his enthusiasm. It's only when the British Freemen come to power that he'll realize that the word was really used in an entirely different sense. Divide and conquer. I conquered. *P.S.* – Or rather one part of me conquered. I've got into

344

the habit of associating myself with that part and applauding when it triumphs. But, after all, is it the best part? In these particular circumstances, perhaps yes. It's probably better to be dispassionately analytical than to be overwhelmed by Everard's stage-managing and eloquence into becoming a British Freeman. But in other circumstances? Rampion's probably right. But having made a habit of dividing and conquering in the name of the intellect, it's hard to stop. And perhaps it isn't entirely a matter of second nature; perhaps first nature comes in too. It's easy to believe one ought to change one's mode of living. The difficulty is to act on the belief. This settlement in the country, for example; this being rustic and paternal and a good neighbour; this living vegetably and intuitively – is it really going to be possible? I imagine it; but in fact, in fact …? Meanwhile, it might be rather interesting to concoct a character on these lines. A man who has always taken pains to encourage his own intellectualist tendencies at the expense of all the others. He avoids personal relationships as much as he can, he observes without participating, doesn't like to give himself away, is always a spectator rather than an actor. Again, he has always been careful not to distinguish one day, one place from another; not to review the past and anticipate the future at the New Year, not to celebrate Christmas or birthdays, not to revisit the scenes of his childhood, not to make pilgrimages to the birthplaces of great men, battlefields, ruins and the like. By this suppression of emotional relationships and natural piety he seems to himself to be achieving freedom – freedom from sentimentality, from the irrational, from passion, from impulse and emotionalism. But in reality, as he gradually discovers, he has only narrowed and desiccated his life; and what's more, has cramped his intellect by the very process he thought would emancipate it. His reason's free, but only to deal with a small fraction of experience. He realizes his psychological defects, and desires, in theory, to change. But it's difficult to break life-long habits; and perhaps the habits are only the expression of an inborn indifference and coldness, which it might be almost impossible to overcome. And for *him* at any rate, the merely intellectual life is easier; it's the line of least resistance, because it's the line that avoids other human beings. Among them his wife. For he'd have a wife and there would be the elements of drama in the relations between the woman, living mainly with her emotions and intuitions, and the man whose existence is mainly on the abstracted intellectual plane. He loves her in his way and she loves him in hers. Which

345

means that he's contented and she's dissatisfied; for love in his way entails the minimum of those warm, confiding human relationships which constitute the essence of love in her way. She complains; he would like to give more, but finds it hard to change himself. She even threatens to leave him for a more human lover; but she is too much in love with him to put the threat into effect.

*

That Sunday afternoon Elinor and Everard Webley drove down into the country.

'Forty-three miles in an hour and seven minutes,' said Everard looking at his watch as he stepped out of the car. 'Not bad considering that includes getting out of London and being held up by that filthy charabanc in Guildford. Not at all bad.'

'And what's more,' said Elinor, 'we're still alive. If you knew the number of times I just shut my eyes and only expected to open them again on the Day of Judgement. ...'

He laughed, rather glad that she should have been so frightened by the furiousness of his driving. Her terrors gave him a pleasing sense of power and superiority. He took her arm protectively and they walked away down the green path into the wood. Everard drew a deep breath.

'This is better than making political speeches,' he said, pressing her arm.

'Still,' said Elinor, 'it must be rather wonderful to sit on a horse and make a thousand people do whatever you want.'

Everard laughed. 'Unfortunately there's a bit more in politics than that.' He glanced at her. 'You enjoyed the meeting?'

'I was thrilled.' She saw him again on his white horse, heard his strong vibrating voice, remembered her exultation and those sudden tears. Magnificent, she said to herself, magnificent! But there was no recapturing the exultation. His hand was on her arm, his huge presence loomed almost threateningly over her. 'Is he going to kiss me?' she nervously wondered. She tried to drive out the questioning dread and fill its place with yesterday's exultation. Magnificent! But the dread would not be exorcised. 'I thought your speech was splendid,' she said aloud and wondered parenthetically as she spoke what it had been about. She remembered the sound and timbre of the words, but not their significance. Hopeless! 'Oh, what lovely honeysuckle!'

Everard reached up, enormous, and picked a couple of blossoms.

'Such beauty, such loveliness!' He quoted Keats, fumbled in his memory for a line in the *Midsummer Night's Dream*. He wondered lyrically why one lived in towns, why one wasted one's time in the pursuit of money and power, when there was all this beauty waiting to be known and loved.

Elinor listened rather uncomfortably. He seemed to turn it on, this love of beauty, like an electric light – turn out the love of power, turn out efficiency and political preoccupations and turn on the love of beauty. But why shouldn't he, after all? There was nothing wrong in liking beautiful things. Nothing, except that in some obscure indescribable way Everard's love of beauty wasn't quite right. Too deliberate was it? Too occasional? Too much for holidays only? Too conventional, too heavy, too humourlessly reverent? She preferred him as a lover of power. As a power-lover he was somehow of better quality than as a beauty-lover. A poor beauty-lover, perhaps, because he was such a good power-lover. By compensation. Everything has to be paid for.

They walked on. In an open glade between the trees the foxgloves were coming into flower.

'Like torches burning upwards from the bottom,' said Everard poetically.

Elinor halted in front of one tall plant whose first flower-bells were on a level with her eyes. The red flesh of the petals was cool and resilient between her fingers. She peeped into the open bell-mouth.

'Think of the discomfort of having freckles in one's throat,' she said. 'Not to mention little beetles.'

They moved away in silence through the trees. It was Everard who first spoke.

'Will you ever love me?' he asked suddenly.

'You know how fond I am of you, Everard.' Her heart sank; the moment had come, he would want to kiss her. But he made no gesture, only laughed, rather mournfully.

'Very fond of me,' he repeated. 'Ah, if only you could be a little less reasonable, a little more insane! If only you knew what loving was!'

'Isn't it a good thing somebody should be sane?' said Elinor. 'Sane beforehand, I mean. For everybody can be sane afterwards. Much too sane, when the fit's over and the lovers begin to wonder whether, after all, the world *was* well lost. Think, Everard, think first. Do you want to lose the world?'

347

'I shouldn't lose it,' Everard answered, and his voice had that strange thrilling vibration which she seemed to hear, not with her ears, but with her body, in the very midriff. 'They couldn't take it away from me. Times have changed since Parnell's day. Besides I'm not Parnell. Let them try to take it away!' He laughed. 'Love *and* the world – I'm going to have both, Elinor. Both.' He smiled down at her, the power-lover triumphant.

'You're asking too much,' she answered laughing, 'you're greedy.' The exultation tingled again through her, was like the breath-taking warmth of hot wine.

He bent down and kissed her. Elinor did not shrink.

Another car had pulled up at the roadside, another couple strolled along the green path into the wood. Through the glaring pink and white of her cosmetics the woman's face was old; the weary flesh had sagged out of its once charming shape.

'Oh, isn't it lovely!' she kept exclaiming as she walked along, carrying her heavy body rather unsteadily on very high-heeled shoes over the uneven ground. 'Isn't it lovely!'

Spandrell – for it was he – did not answer.

'Pick me some of that honeysuckle there!' she begged.

He pulled down a flowered spray with the crook of his stick. Through the reek of chemical perfumery and not very clean under-linen the scent of the flowers came cool and delicious to his nostrils.

'Don't they smell simply divine!' she exclaimed, rapturously sniffing. 'Too divine!'

The corners of Spandrell's mouth twitched into a smile. It amused him to hear the cast-off locutions of duchesses in the mouth of this ageing prostitute. He looked at her. Poor Connie! She *was* a skeleton at the feast – more gruesomely deathly for being covered with so much loose and sagging flesh. Really gruesome. There was no other word. Here, in the sun, she was like a piece of stage scenery seen by daylight and from close at hand. That was why he had gone to the expense of hiring the Daimler and taking her out – just because the poor superannuated punk was so gruesome. He nodded. 'Quite nice,' he said. 'But I prefer your scent.'

They walked on. A little uncertain already of the distinction between a second and a minor third, a cuckoo was calling. In the slanting corridors of sunlight tunnelled through the green and purple of the forest shadows the little flies jerkily danced and zigzagged. There was no wind, the leaves hung down heavy with greenness.

The trees were as though gorged with sap and sunshine.

'Lovely, lovely,' was Connie's refrain. The place, the day reminded her, she said, of her childhood in the country. She sighed.

'And you wish you'd been a good girl,' said Spandrell sarcastically. ' "The roses round the door make me love mother more." I know, I know.' He was silent for a moment. 'What I hate about trees in the summer,' he went on, 'is their beastly fat complacency. Bulging – that's what they are; like bloated great profiteers. Bulging with insolence, passive insolence.'

'Oh, the foxgloves!' cried Connie, who hadn't even been listening. She ran towards them, grotesquely unsteady on her high heels. Spandrell followed her.

'Pleasingly phallic,' he said, fingering one of the spikes of unopened buds. And he went on to develop the conceit, profusely.

'Oh, be quiet, be quiet,' cried Connie. 'How can you say such things?' She was outraged, wounded. 'How can you – here?'

'In God's country,' he mocked. 'How can I?' And raising his stick he suddenly began to lay about him right and left, slash, slash, breaking one of the tall proud plants at every stroke. The ground was strewn with murdered flowers.

'Stop, stop!' She caught at his arm. Silently laughing, Spandrell wrenched himself away from her and went on beating down the plants. 'Stop! Please! Oh, don't, don't.' She made another dash at him. Still laughing, still laying about him with his stick, Spandrell dodged away from her.

'Down with them,' he shouted, 'down with them.' Flower after flower fell under his strokes. 'There!' he said at last, breathless with laughter and running and slashing. 'There!' Connie was in tears.

'How could you?' she said. 'How could you do it?'

He laughed again, silently, throwing back his head. 'Serve them right,' he said. 'Do you think I'm going to sit still and let myself be insulted? The insolence of the brutes! Ah, there's another!' He stepped across the glade to where one last tall foxglove stood as though hiding among the hazel saplings. One stroke was enough. The broken plant fell almost noiselessly.

'Damn their insolence! It serves them right. Let's come back to the car.'

Chapter Thirty

RACHEL QUARLES had no sympathy with those sentimental philanthropists who blur the distinction between right and wrong, between wrongdoers and the righteous. Criminals, in her eyes, and not the society in which they lived, were responsible for their crimes. Sinners committed their own sins; their environment did not do it for them. There were excuses, of course, palliations, extenuating circumstances. But good was always good, bad remained bad. There were circumstances in which the choice of good was very difficult; but it was always the individual who made the choice and who, having made, must answer for it. Mrs Quarles, in a word, was a Christian and not a humanitarian. As a Christian she thought that Marjorie had done wrong to leave her husband – even such a husband as Carling – for another man. She disapproved the act, but did not presume to judge the person, the more so since, in spite of what she had done, Marjorie's heart and head were still, from Mrs Quarles's Christian point of view, 'in the right place.' Rachel found it easier to like a person who had acted wrongly, while continuing to think rightly, than one who, like her daughter-in-law, Elinor, thought wrongly, while acting, so far as she knew, in a manner entirely blameless. There were circumstances, too, in which wrong action seemed to her almost less reprehensible than wrong thought. It was not that she had any sympathy for hypocrisy. The person who thought and spoke well while consistently and consciously acting ill was detestable to her. Such people, however, are rare. Most of those who do wrong, in spite of their sound beliefs, do so in a moment of weakness and afterwards regret their wrongdoing. But the person who thinks wrongly does not admit the wrongness of bad actions. He sees no reason why he should not commit them or why, having committed them, he should repent and mend his ways. And even if he in fact behaves virtuously, he may be the means, by his wrong thinking, of leading others into wrong action.

'An admirable woman,' had been John Bidlake's verdict; 'but rather too fond of fig-leaves – especially over the mouth.'

Herself, Rachel Quarles was only conscious of being a Christian. She could never imagine how people contrived to live without being Christians. But a great many, she sadly had to admit, did so contrive. Almost all the young people of her acquaintance. 'It's as though one's children talked a different language,' she had once complained to an old friend.

In Marjorie Carling she discovered someone who spoke and understood her own spiritual idiom.

'You'll find her, I'm afraid, a bit of a bore,' Philip had warned her, when he announced his intention of lending his little house at Chamford to Walter and Marjorie. 'But be nice to her, all the same. She deserves it, poor woman. She's had a very thin time of it.' And he detailed a story that made his mother sigh to listen to.

'I shouldn't have expected Walter Bidlake to be like that,' she said.

'But in these matters one doesn't *expect* anything of anybody. Things happen to them, that's all. They don't do them.'

Mrs Quarles did not answer. She was thinking of the time when she had first discovered one of Sidney's infidelities. The astonishment, the pain, the humiliation. ...'But still,' she said aloud, 'one wouldn't have thought he'd knowingly have made somebody unhappy.'

'Still less that he'd knowingly have made himself unhappy. And yet I think he's really made himself quite as wretched as Marjorie. Perhaps that's his chief justification.'

His mother sighed. 'It all seems so extraordinarily unnecessary.'

Mrs Quarles called on Marjorie almost as soon as she had settled in.

'Come and see me often,' she said, as she took her leave. 'Because I like you,' she added, with a sudden smile, for which poor Marjorie was quite pathetically grateful. It wasn't often that people liked her. That she had fallen so deeply in love with Walter was due, above everything, to his having been one of the few people who had ever shown any interest in her. 'And I hope you like me,' Mrs Quarles added.

Marjorie could only blush and stammer. But she already adored.

Rachel Quarles had spoken in all sincerity. She did like Marjorie – liked her, even, for the very defects which made other people find her such a bore; for her stupidity – it was so good and well-meaning; for her lack of humour – it was the mark of such earnestness. Even those intellectual pretensions, those deep or informative remarks dropped portentously out of a meditative silence, did not displease her. Mrs Quarles recognized in them the rather absurd symptoms of a genuine love of the good, the true, and the beautiful, of a genuine desire for self-improvement.

At their third meeting Marjorie confided all her story. Mrs Quarles's comments were sensible and Christian. 'There's no miraculous cure for these things,' she said; 'no patent medicine for unhappiness. Only the old dull virtues, patience, resignation, and the rest; and the old consolation, the old source of strength – old, but not dull. There's nothing less dull than God. But most young people won't believe me when I tell them so, even though they're bored to death with jazz bands and dancing.'

Marjorie's first adoration was confirmed and increased – increased so much, indeed, that Mrs Quarles felt quite ashamed, as though she had extorted something on false pretences, as though she had fraudulently acted a part.

'You're such a wonderful help and comfort,' Marjorie declared.

'No, I'm not,' she answered almost angrily. 'The truth is that you were lonely and unhappy and I was conveniently there at the right moment.'

Marjorie protested; but the older woman would not permit herself to be praised or thanked.

They talked a good deal about religion. Carling had given Marjorie a horror for all that was picturesque or formal in Christianity. Piran of Perranzabuloe, vestments, ceremonials – everything remotely connected with a saint, a rite, a tradition was hateful to her. But she preserved a vague inchoate faith in what she regarded as the essentials; she had retained from girlhood a certain habit of Christian feeling and thought. Under the influence of Rachel Quarles the faith became more definite, the habitual emotions were reinforced.

'I feel so enormously much happier since I've been here, with you,' she announced hardly more than a week after her arrival.

'It's because you're not trying to be happy or wondering why you should have been made unhappy, because you've stopped thinking in terms of happiness or unhappiness. That's the enormous stupidity of the young people of this generation,' Mrs Quarles went on; 'they never think of life except in terms of happiness. How shall I have a good time? That's the question they ask. Or they complain. Why am I not having a better time? But this is a world where good times, in their sense of the word, perhaps in any sense, simply cannot be had continuously, and by everybody. And even when they get their good times, it's inevitably a disappointment – for imagination is always brighter than reality. And after it's been had for a little, it becomes a bore. Everybody strains after happiness, and the result is that nobody's happy. It's because they're on the wrong road. The question they ought to be asking themselves isn't: Why aren't we happy, and how shall we have a good time? It's: How can we please God, and why aren't we better? If people asked themselves those questions and answered them to the best of their ability in practice, they'd achieve happiness without ever thinking about it. For it's not by pursuing happiness that you find it; it's by pursuing salvation. And when people were wise, instead of merely clever, they thought of life in terms of salvation and damnation, not of good times and bad times. If you're feeling happy now, Marjorie, that's because you've stopped wishing you were happy and started trying to be better. Happiness is like coke – something you get as a by-product in the process of making something else.'

*

At Gattenden, meanwhile, the days passed gloomily.

'Why don't you do a little painting?' Mrs Bidlake suggested to her husband on the morning that followed his arrival.

Old John shook his head.

'You'd enjoy it so much once you started,' coaxed Elinor.

But her father would not allow himself to be persuaded. He didn't want to paint, precisely because painting would have been so enjoyable. His very dread of pain, sickness, and death made him perversely refuse to let his mind be distracted from their abhorred contemplation. It was as though some part of him obscurely desired to accept defeat and misery, were anxious to make abjection yet more abject. His courage, his Gargantuan power, his careless high spirits had been the fruits of a deliberate and life-long ignorance. But now that to ignore was no longer possible, now that the enemy was installed in his very vitals, the virtue had gone out of him. He was afraid and could not conceal his terrors. He no longer even desired to conceal them. He somehow wanted to be abject. And abject he was. Mrs Bidlake and Elinor did their best to rouse him from the apathetic misery in which he spent the greater part of his days at Gattenden. But he would not be roused except to complain and occasionally fly into a querulous rage.

'Deplorable,' wrote Philip in his notebook, 'to see an Olympian reduced by a little tumour in his stomach to a state of sub-humanness. But perhaps,' he added a few days later as an afterthought, 'he was always sub-human, even when he seemed most Olympian; perhaps being Olympian was just a symptom of sub-humanity.'

It was only with little Phil that John Bidlake would occasionally rouse himself from his abjection. Playing with the child, he would sometimes forget for a little to be wretched.

'Draw something for me,' he would say.

And with his tongue between his teeth little Phil would draw a train, or a ship, or the stags in Gattenden Park fighting, or the old marquess in his donkey-drawn chair.

'Now you draw me something, grandfather,' he would say, when he was tired.

And the old man would take the pencil and make half a dozen marvellous little sketches of T'ang, the Pekingese dog, or Tompy, the kitchen cat. Or sometimes, in a fit of naughtiness, he would scribble a caricature of poor Miss Fulkes writhing. And sometimes, forgetting all about the child, he would draw for his own amusement – a group of bathers, two men wrestling, a dancer.

'But why have they got no clothes on?' the child would ask.

'Because they're nicer without.'

'I don't think so.' And losing interest in drawings that had so little in the way of a story to tell him, he would ask for the pencil back again.

But it was not always that John Bidlake responded so happily to his grandson. Sometimes, when he was feeling particularly wretched, he felt the child's mere presence as an outrage, a kind of taunting. He would fly into a rage, would shout at the boy for making a noise and disturbing him.

'Can't I ever be left in peace?' he would shout, and then would go on to complain with curses of the general inefficiency of everybody. The house was full of women, all supposed to be looking after that damned brat. But there he always was, rampaging round, kicking up hell's own din, getting in the way. It was intolerable. Particularly when one wasn't well. Absolutely intolerable. People were without any consideration. Flushed and writhing, poor Miss Fulkes would lead her howling charge back to the nursery.

The most trying scenes were at meal-times. For it was at meals (now reduced, so far as he was concerned, to broth and milk and Benger's food) that John Bidlake was most disagreeably reminded of the state of his health. 'Disgusting slops!' he grumbled. But if he ate anything solid, the results were deplorable. Meal-times were the stormiest and most savage moments of John Bidlake's day. He vented his anger on the child. Always a reluctant eater, little Phil was

354

peculiarly difficult about his food all that spring and early summer. There were tears at almost every meal.

'It's because he isn't really very well,' Miss Fulkes explained apologetically. And it was true. The boy looked sallow and peaked, slept uneasily, was nervous and quickly tired, suffered from headaches, had ceased to put on weight. Dr Crowther had ordered malt and cod-liver oil and a tonic. 'Not well,' insisted Miss Fulkes.

But John Bidlake would not hear of it. 'He's simply naughty, that's all. He just won't eat.' And turning to the boy, 'Swallow, child, swallow!' he shouted. 'Have you forgotten how to swallow?' The spectacle of little Phil chewing and chewing interminably on a mouthful of something he did not like exasperated him. 'Swallow, boy! Don't go on ruminating like that. You're not a cow. Swallow!' And, very red in the face, with tears welling up into his eyes, little Phil would make a terrible effort to swallow the abhorred cud of five minutes' queasy mastication. The muscles of his throat would heave and ripple, an expression of invincible disgust would distort his small face, there would be an ominous sound of retching. 'But it's simply revolting!' stormed the old man. 'Swallow!' His shouting was an almost infallible recipe for making the child sick.

*

Burdens fell, darkness gave place to light, Marjorie apocalyptically understood all the symbols of religious literature. For she herself had struggled in the Slough of Despond and had emerged; she too had climbed laboriously and without hope and had suddenly been consoled by a sight of the promised land.

'All these phrases used to sound so conventional and meaninglessly pious,' she said to Mrs Quarles. 'But now I see they're just descriptions of facts.'

Mrs Quarles nodded. 'Bad descriptions, because the facts are indescribable. But if you've had personal experience of them, you can see what the symbols are driving at.'

'Do you know the Black Country?' said Marjorie. 'I feel as though I'd come out of one of those mining towns on to the moors. Out into the great open spaces,' she added in her earnest, rather drawlingly childish voice. (The voice, Mrs Quarles couldn't help thinking, and repented immediately of the thought – for after all the poor girl couldn't help her voice – made the great open spaces seem curiously stuffy.) 'And when I look back, the black town seems so small and insignificant compared with the space and the enormous sky. As though one were looking at it through the wrong end of a pair of field-glasses.'

Mrs Quarles frowned slightly. 'Not so insignificant as all that,' she said. 'For after all, there are people living in the town, however black it may be. And the wrong end of the field-glasses is the wrong end. One isn't meant to look at things so that they appear small and insignificant. That's one of the dangers of getting out under the sky; one's too apt to think of the towns and the people in them as small and remote and unimportant. But they aren't, Marjorie. And it's the business of the lucky ones who have got out into the open to help the others to come too.' She frowned again, at herself this time; she hated anything like preaching. But Marjorie mustn't imagine herself superior, promoted out of the world. 'How's Walter?' she asked with an irrelevance that was no irrelevance. 'How are you getting on together now?'

'The same as ever,' said Marjorie. The admission, a few weeks ago, would have made her utterly wretched. But now even Walter had begun to seem small and rather remote. She loved him still, of course; but somehow through the wrong end of the field-glasses. Through the right end she saw only God and Jesus; they loomed overwhelmingly large.

Mrs Quarles looked at her, and an expression of sadness passed quickly over her sensitive face. 'Poor Walter!' she said.

'Yes, I'm sorry for him too,' said Marjorie. There was silence.

Old Dr Fisher had told her to come and report progress every few weeks, and Marjorie took advantage of that Wednesday's cheap excursion tickets to run up to town, do some necessary shopping, and tell the doctor how well she felt.

'You look it too,' said Dr Fisher, peering at her first through his spectacles, then over the top of them. 'Extraordinarily much better than when you were here last. It often happens in the fourth month,' he went on to explain. Dr Fisher liked to make his patients take an intelligent interest in their own physiology. 'Health improves. So do spirits. It's the body settling down to the new state of affairs. The changes in the circulation no doubt have something to do with it. The foetal heart begins to beat about this time. I've known cases of neurasthenic women who wanted to have one baby after another, as quick as ever it could be managed. Pregnancy was the only thing that could cure them of their melancholy and obsessions. How little as yet we understand about the relations between body and mind!'

Marjorie smiled and said nothing. Dr Fisher was an angel, one of the best and kindest men in the whole world. But there were things he understood even less of than the relations between body and mind. What did he understand about God, for example? What did he understand about the soul and its mystical communion with spiritual powers? Poor Dr Fisher! All that he could talk about was the fourth month of pregnancy and the foetal heart. She smiled inwardly, feeling a kind of pity for the old man.

Burlap that morning was affectionate. 'Old man,' he said, laying a hand on Walter's shoulder, 'shouldn't we go out and eat a chop together somewhere?' He gave Walter's shoulder a little squeeze and smiled down at him with the wistful enigmatic tenderness of one of Sodoma's saints.

'Alas,' said Walter, trying to simulate an answering affection, 'I'm lunching with a man at the other end of London.' It was a lie; but he couldn't face the prospect of an hour with Burlap in a Fleet Street chop-house. Besides, he wanted to see if there was a letter from Lucy waiting for him at the club. He looked at his watch. 'Lord!' he added, not wishing to prolong the conversation with Burlap, 'I must be off.'

Outside it was raining. The umbrellas were like black mushrooms that had suddenly sprouted from the mud. Gloomy, gloomy. In Madrid the sunshine would be ferocious. 'But I love the heat,' she had said. 'I blossom in ovens.' He had imagined Spanish nights, dark and hot, and her body pale in the starlight, a ghost, but tangible and warm; and love as patient and relentless as hatred, and possessions like slow murder. His imaginations had justified every conceivable lie and outrage. It mattered not what might be done or left undone, provided the imaginations were realized. He had prepared the ground, he had invented a series of elaborate lies, one set for Burlap, another for Marjorie; he had made enquiries about the price of tickets, he had arranged for an overdraft at the bank. And then came Lucy's letter with the news that she had changed her mind. She was going to stay in Paris. Why? There was only one possible reason. His jealousy, his disappointment, his humiliation had overflowed into six pages of reproach and fury.

'Any letters?' he asked off-handedly of the porter as he entered the club. His tone was meant to imply that he expected nothing more interesting than a publisher's circular or a philanthropic offer to lend five thousand pounds without security. The porter handed him the familiar yellow envelope. He tore it open and unfolded three sheets of pencilled scribble. 'Quai Voltaire. Monday.' He pored over the writing. It was almost as difficult to read as an ancient manuscript. 'Why do you always write to me in pencil?' He remembered Cuthbert Arkwright's question and her answer. 'I'll kiss the ink away,' he had replied. The lout! Walter entered the dining-room and ordered his lunch. Between the mouthfuls he deciphered Lucy's letter. 'Quai Voltaire. Insufferable, your letter. Once and for all, I refuse to be cursed at or whined at; I simply won't be reproached, or condemned. I do what I like and I don't admit anybody's right to call my doings into question. Last week I thought it would be amusing to go to Madrid with you; this week I don't. If my changing my mind has put you to any inconvenience, I'm sorry. But I'm not in the least apologetic for having changed my mind, and if you think your howlings and jealousies make me feel sorry for you, you're much mistaken. They're intolerable, they're inexcusable. Do you really want to know why I'm not leaving Paris? Very well. "I suppose you've found some man you like more than me." Marvellous, my dear Holmes! And guess where I found him? In the street. Strolling along the Boulevard Saint-Germain, looking at the bookshops. I noticed I was being followed from window to window by a young man. I liked his looks. Very black, with an olive skin, rather Roman, no taller than I. At the fourth window he began to talk to me in extraordinary French, with accents on all the mute E's. "Ma Lei è italiano." He was; huge delight. "Parla italiano?" And he began pouring out his admiration in the choicest Tuscan. I looked at him. After all, why not? Someone one has never seen before and knows nothing about – it's an exciting idea. Absolute strangers at one moment and as intimate at the next as two human beings can be. Besides, he was a beautiful creature. "Vorrei e non vorrei," I said. But he'd never heard of Mozart – only Puccini, so I cut the cackle. "All right." We hailed a taxi and drove to a little hotel near the Jardin des Plantes. Rooms by the hour. A bed, a chair, a cupboard, a washstand with a tin basin and jug, a towel-horse, a bidet. Sordid, but that was part of the fun. "Dunque," I said. I hadn't let him touch me in the cab. He came at me as though he were going to kill me, with clenched teeth. I shut my eyes, like a Christian martyr in front of a lion. Martyrdom's exciting. Letting oneself be hurt, humiliated, used like a doormat – queer. I like it. Besides, the doormat uses the user. It's complicated. He'd just come back from a seaside holiday by the Mediterranean and is body was all brown and polished by the sun. Beautifully savage he looked, a Red Indian. And as savage as his looks. The marks are till there where he bit me on the neck. I shall have to wear a scarf for days. Where did I see that statue of Marsyas being skinned? His face was like that. I dug my nails into his arm so that the blood came. Afterwards I asked him what he was called. His name's Francesco Allegri and he's an aeronautical engineer, and comes from Siena, where his father's a professor of medicine at the university. How curiously irrelevant that a brown savage should design aircraft engines and have a father who's a professor! I'm going to see him again to-morrow. So now you know, Walter, why I've changed my mind about going to Madrid. Don't ever send me another letter like the last. L.'

*

Marjorie caught the three-twelve back to Chamford. The rain had stopped when she arrived. The hills on the other side of the valley were touched with sunlight and seemed to shine with their own radiance against the smoke and indigo of the clouds. Drops still hung from the twigs and every cup of leaves and petals was full. The wetted earth gave out a cool delicious fragrance; there was a noise of birds. As she passed under the overhanging branches of the great oak tree half-way up the hill, a puff of wind shook down a cold and sudden shower on her face. Marjorie laughed with pleasure.

She found the cottage untenanted. The maid was out and wouldn't be back till a little before bedtime. The silence in the empty rooms had a quality of crystalline and musical transparency; the solitude seemed friendly and kind. When she moved about the house, she walked on tiptoe, as though she were afraid of waking a sleeping child.

Marjorie made herself a cup of tea, sipped, ate a biscuit, lighted a cigarette. The flavour of the food and drink, the aroma of the tobacco seemed peculiarly delicious and somehow novel. It was as if she had discovered them for the first time.

She turned the arm-chair so that it faced the window and sat there looking out, over the valley towards the bright hills with their background of storm. She remembered a day like this when they were living in their cottage in Berkshire. Sunshine the brighter for being so precarious in the midst of darkness; a shining and transfigured earth. Walter and she had sat together at the open window. He had loved her then. And yet she was happier now, much happier. She

359

regretted nothing of what had happened in the interval. The sufferin[g] had been necessary. It was the cloud that enhanced the shining of he[r] present felicity. A dark cloud, but how remote now, how curiousl[y] irrelevant! And that other happy brightness before the coming of th[e] cloud – that too was tiny and far away, like an image in a curve[d] mirror. Poor Walter! she thought, and remotely she was sorry fo[r] him. Pursuing happiness, he had made himself miserable. Happines[s] is a by-product, Mrs Quarles had said. It was true. 'Happines[s] happiness.' Marjorie repeated the word to herself. Against the blac[k] vapours the hills were like emeralds and green gold. Happiness an[d] beauty and goodness. 'The peace of God,' she whispered, 'the peac[e] of God that passeth all understanding. Peace, peace, peace ...' Sh[e] felt as though she were melting into that green and golden tranquil[l]ity, sinking and being absorbed into it, dissolving out of separate[e]ness into union. Stillness flowed into stillness, the silence withou[t] became one with the silence within her. The shaken and turbid liquo[r] of existence grew gradually calm, and all that had made it opaque – a[ll] the noise and uproar of the world, all the personal anxieties an[d] desires and feelings – began to settle like a sediment, fell slowl[y], slowly and noiselessly, out of sight. The turbid liquor became cleare[r] and clearer, more and more translucent. Behind that gradually van[n]ishing mist was reality, was God. It was a slow, progressive revela[-] tion. 'Peace, peace,' she whispered to herself; and the last faint rippl[e] died away from the surface of life, the opacities churned up by th[e] agitation of living dropped away through the utter calm. 'Peac[e], peace.' She had no desires, no more preoccupations. The liquo[r] which had been turbid was now quite clear, clearer than crystal, mor[e] diaphanous than air; the mist had vanished and the unveiled realit[y] was a wonderful emptiness, was nothing. Nothing – the only pe[r]fection, the only absolute. Infinite and eternal nothing. The gradua[l] revelation was now complete.

Marjorie was roused by the click of the front-door latch and th[e] sound of footsteps in the passage. Reluctantly and with a kind of pai[n] she rose from the depths of divine vacancy; her soul swam up agai[n] to the surface of consciousness. The sunlight on the hills had deep[-] ened its colour, the clouds had lifted and the sky was a pale greenis[h] blue, like water. It was almost evening. Her limbs felt stiff. She mus[t] have been sitting there for hours.

'Walter?' she called questioningly to the source of the noises i[n] the passage.

The voice in which he answered was dead and flat. 'Why is he so unhappy?' she wondered at the sound of it, but wondered from a great distance and with a kind of far-away resentment. She resented his disturbing and interrupting presence, his very existence. He entered the room and she saw that his face was pale, his eyes darkly ringed.

'What's the matter?' she asked, almost against her will. The nearer she came to Walter, the further she moved from the marvellous nothingness of God. 'You don't look at all well.'

'It's nothing,' he answered. 'Rather tired, that's all.' Coming down in the train he had read and re-read Lucy's letter, till he almost knew it by heart. His imagination had supplemented the words. He knew that sordid little room in the *hôtel meublé*; he had seen the Italian's brown body and her whiteness, and the man's clenched teeth and his face like the face of a tortured Marsyas, and Lucy's own face with that expression he knew, that look of grave and attentive suffering, as though the agonizing pleasure were a profound and difficult truth only to be grasped by intense concentration.

Ah well, Marjorie was thinking; he had said it was nothing; that was all right; she needn't worry any further. 'Poor Walter!' she said aloud and smiled at him with a pitying tenderness. He wasn't going to make any demands on her attention or her feelings; she resented him no longer. 'Poor Walter!'

Walter looked at her or a moment, then turned away. He didn't want pity. Not that sort of superior angel's pity, at any rate, and not from Marjorie. He had accepted pity from her once. The memory of the occasion made his whole flesh creep with shame. Never again. He walked away.

Marjorie heard his feet on the stairs and the banging of a door.

'All the same,' she thought, reluctantly solicitous, 'there *is* something wrong. Something *has* made him specially miserable. Perhaps I ought to go up and see what he's doing.'

But she didn't go. She sat where she was, quite still, deliberately forgetting him. The little sediment that Walter's coming had stirred up in her quickly settled again. Through the vacant lifelessness of trance her spirit sank slowly down once more into God, into the perfected absolute, into limitless and everlasting nothing. Time passed; the late afternoon turned into summer twilight; the twilight thickened slowly into darkness.

Daisy, the maid, came back at ten.

'Sittin' in the dark, mum?' she asked, looking into the sitting-room. She turned on the light. Marjorie winced. The glare brought back to her dazzled eyes all the close immediate details of the material world. God had vanished like a pricked bubble. Daisy caught sight of the unlaid table. 'What, 'aven't you 'ad no supper?' she exclaimed in horror.

'Why, no,' said Marjorie. 'I quite forgot about supper.'

'Not Mr Bidlake neither?' Daisy went on reproachfully. 'Why, pore man, 'e must be perished.'

She hurried away towards the kitchen in search of cold beef and pickles.

Upstairs in his room Walter was lying on the bed, his face buried in the pillows.

Chapter Thirty-one

A CROSSWORD problem had brought Mr Quarles to the seventeenth volume of the *Encyclopaedia Britannica*. Idle curiosity detained him. The Lord Chamberlain, he learned, carries a white staff and wears a golden or jewelled key. The word lottery has no very definite signification; but Nero gave such prizes as a house or a slave, while Heliogabalus introduced an element of absurdity – one ticket for a golden vase, another for six flies. Pinckney B. S. Pinchback was the acting Republican governor of Louisiana in 1873. To define the lyre, it is necessary clearly to separate it from the allied harp and guitar. In one of the northern ravines of Madeira some masses of a coarsely crystalline Essexite are exposed to view. But there is also a negative side to magic. And terrestrial magnetism has a long history. He had just started to read about Sir John Blundell Maple, Bart. (1845–1903), whose father, John Maple (*d*. 1900) had a small furniture shop in the Tottenham Court Road, when the parlour-maid appeared at the door and announced that there was a young lady to see him.

'A young ladah?' he repeated with some surprise, taking off his pince-nez.

'Yes, it's me,' said a familiar voice and Gladys pushed past the maid and advanced into the middle of the room.

At the sight of her, Mr Quarles felt a sudden spasm of apprehension. He got up. 'You can go,' he said with dignity to the maid. She went. 'My dyah child!' He took Gladys's hand; she disengaged it. 'But what a surprise!'

'Ow, a pleasant surprise!' she answered sarcastically. Emotion always resuscitated the cockney in her. She sat down, planting herself with force and determination in the chair. 'Here I am,' that determined down-sitting seemed to imply, 'and here I stay' – perhaps even, 'here I bloody well stay.'

'Pleasant indeed,' said Mr Quarles mellifluously, for the sake of saying something. This was terrible, he was thinking. What could she want? And how should he get her out of the house again? But if necessary, he could say he'd sent for her to do some specially urgent typing for him. 'But very unexpected,' he added.

'Very.' She shut her mouth firmly and looked at him – with eyes

that Mr Quarles didn't at all like the expression of – as if in expecta-
tion. Of what?

'I'm delighted to see you, of course,' he went on.

'Ow, are you?' She laughed dangerously.

Mr Quarles looked at her and was afraid. He really hated the girl.
He began to wonder why he had ever desired her. 'Very glad,' he
repeated, with dignified emphasis. The great thing was to remain
dignified, firmly superior. 'But ...'

'*But,*' she echoed.

'Well, ryahlly, I think it was rather rash to come here.'

'He thinks it rather rash,' said Gladys, as though passing on the
information to an invisible third party.

'Not to say unnecessarah.'

'Well, I'm the judge of *that.*'

'After all, you know quite well that if you'd wanted to see me,
you'd only got to write and I'd have come at once. So why run the
risk of coming hyah?' He waited. But Gladys did not answer, only
looked at him with those hard green eyes of hers and that close-lipped
smile that seemed to shut in enigmatically heaven only knew what
dangerous thoughts and feelings. 'I'm ryahlly annoyed with you.'
The manner of Mr Quarles's rebuke was dignified and impressive,
but kind – always kind. 'Yes, ryahlly annoyed.'

Gladys threw back her head and uttered a shrill, short, hyena-like
laugh.

Mr Quarles was disconcerted. But he preserved his dignity. 'You
may laugh,' he said. 'But I speak syahriously. You had no right to
come. You knew quite well how important it is that nothing should
be suspected. Especially hyah – hyah, in my own house. You knew
it.'

'Yes, I knew it,' Gladys repeated, nodding her head truculently.
'And that's exactly why I came.' She was silent for a moment. But
the pressure of her feelings made silence no longer bearable. 'Because
I knew you were frightened,' she went on, 'frightened that people
might find out what you were reelly like. You dirty old swine!' And
suddenly losing all control of her fury, she sprang to her feet and
advanced on Mr Quarles so menacingly, that he recoiled a step. But
her attack was only verbal. 'Giving yourself such airs, as though you
was the Prince of Wales. And then taking a girl to dinner at the
Corner House. And blaming everybody else, worse than a parson,
when you're no better than a dirty old pig yourself. Yes, a dirty old

364

pig, that's what you are. Saying you loved me, indeed! I know what that sort of love is. Why, a girl isn't safe with you in a taxi. No, she isn't. You filthy old beast! And then ...'

'Ryahlly, ryahlly!' Mr Quarles had sufficiently recovered from his first shock of horrified surprise to be able to protest. This was terrible, unheard of. He felt himself being devastated, laid waste to, ravaged.

'"Ryahlly, ryahlly,"' she mimicked derisively. 'And then not even taking a girl to a decent seat at the theatre. But when it was a question of your having a bit of fun in your way – oh, lord! Nasty fat old swine! And carrying on all the time like Rudolph Valentino, with your chatter about all the women that had been in love with you. With *you*! You just look at yourself in the glass. Like a red egg, that's what you are.'

'Too unseemlah!'

'Talking about love with a face like that!' she went on, more shrilly than ever. 'An old swine like you! And then you only give a girl a rotten old watch and a pair of ear-rings, and the stones in them aren't even good ones, because I asked a jeweller and he said they weren't. And now, on top of everything I'm going to have a baby.'

'A babah?' repeated Mr Quarles incredulously, but with a deeper and more dreadful sinking of apprehension. 'Surely not a babah.'

'Yes, a baby!' Gladys shouted, stamping her foot. 'Can't you hear what I say, you old idiot? A baby. That's what I've come here about. And I won't go away till ...'

It was at this moment that Mrs Quarles walked in through the French window from the garden. She had been having a talk with Marjorie at the cottage and had come to tell Sidney that she had asked the two young people to dinner that evening.

'Oh, I'm sorry,' she said, halting on the threshold.

There was a moment's silence. Then, addressing herself this time to Mrs Quarles, Gladys began again with uncontrollable fury. Five minutes later she was no less uncontrollably sobbing and Mrs Quarles was trying to console her. Sidney took the opportunity to sneak out of the room. When the gong sounded for lunch, he sent down word to say that he was feeling very ill and would they please send up two lightly boiled eggs, some toast and butter, and a little stewed fruit.

Meanwhile in the study Mrs Quarles had hung solicitously over Gladys's chair. 'It's all right,' she kept repeating, patting the girl's shoulder, 'It's all right. You mustn't cry.' Poor girl! she was thinking. And what a dreadful scent! And how *could* Sidney? And again, poor girl, poor girl! 'Don't cry. Try to be brave. It'll be all right.'

Gladys's sobbing gradually subsided. Mrs Quarles's calm voice talked on consolingly. The girl listened. Then suddenly she jumped up. The face that confronted Mrs Quarles was savagely derisive through the tear stains.

'Ow, shut it!' she said, sarcastically, 'shut it! What do you take me for? A baby? Talking like that! You think you can talk me quiet, do you? Talk me out of my rights. Talky talky; baby's going to be good, isn't she? But you're mistaken, I tell you. You're damned well mistaken. And you'll know it soon enough, I can tell you.'

And with that she bounced out of the room into the garden and was gone.

Chapter Thirty-two

IN the little house at the end of the mews Elinor was alone. Faint rumblings of far-away traffic caressed the warm silence. A bowl of her mother's pot-pourri peopled the air for her with countless potential memories of childhood. She was arranging roses in a vase; huge white roses with petals of malleable porcelain, orange roses like whorls of congealed and perfumed flame. The chiming clock on the mantelpiece made a sudden and startling comment of eight notes and left the accorded vibrations to tinkle mournfully away into nothingness, like music on a departing ship. Half past three. And at six she was expecting Everard. Expecting Everard for a cocktail, she was at pains to explain to herself, before he took her out to dinner and the play. Just an evening's entertainment, like any other evening's entertainment. She kept telling herself so, because she knew, underneath, she was prophetically certain, that the evening wouldn't be in the least like other evenings, but cardinal, decisive. She would have to make up her mind, she would have to choose. But she didn't want to choose; that was why she tried to make herself believe that the evening was to be merely trivial and amusing. It was like covering a corpse with flowers. Mountains of flowers. But the corpse was always there, in spite of the concealing lilies. And a choice would have to be made, in spite of dinner at Kettner's and the theatre. Sighing, she picked up the heavy vase in both hands and was just lifting it on to the mantelpiece, when there was a loud knock at the door. Elinor started so violently that she almost dropped her burden. And the terror persisted, even when she had recovered from the first shock of surprise. A knock at the door, when she was alone in the lonely house, always set her heart uncomfortably beating. The idea that there was somebody there, waiting, listening, a stranger, an enemy perhaps (for Elinor's fancy was pregnant with horrible hairy faces peering round corners, with menacing hands, with knives and clubs and pistols) or perhaps a madman, listening intently for any sound of life within the house, waiting, waiting like a spider for her to open – this was a nightmare to her, a terror. The knock was repeated. Setting down the vase, she tiptoed with infinite precautions to the window and peeped between the curtains. On days when she was feeling particularly nervous she lacked the courage even to do this, but sat motionless, hoping that the noise of her heart might not be audible in the street, until the knocker at last wore out his patience and walked away. Next day the man from Selfridge's would heap coals of fire upon her by apologizing for the retarded delivery. 'Called yesterday evening, madam, but there was nobody at home.' And Elinor would feel ashamed of herself and a fool. But the next time she was alone and nervous, she would do exactly the same thing.

This afternoon she had courage; she ventured to look at the enemy – at as much of him, that is to say, as she could see, peeping sideways through the glass towards the door. A grey trouser-leg and an elbow were all that entered her field of vision. There was yet another knock. Then the trouser-leg moved back, the whole coat came into view, the black hat and, with a turn of the head, Spandrell's face. She ran to the door and opened.

'Spandrell!' she called, for he had already turned to go. He came back, lifting his hat. They shook hands. 'I'm so sorry,' she explained. 'I was alone. I thought it was at least a murderer. Then I peeped hrough the window and saw it was you.'

Spandrell gave vent to brief and noiseless laughter. 'But it might still be a murderer, even though it *is* me.' And he shook his knobbed stick at her with a playfulness which was, however, so dramatically like her imaginings of the genuinely homicidal article, that Elinor was made to feel quite uncomfortable.

She covered her emotion with a laugh, but decided not to ask him into the house. Standing on the doorstep she felt safer. 'All the same,' she said, 'it would be better to be murdered by somebody one knows than by a stranger.'

'Would it?' He looked at her; the corners of his wide weal-like mouth twitched into a curious smile. 'It needs a woman to think of those refinements. But if you should ever feel like having your throat cut in a thoroughly friendly fashion …'

'My dear Spandrell!' she protested, and felt gladder than ever that she was still on the doorstep and not inside the house.

' … Don't hesitate to send for me. No matter what the inconvenience,' he laid his hand on his heart, 'I'd fly to your side. Or rather to your neck.' He clicked his heels and bowed. 'But tell me,' he went on in another tone, 'is Philip anywhere about? I wanted him to come and dine to-night. At Sbisa's. I'd ask you too. Only it's a purely masculine affair.'

She thanked him. 'But I couldn't come in any case. And Philip's gone down into the country to see his mother. And will only be back just in time for Tolley's concert at the Queen's Hall. But I know he said he was going round to Sbisa's afterwards, on the chance of meeting someone. You'll see him then. Late.'

'Well, better late than never. Or at least,' he uttered another of his soundless laughs, 'so one piously hopes, where one's friends are concerned. Pious hopes! But to tell you the truth, the proverb needs changing. Better never than early.'

'Then why go to the trouble of asking people to dine?'

Spandrell shrugged his shoulders. 'Force of habit,' he said. 'And besides, I generally make them pay, when I ask them out.'

They were both laughing, when a loud ringing made them turn. A telegraph boy on a red bicycle was shooting down the mews towards them.

'Quarles?' he asked, as he jumped off.

Elinor took the telegram and opened it. The laughter went out of her face as she read. 'No answer.' The boy remounted and rode away. Elinor stood staring at the telegram as though its words were written in an unfamiliar language difficult to interpret. She looked at the watch on her wrist, then back at the flimsy paper.

'Will you do something for me?' she said at last, turning to Spandrell.

'But of course.'

'My baby's ill,' she explained. 'They want me to come. If I hurry' (she looked again at her watch), 'I can just catch the four-seventeen at Euston. But there'll be no time for anything else. Will you ring up Everard Webley for me and explain why I can't dine with him this evening?' It was a warning, she thought; a prohibition. 'Before six. At his office.'

'Before six,' he repeated slowly. 'At his office. Very well.'

'I must rush,' she said, holding out her hand.

'But I'll go and get you a cab, while you put on your hat.'

She thanked him. Spandrell hurried away along the mews. A prohibition, Elinor repeated to herself, as she adjusted her hat in front of the Venetian mirror in the living-room. The choice had been made for her. It was at once a relief and a disappointment. But made, she went on to reflect, at poor little Phil's expense. She wondered what was the matter with him. Her mother's telegram – such a characteristic one, that she could not help smiling now that she thought of it again – said nothing. 'PHILIP RATHER SOUFFRANT AND THOUGH UNALARMINGLY SHOULD ADVISE PROMPT HOME-COMING

MOTHER.' She remembered how nervous and difficult the child had been of late, how easily fatigued. She reproached herself for not having realized that he was working up for an illness. Now it had come. A touch of influenza, perhaps. 'I ought to have taken more care,' she kept repeating. She scribbled a note for her husband. 'The accompanying telegram explains my sudden departure. Join me at Gattenden to-morrow morning.' Where should she put it so that Philip should be sure to see it when he came in? Leaning against the clock on the mantelpiece? But would he necessarily want to know the time? Or on the table? No; pin it to the screen; that was the thing! He couldn't miss it. She ran upstairs in search of a pin. On Philip's dressing-table she saw a bunch of keys. She picked them up and looked at them, frowning. 'The idiot's forgotten his latch-key. How will he get in to-night?' The noise of a taxi under the window suggested a solution. She hurried down, pinned the note and the telegram conspicuously to the screen that shut off the drawing-room part of the living-room from the door and let herself out into the mews. Spandrell was standing at the door of the cab.

'That *is* kind of you,' she said. 'But I haven't finished exploiting you even now.' She held up the keys. 'When you see Philip this evening, give him these and tell him with my love that he's an imbecile. He wouldn't have been able to get in without them.' Spandrell took the keys in silence. 'And tell him why I've gone and that I'm expecting him to-morrow.' She got into the cab. 'And don't forget to ring up Webley. Before six. Because he was supposed to be meeting me here at six.'

'Here?' he asked with an expression of sudden interest and curiosity which Elinor found rather offensive and embarrassing. Was he imagining something, was he daring to suppose …?

'Yes, here,' she nodded curtly.

'I won't forget,' he assured her emphatically, and there was still something about his expression which made her suspect a private significance behind the obvious words.

'Thank you,' said Elinor, without cordiality. 'And now I must fly.' She gave the word to the driver. The taxi backed up the mews, under the archway, turned and was gone.

Spandrell walked slowly up to Hyde Park Corner. From the public call-box in the station he telephoned to Illidge.

*

Everard Webley was striding about the room, dictating. Sedentary composition he found impossible. 'How do people write when they're grafted to chairs all day long, year in year out?' He found it incomprehensible. 'When I'm sitting in a chair, or lying on a bed, I become like the furniture I've combined myself with – mere wood and stuffing. My mind doesn't move unless my muscles move.' On days when his correspondence was large, when there were articles to dictate, speeches to compose, Everard's working day was an eight-hour walking tour. 'Doing the lion,' was how his secretaries described his methods of dictation. He was doing the lion now – the restless lion, a little before feeding time – pacing from wall to wall of his big bare office.

'Remember,' he was saying, frowning, as he spoke, at the grey carpet; under his secretary's pencil the shorthand scurried across the page, 'remember that the final authority is in all cases mine and that, so long as I remain at the head of the B.B.F., every attempt at insubordination will be promptly and ruthlessly suppressed. Yours etcetera.' He was silent and, walking back to his desk from the spot where the conclusion of his thoughtful and leonine pacing had left him, he turned over the scattered papers. 'That seems to be all,' he said and looked at his watch. It was just after a quarter to six. 'Have these last letters ready for me in the morning,' he went on. 'I'll sign them then.' He took his hat from the peg. 'Good evening.' And slamming the door, he descended the stairs two at a time. Outside the house he found his chauffeur waiting with the car. It was a powerful machine (for Everard was a lover of furious driving) and, since he also enjoyed the sensation of battling with the weather and the wind of his own speed, open. A tightly-stretched waterproof sheet covered the whole of the back part of the touring body like a deck, leaving only the two front seats available for passengers. 'I shan't need you any more this evening,' he said to the chauffeur, as he settled into the driver's seat. 'You can go.'

He touched the self-starter, threw the car into gear and shot off with a violent impetuosity. Several dozens of horses were bottled in the three litres of Everard's cylinders; he liked to make them work their hardest. Full speed ahead and then, a yard from the impending accident, jam on the brakes, that was his method. Driving with Everard in town was almost too exciting. Elinor had protested the last time he took her out. 'I don't so much mind dying,' she had said. 'But I really should object to passing the rest of my life with two wooden legs and a broken nose.' He had laughed. 'You're quite safe with me. I don't have accidents.' 'You're above such things, are you?' she had mocked. 'Well, if you like to put it like that ...' The brakes were applied with such violence that Elinor had had to clutch at the arms of her seat to prevent herself from being thrown against the wind-screen. 'Imbecile,' he had shouted at the bewildered old gentleman whose hen-like indecisions in the roadway had so nearly landed him under Everard's Dunlops. 'If you like to put it like that –' and the car had shot forward again with a jerk that flattened Elinor against the back of her seat –'you may. I don't have accidents. I manufacture my own luck.'

Remembering the incident, Everard smiled to himself as he drove along Oxford Street. A railway delivery van held up his progress. Horses oughtn't to be allowed in the streets. 'Either you take me,' he would say to her, 'and in the end that means you'll have to make the thing public – leave Philip and come to me ' – (for he intended to be entirely honest with her; there were to be no false pretences of any kind); 'either that, or else ...' There was an opportunity to pass the delivery van; he pressed the accelerator and darted forward with a swerve to the right and another, past the nose of the old and patiently trotting horse, to the left again. 'Or else we don't see one another again.' It was to be an ultimatum. Brutal. But Everard hated situations that were neither one thing nor the other. He preferred definite knowedge, however unpleasant, to even the most hopefully blissful of uncertainties. And in this case the uncertainty wasn't at all blissful. At the entry to Oxford Circus a policeman lifted his hand. It was seven minutes to six. She was too squeamish, he thought, looking round, too sensitive about these new buildings. Everard found nothing displeasing in the massively florid baroque of modern commerce. It was vigorous and dramatic; it was large, it was expensive it symbolized progress. 'But it's so revoltingly vulgar!' she had protested. 'But it's difficult,' he had answered, 'not to be vulgar, when one isn't dead. You object to these people doing things. And I agree. doing things *is* rather vulgar.' She had the typical consumer's point of view, not the producer's. The policeman dropped his hand. Slowly, at first, but with gathering impetus, the pent-up flood of traffic rumbled forward. A luxury mind – that was what she had; not a necessity mind. A mind that thought of the world only in terms of beauty and enjoyment, not of use; a mind preoccupied with sensations and shades of feeling, and preoccupied with them for their own sake, not because sharp eyes and intuition are necessary in the struggle for life. Indeed, she hardly knew that there was a struggle. He ought to have disapproved of her; and he would have disapproved (Everard smiled to himself as he made the reflection) if he hadn't been in love with her. He would have ... Flop! from the roof of a passing bus a banana skin fell like a draggled star-fish on to the bonnet in front of him. A whoop of laughter sounded through the roaring. Lifting his eyes he saw two young girls looking down at him over the rail, open-mouthed, like a pair of pretty little gargoyles, and laughing, laughing as though there had never been a joke in the world before that moment. Everard shook his fist at them and laughed too. How much Elinor would have enjoyed that! he thought. She who so loved the streets and their comedies. What an eye she had for the odd, the amusing, the significant! Where he perceived only a mass of undifferentiated humanity, she distinguished individuals. And her talent for inventing life histories for her once-glimpsed oddities was no less remarkable than her detecting eye. She would have known all about those young girls – their class, the sort of homes they came from, where they bought their clothes and how much they paid for them, whether they were still virtuous, what books they read, and which were their favourite cinema actors. Imagining to himself what Elinor would have said, remembering her laughter and the look in her eyes and her tricks of speech, he was suddenly filled with so much tenderness, such a violent yet delicately affectionate longing to be with her, that he could hardly bear to be separated from her for even a moment longer. He hooted at the taxi in front of him, he tried to thrust past on the right. An obstructing street island compelled him to fall back, but not before the taxi-driver had had time to throw doubts on his legitimacy, his heterosexuality, and his prospects of happiness in another world. With as much gusto and incomparably more originality, Everard swore back. He felt himself overflowing with life, extraordinarily vigorous and strong, inexplicably and (but for the fact that it would be at least five minutes before he saw Elinor) perfectly happy. Yes, perfectly happy; for he knew (with what calm conviction!) that she would say yes, that she loved him. And his happiness became more intense, more poignant and at the same time more serene, as he swung round past the Marble Arch into the Park. His prophetic conviction deepened into something like remembered certainty, as though the future were already history. The sun was low and wherever its rosily golden light touched earth, it was as if a premature and more luminous autumn had fired the leaves and grass. Great shafts of powdery radiance leaned down from the west between the trees and in the shadows the twilight was a mist of lavender, a mist of blue and darkening indigo, plane after plane into the hazy London distance. And the couples strolling across the grass, the children playing were alternately eclipsed and transfigured as they passed from shade to sunlight, were alternately insignificant and brilliantly miraculous. It was as though a capricious god, now bored and now enchanted by his creatures, had turned upon them at one moment an eye of withering indifference and at the next, with his love, had bestowed upon them some of his own divinity. The road stretched clear and polished before him; but Everard hardly exceeded the speed limit – in spite of his longing; in a sense because he loved her so much. For it was all so beautiful; and where beauty was, there too, for Everard, by some private logic, some personal necessity, was Elinor. She was with him now, because she would have enjoyed this loveliness so much. And because she would have wanted to prolong the pleasure, he crept along. The engine was turning at a bare fifteen hundred revolutions a minute; the dynamo was hardly charging. A Baby Austin passed him as though he were standing still. Let them pass! Everard was thinking of the phrases in which he would describe to her this marvel. Through the railings, the buses in Park Lane blazed scarlet and glittered like triumphal cars in a pageant. Faintly through the noise of the traffic, a clock struck six; and before it had finished, another chimed in, melodious, sweet, and with a touch of melancholy – the very voice of the bright evening and of his happiness. And now, for all his creeping, the marble gateways of Hyde Park Corner were before him. Offered, in spite of the nakedness and the more than Swedish development of his abdominal muscles, by the Ladies of England to the Victor of Waterloo, the bronze Achilles, whose flesh had once been Napoleon's cannons, stood with shield raised, sword brandished, menacing and defending himself against the pale and empty sky. It was almost regretfully, though he longed to be at his journey's end, that Everard left the Park. Once more the towering buses roared before him and behind. Rounding the archipelago of islands he vowed that to-morrow, if Elinor said Yes, he would send five pounds to St George's Hospital. He knew she would. The money was as good as given already. He turned out of Grosvenor Place; the roaring faded behind him. Belgrave Square was an oasis of trees; the starlings chattered in a rural silence. Everard turned once,

374

vice, and yet again. On the left, between the houses was an archway. He passed it by a yard or two, stopped and, pulling the wheel over, backed under it into the mews, back, back to the very end of the blind alley. He stopped the car and got out. How charming the yellow curtains looked! His heart was beating very fast. He felt as he had felt when he made his first speech, half-frightened, half-exultant. Mounting the doorstep, he knocked and waited twenty heart-beats; the house gave forth no answering sound. He knocked again and, remembering what Elinor had told him of her terrors, accompanied the rap with a whistle and, as though in answer to the unspoken challenge of her fears, a call of 'Friend!' And then, suddenly, he noticed that the door was not latched, but only ajar. He pushed; it swung open. Everard stepped over the threshold.

'Elinor!' he called, thinking that she must be upstairs. 'Elinor!'

There was still no answer. Or was she playing a joke? Would she suddenly pounce out at him from behind one of the screens. He smiled to himself at the thought and was advancing to explore the silent room, when his eye was caught by the papers pinned so conspicuously to a panel of the screen on the right. He approached and had just begun to read, 'The accompanying telegram will explain ...' when a sound behind him made him turn his head. A man was standing within four feet of him, his hands raised; the club which they grasped had already begun to swing sideways and forward from over the right shoulder. Everard threw up his arm, too late. The blow caught him on the left temple. It was as though a light had suddenly been turned out. He was not even conscious of falling.

*

Mrs Quarles kissed her son. 'Dear Phil,' she said. 'It's good of you to have come so quickly.'

'You're not looking very well, mother.'

'A little tired, that's all. And worried,' she added after a moment's pause and with a sigh.

'Worried?'

'About your father. He's not well,' she went on, speaking slowly and as if with reluctance. 'He wanted very specially to see you. That was why I wired.'

'He isn't dangerously ill?'

'Not physically,' Mrs Quarles replied. 'But his nerves. ... It's a kind of breakdown. He's very excited. Very unstable.'

'But what's the cause?'

Mrs Quarles was silent. And when at last she spoke it was with an obvious effort, as though each word had to force its way past some inward barrier. Her sensitive face was fixed and strained. 'Something has happened to upset him,' she said. 'He's had a great shock.' And slowly, word by word, the story came out.

Bent forward in his chair, his elbows on his knees, his chin in his hands, Philip listened. After a first glance at his mother's face, he kept his eyes fixed on the ground. He felt that to look at her, to meet her eyes would be the infliction of an unnecessary embarrassment. Speaking was already a pain to her and a humiliation; let her at least speak unseen, as though there were nobody there to witness her distress. His averted eyes left her a kind of spiritual privacy. Word after word, in a colourless soft voice, Mrs Quarles talked on. Incident succeeded sordid incident. When she began to tell the story of Gladys's visit of two days before, Philip could not bear to listen any longer. It was too humiliating for her; he could not permit her to go on.

'Yes, yes, I can imagine,' he said, interrupting her. And jumping up, he limped with quick nervous steps to the window. 'Don't go on.' He stood there for a minute, looking out at the lawn and the thick yew tree walls and the harvest-coloured hills beyond, on the further side of the valley. The scene was almost exasperatingly placid. Philip turned, limped back across the room and standing for a moment behind his mother's chair laid a hand on her shoulder; then walked away again.

'Don't think about it any more,' he said. 'I'll do whatever has to be done.' He looked forward with an enormous distaste to loud and undignified scenes, to disputes and vulgar hagglings. 'Perhaps I'd better go and see father,' he suggested.

Mrs Quarles nodded. 'He was very anxious to see you.'

'Why?'

'I don't know. But he's been insisting.'

'Does he talk about … well, this business?'

'No. Never mentions it. I have the impression that he forgets about it deliberately.'

'Then I'd better not speak about it.'

'Not unless he begins,' Mrs Quarles advised. 'Mostly he talks about himself. About the past, about his health – pessimistically. You must try to cheer him.' Philip nodded. 'And humour him,' his mother went on; 'don't contradict. He easily flares up. It isn't good for him to get excited.'

Philip listened. As though he were a dangerous animal, he was thinking; or a naughty child. The misery of it, the anxiety, the humiliation for his mother!

'And don't stay too long,' she added.

Philip left her. The fool, he said to himself as he crossed the hall, the damned fool! The sudden anger and contempt with which he thought of his father were tempered by no previous affection. Neither, for that matter, were they exacerbated by any previous hatred. Up to this time Philip had neither loved nor disliked his father. Unreflectingly tolerant or, at the worst, with a touch of amused resignation, he had just accepted his existence. There was nothing in his memories of childhood to justify more positive emotions. As a father, Mr Quarles had shown himself no less erratic and no less ineffectual than as a politician or as a man of business. Brief periods of enthusiastic interest in his children had alternated with long periods, during which he almost ignored their existence. Philip and his brother had preferred him during the seasons of neglect; for he had ignored them benevolently. They liked him less when he was interested in their well-being. For the interest was generally not so much in the children as in a theory of education or hygiene. After meeting an eminent doctor, after reading the latest book on pedagogical methods, Mr Quarles would wake up to the discovery that, unless something were drastically done, his sons were likely to grow up into idiots and cripples, weak-minded and with bodies poisoned by the wrong food and distorted by improper exercise. And then, for a few weeks, the two boys would be stuffed with raw carrots or overdone beef (it depended on the doctor Mr Quarles happened to have met); would be drilled, or taught folk-dancing and eurhythmics; would be made to learn poetry by rote (if it happened to be the memory that was important at the moment) or else (if it happened to be the ratiocinative faculties) would be turned out into the garden, told to plant sticks in the lawn and, by measuring the shadow at different hours of the day, discover for themselves the principles of trigonometry. While the fit lasted, life for the two boys was almost intolerable. And if Mrs Quarles protested, Sidney flew into a rage and told her that she was a selfishly doting mother, to whom the true welfare of her children meant nothing. Mrs Quarles did not insist too strongly; for she knew that, thwarted, Sidney would probably become more obstinate; humoured, he would forget his enthusiasm. And in fact, after a few weeks, Sidney would duly tire of labours which produced no quick and obvious results. His hygiene had not made the boys perceptibly larger or stronger; they had not grown appreciably more intelligent for his pedagogy. All that they quite indubitably were was a daily and hourly bore. 'Affairs of greater moment' would occupy more and more of his attention, until gradually, like the Cheshire cat, he had faded altogether out of the world of the schoolroom and the nursery into higher and more comfortable spheres. The boys settled down again to happiness.

Arrested at the door of his father's room by the sounds from within, Philip listened. His face took on an expression of anxiety, even of alarm. That voice? And his father, he had been told, was alone. Talking to himself? Was he as bad as all that? Bracing himself, Philip opened the door and was immediately reassured to find that what he had taken for insanity was only dictation to the dictaphone. Propped up on pillows, Mr Quarles was half-sitting, half-lying in his bed. His face, his very scalp were flushed and shining, and his pink silk pyjamas were like an intensified continuation of the same fever. The dictaphone stood on the table by his bed; Mr Quarles was talking into the mouthpiece of its flexible speaking-tube. 'True greatness,' he was saying sonorously, 'is inversely proportional to myahr immediate success. Ah, *hyah* you are!' he cried, looking round as the door opened. He stopped the clockwork of the machine, hung up the speaking-tube and stretched out a welcoming hand. Simple gestures. But there was something, it seemed to Philip, extravagant about all his movements. It was as though he were on the stage. The eyes which he turned on Philip were unnaturally bright. 'I'm so glad you've come. So glad, dyah boy.' He patted Philip's hand; the loud voice suddenly trembled.

Unused to such demonstrations, Philip was embarrassed. 'Well, how are you feeling?' he asked with an assumption of cheeriness.

Mr Quarles shook his head and pressed his son's hand without speaking. Philip was more than ever embarrassed at seeing that the tears had come into his eyes. How could one go on hating and being angry?

'But you'll be all right,' he said, trying to be reassuring. 'It's just a question of resting for a bit.'

Mr Quarles tightened the clasp of his hand. 'Don't tell your mother,' he said. 'But I feel that the end's nyah.'

'But that's nonsense, father. You mustn't talk like that.'

'Nyah,' Mr Quarles repeated, obstinately nodding, 'very nyah.

That's why I'm so glad you're hyah. I should have been unhappah to die when you were at the other end of the wahld. But with you hyah, I feel I can go' – his voice trembled again – 'quite contentedlah.' Once more he squeezed Philip's hand. He was convinced that he had always been a devoted father, living for nothing but his children. And so he had been, every now and then. 'Yes, quite contentedlah.' He pulled out his handkerchief, blew his nose, and while he was doing so surreptitiously wiped his eyes.

'But you're not going to die.'

'Yes, yes,' Mr Quarles insisted. 'I can feel it.' He genuinely did feel it; he believed he was going to die, because there was at least a part of his mind that desired to die. These complications of the last weeks had been too much for him; and the future promised to be worse, if that were possible. To fade out, painlessly – that would be the best solution of all his problems. He wished, he believed; and, believing in his approaching death, he pitied himself as a victim and at the same time admired himself for the resigned nobility with which he supported his fate.

'But you're not going to die,' Philip dully insisted, not knowing what consolation, beyond mere denial, to offer. He had no gift for dealing extempore with the emotional situations of practical life. 'There's nothing … ' He was going to say, 'There's nothing the matter with you'; but checked himself, reflecting, before it was too late, that his father might be offended.

'Let's say no more about it.' Mr Quarles spoke tartly; there was a look of annoyance in his eye. Philip remembered what his mother had said about humouring him. He kept silence. 'One can't quarrel with Destinah,' Mr Quarles went on in another tone. 'Destinah,' he repeated with a sigh. 'You've been fortunate, dyah boy; you discovered your vocation from the farst. Fate has treated you well.'

Philip nodded. He had often thought so himself, with a certain apprehension even. He had an obscure belief in nemesis.

'Whereas in my case …' Mr Quarles did not finish the sentence, but raised his hand and let it fall again, hopelessly, on to the coverlet. 'I wasted yahs of my life on false scents. Yahs and yahs before I discovered my ryahl bent. A philosopher's wasted on practical affairs. He's even absard. Like what's-his-name's albatross. You know.'

Philip was puzzled. 'Do you mean the one in *The Ancient Mariner?*'

'No, no,' said Mr Quarles impatiently. 'That Frenchman.'

'Oh, of course.' Philip had caught the reference. 'Le Poète est semblable au prince des nuées. Baudelaire, you mean.'

'Baudelaire, of course.'

> 'Exilé sur le sol au milieu des huées,
> Ses ailes de géant l'empêchent de marcher,'

Philip quoted, glad to be able to divert the conversation if only for a moment from personalities to literature.

His father was delighted. 'Exactlah!' he cried triumphantly. 'It's the same with philosophers. Their wings prevent them from walking. For tharty yahs I tried to be a walker – in politics, in business. I didn't ryahlize that my place was in the air, not on the ground. In the air!' he repeated, raising his arm. 'I had wings.' He agitated his hand in a rapid tremolo. 'Wings, and didn't know it.' His voice had grown louder, his eyes brighter, his face pinker and more shiny. His whole person expressed such an excitement, such restlessness and exaltation, that Philip was seriously disquieted.

'Hadn't you better rest a little?' he anxiously suggested.

Mr Quarles disregarded the interruption. 'Wings, wings,' he cried. 'I had wings and if I'd ryahlized it as a young man, what heights I might have flown to! But I tried to walk. In the mud. For tharty yahs. Only after tharty yahs did I discover that I was meant to be flying. And now I must give up almost before I've begun.' He sighed and, leaning back against his pillows, he shot the words almost perpendicularly up into the air. 'My work unfinished. My dreams unryahlized. Fate's been hard.'

'But you'll have all the time you need to finish your work.'

'No, no,' Mr Quarles insisted, shaking his head. He wanted to be one of fate's martyrs, to be able to point to himself and say: There, but for the malignity of providence, goes Aristotle. Destiny's unkindness justified everything – his failure in sugar, in politics, in farming, the coldness with which his first book had been received, the indefinite delay in the appearance of the second; it even justified in some not easily explicable fashion his having put Gladys in a family way. To be a seducer of servants, secretaries, peasant girls was part of his unhappy destiny. And now that, to crown the edifice of his misfortune, he was about to die (prematurely but stoically, like the noblest Roman of them all), how trivial, how wretchedly insignificant was this matter of lost virginities and impending babies! And how unseemly, at the philosophic death-bed, was all the outcry! But he could only ignore it on condition that this was genuinely his death-bed and that destiny was universally admitted to have been cruel. A martyred philosopher on the point of death was justified in refusing to be bothered with Gladys and her baby. That was why (though the reason was felt and not formulated) Mr Quarles repudiated, so vigorously and even with annoyance, his son's consoling assurances of long life; that was why he arraigned malignant providence and magnified with even more than his ordinary self-complaisance the talents which providence had prevented him from using.

'No, no, dyah boy,' he repeated. 'I shall never finish. And that was one of the reasons why I wanted to have a talk with you.'

Philip looked at him with a certain apprehension. What was coming next? he wondered. There was a little silence.

'One doesn't want to shuffle off entirely unrecorded,' said Mr Quarles in a voice made husky by a recrudescence of self-pity. 'Shyahr extinction – it's difficult to face.' Before his mind's eye the void expanded, lampless and abysmal. Death. It might be the end of his troubles; but it was none the less appalling. 'You understand the feeling?' he asked.

'Perfectly,' said Philip, 'perfectly. But in your case, father ...' Mr Quarles who had been blowing his nose again raised a protesting hand. 'No, no.' He had made up his mind that he was going to die; it was useless for anyone to attempt to dissuade him. 'But if you understand my feeling, that's all that matters. I can depart in peace with the knowledge that you won't allow all memory of me to disappyah completely. Dyah boy, you shall be my literary executor. There are some fragments of my writing. ...'

'The book on democracy?' asked Philip, who saw himself being called upon to complete the largest work on the subject yet projected. His father's answer took a load off his mind.

'No, not that,' Mr Quarles hastily replied. 'Only the bare matyahrials of that book exist. And to a great extent not on paper. Only in my mind. In fact,' he went on, 'I was just going to tell you that I wanted all my notes for the big book destroyed. Without being looked at. They're myah jottings. Meaningless except to me.' Mr Quarles was not anxious that the emptiness of his files and the prevailing blankness of the cards in his card-index should be posthumously discovered and commented on. 'They must all be destroyed, do you understand?'

Philip made no protest.

'What I wanted to entrust to you, dyah boy,' Mr Quarles went on, 'was a collection of more intimate fragments. Reflections on life, records of pahsonal expyahriences. Things like that.'

Philip nodded. 'I see.'

'I've been jotting them down for a long time past,' said Mr Quarles. 'Memories and Reflections of Fifty Yahs – that might be a good title. There's a lot in my notebooks. And these last days I've been recording on this.' He tapped the dictaphone. 'When one's ill, you know, one thinks a lot.' He sighed. 'Syahriously.'

'Of course,' Philip agreed.

'If you'd care to listen …' he indicated the dictaphone.

Philip nodded. Mr Quarles prepared the machine. 'It'll give you an idyah of the kind of thing. Thoughts and memories. Hyah.' He pushed the machine across the table and, pushing, sent a piece of paper fluttering to the ground. It lay there on the carpet, chequered, a puzzle. 'This is where you listen.'

Philip listened. After a moment of scratchy roaring, the Punch and Judy parody of his father's voice said, 'The key to the problem of sex: – passion is sacred, a manifestation of the divinitah.' And then, without stop or transition, but in a slightly different tone: 'The wahrst thing about politics is the frivolitah of politicians. Meeting Asquith one evening at dinner, I forget now where, I took the opportunitah of ahrging on him the necessitah of abolishing capital punishment. One of the most syahrious questions of modern life. But he myahrly suggested that we should go and play bridge. Unit of measure seven letters long: Verchok. Fastidious men do not live in pigsties, nor can they long remain in politics or business. There are nature's Greeks and nature's Mrs Grundies. I never shared the mob's high opinion of Lloyd George. Every man is born with a natural right to be happy; but what ferocious repression when anybody tried to claim his right! Brazilian stork, six letters: jabiru. True greatness is invarsely proportional to myahr immediate success. Ah, *hyah* you …!' The scratchy roar supervened.

'Yes, I see the style of the thing,' said Philip, looking up. 'How does one stop this affair? Ah, that's it.' He stopped it.

'So many thoughts occur to me as I lie hyah,' said Mr Quarles, aimed upwards, as though speaking against aircraft. 'Such a wealth! I could never record them all but for the machine. It's wonderful. Ryahly wonderful!'

Chapter Thirty-three

ELINOR had had time to telegraph from Euston. On her arrival, she found the car waiting for her at the station. 'How is he?' she asked the chauffeur. But Paxton was vague, didn't rightly know. Privately, he thought it was one of these ridiculous fusses about nothing, such as the rich are always making, particularly where their children are concerned. They drove up to Gattenden and the landscape of the Chilterns in the ripe evening light was so serenely beautiful, that Elinor began to feel less anxious and even half wished that she had stayed till the last train. She would have been able in that case to see Webley. But hadn't she decided that she was really almost glad not to be seeing him? One can be glad and sorry at the same time. Passing the north entrance to the Park, she had a glimpse through the bars of Lord Gattenden's bath-chair standing just inside the gate. The ass had stopped and was eating grass at the side of the road, the reins hung loose and the marquess was too deeply absorbed in a thick red morocco quarto to be able to think of driving. The car hurried on; but that second's glimpse of the old man sitting with his book behind the grey donkey, as she had so often seen him sitting and reading; that brief revelation of life living itself regularly, unvaryingly in the same old familiar way, was as reassuring as the calm loveliness of beech-trees and bracken, of green-golden foreground and violet distances.

And there at last was the Hall! The old house seemed to doze in the westering sun like a basking animal; you could almost fancy that it purred. And the lawn was like the most expensive green velvet; and in the windless air the huge Wellingtonia had all the dignified gravity of an old gentleman who sits down to meditate after an enormous meal. There could be nothing much wrong here. She jumped out of the car and ran straight upstairs to the nursery. Phil was lying in bed, quite still and with closed eyes. Miss Fulkes, who was sitting beside him, turned as she entered, rose and came to meet her. One glance at her face was enough to convince Elinor that the blue and golden tranquillity of the landscape, the dozing house, the marquess and his ass had been lying comforters. 'All's well,' they had seemed to say. 'Everything's going on as usual.' But Miss Fulkes looked pale and frightened, as though she had seen a ghost.

'What's the matter?' Elinor whispered with a sudden return of all her anxiety, and before Miss Fulkes had time to answer, 'Is he asleep?' she added. If he were asleep, she was thinking, it was a good sign; he looked as though he were asleep.

But Miss Fulkes shook her head. The gesture was superfluous. For the question was hardly out of Elinor's mouth, when the child made a sudden spasmodic movement under the sheets. His face contracted with pain. He uttered a little whimpering moan.

'His head hurts him so much,' said Miss Fulkes. There was a look of terror and misery in her eyes.

'Go and have a rest,' said Elinor.

Miss Fulkes hesitated, shook her head. 'I'd like to be useful. ...'

Elinor insisted. 'You'll be more useful when you've rested. ...' She saw Miss Fulkes's lips trembling, her eyes growing suddenly bright with tears.

'Go along,' she said and pressed her arm consolingly.

Miss Fulkes obeyed with a sudden alacrity. She was afraid that she might start crying before she got to her room.

Elinor sat down by the bed. She took the little hand that lay on the turned-back sheet, she passed her fingers through the child's pale hair caressingly, soothingly. 'Sleep,' she whispered, as her fingers caressed him, 'sleep, sleep.' But the child still stirred uneasily; and every now and then his face was distorted with sudden pain; he shook his head, as though trying to shake off the thing that was hurting him, he uttered his little whimpering moan. And bending over him, Elinor felt as though her heart were being crushed within her breast, as though a hand were at her throat, choking her.

'My darling,' she said beseechingly, imploring him not to suffer, 'my darling.'

And she pressed the small hand more tightly, she let her palm rest more heavily on his hot forehead, as if to stifle the pain or at least to steady the shuddering little body against its attacks. And all her will commanded the pain to cease under her fingers, to come out of him – out of him, through her fingers, into her own body. But still he fidgeted restlessly in his bed, turning his head from one side to the other, now drawing up his legs, now straightening them out with a sharp spasmodic kick under the sheets. And still the pain returned, stabbing; and the face made its grimace of agony, the parted lips gave utterance to the little whimpering cry, again and again. She stroked his forehead, she whispered tender words. And that was all she could do. The sense of her helplessness suffocated her. At her

384

throat and heart the invisible hands tightened their grip.

'How do you find him?' asked Mrs Bidlake, when her daughter came down.

Elinor did not answer, but turned away her face. The question had brought the tears rushing into her eyes. Mrs Bidlake put her arms round her and kissed her. Elinor hid her face against her mother's shoulder. 'You must be strong,' she kept saying to herself. 'You mustn't cry, mustn't break down. Be strong. To help him.' Her mother held her more closely. The physical contact comforted her, gave her the strength for which she was praying. She made an effort of will and with a deep intaken breath swallowed down the sobs in her throat. She looked up at her mother and gratefully smiled. Her lips still trembled a little; but the will had conquered.

'I'm stupid,' she said apologetically. 'I couldn't help it. It's so horrible to see him suffer. Helplessly. It's dreadful. Even if one knows that it'll be all right in the end.'

Mrs Bidlake sighed. 'Dreadful,' she echoed, 'dreadful,' and closed her eyes in a meditative perplexity. There was a silence. 'By the way,' she went on, opening them again to look at her daughter, 'I think you ought to keep an eye on Miss Fulkes. I don't know whether her influence is always entirely good.'

'Miss Fulkes's influence?' said Elinor, opening her eyes in astonishment. 'But she's the nicest, the most conscientious ...'

'Oh, not that, not that!' said Mrs Bidlake hastily. 'Her artistic influence, I mean. When I went up to see Phil the day before yesterday I found her showing him such dreadfully vulgar pictures of a dog.'

'Bonzo?' suggested Elinor.

Her mother nodded. 'Yes, Bonzo.' She pronounced the word with a certain distaste. 'If he wants pictures of animals, there are such excellent reproductions of Persian miniatures at the British Museum. It's so easy to spoil a child's taste. ... But Elinor! My dear!'

Suddenly and uncontrollably, Elinor had begun to laugh. To laugh and to cry, uncontrollably. Grief alone she had been able to master. But grief allied with Bonzo was irresistible. Something broke inside her and she found herself sobbing with a violent, painful, and hysterical laughter.

Mrs Bidlake helplessly patted her shoulder. 'My dear,' she kept repeating. 'Elinor!'

Roused from uneasy and nightmarish dozing, John Bidlake shouted furiously from the library. 'Stop that cackling,' commanded the angry-plaintive voice. 'For God's sake.'

But Elinor could not stop.

'Screaming like parrots,' John Bidlake went on muttering to himself.

'Some idiotic joke. When one isn't well. ...'

*

'Now, for God's sake,' said Spandrell roughly, 'pull yourself together.'

Illidge pressed his handkerchief to his mouth; he was afraid of being sick. 'I think I'll lie down for a moment,' he whispered. But when he tried to walk, it was as though his legs were dead under him. It might have been a paralytic who dragged himself to the sofa.

'What you need is a mouthful of spirits,' said Spandrell. He crossed the room. A bottle of brandy stood on the sideboard, and from the kitchen he returned with glasses. He poured out two fingers of the spirit. 'Here. Drink this.' Illidge took and sipped. 'One would think we were crossing the Channel,' Spandrell went on with ferocious mockery, as he helped himself to brandy. 'Study in green and ginger – that's how Whistler would have described you now. Apple-green. Moss-green.'

Illidge looked at him for a moment, then turned away, unable to face the steady glance of those contemptuous grey eyes. He had never felt such hatred as he now felt for Spandrell.

'Not to say frog-green, slime-green, scum-green,' the other went on.

'Oh, shut up!' cried Illidge in a voice that had recovered some of its resonance and hardly wavered. Spandrell's mockery had steadied his nerves. Hate, like brandy, is a stimulant. He took another burning gulp. There was a silence.

'When you feel like it,' said Spandrell, putting down his emptied glass, 'you can come and help me clear up.' He rose and walked round the screen, out of sight.

Everard Webley's body was lying where it had fallen, on its side, with the arms reaching out across the floor. The chloroform-soaked handkerchief still covered the face. Spandrell bent down and twitched it away. The temple which had been struck was against the floor; seen from above the face seemed unwounded.

His hands in his pockets, Spandrell stood looking down at the body.

'Five minutes ago,' he said to himself, formulating his thoughts in words, that his realization of their significance might be the more complete, 'five minutes ago, it was alive, it had a soul. Alive,' he repeated and balancing himself unsteadily on one leg, with the other foot he touched the dead cheek, he pushed forward the ear and let it flick back again. 'A soul.' And for a moment he allowed some of his weight to rest on what had been Everard Webley's face. He withdrew his foot; the print of it remained, dust-grey, on the white skin. 'Trampling on a dead face,' he said to himself. Why had he done it? 'Trampling.' He raised his foot again and pressed his heel into the socket of the eye, gently, tentatively, as though experimenting with outrage. 'Like grapes,' he thought. 'Trampling wine out of the grapes.' It was in his power to trample this thing into a pulp. But he had done enough. Symbolically, he had trodden out the essential horror from his murder; it flowed from under his trampling feet. The essential horror? But it was more stupid and disgusting than horrible. Pushing the toe of his boot under the chin, he rolled the head over until the face was looking up, open-mouthed and with half-shut eyes, at the ceiling. Above and behind the left eye was a huge red contusion. There were trickles of blood on the left cheek, already dry, and where the forehead had rested on the floor, a little pool – hardly even a pool – a smear.

'Incredibly little blood,' said Spandrell aloud.

At the sound of his calm voice Illidge violently started.

Spandrell withdrew his supporting foot. The dead face fell back with a little thump on to its side.

'It's a complete justification for Bishop Odo's mace,' he went on dispassionately. That he should find himself recalling, at this of all moments, the comical prancings of that conscientious churchman in the Bayeux tapestry – that too was part of the essential horror. The frivolousness of the human mind! The wandering irrelevance! Evil might have a certain dignity. But silliness ...

Illidge heard him walk into the kitchen. There was the gradually sharpening note of water running into a pail. The tap was turned off; there were foot-falls; the bucket was set down with a metallic clink.

'Luckily,' Spandrell went on, in comment on his last remark. 'Or else I don't know what we should have done about the mess.'

Illidge listened with a strained and horrified attention to the sounds that came to him from the other side of the screen. A limp and meaty thud; was that an arm lifted and dropped? The sibilant sliding of a soft and heavy object across the floor. Then the splash of water, the homely noise of scrubbing. And at these sounds, so incomparably more horrible, more profoundly significant than any words, however brutal, however calmly cynical, that Spandrell could say, he felt a recrudescence of that sinking, that heart-fluttering faintness of the first minutes, when the dead man was lying there, still twitching, at his feet. He remembered, he lived over again those moments of breathless and sick anticipation before the horrible event. The noise of the car backing down the street; the gritty scrape of feet on the doorstep, and then the knock, and then a long, long silence of heart-beats and visceral creepings and imaginative forebodings, of justifying thoughts of revolution and the future, justifying hatred of oppression and the vileness of wealth. And at the same time ridiculous, incongruous recollections, as he crouched behind the screen, of those childish games of hide-and-seek on school-treat days, among the gorse and juniper bushes of the common. 'One, two, three ...'; the seekers covered their faces and began to count their hundred, aloud; the hiders scattered. You thrust yourself into a prickly bush, you lay in the bracken. Then came the shout of 'ninety-nine, a hundred, Cooee!'; and the seekers were off, were after you. And the excitement was so painfully intense, as you crouched or squatted in your lair, peeping, listening for a chance to make a bolt for Home, that you felt an almost irrepressible desire to 'do something,' though something had been done, behind the junipers, only five minutes before. Absurd memories! And because absurd, dreadful! For the hundredth time he felt in his pocket to make sure that the bottle of chloroform was still there and safely corked. The second knock startlingly resounded and, with it, the whistle and that humorous call (you could *hear*, from the tone of his voice, that he was smiling) of 'Friend!' Behind his screen Illidge had shuddered. 'Friend!' And remembering now, he shuddered again, more violently, with all the shame and horror and humiliation which he had had no time then to feel. No time; for before his mind could realize all the implications upon implications of that laughing call, the door had creaked on its hinges, there was the noise of feet on the boards, and Webley was shouting Elinor's name. (Illidge suddenly found himself wondering if he had been in love with her.) 'Elinor!' There followed a silence; Webley had seen the note. Illidge had heard his breathing, only a foot or two away, on the other side of the screen. And then there was the rustle of a quick movement, the beginning of an exclamation and that sudden dry concussion, like the noise of a slap, but duller, deader and at the same time much louder. There followed a fraction of a second's silence, then the noise of falling – not a single sound, but a series of noises spread over an appreciable period of time; the bony collapse of the knees, the scrape of shoes sliding away across the polished floor, the muffled thud of the body and arms, and the sharp hard rap of the head against the boards. 'Quick!' had come the sound of Spandrell's voice, and he had darted out of his hiding-place. 'Chloroform.' Obediently, he had soaked the handkerchief, he had spread it over the twitching face. ... He shuddered again, he took another sip of brandy.

The sound of scrubbing was succeeded by the squelch of a wetted cloth.

'There,' said Spandrell, appearing round the screen. He was drying his hands on a duster. 'And how's the invalid?' he added in the parody of a bedside manner, smiling ironically.

Illidge averted his face. The hatred flared up in him, expelling for the moment every other emotion. 'I'm all right,' he said curtly.

'Just taking it easy while I do the dirty work. Is that it?' Spandrell threw the duster on to a chair and began to turn down his shirt cuffs.

In two hours the muscles of the heart contract and relax, contract again and relax only eight thousand times. The earth travels less than an eighth of a million miles along its orbit. And the prickly pear has had time to invade only another hundred acres of Australian territory. Two hours are as nothing. The time to listen to the Ninth Symphony and a couple of the posthumous quartets, to fly from London to Paris, to transfer a luncheon from the stomach to the small intestine, to read *Macbeth*, to die of snake bite or earn one-and-eightpence as a charwoman. No more. But to Illidge, as he sat waiting, with the dead body lying there behind the screen, waiting for the darkness, they seemed unending.

'Are you an idiot?' asked Spandrell, when he had suggested that they should go away at once and leave the thing lying there. 'Or are you particularly anxious to die of hanging?' The sneer, the cool ironic amusement were maddening to Illidge. 'It would be found to-night when Philip came home.'

'But Quarles hasn't got a key,' said Illidge.

'Then to-morrow, as soon as he'd got hold of a locksmith. And three hours later, when Elinor had explained what she had done with the key, the police would be knocking at my door. And I promise you, they'd knock at yours very soon afterwards.' He smiled at

Illidge, who averted his eyes. 'No,' Spandrell went on, 'Webley's got to be taken away. And with his car standing outside, it's child's play, if we wait till after dark.'

'But it won't be dark for another two hours.' Illidge's voice was shrill with anger and complaint.

'Well, what of it?'

'Why ...' Illidge began and checked himself; he realized that if he was going to answer truthfully, he would have to say that he didn't want to stay those two hours because he was frightened. 'All right,' he said. 'Let's stay.' Spandrell picked up the silver cigarette box, opened and sniffed. 'They smell very nice,' he said. 'Have one.' He pushed the box across the table. 'And there are lots of books. And *The Times*. And the *New Statesman*. And the latest number of *Vogue*. It's positively a dentist's waiting-room. And we might even make ourselves a cup of tea.' The time of waiting began. Heart-beat followed heart-beat. Each second the earth travelled twenty miles and the prickly pears covered another five rods of Australian ground. Behind the screen lay the body. Thousands upon thousands of millions of minute and diverse individuals had come together and the product of their mutual dependence, their mutual hostility had been a human life. Their total colony, their living hive had been a man. The hive was dead. But in the lingering warmth many of the component individuals still faintly lived; soon they also would have perished. And meanwhile, from the air, the invisible hosts of saprophytics had already begun their unresisted invasion. They would live among the dead cells, they would grow, and prodigiously multiply and in their growing and procreation all the chemical building of the body would be undone, all the intricacies and complications of its matter would be resolved, till by the time their work was finished a few pounds of carbon, a few quarts of water, some lime, a little phosphorus and sulphur, a pinch of iron and silicon, a handful of mixed salts – all scattered and recombined with the surrounding world – would be all that remained of Everard Webley's ambition to rule and his love for Elinor, of his thoughts about politics and his recollections of childhood, of his fencing and good horsemanship, of that soft strong voice and that suddenly illuminating smile, of his admiration for Mantegna, his dislike of whisky, his deliberately terrifying rages, his habit of stroking his chin, his belief in God, his incapacity to whistle a tune correctly, his unshakeable determinations and his knowledge of Russian.

Illidge turned over the advertisement pages of *Vogue*. A young lady in a fur coat priced at two hundred guineas was stepping into a motor car; on the opposite page another young lady in nothing but a towel was stepping out of a bath impregnated with Dr Verbruggen's Reducing Salts. There followed a still-life of scent bottles containing *Songe Nègre* and the maker's latest creation, *Relent d'Amour*. The names of Worth, Lanvin, Patou sprawled across three more pages. Then there was a picture of a young lady in a rubber reducing belt, looking at herself in the glass. A group of young ladies admired one another's slumber wear from Crabb and Lushington's lingerie department. Opposite them another young lady reclined on a couch at Madame Adrena's Beauty Laboratory, while the hands of a masseuse stroked the menace of a double chin. Then followed a still-life of rolling pins and rubber strigils for rolling and rubbing away young ladies' superfluous fat, and another still-life of jars and gallipots containing skin foods to protect their faces from the ravages of time and the weather.

'Revolting!' Illidge said to himself as he turned the pages. 'Criminal!' And he cherished his indignation, he cultivated it. To be angry was a distraction, and at the same time a justification. Raging at plutocratic callousness and frivolity, he could half forget and half excuse to himself the horrible thing that had happened. Webley's body was lying on the other side of the screen. But there were women who paid two hundred guineas for a fur coat. Two hundred guineas! His Uncle Joseph would have thought himself happy if he could have made as much in eighteen months of cobbling. And they bought scent at twenty-five shillings the quarter-pint. He remembered the time when his little brother Tom had had pneumonia after influenza. Ghastly! And when he was convalescent, the doctor had said he ought to go away to the sea for a few weeks. They hadn't been able to afford it. Tom's lungs had never been too strong after that. He worked in a motor factory now (making machines for those bitches in two-hundred-guinea coats to sit in); Illidge had paid for him to go to a technical school – paid, he reflected, beating up his anger, that the boy might have the privilege of standing eight hours a day in front of a milling machine. The air of Manchester wasn't doing Tom any good. There was no superfluous fat to be rolled off him, poor devil. Swinish guzzling! Why couldn't they do a little useful work instead of squee-geeing their hams and bellies? That would take the fat off all right. If they worked as his mother had done. ... She had no fat to rub off with rolling-pins, or sweat off under a rubber belt, or stew off in hot baths and brine. He thought indignantly of that endless dreary labour of housework. Day after day, year after year. Making beds, that they might be unmade. Cooking to fill bellies eternally empty. Washing up what the next meal was to make dirty again. Scrubbing the floor for muddy boots to defile. Darning and patching that yet more holes might be made. It was like the labouring of Sisyphus and the Danaids, hopeless and interminable – or would have been interminable (except by his mother's death), if he hadn't been able to send her those two pounds a week out of his salary. She could get a girl in now to help with the hardest work. But she still did more than enough to make rubber belts unnecessary. What a life! And in the world of fur coats and *Songe Nègre* they complained of boredom and fatigue, they had to retire into nursing homes for rest cures. If they could lead *her* life for a bit! And perhaps they'd be made to, one of these days (he hoped so), even in England. Illidge thought with satisfaction of those ex-officers of the Tsar driving taxis and working in factories, those ex-countesses with their restaurants and cabarets and hat-shops; of all the ex-rich of Russia, all over the world, from Harbin and Shanghai to Rome and London and Berlin, bankrupt, humiliated, reduced to the slavish estate of the common people on whom they had once parasitically lived. That was good, that served them right. And perhaps it might happen here too. But they were strong here, the fat-reducers and the fur-coated; they were numerous, they were an organized army. But the army had lost its chief. He had got his packet. Embodied beastliness and plutocracy, he lay there behind the screen. But his mouth had been open and the muscles of his face, before the reeking handkerchief had covered it, had twitched grotesquely. Illidge shuddered. He looked again for indignant distraction and justification at the picture of the young lady in the two-hundred-guinea fur, of the young lady stepping, naked but coyly towelled, out of her reducing bath. Strumpets and gluttons! They belonged to the class that Webley had fought to perpetuate. The champion of all that was vile and low. He had got what he deserved, he had …

'Good Lord!' exclaimed Spandrell suddenly, looking up from his book. The sound of his voice in the silence made Illidge start with an uncontrollable terror. 'I'd absolutely forgotten. They get stiff, don't they?' He looked at Illidge. 'Corpses, I mean.'

Illidge nodded. He drew a deep breath and steadied himself with an effort of will.

'What about getting him into the car, then?' He sprang up and walked quickly round the screen, out of sight. Illidge heard the latch of the house door rattling. He was seized with a sudden horrible terror: Spandrell was going to make off, leaving him locked in with the body.

'Where are you going?' he shouted and darted off in panic pursuit. 'Where are you going?' The door was open, Spandrell was not to be seen, and the thing lay on the floor, its face uncovered, open-mouthed and staring secretly, significantly, as though through spy-holes, between half-closed eyelids. 'Where are you going?' Illidge's voice had risen almost to a scream.

'What *is* the excitement about?' asked Spandrell as the other appeared, pale and with desperation in his looks, on the doorstep. Standing by Webley's car, he was engaged in undoing the tightly stretched waterproof which decked in all that part of the open body lying aft of the front seats. 'These thingumbobs are horribly hard to unfasten.'

Illidge put his hands in his pockets and pretended that it was merely an idle curiosity that had brought him out with such precipitation.

'What are you doing?' he asked off-handedly.

Spandrell gave a final tug; the cover came loose along the whole length of one side of the car. He turned it back and looked in. 'Empty, thank goodness,' he said and, stretching his hand, he played imaginary octaves, span after span, over the coach-work. 'Say four feet wide,' he concluded, 'by about the same in length. Of which half is taken up by the seat. With two foot six of space under the cover. Plenty of room to curl up in and be very comfortable. But if one were stiff?' He looked inquiringly at Illidge. 'A man could be got in, but not a statue.'

Illidge nodded. Spandrell's last words had made him suddenly remember Lady Edward's mocking commentary on Webley. 'He wants to be treated like his own colossal statue – posthumously, if you see what I mean.'

'We must do something quickly,' Spandrell went on. 'Before the stiffness sets in.' He pulled back the cover and laying a hand on Illidge's shoulder, propelled him gently into the house. The door slammed behind them. They stood looking down at the body.

'We shall have to pull the knees up and the arms down,' said Spandrell.

393

He bent down and moved one of the arms towards the side. It returned, when he let go, half-way to its former position. Like a puppet, Spandrell reflected, with elastic joints. Grotesque rather than terrible; not tragical, but only rather tiresome and even absurd. That was the essential horror – that it was all (even *this*) a kind of bad and tedious jape. 'We shall have to find some string,' he said. 'Something to tie the limbs into place.' It was like amateur plumbing, or mending the summer-house oneself; just rather unpleasant and ludicrous.

They ransacked the house. There was no string to be found. They had to be content with three bandages, which Spandrell found among the aspirin and iodine, the boracic powder and vegetable laxatives of the little medicine cupboard in the bathroom.

'Hold the arms in place while I tie,' commanded Spandrell.

Illidge did as he was told. But the coldness of those dead wrists against his fingers was horrible; he felt sick again, he began to tremble.

'There!' said Spandrell, straightening himself up. 'Now the legs. Thank goodness we didn't leave it much longer.'

'Treated like his own statue.' The words reverberated in Illidge's memory. 'Posthumously, if you see what I mean.' Posthumously … Spandrell bent one of the legs till the knee almost touched the chin.

'Hold it.'

Illidge grasped the ankle; the socks were grey and clocked with white. Spandrell let go, and Illidge felt a sudden and startlingly powerful thrust against his retaining hand. The dead man was trying to kick. Black voids began to expand in front of his eyes, eating out holes in the solid world before him. And the solid world itself swayed and swam round the edges of those interstellar vacancies. His gorge turned, he felt horribly giddy.

'Look here,' he began, turning to Spandrell, who had squatted down on his heels and was tearing the wrapping off another bandage. Then shutting his eyes, he relinquished his grasp.

The leg straightened itself out like a bent spring, and the foot, as it shot forward, caught Spandrell on the shoulder and sent him, unsteadily balanced as he was, sprawling backwards on to the floor.

He picked himself up. 'You bloody fool!' But the anger aroused by that first shock of surprise died down. He uttered a little laugh. 'We might be at the circus,' he said. It was not only not tragic; it was a clownery.

By the time the body was finally trussed, Illidge knew that Tom's weak lungs and two-hundred-guinea coats, that superfluous fat and his mother's life-long slaving, that rich and poor, oppression and revolution, justice, punishment, indignation – all, as far as he was concerned, were utterly irrelevant to the fact of these stiffening limbs, this mouth that gaped, these half-shut, glazed and secretly staring eyes. Irrelevant, and beside the point.

*

Philip was dining alone. In front of his plate half a bottle of claret and the water-jug propped up an open volume. He read between the mouthfuls, as he masticated. The book was Bastian's *On the Brain*. Not very up to date, perhaps, but the best he could find in his father's library to keep him amused in the train. Halfway through the fish, he came upon the case of the Irish gentleman who had suffered from paraphasia, and was so much struck by it that he pushed aside his plate and, taking out his pocket-book, made a note of it at once. The physician had asked the patient to read aloud a paragraph from the statutes of Trinity College, Dublin. 'It shall be in the power of the College to examine or not examine every Licentiate previous to his admission to a fellowship, as they shall think fit.' What the patient actually read was: 'An the bee-what in the tee-mother of the trotho-doodoo, to majoram or that emidrate, eni eni krastrei, mestreit to ketra totombreidei, to ra from treido as that kekritest.' Marvellous! Philip said to himself as he copied down the last word. What style! what majestic beauty! The richness and sonority of the opening phrase! 'An the bee-what in the tee-mother of the trothodoodoo.' He repeated it to himself. 'I shall print it on the title-page of my next novel,' he wrote in his notebook. 'The epigraph the text of the whole sermon.' Shakespeare only talked about tales told by an idiot. But here was the idiot actually speaking – Shakespeareanly, what was more. 'The final word about life,' he added in pencil.

At the Queen's Hall Tolley began with Erik Satie's *Borborygmes Symphoniques*. Philip found the joke only moderately good. A section of the audience improved it, however, by hissing and booing. Ironically polite, Tolley bowed with more than his usual grace. When the hubbub subsided, he addressed himself to the second item on the programme. It was the *Coriolan* overture. Tolley prided himself on a catholic taste and omnicompetence. But, oh dear! thought Philip as he listened, how abominably he conducted real music! As though he were rather ashamed of Beethoven's emotions and were trying to

395

apologize for them. But fortunately Coriolanus was practically Tolley-proof. The music was heroically beautiful, it was tragic and immense in spite of him. The last of the expiring throbs of sound died away, a demonstration of man's indomitable greatness and the necessity, the significance of suffering.

In the interval Philip limped out for a smoke in the bar. A hand plucked at his sleeve.

'The melomaniac discovered!' said a familiar voice. He turned and saw Willie Weaver twinkling all over with good-humour, kindliness, and absurdity. 'What did you think of our modern Orpheus?'

'If you're referring to Tolley, I don't think he can conduct Beethoven.'

'A shade too light and fantastic for old man Ludwig's portentiosities?' suggested Willie.

'That's about it,' said Philip smiling. 'Not up to him.'

'Or too far up. Portentiosity belongs to the prepositivistic epoch. It's bourgeois, as Comrade Lenin would say. Tolley's nothing if not contemporaneous. Didn't you like him in the Satie? Or did you,' he went on, in response to Philip's contemptuous shrug, 'did you wish he'd committed it?' He coughed his own appreciation of the pun.

'He's almost as modern as the Irish genius whose works I discovered this evening.' Philip took out his pocket-book and, after a word of explanation, read aloud. 'An the bee-what in the tee-mother of the trothodoodoo ...' At the foot of the page were his own comments of an hour before. 'The text of the whole sermon. The final word about life.' He did not read them out. He happened to be thinking quite differently now. 'The difference between portentiosity and Satie-cum-Tolleyism,' he said, 'is the same as the difference between the statutes of Trinity College, Dublin, and this bee-what in the tee-mother of the trothodoodoo.'

He was blankly contradicting himself. But, after all, why not?

*

Illidge wanted to go home and to bed; but Spandrell had insisted that he should spend at least an hour or two at Tantamount House.

'You must get yourself seen,' he said. 'For the sake of the alibi. I'm going on to Sbisa's. There'll be a dozen people to vouch for me.'

Illidge agreed only under the threat of violence. He dreaded the ordeal of talking with anyone – even with someone so incurious, preoccupied, and absent as Lord Edward. 'I shan't be able to stand it,' he kept repeating, almost in tears. They had had to carry the body trussed into the posture of a child in the womb – carry it amorously pressed in a close and staggering embrace – out of the door, down the steps into the roadway. A single greenish gas-lamp under the archway threw but a feeble light up the mews; enough, however, to have betrayed them, if anyone had happened to be passing the entrance as they carried their burden out and lifted it into the car. They had begun by dumping the thing on its back on the floor; but the up-drawn knees projected above the level of the carriage-work. Spandrell had to climb into the car and push and lug the heavy body on to its side, so that the knees rested on the edge of the back seat. They shut the doors, pulled the cover over and fastened it tautly into place. 'Perfect,' said Spandrell. He took his companion by the elbow. 'You need a little more brandy,' he added. But in spite of the brandy Illidge was still faint and tremulous when they drove away. Nor was Spandrell's bungling with the mechanism of the unfamiliar car at all calculated to soothe his nerves. They had begun by backing violently into the wall at the end of the mews; and before he discovered the secret of the gears, Spandrell twice inadvertently stopped the engine. He relieved his irritation by a few curses and laughed. But to Illidge these little mishaps, entailing as they did a minute's delay in escaping from that horrible and accursed place, were catastrophes. His terror, his anxious impatience became almost hysterical.

'No, I can't, I really can't,' he protested when Spandrell had told him that he must spend the evening at Tantamount House.

'All the same,' said the other, 'you're damned well going to,' and he headed the car into the Mall. 'I'll drop you at the door.'

'No, really!'

'And if necessary kick you in.'

'But I couldn't stand being there, I couldn't stand it.'

'This is an extremely nice car,' said Spandrell pointedly changing the subject. 'Delightful to drive.'

'I couldn't stand it,' Illidge whimperingly repeated.

'I believe the makers guarantee a hundred miles an hour on the track.'

They turned up past St James's Palace into Pall Mall.

'Here you are,' said Spandrell, drawing up at the kerb. Obediently, Illidge got out, crossed the pavement, climbed the steps and rang the bell. Spandrell waited till the door had closed behind him, then drove on into St James's Square. Twenty or thirty cars were parked round

397

the central gardens. He backed in among them, stopped the engine, got out and walked up to Piccadilly Circus. A penny bus-ride took him to the top of the Charing Cross Road. The trees of Soho Square shone green in the lamplight at the end of the narrow lane between the factory buildings. Two minutes later he was at Sbisa's, apologizing to Burlap and Rampion for being so late.

*

'Ah, here you are,' said Lord Edward. 'So glad you've come.'

Illidge mumbled vague apologies for not having come sooner. An appointment with a man. About business. But suppose, he wondered in terror while he spoke, suppose Lord Edward should ask what man, what business? He wouldn't know what to answer; he would utterly break down. But the Old Man seemed not even to have heard his excuses.

'Afraid I must ask you to do a little arithmetic for me,' he said in his deep blurred voice. Lord Edward had made himself a tolerably good mathematician; but 'sums' had always been beyond his powers. He had never been able to multiply correctly. And as for long division – it was fifty years since he had even attempted it. 'I've got the figures here.' He tapped the notebook that lay open in front of him on the desk. 'It's for the chapter on phosphorus. Human interference with the cycle. How much P_2O_5 did we find out was dispersed into the sea in sewage?' He turned a page. 'Four hundred thousand tons. That was it. Practically irrecoverable. Just thrown away. Then there's the stupid way we deal with cadavers. Three-quarters of a kilo of phosphorus pentoxide in every body. Restored to the earth, you may say.' Lord Edward was ready to admit every excuse, to anticipate, that he might rebut, every shift of advocacy. 'But how inadequately!' he swept the excuses away, he blew the special pleaders to bits. 'Huddling bodies together in cemeteries! How can you expect the phosphorus to get distributed? It finds its way back to the life cycle in time, no doubt. But for *our* purposes it's lost. Taken out of currency. Now, given three-quarters of a kilo of P_2O_5 for every cadaver and a world population of eighteen hundred millions and an average death-rate of twenty per thousand, what's the total quantity restored every year to the earth? You can do sums, my dear Illidge. I leave it to you.' Illidge sat in silence, shielding his face with his hand. 'But then one has to remember,' the Old Man continued, 'that there are a lot of people who dispose of the dead more sensibly than we do. It's really only among the white races that the phosphorus is taken out of circulation. Other people don't have necropolises and watertight coffins and brick vaults. The only people more wasteful than we are the Indians. Burning bodies and throwing the ashes into rivers! But the Indians are stupid about everything. The way they burn all the cow-dung instead of putting it back on the land. And then they're surprised that half the population hasn't enough to eat. We shall have to make a separate calculation about the Indians. I haven't got the figures, though. But meanwhile will you work out the grand total for the world? And another, if you don't mind, for the white races. I've got a list of the populations here somewhere. And of course the death-rate will be lower than the average for the whole world, at any rate in Western Europe and America. Would you like to sit here? There's room at this end of the table.' He cleared a space. 'And here's paper. And this is quite a decent pen.'

'Do you mind,' said Illidge faintly, 'if I lie down for a minute. I'm not feeling well.'

Chapter Thirty-four

It was nearly eleven before Philip Quarles appeared at Sbisa's. Spandrell saw him as he was entering and beckoned him to the table where he was sitting with Burlap and Rampion. Philip came limping across the room and sat down beside him.

'I've got messages for you,' said Spandrell, 'and, what's more important,' he felt in his pocket, 'the key of your house.' He handed it over, explaining how he had come into possession of it. If the man knew what had happened in his house that evening. … 'And Elinor's gone down to Gattenden,' he went on. 'She had a telegram. The child doesn't seem to be well. And she expects you to-morrow.'

'The devil she does!' said Philip. 'But I have at least fifteen engagements. What's wrong with the boy?'

'Unspecified.'

Philip shrugged his shoulders. 'If it had been serious, my mother-in-law wouldn't have telegraphed,' he said, yielding to the temptation to say something amusing. 'She's like that. She'll take a case of double pneumonia with perfect calm and then get terribly excited about a headache or a pain in the belly.' He interrupted himself to order an omelette and half a bottle of Moselle. Still, Philip reflected, the boy hadn't been very flourishing these last weeks. He rather wished he hadn't yielded to the temptation. And what he had said hadn't really been in the least amusing. Wanting to be amusing – that was his chief literary defect. His books would be much better if he would allow them to be much duller. He sank into a rather gloomy silence.

'These children!' said Spandrell. 'If you will go in for them. …'

'Still, it must be wonderful to have a child,' said Burlap with proper wistfulness. 'I often wish …'

Rampion interrupted him. 'It must be still more wonderful to *be* one. When one's grown up, I mean.' He grinned.

'What do you do about *your* children?' asked Spandrell.

'As little as I can. Unfortunately they have to go to school. I only hope they won't learn too much. It'd be really awful if they emerged as little professors stuffed with knowledge, trotting out their smart little abstract generalizations. They probably will. Just to spite me. Children generally do spite their parents. Not on purpose, of course, but unconsciously, because they can't help it, because the parents have probably gone too far in one direction and nature's reacting, trying to get back to the state of equilibrium. Yes, yes, I can feel it in my bones. They'll be professors, the little devils. They'll be horrid little scientists. Like your friend Illidge,' he said, turning to Spandrell, who started uncomfortably at the name and was annoyed that he should have started. 'Horrid little brains that do their best to suppress the accompanying hearts and bowels.'

Spandrell smiled his significant, rather melodramatically-ironic smile. 'Young Illidge hasn't succeeded in suppressing his heart and bowels,' he said. 'Not by a long chalk.'

'Of course not. Nobody can suppress them. All that happens in the process is that they're transformed from living organs into offal. And why are they transformed? In the interests of what? Of a lot of silly knowledge and irrelevant abstractions.'

'Which are after all quite amusing in themselves,' said Philip, breaking his silence to come to the rescue of the intellect. 'Making generalizations and pursuing knowledge are amusements. Among the most entertaining, to my mind.' Philip went on to develop his hedonistic justification of the mental life. 'So why be so hard on our little diversions?' he concluded. 'You don't denounce golf; so why should you denounce the sports of the highbrows?'

'That's fairly rudimentary, isn't it?' said Rampion. 'The tree shall be known by its fruits. The fruits of golf are either non-existent, harmless, or positively beneficial. A healthy liver, for example – that's a very fine fruit. Whereas the fruits of intellectualism – my God!' He made a grimace. 'Look at them. The whole of our industria civilization – that's their fruit. The morning paper, the radio, the cinema, all fruits. Tanks and trinitrotoluol; Rockefeller and Mond – fruits again. They're all the result of the systematically organized, professional intellectualism of the last two hundred years. And you expect me to approve of your amusements? But, I tell you, I prefer bull-fighting. What's the torture of a few animals and the brutalizing of a few hundred spectators compared to the ruining and befouling and degrading of a whole world? Which is what you highbrows have done since you professionalized and organized your amusements.'

'Come, come,' said Philip. 'The picture's a little lurid. And anyhow, even if it were accurate, the highbrows can't be held responsible for the applications other people have made of their results.'

'They *are* responsible. Because they brought the other people up in their own damned intellectualist tradition. After all, the other people are only highbrows on another plane. A business man is just a man of science who happens to be rather stupider than the real man of science. He's living just as one-sidedly and intellectually, as far as his intellect goes, as the other one. And the fruit of that is inner psychological degeneration. For of course,' he added parenthetically, 'the fruits of your amusements aren't merely the external apparatus of modern industrial life. They're an inward decay; they're infantilism and degeneracy and all sorts of madness and primitive reversion. No, no, I have no patience with your precious amusements of the mind. You'd be doing far less harm if you were playing golf.'

'But truth?' queried Burlap, who had been listening to the discussion without speaking. 'What about truth?'

Spandrell nodded approval. 'Isn't that worth looking for?'

'Certainly,' said Rampion. 'But not where Philip and his scientific and scholarly friends are looking for it. After all, the only truth that can be of any interest to us, or that we can know, is a human truth. And to discover that, you must look for it with the whole being, not with a specialized part of it. What the scientists are trying to get at is non-human truth. Not that they can ever completely succeed; for not even a scientist can completely cease to be human. But they can go some way towards abstracting themselves from the human world of reality. By torturing their brains they can get a faint notion of the universe as it would seem if looked at through non-human eyes. What with their quantum theory, wave mechanics, relativity and all the rest of it, they do really seem to have got a little way outside humanity. Well, what the devil's the good of that?'

'Apart from the fun of the thing,' said Philip, 'the good may be some astonishing practical discovery, like the secret of disintegrating the atom and the liberation of endless supplies of energy.'

'And the consequent reduction of human beings to absolute imbecility and absolute subservience to their machines,' jeered Rampion. 'I know your paradises. But the point for the moment is truth. This non-human truth that the scientists are trying to get at with their intellects – it's utterly irrelevant to ordinary human living. Our truth, the relevant human truth is something you discover by living – living completely, with the whole man. The results of your amusements, Philip, all these famous theories about the cosmos and their practical applications – they've got nothing whatever to do with the only truth that matters. And the non-human truth isn't merely irrelevant; it's dangerous. It distracts people's attention from the important human truth. It makes them falsify their experience in order that lived reality may fit in with abstract theory. For example, it's an established non-human truth – or at least it was established in my young days – that secondary qualities have no real existence. The man who takes that seriously denies himself, destroys the whole fabric of his life as a human being. For human beings happen to be so arranged that secondary qualities are, for them, the only real ones. Deny them and you commit suicide.'

'But in practice,' said Philip, 'nobody does deny them.'

'Not completely,' Rampion agreed. 'Because it can't be done. A man can't abolish his sensations and feelings completely without physically killing himself. But he can disparage them after the event. And, in fact, that's what a great number of intelligent and well-educated people do – disparage the human in the interests of the non-human. Their motive's different from that of the Christians; but the result's the same. A sort of self-destruction. Always the same,' he went on with a sudden outburst of anger in his voice. 'Every attempt at being something better than a man – the result's always the same. Death, some sort of death. You try to be more than you are by nature and you kill something in yourself and become much less. I'm so tired of all this rubbish about the higher life and moral and intellectual progress and living for ideals and all the rest of it. It all leads to death. Just as surely as living for money. Christians and moralists and cultured aesthetes, and bright young scientists and Smilesian business men – all the poor little human frogs trying to blow themselves up into bulls of pure spirituality, pure idealism, pure efficiency, pure conscious intelligence, and just going pop, ceasing to be anything but the fragments of a little frog – decaying fragments at that. The whole thing's a huge stupidity, a huge disgusting lie. Your little stink-pot of a St Francis, for example.' He turned to Burlap, who protested. 'Just a little stink-pot,' Rampion insisted. 'A silly vain little man trying to blow himself up into a Jesus and only succeeding in killing whatever sense or decency there was in him, only succeeding in turning himself into the nasty smelly fragments of a real human being. Going about getting thrills of excitement out of licking lepers! Ugh! The disgusting little pervert! He thinks himself too good to kiss a woman; he wants to be above anything so vulgar as natural healthy pleasure, and the only result is that he kills whatever core of human decency he ever had in him and becomes a smelly little pervert who can only get a thrill out of licking

403

lepers' ulcers. Not curing the lepers, mind you. Just licking them. For his own amusement. Not theirs. It's revolting!'

Philip leaned back in his chair and laughed. But Rampion turned on him in a fury.

'You may laugh,' he said. 'But don't imagine you're any better, really. You and your intellectual, scientific friends. You've killed just as much of yourselves as the Christian maniacs. Shall I read you your programme?' He picked up the book that was lying beside him on the table and began to turn the pages. 'I came upon it just now, as I was coming here in the bus. Here we are.' He began to read, pronouncing the French words carefully and clearly. '*Plus un obstacle matériel, toutes les rapidités gagnées par la science et la richesse. Pas une tare à l'indépendance. Voir un crime de lèse-moi dans toute fréquentation, homme ou pays, qui ne serait pas expressément voulu. L'énergie, le recueillement, la tension de la solitude, les transporter dans ses rapports avec de vrais semblables. Pas d'amour peut-être, mais des amitiés rares, difficiles, exaltées, nerveuses; vivre comme on revivrait en esprit de détachement, d'inquiétude et de revanche.*' Rampion closed the book and looked up. 'That's your programme,' he said to Philip. 'Formulated by Marie Lenéru in 1901. Very brief and neat and complete. And, my God, what a horror! No body, no contact with the material world, no contact with human beings except through the intellect, no love ...'

'We've changed *that* a little since 1901,' said Philip, smiling.

'Not really. You've admitted promiscuous fornication, that's all. But not love, not the natural contact and flow, not the renunciation of mental self-consciousness, not the abandonment to instinct. No, no. You stick to your conscious will. Everything must be *expressément voulu*, all the time. And the connexions must be purely mental. And life must be lived, not as though it were life in a world of living people, but as though it were solitary recollection and fancy and meditation. An endless masturbation, like Proust's horrible great book. That's the higher life. Which is the euphemistic name of incipient death. It's significant, it's symbolic that that Lenéru woman was deaf and purblind. The outward and visible sign of an inward and spiritual truth. Poor creature! She had some excuse for spirituality. But the other Higher-Lifers, the ones who haven't any physical defect – they're not so forgivable. They've maimed themselves deliberately, for fun. It's a pity they don't develop visible hunch-backs or wall-eyes. One would know better who one was dealing with.'

'Quite,' said Philip, nodding, and laughed with an affectation of amusement that was meant to cover the embarrassment he felt at Rampion's references to physical disability. 'Quite.' Nobody should think that, because he had a game leg, he didn't entirely appreciate the justice of Rampion's remarks about deformity.

The irrelevant loudness of his laugh made Rampion glance questioningly at him. What was up? He couldn't be bothered to discover.

'It's all a damned lie,' he went on, 'and an idiotic lie at that – all this pretending to be more than human. Idiotic because it never comes off. You try to be more than human, but you only succeed in making yourself less than human. Always …'

'Hear, hear!' said Philip. ' "We walk on earth and have no need of wings." ' And suddenly he heard his father's loud voice saying, 'I had wings. I had wings'; he saw his flushed face and feverishly pink pyjamas. Ludicrous and deplorable. 'Do you know who that's by?' he went on. 'That's the last line of the poem I wrote for the Newdigate prize at Oxford, when I was twenty-one. The subject was "King Arthur," if I remember rightly. Needless to say I didn't get the prize. But it's a good line.'

'A pity you didn't live up to it,' said Rampion, 'instead of whoring after abstractions. But of course, there's nobody like the lover of abstraction for denouncing abstractions. He knows by experience how life-destroying they are. The ordinary man can afford to take them in his stride. He can afford to have wings too, so long as he also remembers that he's got feet. It's when people strain themselves to fly all the time that they go wrong. They're ambitious of being angels; but all they succeed in being is either cuckoos and geese on the one hand or else disgusting vultures and carrion crows on the other.'

'But all this,' said Spandrell, breaking a long silence, 'is just the gospel of animalism. You're just advising us to behave like beasts.'

'I'm advising you to behave like human beings,' said Rampion. 'Which is slightly different. And anyhow,' he added, 'it's a damned sight better to behave like a beast – a real genuine undomesticated animal, I mean – than to invent a devil and then behave like one's invention.'

There was a brief silence. 'Suppose I were to tell them,' Spandrell was thinking, 'suppose I were to tell them that I'd just jumped out on a man from behind a screen and hit him on the side of the head with an Indian club.' He took another sip of brandy. 'No,' he said aloud, 'I'm not so sure of what you say. Behaving like an animal is

405

behaving like a creature that's below good and evil. You must know what good is before you can start behaving like the devil.' And yet it had all been just stupid and sordid and disgusting. Yes, and profoundly silly, an enormous stupidity. At the core of the fruit from the tree of the knowledge of good and evil he had found, not fire and poison, but only a brown disgusting putrefaction and a few small maggots. 'Things exist only in terms of their opposites,' he went on, frowning at his own thoughts. 'The devil implies God.'

'No doubt,' said Rampion impatiently. 'A devil of absolute evil implies a God of absolute good. Well, what of it? What's that got to do with you or me?'

'A good deal, I should have thought.'

'It's got about as much to do with us as the fact of this table being made of electrons, or an infinite series of waves undulating in an unknown medium, or a large number of point-events in a four-dimensional continuum, or whatever else Philip's scientific friends assure us it is made of. As much as that. That is to say, practically nothing. Your absolute God and absolute devil belong to the class of irrelevant non-human facts. The only things that concern us are the little relative gods and devils of history and geography, the little relative goods and evils of individual casuistry. Everything else is non-human and beside the point; and if you allow yourself to be influenced by non-human, absolute considerations, then you inevitably make either a fool of yourself, or a villain, or perhaps both.'

'But that's better than making an animal of oneself,' insisted Spandrell. 'I'd rather be a fool or a villain than a bull or a dog.'

'But nobody's asking you to be a bull or a dog,' said Rampion impatiently. 'Nobody's asking you to be anything but a man. A man, mind you. Not an angel or a devil. A man's a creature on a tight-rope, walking delicately, equilibrated, with mind and consciousness and spirit at one end of his balancing pole and body and instinct and all that's unconscious and earthy and mysterious at the other. Balanced. Which is damnably difficult. And the only absolute he can ever really know is the absolute of perfect balance. The absoluteness of perfect relativity. Which is a paradox and nonsense intellectually. But so is all real, genuine, living truth – just nonsense according to logic. And logic is just nonsense in the light of living truth. You can choose which you like, logic or life. It's a matter of taste. Some people prefer being dead.'

'Prefer being dead.' The words went echoing through Spandrell's mind. Everard Webley lying on the floor, trussed up like a chicken. Did he prefer being dead? 'All the same,' he said slowly, 'some things must always remain absolutely and radically wrong. Killing, for example.' He wanted to believe that it was more than merely low and sordid and disgusting. He wanted to believe that it was also terrible and tragic. 'That's an absolute wrong.'

'But why more absolute than anything else?' said Rampion. 'There are circumstances when killing's obviously necessary and right and commendable. The only absolutely evil act, so far as I can see, that a man can perform, is an act against life, against his own integrity. He does wrong if he perverts himself, if he falsifies his instincts.'

Spandrell was sarcastic. 'We're getting back to the beasts again,' he said. 'Go ravening round fulfilling all your appetites as you feel them. Is that the last word in human wisdom?'

'Well, it isn't really so stupid as you try to make out,' said Rampion. 'If men went about satisfying their instinctive desires only when they genuinely felt them, like the animals you're so contemptuous of, they'd behave a damned sight better than the majority of civilized human beings behave to-day. It isn't natural appetite and spontaneous instinctive desire that make men so beastly – no, "beastly" is the wrong word; it implies an insult to the animals – so all-too-humanly bad, and vicious, then. It's the imagination, it's the intellect, its principles, its tradition and education. Leave the instincts to themselves and they'll do very little mischief. If men made love only when they were carried away by passion, if they fought only when they were angry or terrified, if they grabbed at property only when they had need or were swept off their feet by an uncontrollable desire for possession – why, I assure you, this world would be a great deal more like the Kingdom of Heaven than it is under our present Christian-intellectual-scientific dispensation. It's not instinct that makes Casanovas and Byrons and Lady Castlemaines; it's a prurient imagination artificially tickling up the appetite, tickling up desires that have no natural existence. If Don Juans and Don Juanesses only obeyed their desires, they'd have very few affairs. They have to tickle themselves up imaginatively before they can start being casually promiscuous. And it's the same with the other instincts. It's not the possessive instinct that's made modern civilization insane about money. The possessive instinct has to be kept artificially tickled by education and tradition and moral principles. The money-grubbers have to be told that money-grubbing's natural and noble, that thrift and industry are virtues, that persuading people to buy things they don't want is Christian Service. Their possessive instinct would never be strong enough to keep them grubbing away from morning till night all through a lifetime. It has to be kept chronically gingered up by the imagination and the intellect. And then, think of civilized war. It's got nothing to do with spontaneous combativeness. Men have to be compelled by law and then tickled up by propaganda before they'll fight. You'd do more for peace by telling men to obey the spontaneous dictates of their fighting instincts than by founding any number of Leagues of Nations.'

'You'd do still more,' said Burlap, 'by telling them to obey Jesus.'

'No, you wouldn't. Telling them to obey Jesus is telling them to be more than human. And, in practice, trying to be more than human always means succeeding in being less than human. Telling men to obey Jesus literally is telling them, indirectly, to behave like idiots and finally like devils. Just consider the examples. Old Tolstoy – a great man who deliberately turned himself into an idiot by trying to be more than a great man. Your horrid little St Francis.' He turned to Burlap. 'Another idiot. But already on the verge of diabolism. With the monks of Thebaid you see the process carried a step further. They went over the verge. They got to the stage of being devils. Self-torture, destruction of everything decent and beautiful and living. That was their programme. They tried to obey Jesus and be more than men; and all they succeeded in doing was to become the incarnation of pure diabolic destructiveness. They could have been perfectly decent human beings if they'd just gone about behaving naturally, in accordance with their instincts. But no, they wanted to be more than human. So they just became devils. Idiots first and then devils, imbecile devils. Ugh!' Rampion made a grimace and shook his head with disgust. 'And to think,' he went on indignantly, 'that the world's full of these creatures! Not quite so far gone as St Anthony and his demons or St Francis and his half-wits. But of the same kind. Different only in degree. And all perverted in the same way – by trying to be non-human. Non-humanly religious, non-humanly moral, non-humanly intellectual and scientific, non-humanly specialized and efficient, non-humanly the business man, non-humanly avaricious and property-loving, non-humanly lascivious and Don Juanesque, non-humanly the conscious individual even in love. All perverts. Perverted towards goodness or badness towards spirit or flesh;

but always away from the central norm, always away from humanity. The world's an asylum of perverts. There are four of them at this table now.' He looked round with a grin. 'A pure little Jesus pervert.' Burlap forgivingly smiled. 'An intellectual-aesthetic pervert.'

'Thanks for the compliment,' said Philip.

'A morality-philosophy pervert.' He turned to Spandrell. 'Quite the little Stavrogin. Pardon my saying so, Spandrell; but you really are the most colossal fool.' He looked intently into his face. 'Smiling like all the tragic characters of fiction rolled into one! But it won't do. It doesn't conceal the simple-minded zany underneath.'

Spandrell threw back his head and noiselessly laughed. If he knew, he was thinking, if he knew ... But if he knew, would he think him any less of a fool?

'Laugh away, old Dostoievsky! But let me tell you, it's Stavrogin who ought to have been called the Idiot, not Myshkin. He was incomparably the bigger fool, the completer pervert.'

'And what sort of a fool and pervert is the fourth person at this table?' asked Philip.

'What indeed!' Rampion shook his head. His fine hair floated up silkily. He smiled. 'A pedagogue pervert. A Jeremiah pervert. A worry-about-the-bloody-old-world pervert. Above all a gibber pervert.' He got up. 'That's why I'm going home,' he said. 'The way I've been talking – it's really non-human. Really scandalous. I'm ashamed. But that's the trouble: when you're up against non-human things and people, you invariably become non-human yourself. It's all your fault.' He gave a final grin, waved good-night and was gone.

*

Burlap came home to find Beatrice, as usual, waiting up for him. Sitting – for such was the engagingly childlike habit he had formed during the last few weeks – on the floor at her feet, his head, with the little pink tonsure in the middle of the dark curls, against her knee, he sipped his hot milk and talked of Rampion. An extraordinary man, a great man, even. Great? queried Beatrice, disapprovingly. She didn't like to hear greatness attributed to any living man (the dead were a different matter; they were dead), unless it was to Denis himself. Hardly *great*, she insisted jealously. Well, perhaps not quite. But very nearly. If he hadn't that strange insensitiveness to spiritual values, that prejudice, that blind spot. The attitude was comprehensible. Rampion was reacting against something which had gone too far in one direction; but in the process of reacting he had gone too far in the other. His incapacity to understand St Francis, for example. The grotesque and really hideous things he could say about the saint. That was extraordinary and deplorable.

'What does he say?' asked Beatrice severely. Since knowing Burlap, she had taken St Francis under her protection.

Burlap gave her an account, a little expurgated, of what Rampion had said. Beatrice was indignant. How could he say such things? How did he dare? It was an outrage. Yes, it was a defect in him, Burlap admitted, a real defect. But so few people, he added in charitable palliation, were born with a real feeling for spiritual beauty. Rampion was an extraordinary man in many ways, but it was as though he lacked that extra sense-organ which enables men like St Francis to see the beauty that is beyond earthly beauty. In a rudimentary form he himself, he thought, had the power. How rarely he met anyone who seemed to be like him! Almost everybody was in this respect a stranger. It was like seeing normally in a country where most people were colour blind. Didn't Beatrice feel that too? For of course she was one of the rare clear-seeing ones. He had felt it at once, the first time he met her. Beatrice nodded gravely. Yes, she too felt like that. Burlap smiled up at her; he knew it. She felt proud and important. Rampion's idea of love, for example; Burlap shook his head. So extraordinarily gross and animal and corporeal.

'Dreadful,' said Beatrice feelingly. Denis, she was thinking, was so different. Tenderly she looked down at the head that reposed, so trustingly, against her knee. She adored the way his hair curled, and his very small, beautiful ears, and even the pink bare spot on the top of his crown. That little pink tonsure was somehow rather engagingly pathetic. There was a long silence.

Burlap at last profoundly sighed. 'How tired I am!' he said.

'You ought to go to bed.'

'Too tired even to move.' He pressed his cheek more heavily against her knee and shut his eyes.

Beatrice raised her hand, hesitated a moment, dropped it again, then raised it once more and began to run her fingers soothingly through his dark curls. There was another long silence.

'Ah, don't stop,' he said, when at last she withdrew her hand. 'It's so comforting. Such a virtue seems to go out from you. You'd almost cured my headache.'

'You've got a headache?' asked Beatrice, her solicitude running as usual to a kind of anger. 'Then you simply must go to bed,' she commanded.

'But I'm so happy here.'

'No, I insist.' Her protective motherliness was thoroughly aroused. It was a bullying tenderness.

'How cruel you are!' Burlap complained, rising reluctantly to his feet. Beatrice was touched with compunction. 'I'll stroke your head when you're in bed,' she promised. She too now regretted that soft warm silence, that speechless intimacy, which her outburst of domineering solicitude had too abruptly shattered. She justified herself by an explanation. The headache would return if he didn't go to sleep the moment it was cured. And so on.

Burlap had been in bed nearly ten minutes when she came to keep her promise. She was dressed in a green dressing-gown and her yellow hair was plaited into a long thick pigtail that swung heavily as she moved, like the heavy plaited tail of a cart-horse at a show.

'You look about twelve with that pigtail hanging down your back,' said Burlap, enchanted.

Beatrice laughed, rather nervously, and sat down on the edge of the bed. He raised his hand and took hold of the thick plait. 'Too charming,' he said. 'It simply invites pulling.' He gave a little tug at it, playfully.

'Look out,' she warned. 'I'll pull back, in spite of your headache.' She took hold of one of his dark curls.

'Pax, pax!' he begged, reverting to the vocabulary of the preparatory school. 'I'll let go. The real reason,' he added, 'why little boys don't like fighting with little girls is simply that little girls are so much more ruthless and ferocious.'

Beatrice laughed again. There was a silence. She felt a little breathless and fluttering, as one feels when one is anxiously expecting something to happen. 'Head bad?' she asked.

'Rather bad.'

She stretched out a hand and touched his forehead.

'Your hand's magical,' he said. With a quick unexpected movement he wriggled round sideways under the sheets and laid his head on her lap. 'There,' he whispered and, with a sigh of contentment, closed his eyes.

For a moment Beatrice was taken aback, almost frightened. That dark head lying hard and heavy on her thighs – it seemed strange, terrifying. She had to suppress a little shudder before she could feel

411

glad at the confiding childishness of his movement. She began stroking his forehead, stroking his scalp through the thick dark curls. Time passed. The soft warm silence enveloped them once more, the dumb intimacy of contact was re-established. She was no longer domineering in her protective solicitude, only tender. The armour of her hardness was as though melted away from her, melted away in this warm intimacy along with the terrors which made it necessary.

Burlap sighed again. He was in a kind of blissful doze of sensual passivity.

'Better?' she asked in a soft whisper.

'Still rather bad on the side,' he whispered back. 'Just over the ear.' And he rolled his head over so that she could more easily reach the painful spot, rolled it over so that his face was pressed against her belly, her soft belly that stirred so livingly with her breathing, that was so warm and yielding against his face.

At the touch of his face against her body Beatrice felt a sudden renewal of those spasmodic creepings of apprehension. Her flesh was terrified by the nearness of that physical intimacy. But as Burlap did not stir, as he made no dangerous gesture, no movement towards a closer contact, the terrors died gradually down and their flutterings served only to enhance and intensify that wonderful warm emotion of tenderness which succeeded them. She ran her fingers through his hair, again and again. The warmth of his breathing was against her belly. She shivered a little; her happiness fluttered with apprehensions and anticipations. Her flesh trembled, but was somehow joyful; was afraid and yet curious; shrank, but took warmth at the contact and even, through its terrors, timidly desired.

'Better?' she whispered again.

He made a little movement with his head and pressed his face closer to her soft flesh.

'Shall I stop now?' she went on, 'shall I go away?'

Burlap raised his head and looked at her. 'No, no,' he implored. 'Don't go. Not yet. Don't break the magic. Stay here for a moment longer. Lie down here for a moment under the quilt. For a moment.'

Without speaking she stretched herself out beside him and he drew the quilt over her, he turned out the light.

The fingers that caressed her arm under its wide sleeve touched delicately, touched spiritually and as it were disembodiedly, like the fingers of those inflated rubber gloves that brush so thrillingly against one's face in the darkness of séances, bringing comfort from the Great Beyond and a message of affection from the loved ones who have passed over. To caress and yet be a spiritualized rubber glove at a séance, to make love but as though from the Great Beyond – that was Burlap's talent. Softly, patiently, with an infinite disembodied gentleness he went on caressing. Beatrice's armour was melted quite away. It was the soft young-girlish, tremulous core of her that Burlap caressed with that delicate touch of spirit fingers from the Great Beyond. Her armour was gone; but she felt so wonderfully safe with Denis. She felt no fears, or at least only such faint breathless flutterings of her still almost childish flesh as served to quicken her happiness. She felt so wonderfully safe even when – after what had seemed a delicious eternity of patiently repeated caresses from wrist to shoulder and back again – the spirit hand reached out of the Beyond and touched her breast. Delicately, almost disembodiedly it touched, like a skin of rubber stuffed with air; spiritually it slid over the rounded flesh, and its angelic fingers lingered along the skin. At the first touch the round breast shuddered; it had its private terrors within Beatrice's general happiness and sense of security. But patiently, gently, unalarmingly, the spirit hand repeated its caress again, again, till the reassured and at last eager breast longed for its return and her whole body was alive with the tingling ramifications of the breast's desires. In the darkness the eternities prolonged themselves.

Chapter Thirty-five

NEXT day, instead of whimpering with every return of pain, the child began to scream – cry after shrill cry, repeated with an almost clockwork regularity of recurrence for what seemed to Elinor an eternity of hours. Like the scream of a rabbit in a trap. But a thousand times worse; for it was a child that screamed, not an animal; *her* child, trapped and in agony. She felt as though she too were trapped. Trapped by her own utter helplessness to alleviate his pain. Trapped by that obscure sense of guilt, that irrational belief (but haunting in spite of its irrationality), that ever more closely pressing and suffocating conviction that it was all, in some inscrutable fashion, *her* fault, a punishment, malevolently vicarious, for *her* offence. Caged within her own snare, but outside his, she sat there holding the small hand as it were between invisible bars, unable to come to his aid, waiting through the child's quick-breathed and feverish silence for the recurrence of that dreadful cry, for yet another sight of that suddenly distorted face, that shuddering little body racked by a pain which was somehow of her own inflicting.

The doctor came at last with his opiates.

Philip arrived by the twelve-twenty. He had been in no hurry to get up and come by an earlier train. It annoyed him to have to leave town. His late arrival was in the nature of a protest. Elinor must really learn not to make such a fuss every time the child had a stomach-ache. It was absurd.

She met him at the door as he stepped out of the car, so white and haggard, and with such dark-circled and desperate eyes, that he was shocked to see her.

'But you're the one who's ill,' he said anxiously. 'What is it?'

She did not answer for a moment, but stood holding him, her face hidden on his shoulder, pressing herself against him. 'Dr Crowther says it's meningitis,' she whispered at last.

At half past five arrived the nurse for whom Mrs Bidlake had telegraphed in the morning. The evening papers came by the same train; the chauffeur returned with a selection of them. On the front page was the announcement of the discovery, in his own motor car, of Everard Webley's body. It was to old John Bidlake, dozing listlessly in the library, that the papers were first brought. He read and was so excited by the news of another's death that he entirely forgot all his preoccupations with his own. Rejuvenated, he sprang to his feet and ran, waving the paper, into the hall. 'Philip!' he shouted in the strong resonant voice that had not been his for weeks past. 'Philip! Come here at once!'

Philip, who had just come out of the sick-room and was standing in the corridor, talking to Mrs Bidlake, hurried down to see what was the matter. John Bidlake held out the paper with an expression almost of triumph on his face. 'Read that,' he commanded importantly.

When Elinor was told the news, she almost fainted.

*

I believe he's better this morning, Dr Crowther.'

Dr Crowther fingered his tie to feel if it were straight. He was a small man, brisk and almost too neatly dressed. 'Quieter, eh? Sleeps?' he inquired telegraphically. His conversation had been reduced to bed-rock efficiency. It was just comprehensible and nothing more. No energy was wasted on the uttering of unnecessary words. Dr Crowther spoke as Ford cars are made. Elinor disliked him intensely, but believed in him for just those qualities of perky efficiency and self-confidence which she detested.

'Yes, that's it,' she said. 'He's sleeping.'

'He would be,' said Dr Crowther, nodding, as though he had known everything in advance – which indeed he had; for the disease was running its invariable course.

Elinor accompanied him up the stairs. 'Is it a good sign?' she asked in a voice that implored a favourable answer.

Dr Crowther pushed out his lips, cocked his head a little on one side, then shrugged his shoulders. 'Well ...' he said non-committally and was silent. He had saved at least five foot-pounds of energy by not explaining that, in meningitis, a phase of depression follows the initial phase of excitement.

The child now dozed away his days in a kind of stupor, suffering no pain (Elinor was thankful for that), but disquietingly unrespons-ive to what was going on about him, as though he were not fully alive. When he opened his eyes she saw that the pupils were so enor-mously dilated that there was hardly any iris left. Little Phil's blue and mischievous regard had turned to expressionless blackness. The light which had caused him such an agony during the first days of his illness no longer troubled him. No longer did he start and tremble at every sound. Indeed, the child did not seem to hear when he was spoken to. Two days passed and then, quite suddenly and with a horrible sinking sense of apprehension, Elinor realized that he was almost completely deaf.

'Deaf?' echoed Dr Crowther, when she told him of her dreadful discovery. 'Common symptom.'

'But isn't there anything to be done about it?' she asked. The trap was closing on her again, the trap from which she had imagined herself free when that terrible screaming had quieted into silence.

Dr Crowther shook his head, briskly, but only once each way. He did not speak. A foot-pound saved is a foot-pound gained.

'But we can't let him be deaf,' she said, when the doctor was gone, appealing with a kind of incredulous despair to her husband. 'We can't let him be deaf.' She knew he could do nothing; and yet she hoped. She realized the horror; but she refused to believe in it.

'But if the doctor says there isn't anything to be done ...'

'But deaf?' she kept repeating, questioningly. 'Deaf, Phil? Deaf?'

'Perhaps it'll pass off by itself,' he suggested consolingly and wondered, as he spoke the words, whether she still imagined that the child would recover.

Early next morning when, in her dressing-gown, she tiptoed upstairs for nurse's report on the night, she found the child already awake. One eyelid was wide open and the eye, all pupil, was looking straight up at the ceiling; the other was half shut in a permanent wink that imparted to the thin and shrunken little face an expression of ghastly facetiousness.

'He can't open it,' the nurse explained. 'It's paralysed.'

Between those long and curly lashes, which she had so often envied him, Elinor could see that the eyeball had rolled away to the exterior corner of the eye and was staring out sideways in a fixed unseeing squint.

*

'Why the devil,' said Cuthbert Arkwright, in the tone of one who has a personal grievance, 'why the devil doesn't Quarles come back to London?' He hoped to extort from him a preface to his new illustrated edition of the Mimes of Herondas.

The rustication, Willie Weaver explained polysyllabically, was not voluntary. 'His child's ill,' he added, uttering his little cough of self-applause; 'it seems very reluctant, as they would say in Denmark, to absent itself from felicity much longer.'

'Well, I wish it would hurry up about it,' grumbled Arkwright.

He frowned. 'Perhaps I'd better try to get hold of someone else for my preface.'

At Gattenden the days had been like the successive stages of an impossibly horrible dream. When he had been deaf for a couple of days, little Phil ceased also to see. The squinting eyes were quite blind. And after nearly a week's respite there was a sudden recurrence of the pain of the first days; he began to scream. Later he was seized several times with violent attacks of convulsions; it was as though a devil had entered into him and were torturing him from within. Then, one side of his face and half his body became paralysed and the flesh began to waste almost visibly from off his bones, like wax melting away in the heat of some inward and invisible fire. Trapped by her helplessness and by that horrible sense of guilt, which the news of Everard's murder had enormously intensified, Elinor sat by her child's bed and watched the phases of the malady succeeding one another – each one worse, it seemed to her, than the last, each more atrociously impossible. Yes, impossible. For such things could not, did not happen. Not to oneself at any rate. One's own child was not gratuitously tortured and deformed before one's eyes. The man who loved one and whom one had (oh wrongly, guiltily, and as it had turned out, fatally!) almost made up one's mind to love in return, was not suddenly and mysteriously murdered. Events like that simply did not occur. They were an impossibility. And yet, in spite of this impossibility, Everard was dead and for little Phil each day reserved a new and more excruciating torment. As in a nightmare, the impossible was being actualized.

Outwardly Elinor was very calm, silent, and efficient. When Nurse Butler complained that the meals brought up to the sick-room got very cold on the way (and might she have Indian tea, as China didn't agree with her digestion?), she ordered Lipton and arranged, in spite of Dobbs's passionate objections, that lunch and dinner should be brought up in the water-heated breakfast dishes. All that Dr Crowther telegraphically ordered her to do, she did, punctually, except to take more rest. Even Nurse Butler had grudgingly to admit that she was thorough and methodical. But she backed up the doctor, partly because she wanted to rule alone and undisputed in the sick-room and partly disinterestedly, for Elinor's own sake. That calmness, she could see, was the result of effort; it was the rigidity of extreme tension. Philip and Mrs Bidlake were no less insistent that she should rest; but Elinor would not listen to them.

'But I'm perfectly all right,' she protested, denying the evidence of her pallor and of those dark circles round her eyes.

She would have liked, if it had been humanly possible, never to eat or sleep at all. With Everard dead and the child in torture before her eyes, eating and sleeping seemed almost cynical. But the very possession of a body is a cynical comment on the soul and all its ways. It is a piece of cynicism, however, which the soul must accept whether it likes it or no. Elinor duly went to bed at eleven and came down to meals – if only that she might have strength to endure yet more unhappiness. To suffer was the only thing she could do; she wanted to suffer as much and intensely as she could.

'Well, how's the boy?' her father would ask perfunctorily, over his chicken-broth, when they met at lunch. And when she had given some vague reply, he would hastily pass on to another topic.

John Bidlake had steadily refused, throughout his grandchild's illness, to come near the sick-room. He had always hated the spectacle of suffering and disease, of anything that might remind him of the pain and death he so agonizingly dreaded for himself. And in this case he had a special reason for terror. For, with that talent for inventing private superstitions which had always distinguished him, he had secretly decided that his own fate was bound up with the child's. If the child recovered, so would he. If not ... Once formulated, the superstition could not be disregarded. 'It's absurd,' he tried to assure himself. 'It's utterly senseless and idiotic.' But every unfavourable bulletin from the nursery made him shudder. To have entered the room might have been to discover, quite gratuitously, the most horrible confirmation of his forebodings. And perhaps (who knows?) the child's sufferings might in some mysterious way infect himself. He did not even wish to hear of the boy. Except for that single brief inquiry at lunch-time, he never alluded to him, and whenever some one else spoke of him, he either changed the subject of conversation (surreptitiously touching wood as he did so) or else withdrew out of earshot. After a few days the others learned to understand and respect his weakness. Moved by that sentiment which decrees that condemned criminals shall be treated with a special kindness, they were careful, in his presence, to avoid any allusion to what was happening upstairs.

Philip, meanwhile, hovered uneasily about the house. From time to time he went up to the nursery; but after having made an always vain attempt to persuade Elinor to come away, he would go down again in a few minutes. He could not have borne to sit there for long at a time. The futility of Elinor's helpless vigil appalled him; he had at all times a dread of doing nothing and in circumstances like these a long spell of mental disoccupation would have been a torture. In the intervals between his visits to the sick-room, he read, he tried to write. And then there was that affair of Gladys Helmsley to be attended to. The child's illness had made a journey to London impossible and so absolved him from the necessity of personally interviewing Gladys. It was to Willie Weaver — Willie, who was a solicitor as well as the most reliable of friends — that he delegated the business. With what immense relief! He had really dreaded the encounter with Gladys. Willie, on the contrary, seemed to enjoy the business. 'My dear Philip,' he wrote, 'I have been doing my best for your Aged Parent; but even my best promises to be somewhat expensive. The lady has all the endearing young charms (only professional etiquette prevented me from attempting a little playful superfoetation on my own account); but she is also a business woman. Moreover, her feelings about the Aged P. are ferocious. Rather justifiably so, I must confess to thinking, after what I heard from her. Do you know where he feeds his paramours? Chez Lyons. The man must be a barmecidal maniac, as I said to the young lady when she told me. (Needless to say, she didn't understand the witticism; so I offer it to you, on the basis of a five per cent commission on all royalties accruing from the sales of any work or works into which you may introduce it.) Tell the Aged P. that, next time, he must really spend a little more on his amusements; it'll probably be cheaper in the long run. Advise him to indulge his gulosity as well as his lubricity; bid him control his thrift and temperance. I return to the attack to-morrow, when I hope to get the terms of the peace treaty set down in black and white. So sorry to hear your offspring's not well. Yours, W. W.'

Philip smiled as he read the letter, and 'Thank goodness,' he thought, 'that's settled.' But the last phrase made him feel ashamed of his amusement and his sense of relief. 'What bottomless selfishness' he reproached himself. And as though to make some amends, he limped upstairs to the nursery to sit for a while with Elinor. Little Phil lay in a stupor. His face was almost unrecognizably fleshless and shrunken, and the paralysed side of it was twisted into a kind of crooked grin. His little hands plucked unceasingly at the bed-clothes. He breathed now very quickly, now so slowly that one began to wonder whether he was breathing at all.

Nurse Butler had gone to take a nap; for her nights were half sleepless. They sat together in silence. Philip took his wife's hand and held it. Measured by that light irregular breathing from the bed, time slowly passed.

In the garden John Bidlake was painting – his wife had finally induced him to make the experiment – for the first time since his arrival at Gattenden. And for the first time, forgetting himself and his illness, he was happy. What an enchantment! he was thinking. The landscape was all curves and bulges and round recessions, like a body. Orbism, by God, orbism! The clouds were cherubic backsides; and that sleek down was a Nereid's glaucous belly; and Gattenden Punch Bowl was an enormous navel; and each of those elms in the middle distance was a paunchy great Silenus straight out of Jordaens; and these absurd round bushes of evergreen in the foreground were the multitudinous breasts of a green Diana of the Ephesians. Whole chunks of anatomy in leaves and vapour and swelling earth. Marvellous! And by God, what one could make of it! Those seraphic buttocks should be the heavenly reflection of Diana's breasts; one orbic theme, with variations; the buttocks slanting outwards and across the canvas towards the surface of the picture; the breasts slanting inwards, towards the interior. And the sleek belly should be a transverse and horizontal reconciliation of the two diagonal movements, with the great Sileni, zigzagging a little, disposed in front of it. And in the foreground on the left there'd be the silhouetted edge of the Wellingtonia, imaginatively transplanted there to stop the movements from running right out of the picture; and the stone griffon would come in very nicely on the right – for this was to be a closed composition, a little universe with boundaries beyond which the imagination was not to be allowed to stray. And the eye was to gaze as through an imaginary tunnel, unable to stray from the focal point in the middle of the great navel of Gattenden Punch Bowl, round which all the other fragments of divine anatomy would be harmoniously grouped. 'By God,' John Bidlake said to himself, swearing aloud in pure satisfaction of spirit, 'by God!' And he began to paint with a kind of fury.

Wandering through the garden in her endless crusade against weeds, Mrs Bidlake halted for a moment behind him and looked over his shoulder.

'Admirable,' she said, as much in comment on her husband's activity as on its pictorial results.

She moved away and, having uprooted a dandelion, paused and, with eyes shut, began to repeat her own name, 'Janet Bidlake, Janet Bidlake, Janet Bidlake,' again and again, until the syllables had lost all significance for her and had become as mysterious, meaningless, and arbitrary as the words of a necromancer's spell. Abracadabra, Janet Bidlake – was she really herself? did she even exist? and the trees? and people? this moment and the past? everything …?

Meanwhile, in the nursery, an extraordinary thing had happened. Suddenly and without warning, little Phil had opened his eyes and looked about him. They met his mother's. As well as his twisted face would permit him, he smiled.

'But he can see!' cried Elinor. And kneeling down by the bed, she put her arms round the child and began to kiss him with a love that was quickened by an outburst of passionate gratitude. After all these days of squinting blindness, she was thankful to him, she was profoundly grateful for that look of answering intelligence in his eyes, that poor twisted essay at a smile. 'My darling,' she repeated and, for the first time for days, she began to cry. She averted her face, so that the child should not see her tears, got up and walked away from the bed. 'Too stupid,' she said apologetically to her husband, as she wiped her eyes. 'But I can't help it.'

'I'm hungry,' said little Phil suddenly.

Elinor was down on her knees again beside the bed. 'What would you like to eat, my darling?' But the child did not hear her question.

'I'm hungry,' he repeated.

'He's still deaf,' said Philip.

'But he can see again, he can speak.' Elinor's face was transfigured. She had known all the time, in spite of everything, that it was impossible he shouldn't get well. Quite impossible. And now she was being proved right. 'Stay here,' she went on. 'I'll run and get some milk.' She hurried out of the room.

Philip remained at the bedside. He stroked the child's hand and smiled. Little Phil smiled back. He too began to believe that there really might have been a miracle.

'Draw me something,' the child commanded.

Philip pulled out his fountain pen and, on the back of an old letter, scribbled one of those landscapes full of elephants and airships, trains and flying pigs and steamers, for which his son had such a special partiality. An elephant came into collision with a train. Feebly, but with a manifest enjoyment, little Phil began to laugh. There could be no doubt of it; the miracle had really happened.

Elinor returned with some milk and a plate of jelly. There was colour in her cheeks, her eyes were bright and the face which, all these days, had been drawn and rigidly set had in a moment recovered all its mobility of expression. It was as though she had suddenly come to life again.

'Come and look at the elephants,' said little Phil. 'So funny!' And between each sip of milk, each spoonful of jelly, Philip had to show him the latest additions to his crowded landscape – whales in the sea, and divers being pinched by lobsters, two submarines fighting and a hippopotamus in a balloon; a volcano in eruption, cannons, a lighthouse, a whole army of pigs.

'Why don't you ever say anything?' the child suddenly asked.

They looked at one another. 'He can't hear us,' said Philip.

Elinor's expression of happiness was momentarily clouded. 'Perhaps to-morrow,' she said. 'If the blindness has gone to-day why shouldn't he hear to-morrow?'

'Why do you whisper?' said the child.

The only answer she could make was to kiss him and stroke his forehead.

'We mustn't tire him,' said Elinor at last. 'I think he ought to go to sleep.' She shook up his pillow, she smoothed the sheets, she bent over him. 'Good-bye, my little darling.' He could answer at least to her smile.

Elinor drew the curtains and they tiptoed out. In the passage she turned and waited for her husband to come up to her. Philip put his arm round her and she pressed herself against him with a great sigh.

'I was beginning to be afraid,' she said, 'that the nightmare was going on for ever. To the end.'

Luncheon that day was like a festival of resurrection, an Easter sacrament. Elinor was unfrozen, a woman of flesh again, not of stone. And poor Miss Fulkes, in whom the symptoms of misery had been identical with those of a very bad cold in the head accompanied by pimples, reassumed an almost human appearance and was moved to all but hysterical laughter by the jokes and anecdotes of the resuscitated John Bidlake. The old man had come in, rubbing his hands.

'What a landscape!' he exclaimed as he took his seat. 'So juicy, so succulent, if you know what I mean, so fleshy – there's no other word. It makes one's mouth water to look at it. Perhaps that's why I'm so ravenously hungry.'

'Here's your broth,' said Mrs Bidlake.

'But you can't expect me to do a morning's painting on slops!' And in spite of protests, he insisted on eating a cutlet.

The news that little Phil was better increased his satisfaction. (He touched wood three times with both hands at once.) Besides, he was really very fond of his grandchild. He began to talk, and it was the old Gargantuan Bidlake who spoke. Miss Fulkes laughed so violently at one of his anecdotes about Whistler that she choked and had to hide her face in her napkin. In the vague benevolence even of Mrs Bidlake's smile there was a hint of something like hilarity.

At about three o'clock John Bidlake began to feel a familiar discomfort, growing momently more acute, in the region of his midriff. He was shaken by spasmodic hiccoughs. He tried to go on painting; but all his pleasure in the work had evaporated. Diana's breasts and the angel's hind-quarters had lost all their charm for him. 'A slight obstruction at the pylorus.' Sir Herbert's medical phrases re-echoed in his memory. 'The contents of the stomach … a certain difficulty in passing into the duodenum.' After a particularly violent hiccough, he put down his brushes and walked into the house to lie down.

'Where's father?' Elinor inquired, when she came down to tea.

Mrs Bidlake shook her head. 'He's not feeling very well again.'

'Oh, dear.'

There was a silence, and it was as though death were suddenly in the room with them. But, after all, he was old, Elinor reflected; the thing was inevitable. He might be worse, but little Phil was better; and that was all that really mattered. She began to talk to her mother about the garden. Philip lighted a cigarette.

There was a knock at the door. It was the housemaid with a message from Nurse Butler: would they please come up at once.

The convulsions had been very violent; the wasted body was without strength. By the time they reached the nursery, little Phil was dead.

Chapter Thirty-six

The Webley Mystery, as the papers lost no time in calling it, was complete. There was no clue. At the offices of the British Freemen nobody knew anything. Webley had left at the usual hour and by his usual mode of conveyance. He was not in the habit of talking to his subordinates about his private affairs; nobody had been told where he was going. And outside the office nobody had observed the car from the time Webley had told his chauffeur he could go and the time when the policeman in St James's Square began to wonder, at about midnight, how much longer it was going to be left there unattended. Nobody had noticed the car being parked, nobody had remarked the driver as he left it. The only finger-prints on the paintwork and the steering wheel were those of the dead man. The person who drove the car after the murder had evidently worn gloves. No, there was no clue. Direct evidence was absolutely lacking. The police did what they could with the indirect. The fact that the body had not been robbed seemed obviously to point to a political motive for the crime. At the offices of the British Freemen reposed a whole collection of threatening letters. Webley received two or three of them every week. 'They're my favourite reading,' he was fond of saying. A search was made for the writers. Two Russian Jews from Hounds-ditch, a Nottingham typist, and an ardent young undergraduate of Balliol were identified as the authors of the most menacing and arrested, only to be released again almost immediately. The days passed. The murderers remained at large. Public interest in the crime was not allowed to abate. In part of the conservative press it was openly affirmed that the Liberal-Labour Government had given orders to the police that the affair was not to be too closely looked into. 'Screening the Murderers.' 'Socialists fear the Light.' 'Politics before the Ten Commandments.' The headlines were lively. The crime was a godsend to the opposition. The *Daily Mail* offered ten thousand pounds reward to any person who would give information leading to the arrest of Webley's murderers. Meanwhile, the British Freemen had almost doubled their numbers in a week. 'Are you on the side of Murder? If not, join the British Freemen.' The poster glared from every hoarding. Troops of Freemen in uniform and plain clothes scoured London canvassing for recruits, making patri-otic demonstrations, doing amateur detective work. They also took the opportunity to beat a number of people with whose opinions they disagreed. In Tottenham and East Ham they fought pitched battles with hostile crowds and damaged numerous policemen. At Everard's funeral a green procession more than three miles long followed the coffin to the grave.

Spandrell read all the papers every morning. They amused him. What a farce! What knockabout! What an incomparable idiocy! To Illidge, who had gone down to Lancashire to stay with his mother, he sent a picture post-card of Everard in uniform on his white horse – the shops were full of them now; hawkers peddled them in the streets. 'The dead lion seems likely to do much more damage than the live dog,' he wrote on the back. 'God was always a joker.'

God's best joke, so far as he himself was concerned, was not being there. Simply not there. Neither God nor the devil. For if the devil had been there, God would have been there too. All that was there was the memory of a sordid disgusting stupidity and now an enormous knockabout. First an affair of dust-bins and then a farce. But perhaps that was what the devil really was: the spirit of dust-bins. And God? God in that case would be simply the absence of dust-bins.

'God's not apart, not above, not outside.' He remembered what Rampion had once said. 'At any rate, no relevant, humanly important aspect of God's above and outside. Neither is God inside, in the sense that the Protestants use the phrase – safely stowed away in the imagination, in the feelings and intellect, in the soul. He's there, of course, among other places. But he's also inside in the sense that a lump of bread's inside when you've eaten it. He's in the very body, in the blood and bowels, in the heart and skin and loins. God's the total result, spiritual and physical, of any thought or action that makes for life, of any vital relation with the world. God's a quality of actions and relations – a felt, experienced quality. At any rate, he's that for *our* purposes, for purposes of living. Because, of course, for purposes of knowing and speculating he may be dozens of other things as well. He may be a Rock of Ages; he may be the Jehovah of the Old Testament; he may be anything you like. But what's that got to do with us as living corporeal beings? Nothing, nothing but harm, at any rate. The moment you allow speculative truth to take the place of felt instinctive truth as a guide to living, you ruin everything.'

Spandrell had protested. Men must have absolutes, must steer by fixed external marks. 'Music exists,' he concluded, 'even though you personally happen to be unmusical. You must admit its existence, absolutely, apart from your own capacity for listening and enjoying.'

'Speculatively, theoretically, yes. Admit it as much as you like. But don't allow your theoretical knowledge to influence your practical life. In the abstract you know that music exists and is beautiful. But don't therefore pretend, when you hear Mozart, to go into raptures which you don't feel. If you do, you become one of those idiotic music-snobs one meets at Lady Edward Tantamount's. Unable to distinguish Bach from Wagner, but mooing with ecstasy as soon as the fiddles strike up. It's exactly the same with God. The world's full of ridiculous God-snobs. People who aren't really alive, who've never done any vital act, who aren't in any living relation with anything; people who haven't the slightest personal or practical knowledge of what God is. But they moo away in churches, they coo over their prayers, they pervert and destroy their whole dismal existences by acting in accordance with the will of an arbitrarily imagined abstraction which they choose to call God. Just a pack of God-snobs. They're as grotesque and contemptible as the music-snobs at Lady Edward's. But nobody has the sense to say so. The God-snobs are admired for being so good and pious and Christian. When they're merely dead and ought to be having their bottoms kicked and their noses tweaked to make them sit up and come to life.'

Spandrell thought of the conversation now, as he addressed his post-card to Illidge. God was not there, the devil was not there; only the memory of a piece of squalid knockabout among the dust-bins, a piece of dirty dung-beetle's scavengering. A God-snob – that's what Rampion would call him. Dung-beetling in search of a non-existent God. But no, but no, God was there, outside, absolute. Else how account for the efficacy of prayer – for it *was* efficacious; how explain providence and destiny? God was there, but hiding. Deliberately hiding. It was a question of forcing him to come out of his lair, his abstract absolute lair, and compelling him to incarnate himself as a felt experienced quality of personal actions. It was a matter of violently dragging him from outsideness and aboveness to insideness. But God was a joker. Spandrell had conjured him with violence to appear; and out of the bloody steam of the magically compelling sacrifice had emerged only a dust-bin. But the very failure of the incantation had been a proof that God *was* there, outside. Nothing happens to a man except that which is like himself. Dust-bin to dust-bin, dung to dung. He had not succeeded in compelling God to pass

426

from outsideness to insideness. But the appearance of the dust-bin confirmed the reality of God as a providence, God as a destiny, God as the giver or withholder of grace, God as the predestinating saviour or destroyer. Dust-bins had been his predestined lot. In giving him dust-bins yet again, the providential joker was merely being consistent.

One day, in the London Library, he met Philip Quarles.

'I was very sorry to hear about your little boy,' he said.

Philip mumbled something and looked rather uncomfortable, like a man who finds himself involved in an embarrassing situation. He could not bear to let anyone come near his misery. It was private, secret, sacred. It hurt him to expose it, it made him feel ashamed.

'It was a peculiarly gratuitous horror,' he said, to bring the conversation away from the particular and personal to the general.

'All horrors are gratuitous,' said Spandrell. 'How's Elinor standing it?'

The question was direct, had to be answered. 'Badly.' He shook his head. 'It's quite broken her down.' Why did his voice, he wondered, sound so strangely unreal and, as it were, empty?

'What are you going to do now?'

'We shall go abroad in a few days, if Elinor feels up to the journey. To Siena, I'd thought. And then perhaps to the seaside somewhere in the Maremma.' It was a comfort to be able to go into these geographical details.

'No more English domesticity then,' said Spandrell after a little pause.

'The reason of it has been taken away.'

Spandrell nodded slowly. 'Do you remember that conversation we had at the Club, with Illidge and Walter Bidlake? Nothing ever happens to a man except what's like him. Settling down in the country in England wasn't at all like you. It didn't happen. It's been prevented. Ruthlessly, by God! But providence uses foul means as well as fair. Travelling about, being unfixed, being a spectator – that was like you. You're being compelled to do what's like you.' There was a silence. 'And living in a kind of dust-heap,' Spandrell added, 'that's like me. Whatever I do, however hard I try to escape, I remain on the dust-heap. I suppose I always shall.' Yes always, he went on thinking. He had played the last card and lost. No, not the last card; for there was one other. The last but one. Would he also lose with the last?

Chapter Thirty-seven

S PANDRELL was very insistent that they should come without delay. The *heiliger Dankgesang eines Genesenen an die Gottheit, in der lydischen Tonart* simply must be heard.

'You can't understand anything until you have heard it,' he declared. 'It proves all kinds of things – God, the soul, goodness – unescapably. It's the only real proof that exists; the only one, because Beethoven was the only man who could get his knowledge over into expression. You *must* come.'

'Most willingly,' said Rampion. 'But ...'

Spandrell interrupted him. 'I heard quite by accident yesterday that the A minor quartet had been recorded for the gramophone. I rushed out and bought a machine and the records specially for you.'

'For me? But why this generosity?'

'No generosity,' Spandrell answered laughing. 'Pure selfishness. I want you to hear and confirm my opinion.'

'But why?'

'Because I believe in you and, if you confirm, I shall believe in myself.'

'What a man!' mocked Rampion. 'Ought to join the Church of Rome and have a confessor.'

'But you *must* come.' He spoke earnestly.

'But not now,' said Mary.

'Not to-day,' her husband echoed, wondering as he spoke why the man was so strangely insistent. What was the matter with him? The way he moved and spoke, the look in his eyes. ... So excited. 'I have innumerable things to do this afternoon.'

'Then to-morrow.'

As though he were drunk, Rampion was reflecting. 'Why not the day after?' he said aloud. 'It would be much easier for me. And the machine won't fly away in the interval.'

Spandrell uttered his noiseless laugh. 'No, but *I* may,' he said. 'I shall probably be gone by the day after to-morrow.'

'You hadn't told us you were going away,' said Mary. 'Where?'

'Who knows?' Spandrell answered, laughing once more. 'All *I* know is that I shan't be here any more.'

'All right,' said Rampion, who had been watching him curiously, 'I'll make it to-morrow.' Why is he so melodramatic? he wondered.

Spandrell took his leave.

'What was wrong with him?' said Rampion, when he was gone.

'I didn't notice anything particularly wrong with him,' Mary answered.

Rampion made a gesture of impatience. 'You wouldn't notice the Last Judgement,' he said. 'Didn't you see that he was holding down his excitement. Like the lid of a saucepan on the boil – holding it down. And that melodramatic way of laughing. Like the conscious villain in the play. ...'

'But was he acting?' said Mary, 'was he playing the fool for our benefit?'

'No, no. He was genuine all right. But when you're genuinely in the position of the conscious villain in the melodrama, you inevitably begin to behave like the conscious villain. You act in spite of yourself.'

'But what's he being a conscious villain about?'

'How on earth should I know?' said Rampion impatiently. Mary always expected him, by some mysterious and magical intuition, to know everything. Her faith sometimes amused and sometimes pleased, but sometimes also annoyed him. 'Do you take me for Spandrell's father confessor.'

'There's nothing to fly in a rage about.'

'On the contrary,' said Rampion, 'there's practically nothing not to fly in a rage about. If one keeps one's temper, it's because one lives most of the time with one's eyes shut, half asleep. If one were always awake, my God! There wouldn't be much crockery unsmashed.' He stalked off to his studio.

Spandrell walked slowly eastwards from Chelsea along the river whistling to himself over and over again the opening phrases of the Lydian melody from the *heiliger Dankgesang*. Over and over again. The river stretched away into the hot haze. The music was like water in a parched land. After so many years of drought, a spring, a fountain. A watering-cart rumbled past trailing its artificial shower. The wetted dust was fragrant. That music was a proof, as he had said to Rampion. In the gutter a little torrent was hurrying a crumpled cigarette packet and a piece of orange peel towards the drain. He stopped whistling. The essential horror. Like carting garbage; that was what it had been. Just nasty and unpleasant, like cleaning a latrine. Not terrible so much as stupid, indescribably stupid. The music was a proof; God existed. But only so long as the violins were

429

playing. When the bows were lifted from the strings, what then? Garbage and stupidity, the pitiless drought.

In the Vauxhall Bridge Road he bought a shilling packet of writing-paper and envelopes. For the price of a cup of coffee and a bun he hired a table in a tea-shop. With a stump of pencil he wrote. 'To the Secretary-General, Brotherhood of British Freemen. Sir, To-morrow, Wednesday, at five p.m., the murderer of Everard Webley will be at 37 Catskill Street, S.W.7. The flat is on the second floor. The man will probably answer the bell in person. He is armed and desperate.'

He read it through and was reminded of those communications (written in red ink, to imitate blood, and under the influence of the serial stories in *Chums* and the *B.O.P.*) with which he and Pokinghorne Minor had hoped, at nine years old, to startle and terrify Miss Veal, the matron of their preparatory school. They had been discovered and reported to the head master. Old Nosey had given them three cuts apiece over the buttocks. 'He is armed and desperate.' That was pure Pokinghorne. But if he didn't say it, they wouldn't carry revolvers. And then, why, then it wouldn't happen. Nothing would happen. Let it go. He folded the paper and put it into the envelope. There was an essential silliness, as well as an essential nastiness and stupidity. He scribbled the address.

'Well, here we are,' said Rampion, when Spandrell opened his door to them the next afternoon. 'Where's Beethoven? Where's the famous proof of God's existence and the superiority of Jesus's morality?'

'In here.' Spandrell led the way into his sitting-room. The gramophone stood on the table. Four or five records lay scattered near it. 'Here's the beginning of the slow movement,' Spandrell went on, picking up one of them. 'I won't bother you with the rest of the quartet. It's lovely. But the *heiliger Dankgesang* is the crucial part.' He wound up the clockwork; the disc revolved; he lowered the needle of the sound-box on to its grooved surface. A single violin gave out a long note, then another a sixth above, dropped to the fifth (while the second violin began where the first had started), then leapt to the octave, and hung there suspended through two long beats. More than a hundred years before, Beethoven, stone deaf, had heard the imaginary music of stringed instruments expressing his inmost thoughts and feelings. He had made signs with ink on ruled paper. A century later, four Hungarians had reproduced from the printed

430

reproduction of Beethoven's scribbles that music which Beethoven had never heard except in his imagination. Spiral grooves on a surface of shellac remembered their playing. The artificial memory revolved, a needle travelled in its grooves and through a faint scratching and roaring that mimicked the noises of Beethoven's own deafness, the audible symbols of Beethoven's convictions and emotions quivered out into the air. Slowly, slowly, the melody unfolded itself. The archaic Lydian harmonies hung on the air. It was an unimpassioned music, transparent, pure and crystalline, like a tropical sea, an Alpine lake. Water on water, calm sliding over calm; the according of level horizons and waveless expanses, a counterpoint of serenities. And everything clear and bright; no mists, no vague twilights. It was the calm of still and rapturous contemplation, not of drowsiness or sleep. It was the serenity of the convalescent who wakes from fever and finds himself born again into a realm of beauty. But the fever was 'the fever called living' and the rebirth was not into this world; the beauty was unearthly, the convalescent serenity was the peace of God. The interweaving of Lydian melodies was heaven.

Thirty slow bars had built up heaven, when the character of the music suddenly changed. From being remotely archaic, it became modern. The Lydian harmonies were replaced by those of the corresponding major key. The time quickened. A new melody leapt and bounded, but over earthly mountains, not among those of paradise.

'*Neue Kraft fühlend*,' Spandrell quoted in a whisper from the score. 'He's feeling stronger; but it's not so heavenly.'

The new melody bounded on for another fifty bars and expired in scratchings. Spandrell lifted the needle and stopped the revolving of the disc.

'The Lydian part begins again on the other side,' he explained, as he wound up the machine. 'Then there's more of this lively stuff in A major. Then it's Lydian to the end, getting better and better all the time. Don't you think it's marvellous?' He turned to Rampion. 'Isn't it a proof?'

The other nodded. 'Marvellous. But the only thing it proves, so far as I can hear, is that sick men are apt to be very weak. It's the art of a man who's lost his body.'

'But discovered his soul.'

'Oh, I grant you,' said Rampion, 'sick men are very spiritual. But that's because they're not quite men. Eunuchs are very spiritual lovers for the same reason.'

'But Beethoven wasn't a eunuch.'

'I know. But why did he try to be one? Why did he make castration and bodilessness his ideal? What's this music? Just a hymn in praise of eunuchism. Very beautiful, I admit. But couldn't he have chosen something more human than castration to sing about?'

Spandrell sighed. 'To me it's the beatific vision, it's heaven.'

'Not earth. That's just what I've been complaining of.'

'But mayn't a man imagine heaven if he wants to?' asked Mary-

'Certainly, so long as he doesn't pretend that his imagination is the last word in truth, beauty, wisdom, virtue and all the rest. Spandrell wants us to accept this disembodied eunuchism as the last word. I won't. I simply won't.'

'Listen to the whole movement, before you judge.' Spandrell reversed the disc and lowered the needle. The bright heaven of Lydian music vibrated on the air.

'Lovely, lovely,' said Rampion, when the record was finished. You're quite right. It *is* heaven, it *is* the life of the soul. It's the most perfect spiritual abstraction from reality I've ever known. But why should he have wanted to make that abstraction? Why couldn't he be content to be a man and not an abstract soul? Why, why?' He began walking up and down the room. 'This damned soul,' he went on, 'this damned abstract soul – it's like a kind of cancer, eating up the real, human, natural reality, spreading and spreading at its expense. Why can't he be content with reality, your stupid old Beethoven? Why should he find it necessary to replace the real, warm, natural thing by this abstract cancer of a soul? The cancer may have a beautiful shape; but, damn it all, the body's more beautiful. I don't want your spiritual cancer.'

'I won't argue with you,' said Spandrell. He felt all at once extraordinarily tired and depressed. It had been a failure. Rampion had refused to be convinced. Was the proof, after all, no proof? Did the music refer to nothing outside itself and the idiosyncrasies of its inventor? He looked at his watch; it was almost five. 'Hear the end of the movement at any rate,' he said. 'It's the best part.' He wound up the gramophone. Even if it's meaningless, he thought, it's beautiful, so long as it lasts. And perhaps it isn't meaningless. After all, Rampion isn't infallible. 'Listen.'

The music began again. But something new and marvellous had happened in its Lydian heaven. The speed of the slow melody was doubled; its outlines became clearer and more definite; an inner part

432

began to harp insistently on a throbbing phrase. It was as though heaven had suddenly and impossibly become more heavenly, had passed from achieved perfection into perfection yet more deeper and more absolute. The ineffable peace persisted; but it was no longer the peace of convalescence and passivity. It quivered, it was alive, it seemed to grow and intensify itself, it became an active calm, an almost passionate serenity. The miraculous paradox of eternal life and eternal repose was musically realized.

They listened, almost holding their breaths. Spandrell looked exultantly at his guest. His own doubts had vanished. How could one fail to believe in something which was there, which manifestly existed? Mark Rampion nodded. 'Almost thou persuadest me,' he whispered. 'But it's *too* good.'

'How can anything be too good?'

'Not human. If it lasted, you'd cease to be a man. You'd die.'

They were silent again. The music played on, leading from heaven to heaven, from bliss to deeper bliss. Spandrell sighed and shut his eyes. His face was grave and serene, as though it had been smoothed by sleep or death. Yes, dead, thought Rampion as he looked at him. 'He refuses to be a man. Not a man – either a demon or a dead angel. Now he's dead.' A touch of discord in the Lydian harmonies gave an almost unbearable poignancy to the beatitude. Spandrell sighed again. There was a knocking at the door. He looked up. The iines of mockery came back into his face, the corners of the mouth became once more ironic.

'There, he's the demon again,' thought Rampion. 'He's come to life and he's the demon.'

'There they are,' Spandrell was saying and without answering Mary's question, 'Who?' he walked out of the room.

Rampion and Mary remained by the gramophone, listening to the revelation of heaven. A deafening explosion, a shout, another explosion and another, suddenly shattered the paradise of sound.

They jumped up and ran to the door. In the passage three men in the green uniform of British Freemen were looking down at Spandrell's body. They held pistols in their hands. Another revolver lay on the floor beside the dying man. There was a hole in the side of his head and a patch of blood on his shirt. His hands opened and shut, opened again and shut, scratching the boards.

'What *has* …?' began Rampion.

'He fired first,' one of the men interrupted.

433

There was a little silence. Through the open door came the sound of music. The passion had begun to fade from the celestial melody. Heaven, in those long-drawn notes, became once more the place of absolute rest, of still and blissful convalescence. Long notes, a chord repeated, protracted, bright and pure, hanging, floating, effortlessly soaring on and on. And then suddenly there was no more music; only the scratching of the needle on the revolving disc.

*

The afternoon was fine. Burlap walked home. He was feeling pleased with himself and the world at large. 'I accept the Universe,' was how, only an hour before, he had concluded his next week's leader. 'I accept the Universe.' He had every reason for accepting it. Mrs Betterton had given him an excellent lunch and much flattery. The *Broad Christian's Monthly* of Chicago had offered him three thousand dollars for the serial rights of his *St Francis and the Modern Psyche.* He had cabled back demanding three thousand five hundred. The *Broad Christian*'s answer had arrived that afternoon; his terms were accepted. Then there were the Affiliated Ethical Societies of the North of England. They had invited him to deliver four lectures each in Manchester, Bradford, Leeds, and Sheffield. The fee would be fifteen guineas per lecture. Which for England wasn't at all bad. And there'd be very little work to do. It would just be a matter of re-hashing a few of his leaders in the *World.* Two hundred and forty guineas plus three thousand five hundred dollars. The best part of a thousand pounds. He would go and have a talk with his broker about the position and prospects of rubber. Or what about one of these Investment Trusts? They gave you a very safe six or seven per cent. Burlap whistled softly as he walked. The tune was Mendelssohn's 'On Wings of Song.' The *Broad Christian* and the Affiliated Ethicals had made him spiritually musical. He whistled with no less satisfaction when he thought of the day's other triumph. He had definitely got rid of Ethel Cobbett. The moment had been auspicious. Miss Cobbett had gone away for her holiday. These things are easier to do by post than face to face. Mr Chivers, the business manager, had written a business-like letter. For financial reasons a reduction of the staff of the *Literary World* was urgently necessary. He regretted, but ... One month's notice would have been legally sufficient. But as a token of the directors' appreciation of her services he was enclosing a cheque for three months' salary. Any references she might require would

434

always be forthcoming and he was hers faithfully. Burlap had tempered Mr Chivers's business-likeness with a letter of his own, full of regrets, and friendship, and jeremiads against a public that wouldn't buy the *Literary World*, and lamentations over the defeat of God, incarnated in literature and himself, by Mammon in the person of Mr Chivers and all business men. He had spoken of her to his friend Judd of the *Wednesday Review*, as well as to several other people in the journalistic world and would, of course, do everything in his power to etcetera.

Thank goodness, he reflected, as he walked along whistling 'On Wings of Song' with rich expression, that was the end of Ethel Cobbett so far as he was concerned. It was the end of her also as far as everybody was concerned. For some few days later, having written him a twelve-page letter which he put in the fire after reading the first scarifying sentence, lay down with her head in an oven and turned on the gas. But that was something which Burlap could not foresee. His mood as he walked whistling homewards was one of unmixed contentment. That night he and Beatrice pretended to be two little children and had their bath together. Two little children sitting at opposite ends of the big old-fashioned bath. And what a romp they had! The bathroom was drenched with their splashings. Of such is the Kingdom of Heaven.

*Some more Penguin
fiction is described on the
following pages*

THE SNOWS OF KILIMANJARO
and Other Stories

ERNEST HEMINGWAY

1882

Where Somerset Maugham had been clinical and dispassionate and Katherine Mansfield passive and poetical, Hemingway seized the short story and injected violence, brutality, passion, blood, and death into it. As a journalist he had learned to pare his style down to a verbal photography of action. His threading of strong and simple words into short, staccato sentences became the envy of a whole school of imitators. But very few managed to suggest the compassion that lies between the lines of clipped action and laconic dialogue in Hemingway's stories.

'The Snows of Kilimanjaro' is probably the best short story he ever wrote. Face to face with death, a writer on safari contemplates all the stories there will now be no time to write. The other stories in this volume are all early ones, and those which feature Nick Adams are at least in part autobiographical.

'Unforgettable reporting of the world in which blood is the argument ... they are stamped with the urgency of Mr Hemingway's style. That style, at its best, is a superb vehicle for revealing tenderness beneath descriptions of brutality' – Ivor Brown in the *Guardian*

AS I LAY DYING

WILLIAM FAULKNER

1940

'The one unchallengeable and unquestionable genius at present functioning at the full tide of his creative powers on the American literary scene.'

In such terms Nobel Prizewinner William Faulkner was described, by Anthony West, prior to his death in 1962. When he wrote *As I Lay Dying* – in six summer weeks in 1929 during night-shifts at the local power station – Faulkner had already shaken off the influence of Huxley and Joyce. This story is one of his simplest and is considered by many critics to be his masterpiece.

The succeeding episodes of the death and burial of Addie Bundren are recounted by various members of the family circle, principally as they are carting their mother's coffin to Jefferson, Mississippi, in order to bury her among her people. As the desires and fears and rivalries of the family are revealed in the vernacular speech of the South, the author builds up an impression as epic as the Old Testament, as earthy and comic as Chaucer, as American as *Huckleberry Finn*.

'Often brilliant and compelling, and one is constrained to follow to the end' – *Spectator*

THE ROCK POOL

CYRIL CONNOLLY

1891

This, the only novel by the well-known critic, was published in Paris before the war, after being refused by two London publishers on the grounds of obscenity. It was subsequently published in America and England without alteration.

Edmund Wilson described the book as follows: 'A snobbish and mediocre young literary man from Oxford, with a comfortable regular income, spends the summer on the Riviera with an artists' and writers' colony. His first attitude is interested but patronizing: he tells himself that he has come as an observer and will study the community like a rock pool. But the denizens of the pool drag him down into it ... The story, which owes something to *South Wind* and Compton Mackenzie's novels of Capri, differs from them through its acceleration, which, as in the wildly speeded-up burlesques, has something demoniacal about it.'

And Desmond MacCarthy, the famous *Sunday Times* critic, wrote: 'I have read it twice, and I shall read it again, remembering it between whiles as a theme admirably and seriously handled, and as a novel written with a peremptory, witty precision, and a spirited, off-hand elegance extremely pleasing.'

Also available:

ENEMIES OF PROMISE (1573)

PENGUIN MODERN CLASSICS

NOT FOR SALE IN THE U.S.A.

GRAHAM GREENE

'Mr Greene is a story-teller of genius' – Evelyn Waugh

Five more books by Graham Greene are now available in Penguins, in addition to his five great novels which appeared together in Penguins in the autumn of 1962. These include his most recent major novel.

A Burnt-out Case

Philip Toynbee described his latest novel, set at a leper colony in the Congo, as being 'perhaps the best that he has ever written' (1894)

The Confidential Agent

One of his pre-war thrillers, in which the agent of a government engaged in a civil war is on the run in England (1895)

A Gun for Sale

This exciting story of a professional gunman's revenge was an immediate forerunner of *Brighton Rock* (1896)

The Ministry of Fear

In this, his most phantasmagoric study, the story, largely set in the London 'blitz', passes 'through twilit corridors of horror' – *Observer* (1897)

Stamboul Train

Good writing, intense excitement, and excellent characterization mark this early story which takes place on the Orient Express (1898)

Also available:

BRIGHTON ROCK (442)

THE LOST CHILDHOOD AND OTHER ESSAYS (1695)

THE END OF THE AFFAIR (1785)

THE HEART OF THE MATTER (1789)

OUR MAN IN HAVANA (1790)

THE POWER AND THE GLORY (1791)

THE QUIET AMERICAN (1792)

NOT FOR SALE IN THE U.S.A.

DORIS LESSING

Five

A collection of five short novels that won the Somerset Maugham award, for the best literary work of the year by a British author under thirty-five, in 1954.

'Miss Lessing is a powerful writer; her narrative flows with such impetus and colour that it is never dull or gloomy' – *Sunday Times* (1446)

The Grass is Singing

This was Doris Lessing's first novel and brought her immediate recognition. A story of white people in Rhodesia, it is both an accurate picture of Africa as it appears to the average settler and a subtle study of doomed marriage.

'Original and striking' – *New Statesman* (1525)

The Habit of Loving

'Each story has Doris Lessing's touch, warm in feeling but tough at the same time ... her writing is superbly readable and self confident' – *Daily Express*

'Remarkable variety of subject, scene, mood and treatment, ... a very distinguished collection' – *Spectator* (1473)

ANGUS WILSON

Anglo-Saxon Attitudes

'This brilliant and ambitious novel is about the conscience as it worries two generations of a middle-class family' – *New Statesman* (1311)

Hemlock and After

'It establishes him immediately as the most important novelist to come forward since the last war' – *Listener* (1086)

The Middle Age of Mrs Eliot

'What makes this novel tower above the fiction of a decade is the full-length presentation of Mrs Eliot herself ... She may be one of fiction's great female creatures' – *Daily Telegraph* (1502)

Such Darling Dodos

A frighteningly vivid picture of decaying gentlepeople and outmoded idealists, and of the ambitious 'new-look' young intelligentsia of the late 1940s. (1508)

The Wrong Set

His first published work, these twelve stories contain some of his most perfectly observed characters. (1355)

NOT FOR SALE IN THE U.S.A.

E. M. FORSTER

Collected Short Stories

These are fantasies and more light hearted than the major novels; but behind the comedy are glimpses of more profound themes. (1031)†

Howards End

A closely constructed novel about the lives of two sisters, both women of intense individuality, around whom a strange fabric of events is woven. (311)*

The Longest Journey

'Perhaps the most brilliant, the most dramatic, and the most passionate of his works' – Lionel Trilling (1470)†

A Passage to India

In this dramatic story E. M. Forster depicts, with sympathy and discernment, the complicated Oriental reaction to British rule in India, and reveals the conflict of temperament and tradition involved in that relationship. (48)*

A Room with a View

The typical behaviour of the English abroad is observed with E. M. Forster's shrewd eye and the result is, among other things, a first-rate piece of social comedy. (1059)*

Where Angels Fear to Tread

A sophisticated comedy about a group of well-bred English people exposed to a situation which rouses each of them to violent and unexpected reactions. (1344)†

D. H. LAWRENCE

D. H. Lawrence is now acknowledged as one of the greatest writers of the twentieth century. Nearly all his works have been published in Penguins and the following are available:

Novels

THE BOY IN THE BUSH (with M. L. Skinner) (1953)
LADY CHATTERLEY'S LOVER (1484)
THE LOST GIRL (752)
THE PLUMED SERPENT (754)
THE RAINBOW (692)
SONS AND LOVERS (668)
THE TRESPASSER (1480)
THE WHITE PEACOCK (760)
WOMEN IN LOVE (1485)

Short Stories

ENGLAND, MY ENGLAND (1482)
THE LADYBIRD (1483)
LOVE AMONG THE HAYSTACKS *and* OTHER STORIES
(1512)

Travel Books and Other Works

MORNINGS IN MEXICO *and*
ETRUSCAN PLACES (1513)
TWILIGHT IN ITALY (1481)
SELECTED ESSAYS (753)
SELECTED LETTERS (759)
SELECTED POEMS (D11)
À PROPOS OF LADY CHATTERLEY'S LOVER (1668)

NOT FOR SALE IN THE U.S.A. OR CANADA

EVELYN WAUGH

This *enfant terrible* of English letters in the 1930s became a best-seller with the publication in 1928 of his first novel, *Decline and Fall*. Many of the characters in this masterpiece of derision reappear in the subsequent novels, which, culminating in *Put Out More Flags*, present a satirical and entertaining picture of English leisured society between the wars.

Evelyn Waugh books available are:

NOT FOR SALE IN THE U.S.A.

ALDOUS HUXLEY

The name of Aldous Huxley, which became known in the twenties, rapidly developed into a password for his generation. At cocktail parties, which were becoming fashionable in the same period, it was bandied about as if the mere mention of it were enough to show that one was brilliant, witty, and cynically up to date. To start with, as Cyril Connolly has written, 'witty, serious, observant, well-read, sensitive, intelligent, there can have been few young writers as gifted as Huxley'. But the accusations of his less perceptive critics were completely off the mark, for in spite of Huxley's brilliant sense of light comedy, he has always been fundamentally serious. Too good an artist to become a preacher, he has never disguised his disillusionment, which in one form or another has been the basis of his satire, while he showed himself to be a mystic – a role with which he has been preoccupied since he went to live in California in 1937. As a result he has become more and more concerned in his books with contrasting reality and illusion. Those of his books available as Penguins are:

AFTER MANY A SUMMER · 1049

ANTIC HAY · 645

BRAVE NEW WORLD · 1052

CROME YELLOW · 41

THE DOORS OF PERCEPTION *and*

HEAVEN AND HELL · 1351

EYELESS IN GAZA · 1050

MORTAL COILS · 1051

POINT COUNTER POINT · 1047

THOSE BARREN LEAVES · 832

* NOT FOR SALE IN THE U.S.A.